MW01096814

HEARTACHE AND HOPE

HEARTACHE

FIRST AND FOREVER

Duet

HEARTACHE AND HOPE

HEARTACHE

FIRST AND FOREVER

Duet

JAY McLEAN

HEARTACHE AND HOPE

HEARTACHE DUET BOOK ONE

For Jordan McLean

ONE MINUTE you're sipping on your first beer at your first bonfire party, wearing a hoodie provided by a boy you've been crushing on for months. He slips his hand around your waist, pulls you closer to him. Then he dips his head, whispers into your neck, "You're beautiful, Ava."

It's your fifteenth birthday, and you have the world at your feet, and you watch the fire blaze in front of you, watch the embers rise, float to a new existence, and you think to yourself, *This is life.*

Your phone rings, and you pull it out of your back pocket, see your stepfather's name flashing on the screen, and you end the call, pocket the phone again.

The boy kisses your neck, and you take another sip, your eyes drifting shut at the feel of his lips against your skin.

Your phone rings again.

And again.

And you ignore it every time.

Every single time.

You move to the bed of a truck, your hands in his hair, his hands on your breasts, and you're so drunk on desire it makes you high on this life.

This life.

This perfect life.

It's 3:00 a.m. when you stumble home, drunk and delusional. Your stepfather is slouched on the couch in the living room, a single lamp casting the only shadows of the night. "I've been calling you," he says, and you're too out of it to care. "It's your mother."

At fifteen and one day, you sit with your stepfather in the same living room where he waited all night for you. Night has turned to day, and unlike him, you don't look at the door, waiting. No. You look at the phone.

Waiting.

At fifteen and two days, the call comes through, and neither you nor your stepdad has slept a wink. Your stepbrother is on his way home from Texas, and you wring your hands together.

Waiting.

At fifteen and three days, you find out that the situation is so bad, they're bypassing Germany and bringing your mother right home. To you. To her family.

At fifteen and four days, your stepbrother comes home, and you look to him for courage, find it in his eyes, in the way he holds your hand while you can do nothing but wait.

At fifteen and five days, you fly to DC, and see your mother for the first time in five months. The last words she said to you were "Be careful." She smiled at you the way mothers smile at their children, and you hid the pain and fear in your chest, replaced weakness for courage, and offered her a smile of your own.

At fifteen and six days, you try to search for that smile on her face while you sit by her hospital bed, but you don't find it. *Can't* find it. Because half of her face is gone. Half of her arm is, too.

A grenade, they told you.

At fifteen and seven days, you say to yourself, "This is life." And it only took seven days for you to realize how imperfect it is.

ONE

connor

LEBRON JAMES GREW up poor as hell with a single mother and zero privilege. His high school was completely unheard of before he showed up with three of his buddies and took over the league. At eighteen, a senior, he went prep to pro and was drafted by the Cleveland Cavaliers. His initial contract was $18.8 million over four years. Nike had offered him more than one hundred million off the court. This was before he played a single second of professional ball.

Talk about a game changer.

Obviously, I'm no LeBron James.

No one is.

Besides being raised by a single parent, comparing myself to LeBron would be like chasing rainbows.

Also, LeBron didn't have to change schools senior year just for the slight hope of getting noticed.

I walk back down the driveway for the millionth time, sweat pouring from every inch of my body, and blink away the fatigue from driving all night. Dad's at the rear of the rental truck unloading the last of the boxes we managed to stuff in there. After this, we only have *all* the furniture to unload. Fun times. I pick up a large, heavy box and ask, "Where to?"

"What does it say on the box?" Dad huffs. He's struggling more than I am.

I look down at the box, at the *somewhere* written in Dad's handwriting. "It says *somewhere*," I tell him, rolling my eyes.

He chuckles. "That must have been when I started to lose my mind. If only I'd had someone to help me pack."

I shrug. "I was busy." *Lazy.*

"Just dump it in the living room, and we'll go through it later, but I gotta go."

"Where?" I stop halfway to the house and look at the truck, then him, and back again. "Who's going to help me unload the furniture?"

"Just take the small stuff for now. I'll be back in a couple hours."

Sweat drips into my eyeballs. "A couple *hours*?" I drop the box, use the bottom of my shirt to wipe at my eyes, then search for a hose so I can drown myself. Maybe I don't even need the water. I could just use my own self-pity. There's sure as shit an abundance of it. I look over at my dad as he struggles to open the front door with his foot while carrying *two* boxes. *Shit.* I need to suck it up and quit complaining. He's given up a hell of a lot more than I have, and besides, he's here for me, no other reason. I rush to hold the door open, then I plaster on the most genuine smile I can muster. "No worries, Pops. Take your time. I got it."

"Don't overdo it, Connor. Just the small stuff."

When he leaves, the first thing I do is try to lift a three-seater couch on my own. Because I'm a shit of a kid and I don't listen apparently.

"Yo, you need a hand?" a guy calls from behind, rushing to lift the other end of the couch before it falls off the back of the truck. He asks, "You thought you could lift this on your own?"

I'd be annoyed by his words if he wasn't laughing when he said them. Besides, the guy's huge. If Shaq had a long-lost son, he would be it... so it's probably best not to start off on the wrong foot.

"Apparently so," I murmur.

With his help, we get the couch into the living room within seconds.

"Hey, man. Thanks for that." I throw out my fist for a bump as we walk out of the house.

"Nah, it's nothing." I expect him to leave, to go back to wherever the hell he appeared from, but he simply walks back to the truck, jumps in, and comes out with a mattress.

"Dude, honestly, you don't need to help."

He jumps down, then lifts the mattress onto his back as if it's air. "I got nothing going on."

"I can't, like, *pay you*... or anything."

He shakes his head. "Man, shut up with that." Then he motions to the rest of our shit in the truck. "But I'm not doing this on my own."

"Right."

An hour later and the entire truck is empty. I'm completely drenched in sweat. So is Trevor—whose name I just asked a minute ago. "I'd offer you a drink," I tell him, rolling down the truck door, "but we don't really have anything."

He looks over at my house. "You got AC?"

I nod. "I assume so."

He slaps my arm. "Get it on. I'll be back."

A minute later, AC blowing in the living room, he returns with two beers and hands me one. I take it without a second thought, down half of it in one go while he makes himself comfortable on the couch. Legs kicked up on the *somewhere* box, he says, "I live next door by the way."

I sit on a desk chair opposite him. "I figured. Hey, I can't thank you enough. My dad had to run out, so you showed up at the right time. Or wrong time for you, I guess."

He chuckles, his voice deep, low, when he says, "I wouldn't have offered if I didn't want to."

"Well, thank you. *Again.*"

He lifts his beer bottle in a salute motion, looking around the room. "So, you're here with your parents?"

"Just my dad."

"That him walking up your porch steps right now?"

I look through the window behind me, and sure enough... and I'm too late to remember the beer in my hand because it's the first thing Dad spots when he walks into the house.

The second is Trevor.

"This is Trevor," I tell Dad, standing, trying to hide the beer in plain sight. "He lives next door."

Dad clears his throat, takes the beer from my grasp. "Nice to meet you, Trevor," Dad says. "And I assume my son didn't mention he was a *minor*."

"Oh, my bad." Trevor gets up to shake Dad's hand. "To be fair, I didn't ask."

Dad simply nods, enjoying the ice-cold beer that I once called mine. "You help him bring all this furniture in?"

"Yes, sir."

Dad opens his wallet.

I cringe a little on the outside, and a *whole lot* on the inside.

Dad tries to hand him a twenty, but Trevor shoves his hands in his pockets, declining. "You're good, sir. I just saw him trying to lift more than all our weights combined. Didn't want him hurting himself, you know?"

"Well, thank you. I appreciate it."

Trevor eyes me. "A *minor*, huh?"

I nod, face heating with embarrassment.

"High school?"

"Yep."

"West High?"

"Nah. St. Luke's Academy."

Trevor's eyes widen. "Oh yeah? That's my old stomping ground." He takes a quick glance around our two bed, one bath, paint-peeling-off-the-walls rental, and all our belongings, focusing a few seconds on the framed Larry Bird jersey. When his eyes meet mine again, he's smirking. "Let me guess. Basketball scholarship?"

"Yeah," Dad and I answer at the same time. Dad asks, "You play ball?"

Trevor looks down at his feet. "Football. Well, I used to. Not so much anymore."

"You in college?" Dad asks him, and I hold back from doing the whole *ohmygod Dad stahhp, you're so embarrassing!* thing and keep my mouth shut.

"Nah," says Trevor. "I just work full-time now. Got my own company." He pulls out a card from his wallet and hands it to Dad. "Electrician. If you need anything, my number's on there."

"You got it," Dad asserts.

Trevor smiles at the both of us. "It's been fun, but I gotta get going. Hope y'all settle in all right."

"Hey, thanks again," I tell him.

Dad says, "Are you sure you won't take any—"

Trevor lifts his hand, already halfway to the door. "I'm good."

"Well, if you won't take money, maybe come around later this week. I'll grill some steaks for us."

Trevor stops, his hand on the door, and turns to us, his grin from ear-to-ear. "Now *that* is an offer too good to refuse."

He's gone a second later, his footsteps heavy on the porch.

Dad waits for him to be out of earshot before stating, "Good kid."

"Yeah."

"Good beer, too."

I clamp my lips together.

He laughs. "Come with me?"

"Where?"

He places the empty bottle on a box labeled *Boy Spawn* and heads out the door.

I follow as he leads me to a hunk of metal on four wheels.

"So...?" Dad asks, his eyes wide and waiting. It doesn't take long for his face to switch from his usual overtired, overworked, over-the-every-day-struggles-of-life frown into a full-blown grin. All it took was a twitch of my lips, a semblance of a smile. "Do you like it?"

He's asking the wrong question, because honestly? Do I *like* it? No. The car's a piece of shit. Way beyond its expiration. Beaten to death and then brought back to life only to be beaten again. Rust forms the majority of the two-door's roof. Door handles have been replaced with what I assume are coat hangers. The rear windshield... well, there is no rear windshield. There's just black plastic in its place, so... again... do I *like* it? Fuck no.

Do I *appreciate* it? Hell yes. "Dad, are you serious?" My grin matches his now. "You didn't have to. I mean, you shouldn't have. Things are hard enough with the move and—"

"Connor," he cuts in, shushing me with one hand, while a finger of the other runs along the dirt of the car's hood. "It's my job to worry about what's too hard and what isn't." His shoulders heave with his inhale as he focuses on the perfectly clean line he's just created. When his gaze meets mine again, I can see the exhaustion in his eyes. He's worn out. *Done.* He tries to cover it up with the same smile he's kept on, but I can tell it's waning. Slowly. Surely.

I inspect the car closer. Or at least pretend to. Because my mind is elsewhere, running on empty, doing a play-by-play of every possible scenario my future has waiting for me. And not even my entire future. Just *tomorrow.*

The first day of senior year is daunting for anyone, but the first day as the new guy in a new school full of rich kids who I'm sure can sniff a poor, scholarship kid from a mile away? Yeah, tomorrow's going to suck. And showing up in this car? It's going to be hell... but there's no way I'm telling Dad that. Or anyone else. Because the truth is, I don't *have* anyone else. It's 598 miles from Tallahassee, Florida, to Shemeld, North Carolina. Physically. But for my so-called friends and teammates back there, I may as well have moved to Mars. The second rumors started to spread about my moving for a better chance at my dreams was the exact second the invites and phone calls stopped. In one breath I was the team hero, and in the next, I was getting a stream of *Fuck you, Traitor* text messages.

What a time to be alive.

I grip the makeshift handle and pull up, cringing at the sound of metal scraping metal.

"She'll get better. Don't think she's been used in a while," Dad says, kicking at the tire. The hubcap separates from the wheel and falls to the ground in a circular motion—around and around—and I watch it, feel the chuckle building in my chest. I clamp my lips shut and try to contain it because the last thing I want to do is offend him.

His laughter starts low from somewhere deep inside him, and a moment later, he's in hysterics, a belly-rumble type sound that has me doing the same. "Goddamn, it's a piece of shit," he murmurs, trying to compose himself.

"It's not," I assure.

It is.

"At least this way, you'll be sure to get to school and games on time. Besides, it's all for the end game, right?"

I nod. The "end game" is what we call the plan for my future, and St.

Luke's Academy is the first step. My agent, Ross, suggested the move, and Dad and I agreed early on that whatever Ross says goes, and he says to "trust in the process."

So... I trust in the process.

Ross had organized everything. All I had to do was show up, play ball, keep my grades up, and he'd make sure I'd get into a D1 college.

Four years.

Graduate.

NBA.

End game.

Ross—he's not big on the four-year part of the plan, but Dad's adamant on it and in a way, so am I. A pro-athlete can only maintain the physical demands for so long. Besides, one injury could end it all and then what?

I catch the keys Dad throws at my chest.

"You need to drive me back to my car."

"What? You ain't worried about ruining your street cred by being seen in this?" I joke.

"Boy," he mocks, pulling open the passenger door. "Being seen with *you* ruined my street cred a long time ago."

THE CORRIDORS of school are deserted, first period already in progress. Through thin walls and solid doors, teachers speak loudly, authoritative tones used to impart their knowledge and wisdom on the students in front of them.

St. Luke's Academy is the most prestigious school within a fifty-mile radius, and I'm lucky to be here—just ask the faculty.

I descend the main staircase, past the words etched into the mahogany above the doorway: *Vincit qui se vincit.* Translation: He conquers who conquers himself.

Basically: master yourself, and then master the world around you. What's written between the lines, though, is this: St. Luke's will mold you to perfection, then throw you out into the real world and hope you know what the hell you're doing.

On the ground floor, I look left, look right. It's the same down here as it was above: deserted. The air conditioner above me whirs to life, blowing chills across my skin. Posters and flyers flap at the edges. The largest one spans across an entire wall, from one classroom door to another. *Wildcats! Wildcats! Wildcats!* There's a significant divide in this school, with only two segments: jocks and academics.

My stepbrother fell into the jock category.

Two years ago, so did I.

Kind of.

Now, I don't fit in either. I'm a loner, floating on the outskirts, discarded and unseen.

Invisible... until I'm not.

The long, narrow, empty hall stretches in front of me. Even with the air conditioning creating goosebumps on my flesh, making the hairs on my arms rise, sweat builds on my neck, at my hairline. I hold my psychology book to my chest and keep my head lowered. One step. Two. The walls seem to close in, but there's no exit in sight. I stop just outside the classroom door and freeze. I pray for an escape while I will myself not to press my ear against the heavy timber and listen in. A short breath in, out. I ball the note in my hand: a message from the school's psychologist excusing me from my tardiness with words so articulate, I struggle to understand them even though they're written about me. It's as if she tries to hide the truth that everyone already knows. It should just say: *Be nice. Y'all know what she's been through.*

I take one more deep, calming breath before I press my shoulder to the door and start to push, but the door gives way, and I'm falling forward, my shoes squeaking against the marble floor as I try to brace myself.

"Miss Diaz," Mr. McCallister booms, his hand on my arm to help keep me upright. Heat forms in my cheeks as I quickly hand him the note. Around me: silence. Not a single word, not even a whisper. Mr. McCallister doesn't bother reading the note; he simply places it on his desk and motions to the class-room. "Please swiftly find a seat so we can continue."

My phone vibrates in the hidden pocket of my school skirt.

Ignore it.

But I can't. I start to reach for it at the same time Mr. McCallister clears his throat. "Now, Miss Diaz."

I swallow my nerves and glance up through my lashes. I can feel every set of eyes on me, but I refuse to meet them.

It's a miracle my feet move at all, and they lead me to the only empty seat left in the room.

I drop my bag by the desk and climb into the chair, the lump in my throat the size of the random basketball by my feet.

Mr. McCallister turns his back, his focus already on writing down the semester's syllabus on the whiteboard. It takes a second for the class to follow, fingers busy tap, tap, tapping on their keyboards.

"Hey," a male voice whispers from next to me. I have no idea who he is, and I don't look up when he says, "I'm Connor."

I open my textbook to the first page, ignoring the dampness on the side of the pages from where I'd been gripping it.

"I'm new here..." my desk-mate says, his voice trailing as if waiting for a response.

In my mind, I say, "*Hi, I'm Ava. Welcome to my personal hell. The only reason I'm here is because guilt forces me to be.*"

Out loud, I say nothing.

Soon enough, he'll know everything there is to know about me.

connor

THE CAR DIDN'T STALL ONCE.

A miracle, really.

I got to school early this morning, about a half hour before I was supposed to be here. I thought it might help with the whole car situation. Not that I'm embarrassed by it, because I'm not. But you know what they say about first impressions. I didn't want to go into the year being "that kid."

It was pointless, though. One car in the parking lot, one kid on campus. Put two and two together, and you get my dumb ass.

I spent some time on the court alone, getting used to the hardwood that would become my playground for the next year. About twenty minutes in, my new teammates started to show.

Rhys, the team captain, was the first to greet me. His lackey, Mitch, was next, and then the rest of the guys. Everyone but Rhys seemed more interested in my car than in me, and when Rhys told them to quit raggin' on me, they didn't listen.

The first official practice of the season sucked. I'd spent so many hours during the summer learning the plays and memorizing my positions. I thought I had it down. I was wrong, so fucking wrong. I lagged. Hard. Balls flew past my head faster than I could catch them, names were called, threats were made. And that was just from Coach Sykes. Besides Rhys, no one said a word to me in the locker room afterward. This was all before the first bell, and my introduction to the shitty elite side of St. Luke's Academy.

And then first period started, psychology, and things just went downhill from there. No one sat next to me, and other than a few girls with coy smiles, I was ignored.

Then *she* walked in, like a baby bird leaving its nest for the first time—a discombobulation of limbs flapping around. Thing is—after the morning I had—I thought people would laugh at her, but no one did. Maybe because things were taken more seriously off the court, or maybe it was because the girl was crazy hot; all naturally tanned skin and legs upon legs beneath her school-issued skirt, and I never thought I'd have a kink for the whole school-girl uniform thing, but hey...

She made an entrance, that's for sure, or maybe it was just me that was paying attention. Maybe a little *too much* attention. She sat next to me, the only available seat... and said and did nothing. Even when I calmed my thoughts enough to introduce myself... nothing. While the entire class was busy taking notes, she stared ahead, picking at the desktop with her fingernail.

It's not until the bell rings forty odd minutes later that she finally moves. We face each other as we gather our things. Our eyes meet. Hold. Her irises catch the sunlight streaming through the windows, a light brown—so similar to the maple I spend my days shredding. Her lips part and my gaze glues to the motion. I try again, this time extending a hand. "I'm Connor. It's my first..." I trail off because she's already making her way to the door.

I turn at the hand landing on my shoulder. Rhys is behind me, his gaze following mine. "She's unavailable."

With a shrug, I tell him, "I wasn't interested."

He shakes his head. "No. I don't mean she's unavailable because she's seeing someone. I mean, she's unavailable"—he taps at his temple—" because she's checked out."

"No longer part of this world," Mitch adds, stepping up behind him. He rotates a finger around his ear—the universal sign for crazy—and whispers, "Certifiable." He eyes me up and down, stopping at my worn-out sneakers. "Actually, you'd do just fine together. Ghetto with ghetto. A perfect match."

I should punch him. Once for me. Then two more for the girl-with-no-name. Instead, I walk away, convince myself that people, in general, can be dicks, but people in high school? They fucking thrive on it.

Besides, I'm not here to make friends.

I'm here to make plays.

FOUR

ava

HEALTHY WAYS *of Coping with PTSD and Anxiety.*

I read the title of the pamphlet for the umpteenth time, shaking my head in disbelief. I'm not the one with PTSD, and maybe if the school psychologist had given me reading material about how to cope *with* people suffering *from* PTSD, I'd have a different reaction. I didn't feel like I needed to see her, but Trevor had spoken to the principal about how to "make sure my final year runs as smoothly as possible" and this was one of the many, many things on the list. So, every Monday and Wednesday I had to sit in an uncomfortable chair for a half hour and spill my guts about everything that was going on, all the emotions I was experiencing, and what I was doing to *cope* with it all.

I had nothing to say regarding any of those things, so I spent the entirety of our appointment trying to convince Miss Turner—a woman not much older than myself—that I was *fine*. Perfect, even. That my home life did not affect my school life, my grades, my future.

Vincit qui se vincit: He conquers who conquers himself.

I am a conqueror.

I am.

I am.

I flick the ring around my thumb.

I am.

I am.

I wish it to be true because those are the last words my stepdad, William, said to me before he walked out the door. *"You're a conqueror, Ava. You got this."* I didn't respond to him. I simply held the front door open and watched his truck pull out of the driveway and disappear down the road. I didn't ask where he was going. I didn't care. And I didn't ask why he was leaving me, leaving *us*. I already knew. He didn't love us, so he left. Love should make people stay. Love should make you want to keep the people who hold that love near.

Until one day when you open the bathroom door, and the scream that erupts from your throat forces you to understand. At that moment, I fell to my knees, soaking in crimson while clinging to hope—and I knew why William left. Because sometimes, love isn't enough. And neither is a school motto that teaches you from the day you enroll to the day you graduate that you must *conquer all*. Always. And when the tears blur your vision and your hands shake uncontrollably, and your throat aches with the cries that have consumed you, and you pick up the phone and question who to call, who to save you... you fail.

You don't dial 911 as you should.

Guilt seeps into my veins and through my airways, making breathing a task.

I flick the ring again.

I am not a conqueror.

I am a fucking failure.

I am.

I am.

* * *

At around five thirty a car door slams, and I pack up my homework scattered on the kitchen table and get started on dinner. Heavy footsteps enter the house, his head lowered, tools in one hand, work hat in the other. I watch from the kitchen doorway as he slumps down on the couch by the front door of our tiny three-bedroom house and starts unlacing his boots. Shoulders slouched, messy hair and tired eyes, the man is a picture of exhaustion and responsibility, and I hate that he's here. Hate that he's taken us on when he should be living his dream: playing football and finishing his degree at Texas A&M.

I don't ask him how his day was; I already know.

"How was your first day?" he asks, never once looking up.

"Good," I lie.

He nods, not asking anything more. He looks across the living room at a bedroom door—behind it: *our* reason and *his* responsibility. He murmurs words I can't decipher. When he looks up at me, he offers a smile that shatters my heart and adds layers to the constant knot in my throat. Heat burns behind my eyes, and I choke back my weaknesses. "Dinner will be ready in ten minutes."

He sighs, "Thank you, Ava."

I want to yell at him. I want to tell him that he shouldn't be thanking me for anything. That I'm the one who's thankful, that I'm forever in his debt. I want to tell him that I love him.

But if my stepdad leaving has taught me anything—it's this:

Love is not a noun.

Love is something you *do*.

Something you *prove*.

Something you work hard to *create*.

Love is not something that simply exists because you say it.

Love is not a noun.

Love is a verb.

IT'S ONLY BEEN a week since school started, and I'm already counting down the days until it's over. I'm sure things will get better. They have to. Once the season starts, I'll be able to focus all my energy on ball. But right now, I'm feeling... stuck. Somewhere between my old life and my new one. I'm struggling to navigate the hallways, not just geographically but socially, too. The kids are different, the classes are harder, the teachers are stricter, and the girls... the girls are on another level. I've been approached more in the past week than I have in my entire life. They know what they want, and I'm sure they're used to getting it. I could lie—tell them that I have a girl back home. Truth is, I'm out of my damn element, and every morning when I wake up, I feel like I'm drowning.

I tell Dad all this while lifting weights in our garage.

"It could be worse," Dad offers.

"Yeah? How?"

He helps me settle the bar onto the rack before handing me a water bottle. Then he raises his eyebrows at me as if to ask *do you really want to know*?

I down half the bottle and shake my head. No, I don't want to know. I've heard it too many times before. Dad's a paramedic, so he's seen it all. He was lucky enough to get a job here doing the same. The downside? He works nights.

I admire him for what he does. Honestly, I do. But sometimes I wish I could just complain about things and not have it thrown in my face. Sometimes I want to vent without feeling guilty for having those thoughts.

And sometimes I want to go back to my old school and play ball as if our future wasn't riding on it. To be fair, he's never made me feel as though that responsibility was mine.

But that doesn't mean I don't think it.

Going pro isn't just the end game. It's our ticket out. Our saving grace. Being a single parent is tough enough but raising a kid whose goal in life is to be a paid athlete—that's a whole other level. Training camps, uniforms, gear, gas to and from practices and games—games that up until a couple years ago he never missed, the time off work, the food. Goddamn, I eat *a lot*. I'm surprised he still somehow affords the roof over our heads.

"It's just a year, Connor. Do the work. Stay focused. No distractions—"

"Like girls?" I cut in, smirking.

"It only takes one," he mumbles, removing a weight off the bar.

His words hit me hard and fast. I lower my gaze and say, repeating his words from earlier, "It could be worse."

He crosses his arms. "Yeah? How?"

I shrug. "I could be nothing more than a stain on your bedsheets."

He says, his tone filled with regret, "That's not what I meant, son."

"Yeah? Because that's not what I heard, *Dad*."

connor

I WAS AN AWKWARD KID, a loner, anxious, with barely any social skills. On the advice of my teachers, Dad had me trying a bunch of things to help build my confidence and make me feel like I was part of something. Anything. Looking back, I know he went above and beyond to help me find my place in this world, to make me feel as comfortable as I could in my own skin. For most of my life, he'd played the part of both parents, which I'm sure comes with a level of difficulty I can't even imagine. He'd always been there for me. *Always.* Which I guess is why when he says things like he did last night —things in passing that aren't meant to offend—it cuts deep.

Deeper than I'll ever let show.

Anyways, the point is I spent a good year of my life trying everything: baseball, football, soccer, karate, Scouts, *sewing.* You name it, I was there. But I didn't love any of them, and nothing stuck. Not until I touched a basketball for the first time when I was ten years old, and something just... clicked.

My coaches said I was a natural-born athlete, which makes sense, I guess, given my genetics.

A lot changed in the years that followed.

The harder I worked on the court; the easier things became off of it. Throw in a growth spurt that didn't seem to end, and I started to get attention from all over. Girls included. Luckily for me, Dad was always there to remind me of my never-ending list of priorities, and dating... it wasn't even in the footnotes.

So, with that said, it's no real surprise that my experience with those of the opposite sex is limited to a few make-out sessions at post-win celebrations. I'd never been in a relationship. Never even dated. And so the aggressiveness of the attention I was suddenly getting was intimidating, to say the least, and uncomfortable as hell. Especially when it's constant. Like this girl, Karen, who's somehow managed to find me at my locker every single morning. There's no doubt she's cute, in the kind of way that money can buy attractiveness. Perfect make-up to go with her perfect skin and perfect hair and perfect attitude. And I'm sure she's perfect for a guy who's just as perfect for her. But for me? I'm not interested in her, at least not in that way, and I sure as hell don't have the time to try to match that level of perfection. Or the time at all... just ask my dad.

Monday morning. First period. Psychology. And guess who's in my class? Karen.

Karen... who's currently staring at me from across the room. Or maybe she's looking at the girl next to me; Ava—whose name I worked out through other people because she still won't talk to me even though she sits next to me every psych class.

She's a goddamn enigma.

I've never seen her outside of this class, not even in the cafeteria. Not that I've been looking. *Lie.* Unless she's conspicuously making a grab for her phone under the desk, she shows no other signs of life. It's as if she lives in a bubble, and everyone accepts that.

Sometimes, sitting next to her like we are, I wonder what it would be like to burst that bubble.

"One thing I forgot to mention—" Mr. McCallister's voice booms, pulling me from my thoughts, "the nature versus nurture paper you're all going to submit will be done in pairs. You have three seconds to choose your partners."

Across the room, Karen's eyes widen and zone in on me. Chairs scrape, students move, and panic fills my bloodline. Instantly—*stupidly*—I reach for Ava's arm at the same time she stands. Not a second later, Karen's in front of us, her gaze switching from me to Ava to my hand on Ava's arm. Ava's wide-eyed as she looks up at me, then at Karen, then to our touch. Behind me, a throat clears. It's Rhys, and he's looking at all three of us with unmasked confusion.

"Ava," Karen says, motioning to me. Ava's shoulders rise with her intake of breath, and she pulls her arm from my grasp. My eyes drift shut, embarrassment heating my cheeks. *What the hell was I thinking?*

"Ava?" Karen repeats. Firmer. Stronger. There's a hidden question there, one I can't decipher.

Rhys asks, "You good, A?" It's the first time I've heard a student speak to Ava this way, as if they care, and I sure as shit didn't expect it from him.

Ava swallows, nervous, her eyes flitting to mine quickly before moving away. "I'd rather work with Rhys," she says, so quiet I barely hear her. But I do, and there's a sudden knot in my gut, a flashback to my past. Awkward, anxious, loner. I bite my tongue, physically and metaphorically, and try to push down my insecurities. I feel like I'm being judged, and it sucks that the one person in the entire school who's paid absolutely no attention to me in the past is the one doing the judging.

"Groups of two, not four," the teacher yells, waving a hand toward us. "And since none of you can take basic direction, I'll make the choice for you. Ava and Connor. Rhys and Karen."

Rhys curses under his breath, his lips pressed tight as he eyes Ava. "You going to be okay?"

"Jesus Christ," I murmur. "Way to make a guy feel good."

I watch Ava for a response, but I don't get one. At least not to me. Rhys does, though, in the form of a painstakingly slow nod from her.

In front of me, Karen stomps her foot, spins and walks back to her seat, Rhys following after her.

I turn to the girl next to me, my insecurities switching to annoyance. "I'm not stupid."

Her gaze locks on mine, her head shaking slowly. "I'm sor—"

I interrupt because I don't need her sympathy. "No, *I'm* sorry. I'm sorry to disappoint you before you even get to know me." I take a breath, try to regain some composure. "I'm not stupid," I repeat, calmer. "Just because I'm new and I'm here on an athletic scholarship doesn't mean I'm a dumbass. I'll work just as hard as you, if not more, because I have something to prove. I don't expect you to carry the weight if that's what you're thinking." I keep my eyes trained on her, watching the confusion settle across her face.

"It's Connor, right?"

"Yeah...?"

"Let's just get this clear, *Connor*." She spits my name. "I have no assumptions about you at all because I haven't thought of you once. Not even for a second. And I don't care enough about you to judge you. So, let's just get to work." She slaps a sheet of paper between us and scrawls my name and hers across the top, then glares up at me. Daggers upon daggers. "Do you think it's nature or nurture that has you believing that your woe-is-me attitude isn't just another form of self-entitlement?"

My head spins, but I can't come up with a retort. Not even a decent response. All this time I spent wondering what it would be like to burst her bubble, and now here she was... completely obliterating mine.

ONE OF THE only two friends I have left belongs to my brother. He was there the first day I met Trevor—when I was nothing but a kindergartener in a bright purple dress and rainbow-colored socks. He's been there pretty much every day since. From grade school to middle school to high school, wherever Trevor Knight was, so was Peter Parker. Yes, that's his real name.

When he and Trevor graduated, they both took off to Texas A&M. It's safe to say we all grew up together, but the four-year age difference meant we experienced things at different times. While they hit freshman year of high school, I was in fifth—and back then, I was trying to decide between Harry Styles and Justin Bieber while the *Glee* soundtrack blasted from my bedroom.

The point is, now that I'm older, wiser, and the experiences of my life have forced me to grow up, the four years between us don't seem so vast anymore.

Peter comes from the "right" side of town, the same side where Trevor and I grew up before we had to sell the house to cover my mother's medical bills. The same side with the fancy, big houses and boats in their yards. His parents usually go away for the summer, a new country every year, and every year he'd join them. Until last year. Last year, he spent his summer helping Trevor with his business. Trevor's offered to pay him what little he can. Peter refuses every cent, knowing we need it more than he does. He's become a good friend to me, a solid wall of dependency that for so long, I refused to believe I needed.

And that's the difference between Trevor's friends and mine: when our worlds came crashing down, Peter stood by our sides. My so-called friends stopped coming around, too afraid of the woman with the half face and stub for an arm.

Soon enough, they stopped calling altogether.

"I like what you've done with the place," Peter jokes, throwing his entire weight on the couch next to me. "It's very—"

"Thrift store chic?" I finish for him.

He shakes his head, placing the bowl of popcorn on my lap. He's home for the week, and when he found out Trevor was out quoting jobs after hours, he offered to come over so I wouldn't be home alone. "No," he says, "It's got bits of your personality all over the place." He grabs a blanket from behind us and places it over his lap. "Like this." He rubs the blanket between his fingers. "It's very... *boho*."

"You mean homeless?"

With a chuckle, he throws his arm on the couch behind me and gets comfortable. "So, Ava. Tell me everything. What's been going on with you?"

"Same old, really. Just counting down the days until school's over." I hit play on the remote, but keep the volume muted.

"You'll miss high school when it's over," he tries to assure.

I scoff. "I think your version of high school and mine are very different, Peter."

"Yeah, I guess." After grabbing a handful of popcorn, he asks, "You still friends with that Rhys kid?"

Nodding, I stare at the opening scene of the horror movie he's got us watching.

"Is he still helping you out at school? Getting you notes for your missed classes?"

"Yeah," I reply through a slow exhale.

On TV, a blonde girl climbs the stairs toward the killer.

"Good," Peter says, nodding. Then adds, "He's a good guy, Ava. He's just not good enough for *you*."

"Okay," I mumble because it doesn't really matter what he thinks.

"Ava?" Peter asks, his leg brushing against mine. He's closer than he was only minutes ago, and discomfort swarms in my veins, beating against my flesh.

I manage a "Yeah?"

The warmth of his breath floats against my cheek as his heated fingers brush along the skin of my shoulder. It's not the first time he's acted like this. It won't be the last. And it would be so easy to use him this way, to be with someone who understands without explanations, who forgives without excuses.

I swallow, nervous. "If Trevor knew what you were thinking right now, he'd kill you with his bare hands."

THE WAY STEPHEN CURRY puts his defenders off balance with a simple behind-the-back crossover is history-making. He's proven that a killer jump shot can make or break a team's final score, making him arguably the best ball handler in the NBA.

Me?

I can't even catch the fucking ball when it's thrown directly at my chest.

It's the day after Ava tore me to shreds, and I'm in the locker room following another pathetic practice, staring down at my hands trying to reason with them. For years, I've lived and breathed this sport. I dreamed about it even when I was awake. The amount of shit I've broken in the house because I couldn't *stop* thinking about it is enough to fill a whole other house. Every lawn I mowed to earn money to replace those things—worth it. Every grounding—worth it. Every single hour I spent watching game tape or studying plays or fantasizing about what it would be like to play at Madison Square Garden was *worth it.*

But here? Now? I'm second-guessing it all.

"You ever watch that movie *Little Giants*?" Rhys asks, flopping down on the bench next to me. I thought I was the only one left in the locker room, but apparently, I was wrong.

I slam my locker shut and face him. "That one with the reject kids playing football?"

He nods. "There's this line in it that I always think about whenever I have bad days. Football is 80% mental and 40% physical."

I glare at him, my brow bunched in confusion. "That makes no sense."

He taps at his temple. "Get out of your head," he says, squeezing my shoulder. "The rest will follow." I force out a breath as he comes to a stand. He adds, "You know Miss Turner?"

"No."

"She's the school psychologist."

I shake my head. *Is this kid serious?* "I'm fine."

"I've made an appointment for you after school tomorrow."

Frustration knocks on my flesh from the inside. "Dude, I don't need—"

"Trust in the process," he cuts in, and I'm reminded of Ross, of my dad, of the weight of expectation balancing on my shoulders.

He starts to walk away but stops just by the door. "And hey. Not that I'm assuming this has anything to do with you sucking—because you might just be a shitshow—but the whole Ava thing? Try not to take it personally, okay?"

* * *

Try not to take it personally.

It's 3:00 a.m., and Rhys's final words are plaguing my mind. Like a scratched record stuck on repeat. Over and over. Again, and again.

The thing is, I *did* try.

Just like I tried to forget what Dad had said.

And just like I tried to ignore the fact that I've made zero connection whatsoever with my new life.

* * *

The next day drags, every second filled with anxiety. By the time I sit my ass outside the psych office, I'm a ball of nerves. My knee bounces, my palms sweat, and there's a throbbing between my eyes that won't fucking quit. Elbows on my knees, I lower my head and pinch the bridge of my nose for some form of reprieve. I try to blame it on the lack of sleep, but I know the truth. I've been here too many times not to know.

The door opens, and I look up just in time to see Ava standing in the doorway.

"My door is always open," a younger woman who I assume is Miss Turner tells Ava. "Whatever you need."

Ava doesn't respond to her because she's too focused on me, her head cocked, eyes narrowed.

Great, now I'm the "self-entitled" new guy with *issues*. But she's here, too, which means...

I try to offer a smile.

She returns it with a scowl.

Awesome.

* * *

"Tell me why you're here," Miss Turner asks.

I settle my hands on my knees to stop the shaking and take a breath. Her office is nothing but white walls and empty bookshelves. I squirm in my seat, unease filling my bloodlines.

"Sorry," she says. "The seats aren't very comfortable." She waves a hand around the room. "As you can tell, I'm waiting on more funding to get my office up to scratch."

"I'm sure the parents of a few kids here could throw you some loose change," I remark, my gaze catching the files on the desk in front of her.

Connor Ledger. Beneath that: *Ava Diaz.*

"Sure," she says, swiping both files together and placing them roughly in a draw. "But the parents here aren't as interested in their kids' mental health so much as their grades, or in some cases their triple-double stats."

My eyes lift to hers.

She smirks. "So why are you here?"

I shrug. "My stats suck, and I guess my team captain wants to figure out why the hell I'm at this school."

"Do you ever wonder why you're here, Connor?"

Every damn minute of every day. "Nope. I *know* why I'm here."

"Enlighten me then."

"Because some people think I'm good enough."

"And you don't?"

Another shrug.

Her sigh echoes off the empty walls. "Let's start from the beginning," she says, grabbing a pen from a cup in the shape of a unicorn. "Tell me about your home life."

Here we go...

* * *

The time with Miss Turner did nothing for my nerves. If anything, it just made things worse. By the time I finally make it out of the damn building, my heart is racing, sinking, and my mind? My mind is questioning what all she had to say about me in her too-messy-to-make-out notes that went on for *five* goddamn pages. I'm almost positive it'll be the same generic diagnosis of everyone else before her.

Connor Ledger has a good head on him, but he lacks self-confidence due to his fear of abandonment.

At the end, she asked if I wanted to schedule another appointment. I imagined getting out of my chair and throwing it out the window, I was that exasperated. Instead, I politely declined, told her I'd do "better." I don't even know what I meant by "better," but it sure as shit seemed to suffice.

In the student parking lot, my car is the only one left. By now, every single person knows who it belongs to, so there's no shame left, and even if there was, I have absolutely zero fucks left to give.

I make it halfway to my car before I hear a "Hey!" from somewhere behind me. I assume it's Miss Turner, but it's not.

It's Ava.

She's standing a few feet away, her hands gripping the straps of her bag. I stop in my tracks as I watch her approach. And I mean *watch* in every sense because as much as she might despise me, *goddamn,* there's still an attraction to her I can't seem to shake, and maybe...

Maybe Rhys is onto something. Because as hard as I've tried to deny it, what Ava said affected me in ways I don't truly understand.

"Is that your car?" she asks, looking over my shoulder.

So those fucks that had disappeared? They're back, and they're plentiful, and they're causing the heat forming in my face.

"Yes," I answer, but it comes out a whisper. *Jesus.* I clear my throat, try again. "Yeah, it's mine."

"Cool..."

Then I pull out the last remaining semblance of confidence I have left. "Do you... I mean, do you need a ride somewhere?"

* * *

Sitting next to Ava in class is one thing. Having her sit in the tiny space of my car? Whole other story. Besides giving me directions, she doesn't speak, but I hear every sound. Every breath, every swallow, every shift of her skirt against her thighs...

And my eyes... my eyes can't seem to focus on the road because they're too busy focusing on her.

"Just here," she says, her voice pulling me back to reality.

I pull over in front of a diner and watch her looking out the window, her index finger flicking the ring around her thumb. It's too big for such small, delicate fingers, and I wonder who it belongs to. The sun reflects off the bright red stone, and when I look closer, I see the words *United States*—She closes her fingers around her thumb, blocking the ring entirely. With her other hand, she reaches into the pocket of her skirt and pulls out her phone. Her thumb moves swiftly across the screen as she types out a text, but she doesn't make a move to get out.

I strum my fingers on the steering wheel.

"You got somewhere you need to be?" she asks, not looking up.

"I'm good," I tell her, then swallow my nerves. "Listen, about yesterday..."
I wait for her to say something, and when nothing comes, I continue, "I think
we got off to a bad start. I shouldn't have snapped at you the way I did, and I
guess I just wanted to apologize." *There.* I said it. And as soon as the words are
out of my mouth, I feel the tension lift off of my shoulders.

"We all say things we don't mean," she mumbles, shrugging, and it's as
genuine as the slight smile she offers me. A smile that has my stomach twisting. She adds, "That includes me. I shouldn't have said what I did, either."

I bite my lip, contain my grin, and take the apology one step further. "So...
friends?"

She turns to me, and the corner of her lips lift just a tad. "I'd make a
horrible friend."

I settle in my seat, my back against the door to give her my full attention.
"To be honest, you could be the absolute worst friend in the world, and you'd
still be the best one I have."

Her smile fades, concern dripping in her words. "But you have the team,
right?"

My eyes widen in shock. *Busted.* Caught in a lie. "I thought you hadn't
thought about me, not even for a second?" I tease.

"Just because I don't listen, it doesn't mean people don't talk," she rushes
out, a blush forming on her cheeks. Shaking her head, she blinks hard. Once.
Twice. "Anyway," she says, scrambling for words. "You're a good-looking jock.
You don't need friends when you can have girls."

"Wait." I sit up higher, my heart racing. "You think I'm good-looking?"

Those small hands of hers cover her entire face. "Jesus. That's not—I
didn't mean—what I meant is that... I gotta go!"

I PRACTICALLY RUN AWAY from Connor's car, past Trevor's truck with the *Knight Electrical* decal plastered on the side. When I enter the diner, I keep my head down but my eyes up, searching. I spot Trevor almost immediately, working on an old jukebox. Pressing my hands to my cheeks, I try to feel for any visible signs of the blush I'm positive I'm wearing. I could blame it on all the people I'm sure are staring, but it's not them. The *real* reason just drove away after letting me escape so I could yank the foot out of my mouth. *You're a good-looking jock...* God! What an idiot! Who even says that?

I kick the heel of Trevor's shoe when I get to him and wait the few seconds for him to pop his head out from behind the jukebox. His eyes widen when he sees me, and I tap my imaginary watch on my wrist. "Did you forget about me?"

"Shit, Ava. My bad. I got caught up."

I drop my bag and sit in the booth next to his tool bag. "It's cool. I just hitched a ride from some beefy dude with full-sleeve tats and a ferret named Roger."

Trevor rolls his eyes. "I'm guessing he had a blacked-out van?"

"Motorcycle actually. Cool guy."

He focuses on his work again. "Where was the ferret riding?"

"Shirt pocket. *Obviously.*"

Chuckling, he swaps one tool for another. "I'm almost done here. Grab a drink if you want."

"I'm good."

A few minutes later, Trevor's being handed a check by the diner owner, and we're on our way. Walking side by side toward his truck, he nudges my shoulder. "Guess what?"

"What?"

"We got the Preston job."

"Trevor!" I squeal, stopping in the middle of the sidewalk. "Are you serious? That's amazing!" I wrap my arms around him, my laughter unconfined. God, we needed this. Even without the extra money or job security, we *needed* this; a tiny ray of light to help clear the darkness.

He returns my embrace with the same enthusiasm, and when he releases me, he asks, "Honestly, though, how did you get here?"

"Some guy from school gave me a ride."

"Some guy?" he asks, eyebrow quirked.

I shrug, try to play it cool. "Apparently, I'm his new best friend."

* * *

I haven't stopped smiling since Trevor delivered the news, and neither has he. "So, tell me everything!" I all but shout, moving around the kitchen like it's my job. Around us, music blares, filling our souls with a semblance of hope.

Tomorrow we'll go back to worrying, to eating ramen and potatoes. But tonight? We celebrate. Tonight, it's a three-course meal with all of Trevor's favorites. He deserves it every day, but we've never been in a position to splurge like we are now.

Trevor sits on the counter, his legs swinging as he licks the wooden spoon from the cake mix I've just made. "The contractor they used for all their electrical work retired, so they were after someone new. I applied, went in for the interview with Tom Preston, told him about our situation—"

"You used our sob story to land the job?"

His brow bunches. "I did what I had to do, Ava. This job gives us an iota of breathing room, and it's something we really need right now."

"Oh, I know," I assure. "I don't blame you. I would've done the same." Hell, I would've thrown in some waterworks if it guaranteed us the job. Everyone in town knows Tom Preston is a giant softy, especially when it comes to matters of family.

I shove the cake tin in the oven, slam the door, and turn to Trevor. He's wearing a shit-eating grin, and I think I know why. "So..." he sing-songs, rocking back and forth. "Who's the guy?"

I turn my back to him, pretend to be engrossed in the salad I'm spinning. "What guy?"

"What guy?" He repeats, mocking. "The guy who's got you in a daze since you walked into the diner."

"Pshh. What are you talking about?"

He points at me. "You think I don't know you, Ava..."

True. He knows me well. Too well. I throw a piece of lettuce at his head. He ducks it, of course, and doesn't bother with the cleanup.

"So?" he pushes.

"Trust me, there is no guy. And even if I were interested in someone, it's not like I could—"

"You could."

"Could what?"

"Date."

"No." I shake my head.

"Why not?"

"Because," I snap. And even though I know he's just teasing; I can't ignore the microscopic ball of disappointment settling at the pit of my stomach. "Because I'd be the world's flakiest girlfriend, that's why." And I can't help comparing myself to the type of girl Connor could easily attain. I mean, the guy's a god. And I don't know why I've never noticed him in that way before because his presence is pretty hard to ignore. Well over six foot, eyes so blue you'd mistake them for puddles. His hair, that unintentional blend of messy perfection, parted in ways that let you know he spends many seconds running his fingers through it. His body—God, it's a wonder the girls at school haven't devoured him to pieces and spat out his remains. And don't even get me started on his dimples. I didn't even know he had them until I was riding in his car. But I think the thing I'm most drawn to is the way the blood rushed to his cheeks and his eyes lit up when I mentioned he was good-looking. I mean, he has to know, right? If the mirror doesn't show him, then there are plenty of girls, and even guys, who would tell him, who would be more than happy to *prove* it to him.

When I saw the car in the lot, I put two and two together and assumed it was his. In a way, I was kind of hoping it was. I imagined what it would be like to sit with someone who (hopefully) knew nothing about me or my past or the moments that led me here. It felt like a blessing. Until I was sitting in that confined space with no way out, and I couldn't ignore the way his fore-arms looked beneath his rolled-up sleeves or the way his large hands wrapped around the wheel. And I definitely couldn't ignore the way his eyes drifted from the road, lower, lower, until they focused on my legs, and guh!

It's so pointless. Stupid, really.

"No, you wouldn't, Ava," Trevor says, hopping down from the counter, and I can feel his pity from across the room. "You'd make a great girlfriend because you're a great girl. You just—"

"I just what?" I interrupt. "I just need to find a few extra hours in the week, so I can make time to hang out, go on dates... no. It wouldn't work. And I don't *want* it to, so there's that."

Trevor watches me warily. One second. Two. Then he nods, slow, as if afraid to say anything else.

I make my way over to him and place my hands on his back, pushing him toward the living room. "Will you please go and relax. Let me do something for once."

He grabs a beer from the fridge before taking my instructions.

We eat dinner at the table—just Trevor and me—and we laugh, and we talk, and we go back to who we were *before*. Before the weight of uncertainty and responsibility crashed into us, wave after wave of hopelessness and desperation. We become people again, individualized by what little hopes and dreams we have for the future. And when we're washing up at the sink once we're done eating, I look outside, see the fireflies glowing like embers searching for freedom.

"They'll be gone soon," I murmur, motioning toward them. "They're so beautiful."

Trevor takes a moment, watching them with me. Then he settles his hand on my shoulder, presses his lips to my temple. "I'm glad she was here to see them this year, Ava. I'm glad we all were."

* * *

Trevor's fallen asleep on the couch, hands on his chest as he breathes to a steady rhythm. But even with his eyes closed, muscles relaxed, his brow is bunched, as if his troubles never truly leave him. There are electrical plans scattered on the coffee table, his laptop sitting atop them. I go to close it but freeze when my gaze catches on the screen. There's a picture of his ex, Amy, with another guy's arms wrapped around her. She's smiling as if their heart-break had no history. I look over at Trevor again, at the stress lines that mar his youthful face, and my chest tightens. Heat burns behind my eyes, my nose, and I cover my mouth, so my single sob doesn't wake him.

Amy had been his girl two weeks into college, and if I ever doubted that true love existed, I'd go to them. When my fourteen-year-old self questioned life, I'd go to them. Not just one or the other. But both of them. They were a team, a fortress, a love so strong I thought nothing could break them. But *I* did. *I* broke them. I still remember listening in on Trevor's call to her—he here and she in Texas—the way he struggled to get through his words without his voice cracking. "I can't come back," he'd told her. "And I can't hold *you* back because of it."

I sat in my room that night, tear after tear, cry after cry. Hopelessness swam through my veins, pulsed through my airways.

I see the empty bottles of beer on the floor, and I fight to keep it together, to contain my emotions. To *conquer* them. Tears stream down my cheeks, and

I hold back my cries. But it's useless. I'm too far gone, and I wasn't built with the strength my mother holds. Trevor wakes, and he's quick to sit up. To notice my anguish. "Hey," he coos, his arms around me like a shield. A protector. Always. "Ava, it's okay. What happened?" I cry into his chest, tears of self-loathing soaking into his T-shirt. I can't speak; I can't say the words.

Remorse.

Regret.

Guilt.

He holds on to me—my *Knight*—and I try to remember why it was I called him. Why amid the darkest and most terrifying moment of my life, I couldn't fight my need for him, for anyone, just so I wouldn't have to go it alone. It had been a year since his father had walked out, a year of Trevor calling every other day to check in on me when he had no real reason to. And so when I look back on it—at the crimson life seeping into my hands, the way the liquid pooled on the glass layer of my phone, making it impossible to see—as if the tears weren't enough, as if the scene in front of me wasn't enough to force my eyes shut... I know I should've called 911.

But instead, I called Trevor. And I gave him no other choice but to come home and carry the burden of what should have been his father's. The difference is, Trevor stayed.

Because for Trevor, love is enough.

Love is everything.

He is the conqueror.

He is.

He is.

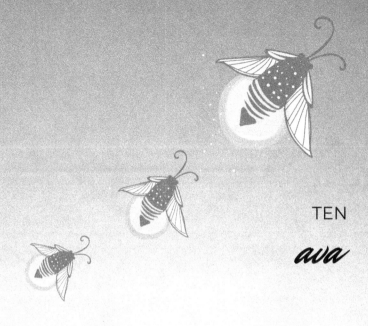

ava

IN MY DESK drawer lives a check.
    A check for six figures.
    Signed by Peter Parker.
    The sum is enough to put my mom in a treatment center full-time.
    In my mind,
    I wonder what it would be like not to have to worry as much as we do.
    In my heart,
    I try to imagine what it would feel like to *abandon* her like that.
    The check is made out to me.
    I can take care of you, Ava,
    Peter said.
    But it's our little secret.
    In my mind,
    I wonder why he didn't offer it to Trevor.
    But in my heart,
    I already know.
    In my desk drawer lives a picture.
    Me and Mom surrounded by fireflies.
    When the world is at its darkest,
    that's when the magic appears,
    my mom says.
    So, in my mind,
    I question if the check is a form of magic.
    But in my heart,
    I believe that *hope* creates the magician.

connor

I'D BEEN KILLING it during practice. Every shot, every play, every move of my feet had been perfect. I was back to the old me, or as the team saw it—a *new* me. And then *she* walked into the gym, and I forget who I am and why I'm here.

The girl is something else. Even beneath her school blazer, those knee-high socks and completely modest skirt, I could tell she was hiding things some girls go above and beyond to flaunt.

I'm staring.

"Ledger!" someone calls out a split second before a ball hits the side of my head, knocking what little sense I had right out of me.

I take a time-out and head for my water bottle.

Still staring.

Because I can't not.

"How's that going for ya?" Rhys asks, motioning to Ava as he slumps down next to me.

She's at the corner of the gym now, picking up a random backpack I didn't know was there. "Huh?"

"You got a little drool," he says, chuckling, and hands me a towel.

I wipe at my mouth because I'm too far gone.

Bending down to tie his laces, he says, "She told me you gave her a ride yesterday."

"She did?" So, she and Rhys are friends. *Noted.* I clear my throat, try not to sound too... inquisitive. "What—I mean, what else did she say about me?"

He all out laughs now, coming to a stand. Shaking his head, his gaze floats between Ava and me. His hand on my shoulder tells me *"You poor, pathetic little dude"* but his words—his words say, "She said you make her uncomfortable."

* * *

The first class I ever had at this school was psychology. After doing everything I needed at the office to register, I was late. It was only a minute, but it was enough to make my already anxious mind go into overdrive. When I walked into the room, there was only one desk free, two chairs, and so I took what was offered. A few people watched me walk through the rows, but no one said a word. It was a relief. A few minutes after that, Ava walked in. Initially, I thought she might be new, too, but I didn't see her in the office and going by how the teacher spoke, I figured she was just late.

Now, I was walking toward that same room, and I wish I were late again. Or better yet, I wish the floor would swallow me whole. Unfortunately, I can't come up with an excuse or some form of sudden chronic illness that would excuse me from attending classes for the rest of the year, so I grab the door that someone holds open for me and make my way into the room.

She's here, in her seat, a textbook in front of her, staring into the abyss. You know, *Classic-Ava*. I walk painstakingly slow, but not slow enough because I still end up next to her. My chair drags as I pull it out, causing her to glance up, then right back down.

I clear my throat, and with my voice low, I ask, "Is it okay if I sit here?"

Her eyes lock on mine. Hold. She offers a smile filled with pity and laced with what I'm sure is disgust. "Of course," she murmurs. "Why wouldn't it be?"

"I don't know," I breathe out, taking the seat. "The last thing I want to do is make you *uncomfortable.*"

A sound falls from her lips; a squeak of sorts. And she turns in her seat to the person behind us.

Rhys.

She shakes her head at him, her eyes wide.

Rhys laughs. *Fucker.*

And me? I spend the rest of the day in *Classic-Ava* mode.

TWELVE

ava

"YOUR GRADES ARE FANTASTIC, Ava. Your GPA hasn't dropped once since you started here. There are a lot of colleges that would be lucky to have you," Miss Turner says, an assortment of catalogs spread out on her desk. "UNC, Duke, NC State. Given your circumstance, I assume you'd like to stay local?"

She's only half right. I do plan on staying local; I just don't plan on furthering my education—much to Trevor's dismay.

I don't tell her this, though. I simply nod, watch the minutes tick by. I don't want to be here a second longer than I have to. I want to get to first-period psychology early enough to get a few words in with Connor, if he'll even listen to me.

"Have you thought more about where you're going to apply?"

One minute until the warning bell.

"Everywhere, anywhere," I rush out.

"Well, that's great, Ava!" She beams. "I'm glad you're—"

"I have to go," I say, cutting her off. I stand quickly. "I have a thing I need to do."

* * *

Connor's already in his seat when I walk in, his head on the desk, arms folded beneath it—a vision of hopelessness.

There's a sudden sinking in my gut. An ache so strong it has me frozen to my spot. Around me, students swarm, bumping into me with zero apologies.

My feet drag when I make my way over to him. Standing beside him, I whisper, "Hey."

Tired, tormented eyes lock on mine. One second. Two. Then he goes back to his original position.

My heart drops.

"Take a seat, Ava," Mr. McCallister says, walking into the room. "Are you with us, Connor?"

Connor sits up, grumbles under his breath, "Unfortunately."

Mr. McCallister waits for the rest of the class to settle in, and when enough silence descends, he announces, "It's your lucky day, people. My laptop has decided to die, so you'll be working on your nature versus nurture assignment, and since it's such a lovely day out, I'm going to let you partner up and work wherever you like. Within reason, of course."

A flurry of excitement fills the room. Beside me, Connor groans. "Jesus. No."

Connor silently, reluctantly, agrees to follow me outside. With his backpack in one hand, a basketball in the other, his feet drag as he tracks behind me.

I take him to the school gym.

"Here?" he asks, moving to the center circle. "You want to work *here?*"

I shrug. "I figured it's where you're most comfortable."

Dropping his bag by his feet, his eyes take in the surroundings: from the championship flags strung off the ceiling to the retired jerseys hanging on the walls. I try to make small talk. "First game of the season's in a few weeks, right?"

He eyes me sideways, a rush of air falling from his lips. I watch the way his shirt shifts beneath the muscles of his broad chest, strong shoulders, and I look away, hoping he isn't witness to the heat forming on my ears, my cheeks, my entire damn body. "So, I think we should talk about—"

"The paper," he interjects.

"—what Rhys said," I finish.

He drops the ball, sweeps it up again, his bottom lip caught between his teeth. "So, this paper..." he says, deflecting. "I've taken some notes. Hopefully, it'll be enough to give us a starting point." After reaching into his bag, he pulls out a few sheets of paper and holds them out between us.

Okay.

So.

He obviously doesn't want to deal with what happened, and I'm clearly not going to get anywhere.

I step into the circle so I can take the notes, flipping through them without actually reading a word. My mind works in overdrive as I try to come up with a way to fix things for us, *for me*. I need a way to settle my guilt. "I was thinking," I start, needing a moment to catch my breath. It's as if we're in his car again. Close. Almost *too* close. And there's no one here but us. "I was thinking..." I repeat, coming up with a plan on the fly. It's a selfish plan, one that will help me find a way to gain his forgiveness. "We should maybe put our own spin on it."

"How?" he asks, and when I look up, I catch him watching me. He averts his gaze a moment later, focuses on the ball in his hand.

"I thought we could make it more personal? Have an actual test subject rather than resources we find online so it's not the same old, same old, you know?"

He bounces the ball. Again and again. Contemplating. "You have a subject in mind?"

"You."

His eyes widen. "Me?"

I nod.

"And what exactly would that entail?"

"You have to tell me about you. Genetics versus upbringing."

He takes a step back, shaking his head. Jaw tense, a fierceness flickers in his gaze, a wall dropping down between us. It's as instant as it is intense. He closes his eyes, slowly, his dark lashes fanning across his cheeks. By the time he opens them again, all emotions have been wiped. "I wouldn't be the best subject for this," he says, his voice flat. "We should use you."

"Hell no." A giant *Fuck No*. There's no way I'm willing to reveal the details of my life.

Not yet.

Not to him.

"Well, I'm out."

"But—"

"But nothing, Ava. We're not doing this," he says, his voice firm.

"But you need the grades, right? To play, I mean. This is the perfect—"

"I said no!" His voice echoes off the walls, and he cringes at the sound. Annoyance fills his every word. "Just leave it alone."

I shrink into myself. I hate being spoken to like this. Being yelled at. "Jesus, what's your deal?" I snap, combative. "I'm just trying to get to know you here, and you're—"

"I'm what?"

"You're fighting me."

"Fine!" he barks, frustrated, and looms over me. "I can't do what you're asking because I don't know shit about my mom." His voice cracks on the last words.

My breath catches on an inhale, my stomach giving out. I lower my gaze, wishing for a damn shovel to dig a hole that I could crawl into. I stumble through my speech. "I'm so sorry, Connor. Did she, umm... did she die or...?"

"No," he breathes out. His voice softer, calmer. "I mean, I don't know. She abandoned me when I was young."

I look up again. Right into his eyes already focused on mine. "As in, she left?"

His lips part, but nothing comes out. A sharp inhale. Steady exhale. His throat moves with his loud swallow, but he doesn't break eye contact. Finally, he speaks. "As in she drove us to the airport parking lot on a hundred-degree day in the middle of July, made sure I was buckled in nice and tight in my car seat, kissed me goodbye, and walked away. She walked away, and she never came back. So no, Ava, she didn't just 'leave me.' She fucking *abandoned* me."

THIRTEEN

Connor

MY EARS FILL with the sound of the ball bouncing off the hardwood, the backboard, the rim. Again and again. Echo echo echo. My shoes scrape. Muscles in my arms, my legs, my heart burning. Sweat pools, drips down my face, but I can't stop. Won't stop. I push harder, further. It's the only way to get out of my head, to stop the memories from flooding in.

I remember looking down at my hands, at the sweat that pooled beneath the two toy cars I held on to. Lightning McQueen in my right. Sally in my left. I took them everywhere with me, even in my sleep. "You're my reason, Connor. Don't ever forget that," she said. She kissed my forehead, and I'd kept my gaze down, watching my three-year-old legs kicking back and forth.

I remember the heat.

The way the sun filtered through the open door, burning my flesh...

Right before she slammed the door shut between us.

No other words.

No warnings.

I watched her walk away, step by step until she disappeared between the rows of cars.

Minutes passed, and I started to worry.

She'd never left me before, not for that long.

I struggled to breathe.

It was so hot.

I kicked at the back of the front seat in frustration, dropping Lightning as I did.

I tried to reach for it, but my belt was on tight.

So tight.

So hot.

That's when the tears came.

I remember the way the belt cut into me when I kept reaching for the car, over and over.

I squirmed.

I screamed.

I remember how my tears felt on the palms of my hands. Warm and wet.

I remember the marks those tears left on the windows. Handprints dragged down in desperation.

I remember the pain in my chest, the ache in my throat from crying her name, over and over.

Mama! Mama! Mama!

I remember the heat.

God, I remember the heat.

Like a fire burning inside me.

I remember the thickness of the air in my throat.

The sweat in my eyes.

And I remember the exact moment my body started to shut down.

To give in.

Give up.

I remember the heaviness of my eyelids.

The weakness in my limbs.

The anguish.

The despair.

I remember those last moments.

The world as a blur.

Right before it was coated in darkness.

I'm in a daze when I come to, eyes wet and weary as I watch the ball bounce away from me and into Ava's arms. *Fuck.* I'd forgotten where I was, and worse? I'd forgotten who I was with.

I fold in on myself, exhausted, every muscle in my body screaming for reprieve.

But I'm not ready.

Not yet.

One hand on my knee to keep me upright, I extend the other. "Give me the ball, Ava."

"No."

I grind my teeth, irked beyond reason. "Not right now, okay?"

She shrugs. "Okay."

I stand taller. "So give me the damn ball."

She holds it behind her back. "Come and get it."

I'm in no fucking mood for these mind games. Shaking my head, my eyes on hers, I take several steps to close in on her. But as soon as I'm near, she throws the ball away, and the next thing I know, her arms are wrapped tightly around me, her nose to my chest. I feel the heat of her breath against me, the way my shirt stretches across my torso from the strength of her hold.

"I'm so sorry, Connor," she whispers, and everything inside me stills.

Breaks.

Shatters.

My inhale is shaky. My exhale the same. I close my eyes, take in the moment. Bask in it. If only for a second. "What's this for?" I ask.

She looks up at me, liquid sorrow coating her eyes. "It just looked like you needed it."

I reach up and palm the back of her head, hold her to me. Because of all the things I hoped could heal the memories of my past, the human touch and a single moment of compassion weren't it. Maybe it was because it was never offered to me before. Or maybe it's because it's coming from her.

When I feel her start to pull away, I bring her closer. Hold her tighter. Because her touch...

...her touch is like fire.

Only this time,

I don't mind the burn.

FOURTEEN

Connor

DAD GREETS me at the door when I get home. It's been a solid two weeks since we've seen each other in more than just passing. By the time I'd get back from school, he'd be asleep, and by the time he'd leave for work, I'd be getting ready for bed. "Can I help you?" he asks, hand pressed to my chest to stop me from going inside.

"What?" Confusion clouds my mind.

"Do I know you? I mean, you *look* like my son, but it's been so long I can't be sure."

Chuckling, I swat his hand away and force my way inside. "Haha. You became a comedian overnight." I start for my room.

"I ordered pizza," he calls out after me.

"Can't wait."

In my room, I drop my bag and ball on the bed, dock my phone on the speakers and hit play on Kendrick Lamar. In my mind, I'm at Toyota Arena wearing number 13, James Harden, and I've just sunk a killer fadeaway against the Nets. In the real game, Harden walked away with one hand out pretending to hold a bowl, the other holding a utensil to mimic stirring the pot—his signature celebration. In my bedroom, I do the same while the imaginary crowd chants my name, *Led-ger! Led-ger! Led-ger!* I nod, hold my hand to my ear to encourage them. *Louder! Louder! Louder!* My eyes close, and I take in the moment, remember the feel of Ava's body against me. The way her eyes locked on mine. *Connor! Connor! Connor!*

A stupid grin sweeps my entire face.

"Connor!"

My eyes snap open. Dad's at my door, his hand on the knob. He eyes me sideways, looking from me, to my speakers, and back again. Shaking my head, I move to the speakers and switch off the music.

Dad says, "Pizza's here."

I walk past him and toward the kitchen.

"I take it you had a good day," he muses.

I shrug. "Same old." Then I ask, only slightly embarrassed, "How much did you see?"

"Enough to know you'll never be able to grow a beard as majestic as Harden's."

I rub my chin, and for a split second, I wonder if Ava likes beards. "I could grow a beard."

"So..." Dad says, settling in the chair opposite me.

I pick up a slice of pizza, take half of it in one bite. "So?" I mumble around a mouthful of food.

He throws a napkin toward me. "So, tell me everything. We haven't had a real conversation since school started. How are the classes?"

I swallow. "Good."

"And the team?"

"Also good."

"Welp. I'm glad we had this talk," he jokes, standing. He opens the fridge, eyeing the drink selection. I watch his every move, waiting for the right time to bring up what went down today. Besides the people who were there that day and my dad's parents, no one else knows what happened to me. Until Ava. I figure I should ease into it, so I say, "So, I met a girl..."

His shoulders tense. "Oh yeah?" he says, refusing to turn to me.

"Yeah," I edge. "She's uh... she's in my psych class. We're working on a paper together."

He moves again, and just when I think I can proceed, he asks, "Psych, huh? What's that like?"

I ignore his question, sit higher in my chair. "Her name's Ava."

"Right." He turns to me now, his eyes trained on the floor. "Just remember we need to keep focused on the end game, Connor."

Irritation fills the emptiness inside me. "*We?*"

"You," he sighs out. "I mean *you*."

Puffing out a breath, I slump in my chair, throw the napkin in the almost full pizza box. I'm frustrated. It's obvious. And the truth is, I've *tried* to under-stand why he's like this. Why he seems to have a distaste for *all* women. In all the years post-Mom, I've never known him to date, or even have a random hook-up. I guess, in a way, I get it. The one woman he loved enough to have his child left, abandoned not just me, but him, too. Only he wasn't there. What happened to me didn't happen to him. I'm the one who should have his level of hatred and distrust. Because in truth, as much as I hate to think about it, she only *left* him. But me? Me she wanted *dead*. And that's a hard fucking pill to swallow no matter how I try to spin it. I inhale deeply and swallow all those thoughts. Bury them deep inside me. Like always. "It doesn't matter," I say, mask back in place. "I'm pretty sure she's not interested in me."

Dad nods. "That's probably for the best."

"Yeah." I stand, done. "Thanks for the pizza... and the talk, I guess." I start to leave.

"Connor," he calls after me.

"It's fine."

* * *

I knew going into this year that the schoolwork would be hard. I thought I was prepared. I was wrong. The workload is insane, which is okay for now, but once the season starts, I'll probably have to give up sleep. It's my only option. Most of my free nights I split between studying game tapes, memorizing plays, and doing homework. But tonight, I can't seem to focus on anything. Well, anything besides the girl who appears to have infiltrated my mind. I know it's wrong to be this infatuated, and I'm not one to be making moves on a girl. And *I won't*, I assure myself.

Unless...

Sitting at my desk, I reach into my bag and pull out the team folder. The first page has a list of numbers, including the coaching staff and all the players. My finger moves down the page until I find the one I want. I stare at the name, flip my phone in my hand. Then I stand. Pace. Convince myself that *surely* even James Harden had moments like these growing up.

I type out a text.

> Connor: Hey.

> Rhys: Who's this?

> Connor: Connor.

> Rhys: Hey man, what's up?

I stop pacing.
Start again.
Drop my phone on the bed.

Pick it up.
Suck it up.

> Connor: Do you have Ava's number? I need to talk to her about the psych paper.

Seconds pass.
Then minutes.
Fricken *eons.*
When he finally responds, he has her number attached and the words:

> Rhys: Remember: whatever she does, don't let it affect you. And whatever you do, don't fucking hurt her.

> Connor: Thanks... I guess?

I go back to pacing. Preparing—*out loud*—the first message I'll send. "Hey... Hi, it's Connor... Hey, it's me, Connor... Yo... Yo, it's Connor from school..."

Dad opens my door without knocking, interrupting my absurdity. "You okay?"

"Yeah."

He taps on the door. "I'm heading out..." he trails off, the tension from earlier hanging between us.

"Okay."

* * *

> Connor: Hey, it's Connor. From psych. I had an idea about the paper.

The swiftness of her response has my stomach flipping.

> Ava: Hi Connor from psych :) What's your idea?

> Connor: I think I've come up with a subject that might set us apart.

> Ava: Go on.

> Connor: Serial Killers.

> Ava: Dude

Connor: No? Too much? Too dark?

Ava: It's fucking genius. I'm obsessed with true crime.

Connor: Me too! You should check out some podcasts. I listen to them on the way to and from school.

Ava: Shut up! Me too. Casefile is my favorite.

Connor: Mine too! The narrator...

Ava: So intense.

Connor: So good.

Ava: Lol

Connor: Cool.

Ava: Cool.

Connor: So.

Ava: So...

Connor: How are you?

Ava: Oh, you know, living the dream.

Connor: Money.

Ava: Money?

Connor: I don't know. I'm trying really hard to sound cool here.

Ava: lol. What are you doing?

Connor: Homework.

Ava: Want me to let you go?

Connor: Hell no.

Connor: Wait.

Connor: Are you busy?

Ava: Not at all. I was doing the same. Could use the break.

Connor: Yeah?

Ava: Yeah.

Connor: So.

Ava: So.

Connor: We're nailing this whole conversation thing.

Ava: I know, right? It's... dare I say... money.

Connor: Are you teasing me?

Ava: A little. Don't hate.

Connor: I couldn't if I tried.

Ava: Yeah? Because for a minute there, I'm pretty sure you did.

Connor: When?

Ava: The whole Rhys thing?

Connor: ...

Ava: About how you make me uncomfortable...

Connor: Ohhhh! You mean *that* thing.

Ava: ...

Connor: So what exactly did you mean by that?

Ava: You don't want to know.

Connor: I mean... I asked, right?

The three dots on the screen appear, disappear. Again and again. My anxiety builds. And builds. To the point of—

Ava: So these serial killers...

Shaking my head, I smile at her response.

Connor: What's your middle name, Ava?

Ava: I have two. Elizabeth Diana.

Connor: Like, the Royal family?

Ava: lol. Yes. My mom was a little obsessed. What about you, Connor? What's your middle name?

Connor: Jordan.

Ava: As in Michael? Lol. Did you have your whole life planned out before you were even born?

Connor: I'd love to say yes, but no. Just a fluke, I guess.

Ava: Got it.

Connor: Yep.

Ava: So...

Connor: So...

Ava: I should probably get back to this homework.

Connor: yeah, I should probably do the same.

Ava: See you at school?

Connor: Yep.

I drop my phone in my desk drawer, slam it shut. Keep it away from temptation. Because sending her useless, one-word texts is the second-best time I've had since I moved here. The best was when she was riding shotgun in my car.

I try to eat.

Try to study.

Try to sleep.

Nothing flies.

Hours pass, and I'm still wide awake, tossing and turning when my phone goes off in my drawer.

A text.

I stare in the general direction of it. It might be Dad, but he calls, not messages.

It goes off again.

And again.

Hope fills my chest—*please be Ava*—and I reach for it without getting out of bed.

Ava: Hey, I hope this doesn't wake you.

Ava: I've just been thinking about you… about what you told me today. And I have a question but feel free not to answer.

Ava: I was just curious. Do you remember any of it… what happened to you?

My response is swift. Easy to formulate. Because I give her the same answer I've given everyone before.

Connor: Not a damn thing.

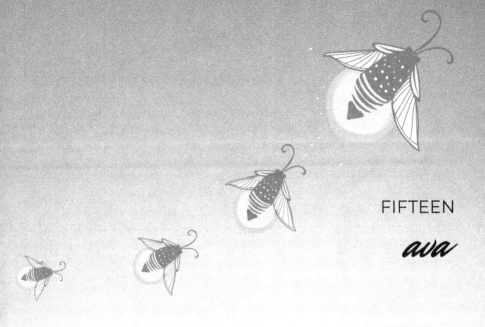

FOUR THIRTY A.M. comes around quick.

After a hurried shower, I check over the notes that Krystal, Mom's in-home caretaker, had provided. She's here Monday through Friday, from 7 a.m. until I get home from school. On the weekends, it's just Trevor and me. Or just me, most of the time. Trevor doesn't like to leave me alone with her so much, but he works, and now and then I force him to go out and live a normal twenty-two-year-old life.

We're so lucky he was able to pick up the family business when his dad left, and it only took him a couple of months to get certified. If he'd let me, I'd have dropped out of school and worked, too, but for him, that wasn't an option. For him, it was vital that we look further into my future than just tomorrow.

Breakfast is already on the table when Mom appears from her bedroom at 5 a.m. sharp. No alarm clock needed. Years in the military can do that. "Mornin'," she greets, kissing me on the cheek. She adjusts the hood of her robe to hide most of her battle scars as she takes a seat at the kitchen table.

"Morning, Mama. Did you sleep well?" I ask, even though I already know the answer. No screams in the night mean no flashbacks or memories of her real-life nightmares, and I'm grateful for that always, but last night especially because I couldn't sleep.

My mind was too inundated with thoughts of Connor.

And me.

Not Connor and me.

At least not like that.

But, I'd thought about him a lot, all day and night, and I kept replaying what he'd told me.

I wondered if everyone remembered traumatic experiences the way I do. Vivid and powerful and intense. As if I were reliving the moment again and again. Maybe he was too young. Or maybe he blocked it out completely. Sometimes I want to ask my mom if she remembers any of it, but I'm too afraid of her answer.

Sometimes, I'm afraid of *her*.

"I slept like a baby," she says, a slice of toast halfway to her mouth. She watches me watching her and places the bread back down. Using her one good arm, she scoots back in the chair and comes to a stand. "Ava?" she asks, her tone flat.

I swallow, apprehensive of her next move. She stops in front of me, her eyes shuffling between each of mine. "Ma?" I whisper.

Her head tilts.

I dig my heels into the floor, my muscles taut.

Ready.

Waiting.

Of all the injuries and affects her "accident" caused, the toughest ones to deal with are the ones no one sees. And while this entire town was running scared from her physical trauma, not one of them ever thought about the invisible scars. PTSD, reassimilation, agoraphobia, and short-term memory loss to name a few. Sometimes I worry that she'll wake up one day and have no idea who I am, that she'll forget about me altogether.

Mom smiles, a vision that has me exhaling with relief and warming me from the inside out. "You look so exhausted," she says, holding my face in her hand. "But you're still so damn beautiful, Ava."

Please, please don't ever forget me.

CONNOR

The sun is just beginning to rise when I finish my weekly six-mile run. Out of breath, I slow to a jog as I turn into my cul-de-sac and take in my surroundings. All the houses on the street are the same, but different in their own right. All in various levels of upkeep. Ours is at the end, one of the more *modest* ones on the block, a simple cottage style with a centered door, a window on each side, and a rotting porch Dad and I plan to fix sooner rather than later.

I spot Trevor's truck in front of his house, the *Knight Electrical* sticker on the side a giveaway. I should follow through on Dad's invitation to have him over for dinner, but when I check the time, it's too damn early to be knocking on doors. I go back to the house, shower, then sit on the couch with *Forensic*

Files on in the background. An hour passes, and all I've done is read through my text conversation with Ava too many times to count.

AVA

One of the more apparent effects of Mom's injuries, besides the physical, is dysarthria. She's still wholly understandable, at least to me, but the trauma to her brain left her with a slight slur and slowed speech. The doctors said that her mind processes everything normally, but the signal from her brain to her mouth is just a little more... crooked.

Mom works on pronouncing the words on her flashcards Krystal had prepared while I start on the meal prep for the upcoming week. She's improved so much since we started the speech therapy, but I can tell how frustrating it is for her. Not only is she relearning a skill she attained while still in diapers, but she has to do it in front of *me*, and I think that's the hardest part for her. For her, being my mother was always the priority. Everything else came second—even the Marines. But for me, she'll always be the woman who held me through my first knee scrape, my first loss of friendship, my first heartbreak. She'll always be the one to teach and guide me with more patience than I deserve. The least I could do is be the same for her.

CONNOR

"Oh, my God, I'm so fucking bored," I whisper, throwing my ball in the air for the fiftieth time. On my back, in my bed, I blindly reach for my phone under the pillow.

> Connor: Yo, are there any pick-up games I can walk in on?

It takes a good ten minutes for him to respond.

> Rhys: Yeah, man. The team's got one going right now.

I balk at his response, read the text again and again.

> Rhys: You want in?

> Connor: The team?? Thanks for the invite.

> Rhys: Want a spoon?

> Connor: What?

Rhys: For your cry-about-it soup?

Connor: Whatever

Rhys: It was a joke. Seriously, you want in?

Connor: I'm good.

AVA

My phone vibrates in my pocket, and I'm quick to check it. I try to hide my smile when I see his name.

Connor: Jeffrey Dahmer, Ted Bundy, Richard Ramirez.

Ava: I'll take men I'd actually be caught *dead* with for two-hundred please, Alex.

Connor: Ah. So you're not just a pretty face. You got jokes, too.

My stupid heart does a stupid pitter-patter, and I bite down on my lip so my grin doesn't split my face in two.

Ava: You think I'm pretty?

Connor: Of course I do. But so would Ted Bundy so...

Ava: I think we change Richard Ramirez for Blanche Tyler Moore.

Connor: Who's that?

Ava: She was a serial killer in the early 1900s who met her victims via newspaper (aka text messages). She promised them love (told them they were good-looking), then when they came to see her (psych class paper), she'd poison them, chop them up into pieces and bury them on her farm. Then she'd take whatever life insurance and money they had.

Connor: Ha! Joke's on you! I have no money :(

I cover my mouth, stifle my laugh.

Ava: What are you doing on this fine day, Connor?

Connor: I have a multitude of dates.

Ava: Do you now?

Connor: Yep. First with my basketball, then with my laptop, and later, if I'm feeling frisky, with some leftover pizza. So, yeah. Not much. You?

Ava: About the same.

Connor: You play basketball?

Ava: Not even close. I can throw a mean spiral, though.

Connor: You're into football?

Ava: It's a family thing. I don't have a choice.

Connor: Right.

"You got that list for me?" Trevor asks, hand out waiting.

Dropping my phone, I quickly fish the list from my pocket and hand it to him.

"What's with your face?"

I touch my cheeks with the back of my hand. *Fire.*

Trevor smirks. "Are you texting *some guy from school?*"

"What guy from school?" Mom asks from her spot on the couch.

I look out the window. "It's such a beautiful day outside..." I deflect, even though it's true. The sun's out, leaves are starting to turn orange. If only I could leave...

"This guy who—" Trevor starts.

But I interrupt, "Don't skimp on my chocolate. I've got cramps."

"Dammit, Ava, I don't need to know this shit," he grunts, recoiling away from me as if he'll catch The Menstruation.

"It's such a heavy flow!" I yell after him.

He slams the front door shut.

I laugh harder.

Mom says, "Don't you think that boy goes through enough?"

I shrug. "I have to get my kicks where I can." Then I turn to her, my smile fading. "You think you might want to try wearing your prosthetic today? Just for a little bit?"

"Not today, Ava."

"But Krystal—"

"No." She turns away from me, her facial scars in full view. "We've been through this before—"

"But—"

"But *nothing.* It's not growing back, so there's no point in pretending like something's there when it's not!" She's quick to stand and march to her room.

Before kicking the door shut, she mumbles, "I have one good arm; it's all I need."

CONNOR

Of all the things my dad and I are, handymen are not it. I searched the entire house and garage for a measuring tape and came up empty-handed. Now I'm on the porch measuring the fucker with a 12-inch ruler. A bunch of kids rides past on their bikes, no older than ten, and I watch them, feeling a pang of childish jealousy. They dump their bikes and start throwing a football around. I check for Trevor's truck, but it's not there. When I'm done with the measuring, I head back inside, get on YouTube and spend the next hour watching old men build porches from scratch. I thought we'd just have to replace the top; turns out, it could be the foundation, which means getting under there. With a grunt, I get my ass back up and out but freeze when I see the kids messing with Trevor's house. Rolls of toilet paper in each of their hands, they make quick work of stringing that shit all over the front chain-link fence, giggling maniacally at their masterpiece.

"Hey!" I shout, at the same time Trevor's truck pulls up to the curb, brakes screeching.

He hops out. "Get the hell out of here!" he yells, chasing after them at a speed much slower than I know he's capable of.

The boys bolt to their bikes, cursing, and I take the steps down to meet him on the sidewalk.

"What the hell was that about?" I ask, helping him remove the toilet paper.

Trevor shakes his head. "Just dumb kids being kids," he murmurs, pulling on a longer piece. I watch his face, the tension in his jaw, the frustration in his brows. "What's been going on? How are you settling in at St. Luke's?"

"As well as can be expected." I hand him all the trash I've collected. "You know anywhere good to eat around here?"

"Yeah." He balls up all the toilet paper with both hands. "Best place on a Saturday is the sports park. They have a bunch of food trucks. Take your pick."

"Sports park?"

"Yeah, there are batting cages, basketball courts, sometimes they put up the rock-climbing thing. It's pretty cool. You should check it out."

Nodding, I push away my awkwardness and ask, "You want to come with?"

His eyes widen, and he offers a crooked grin. "Yeah?"

I shrug. "On me."

Pointing to his truck, he says, "Let me just bring in the groceries." He hands me the toilet paper. "Take care of that for me?"

"Got it."

He gets a few bags from his truck while I get rid of the trash.

When I get back to the sidewalk, I notice a note stuck on his mailbox, no doubt put there by the same kids—*Insane Asylum*. I look at the house again. The blinds are open, but the sheer curtains stop me from seeing much else.

When Trevor comes out, he notices what I'm looking at and rips it off before pocketing it.

"What's that about?" I ask.

"Like I said, dumb kids..."

The sports park is insane, and I've dubbed it my new playground. And Trevor? He's a cool dude. I would even consider him a friend. I learned that he lives with his stepmom and sister and that he used to play college football but blew out his knee and gave up on it. I also learned (the hard way) that Trevor is a natural-born athlete. Put a ball or a bat in his hand, and it's like he was specifically built for it. He even gave me a hard time on the court, almost put me to shame until I realized I was taking it a lot more casually than he was. I amped up my game, gave it a hundred, and he assured me I'd have no problems getting into a D1 school, giving me the confidence I'd been struggling to find.

By the time I drive us back home, the sun's already beginning to set. I would have stayed longer if Trevor didn't have to get back. Hell, I would've stayed all damn night. "Thanks for hanging out," I tell him, standing on the sidewalk. "It hasn't been the easiest making friends, you know?"

He settles with his back against his fence, his hands in his pockets. "It'll get better. You're a good kid with a good head on you." He glances toward his house. "Right now, your team probably sees you as a threat because you're good, Connor. Like, *really* good. And people... people fear what they don't know."

AVA

> Ava: Sleeping?

Connor: It's, like, 9:30. Lol

> Ava: Hey, I don't know. Maybe playing with your balls all day got you tired.

Connor: Dirty girl.

Connor: I like it.

Connor: What's up?

Ava: Nothing, just researching these serial killers. It's a little depressing.

Connor: I know. I had to stop after a while, too. It's kind of messed up that we're so intrigued by it all.

Ava: Because people fear what they don't know.

Connor: You're the second person to tell me that today.

Ava: Really? Strange. But I think that's why it's so intriguing, right? The more we know, the less afraid we are of it all.

Connor: That makes sense. No wonder you're taking this class.

Ava: Why are you?

Connor: Not gonna lie, I thought it would be easy. Why are you taking it?

Ava: I think it might be something I'll want to get into more when I'm older. Not necessarily a career, but... I don't know. It would be nice if I could help turn someone's bad day into just a bad moment.

Connor: That's... that's a really great way to look at things, Ava. For real.

Ava: Also because the human mind intrigues me. Makes me curious...

Connor: Uh oh. Why do I feel like those ellipses are a segue to something else... about me?

Ava: Because they might be...

My eyes widen when Connor's name flashes on the screen. I clear my throat, sit up in bed. "Hello?"

"I figured it was easier to talk than text." His voice... I never really paid attention to it before, but now that I hear it, and it's all that I hear... holy shit. Deep and smooth and so intense... he could easily host a podcast, and I'd listen to it regardless of the topic.

"Ava? You there?"

"Yeah." I swallow. "Yeah, I'm here."

The speaker distorts with his light chuckle. "So what's up? What about me has your curiosity piqued?"

I pick at the blanket covering my thighs and stare at the wall opposite me, trying to find the courage, the words... "It's about what happened to you."

A loud sigh from his end. "Yeah, I figured. I mean, *I hoped* it wasn't that, but here we are."

"Do you not like talking about it?" I ask.

"It's not that I don't *like* it, so much as... it's not really something I've shared with anyone besides professionals, you know?"

"Wait. I'm the first real person you've told?"

"Well, yeah. I guess."

"But why—"

"I don't know, Ava," he says through an exhale. "It just kind of came out in frustration."

"Because I pushed you?"

"A little."

"I'm sorry."

"It's okay."

Moments pass, neither of us saying a word. I listen to him breathe, and I wonder if he's doing the same.

Finally, he says, "I don't know what happened to her if that's what you're wondering."

It was *exactly* what I was wondering.

He adds, "There was no evidence she got on a plane, at least under her name. And there's been no evidence of her existence since."

"Do you—" I start, my voice cracking with emotion. "Do you remember when you stopped looking for her?"

"It happened when I was three. The last time my dad ever mentioned anything about it, I was in third grade. That was probably when we stopped looking. But looking and *hoping* are two very different things."

I want to ask him when he stopped hoping, but I'm almost afraid of the answer. I get through each day searching for hope, so the idea of losing it the way he has...

"Connor?" I whisper.

"Yeah?"

"I just wanted to tell you that I'm sorry."

"For what?"

"For so many things. But mainly... I'm sorry about what happened to you. About *how* it happened, and what that must've felt like. I think, as kids, all we truly need are our parents, and your mom—I think I feel the sorriest for your mom... because she missed out on you."

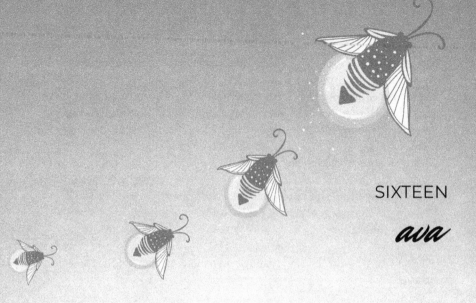

ava

"WHERE THE HELL IS MY WALLET?" Trevor's walking around the house as if we have all the time in the world.

"Did you check your pants pocket from the last time you remember having it?" Krystal offers.

"I don't even know when I had it last!" he grumbles.

I put my hand on the doorknob, twist. "Hurry up!"

"Ava," Mom scolds. "Give him a minute."

Trevor walks out of his room with three different pairs of pants, patting down each pocket.

"I'm going to be so late," I mumble.

Now Trevor's looking behind the TV because *of course* it's going to be there. "Why do you have to get to school so early, anyway?"

"Because *someone*," I say, glaring at him, "made me see the school shrink."

"Ava," Krystal admonishes. "We don't use that term."

"Sorry." I lower my gaze, my voice. "I didn't mean that."

"Where the hell is it!" Trevor utters.

"I'll be outside," I announce to whoever is listening. I open the door.

Freeze.

On my doorstep is Connor, one hand raised, ready to knock.

"Connor?" I shriek.

"Ava?" He looks as confused as I feel.

"What—" My voice is too high, too loud. My pulse thumps wildly, beating on my eardrums. I try again. "What are you doing here?"

Trevor shoves me to the side.

Connor lifts Trevor's wallet, but his eyes are glued to me.

"Thank you," Trevor says, relieved as he grabs for it. "I've been looking all morning."

"You left it in my car," Connor tells him. To me, he asks, "What are *you* doing here?"

I say, "I live here."

Trevor laughs. "I'd introduce you both, but it seems like you've already met."

"Wait," replies Connor, his feet planted on our porch. "You *live* here?"

Now Trevor's pushing me out the door as if he's the one in a rush. I stop inches short of slamming into Connor, while Trevor shuts the door behind him.

I'm practically sniffing Connor's shirt; I'm *that* close to him.

"I told you I lived with my sister," Trevor says, moving past us and down the porch steps.

I ask, "How do you know each other?"

Trevor answers, "I told you about him, no? He just moved in next door."

He told me we had new neighbors. He didn't mention him by name or give *any* other information.

"Your *sister*?" Connor asks, confusion evident in his tone. "But you're..." he trails off.

Trevor quirks an eyebrow, holding back a smile before saying, "Black?"

Connor's cheeks flush red.

"Stepsister," Trevor and I respond at the same time.

"Oh."

We all three make our way down the driveway.

"Hey," Trevor says, turning back to us. "Do me a favor? Drive her to school? I might be able to grab a decent breakfast before work."

"Sure," says Connor.

I reply, trying to get out of it, "No, wait." Because the last time I was in the confines of Connor's car I almost lost all my senses. "His car..." I get stuck for words and idiotically come up with: "His car *smells*..." But it comes out a question, and I wish I could rewind time, or I don't know, disappear into thin air.

"My car does *not* smell," Connor says defensively.

"I'm sorry, I don't know why I said that," I admit. "It doesn't."

Trevor's eyes narrow. "How do you know what his car smells like?" Then his face lights up with a stupid shit-eating grin. "Wait, is Connor *the* Some Guy From School?"

"Trevor!" I screech. "Shut. Up!"

Trevor laughs, his head thrown back as he opens the door of his truck. "Go easy on her," he tells Connor. "She's on her period. Apparently, it's a heavy flow."

I die.

Right there.

On my driveway.

Dead.

* * *

The first thing Connor does when we get into his car is reach for his gym bag in the back and spray deodorant *everywhere*. I die my second death of embarrassment and cover my face with my hands. "Sorry. Your car doesn't smell!" I laugh out.

"Uh huh. Sure," he responds. He's smiling, though, eyeing me sideways as he starts the car. Then he coughs, waves a hand in front of his face, the deodorant getting to him. He winds down the window. I try to do the same. "Yours doesn't work," he says, clearly proud of himself. He sprays the can directly on me.

"Connor!" I squeal.

He does it again. "Sucks to be you."

Another spray.

I attempt to shield myself, but it's useless. "I said I was sorry!"

His chuckle reverberates throughout my entire body. "Okay," he says, dropping the can on his lap. He offers me his pinky, giving me the same deep-dimpled smile that had me losing my mind the first time I saw it. "Truce?"

"Truce," I respond, linking my finger with his. His touch is warm, soft. I'm almost tempted to take his entire hand and hold it in mine. But that... that would be crazy. Right? Right.

We stop at a red light, and he turns to me. "I researched that Blanch Tyler what's-her-face."

"Moore."

"Yeah, her. Man, she's..."

"My hero."

"Your *hero*?" he asks, incredulous.

"I don't know. There's something about having that level of control over men that makes me..."

"Insane?" he finishes, his back pressed against the door, as if afraid of me.

His reaction makes me giggle.

And the spray of deodorant makes me stop. "You called a truce!"

The light turns green, and we're moving again. "I value my life more than a truce," he murmurs, and resprays me.

I reach across the car to grab his forearm, but he's too strong, and he damn well knows it. "Give me that stupid thing!"

"Ava, you're going to make me veer off the fucking road," he laughs.

"No, *you* are. Give it!" I can't stop laughing.

"Fine," he says, handing it over.

I throw it out his open window.

He hits the brakes so fast my seatbelt catches. Then he turns to me with a seriousness that has me clamping my lips together to stop from busting out a cackle. "That's littering, Miss Diaz." He motions his head outside. "Off you go."

He has a point. I roll my eyes but open the door. There are no other cars on the road, thank God, and so I quickly find the can, pick it up, and start back for his car, gripping the can tight. No way I'm letting him have it again. I place my hand on the handle, but the car moves forward a few feet. "Are you serious?" I yell, jogging forward to keep up. I reach for the handle again. He drives off again. This time farther. "Connor!" I can hear him laughing, see him eyeing me in the rearview. This happens three more times, his laughter getting louder, and mine becoming more uncontrollable. It's been years, *years* since I've felt this way. Laughed this hard. Felt this free.

I don't bother moving when he does it again. Instead, I stand still, my hands on my hips, my foot tapping. "I don't mind walking," I shout. A lie. Fuck walking. I'd sooner call Trevor to pick me up.

The car roars to life, and just when I think he's going to bail, I see him reach across the car to open the door for me. "Truce," he yells.

"Your truces mean nothing!" I shout back.

"Triple truce!" he counters.

I walk toward the car slowly, anticipating his next move. When I get to the open door, I see him watching me, his head dipped, his bottom lip between his teeth. I gracelessly sit and quickly shut the door, deodorant still in my hand.

"You're an asshole," I say playfully, spraying him with his chosen weapon.

He chuckles, starts driving again. "What can I say? I like to watch you run."

* * *

It turns out Connor comes to school this time on Mondays because he has a short practice. I tell him the truth about why I do, to see Miss Turner. He simply nods. When I ask if he's curious as to *why* I was seeing her, he shrugs, says, "I mean, it's pretty obvious you're a sociopath."

I spray his entire body.

He laughs it off, cranks his window up, and breathes it in as if it's fresh air.

If anyone's a sociopath here, it's him.

* * *

Connor and I walk together to Miss Turner's office, as it's on the way to the gym. "Thanks for the ride," I say, my hand on the doorknob. I twist. Push. Nothing happens. Connor laughs, peels off a note stuck on the office window.

Miss Turner is ill. No sessions today.

"Seriously?" I groan, slamming my open hand on the door. And because I'm an idiot, I try the door again, my forehead touching the timber. "Doesn't she know about texts or emails?"

Connor says, sticking the note back up, "Yeah, you sure seem like you could've used that extra hour to sleep in, *cranky*."

I narrow my eyes at him, backhand his brick wall of a stomach. "Go to your stupid practice."

He feigns hurt, only for a second, before asking, "What are you going to do?"

"Sit in the stands and shout *boo* every time the ball comes near you."

Laughing, he says, "Why are you so mean to me?"

I hasten my steps to keep up with him. "Defense mechanism."

"For what?" he asks.

To stop me from falling for you, stupid.

I shrug. "I don't know."

CONNOR

Ava comes through on her word. She sits front row center, in the gym stands. And as promised, the second a ball is in my hand, she shouts, "Boo!" Which garners looks from the other players, coaches, and the few spectators crazy enough to watch a half-hour practice session first thing Monday morning.

I shake my head at her, but she simply raises her eyebrows, a smirk on her lips, lips I'd love to—

"Ledger!" Coach Sykes yells. "This isn't a teen soap opera. Get to work."

"Boo, Ledger!" Ava shouts, and now she's laughing, silently, but I know it's there because I can see her shoulders shaking with the force of it. I'm too busy watching her that I don't even notice Coach Sykes approaching me until the ball slams against my chest.

Ava laughs harder.

"You get one," I tell her and decide that if she's here to watch me, then I may as well give her a show.

The practice is nothing more than basic drills. But when the coach asks for suicides, I'm the first on the line. When he wants to work on ball handling, I'm using two balls, behind the back, reverse, between the knees, ankle breakers. When he asks for lay-ups, I'm power dunking—one after another.

"Damn, Ledger! Where the fuck have you been hiding?" Rhys shouts.

"Quit showing off!" Mitch yells. "We get it; you're good."

"He's better than good," Coach Sykes retorts. "In fact, every practice I want you all to come in with the same amount of power and precision that Ledger has! Got it?"

I throw Ava a smirk.

She gives me the finger.

* * *

Psychology may be my favorite subject in the history of forever. Scratch that. *Ava* is my favorite subject. Sitting side by side in class waiting for the teacher to arrive, she asks me questions:

Where am I from?

Why did I move here?

Who do I live with?

What's my favorite murder?

I answer each one with truth, minus the murder one because I don't even know *how* to answer it. Mitch walks past us, sniffing the air. "What the hell is that smell?"

We burst out in childish giggles. She says to me, "You were not *at all* impressive this morning. I just want you to know that in case you think otherwise. In fact, you pretty much sucked."

Mr. McCallister enters the classroom saying, "You may spend the first ten minutes of class discussing your partner paper. Use that time wisely."

Ava and I turn to each other at the same time, our knees knocking painfully. Ava groans, reaching for her knee, but I beat her to it, grimacing. I rub at the spot I think I hit, while we both apologize. Dipping my head closer to hers, I whisper, "So I worked on the outline like we said."

She moves closer again. So close I can feel the heat of her cheek on mine. "Why are we whispering?"

"Because I don't want anyone to hear our plan and steal it."

"Got it."

"Hey, Coach said you have to be at every game from now on. Says you're my lucky charm."

Ava pulls back to look at my face, then rolls her eyes. She says, her voice still low, "You're going to need it if you don't take your hand off my leg."

It's not as if I'd forgotten it was there. I was just hoping *she* wouldn't notice. Or if she did, maybe she wouldn't mind. With a confidence only she brings out of me, I squeeze her knee, tell her, "I'm just trying to give you an *actual* reason."

"For what?"

"To say I make you uncomfortable."

"Oh, I've come to terms with the fact that you're a creep."

"Oh yeah?" I laugh.

She nods, brings her head closer again, our faces almost touching.

I ask, "You want creepy?"

"Oh, no," she backpedals.

If she wants to play, I'm here for it. "Your eyes are possibly the prettiest things I've ever seen." And it's the truth. Whenever I picture her in my mind, her eyes are the first things I see.

I hear her swallow, loud, and I know she's feeling *something*. When she pulls away, her eyes search mine, her cheeks flushed. My heart is racing, my mind spinning. Because never in my life have I wanted a girl more than I want her. And not even in the physical sense. But just talking to her or being around her. To feel *this* all day, every day. It feels like my soul's on fire, and she's holding the match. "Yeah?" she starts, a threatening lilt to her tone. She opens her mouth. Closes it. Opens it again. Finally, she stutters, "Well... well, your smile could melt panties." The second the words are out of her mouth, her eyes widen, and she covers her face. I think she mumbles, "Too far, Ava. Too fucking far." But I can't be sure.

I finally remove my hand from her knee so that I can tug at her wrists and uncover her face. And then I smile my—and I quote—panty-melting smile, just for her.

She shoves my face away with her entire palm. "Stop."

"Psst!" Rhys hisses from behind us.

We both turn to him.

He says, "Quit eye-fucking each other. It's making *me* uncomfortable."

I rip off a sheet of paper from my notebook and draw a large spoon, then hand it to him, my smile widening. "For your cry-about-it soup."

SEVENTEEN

Connor

"SO, HOW'S SCHOOL?" Dad asks.

"Good."

"And the team?"

"Also, good."

Dad looks up from his meal and drops his knife and fork on the plate. "I feel like we have this same conversation every day."

"Because we do," I murmur. "But I don't know what else to tell you."

"Well, I don't know, Connor," he says, running his hands through his hair. "Why don't we talk about something else then? I feel like... I don't know. Ever since we moved here, we've become so disconnected."

Shrugging, I take a sip of my soda. "Remember that girl I told you about?"

Dad inhales, long and slow, and I already know what's coming next. "Don't let a girl distract you from—"

I rub at my eyes, frustrated, cutting him off.

"Connor, this is serious," he says.

"I know, Dad. I *know* how serious this is. I'm the one who feels the pressure of it," I rush out, then take a calming breath and regroup my thoughts. "But you want to sit here and have a non-mundane conversation with me; this is what I want to talk about. This is what's happening in my life right now. This is what I *want* to tell my dad. I'm seventeen, and I'm interested in a girl. And I'm allowed to be. But my wanting to spend time with someone doesn't take away from my other priorities. I know how important *the end game* is. For both of us."

Dad's silent a moment, his heavy breaths filling the small room. Finally, he nods, his eyes locked on mine. "You're right," he sighs out.

And I exhale, relieved.

"You're absolutely right, Connor, and I'm sorry I haven't been what you needed me to be." The corner of his lips lift. "So, this girl... her name?"

"Ava."

He smiles. "That's a pretty name."

I relax in my seat, let the words flow through me. "She's a pretty girl."

"I bet. Does she go to your school?"

"Yeah. Well, we met at school."

"Psych paper, right?"

I nod, shocked that he remembers. "Turns out she lives next door."

"No way!" he says, his enthusiasm genuine. "So, have you been hanging out outside of school?"

"Not really, I mean not yet. But she's a cool girl. Remember that Trevor guy who helped me move in all the furniture?"

"Of course, yeah."

"She's his stepsister."

"Ah, I see." Then his face falls as if his mind suddenly became consumed by something else.

"Dad?"

"Which uh... which house? I mean, which side does she live on?"

I point in the general direction of Ava's house.

"I see," Dad mumbles, his gaze distant.

"What just happened right now?" I ask.

He gets up, picking up his half-eaten meal. "What do you mean?"

"It's like something triggered you about her house. What... what do you know?"

Dad empties his plate in the trash, then dumps it in the sink. With his hands gripped to the edge of the counter, facing away from me, he says, "I've just heard things..."

"What things?"

He huffs out a breath but stays quiet.

"What *things*, Dad?"

He turns to me now, his arms crossed as he leans against the counter. "It's not something I'd normally mention, but if you like this girl as much as you say you do, it's probably important you know—"

"Dad, just spit it out already."

His lips part, but no words form, and he's looking everywhere but at me.

I push my plate away.

Dad rubs the back of his neck.

The clock tick, tick, ticks, the only sound in the room.

"Look," he starts, crossing his ankles. "When I told Tony—"

"The guy you ride with?"

Dad nods. "When I told him where we moved to, he mentioned the house next door. Apparently, there was an incident a while back with the mother there. I don't know if it's your friend's mom or—"

"What *incident?*"

"She's a war veteran, the mom, and I guess she got injured in Afghanistan. A grenade went off too close, and she lost an arm and part of her face."

"Jesus Christ," I whisper, my thoughts racing—every one of them on Ava.

"When she got home, things were pretty bad for her. People around here —they're not used to seeing someone in that state. Anyway—and I'm only going by what he told me..."

I'm all ears now.

All in.

Dad takes a breath. And then another. Preparing. "Apparently, she went into a store one day, and maybe she overheard a couple of guys talking about her... no one really knows. But she lost it. Completely. She went through the aisles knocking products off the shelf, screaming and yelling and threatening people with whatever weapons she could find. They say she was inebriated because she was unintelligible, slurring her words and whatnot, but Tony thinks it might be a side effect of some form of head trauma from her injuries."

I press my palms against my forehead, waiting for the pounding to stop.

"The kids around here call her the town drunk or the loony lady..."

I stand, my fists balled, and recall those punk kids messing with their house. *Insane Asylum.*

Dad adds, "They even call her two-face."

"Enough." I'm angry, furious, but beyond that, I'm fucking devastated. I picture Ava smiling, hear her laughing, and I wonder how the hell it's possible she still manages to do any of that when her life... I don't even know anything about her.

"There's more, Connor," Dad says, but I'm done listening.

"I don't..." *I don't want to know.*

"Look, I just think it's important for you to know everything before you get involved with someone like her."

"*Someone like her?*" I spit. "What the hell is that supposed to mean?"

"It means that if you take things further with her, it can and will get complicated. There's so much more I haven't even told—"

"With all due respect, *if* we decide to take things further, that's *our* decision. And if there's more to the story, I'd rather hear it from Ava."

EIGHTEEN

ava

CHEWING MY LIP, I contain my smile and think twice about letting him know. For a while now, I've been coming to the same spot, living in isolation. I've enjoyed it, so I thought. But I enjoy Connor's company more. I reply with a picture of what's in front of me, set my phone down, and wait.

It only takes a couple of minutes for him to appear, long legs on the bright green grass of the football field. His eyes keep shifting from his phone to the field, again and again, no doubt looking for exactly where I might be.

He spots me within seconds and strides up the steps, taking them two at a time. He sits on the bench in front of me, legs bent, feet next to mine.

I point to the ball under his arm. "You take that with you everywhere?"

He shrugs. "Habit. I sleep with one, too."

"No, you don't," I chide.

Another shrug. "I get lonely at night."

He dribbles the ball next to his knee, higher, lower, again and again. But he doesn't speak, doesn't even look at me.

"What's with you?" I ask.

He doesn't skip a beat. "What do you mean?"

I grab the ball, hold it behind my back. "Is everything okay?"

"Mmm-hmm." He holds out his hand, asking for the ball, but I shake my head.

"Your words say mmm-hmm, but your face says something's going on."

He smiles, but it's fake. "You know my *faces*?"

"I watch you through your bedroom window. I see you more than you know."

A forced chuckle from him to accompany his flat words. "My bedroom's on the opposite side of your house."

"Who says I watch you from my house? I'm standing outside your window," I say, my attempt at a joke that doesn't seem to fly.

"And you say I'm the creep?"

It's our usual back-and-forth, but the tone is off. Even if I couldn't see it in the dullness of his eyes, I can feel it in my heart. "Connor, what's going on?"

He runs his fingers through his hair, then tugs at the end. "I just..." He peeks up at me through his long, dark lashes, his bottom lip caught between his teeth. "I was telling my dad about you last night..."

Said in any other context, I'd be surprised and maybe a little flattered, but here? Now? I just feel... like something horrible is about to happen. "What did he say?" I croak.

He waits a beat, his words unsure. "He told me about your mom or stepmom..."

I nod, already knowing the fate of the conversation. "*My* mom," I tell him, heat burning behind my eyes. "What did he say about her?"

"Nothing bad," he assures. "He just told me what he heard from a guy at his work. And it's not like gossip or anything. When Dad told him where we lived, he mentioned—"

"The guy warned him about her?"

"No," he's quick to say, sitting higher. "Ava, it's not like that."

I look away, afraid he'll see the tears threatening to fall. I just wanted a friend, and I thought I found that in Connor. But I *knew*, as much as I tried to ignore it, I knew he'd find out eventually, and knowing the truth would take him away from me. I push down the lump in my throat. "What did he tell you exactly?"

Connor sighs. "He told me about the incident at the store, about how she... she..."

"Yeah, I'm aware of what happened," I murmur. I remember getting the call at school and rushing to the store to get to her. I remember the stares, the whispers as I walked by the witnesses. By the time I saw her, the cops had her detained in the storeroom. She was crying, belligerent and afraid, and then William appeared, and I could see it in his eyes: he'd lost the fight to fake it. He was gone soon after that incident. And I was left to pick up the pieces. I try hard not to blink, not to let the liquid heat fall from my eyes, but I fail. A single tear rolls down my cheek, and I swipe it with the back of my hand.

"Ava," Connor sighs, and I can feel the breath of sympathy and guilt filling the space between us. I imagine my life two weeks from now, when he starts to make excuses for not returning texts, or not sitting next to me, or not acknowledging my existence at all.

I already miss him, and he's sitting right in front of me.

It's my fault, I tell myself. It was stupid of me to get attached. To crave him when he wasn't around.

"Is it true?" he asks.

I nod. "Whatever you heard, it's all true." I don't bother asking what was said or how he feels. None of it matters. I flick the ring around my thumb, over and over. I say, my heartbreak falling from my closed lids, "You know the court ordered her to be on twenty-four hour supervision after that day, so she has a caregiver while I'm at school, and I have to be there all the other times, so it's not really a big deal that, you know... that you can't—or don't *want* to— be friends anymore. It's probably better that—"

"Wait," he interrupts. "Is that what you think this is about?"

"What else can come of this, Connor?"

He gets up to sit next to me and pulls my chin toward him. I resist, not wanting him to see my complete devastation. He lets me go but moves closer until his arm is touching mine.

I face the field.

He does the same.

"I'd like to meet her," he says, and my heart stills.

My entire body turns to him. "Why?"

He replies, his eyes holding mine, "Because regardless of what you think of me, or how you think I'd react, I'd still like to get to know you more, and I feel like she's a big part of who you are."

I wipe at my cheeks again, feel the wetness soak my palms. My exhale is shaky while I wait for all the broken parts of me to calm, still cracked, but settle. "I don't think that's a good idea."

"Oh," he says, looking away.

He's taken it as a rejection, so I try to explain, "She doesn't really remember it, what happened that day. She has problems with memory loss, but I think she's aware that *something* happened, because afterward, when- ever she'd go out, people would treat her differently. Worse than they did before. It wasn't bad enough that she was ashamed of the way she looked, and the things people said about her and the names they called her..."

Connor nods, listening intently.

"She doesn't leave the house anymore, and she doesn't like having people there."

"I understand," he says, gentle and comforting.

"But... I can ask."

His face lights up. "Really?"

I nod. "I can't promise anything."

He smiles, genuine, for the first time since he got here. "I'd really like that, Ava."

I really like *you*, Connor.

* * *

"So, I have this friend..." I tell Mom when I get home from school. I'm sitting on the couch with her on the floor in front of me while I braid her hair, something she used to do for me.

"Uh huh," she responds.

Today is what Krystal and I call a zero-day. We scale Mom's moods and actions between -5 to +5. When things are good for her, when she's a fragment of the woman I know as my mother, we go into the positive. The negative... well, that's obvious. Today is a zero-day. A day when she scrapes by, barely any emotion or recollection of who she truly is.

A zero-day is probably not the best time to be having this conversation, but waiting for a positive day might take too long, and a negative day... I don't think she even hears me on those days.

"He's new in town..." I say.

"He? So, a boyfriend, huh?" she asks, her tone void of any emotion.

"Not a *boyfriend*, but a friend boy."

"Go on."

"And he said he'd like to meet you."

"When?"

"Whenever you're up for it."

"Hmm."

"You don't have to if you don't want to."

"Not tonight," she mumbles. "But maybe tomorrow."

"Okay," I say, but I don't believe it. Believing would create hope. And hope has no home here. At least not on zero days.

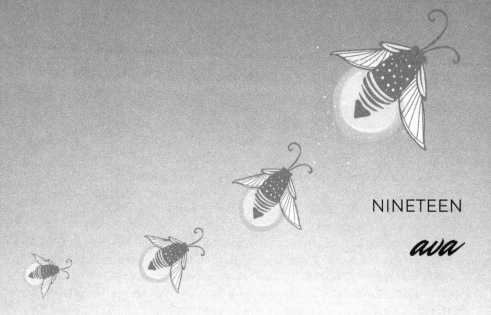

NINETEEN

ava

I TAKE the bus home the next day because Trevor has a job and Connor has practice. I'd love to watch, jeer him from the sidelines, but it's been a long time since I've wanted to do any after-school activities, so Krystal only works the set times I'm at school.

The moment I enter the house, the smell of freshly baked cookies hits my nose, filling my heart with nostalgia. "Ava!" Mom calls from her bedroom.

I drop my bag by the door and rush in to see her, panic swarming my insides. Krystal's sitting on the bed, while Mom stands in front of her dresser. Dressed in a floral skirt and pale pink cardigan, she holds up two different necklaces against her chest. "Which one?" she asks.

"Mama, you look so pretty," I croak out, my pulse settling to a steady strum. "What's the occasion?"

She lowers her hand, eyeing me questioningly. "For your friend's visit? Remember?"

Jaw unhinged, I look over at Krystal. "She's been talking about it all day. She's very excited, Ava. She even baked cookies."

"You did?" I ask, my gaze back on my mother.

She's nodding, smiling.

Pride fills every empty space of my being. "He's at practice right now, but he'll be done soon."

"Okay," Mom chirps. "We can wait."

"Okay," I agree.

"So?" she asks, lifting the necklaces again. "Which one?"

* * *

Ava: CONNOR!

Ava: CALL ME AS SOON AS YOU FINISH.

Ava: IT'S URGENT.

I throw my phone on the bed and strip out of my clothes. Then I stand there in my underwear, trying to decide what to wear because, besides my school uniform, I live in sweats. It's been way too long since I've had to dress for the outside world, and even though I'm still at home, it's Connor... Connor is coming to my house and—

And—

Calm down, Ava.

I slip on a pair of jeans and a Texas A&M T-shirt, and then rip off the T-shirt and get into a fitted tank, something a little more *feminine.*

I tidy up the house a little, ignoring Mom watching me. She's sitting on the couch with a magazine on her lap, smirking, and how is it that she's so calm and I'm the one in a panic?

My phone *barely* rings before I answer it. "Hello?"

"What's wrong?" Connor rushes out. In the background, I can hear a bunch of boys hollering, their voices echoing. He's still at school, in the locker room. "Ava! What happened?"

I run to my room, close the door, and lean against it. "My mom wants to meet you..."

He huffs out a breath, static filling my ears. "Is that it?"

"What do you mean *is that it?* She wants to *meet* you. This afternoon. Like, now, Connor."

"Jesus Christ, Ava, your text sounded like something *bad* happened. Calm the hell down."

"I'm sorry."

"It's fine. Hey, what should I call her? Like... something military or..."

"I don't know. Miss Diaz will do."

"Cool. I'm on my way."

I lower my voice so my mother can't hear me. "Okay, but hurry, because I don't know how long she'll be like this."

Connor chuckles. "I'll break every speed limit."

"And text me when you're leaving your house. Don't knock. Knocking gets her—she gets—"

"I'll text."

"And remember what I said about her short-term memory, she might ask the same—"

"I got it."

"And don't stare when you first see her because—"

"Ava, I'm not a fucking asshole."

My eyes drift shut, my phone held tight to my ear. I release a staggering breath. "I know, I'm just... just..."

"Nervous? And scared?" he asks quietly.

I nod, even though he can't see it.

"It's okay to feel like that. You have every right to. The world hasn't been good to you guys, and I get that. But I wouldn't have asked if I didn't think I could handle it. So, don't worry, okay? I'll see you soon."

I swallow the lump in my throat and whisper, "Please hurry."

"I'll travel through time to get to you."

*   *   *

Connor's on my doorstep, freshly showered, dark jeans and a light blue Henley to match his eyes and *damn, boy.* He ignores me standing right in front of him, his smile purely for my mother. "Ava didn't tell me she had a sister."

Mom giggles—*actually giggles.* "Ava didn't tell me how handsome you were. Come, come," she orders, moving toward the kitchen.

Connor says, stepping into the house, "I should've brought flowers or something. I wasn't thinking."

"It's fine," I assure, the panic over their first meeting lifted. "You being here is enough."

He settles his hand on the small of my back, guiding me in my own house. Dipping his head, his words just for me, he says, "You look nice, Ava."

I pull back so I can take him in again. My initial thoughts haven't changed. "You look... *okay*, I suppose."

"It's milk and cookies," Mom announces proudly, standing behind a chair at the kitchen table. On the table are a giant plate of cookies and three tall glasses of milk. "I used to do this for Ava's friends whenever they'd come around. They were a lot younger then, though." Her eyes shift from Connor to me, a wistfulness in her gaze that sets my soul at ease. "You remember that, Ava?"

"Yeah, Mama," I answer, my voice cracking with emotion. "Of course, I remember."

Please don't ever forget me.

She smiles, but it's sad, and I wonder what's going through her mind. I wonder if the memories of *before* haunt her or heal her. "I know you're seventeen now, but I don't know what else to do..." She looks at Connor. "When I left Ava for my first deployment, she was only ten years old and so..."

Connor rolls up his sleeves, looks directly at her with the same gentle softness in his eyes he carries with him everywhere. If he's at all shocked or deterred by her appearance, he doesn't let it show. "I'm here for it, ma'am," he says. "I mean, who *doesn't* love milk and cookies?"

We sit at the table, all three of us, sipping on milk and munching on cookies while Mom asks Connor about himself. "How tall are you, Connor?"

"Not as tall as I want to be. Six-five right now, but I'm hoping for a growth spurt," he jokes.

Mom says, "Kobe Bryant's only six-five and look at him."

Connor's eyes widen.

Mom adds, "And Chris Paul's six foot even. That never stopped him."

Connor drops his cookie on the plate. "Damn, if I don't like a woman who can talk ball."

Mom laughs.

I tell him, "Mom played college ball."

"No way!" Connor doesn't even try to hide his surprise. He stuffs an entire cookie in his mouth. "These cookies are so good, Miss Diaz."

The conversation moves from him, to the paper we're working on, to me as a kid, me as a baby, and even though some of Mom's stories are embarrassing, I can't wipe the smile off my face. Because I realize that she remembers all the important things, all the events that made me who I am, who *we* are as a family. She remembers the camping trip we took together right before she deployed, the tent leaking, the marshmallows I loved to watch being set ablaze right in front of my eyes. She remembers the fireflies. The magic. "And we sang that song, remember?"

I nod. "'Fireflies' by Owl City."

"I love that song," she hums. "It brings it all back, doesn't it, Ava?"

Another nod, because I can't speak through the knot in my throat. There's an ache in my chest, but the right kind. The kind that reminds me of why I'm here, of why I wake up every day at 4:30, and why I feel absolutely no jealousy when I hear about the parties over the weekend or the games I've missed or see the public displays of affection from the kids at school.

I'm here because *she* is.

Mom refills Connor's milk. "How tall are you, Connor?"

And just like that, my stomach sinks.

Connor says, not skipping a beat, "Not as tall as I want to be. Six-five right now, but I'm hoping for a growth spurt."

Mom smiles. "Kobe Bryant's six-five and look at him."

Under the table, Connor taps his foot against mine. "That's true."

Mom adds, "And Chris Paul, he's only six foot and that never stopped him."

"Also, true," Connor says. Then adds, "Did I mention how good these cookies were?"

Mom's smile widens. "I'm glad you like them."

The front door opens, and Trevor appears, sniffing the air before even stepping foot in the house. "Is that Mama Jo's cookies?" he asks no one in particular. Connor and I watch as Trevor turns his back to slide off his shoes, talking to himself, "I love me some Mama Jo cookies. Mmm-mmm."

Connor stifles his laugh.

When Trevor turns around, he sees Connor at the table and halts momentarily. Slowly, as if stalking his prey, he makes his way over to us and picks up a handful of cookies. His glare shifts between Mom and Connor. Once. Twice. To Connor, he says, "These are *my* favorite cookies.... and you're in *my* seat."

Mom and I bust out a laugh.

Today...

Today is a +infinite day.

* * *

Ava: Thank you.

Connor: For what?

Ava: For giving me a part of my mom I thought I'd lost.

Connor: No, thank you.

Ava: For what?

Connor: For letting me be witness to it.

Ava: You're something else, Connor.

Connor: You're something MORE, Ava.

"IS YOUR DAD TALL?" Ava asks, walking along the bleacher bench, bouncing my basketball.

"He's a few inches shorter than me."

Ava spins, goes back the opposite direction—long, tanned legs moving swiftly. I could watch her all damn day. "Is that where you got your height and athleticism from?"

"Height is from his side, but he doesn't have an athletic bone in his body. Apparently, my mom ran college track, though."

Ava stops completely, the ball held to her waist. Lips parted, she tilts her head, as if contemplating. The girl's got an inquisitive mind, I've realized, and I wonder what questions are floating through her head. "Huh" is all she says.

I laugh under my breath and stand, take the ball from her. "Ask, curious girl."

She snatches the ball back. "I was just thinking, you got split genetics."

"I guess."

"Do you know much else about your mom?"

"I kind of remember what she looks like, but it's a little hazy. And I don't know if it's from memory or because I saw a picture of her once," I admit. "In a drawer in Dad's side table. They were both wearing FSU sweatshirts, so I assume that's where they met."

"He hasn't told you about her?"

"Nah. He doesn't really talk about her or what happened, and to be honest, I kind of prefer it that way."

"Aren't you at all curious?"

"About?"

"God, so many things," she says, eyeing the sky. "Like where she is or what she's doing, or I don't know... *why* she did it."

I run my hands through my hair, replay her words. Lightheartedly, I reply, "Maybe she was a sociopath."

Ava jumps down off the bench and stands in front of me, her head tilted back so she can look me in the eyes. "I'm serious, though, Connor. I mean, if she had some form of mental illness then she should get help."

I swallow, painfully, and try hard to not let her thoughts consume me. "I get where you're going with this, Ava. I do. But my mom and your mom— they're two completely different situations."

"Because something *happened* to my mom to make her that way?"

"I don't know. I guess."

"Maybe your mom was born like that."

"Or maybe..." I start, grabbing my ball. I spin it around on my finger, so I have something else to focus on that isn't her. "Maybe it's a lot simpler than that."

"Like what?" she asks.

"Like maybe she just didn't want me."

* * *

For the next few days, Ava and I ride to school together when our schedules align. She hasn't invited me over again, and besides the few text messages we send to each other at night, we don't really interact. Psych class and lunch are the only times we see each other, so we make the most of what we get. At least I do.

We sit in the bleachers away from the crowds and talk, learn more about each other. She finds new ways to get under my skin, and I find new excuses to touch her.

"Why are you hanging out with me?" she asks out of nowhere.

I push aside the so-called "food" attained from the cafeteria. School this rich, you'd think they'd supply something a little more... edible. "What do you mean?"

She picks up her sandwich—turkey on rye, the same as always—and takes a bite. With her mouth full, she says, "Shouldn't you be hanging out with your team?"

"Eh." I shrug. "You're nicer to look at."

She flicks her shoulder, rolls her eyes. "I mean, *obviously.*"

"Modest, too."

She laughs, the kind that starts deep, comes out low and slowly turns higher and higher. It's my favorite of her laughs, and I pity the world for not hearing it as often as it should. "Honestly, though. Don't they wonder why you're not part of the jock-patrol?"

"I don't really click with anyone on the team as much as I do with you."

"You haven't made friends?" she asks.

"No, *Mom*. I haven't. I told you the first time you were in my car. You could be the suckiest friend in the world, and you'd still be the best one I have. And, to be honest, you're pretty fucking sucky."

"Shut up," she says, shoving my shoulder.

"Nah, the guys aren't too bad. Rhys seems like a decent dude, but talking to him is like talking in circles—which yeah, is basically like talking to *you*—but with Rhys comes Mitch and—"

Ava makes a gagging sound, cutting me off. "Yuck."

"You're not a fan?"

"That guy's a self-entitled dick."

"Hey, remember when you called me self-entitled?"

She stretches her arms in the air, then settles them behind her. "I remember it fondly." Nose in the air, she adds, "It was the morning of August—"

I reach over and cover her mouth, gently push until she's on her back, another new excuse to touch her. "You're such a smart-ass."

"You love it," she mumbles beneath my palm.

With her heavy breath against my hand, our eyes lock, stay. And I don't know why my mind chooses *now* of all times, why the urge I've held on to for so long is at its strongest.

I want to kiss her.

In so many ways.

For so many hours.

My gaze drifts to her throat, the movement sharp as she swallows.

I could kiss her there.

"Connor?" she whispers beneath my touch, her eyes drifting shut.

I could kiss her there, too.

She reaches up, yanks at my wrist to uncover her mouth.

I could kiss her there the most.

"We can't do what you're thinking right now."

My heart sinks. "Why?"

Hand pressed to my chest, she pushes me away and sits up. She refuses to look at me when she says, "Because we *can't*."

And I have no other words but a repetition of "Why?"

"Because," she starts, looking out onto the field, then down at her feet, at her hands, anywhere but at me. "Because my life is complicated enough as it is."

"I'm not here to complicate things, Ava. If anything, I want to help."

"I'm not a charity case."

I shake my head. Sigh out loud. "That's not what I meant."

The warning bell sounds, and I curse under my breath.

Ava's quick to stand. "We should go."

* * *

I don't see Ava for the rest of the day, and she doesn't respond to my texts all afternoon. I'm tempted to go knock on her door to finish our conversation, but I remember what she told me about her mom's reaction to knocking, so I force myself to let it go until the next morning.

Sleep eludes me, and just when I've tossed and turned for the millionth time, legs kicking out in frustration, my phone goes off.

> Ava: I can't date. I don't even know what the meaning of dating is for people our age, but I know that I can't do it. My life outside of school is… my life. My priority. I can't be that girl for you. I can't be the girl on the sidelines cheering you on. I can't be the one you hold hands with when you go out to celebrate all your wins or commiserate all your losses. I can't be the one you bring home to meet your dad or the one you call when you have off days. I can't be anything more than I am right now. Which means *we* can't be anything more. And as much as I hate it, as much as it hurts, I know in my heart that's what you deserve. And it doesn't matter how much I want you or how hard I've fallen for you. Because I have, Connor. In all the possible ways that absolutely terrify me, I've fallen for you. But nothing good can come of this. There'd be no happy ending to our story. There'd be an intense beginning, a shaky middle, and then heartache. And we've both been through enough heartache to last a lifetime.

ava

I SPENT first period in the girls' bathroom because I was too afraid to face Connor.

This is my life now.

After I sent him the wall of text last night, I switched off my phone and managed to get a total of two hours sleep. I didn't want to see what he had to say or fight him on my decision. It had taken me hours to come up with something I felt was worthy enough to send. I gave him the answers he needed, and with it, I gave him every piece of painful truth.

I was falling for him.

And I couldn't do anything about it.

But even saying all that, it still hurt when I turned my phone back on this morning and there wasn't a response from him. I know he'd read it, the proof was there, so maybe that was it for us.

The story of Connor and Ava: *over before it began.*

It's what I wanted; I convince myself. It's what I *asked* for, really. It doesn't mean I won't miss his friendship, or his banter, or the way he puts up with me... or the way he *looks* at me.

My stomach drops as I stare out at the football field. I pick up my phone, see that it's been ten minutes since lunch started, and the ache in my heart doubles. Triples. I lock the phone, stare at the wallpaper: a picture of Trevor, my mom, and me on my last birthday. A zero-day. I can see it in her eyes, remember it like it was yesterday. There were no candles on the cake. No poppers. No singing. But there was *us.* Our mismatched little family; a gradient of skin tones. Trevor being the darkest, then mom, and then me. My *reason.*

"Sorry I'm late," Connor shouts, practically sprinting up the steps. "I was stuck on a stupid conference call with Coach Sykes and my agent, something about UCLA. I don't know; I tuned out."

My mind does a double take.

My heart does a double flip.

"What are you doing here?" I breathe out.

His steps falter. "Are we..." He eyes me sideways. "Are we not allowed to be friends anymore? Because I swear, I read your text, like, eighty times, and there was no mention—"

"I wasn't sure if you'd still want to be," I cut in. "Friends, I mean. I didn't..."

He sits down on the bench in front of me, a step down, his usual spot. "I'm kind of attached to you, Ava." He sniffs at whatever food the cafeteria has supplied him. "You gotta work harder if you want to get rid of me."

I'm *beaming*, and I don't even try to hide it.

He chews the corner of his mouth, his eyes on mine. "Ten bucks says I can wipe that smile off your face in less than five seconds."

Impossible. "Do your best, Ledger."

"I always sit *right here* because I can see up your skirt."

I kick his chest, my mouth open in shock. "You jerk!" Then I cross my legs.

"Red today," he laughs out. "Green yesterday. Did you buy a rainbow-themed bulk pack?"

"I hate you!"

"You owe me ten bucks."

"Fuck you, you didn't earn it." I try to kick him again, but he grabs my ankles, settles them on his lap. I should kick him there, but I don't know... he'd probably make a good dad one day, I suppose.

"Speaking of fuck you," he says, hands still on my ankles. "Rhys invited me to a party this weekend. It's the last chance to let loose before the season starts, so I guess the team is getting drunk and I don't know... trading *yachts*?" He releases my ankles and starts massaging his shoulder.

"What happened?" I ask, motioning to his shoulder.

"I think I tweaked it at practice."

I put my lunch to the side and say, "Come here."

"What?"

"Come here," I repeat.

He leans forward.

"Turn around, you dumbass."

"You have the strangest love language," he mumbles, scooting so his back is facing me.

I press my fingers into his shoulder, feeling the muscles shift beneath my touch. I realize I've never touched him before. Not like *this*. I try to ignore my body's reaction to the heat of his flesh, the strength of his muscles, the sound of his groan when his head rolls forward. I silently clear my throat, reclaim some form of sanity. "Are you going to go?"

"Huh?"

"To the party... are you going to go?"

"I don't know. Do you think I should?"

I keep working his shoulder, below his shirt, skin on skin, up his neck and to his hairline and back again.

He moans. "Ava?"

"Huh?"

"Do you think I should go?"

"Probably. Team building. Blah blah blah."

He chuckles.

I work on both shoulders, watching his muscles contract beneath my touch. Then I move up his neck, run my fingers through his hair.

"Goddammit, Ava," he grunts, his hands covering mine, stopping me. "You're making it really fucking hard."

"What, being *just* friends?"

"Yeah... that, too."

TWENTY-TWO

Connor

I'VE NEVER FELT MORE out of place than I do standing in Rhys's living room. There's a Solo cup in my hand filled with beer, given to me by a server who clearly works for a company that gives zero shits about underage drinking. I thought it was just a team thing, but it looks like the entire school is here. Minus the one girl I wish was.

I sent Ava an SOS two minutes after I got here, but she hasn't responded. And no matter how much I look at my phone, Karen doesn't get the hint. She's on my arm, practically hanging on for dear life, and I don't even know how I got in this situation. "So, you totally should come!" she shouts over the music.

"What?" I yell.

"Next week. To my party. On my boat." She narrows her eyes. "Have you been listening to me at all?"

"Yeah," I lie, point to my ear. "It's just hard to hear you with all the—" My phone vibrates, and I'm quick to check it.

> Dad: No drinking tonight, and if you do, no driving. I mean it, Connor. I don't feel like peeling your brains off the concrete.

> Connor: Don't stress. I'm not drinking.

A tip I learned a while ago is that people tend to leave you alone if you have a drink in your hand. Nobody checks if you're drinking it. And I'm not stupid enough to drink and drive, especially since Dad has enough stories of car accidents to scar me for life.

"So, you'll come?" Karen asks.

"Hey, where's the bathroom?" I need out. Of this conversation *and* this room.

She points in the general direction of a large staircase, and maybe she's beyond drunk, because in a house this big, there has to be at least five down here.

"I'll catch you later, all right?" I don't wait for a response. Instead, I make my way through the already half-drunk party and start for the stairs where I know I can at least get some room to breathe. At the top are two hallways, and honest to God, I wonder if one of them leads to the servant quarters because the house is that big and that lush that it wouldn't surprise me if they had full-time help. And also, where the hell are Rhys's parents? Where the hell is Rhys?

I open door after door looking for the bathroom just so I can shut myself in and get a moment of peace. It's not like I'm not used to partying; I had my fair share back home, but they weren't like this. I find the bathroom, but it's occupied. Mitch has a girl pushed up against the counter, his pants down and her legs around him. "Sorry!" I shout.

"Ledger! What's up, man?" Mitch laughs. "You want in? I don't mind sharing." There's not enough eye bleach in the world to stop me from slamming that door shut.

The next door I open is an empty bedroom, thank fuck. Illuminated by a single lamp on the nightstand, I do a quick sweep of the room before declaring it safe. I close the door behind me. Lock it. And sit on the edge of the bed.

I look at my phone. Still no message.

Then I look around the room again, at the navy-blue paint and the *Wildcats! Wildcats! Wildcats!* poster. My eyes narrow, trying to adjust to the darkness. My gaze catches on a large framed picture on the wall. It's the basketball team, Rhys front and center. Realization sinks in. I'm in his room. And because I'm bored, and maybe a little curious, I start to snoop. I scan the books on his shelf and the clothes in his closet that's the size of my room. The guy's got good taste in kicks, I'll give him that. He owns every pair of Jordans ever released, but only in the classic colorways. Not going to lie, I'm a little jealous. I wonder if he'd notice a pair or two missing...

I look over his desk, boring, and then the massive pinboard above it filled with photographs. Mainly of him. Not surprising. I scan the pictures, one by one. His parents are in them, along with a girl I assume is his sister. And right in the middle, the largest picture there... I look closer, but it's dark, and my eyes... my eyes might be deceiving me. I unpin it from the board and take a closer look. He's in his JV jersey in the middle of the court with a girl in his arms. She's wearing a cheerleader uniform, her hair braided to the side, with his jersey number painted on her cheek. He has his arms around her waist, her arms around his neck, and I fight the urge to rip the picture in half.

A twist in my stomach has me searching for somewhere to sit. I find the edge of his bed again, flop my ass down, my eyes glued to the photograph. She's the same Ava, but she's *different*. Smaller. Younger. Less... *broken*.

My eyes snap up at the sound of the doorknob twisting. I stand, hide the picture behind my back, and gear myself for whoever comes through the door. "Why the fuck is this locked?" I recognize the voice as Rhys's, and I mentally punch myself for getting caught.

The knob jiggles, and a second later the door's open and his head's poking through the gap. "Connor?" he asks, switching on the light.

I blink away the brightness. "Sorry, man. I got lost and... I just needed a little time out."

Stepping into the room, he eyes me suspiciously as he closes the door behind him. "Are you stealing from me?"

"No," I say quickly. "Jesus. *No*."

His eyes span across the room, looking for evidence.

Please don't look at the giant empty space on the board. Please please please.

But he does, and he sighs out loud. "What's the deal with you guys anyway?" he asks, moving closer.

"What's the deal with *you* guys?" I counter.

He chuckles. "I'm not interested in her in that way if that's what you're thinking. At least not anymore. Has she not told you about us?"

And because I suck at hiding my jealousy, I say, "She hasn't mentioned you *at all*."

"That's not surprising," he murmurs. "We didn't exactly have the best timing."

"What does that mean?"

"It means..." He rubs the back of his neck, contemplating. Then he opens his blinds, motions for me to look out the window, to which I comply. "See that house?" he says, pointing to a house only slightly smaller than his.

"Yeah?"

"Three years ago, Ava lived there."

My eyes widen, move to his. "No shit."

He nods. "I was so afraid to talk to her at first, because... well, you know what she looks like. She was so intimidating, and she had this fierceness to her like she wouldn't take shit from anyone. When I found out she was crushing on me, too, I lost my damn mind."

I know that feeling, I don't say.

"We did a lot of back and forth trying to navigate our feelings. We were only fourteen at the time, so it was all kind of new to us."

I don't know if I want to hear anymore, but I nod regardless.

"Anyway, you know Karen?"

"Yeah."

"She and Ava were best friends back then. Karen threw her this rager of a bonfire party for her fifteenth birthday, and I finally found the courage to shoot my shot."

"So, you dated?" If this is all he wants to tell me, he should just say it. I don't need the details.

Rhys shakes his head. "That night we uh... you know..."

Well, now I know, but I wish to fuck I didn't.

"It was the same night they got the call."

"What call?"

"About her mom."

"Oh." *Shit.*

Rhys exhales loudly. "We tried to make it work. Or at least *I* did. I gave her as much as I could, but she... she had *so much* going on, Connor, and then when her stepdad left them and—"

"I uh..." I cut in. "I kind of would prefer to hear her story from her if that's cool."

He nods, understanding. "I just want you to know that whatever goes on between you guys, I'm not your enemy or your threat or whatever. When it comes to Ava, I'm here for the same reason you are. I *care* about her. *Truly.*"

I'm having an out-of-body experience; I'm sure of it. Because I can't seem to process a single thought. It's as if I'm watching Ava's entire life play out and there's no pause button, no rewind. I don't know what to say or how to react, so I mumble, "I appreciate it."

I need to go. I need to get out of here. And I need to go to *her.* "I'm going to take off," I say.

We bump fists, and I start to walk away but stop when he calls my name.

When I turn to him, his hand's out, palm up. "Can I have the picture back?"

I reluctantly hand it back to him and then make for the door. When I go to close it, he's staring at the picture, his mind no doubt filled with memories.

I stand there, watching him, wondering how much time will pass before I start doing the same.

* * *

The second I'm in my driveway and out of my car, I send Ava a text.

> Connor: Everything okay? I haven't heard from you all day. Just checking in.

I'm halfway up my porch steps when I hear the notification, but it's not coming from my phone. I send another one.

Connor: Ava?

I hear it again and hit reverse on my feet. Down the steps and down the driveway, my focus on Ava's house. It's pitch-black, no lights.

I hit dial on her number and hold the phone to my ear. It rings twice on my end before hers goes off, and I follow the sound, see the screen light up.

Ava's sitting on her porch steps, her phone on her lap. She doesn't make a move to answer it, and it's too damn dark to see her clearly.

Slowly, carefully, I make my way up her driveway until I'm standing in front of her.

She's staring straight ahead, her eyes wide.

"Ava," I whisper.

She doesn't respond.

I look up at the house again, but there are no signs of life. So, I sit down next to her, keep my voice low. "What are you doing out here?"

She doesn't look at me when she whispers, "The fireflies are gone."

"What?"

She turns to me now, and lit only by the moonlight, I see her face clearly. Wetness trails down her cheeks, remnants of the tears she's been shedding.

My chest tightens at the sight, and I reach for her hand, link my fingers with hers.

Heartbreak forms in her words even though her features are void of emotion. "Mom says that when the world is at its darkest, that's when the magic appears." Anguish falls from her eyes, and she doesn't make a move to wipe them away. "But there's nothing but empty darkness and negative numbers and... and the fireflies are gone, and I'm finding it really fucking hard to believe in magic right now."

I wish I knew the right thing to say or the right thing to do. But I don't. I let her words settle through me, every single one echoed in my mind. I hold her hand tighter, letting her know that I'm here, with her, for however long she needs me. Time passes without meaning, and I hear every one of her breaths, each one claiming a part of my heart.

"I was dead," I tell her, my voice calm. "There was a couple on their way to their honeymoon who spotted me in the car. A couple who just *happened* to be first responders. Apparently, they tried waking me by knocking on the window, and when I didn't stir, they smashed it open with their luggage. I wasn't breathing..." I pause just so I can push down the knot in my throat. "They got me out of the car, and the man did CPR while his wife called 911. They worked on me for ten whole minutes before I coughed out my first breath. *Ten minutes.* And who knows how long I was out before they got to me. I was barely conscious by the time help arrived."

Ava squeezes my hand, moves closer to me.

"What are the odds? What are the chances that the people who saw me were the right people at the right place and the exact right time? They brought me back to life, Ava." I turn my body to hers and gently place my hand on the back of her head, bring her ear to my chest, right above my heart. "Do you hear it?" I ask. "My heartbeat?"

"Yes," she whispers, her tears soaking through my shirt.

I blink back my own and try to stay strong, for *her*. "If you need proof that magic exists, I'm right here."

TWENTY-THREE

ava

CONNOR'S GRIN IS STUPID, and I wish it didn't give me butterflies like it does. "You made me lunch?"

"It's not a big deal," I say, adjusting my school blazer over my knees, so we don't have a repeat of previous days. "You won't shut up about how bad the food is here, so..."

Swear, his dimples have never been so deep. "So, you made me lunch?"

"I didn't *make* it for you. It's leftovers. It would've just gone to waste."

"Uh-huh," he murmurs, devouring a mouthful of last night's lasagna. "I'm sure Trevor would've loved a second serving."

I wince. "Yeah, maybe don't tell him."

"What? That you *made* me lunch?"

"You're such a pain in my ass."

He chuckles. "And yet, here we are."

I spend a few minutes just watching him eat, a comfortable silence shared only between us. But I have questions. So many of them. And somehow, he picks up on this, because he says, "Yes, I met the couple who saved me. Yes, I keep in contact with them. They're retired now, but they send me a birthday card every year. Dad and the guy became close friends. He actually helped Dad become a paramedic."

Eyes wide in surprise, I open my mouth, but nothing comes.

"I can read you like a book, Ava."

I lean forward, look right into his eyes.

"What are you doing?" he asks, rearing back. "You're creeping me out."

"I'm trying to read your mind," I mumble. "Stay still."

With a laugh, he says, "I don't think that's how it works, but here—" he leans forward, his nose an inch from mine, bright blue eyes staring back at me "—do your best." His hands are on my knees, moving higher and higher. My breath catches, the tension between us building and building. Then his gaze drops, a slight change, but one I notice. One I *feel*.

"You're scared," I whisper.

Defensively, he asks, "Scared of what?"

Of me, I want to tell him. He's afraid of the same things I am. That no matter how hard we try to fight it, we can't stop the momentum. We're getting closer, and these feelings we harbor are just getting stronger and stronger.

I pull away.

Look away.

And come up with a lie. "You're scared about your first game tonight, right?"

Connor huffs out a breath. "Yeah," he admits, sighing heavily. His entire body seems to deflate with that single admission. "I actually am."

Pouting, I say, "I wish I could be there."

He nods. "I know. I understand why you can't."

"Do you want to talk it out?"

With a shrug, he replies, "I'm just nervous, I guess, which is weird because the game has always come so naturally to me. But I feel like I have a lot more riding on it now than I did before. I mean, we picked up our entire lives and moved to another state just for the chance to be seen, and God, Ava, if I don't succeed..."

"I'm sorry," I tell him honestly. Connor was right; I *am* a sucky friend because I'd never really thought about it before. I never stopped to think about the pressures of his life that might weigh him down and keep him up at night. All this time we've spent together and all the stupid questions I ask about his past, I never once asked about his future. Shame fills me. "That must be hard, to feel like all that is riding on *your* shoulders."

"It's all for the end game, right?" he mumbles.

"Well, it's good that your dad supports you with it. He moved here for it so..."

His eyes drop, his hand flexing around his basketball. "Yeah, I guess," he says, but his eyebrows are drawn, and there's a sadness in his expression that has me scooting forward just to be closer to him.

"Is he, like, pressuring you to be something you don't want to be?"

"No." He shakes his head, adamant. "No," he repeats. "I want to go pro. Obviously. And it's not like he'd disown me if I didn't make it, but... I don't know." He pauses a beat. "I feel like I have to *be* something. Something greater than average. Something big, because..." he trails off.

"Because why?"

His nostrils flare with his heavy exhale. "Because there has to be a reason I survived that day."

"Connor," I whisper. "You're putting way too much pressure on yourself."

He shakes his head, his eyes on mine. "What if I fuck it up, Ava? What if it was all for nothing?"

I suck in a breath, hold it there. And I think about my life before Connor, and all the emptiness I felt from scraping through each moment in my own version of zero-days. I sit down next to him, facing away from the field. Then I take his hand in mine, squeeze it, and hope that it gives him the same level of comfort he'd offered me. "What if it was something else entirely?"

"What do you mean?" he asks, spreading my fingers with the tips of his. Our hands are mismatched, his too big and mine too small, but when our fingers entwine, there are no empty spaces, no room for anything more.

"What if five hundred miles away, there was a girl... a girl who was barely holding on to hope... a girl so close to giving up. And you just *happen* to move next door to her? Just *happen* to sit next to her in class. And you form this friendship with her, not knowing how badly she needed someone *exactly* like you, at *exactly* that time, to help piece her back together. To help heal her. And to show her that magic exists and... and maybe it's not the NBA," I say, my voice hoarse, throat aching with the force of my withheld sob. "And maybe it's not what you imagined your purpose to be..." I look up at him, at his red, raw eyes holding mine hostage. "Would that be enough?"

He settles his hand on my jaw, then places the gentlest of kisses on my forehead, making my eyes drift shut. "So, this girl you speak of..." he starts, his lips still on me. "Is she hot?"

connor

"YOU GOT EVERYTHING?" Dad asks, poking his head through my bedroom door.

"Yeah." I adjust the strap of my gym bag across my chest and take one more look in the mirror. Nervous anticipation crawls through my skin, and I wish Ava were here. I wish she'd hold my hand like she did today and calm the anxiety inside my chest, building a fortress, creating a home.

"You okay?" Dad asks, walking behind me toward the front door. "Pre-game nerves always get to you, but once you're on the court and the ball's—"

"I'm fine, Dad," I interrupt. I don't need a pep talk, at least not from him. I just need to stay in my head, stay focused.

I open the front door and freeze momentarily. There's a single, sad looking balloon hanging off the porch railing. Bright orange, like the team colors. And written in black marker, a large *#3,* my jersey number. I notice more writing on the other side, and so I flip it between my hands and take a closer look. A laugh erupts from deep in my throat. *BOO!*

* * *

My back squeaks against the hardwood as I slide a few feet, leaving a trail of sweat in my wake. The crowd that'd been deafening all night is suddenly quiet. I start to raise my hand to shield my eyes from the bright gym lights, but Rhys stands over me, blocking them. He offers me his hand, and the crowd goes crazy. His grin matches mine when I use his hand to help me get back on my feet. "They're going to keep knocking you down until you can't get back up!" he shouts into my ear.

I make my way to the free-throw line, hands out for the ball. "They can keep trying," I yell back. "But I can go all damn night!"

I sink both shots without even trying.

"All damn night, baby!" Rhys whoops, ruffling my hair.

From the sidelines, Coach Sykes calls out to me, "Are you done?"

"Not even close!"

My opponent stands beside me, hands on his knees. He's the sixth one to cover me tonight, and he's *done*. Roasted. Me? I haven't even warmed up yet. He turns to me, shaking his head. "Where the hell did you come from, Ledger?"

I shrug. "Florida."

"Well, go the fuck back."

* * *

"You killed it tonight, Ledger," Oscar, a sophomore says, punching my shoulder while I sit in front of my locker.

"Thanks, man."

"Yeah, way to show us up," Mitch calls.

I ignore him, but Rhys doesn't. "Last I checked, basketball was a team sport. Go run track if you want to get noticed, or I don't know... up your fucking game."

Mitch scoffs. "You cup his balls while you're down there kissing his ass?"

Rhys laughs. "No, but your mom does."

I grab my phone from my locker, the post-win adrenaline spiking when I see the text from Ava:

> Ava: Triple double on your first game? Way to show off, #3.

> Connor: Stalk much?

> Ava: What can I say? I'm a fan.

> Connor: I pretended you were there.

> Ava: :(I wish I were.

> Connor: You kind of were.

> Ava: How?

> Connor: I popped that balloon and shoved it down my shorts.

Ava: Gross.

Connor: Yet endearing, right?

Rhys says, "Hey, the team's going to the diner to celebrate. You're coming, right?" at the same time a message comes through from Ava.

Ava: Mom's already asleep. I can probably come outside for a little bit if you want to tell me all about it...

I look up at Rhys, the way his eyes shift from my phone to me. He sighs. "Do your thing, Ledger. But at some point, you're going to have to act like you're a part of the team, too. It's a two-way street, and I can only hold the guys off for so long."

I slam my locker shut, thank Rhys, and text Ava on my way out.

Connor: I'm leaving now.

* * *

Ava rushes down her porch steps, her arms outstretched as she pounces on me. I catch her just in time, falling back a step while she laughs quietly in my ear. "Superstar!" she whispers. There's something to be said about being able to literally sweep a girl off her feet. I spin her around, refusing to let her go. She doesn't seem to want that, either, because even when her feet are planted on the ground, she's still holding on, her arms around my neck. On her toes, she looks up at me, her eyes lit up by the streetlamp. "Tell me everything," she says, her smile contagious. "From the second you walked out until the final buzzer. And don't skimp on the details. I want a play-by-play so I can feel like I was there."

I laugh at her rambling, then say, "It was... was..." I pause, trying to remember the way I felt less than an hour ago, but the details are blurred, the moments insignificant. Because *this*... being with her and seeing her like this, seeing the pride in her eyes, the excitement in her voice—it outweighs everything else. And knowing that all of her, right now, is all for me... I pull her closer. "It was just a game, Ava." And as the words slip from my lips, I feel the heaviness of their truth dig deeper inside me.

"It wasn't just *a game*. It's, like, you're coming out, you know? Your world's about to change, Connor. I hope you're ready for it." She pulls away from me, releasing me completely. Then she smiles, but it's not the same smile she greeted me with. "Don't forget the little people who got you here," she says, only half in jest. "And by that, I mean *me*. Promise you won't forget me?"

With a heavy sigh, I take a step forward, ridding us of the space she so strongly believes she needs. "It's kind of hard for me to forget the one person I can't stop thinking about."

Her eyes lock on mine, her lips parted, and I wonder if she can hear the magic beating wildly inside me. She sucks in a breath, then seems to refocus. A smile plays on her lips as she looks down at her phone and mumbles, "I wonder if they have any game video yet."

She's tapping away at her phone, and I'm tapping away at my mind, my bravado. "Ava?"

"Yeah?"

"You're so fucking beautiful."

And it's killing me.

* * *

> Connor: You asked me yesterday if it would be enough; meeting you and getting to know you, and I cracked a stupid joke when I should have told you the truth. And the truth is this: yes. In the simplest of terms and the most complicated of circumstances, yes. You are enough. I wake up every single morning looking forward to the couple of hours I get to spend with you, to the few minutes I get to see you smile and hear your voice and feel you next to me. Even on the days when our time is limited, just knowing you're there and you exist is worth it. And even if I have to spend the rest of my life wondering what it would be like to kiss you just once… these moments with you… they're worth everything. YOU are worth everything.

TWENTY-FIVE

Connor

THE ENTIRE SCHOOL IS ABUZZ, hallways are filled with orange and black streamers, and everywhere I go, I get swarmed. Pats on the back from the boys, flirtatious compliments from the girls. Even the teachers are pulling me aside to talk about the game. Or more specifically, my performance. Coach has already had me in his office, along with the school paper's sports reporter. The headline for the next issue: "Ledger: The Powerhouse Import." Even the principal wants to meet so we can set up a media schedule for all the local papers wanting to do a story on me. And then there's the team. It's as if I had to prove beyond all our practices that I was actually good enough to garner their respect. Which I get, but at the same time, fuck you.

"You have to eat lunch in the cafeteria today," Rhys says, catching me in between classes.

"What? No. I have lunch with—"

"Ava, I know. But it's kind of a tradition the day after a game. Win, lose or draw we have to show that we're a team. Coach's orders."

"But—"

"It's five minutes, Connor; it's not going to kill you. Besides, the cheerleaders do a *thing* for new players."

"What *thing*?"

He shrugs. "I'll catch you at lunch, okay? Don't be late!"

* * *

I don't think I've ever cringed as hard as I am right now, watching the cheerleaders chant my name only a few feet in front of me. Next to me, Mitch keeps backhanding my shoulder, his eyebrows raised, like "How good is this?" And maybe to other guys this is a wet dream come true, but to me... I just want to be with Ava. And Rhys—fuck Rhys—because the five minutes he said it would take has turned into twenty, and I need to go. As soon as the cheerleaders have finished their routine, I thank them and start to leave. Rhys pulls me down by my arm. "Stay."

"Did you like it?" Karen asks, shooing Mitch out of his seat so she can sit next to me.

Not wanting to be rude, I plaster on the most genuine smile I can muster. "Yeah, it was great."

She nods, takes a bite out of Mitch's leftover apple. "We worked on it all morning."

"Cool." I stand again, and again, Rhys pulls me to sit back down. "I have to piss. You want me to do it right here?"

"Oh. Why didn't you say so?"

This time, I'm allowed to leave, and I practically sprint over to the football field. Ava is waiting in her usual spot, and I race up the steps two at a time. "I had to sit with the stupid team in the cafeteria and the—"

She holds out a container, cutting me off. "I *made* you lunch," she says, pouting. "But it's probably cold now."

"I'm so sorry," I rush out, sitting in front of her. "I got stuck. I had to sit through the cheerleaders—"

"The welcoming routine," she mumbles. "Shoot. I forgot about that."

I want to crack a joke about how she used to be one of them, but she wasn't the one to tell me, and I don't know if she wants me knowing. "It was horrible," I assure.

She rolls her eyes. "Yeah. It's such a *travesty* that you had to watch a bunch of hot girls in super short skirts screaming your name over and over." She mocks fanning herself. "Oh, Connor, Connor, Connor," she moans.

The sound replays in my head for longer than it should, and I stare, unabashed. Her lips are red, wet, and I can't help but lick my own, wonder for the umpteenth time what those lips would feel like against mine, what she'd taste like. I realize she's watching me, too, her focus on my mouth. She's the first to break our trance, looking away and down at her hands. "Are you still okay to give me a ride home later?"

"Of course."

"And um... what you said last night, in your text, did you mean it?"

I swallow, nervous. "Which part?"

"Did you lie about any of it?"

"No."

She nods, slowly, but still doesn't make eye contact. And before I even get a chance to open the lunch she made me, the warning bell goes off. I curse at the same time Ava drops to her knees beside me. She settles her hands on my chest, her gaze intense and locked on mine. Her lips part, her tongue darting out, spreading moisture on the parts of her I've been fixated on for days. Her touch drifts up to my shoulders, my nape, and I'm frozen with fear but melting with desire, and then she moves an inch closer and closer and closer, her eyes drifting shut and mine doing the same, my own hands blindly finding the small bit of skin between her knees and her skirt. She whispers my name, and I groan in response, and then her mouth's on mine, so fucking soft —a complete contrast to the instant reaction in my pants—and my lips part to take hers in. Her hands are in my hair, fingers laced through the strands, and mine are on her thighs, under her skirt, and she's warm... warm enough to light a fire inside me. I need air, but I need her more, and when the tip of my tongue searches for hers, finds it, I squeeze her legs—an impulse—and she tugs at my hair, pulls me closer again. My head tilts one way, hers the other, and we're two jagged pieces of two different puzzles that somehow fit perfectly when we're connected. Her breaths are sharp, short, and I hear every single one through the loud thump, thump, thumping in my chest. She's sitting higher on her knees, and my hands move behind her, to the spot right beneath her ass. She moans out my name, and all I can do is open my mouth wider, kiss her harder. So many fucking hours of fantasizing about this moment, and never—not once—did it ever feel like this. This... this...

The air hits my mouth where she should be, and I open my eyes to see her watching me, her lips red and raw from my assault. "Holy shit," she whispers, and I use her legs to bring her back to me. She falls, almost on top of me now, and I continue where we left off. This time, I go for her neck, her jaw. She holds me to her, her fingers running through my hair and I'm so fucking turned on, I can't see straight. In the distance, the bell rings again, and Ava pulls away, her eyes glazed. "We should go," she says, but I don't want to. I don't want to stop, and I don't want to leave her, and I don't want this moment to end.

She giggles, pulling away completely. She adjusts her clothes, and I adjust the bulge in my pants. She gives me one final kiss. Chaste. Then she smiles. "Now you no longer have to wonder," she says.

"Wonder what?" I breathe out, confused.

"What it would be like to kiss me... *just once.*"

ava

HOW MUCH DAMAGE can *one* kiss possibly do?

A lot, apparently, because it's all I can think about for the rest of the day. His lips, his hands, all the ways he touched me, the ways he made me feel... I can't focus on anything else. Not the classwork in biology. Not a phone ringing somewhere in the distance. Not Rhys hissing my name.

Something nudges my elbow, pulling me from my daydream. I turn to Rhys sitting next to me, my eyes narrowed in annoyance. "What?"

"Your phone's going off," he says, and I look up and around me, and everyone is staring. Then reality hits and hits hard. I reach for my pocket, see Krystal's name on the screen. I answer it without any regard for where I am or what I'm doing.

"Your mom's having an episode, Ava. You should come home right now. Trevor's on his way." I don't even respond before I'm on my feet and heading toward the door.

No one asks what I'm doing or where I'm going; they already know.

The two minutes waiting for Trevor in the school parking lot feels like hours.

I send a quick text to Connor to let him know I had to bail and practically jump into Trevor's moving truck when he arrives.

Dread.

Dread replaces all other emotions, all other thoughts, and my blood heats, rushes through my entire body. I can't sit still, can't stop the worst possible scenarios from circling my mind.

"It's okay," Trevor says, hand on my knee to stop the bouncing. "Everything's going to be okay."

"How do you know?" I whisper.

He doesn't have an answer, so he doesn't respond.

I burst through the front door and can hardly set foot inside. Magazines and broken glass are scattered throughout; picture frames hang crooked on the walls. Krystal is in the middle of the living room, her hands on her hips, and Mom—Mom is sitting in the corner, head in her knees, an arm covering her face. She's rocking back and forth, whispering words too unintelligible, even for my ears.

Krystal inhales a long, sharp breath before turning to me. "She's okay now," she breathes out. "She's in the—"

"Aftermath," I finish for her, taking the steps to get to my mother. Slowly, quietly, I squat down, ignoring the shattering of glass beneath my shoes. I fight back the tears, hold back my cries. "Mama?" *I am a conqueror. I am. I am.* "It's Ava. Remember me?"

Mom stills, looks up at me with eyes glazed, fighting a battle between chaos and calm. "Of course, I remember you," she says, her voice low. Her warm, wet hand settles on my jaw, taps gently. I fight back the urge to recoil. But then she breaks, a single tear falling from her eyes. "My Ava, Ava, Ava." She starts rocking again. "Ava, Ava, Ava."

I take her in my arms, hold her to me, and sway with her motions.

"I'm sorry, Ava, Ava, Ava."

"It's okay, Mama," I assure, looking up at Trevor. The sadness in his smile creates an ache in my chest.

Mom's shoulders start to shake, and I bring her closer, hold her tighter. "They came for me, Ava. They came for me and they found me... and it was so dark and so..."

"Shh," I hush, letting her bury her face in my neck. "It's okay. It's all over now. You're home, Mama. And you're *safe.*"

* * *

Mom has "episodes" and with them comes "aftermaths."

We've experienced more than a few of them since she's returned, and even a couple between deployments. When Krystal writes up her report about this particular episode, she'll call it a "mild" one. Most of the time I'm with Mom, or at the least, I'm near enough that I can be there to help her through it. When the aftermaths are harder to reach, Trevor has to step in, physically. Emotionally, it's all on me.

It took a half hour to get my mom to calm down enough so I could get her into bed. She was asleep within minutes. The episodes take a lot out of her.

"Ava?" Trevor says, standing in my doorway, his shoulder leaning against the frame. "You okay?"

"Yeah." I nod, saving the final changes to Trevor's calendar. Having him leave work for an emergency like today means having to reschedule his appointments. I always offer to make the calls so he doesn't have to. It's one less thing he has to worry about, and the very least I can do.

"Krystal just left," he says, entering my room. He sits on the edge of the bed, his arms outstretched behind him. "But I gotta be honest, Ava. Things aren't the greatest right now, and I really don't think I should be leaving you alone this—"

"Stop it," I cut in, already knowing this was coming. "I'll be fine." *I hope.* "Besides, you *need* to be there. You're the best man." At his old man's wedding. The same man I used to call my stepdad. The same man who split when things got too hard for him and left all the burden on his son because apparently there's no such thing as *too hard* for Trevor.

He sighs, the sound filling the entire room. "I knew you'd say that, which is why I called in a favor..."

I spin in my desk chair and face him completely. "What do you mean?"

"Peter's flying in tonight," Trevor says, and my stomach turns, remembering what it was like the last time he was here. "He'll be over first thing tomorrow morning."

I go to tell him *no*, that I'll be okay and that Peter doesn't need to come, that I don't *want* him here... but then I look at Trevor, see the strain in his shoulders and the torment in his eyes, and my guilt... my guilt forces me to smile, to say, "I can't wait."

* * *

> Connor: You ruined me with a single kiss, Ava Elizabeth Diana.

My lips twitch, but I fight back a smile. After the day I've had, the last thing I need is to be reminded of the one thing I want, the one thing I *can't* have. No matter how desperately I yearn for it.

I squash my selfish desires and reply.

> Ava: You said you were curious. Don't you know that curiosity killed the cat?

> Connor: And a cat has 9 lives, so does that mean you owe me 8 more kisses?

I stare at the text, ignore the slow breaking of my heart. What I'd give for eight more greedy moments with him.

"Ava?" Mom calls from her bedroom and I drop my phone, along with all my delusions, and I go to her.

I'll *always* go to her.

Because she'll always come first.

First and forever.

connor

I'M LEANING up against my car the day after the Just Once Kiss, looking down at my phone, rereading the past few days' worth of text conversations between Ava and me. And without fail, I keep trying to scroll for more after the last one I sent. She didn't reply, and I can't help but overthink all the possible reasons. Maybe she's playing games, or maybe she got distracted or maybe—and this is the conclusion of my own mind games—maybe she doesn't *want* a repeat.

Maybe I'm a shit kisser.

A complete disappointment.

Sighing, I start writing a message to let her know I'm outside, but their front door opens, stopping me.

I wish for Ava.

I get Trevor instead.

He makes his way down the driveway and stops a few feet away. "You okay?" he asks, eyeing me dubiously.

I run my hand over my clothes, try to straighten out my thoughts. "Yeah, why?"

His eyebrows lower, his lips turned up in disgust. "Were you looking at porn?"

"No. What the fuck?" I mumble. "I was just studying some game tape," I lie.

"I heard about your game. Congrats, man."

I stand taller. "Thanks."

"So, listen, my old man's getting remarried..." he says, pausing when my eyes narrow. I remember what Rhys said about him walking out on them, and a flicker of anger fills my thoughts. "I know..." Trevor shrugs. "He's not the greatest man out there, but he's my dad, so I kind of have to be there."

"I get it."

"Anyway," he says, shoving his hands in his pockets, "I'm going to be away for a few days..."

Hope replaces my anger.

"...so, I'm having a friend come stay with Ava while I'm gone."

And hope dies in my chest. I point to myself. "I could stay with her."

He chuckles, pats my shoulder and squeezes. Tight. "You *could*," he replies. Then his eyes harden when they glare into mine, making sure I'm focused on his next words. "But you *won't*."

My lips purse. "Got it."

A car drives past us, turning at the end of the cul-de-sac, and parks behind mine.

"That's him now," Trevor states, already making his way toward it.

I can't ignore the inkling of jealousy when I see the car—a Mercedes G-Wagon—or the guy. He's around Trevor's age with surfer boy good looks that would be there even if money wasn't. And the jealousy turns into animosity at the thought that *this* is the guy who'll be spending the next few days with Ava, seeing her when I can't, talking to her face-to-face and not through a fucking phone screen. He'll see her just woken up, or just before bed. Hell, he'll probably even see her *in* bed. Bile rises to my throat, but I push it away the moment Ava appears on her porch.

"Ava, Peter's here!" Trevor calls out, looking right at her.

Ava's smile seems unrestrained as she rushes down the steps and greets the guy, completely ignoring the fact that I'm here.

My nemesis—aka Peter—wraps his arms around her the moment she's close enough. The hug lasts too long, and I want to clear my throat and yell, *hello, I'm here, too.* But that would be pathetic. More pathetic than me just standing here watching them. Peter pulls back an inch, takes her in from head to breasts and back again.

Yeah, I already don't like this guy, and I know nothing about him.

He holds her face in both his hands, and I want to rip off those hands and beat him to death with them. "Bad night, huh?" he asks, and there's no possible way he would know that just from looking at her.

Ava finally, *finally*, notices me standing on the sidewalk like a lost fucking puppy and releases her embrace. She tells him, "Just give me a second."

I stand, my hands in my pockets and my pride in her grasp. "I'm going to be late this morning."

That's *it*?

Where's my fucking hug?

I know I shouldn't be this upset, so I do my best to hide it. "Everything okay?"

"Yeah," she says, tugging on the lapels of my blazer. "I should be there by lunch."

Nodding, I glance up to see Peter on their porch watching our every move. Ava asks, "I'll meet you at our usual spot?"

Peter crosses his arms, his eyes narrowed.

Ava tugs on my blazer again. "Okay?"

My eyes drift back to the girl in front of me, the morning sun hitting her eyes, turning them orange. I smile when she does. "Yeah. I'll be waiting."

On her toes, she reaches up, plants a kiss on my cheek. It's not the kiss I wanted, the kiss I thought I *needed*, but it's something. And *something* sure beats all the uncertainty I'd been drowning in.

* * *

Lunch comes around, and I skip the cafeteria just so I can get those few minutes more with her. I'm at our spot before she is, so I wait and wait and wait. My excitement turns to confusion, and then confusion turns to worry. I send her a text, ask if everything's okay. Then I wait some more. By the time the warning bell sounds and there's still no reply, that worry turns to envy, to jealousy.

And I hate that it does. Because I realize that this reaction burning a hole inside me isn't because of this guy's car or his looks or even the fact that he gets to spend time with Ava. It's because whoever the hell he is, Trevor trusts him enough to be around her, and more? Ava trusts him enough to be around her mom... something I haven't earned.

And something I'll probably never get a chance to.

connor

IT'S NEARLY MIDDAY SATURDAY, and the only communication I've had with Ava was a text last night with a simple "sorry."

There was nothing else to accompany it, and I don't even know if she's sorry she stood me up yesterday or sorry she didn't let me know or sorry because she's giving one or all of my eight kisses to a guy sleeping in her house.

My brain is broken. Obviously.

Which is probably why I'm sitting on the front porch with my phone in my hand, staring at the unsent message that's been flashing on my screen for the last half hour.

It says:

Hi

Because I don't know what else to say without sounding as desperate as I feel.

I delete the text and pocket my phone, then just stare out into the street as if it's my only care in the world. The guy opposite us is mowing his lawn; a few houses over, someone is painting their porch. A woman is out walking a dog past a guy washing his car. And then some kids show up on their bikes, backpacks on. It's the same punk kids from before who TP'd Ava's house. I sit higher, watch closer. They ride in circles at the end of the road, their voices low. One of them gets off his bike, the biggest of them all, and removes his backpack. Crouched down and staring at Ava's place, he pulls out a water bomb.

I'm on my feet, walking down my steps before he even raises his arm. "You should probably think twice before throwing that!"

All four boys glare at me. The one with the water bomb yells, "Fuck you!"

Fuck me?

No.

I yell, "You suck your paci with that mouth, you little bitch!" Not my greatest moment, but it's all I could come up with. I'm barefoot, but it doesn't stop me from attempting to chase after them. The minute they see me at full height, they're on their bikes, water bombs discarded. Their laughing grates on my nerves, and they don't leave immediately. Instead, they circle the road, waiting for me to make my next move.

I pick up a stick.

The smallest of the rat-pack yells, mocking, "You should probably think twice before throwing that!"

Then from behind me, water flies over my shoulder, just missing me. I turn to see Peter with a power hose, his eyes narrowed. "Get the hell outta here, you shitheads."

The kids start to bail, and Peter follows them with the hose, attacking their backs. They get too far for the water to reach, so they stop, turn to us. One of them shouts, "Oh, look! Your boyfriend came to save you."

"Fuck these kids," Peter mumbles, standing next to me. "How fast can you run with no shoes?"

"Fast," I respond.

"Ready?"

We jet, my feet hitting the pavement hard. The kids take off, one of them shouting, "You need to get your wisdom teeth removed!"

And another adds, "Yeah. So you can fit more dicks in your mouth!"

Peter busts out a laugh, slowing to a stop. I do the same.

"Jesus Christ," he says, watching them turn the corner. "Insults sure have amped up since I was a kid." He offers me his fist for a bump when we turn back toward my house. "I'm Peter, by the way."

For a second, I'd forgotten that he was my enemy. I bump his fist anyway. "Connor."

"I know who you are," he says in a non-threatening tone.

My chest swells at the idea that Ava mentioned me.

"Trevor told me about you. Or *warned* me actually."

"Warned you?" I ask incredulously.

He shakes his head. "Not like that, just that you and Ava have a thing going on."

A Thing. That's what we're calling it? Cool.

"He said to make sure you weren't creeping into her bedroom at night."

I wish. "Nah," I say. "It's not like that." We stop in front of Ava's house, and

I help him wind up the hose. I ask, as nonchalant as I can, "How is she anyway? I haven't heard from her for a couple days."

Peter shrugs. "She's been busy with her mom and all. I think she has a harder time when Trevor's gone, and I'm no back-up Trevor. I'm just here for the muscle."

Nodding, I pretend to understand what he's saying, but the truth is, besides the basics of what Ava's told me, I have no idea what she goes through on the daily.

A car I recognize as Rhys's drives past us, turns, and parks in front of my house. There are a couple guys from the team with him. And Karen. The others stay in the car while he gets out and approaches, his gaze on Peter. To me, he says, "What's up, dipshit?" And to Peter, he says, "Hey, man. Home for a break?" They shake hands as if they've known each other their entire lives.

Peter answers, "Just staying with Ava while Trevor's gone."

"Oh yeah. His dad's wedding, right?"

Peter nods. And my stomach drops. It's like I'm right here but in another dimension. Clueless to the real world. I don't know how Rhys knows Peter or how he knows what goes on in Ava's life, if it's small-town gossip or if Ava's talking to Rhys the same way she talks to me.

But *more*.

More unreserved and open, and I feel... I feel so fucking *insignificant*.

Rhys says, pointing to me, "Get your ass dressed. We're going to the sports park."

"Don't we have that showcase today?"

After a scoff, Rhys mumbles, "Yeah, in like four hours. Let's go."

I sigh, not really in the mood to socialize. "Is Mitch going?"

"Nah, he can't make it."

Good.

Then Peter says, "Maybe he's getting his wisdom teeth removed."

I can't help but chuckle.

"What?" asks Rhys, confused.

And I say, "You know, so he can fit more dicks in his mouth."

Peter laughs, and Rhys glances between us. Then Karen appears from thin air and sidles up next to me. "You coming?" she asks.

"Yes," Rhys answers for me. "Hurry your ass up. I'm hungry as shit."

"I'll go get dressed," I say at the same time Peter tells Karen, "Hi, I'm Peter."

Karen giggles. "I know who you are. You and Trevor used to chase Ava and me around the backyard with piss-filled water pistols."

His eyes widen. "You're that girl?" Then he eyes her up and down. "Damn, talk about a glow up."

"Get dressed already!" Rhys yells, shoving me toward my front door.

I throw my hands up in surrender. "I'm going." I glance toward Ava's house, shocked to see her standing in her doorway watching us all. I lift my hand in a wave. She shuts the door between us.

AVA

"What's going on outside?" Mom asks, agitated.

I close the door, jealousy and resentment forming an ache in my chest too large to ignore. I plaster on a smile and sit back down at the table, moving Mom's speech therapy flashcards around aimlessly. "It's just some kids from school," I mumble.

"Are they messing with the house again?" she asks, her eyes narrowed, fist balled on the table.

"No, Mama. They're just out there talking to Connor."

She snorts. "Who the hell is Connor?"

"He's..." He's a boy who deserves to have the life being offered to him. "He's no one."

CONNOR

In my room, between getting dressed, I text Ava.

> Connor: Rhys is forcing me out of the house, then I have the showcase this afternoon, but I'm free after if you want me to come by.

> Connor: We can sit on your front porch for all of twenty seconds and watch the grass grow. I don't really care. I just want to see you.

I wait a good five minutes for her to respond, ignoring Rhys on my doorstep telling me to hurry the fuck up. I send a text to Dad sleeping in the next room and tell him where I'll be.

Then I send another message to Ava.

> Connor: I just really miss you is all. If you never want to talk about what happened—the kiss thing—that's cool. Just don't shut me out, Ava. Please.

AVA

"So, I met Connor," Peter says, sitting on the couch next to me while Mom sits in her room, alone, staring at the wall because she'd rather be doing that than be around me right now.

Today is a negative day. I just haven't worked out how bad it is yet.

"And?" I ask, reading back the stream of texts Connor had just sent me.

"And he seems like a decent kid."

I think about Connor and how much things will change for him now that he's in the spotlight. He'll have more friends than he knows what to do with, and girls like Karen... and then there's me. And right now, he thinks that I'll be enough, but that won't last forever, and even after an incredible life-changing kiss, nothing's changed. I'll still be me, always, and he'll get sick of the wanting and waiting, and he'll move on. I reread the message: *Just don't shut me out, Ava.* "He's a dreamer," I mumble. *A disbeliever.*

Peter asks, "What do you mean?"

"Nothing." I shake my head, rid the fog. "I don't know what I'm saying."

CONNOR

Sitting in the front seat of Rhys's car, Oscar moans, rests his head on the window. Next to me, Chad, another senior on the team, does the same. "What's up with you guys?" I ask.

"Not so loud," Chad groans.

Karen looks past Chad in the middle of the back seat and tells me, "They're hung-over."

"Oh man," I laugh out. "Big night?"

Karen's lips purse. "Uh-huh. My birthday party last night. I invited you but..."

Shit. I'd completely forgotten. "I had a ton of homework," I lie.

"Sure," she says, offering a painstakingly fake smile.

We get to the sports park and hit the food trucks first. Rhys seems to get one of everything while the other two guys pick at their food. Karen's sitting next to me, and I don't really know why she's here, but the other guys don't seem to mind it so it must be a regular thing. Rhys lets out an ear-piercing belch when he's done, gets up, and smacks the other two guys upside their heads. "Let's hit the cages," he orders, and the two get up groaning, but follow him anyway. I'm still eating my food and so is Karen, so we awkwardly sit in silence. I don't know what to say, and she doesn't speak. I check my phone. Still no Ava.

"Look at those dumbasses," Karen says, pointing to the cages. Oscar's in the cage, his helmet on backward, balls flying at his head. "You know what they say is the best thing to do when balls are coming at your face?"

"What?" I ask.

She faces me and says, smirking, "Don't open your mouth."

A chuckle erupts from deep in my throat. "Hey, how come you don't seem as hung-over as them?"

She shrugs. "I don't drink."

"Serious?" I ask, unable to hide my shock.

She laughs at my response. "We have the same trick, you and me. Walk around with a full cup and no one bothers you..." she says knowingly.

"I drink sometimes," I explain. "I just have to be in the right mood. What's your reason?"

"I don't really know. I tried it once, but it wasn't really enjoyable, and I'm not one to give in to peer pressure and do something just because everyone else does."

"That's... smart. I would've never thought that about you."

She shrugs. "People tend to judge me based on my looks or the way I carry myself. I'm confident, sure, and I like to look nice, but that doesn't mean I don't have brains. I have the third highest GPA in our class." There's a hint of disdain in her tone, and I wonder if she's talking about people in general, or me specifically. Because I sure as shit judged her based on everything she just said, and in this setting, outside of school, she seems like a decent person to be around. She starts packing up both our empty plates. "You ready?"

"Yeah." We stand together, and I follow her to the trash, then to the cages. I say, making sure she can hear me, "Hey, I'm sorry I missed your party. Happy birthday, by the way."

Her smile is as genuine as her response. "Thanks, Connor. I appreciate it."

* * *

"Jesus. She's got a reasonable swing on her," I remark, watching Karen swing a bat as if it came with years of practice.

Rhys fingers the cage, then starts to climb it. "She ain't bad."

"Does she hang around you guys often?" I ask, pulling him down when I see one of the attendants start making his way over to us.

"Karen? Yeah. She's one of the boys. Has been for years."

"Huh."

"Don't let those legs and that pretty smile fool you," he tells me, leaping off the cage and landing in a squat. To be honest, I hadn't noticed either of those things. "She's competitive as hell. That's why she and Ava got along so well. Put those two in a room together, and they could take down the Chinese wall."

"The Great Wall of China?"

"Same thing." He shrugs. Then adds, "So Peter's home?"

"I guess. How do you know him?"

He scoffs. "Everyone knows Peter Parker."

"That *can't* be his real name," I mumble, bewildered.

Chuckling, he says, "Oh, but it is."

In the cage, Oscar asks for the bat, and Karen tosses it toward him, but he's too slow, and it hits him right in the nuts. Oscar howls in pain, folds over himself. I turn to Rhys, ask him something that's been consuming my mind all afternoon. "Hey, do you and Ava talk a lot?"

He faces me, expressionless. "Define *a lot*."

I shrug, look through the cage again. "Just seems like you know a lot about what's going on in her life." *More than I do,* I want to add, but don't.

"I told you it wasn't like that," he says, clearly irked by my question.

"No, I know," I assure. "I'm just... I'm trying to work out what we are exactly—Ava and me—and I can't seem to get it out of her, so... I don't know. I'm just looking for validation, I guess."

Rhys sighs. "My sister graduated two years ago. She took most of the same classes that Ava's taking now, and she kept most of her notes because she's a giant fucking nerd, I guess. She lets me give them to Ava for the classes she misses because that girl misses *a lot* of classes. We talk about that stuff mainly, but yeah, sometimes I'll ask how she's doing, and she'll tell me."

"She must be telling you more than she tells me. I can barely get her on the phone."

"She has a lot going on," he tries to convince. "And it's got to be hard for her."

"Hard how?"

"I don't know, dude." He rubs the back of his neck, frustrated. "I guess, trying to juggle and prioritize school while having to be a parent to your own parent, add to that the normal teenage anxiety and emotions and trying not to get too attached to people." He backhands my chest. "People like you."

"She can attach herself to me," I say. "I won't mind it."

Shaking his head, he laughs under his breath. "You say that now, but it's harder than you think. Trust me, man. You think I don't know your situation, but I do. I *was* you."

* * *

I get home just in time to shower, change and get ready for the showcase—a "fun" afternoon for the fans where the team plays three-on-three, and we do nothing but show off our skills. I'm one foot out the door when I stop in my tracks. It's a different balloon, but the same writing, same number, same insult.

My stupid grin matches my foolish glee.

I bet Rhys never got balloons.

ava

I STARTLE when my alarm goes off, even though I'm wide awake. The biology paper I'm working on has kept me up the entire night—the only time the house has been peaceful enough to work. I set the phone down. I need the A. Not for me, but for Trevor. He works too damn hard to pay for this education, no matter how hard I'd fought him on it. "When it's over," he'd told me —whatever *over* means—"your high school education is going to be important." And then came the argument about college that ended with me promising I'd apply to some even if I had absolutely zero intentions of going. "You can defer," he'd said. "And we'll work out the rest when the time comes."

I'm typing and typing and typing, rushing through the final two paragraphs when I hear Mom's bedroom door open. *Shit.* I look at the time. 5:05. *Shit. Shit. Shit.* I shut the screen, get to my feet. "Sorry, Mama. I lost track of time. I'll get your breakfast going."

Mom's eyes are dead as she stares at me, and I can't stand to see it. I look away, start on her food. Flames heat my face when I turn on the stove. I quickly set the pan on top, drop in some oil. Then I go to the fridge, pull out the bacon and eggs. I rush around the kitchen, dropping bread in the toaster, and she stands at the doorway watching me. "Five a.m., Ava," she says, her voice as chilling as her presence. "I have breakfast at 5 a.m. every goddamn morning."

"I know, I'm sorry." I turn my back to her so I can work over the stove, my heart beating out of my chest. My hands shake as I try to pick up an egg, and then she's beside me, looming over and around me.

"Move!" she orders. "I can make my own damn breakfast."

"No, Mama," I say, trying to keep as calm as possible, but I can feel the darkness wavering above us, the doom and gloom like a ticking time bomb just waiting to explode. I inhale deeply, exhale the same way. "I got it. Please sit down. I'll only—"

"*Move!*" she shouts, grabbing at the pan handle.

I fight to get it back, even though I know I shouldn't. She's too strong, too wired, and I'm weak... God, I'm so fucking weak. Tears spring in my eyes, and I say, refusing to let go, "I'll make it! I'm sorry."

"Goddammit, Ava! I said MOVE!" she screams, pulling at the pan until I finally release it, but she wasn't expecting it, and neither was I, because the pan flips up and burning hot oil catches on my neck, my chest. I shriek, the pain unbearable, and run to the tap. Tears fall from my eyes, mixing with the oil, burning through my flesh.

"What the hell happened?" Peter exclaims, appearing in the kitchen.

I try to splash water on myself, but it's useless.

"Jesus Christ, Ava," Peter says, grabbing me by my shoulders and turning me to him. His eyes widen when he takes me in, and he's quick to grab a dish towel and soak it with cold water. He wraps it around my neck, then runs to the fridge and pulls out the ice tray. He plugs up the sink, fills it with water and ice.

"What the hell did you do, Jo?" he asks my mom.

Mom doesn't respond.

I'm on the floor now, my cries so strong they're silent. My body convulses, the burning flesh heating my insides. Tears. So many tears. Peter finds all the dish towels in the kitchen and dumps them in the filling sink. He grabs a handful and places them wherever he can see the damage. My neck. My shoulders. My chest. "Keep them there," he tells me. Then he leaves, only to return with his phone to his ear.

"Who are you calling?" I manage to get out.

"The crisis team. We can't do this alone, Ava. We need help."

"No, we can't afford—"

"Quit it. You need to go to the hospital."

"I'm fine," I cry out.

"I swear to God—" he starts, but the call must connect. He gives the person on the other end all our details, Mom's case number, and as much information as he knows about what just happened. When he hangs up, he says, "They're sending over two people. They'll be here soon."

He squats down in front of me, wincing when he pulls back a dish towel. "I'm going to call an ambulance."

I want to say no, but the pain is too much, and so I nod, let him gently wipe my tears. He exhales harshly, his breath hitting my face. Then he shakes his head, his eyes on mine. I know what he's saying without saying a word. *The offer still stands.* And I look away, unable to give him what he needs. Then I glance up, find my mother in front of the stove, a spatula in her hand. The smell of bacon fills the room, then the sound of her singing, humming. She stares out the window. "It looks like the sun's going to grace us today."

* * *

Mom sits at the kitchen table, a plate of bacon, eggs, and toast in front of her. Peter stands in the doorway between the kitchen and living room while the paramedics make their way inside. I sit on the couch, covered in wet dish towels to alleviate the pain and any blistering.

The house is silent bar Mom's continuous, joyous singing.

I feel dead inside.

Dead, dead, dead.

One of the paramedics crouches down in front of me, offers me a smile that does nothing for me. "Hi," he says, his voice soft. He glances behind him at Peter and his partner while Peter explains what he thinks happened. I still haven't found my voice or my courage to tell him.

The man in front of me says, "My name's Corey. And you're Ava, right?"

I nod, even though I don't recall Peter mentioning my name, but most people around here know who I am, or at least know of us and where we live. It's a stigma we carry that I wish would just fuck the hell off.

The man—Corey—smiles again. "I uh... I actually live next door," he tells me. "I'm Connor's dad."

"Oh."

Oh, God, no.

"I'm just going to peel these off and see what we're working with, okay?"

I nod, lift my chin for him to gain better access, and wince when he starts to remove the towel. "I know it hurts, and I'm sorry. I'm going to try to make this as painless as possible for you, okay, Ava?" He has the same gentle tone as Connor, the same blue-blue eyes, too.

"You have his eyes," I murmur.

"What's that?"

"Connor. You have his eyes."

His lips form a line. "I think Connor got them from me if we're being technical..."

I stare at my mom, who's still blissfully unaware.

"Do you want to tell me what happened here, Ava?" Corey asks.

A single tear rolls down my cheek. My heart beats, but there's no life inside me. "I like them," I whisper.

"Like what?"

"His eyes. Connor's. And his heart."

Corey's hands freeze mid-movement. "His *heart*?"

My eyes drift shut, melancholy melting inside me. "His heart is full of magic."

* * *

"If you need to sedate her, do it," I hear Peter tell the crisis workers. They're from the same agency as Krystal, but they're better trained for moments like these. They arrived a few minutes before the paramedics left, but I was already in my room with liquid sorrow staining my pillows.

A knock on my door and Peter appears, not waiting for a response. He sits on the edge of my bed, his shoulders hunched. He lets his face fall into his hands, a quiet moan escaping him. It's not the first time he's experienced Mom on a negative day but never this extreme and never directed at me. He looks over at me, his eyes filled with pity. "How are you feeling?"

I blink. I don't know how to respond, what answer to give him that'll alleviate his concern.

Peter sighs. "You look tired, Ava."

I swallow, my eyelids heavy, the painkillers forcing their way through my bloodline. "I haven't slept."

"All night?" he asks, eyebrows raised in disbelief.

"Mmm."

He settles his hand on my hip. "Sleep, baby girl. I'll stay up and take care of things, okay?"

I nod, my entire body too heavy to move. Eyes closed, I feel the bed dip, then his warm lips settle on my temple. "I'll take care of you, Ava. Always."

* * *

I'm in and out of sleep all day, but always in a daze. Even when I feel alert enough to get up, I stay in bed. Peter checks in on me often, and I keep my eyes closed, not wanting to hear what he has to say.

When the world is at its darkest, that's when the magic appears.

It's not magic that enters my room when the stillness of the night creates a silence around us. It's Peter. My eyes squint at the stream of light filtering in from the hallway, and Peter notices because he walks in and switches on my lamp. He settles on the edge of my bed again, his hand on my leg. "Your mom's asleep, the crisis workers are going to take shifts overnight, and they'll be here all of tomorrow."

"Okay," I whisper, not looking at him.

"Have you reapplied your cream?"

I force my body to half sit up. "No, I forgot."

"Well, we better do that. We don't want that flawless skin of yours scarring." He grabs the cream the paramedics left for me and gets more comfortable on the bed. Then he reaches up, pulls the covers down until they're resting at my waist. He removes the dressing, slowly, carefully, and starts applying the cream where needed. Starting at my neck, he moves to my shoulders, taking his time, and then lower, lower, to my chest revealed by the tank top I've been wearing all day. He spends the most time there, just above my breasts. His touch is soft, heated, nurturing.

I can take care of you, Ava. But it's our little secret.

"Your mom's getting worse, Ava," he murmurs.

"Stop it."

"I know you don't want to hear this, but she needs help."

"I just need to get through this year. For Trevor. And then... then..."

He sighs. "Then what?"

I don't know. My shoulders fall with the first sob that consumes me. I keep my cries quiet, but he's there to hold me. To wipe the tears from my eyes. To assure me that everything will be okay, even when he doesn't believe it himself.

He finishes tending to my physical wounds, then gets under the covers with me. "Come here," he whispers, helping me to lie back down. I rest my head on his chest while his fingers stroke my arm. His chest rises and falls with his steady breaths, his heartbeat forming a steady rhythm blasting in my eardrums.

Thump, thump.

Thump, thump.

I close my eyes and listen; try to find what I'm looking for.

But it's not there.

Because he's not The One.

The Holder of Hope.

The Creator of Magic.

He's not Connor.

connor

MONDAY MORNING, Ava sent me a message telling me she wasn't going to be at school, that something came up with her mom. I offered to help however I could, but she didn't reply to my messages.

Tuesday morning, same damn thing.

Finally, on Wednesday, she tells me she's going, but she doesn't need a ride. Peter will take her. Whatever. At least she's going, and I'll get to see her. Five days of no-Ava is too damn long. But when psych class begins and she's not sitting next to me, I start to worry, and that worry starts burning a hole in my gut. Something's... *off*. And I don't know what to do about it. Finally, about twenty minutes into class, the door opens and she appears. That first breath I inhale when I see her, God, it's like I'd been holding on to it for all five days. She hands Mr. McCallister a note and then makes her way over to me, a slight smile on her lips that has me goddamn giddy with excitement. I've missed her. In all the possible ways you can miss someone, I've *craved* her.

Just her presence alone seems to settle my anxiety, and I haven't even spoken to her yet. She sits down next to me, her leg tapping mine beneath the table.

I pull out a notepad as inconspicuously as possible and scribble down: *You're a sight for sore eyes, Ava.*

With a smile, she reads what I wrote and writes back: *It's good to see you, too, I suppose.* Then crosses it out completely and writes: *I've missed you.*

My heart does a stupid flip, and I settle my hand on her knee, praying she won't push me away. As soon as the teacher's turned his back to the class, I face her.

My eyes thirst for her, as lame as that sounds. But it's true. Five fucking days and I'd forgotten how hot she was. I'm staring, breathing her in, and I don't even care. I've missed her hair, a mess of a thing that seems to have a life of its own. And her eyes surrounded by thick, long lashes. She has freckles on her cheeks, right below her eyes, but just a few. And those lips, goddamn those lips. And her jaw... I've thought too long and too hard about that jaw, what it would be like to kiss her there, and then lower, down her neck and to her collarbone... which I can't see because she's wearing a turtleneck beneath her school shirt and it's strange because it's warm out and she's never worn... my thought trails off when I see it. I know exactly what it is because our medicine cabinet's filled with all the ones Dad takes home from work. Sterile dressing to cover a wound.

Ava catches me staring and lifts her shoulder, adjusts her clothes. She's trying to hide whatever is there, and there's only one reason why she'd do that. She doesn't want me to know how it happened.

I scribble on my notepad: *What happened?*

She writes back: *Nothing.*

Bullshit.

I watch the seconds tick by, forming all the minutes until class is over and I can ask her out loud. As soon as the bell rings, she's on her feet, rushing to get out. But she's too slow, or I'm too fast, too desperate. I catch her just outside the door and grasp her arm to stop her from fleeing. "What happened?"

She inhales deeply, before stating, "Nothing. Stop worrying." She tries to pull out of my hold, but I keep her there.

"Ava, I'm not playing. What the fuck happened? You're MIA for five fucking days, and you come back hurt?"

"It's not what you think," she says.

I don't even know what I'm thinking.

"I have to get to my next class. I'll see you at lunch, okay?"

She bails, leaving me standing in the hallway with my heart pounding and my mind racing. Five days. Five fucking days and she hasn't shown up to school once, has barely answered my texts. Ever since Trevor left—

Trevor left, and Peter came....

Peter.

AVA

I'm going to tell Connor the truth.

I decided a few minutes after leaving him in the hall that I would come clean and tell him everything. I wanted to tell him then and there, but the mix of anger and concern in his eyes had me panicking for a way out. I just needed a few minutes to myself so I could collect my thoughts and explain things in a way that would make him understand. The last thing I needed was for him to misplace his emotions and blame my mom for everything. Of all the things that could possibly ruin whatever it was we had going, his misunderstanding of my mom's mental health would be the most heartbreaking.

I sit in the bleachers, our usual spot, and wait for him to show up while I make up pieces of our future conversation. I want to be ready for any questions he has, and I want the answers to be real. To be raw.

Minutes pass, and I start to get antsy. My breathing becomes shallow, my palms begin to sweat, and the burns begin to itch. I try not to think about it as I wait. Stand. Sit again. I check the school website for the basketball roster, thinking maybe he forgot he had some prior engagement. Nothing comes up. I stand again, look over and out and everywhere I can for him. Then my phone rings. It's already in my hand, so I answer without looking.

"Connor?"

"It's Krystal, Ava. I think you might need to come home, honey. A boy is fighting Peter in the front lawn."

I hang up without a word, dial another number and start rushing toward the lot.

Rhys answers on the first ring. "What's up?"

"I need a ride home. It's Connor."

"Meet me at my car."

* * *

Rhys's car screeches to a halt halfway up my driveway. I have one foot on the ground before he comes to a complete stop. "Oh, my God, Connor, stop!"

The two are wrestling on the grass, Peter on top of Connor, his fist raised. He gets a shot at Connor's stomach, but it doesn't seem to faze him. Connor rolls them both over until he's on top, and his fist hitting Peter's jaw sounds like lightning, feels like thunder. There's blood pouring out of Connor's nose and Peter's mouth, splatters of crimson all over their shirts. "Stop!" I cry out, reaching for Connor's arm. He doesn't flinch. Another punch to Peter's gut.

"Enough!" Peter yells, half defending himself while trying to buck Connor off him.

He has his hand on Connor's throat now, while Connor screams, "Is that what Ava said, huh? Enough?"

"Connor stop it!" I squeal.

"I didn't fucking touch her," Peter yells, getting the strength to shove Connor away. Connor rolls to the side, but Peter won't quit. "Who the fuck do you think you are!"

Connor kicks up his legs, gets Peter in his chest with a knee. "That's enough!" Rhys shouts, trying to get between them.

"Ava!" Krystal calls out. "I'm calling the police."

I can't breathe. I can't see through my tears.

Connor pushes Rhys away, and now he and Peter are on their feet, fists raised, both on the attack. "You ever touch her again, I'll fucking kill you."

Peter lunges for him, his shoulder going straight to Connor's stomach. A guttural sound leaves Connor's lips, and he's on the ground, only for a second before he's back up.

"A little help, Ava!" Rhys hollers, struggling. He's holding Peter back, but he won't last long, and fear and frenzy shake me from the inside.

I run as fast as I can from my house to Connor's, my fists balled as I bang on the door. "Help!" I yell. I pound harder, faster, until the door finally opens. Connor's dad looks at me wide-eyed and startled. "It's Connor. You need—"

Corey's racing down the steps and toward my house, and before I even make it back, he has his arms around Connor's waist, trapping his hands to the side. "Knock it off!"

Now the two guys are restrained, and I stand between them, not knowing what to do or how to act. "I swear to God. I don't give a fuck who you are or where you're from, you so much as look at her again and I'll end you," Connor seethes, his face red. I stand in front of him, but he doesn't see me through the rage flaming inside him. He spits blood from his mouth, his chest heaving beneath his shirt.

"Connor," I cry, trying to calm him.

"Get out of my way, Ava."

His dad tightens his hold. "Connor, that's enough!"

Sirens approach, and when I look around, I see our neighbors outside their homes, all watching us, some with their phones out.

The Insane Asylum.

The Looney Bin.

Tears flow, cascade. I lower my gaze, cover my mouth to muffle my cries. "You need to leave, Connor," I beg.

His heavy breath hits the top of my head, and I look up to see him watching me. Beaten and bruised, his eyes hold mine. "Ava," he whispers, shaking his head.

"Please," I urge. "Just go home."

THIRTY-ONE

Connor

I'M LOCKED. Trapped in my own fucking home—my own nightmare—while outside, Ava and Dad speak to the police as if I don't have a voice of my own. An hour passes, and Dad still hasn't returned, and I'm losing my damn mind. I pace. Three steps one way, then three steps the other because it's all the room this shitty house has to offer.

I'm pissed.

Beyond it.

Because she didn't ask *him* to leave. She asked *me*.

Finally, Dad enters, and I stop pacing. Arms down, chest out, I'm ready for it. "I convinced them not to press any charges against you," he says.

"Me?" I shout. "What about that fucker?!"

"Watch your goddamn mouth, Connor!"

I draw back. "You're kidding, right? He's the one hurting her, and you're in here blasting me?"

"He didn't touch her!"

"How do you know?"

"Because I was there, okay! I'm the one who treated her!" he yells. My stomach drops, and everything inside me stills. I take a breath. And then another. I start to speak, but he beats me to it. "Whatever it is that's going on with you and that girl, it ends *now*."

I shake my head, defiant. "No."

"You think this is up for discussion?"

I start to walk away.

"I'm serious, Connor. I *forbid* you from spending time with her."

I turn on my heels, an incredulous laugh bubbling out of me. "You *forbid* me?"

"Yes." He stands in front of me, arms crossed, standing his ground.

I try to calm my thoughts, try to settle my breathing. "You *forbid* me?" I repeat, then take a step forward, tower over him. "For seventeen years I've done nothing, not one damn thing, to ever disobey you. You've never had to punish me or set rules for me. I've always tried so fucking hard to be the perfect kid because I was so afraid you'd abandon me, too—"

"Connor—"

"No!" I scream. "This is the first time in my entire life that I've ever needed your help, and this is what you do? You take away the one good thing I have in my life and—"

His sneer cuts me off. "You're acting like an ungrateful brat. You have plenty of good things in your life!"

"Like what?" I shout. "Basketball?"

"Yes!"

"It's just a game! It's not—"

"It's more than a game! It's a ticket out!"

"For you, Dad! It's a ticket out *for you!*"

His arms unfold, anger pulling at his brow. "What the hell is that supposed to mean?"

I open my mouth but stop myself from saying something I'll regret, something I've held on to for years. It means that he wants me gone, to a college far, far away, so he doesn't have to deal with me anymore. So he can get rid of the unwanted burden that was left to him. "Nothing."

"If you have something to say, say it!"

"I don't," I mumble, looking down at the floor. "But you can't stop me from seeing her."

"Bullshit, I can't," he says, his voice raised again. "She—that family of hers—they're bad news, Connor. And you don't need them in your life. Not now. Not ever!"

"I need to get out of here." I step into my room and grab my ball, then shoulder past him to get to the door.

The moment my hand's on the knob, Dad yells, "That girl is nothing but a bad distraction! She's got problems, problems too big for you to shoulder, and she's tearing you down with her! Look at you! Look at what she's made you do! She has nothing good to offer you, Connor! Not one damn thing!"

I open the door.

Freeze.

Solid.

Ava's standing on my porch, her fist raised, ready to knock. I slam the door shut behind me, my anger deflating. "How much did you hear?"

Eyes glazed, she slowly looks up at me. "All of it."

I sigh. "If you're here to tell me how much of a fuck-up I am, you can save it." I drop the ball, lean against the porch railing. "I've heard it all already."

Ava stands in front of me, her arms shielding her stomach. "Your dad's right, you know?"

"No, he's not," I breathe out, wiping the dried blood from under my nose. I inspect my hand, then wipe it on my pants. "He's right about a lot of things, Ava, but he's wrong about you."

I wince when she reaches up, touches a particularly sore spot on my jaw. I have no idea what I look like. I haven't checked. "How hurt are you?"

"How hurt are *you*?" I retort.

She doesn't respond.

"Come here," I say, my fingertips making contact with hers. I gently tug, hoping she does the rest.

She takes a step toward me, and then another. I close the distance, wrap my arm around her waist and pull her into me, ignoring the pain in my ribs when she leans against me. She settles her cheek on my chest, while I hold her to me completely, not wanting to let her go. My lips pressed to the top of her head, I whisper, "I need to know what happened, Ava."

She nuzzles closer to me, her arms going around me. "My mom happened."

I swallow the truth I knew was coming. "I'm sorry," I tell her. "And I'll go over tomorrow morning and apologize to Peter, too. I fucked up. I don't—just the thought of someone hurting you... I... I lost it. I don't even know what got into me, but..."

"It's okay," she says, looking up at me. Darkness looms in her stare, while sadness falls from her lashes. "I should've told you the truth from the beginning. It's just—"

"Hard," I finish for her. "God, Ava, I can't even imagine how hard things are for you. But I'm here, whatever you need, whenever you need me. I'm *here*."

"I can't," she says, slowly releasing me.

I grasp her hand. "Why?"

"Because—" Her phone rings, cutting her off. She looks at the screen, but I don't want my question to go unanswered.

"Why?"

She ends the call, looks up at me. "Because your dad's right, Connor." Then she jerks out of my hold. "And I have to go."

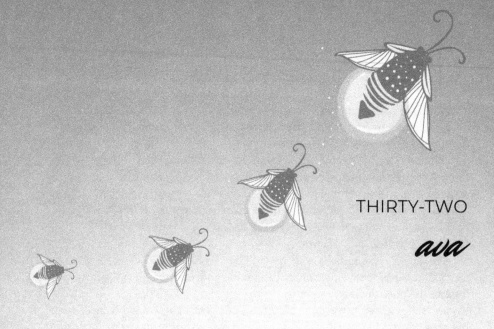

ava

THEY LOOK LIKE FIREFLIES. The way the water falls from the sky, illuminated only by the streetlamps. I stand in the middle of the road, barefoot and barely breathing, my arms out, face to the sky.

I don't know how I got here.

When I climbed out of my window, the sun was just setting and now... now I'm surrounded by dark skies and false hope.

I had to get out of the house. Krystal had left and Peter had called the crisis team to stay overnight again, and there were too many people under one roof. Too much pain and anguish. I couldn't breathe, and yet, I didn't want to. And even though there was so much going on, it felt...*lifeless.*

I messaged Peter once I was far enough away and told him not to look for me, that I was fine and just needed space and time to piece myself back together and prepare for another day.

I know I should go home.

That I should face my fears and tackle them head-on.

My mind travels the right roads at the right time to get me there, but my heart...

My heart takes me to Connor.

Outside his bedroom window, mud seeps between my toes, and the frigid air creates goosebumps along my skin. I raise my fist and tap, tap, tap on the glass.

A moment later, a light turns on. And then nothing. I tap again, my heart racing. The blind lifts and Connor appears, his eyes squinting. It's clear he'd been asleep, or close to it. Hair a mess, he's shirtless, the obvious beginnings of bruises mar parts of his torso, and I look down, shame filling every part of me. I bite down on my lip as he slides the window up. "Jesus Christ, Ava. What the hell are you doing?"

His warm palms meet my soaking wet elbows, and then his entire body is cocooning mine, lifting me off my feet and into his bedroom. My feet land on his soft carpet, and I look down at the mess I've made. "I'm dirty," I tell him.

Inside and out.

Dirty, dazed and damaged.

"You're soaked," he murmurs. "Just wait, okay? Don't go anywhere."

I stand in the middle of his room surrounded by blue walls and basket-balls, raindrops dripping from my hair, my fingers. He returns with a towel and a first-aid box, his movements swift. His towel-covered hands start at my hair, and then down my arms. He squats when he gets to my legs, does each one in turn, and then he stands up again, his touch gentle as he leads me to his desk chair, encourages me to sit. "Your dressing's ruined," he informs. He sits on the edge of his bed and reaches across, rolling me toward him. "I have to change them, or you won't heal properly." Concerned eyes look up at mine, keep them there. His chest rises with his long inhale as if it's the first breath he's taken since he's seen me. He asks, "Can I do that for you, Ava?"

Slowly, I nod, my gaze moving from his eyes to the bruise beneath it, the cut on his nose and the corner of his lips, then down to his collarbone, another bruise, two more on his torso, and I fucking hate myself.

He starts at my neck, slowly peeling off the gauze, his eyes focused, hands steady. "Does it hurt?" he asks, his voice quiet.

I shake my head.

Breaths staggered, his gaze flicks to mine, then back down again. He moves forward, just an inch, his heated breath hitting my jaw. I hear the moment his lips part, and my eyes drift shut when his mouth finds the burn. A moan escapes from deep in my throat.

He repeats the process again and again, each kiss lighting a spark inside me, warming me from the inside out. He pulls back, his eyelids heavy, then he blinks. Once, twice. And his bright blue eyes are focused again. He grabs a tube of cream and starts applying it to the burns, gently, then replaces each of the gauzes he'd removed. When he's done, he exhales loudly, his fingers reaching up to move the hair away from my eyes. He stares at me, eyes flicking between each of mine. "What were you thinking being out in the cold like that?" His fingers trace my arms, up and down, up and down.

"I wasn't," I admit. "But I needed to see you."

His forehead rests against mine when he says, "I'm glad you're here."

I rear back, run my thumb below his eye. "Does this hurt?" I ask.

He nods, his hand circling my wrist and pulling my hand down so he can link our fingers together. "A little."

I lick my lips, kiss away his pain the way he did mine. His palm cups my jaw, his fingertips laced through my hair while his lips find mine, skimming, but not kissing. We exhale at the same time, our breaths merging. I run my hands along his arms, feeling his muscles tense beneath the contact. Then over his bare shoulders, down his chest. I pause just over his heart, wait until I feel his life beating beneath my touch. "Magic," I whisper, my lips still on his. He sucks in a sharp breath, holds it there. I run my hand to his collarbone. "Does this hurt?" I ask, finger tracing the reddish-purple mark.

I pull back so I can look into his eyes—eyes glued to mine. With his bottom lip caught between his teeth, he nods, his head falling back when I lean forward, press my lips to the exact spot. His throat bobs with his heavy swallow, and I kiss him there, smiling at the sound he makes.

I feel... *free.*

Powerful.

For the first time in a long time, I feel like I'm in control of what happens next. I push on his shoulder until he's on his back, his body held up by his elbows, his eyes watching me through his thick lashes. I kiss between his collarbone and down his chest, my tongue darting out, leaving a trail behind me. His hand claims the back of my head, fingers curling as I move lower, lower. I get to my knees, eyes closed, and lick the line between his perfect abs. I find the top of his boxers, fingers playing with the waistband. I start to pull down, but his hand tightens, tugs gently on my hair. "Ava, stop. *Fuck.*"

He sits up, his hand still on my nape, keeping me in place. He buries his face in my neck, his shallow breaths heating me. "Fuck," he says again.

"What's wrong? Do you not want—"

"No, Ava. Jesus Christ, of course I want that. It's just... I don't want *this.*"

"You don't want *what?*"

He settles his forehead against mine, his eyes shut. He takes a few calming breaths, his shoulders heaving. Then he says, "I keep telling myself that I can do this—whatever *this* is. But we keep straddling the line between friendship and *more*... and sure, I can keep doing this with you. I can keep waking up every morning wondering whether that day will be a day I get to hold your hand or kiss you or touch you or just speak to you. I *can* do that every day for the rest of my life, and you'll be worth it, but... but I don't *want* to, Ava. I don't fucking *want* to."

"I can't give you what you want," I whisper, tears pricking behind my eyes.

His forehead drops to my shoulder, his single sigh the sound of defeat. He murmurs, "You keep saying that like you know what I want."

"Then what do you want?"

He looks up now, his eyes locked on mine. "You, Ava. I want you. On your good days and your bad days—*especially* your bad days. I want you to let me in. I want you to come to me and look at me the way you're looking at me now, and know that I'm *all in*. I just want *you*." His voice cracks. "God, Ava. I want you so fucking bad, it's killing me."

"I don't... I don't know what to say."

"Say yes."

My mind tells me that it'll never work, that our paths lead to different roads and the only possible outcome is heartbreak, but my heart...

My heart says, "Yes."

His mouth is on mine before I can take a breath, his strong arms lifting me off my knees and on top of him. Then he rolls us over until he's over me, his weight held up by his elbows. Every inch of him covers every inch of me, and he's so warm. So solid. So *safe*. There's no pain, physical or otherwise, when his hands drift up my side, along my breast, until he's palming my neck. Careful of my burns, he places his mouth on my collarbone, licking, tasting, and I can't breathe, but the good type. The type that comes with excitement and joy and anticipation for what's to come. My foot makes contact with something on his bed, and I lift my head, look at the source. And then I laugh. I shouldn't, but I do. It starts as a giggle and turns into an all-out grandpa wheeze laugh. Connor looks up, his eyebrows drawn. "What's so funny?"

"There's a basketball in your bed," I laugh out.

He gets on his knees between my legs, the bulge in his boxers prominent. I try not to stare. I fail. He says, "I told you I sleep with a basketball."

"I thought you were joking!"

He shakes his head.

My laughter simmers down enough to say, "Show me how you sleep with it."

"Right now?" he asks, and I nod. He adjusts himself, his hand going in his boxers, and I let out a groan as I watch every one of his muscles shift. Disbelief laced in his tone, he adds, "You'd rather watch me pretend to sleep with a ball than continue what we're doing?"

I nod again, unable to hide my grin.

"Fine," he says, standing. He taps my leg. "Get off the bed."

"Sheesh, you're my boyfriend for all of a minute, and you think you can boss me around?"

"Boyfriend?" he asks, smirking. "I like that. A lot. You must refer to me as that for all of eternity."

I push him toward the bed. "Show me how you sleep with the ball, you fucking weirdo."

Chuckling, he fixes the covers, then gets underneath. On his side, one leg bent, he cuddles the ball to his chest and closes his eyes. "Nigh nighs, *girlfriend*," he whispers, then sucks his thumb.

With a short laugh, I ask, "Is it normal to be jealous of a basketball?"

He throws the ball across the room, then lifts the covers. All humor gone, he says, "I'll let you in if you do the same for me."

I don't miss the double meaning in his words, and so I bite my lip, hesitant. "I can't stay."

He smiles. "I'm not asking you to." Because he doesn't want anything more from me than what I have to offer. He wants me. Just me. Exactly as I am.

I get into bed with him and settle in the crook of his arm, my head against his chest. And if magic didn't exist *within* Connor, then it exists all around him. Because moments ago, I was dirty, dazed and damaged, and now...

Now I was falling asleep under a starlit sky, surrounded by tiny glimmers of hope.

connor

Ava: Good morning, boyfriend. My alarm went off at 4:30 and I had to get home. I didn't want to. I could've stayed in your arms forever.

Connor: New phone. Who dis?

Ava: Sorry. Wrong number. I meant to send that to my other boyfriend.

Connor: I'll beat his ass.

Ava: Before or after you get done sucking your thumb, you giant baby.

Connor: Listen here, you little shit.

Ava: I miss you.

Connor: Me too. I'll be around earlier to take you to school. I have a lot of apologizing to do today, remember?

Ava: Oh yeah. Sucks to be you.

Connor: Not really. Last night I had a girl sleep in my bed for the first time ever, so that was kind of cool.

Ava: Yeah? Was she hot?

Connor: Eh.

Ava: Listen here, you little shit.

Connor: I can't wait, Ava.

Ava: For what?

Connor: Everything.

* * *

"DAMN, I DID A NUMBER ON YOU," Peter says, coming down Ava's porch steps.

"Yeah, you got me pretty good," I admit, rubbing the back of my neck. I'm feeling a little ashamed, to say the least, and even though my anxiety had me practicing my apology speech before I got here, I'm stuck on how to start.

He backhands my stomach, and I wince at the sudden pain. "If it makes you feel any better, you got in a few good shots, too."

"I wish it did, but no." Groaning, I look at him but keep my head down. "Look, I'm sorry, man. I wish I had more to say than that, but..." I trail off.

He lets out a heavy sigh, then motions for me to follow him. He walks down the driveway and onto the sidewalk, far enough that Ava can't hear us from the house. Leaning against his car, he shoves his hands in his pockets. "I'm not going to lie; I spent most of yesterday pissed. But I think it was more that you messed up my pretty face than the fact that you did it at all."

"So, you're not pissed at *me*, specifically?" I ask.

"No."

I exhale, relieved.

"Why?"

"I don't know. I feel like that would be worse. You're obviously important to Ava, and she's important to me, so the last thing I want is to jeopardize that by becoming your enemy."

"You're not my enemy," he laughs out. "And even though you were dead wrong about what happened, your intentions were in the right place. And I can't be mad at you for thinking you were protecting Ava. That's..." He looks toward the house. "That's kind of why we're all here, right?"

I nod, though my gut tells me there's an underlying meaning to his words that has me questioning *his* intentions.

"Look," he starts, standing taller. "Ava's had it rough, and she might come across as tough, as though she's *fine*, and sure there are days when she might be, but those days, Connor, those days are rare. And if you want her in your life the way I know you do, you have to prepare yourself to care about her during all the times in between. Because you don't get to pick and choose."

"I know," I reply, my voice hoarse. "I'm aware of all of this."

Nodding, he asks, "She stay with you last night?"

I return his nod.

He smirks. "Five hundred bucks and I won't tell Trevor."

"Dude, I don't have five hundred." I don't even have *five*.

He chuckles. "I'm kidding, man."

Ava opens the door, saying bye to Krystal and her mom over her shoulder. Then she turns to us, her eyebrows raised. Her grin warns me of what's to come. "You guys are so cute," she hollers. "Now kiss!"

Peter shakes his head. "It's good to have you back, Ava," he says, widening his arms for her to embrace him, which she does. "I'll be gone when you get back from school, so this is goodbye."

Ava pouts, looks up at him. "I'll see you soon, though, right?"

"I'm a phone call away if you need anything." He kisses the top of her head, but his eyes are on me. "Anything, Ava. I mean it."

* * *

"What's with you?" Ava asks, squeezing my hand that's settled on her lap as we ride to school.

I ask, distracted, "What do you mean?"

"You're being weird. Distant." She starts to release my hand, but I hold hers tighter.

"Sorry. It's just..." I struggle with my phrasing, then just come out and say it. "Peter gives me the creeps."

She giggles. "Maybe you should go beat him up."

"Maybe," I say, pushing away those thoughts. "Hey, just curious. If you had to score that fight, who do you think came out on top?"

She doesn't skip a beat. "Me."

"You?"

She shrugs. "I got the guy."

* * *

I barely sit my ass down for first period when the teacher calls my name. "You're needed in the principal's office. Now."

Rhys is already in the office, along with Coach Sykes, and there's a sinking in my gut because I know where this is going.

Principal Brown says, "Due to your lack of class attendance yesterday, I'm suspending you both for tomorrow's game."

Coach swears under his breath, throws his hat across the room. "Dagnammit, gentlemen!"

"Ooh, he maaaad," Rhys sings, and I can't stifle my chuckle in time.

"You think this is a joke, Ledger?" Coach says, getting in my face.

I flatten my features. "No, sir."

"It's probably for the best," Coach retorts. "We don't need a face like yours representing the team."

I flinch and turn to Rhys. "How bad do I look?"

He shrugs. "Nothing a little trip to Sephora can't fix."

"I'm glad you gentlemen are finding this amusing," says Brown. "But I'll have you know that a scout from Duke is attending the next game, and while he'll be looking for boys to hand acceptance letters to, you two will be riding the bench."

* * *

When you think college ball, you think Duke. For so long, the idea of going to Duke had been exactly that: an idea. A pipe dream, really. But now... now I was here and *fuck*.

Rhys doesn't care as much as I do. Sure, he's the team captain, but college ball is as far as he wants to go with it. Plus, he has the finances to get into most places. And yeah, I'm sure more opportunities will present themselves, but they won't be Duke.

I try to push all those thoughts aside as I make my way up the bleacher steps, toward a waiting Ava.

"Is it true?" she asks the second I'm in earshot. "That you were suspended for a game and Duke is going to be there?"

"How do you know?"

"Rhys."

"Rhys has a big mouth."

"Connor, I'm serious," she whines, tugging on my arm so I sit down next to her. "Maybe I can talk to Principal Brown. It's the least I could do considering it was my fault you both—"

I grab her legs, cutting her off, and settle them over mine. I place my hand on her thigh, just below her skirt. "You didn't force me to skip class and act like a Neanderthal. It's on me, and I'll bear the consequences."

"But—"

"Ava, *please*, let it go. I get this half hour with you, and I don't want to waste it arguing about dumb shit. Now kiss me already."

"Okay," she says, kissing me once. Her lips lift at the corners, and my eyes drift shut when she runs her fingers through my hair.

"Ava?"

"Yeah?" she murmurs, her mouth pressed to my neck.

I pull her closer. "Promise not to tell anyone about the whole sleeping with a basketball thing?"

She laughs but doesn't pull away. Her lips skim along my jaw, stop just below my ear. "But then the whole flashing my boobs to the AV guys so they'd broadcast it at the next game would be for nothing."

I grunt when she bites down on my earlobe and bring my hand higher up her leg. "Don't fucking joke." Then I pull away, capture her mouth with mine, kissing her with a possessiveness I didn't know was in me.

She giggles into my mouth.

"I'm not playing, Ava."

She just laughs harder.

* * *

Trevor hisses the moment I open my front door. "Damn, kid. You took a beating."

I step onto my porch and close the door behind me. "You should see the other guy."

"I did, dude, and he doesn't look anywhere near as bad as you."

I shrug. "What's up?"

"Can we maybe walk, talk about what happened?"

"There's not much to say. I thought Peter was the reason Ava got hurt and I wanted to kill him."

Trevor's lips thin to a line, and he jerks his head toward the road. "Let's walk anyway." It's not a question this time, so I reopen the door, tell Dad I'm heading out for a bit. We haven't said much to each other since yesterday's blow up, and I don't plan on being the first to break. I have nothing to add to the conversation, and if he genuinely thinks he can stop me from seeing Ava, he obviously doesn't know me as well as he thought he did.

Trevor walks beside me with his hands in his pockets. I do the same. We're two blocks away from our houses, and he hasn't said a word. I've got shit to do, so I say, "So... how was your trip?"

"You know it's not the first time this has happened," he says.

"What?" I ask, turning to him. "That one of Ava's friends has started a fight with your friend on your front lawn?"

It's supposed to be a joke, but Trevor shakes his head, his eyes on mine, not even a hint of humor in them. "That Ava's mom has hurt her." Oh, so we're *not* here to talk about Peter and me. *Noted.* "It's not the first time," he repeats. "And it won't be the last."

Oh. "Right." I didn't know, and the way Ava explained it, she made it sound like an accident. Or maybe I chose to hear it that way.

I follow behind him as he walks up a steep hill. At the top is a little playground. One set of swings and a single slide.

He sits down on a swing, the entire frame bending with his weight. I stay standing... because I'm pretty sure the entire thing would collapse with both our loads. Trevor's legs bend, then outstretch. He's not really going for air; he's just kind of... swaying. He exhales a sharp breath, his eyes to the ground. It's clear that whatever he plans on saying next is hard for him, and so I focus, give him all my attention. "What's going on?"

He scratches at his jaw, his brow furrowed. "Ava's mom..."

"Yeah?"

"She's been through a lot."

"I mean, that's pretty obvious, right?"

"No, Connor." He shakes his head, his shoulders slumped. "You don't even know the half of it." He pauses a beat, and I let him gather his words. "She's a POW. Do you know what that means?"

Swallowing, I nod. "Prisoner of war, right?"

"Yeah," he says, his voice cracking. He clears his throat, looks up at me, his eyes clouded. "I don't want to get into too much detail, but her unit was under fire and uh... they caught her. They caught her and they..." He takes a breath, and then another, and I can see the struggle in his eyes, hear the weakness in his voice. "Jesus, Connor, do you know what they do to *women*—"

He can't finish and I don't want him to.

"They kept her for months, and when she finally managed to escape—that's when the grenade..." A single tear falls from his eye, and he swipes at it quickly, sniffing back his emotions.

My legs give out beneath me, and so I sit on the stupid swing next to him, my stomach in knots. There's an ache in my chest, a burn so intense it has me groaning. Tears prick behind my eyes, and I rub at them, sniff once to keep my rage in check.

"I'm sorry," I manage to say through the lump in my throat.

Trevor shakes his head. "Ava doesn't know any of this. My dad told me, and I made the decision not to tell her. So this is between us. Man to man. Okay?"

"Of course."

"Look," he says, a sigh escaping him. "There are going to be times when you'll hate her for the way she treats Ava, and for the way she acts and the way she feels, but you have to keep perspective, Connor. You *have to*. For Ava. Because you only know her now, but you didn't know her as Ava's mom, back when she was able to *be* Ava's mom."

"I got it," I assure.

Two little kids approach the swings, toy trucks in their hands. They stop when they see us and run back to their parents. I can only imagine what we look like: two big-ass dudes on tiny swings, trying to hold back tears.

"I'm just letting you know," Trevor informs, "because Ava's flitting around the house with a stupid smile on her face that she can't seem to wipe off, and I'm assuming maybe *you're* the reason for it."

I think about the strength Ava must possess, far greater than I had initially assumed, and I say, "I guess."

"So, you guys are a *thing* now."

"Yeah."

"Good," Trevor acknowledges, standing. "I mean, it's good for her to have something in her life that brings her happiness." Pride fills me, but there's a nagging in my gut that tells me I'm not worthy. "But you can't go beating people up every time Ava gets hurt, especially when there's no source to that pain."

"Yeah," I say, because it's all I *can* say.

"Okay," he declares, eyes on mine, cheesy smile in place. Back to the old Trevor, he squeezes my shoulder, his thumb digging into the bruise on my collarbone. "You get her pregnant, and I'll fucking kill you."

connor

"I LOOK like I'm going to a funeral," I say, glaring at myself in the mirror. I'm wearing the school-issued suit that the team has to wear when we're attending the games but are ineligible to play.

Dad sighs, watching me from my bedroom doorway. "I can't believe you got suspended. And tonight, of all nights, Connor. What the hell—"

"Stop," I tell him. "Just stop, okay? I *know*."

"Well, you have to show up, right? Maybe you can catch the scout before he leaves."

"Okay," I say, my eyes drifting shut, shoulders tense, hands balled in frustration.

My phone dings with a text, and I pick it up off my desk.

> Ava: BOYS!!

> Connor: ?

> Rhys: A little early in your relationship for a three-way, but I'm down.

> Connor: Gross.

> Ava: Hot.

> Connor: What's up?

> Ava: Suit up, boys!

> Rhys: Huh?

> Connor: What?

> Ava: Suit up! Or whatever the term is. Get in your uniforms. You guys are playing tonight.

> Connor: No fucking way.

I rip off my tie and slip out of my shoes, my grin unconfined.

> Rhys: Are you serious?

> Connor: How?

> Rhys: ^^ what he said.

"What's going on?" Dad asks.
"Ava got me back in."
"Good. It's the least she could do," he murmurs.
I ignore him. Read the next message.

> Ava: I just had to show Brown my boobs. He was very appreciative.

> Connor: Dammit, Ava!!!

> Rhys: Noice!

> Ava: Does it matter how? Just go!!! Get ready!!! You'll be late.

> Rhys: Thanks, A.

Another message shows up in a different box, just mine and Ava's.

> Ava: So... is this what they call coming in clutch?

> Connor: It is! You're amazing. I don't know what you did, but thank you, Ava. THANK YOU.

> Ava: You're welcome, baby.

> Ava: Now go!!

> Connor: I'm going!

I change as quickly as I can and rush Dad out the door so I can make it for pregame and warm-ups. I practically sprint to Dad's car, and with my fingers on the door handle, I stop when I hear Ava call my name. I turn to see her running toward me, barefoot and beautiful. Her hair's wet and free of its usually messy knot. It's the first time I've seen it like that. The curls flow behind her as she races toward me. She's holding a bright orange balloon and the marker used to write her usual words. She stops when she gets to me, her breathing heavy. "Boo!" she jeers, handing me the balloon.

I take it from her grasp, my cheeks aching with the force of my smile. One hand on her waist, the other shifting her hair. "I like your hair down."

"You do? I just got out of the shower to answer Brown's call and messaged you as soon as I could." She glances over my shoulder to my dad, who no doubt watches us. Her smile falls, and she takes a step back. "Good luck, okay?"

I pull her back to me, not caring who's watching, and plant a kiss on her lips, passionate and painfully perfect.

Just like her.

* * *

Sweat drips down my forehead and into my eyes, and I blink it back, pour water over my face. It's our last timeout of the game, and I've given it everything I have. Our score reflects that, and so does the burn in every one of my muscles. My chest heaves, my shoulders, too. Flames fire in my lungs, and Coach looks at me. "You want out?"

"No, sir."

"You haven't had a minute off, Ledger. It won't break you."

I swallow between shallow breaths. "I'm good." Then I look up at Dad watching from the stands, his arms crossed. He nods, a show of encouragement. And then he smiles at me, and I'm reminded of all the times he's been there, all the times he's done exactly this—even before the end game. "You got it, son!" he shouts loud enough to hear over the chanting of the crowd.

"You okay, man?" Rhys asks.

"Yeah." I shake off all other thoughts. "I'm good. Let's do this."

We're only on the court for another two minutes before the final buzzer sounds. I shake hands with the other team and then rush to the bench so I can sit down, give my body time to recover. Elbows on my knees, I hunch over myself and towel the sweat off my face. "Good job, Ledger," Coach says. "You really turned it on tonight."

"Thanks, Coach."

I stay on the bench longer than the rest of the team. While they leave to hit the showers and the crowd starts to depart, I let my muscles start to solidify again. I'd been weak, weaker than I should be, and I make a promise to start hitting the gym more and working on my stamina. I should be focusing on sprint sets rather than long distance.

"Connor?"

I look up to see Principal Brown and a man I've never met before standing over me. I get to my feet. "Yes, sir?"

Brown smiles, waving a hand to the man next to him. "This is Tony Parsons. From Duke. He wanted a word with you."

My pulse picks up pace, as if I'm on the court again, overtime, two points down and I'm at the three-point line, ball in my hand. "It's good to meet you, sir," I say, shaking his hand.

"Likewise," he responds. "That's quite a shiner you've got there."

"Yeah, it's..."

"It's one of the hazards of basketball, right, son?" Brown says.

I nod, grateful for his response.

Parsons continues, "Well, Connor, have you ever thought about playing for Duke?"

"Only when I'm breathing."

He smiles, then opens his mouth, but I interrupt, my finger up between us. "Sorry, just one second."

I look up at the stands, at one of the only people left—my dad. His eyes are wide, clear. "Dad!" I wave him over and watch as he makes his way toward us. Then I turn back to the scout. "This is my dad," I tell him. "I uh..." I give him the truth that, lately, I'd been too stubborn to realize. "I just like to have him around."

* * *

"It's not like I'm going to get my hopes up or anything," I say into the phone, pacing my room, the adrenaline inside me still pulsing.

"You should totally get your hopes up," Ava encourages. "I mean, it's *Duke*."

"Yeah, but do you know how many scouts they have looking for high school ballers? I'm, like, one in hundreds these scouts would be talking to."

"Connor," she laughs out. "You're looking at it wrong. You're one in *only* hundreds that they're talking to. That's a big deal no matter how much you try to downplay it."

I hold the phone to my ear, and pick up a ball, then spin it on the tip of my finger. "I guess."

"I'm proud of you," she says, and I can hear the genuine honesty in her voice.

I drop the ball to the floor and sit on the edge of the bed. "It wouldn't have happened without you."

"Well, technically, if you think about it..." she trails off.

"How did you get us back in, anyway?"

"I told you."

"Ava..."

She giggles into the phone, causing my chest to ache in longing. I wish she were here. In my bed. So I could see her. So I could run my hands through her curls and kiss her and hold her and maybe fool around a little. "I just wrote him a heartfelt letter about what had been going on and how you and Rhys were my saviors, and that you didn't deserve to be punished for it. Vincit qui se vincit."

"What does that mean? The last part?"

"It's the school motto. It means *He conquers who conquers himself.*"

"What does that have to do with anything?"

"Well," she says, mocking. "How the hell is Brown supposed to let you conquer the world if you're on the sidelines for being chivalrous?"

"I can't believe you managed to work that in there."

"Your girl can be quite convincing, Connor."

I smile into the phone, let the silence fill the space between us.

"I wish I were there," she says quietly, reading my mind.

"I know. Me too."

Dad knocks on my door, enters.

I lower the phone to my lap.

"I'm heading off," he says, smiling. "You did real good tonight, Connor. I'm proud of you. You're one step closer."

"Thanks, Dad," I reply, genuine. "And thanks for being there. I would've been a nervous wreck if you weren't."

His smile widens. "Anytime, son. We'll call Ross tomorrow and fill him in on what happened."

"Okay."

"Don't stay up too late, all right? You've had a long day."

"Yes, sir."

I wait until he's out of my room and out of the house before lifting the phone to my ear again. "Hey, sorry."

"You and your dad are talking again?" Ava asks.

"Yeah, I guess."

"That's good," she says, but I can hear the uncertainty in her voice.

"Look, about what my dad said about you..." I sigh. "It's not as if he has something personal against you. It's just, he's being protective, you know? And it's not like he *knows* you, because if he did..." I trail off, not knowing what to say.

"You don't need to explain," she assures. "It's okay. I know what we are— my family—and I know how it seems from the outside looking in. But just... if it ever gets too much for you—being with me—just say so."

"Ava, stop." I flop down on the bed, cover my eyes with my forearm. "We don't need to be having this conversation."

She's silent a beat too long.

"Ava?" I sit up.

"Sorry," she says. "Someone's just uploaded the game, and I'm trying to download it as fast as I can. Oh, my God, I'm so giddy. *Hurry up!*"

"I can probably get you a copy tomorrow."

"Guh! Tomorrow's too late. I need it *now*!"

"You're not—"

"It's here," she cuts in. "Blah blah blah, people I don't care about! Hey, it's you! Okay, I'm going to watch it. Bye!"

She hangs up before I get a chance to respond. But no more than five minutes later, she sends me a text.

Ava: Damn, Connor. You look good on camera.

Connor: Stop it.

Ava: You think I'm joking? *unzips*

Connor: Hey. No unzipping unless I'm with you.

Ava: Hmm. The thought of you unzipping me…
unzips twice

Connor: You could come here… if you want to. I can leave my window open. Dad doesn't get back until morning.

Ava: I wish I could, but the doctors came by today and changed Mom's meds. I have to be here in case she has a reaction.

Connor: How is she?

Ava: She's doing much better. She just had a few bad days, that's all. Thanks for asking.

Connor: Of course.

Ava: Okay, I'm going to go watch now. Bye, boy, bye!

An hour passes, and I'm already in bed when the next message comes through.

Ava: Welp. It's decided. Sorry to tell you, but you kind of suck, #3.

Connor: I know.

Ava: Feel like giving me a goodnight kiss?

Connor: ...

Ava: ?

Connor: Sorry, I didn't realize that was a question.
How? When? Where?

Ava: Now. Left side of the house. Second window.

I'm out of bed and into sweats and out the door in less than ten seconds. I smile when I see Ava waiting for me, half leaning out her window. She brings her finger to her lips in a shushing motion, and I slow my steps, go lighter on my bare feet.

"You're crazy fast," she whispers.

"I wasn't sure how long the offer would stand."

She rolls her eyes, leaning farther forward to grasp my shoulders. Pulling me as close as I can get, she kisses my forehead. "Goodnight, boyfriend."

"That's it?" I deadpan. "You made me come over—"

Her lips meet mine, soft and warm, while her arms wrap around my neck. I reach up, fingers threading through her curls, and hold her to me. She tilts her head, her tongue swiping against mine, and I let out a guttural moan. Then she gently bites down on my bottom lip, and no joke, my knees give out beneath me. I catch myself, one hand on her window ledge, the other grasping her hair, tugging with enough force that her head rolls back, giving me access to her jaw, her neck. I release the window ledge and bring my hand to her shoulder, down her chest, the backs of my fingers skimming a part of her I've fantasized about for so long. *Too* long. She moans, taking my mouth again. Then my jaw. My throat. God, I love her there. She nuzzles into my neck, her breaths heavy. My heart races, blood rushing to an organ I'll no doubt be paying attention to as soon as I'm back in bed. "I could do this all night," she whispers.

I grunt. Because I'm incapable of forming words, apparently.

"But we can't," she says, laughing silently. "Another minute, and what we're doing will be illegal."

I take a few calming breaths, let my pulse settle. "Yeah, you're probably right."

She rears back, my hand still in her hair. Then she offers one last kiss. Chaste. Her eyes lock on mine, a smile playing on her lips. "Goodnight, boyfriend."

connor

WITH MY BASKETBALL schedule and school and Ava's *life*, we don't get anywhere near as much time together as I want. And with the team doing as well as it has been, there are more commitments I have to deal with. Pep rallies, meetings, and media interviews. It's not a *bad* thing. It means more chances of being noticed, but it sucks that I barely get to even speak to my girlfriend. And we're only ten days into the relationship.

> Ava: Hey, can you ask your dad when my dressing is supposed to come off? I can't remember whether he said ten or fourteen days.

I peel myself off the couch and go to the kitchen, where Dad's starting on dinner. "Hey, Ava wants to know when she should take the dressing off her burns."

Dad looks up from whatever he's doing. "It depends on how well it's healed."

"Okay, I'll tell her," I say, starting to type out a text.

"She can come around if she wants me to have a look at it."

I pause, my thumbs hovering over the screen. I look at Dad again, my eyebrows raised. "Yeah?"

He nods.

"Are you sure?"

"I'm sure."

> Connor: Dad says it depends on how it's healed, but you can come over, and he can take a look at it.

Ava: ...

Connor: ?

Ava: Are you sure?

Connor: That's what he said.

Ava: Okay, I'll be over in a bit.

"She says she'll be around soon," I tell Dad.

"Good."

Something's off with Dad's reaction, but I can't quite put my finger on it. Regardless, I find my home back on the couch and wait. Fifteen minutes later, there's a knock on the door, and I'm on my feet and swinging that bitch open. The door. Not Ava. She's not a bitch. She's The Best. I lean down to kiss her, but she presses her hands to my chest, stopping me. She shakes her head, and I smell... perfume? Ava never wears perfume, at least not that I know of. I take a step back to let her in. She's dressed *nice*, but like, if she were going-to-church type nice. I like Ava in tank tops and sweats, and yeah, her school uniform, but that's a *whole* other conversation. "Why are you dressed like that?" I whisper.

She elbows my gut. "Shut up."

"Hi, Ava," Dad calls from the kitchen. He points a knife at the couch. "Just take a seat, and I'll be with you in a moment." He's all sweetness and smiles, and I'm suspect.

My eyes narrow at him and then Ava when she says, "Thank you, sir. I appreciate this a lot."

I flop down next to her, throw my arm over her shoulders. She pushes my hand away. "What's *with* you?"

"Not now," she hisses without moving her lips.

Dad comes into the living room drying his hands on a dish towel. He sits on the coffee table, dish towel beside him, and asks, "Can I take a look?"

Ava cranes her neck. "Sure."

While Dad's focused on peeling off the dressing, I put my hand on Ava's knee. She pushes it away again.

"It looks like it's healed just fine," Dad says. "No more dressing, but be sure to use the cream I gave you until it's all gone, okay?"

Ava nods. "Thanks again, Mr. Ledger."

He gathers all the dressing and stands. "No problem."

Ava stands, too, and I take her hand. This time, she lets me. "I'll walk you back."

I open the door at the same time Dad calls Ava's name. Ava turns to him, her eyes wide, shoulders rigid. Dad stands between the kitchen and the living room. "I'm just starting on dinner. You're welcome to stay if you'd like."

Ava does her best not to let her shock show, but I see it even if Dad doesn't. "I appreciate the invitation, but I have to get back home."

"Oh." Dad drops his gaze, his shoulders. "Okay, sure."

"It's just..." Ava starts, sensing Dad's disappointment. "I can't really leave my mom, so..."

Dad tilts his head. "Isn't your stepbrother home with her?"

Ava nods, her grip on my hand tightening. "Yeah, he is, but he's really only there for when things with her get uh..." She glances up at me, and I try to offer an encouraging smile. If this is Dad's attempt at getting to know her, then we *have* to try. "Sometimes she gets physical and he—he has to restrain her." I can hear her voice weaken with every word, so I release her hand, place mine on the back of her head and bring her to my chest, her ear to my heart. Ava exhales slowly, her eyes drifting shut. When she opens them again, she says, "I have to be there, because I'm the only one who can really *talk* her through whatever she's experiencing."

It takes a moment for Dad to respond. "Right. And... Trevor's father? Where is he?"

I speak up. "Dad, what's with the twenty questions?"

Dad shakes his head as if clearing the fog. "You're right. I'm sorry."

"No, it's okay," Ava says. "He left a while back."

"So, it's just you kids taking care of her and the house and all the bills?"

Ava nods, then shakes her head. "No, we have a caregiver stay with her when Trevor's at work and I'm at school. But yeah, on the evenings and weekends it's just us."

"Oh, good," Dad says. "I assume that's all done through your health insurance?"

"I wish, but no. Insurance doesn't cover nearly enough of it. The military only really covered her physical injuries, and even though we still get her full benefits it's not even close to..." Ava pulls away. Just a tad. "I sound like I'm complaining, but I'm not. I promise. Things could be a lot worse," she says, looking up at me. She faces my dad again, a frown on her lips. "At least she's alive, and we can be a family. And I'm sure you and I can both agree that there's nothing more important in this world than family. That's why we sacrifice the things we do and protect the people we love."

Dad sucks in a sharp breath, exhales slowly. "You're absolutely right, Ava."

Ava smiles at him, then, on her toes, she kisses me once. "Stay," she tells me. "Have dinner with your dad. I'll call you later."

"Ava," Dad calls again. "If you or your brother or your mom... if you need anything that I can help with, please..." he trails off, nodding, before disappearing into the kitchen.

* * *

"Jeez, Connor. I had no idea how bad things were for her," Dad says, setting the table for us. "I feel horrible for the things—"

"I appreciate it," I tell him. "But I'm not the one you should be saying this to."

With a nod, he sits opposite me at the table, his hands clasped under his chin. "I'm going to make a few calls in the morning, see what I can find out about getting her some financial help for her mother's care."

My brow lifts. "Yeah?"

"It's the least I can do."

I sit back in my chair, watching him closely. "What's with you?"

"What do you mean?"

"It's like you've done a complete 180. Your attitude's changed, and now you're acting... I don't know."

Dad's chest lifts with his inhale. "I reconnected with an old friend today, and they gave me a little perspective. That's all."

"Anyone I know?" I ask.

He shakes his head. "No."

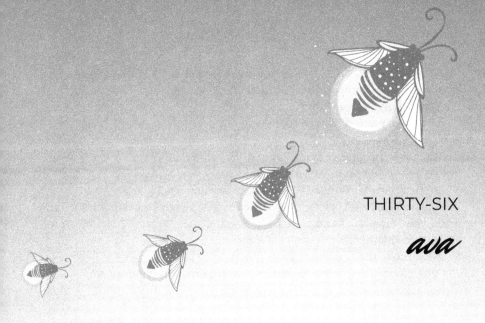

THIRTY-SIX

ava

CONNOR SAYS, downing last night's pasta as he sits on the bench in front of me, "It sucks that our paper's done. Now we don't have an excuse to whisper dirty things in each other's ears during class."

My eyes narrow. "You've never whispered dirty things in my ear."

He chuckles while chewing. "Shit. Different class. Different girl."

"Hmm. Now I'm *really* glad I put cyanide in your food."

He eyes me a moment, then slowly lowers the container next to him.

"I'm kidding," I laugh out.

Shaking his head, he says, "I'm not willing to risk it."

"Speaking of murders..."

"It's such a turn-on when your girlfriend talks about killing people." I push on his shoulder with my foot and regret it the moment he grabs hold of my ankle and then my waist, effortlessly lowering me until I'm sitting across his thighs. "Go on."

I get comfortable in my new position and throw my arm around his neck, fingernails scratching the back of his head. He moans, drops his head between his shoulders. I say, "So I read a story this morning about this twenty-nine-year-old man who saw his dad kill his mom and bury her in their yard when he was three years old. Apparently, when she 'disappeared,' he told the cops his dad hurt his mom, but the cops didn't believe him. Because, like, he's *three*, right?"

He's quiet a moment, then, "Huh."

"And who remembers stuff like that when they're *three*."

His eyes are on mine, searching.

"Anyway," I continue, "he moved back to that same home twenty years later and dug up the spot where he remembers seeing it and guess what?"

"They found her remains."

I nod, lips pressed tight.

"That's crazy."

"I know! Imagine carrying around those memories for so many years, from when he was *three*."

He swallows, looks away. "That'd be pretty horrible."

"Right?" I exhale harshly. "Thank God you don't remember anything from when your mom—" I cut myself off, because *shit*. "Sorry," I say, my voice quiet. "I wasn't thinking."

He shrugs. "It's okay."

"No, it was insensitive," I admit. "I just had a brain fart moment."

"Speaking of brain farts," he says, "what the hell were you wearing when you came over last night?"

My eyes go huge, my breath catching. I pull on his hair, ignore his screech of pain. "I was trying to make a good impression. The first time I met your dad wasn't exactly under the best circumstances!"

"You looked like my grandma."

I laugh. I can't help it. "You make out with your grandma?"

"I barely make out with you," he mumbles.

"Aww." I settle my hands on the sides of his head and make him face me. "You want to make out with me?"

"I'd like to do more than make out with you, but..." He looks around us. "Here?"

I quirk an eyebrow. "You got your car keys?"

He nods, biting down on his lip. Then he's practically throwing me off of him and taking my hand, dragging me down the steps. I giggle the entire way to the parking lot.

Five minutes later and he has my back pressed to the inside of his car door. His mouth is on my neck, lips warm, tongue wet. His hands are everywhere, all at once. I untuck his shirt from his pants and feel the muscles on his stomach, then bring my hands to his back, clawing him closer to me. I can't get enough, and neither can he because he whispers my name as if it's air in his lungs. He covers my mouth again, his tongue sliding against mine, and I wish he had a bigger car, or I had a car *at all* because he's too large for such a small space and I want to feel him all over me and around me, and God... *inside* me. My legs part when his hand slides up from my knee to my bare thigh. He pauses an inch below where I want him the most, his forehead going to my shoulder. He curses, and I look at the roof of his car, my breaths shallow. And then he covers that inch, his thumb stroking. Just once. I buck beneath his touch, and he curses again. And then he's pulling away completely, his eyes glazed, hooded, leaving me cold and confused. He settles back in his seat, adjusting himself, his chest rising and falling. "We can't do it like this..." he murmurs, looking at me. I adjust my clothes and sit up. "In my car? At school?" He sighs heavily.

"I know," I whisper.

"But I want to, Ava. God, I want to do everything with you."

"I know," I say again.

And then we let the silence linger between us because we both know what the next question will be. *How?*

* * *

Connor: Send me a picture of you.

Ava: Are you... are you asking for nudes? Because you can fuck right off, please and thank you.

Connor: Lol. No. I just don't have any pics of you that aren't taken from outside your bedroom window while you're sleeping.

Ava: Dude...

Connor: Hi, I'm Connor. Pleased to creep you.

Connor: But seriously send me a pic. I don't have any of you, and I want it as my home screen.

I bite down on my lip, scandalous thoughts running through my mind. In the month we've been together, we've not shared anything more than a slight touch to the wrong—or *right*—places. I switch off my bedroom light and turn on the lamp, then I get into bed, lower the thin strap of my tank top to reveal my bare shoulder. Eyes on the lens, I lick my lips, take a snapshot. I send it to him without a second thought.

Connor: Jesus Christ, Ava. That's not home screen material, that's...

Ava: You want another one?

Connor: Maybe move your top down a little more? Just an inch.

I comply, shifting until the neckline barely covers the top of my breasts. I take another photo, send it to him.

Minutes pass with no response.

> Ava: Are you there?

> Connor: Can I call you?

> Ava: Yeah.

My phone vibrates in my hand, and I quickly answer. "Give me a sec. I'll just plug in my headphones."

"Mmm."

After grabbing my headphones from my nightstand, I connect them wirelessly and put one in my ear, needing the other free so I can hear the rest of the house. "What's up?" I ask.

"Ava," he says, his voice low. Rough. "I need you to send me another one."

I swallow, knowing what he's asking for. "You first."

My phone vibrates almost instantly. He's lying on his back, his hair a mess, eyes half-hooded. And he's shirtless, his collarbone and muscled chest on full display.

"Your turn," he insists, his voice barely audible.

I hesitate a beat, before lifting my shirt and angling the camera so my stomach and the underside of my breasts are in view. I quickly hit send, my body heating, pulse throbbing between my legs.

"Fuck, Ava," he groans, his voice muffled by what I assume is his pillow. "You're killing me."

"Send me another one," I whisper, gasping for air.

I hear him shift, and a moment later, his picture comes through. This one's similar to the one I sent, an image of his perfect six-pack, each one defined by deep dips. There's a scattering of dark hair between that V that drives women wild. It leads to a spot covered by the waistband of his boxers, an inch above his basketball shorts.

My mouth is dry. So dry. And I squeeze my legs together to try to increase the sensation there. I'm breathing heavy, so heavy I'm sure he can hear it. I force a swallow, try to regain some composure, but I can't. My entire body is on fire, and I'm squirming, trying to find some form of reprieve from the powerful ache building inside me.

"Babe," he says, but it comes out a moan. I can hear him shifting, moving, and I imagine him in his bed, eyes closed, chest rising and falling, his hand in his shorts... thinking of me. "Your turn."

I shove my hand beneath my underwear, the tip of my finger pressing down on my nub. I let out a moan before picking up my phone and hitting the button. I check the picture, just enough for him to know what I'm doing without revealing too much.

I hit send.

"Fuck, Ava."

I close my eyes, listen to the sounds of our breaths. Short. Sharp. Shallow. Amplified by the silence around us. I move my hand faster, faster, my back arching off the bed as I climb, climb, climb.

The phone vibrates again, and I open his next picture. A whimper escapes when I see it. His hand's in his boxers, the outline of his knuckles clear, his hand circling his rock-hard—

Connor grunts, and I close my eyes again, my pleasure soaking my fingers. We don't say another word. We're nothing but heavy breaths and grunts and whimpers. I listen intently. Every sound, every movement. Every rapid, rhythmic shift. I know he's doing the same as what I'm doing, and I imagine that we're doing it to each other. The vision pushes me over the edge, a muted scream bursting from my throat. I bite down on my lip, my entire body convulsing as he moans with each of his breaths, louder and louder until one last, long grunt.

I listen to his breathing settle while mine does the same. An entire minute passes before I hear him chuckle. "Holy shit, Ava."

I sigh, long and loud. "Teenage hormones are one hell of a drug."

THIRTY-SEVEN

Connor

"SO... LAST NIGHT WAS..." I say, looking down at Ava's legs. Her skirt seems higher today, or maybe it's the way she's sitting, or maybe she's doing it just to mess with me.

"Intense?" she asks and lifts her skirt another inch. Yeah. She's definitely messing with me. I grip the steering wheel tighter, and she giggles when I moan and adds, "Keep your eyes on the road, stud."

"Fine." I do as she says and tell her, "You know I have that pep rally in the cafeteria today, so I can't meet you at lunch."

"Oh really? I must've missed the six hundred posters plastered all over school."

"Funny. Maybe you should get your eyes checked."

"Eh," she says, shrugging. "I think my eyes are just fine. I mean, I *do* have the hottest boyfriend in school."

I can't help but smile. "You think I'm hot?"

She scoffs. "As if you don't know."

I shrug.

"Connor! Have your exes never told you?"

Another shrug. "I don't have any exes."

"Shut up!"

"I don't," I laugh out. "You're my first, Ava."

"First girlfriend?"

"Uh huh."

"But you've, like, kissed girls before?"

"Yeah," I nod. "I touched the side of a boob once, too."

"Connor!" she squeals, laughing. She pushes my side, and I straighten the steering wheel. "Ew. I don't want to know that!"

I settle my hand on her leg and gather the courage to ease into the next question. "So, I was thinking... maybe... if you wanted to... you could come to the pep rally today."

She tenses beneath my touch, then whispers my name.

"I know it's not really your thing," I tell her, doing my best to mask my disappointment. "But I just thought I'd ask. It'd be nice if you were there to support me, but it's cool."

"I would if I could," she says quietly.

I glance at her. "So why can't you?"

She sucks in a breath and then exhales slowly. But she doesn't answer my question. In fact, she doesn't say anything else for the rest of the drive.

* * *

I stand between Coach Sykes and Rhys while the school band plays, and the rest of the students are chanting *Wildcats! Wildcats! Wildcats!* The team has been doing well, amping up the school spirit, and I wish I could join them in their hysteria, but I'm too busy looking at the entrance, my hopes rising and dying every time the sliding doors open and it isn't Ava. Don't get me wrong. I appreciate the amount of support she's shown, and I understand why she can't go to the games, but this —this is *in* school—the few hours a day when we actually exist in the same space.

The band finishes their performance, and one of the AV guys appears out of nowhere to hand Coach a microphone. "Thanks for that. What a great intro!" There's a sarcasm in his tone that's readily forgiven because he's old and cantankerous, but he's a staple in the school and the reason why the program runs so well.

He starts going through the team's roster for tonight's game, calling names one after the other, waiting a few seconds for the cheers after each one. Then he gets to my name, and the screams are loud, louder than with Rhys, but beneath all those screams I hear a single sound that has my heart racing, my lips lifting. "Boo!"

My eyes dart everywhere, looking for the sound, and then I spot her. She's standing in front of the students milling by the entrance, and she must've forced her way through because she wasn't there only seconds ago. I thought it would be impossible for my grin to widen, but here I am. I raise my hand, a small wave, and she does the same, a proud smile playing on her lips.

The rally's over as soon as Coach is done talking. I start to make my way over to her, but Coach stops me with his hand on my chest. "One minute, Ledger," he says, and I look at Ava and mouth, "Hang on." She nods, points to the cafeteria line. She gets to the end of the line and picks up a tray. I don't know how long it's been since she's had cafeteria food, but boy, is she in for a treat.

"Ledger," Coach says again, and I turn away, give him all my attention.

"Yeah, Coach?"

Rhys is next to him, wearing a shit-eating grin.

I start to panic.

"Rhys and I got to talking," Coach starts. "And we were wondering if you'd be interested in co-captaining for the rest of the season?"

My jaw drops as I look between them. "Are you serious?"

Rhys shrugs. "It'll look good on your college applications."

"Yeah." I nod incessantly. "Hell, yeah. Thank you."

Coach offers me his hand, and I shake it, unable to hide my elation. The cafeteria breaks out into small giggles, and then all-out laughter. I'm still holding his hand when I turn around to see Ava at the start of the line, her tray of food held at her waist. In front of her, a punk kid has his arm pulled out of the sleeve, his long hair flipped to one side, covering half his face. He's talking to her—no, he's *shouting noises* at her, and then he's swaying his body, using his armless sleeve to knock the food off her tray, his shouts getting louder, and I see red.

Red.

Hot.

Rage.

I release Coach's hand and start toward him, but Coach and Rhys are both holding me back. "I'll take care of him," Coach says.

"Calm down," Rhys tells me, as if I can. As if it's possible. And then I look at Ava. At the way her lips part, the way her eyes are wide open but filled with tears, as if she refuses to blink because if she does, her tears will fall and she doesn't want to give this asshole the satisfaction. Slowly, she places the tray back on the rail and turns, the crowd around her parting as she walks away. People are still laughing and my heart... my heart is sinking.

And then I blink.

Come to.

I chase after her, calling her name. Her steps are fast, but mine are faster. I try to grasp her arm, but she shrugs me off. Within seconds, we're at her locker, and she's stuffing books into her bag, refusing to speak, refusing to look at me.

"Ava!"

She slams her locker shut, and then she runs... a slow run, but still a run. The first sound of her cry comes just as we pass the office. I manage to get her around the waist, force her to stop and face me. "I'm sorry," I say, "I'm sorry." It's all my brain can come up with.

She squeezes her arms between us, her hands on my chest, and then she pushes. She pushes me away, swiping at her tear-stained cheeks. Her cries echo through the empty halls as she holds her bag to her chest and takes the few steps to the psych office. I follow after her, but I don't touch her, too afraid of her reaction.

She opens the door without knocking, and I'm right behind, stopping just inside. Miss Turner stands as soon as she sees Ava, dropping her sandwich on her desk. "Ava?" she whispers, then looks at me. "What happened?"

Ava's cries are louder now, uncontrollable, and there's an ache in my chest that prevents me from answering.

"Ava?" Miss Turner says again, moving around the desk to get to her. "Sweetheart?"

"You said!" Ava cries, the loudness of her voice shaking me to my core. I pull out of my daze, only to realize she's talking to me. "You said, Connor! You said you didn't want anything more from me!"

My heart squeezes, flatlines. A lump forms in my throat. "I didn't..." I look between Ava and Miss Turner. "I didn't know."

"Of course you didn't know!" she screams. "They don't do it in front of you or Rhys, but they do it. And they do it to me. And to *her!*" She takes a breath. "You said..." she repeats, quieter this time. She leans against the wall and then slides down until her ass hits the floor. "You pressured me to be there, to face *that...* You said you just wanted *me,* but you lied!" She lifts her knees to her chest, her face going between them, arms covering her head, shielding her from... from *me.* "You lied, Connor."

She's rocking now, back and forth, and I haven't taken a breath. Haven't felt a single beat in the place I keep just for her. "Ava, I don't—" I choke on my words. "I don't know what to say."

Her cries are silent, the sound replaced by hiccups, and she won't look up, won't stop rocking. And then her breaths get louder, faster, escalating to a point harsh enough that Miss Turner curses, grabs a paper bag from her desk drawer. She drops to her knees in front of Ava and strokes her hair, imploring her to look up.

Tears fill my eyes while the knot in my stomach grows and grows and grows some more. Ava takes the bag from Miss Turner and breathes into it, her breaths slowing, but her cries still steady. Her shoulders shake with every one of her hiccups, and all I can do is stand.

Watch.

Wait.

Worry.

The bell rings, and Miss Turner looks up at me. "Go to class, Connor."

I widen my stance, my arms at my sides. "I'm not leaving her."

Ava's single whimper shatters every living cell inside of me.

Miss Turner's voice hardens. "That wasn't a suggestion, Mr. Ledger. Get to class. *Now!*"

* * *

I don't know how I make it through the rest of the afternoon, but as soon as the bell rings, I go searching for Ava. First her locker, then my car, then Miss Turner's office. She's nowhere to be found, and so I call her. Again and again and each time there's no answer. I try messaging her:

> Connor: Where are you?

And then Rhys:

> Connor: Do you know where she is?

And then I go to send one to Trevor, but I realize I don't even have his number. Hands pulling at my hair, I look up at the sky for answers—answers that aren't there. I check the basketball court, the locker rooms, and then Miss Turner's office again. It's locked.

I knock. "Ava?"

There's no response, so I go to the office and ask where Miss Turner is. Apparently, she's clocked out for the day. I give up on school and am almost home, my phone continually dialing Ava's number as I drive. And then a text comes through:

> Rhys: She's here.

I pull over.

> Connor: With you?

> Rhys: Yeah.

Jealousy burns a hole in my chest.

> Connor: At your house?

> Rhys: No, but yeah. Just drive to my house. You'll see us.

Rhys rushes to my open window the second he sees my car. I spot Ava sitting on the sidewalk, her legs crossed, staring up at her old house. "She won't talk," Rhys says, his voice low as he pulls on the car door to get me out faster. "I tried, man, but... I don't know. I don't know what to do."

"All right," I tell him, calm. As if I have all the answers. I'm as lost as he is, if not worse, because I *should* know what to say. Or do. But I don't. And maybe it's worse that I'm here, because maybe I'm the one who caused all of this, but I'm not willing to walk away like I did before. "Just go home; I'll take care of her."

He leaves without another word, and I gather what little strength I have left and slowly go to her. Her cheeks are wet, but there are no tears in her eyes. At least not yet. "Ava?" I whisper, and she blinks, looks down at her hands. "Can I sit with you?"

She nods slowly but refuses to meet my gaze.

My heart races as I sit behind her, my legs on either side. I wait a moment, pray she doesn't push me away. When enough time passes, I scoot forward until my chest is pressed to her back and wrap my arms around her waist. A single sob escapes her, and she drops her face in her hands. "What's this for?" she whispers.

"I don't know," I say, remembering the first time she'd been there for me. "It just looked like you needed it."

Another whimper, and I'm moving to the side so I can see her. I reach up, hesitant, and cup her jaw. I wait for her response, because if she's done with me, with *us*—if I fucked up beyond forgiveness, I'll hate myself, but I'll have no choice but to wear it.

Right now, the most important thing is her... and I need to make sure she's okay.

Her eyes finally lift to mine, holding more pain than I know what to do with. And then her head tilts, her cheek pressing to my palm. She reaches up, holds my wrist in both her hands to keep me there.

Air fills my lungs, and I exhale, relieved.

I finger the strands of loose hair away from her eyes and bring her face closer to mine. "I'm sorry, baby. I shouldn't have asked you to—"

My hands move with her head shake. "No, I'm sorry, Connor." She releases a staggered breath. "I didn't mean to say all those things to you. I needed someone to blame, and you were there. I'm *so* sorry. And I'm so fucking embarrassed."

"Why? Because of what that asshole—"

"No, because of the way I was." She cries harder, her tears falling fast and free. I swipe them away with my thumbs, kiss them off her lips. "Connor, I never wanted you to see me like that, to see me break and fall apart and... God, why are you here? Why do you still care about me?"

"Ava," I breathe out. "You had every right to feel the way you did... Jesus, I had no idea it was like that for you at school, and I'm sorry. I'm sorry for asking you to do something I knew you weren't comfortable doing. I'm sorry that shit happens to you and to your mom. I'm sorry it happens *period*. But you have to believe me; nothing you said or did today changes the way I feel about you."

She grips my forearms, a single sob falling from her lips.

"Babe, look at me."

Tear-soaked eyes lock on mine.

I kiss her once. "Promise you believe me."

She shakes her head. "You can't possibly tell me that you still look at me the same."

My response is there, on the tip of my tongue, but it's not enough. And even though I want to tell her how I truly feel, that I've fallen so hard and so fast and so deep... that my every thought, every action is consumed by *her*, this isn't the right time or place, and so I take her hand in mine. "Let's get you home. Your mom will be worried."

* * *

I get ready for the game, but my heart's not in it like it's always been. There are too many thoughts flying through my mind, and every single one of them begins and ends with Ava. I peek out the living room window through the gaps of the blinds and wait.

"What are you doing?" Dad asks, slipping on his shoes.

"Waiting for Ava."

"Is she coming to the game?" he asks, a hopeful lilt in his tone.

I shake my head. "No, but she always..." I trail off when I see her on the sidewalk, her steps slow, a single balloon on a string flopping down by her legs. "I'm going to need five minutes," I tell Dad, now waiting by the door.

I wait a few seconds, my ear to the door, listening for the sound of her footsteps on our rickety porch. I count to three, then open the door, and sweep her into my arms from behind. She squeals, and a tiny bubble of laughter comes next, eliminating all prior worries about how she'd be feeling.

"Jeez, Connor, give the girl some room to breathe," Dad jokes.

I close the door between us while I allow Ava to turn into me, her hands pressed to my chest. "Hi," I say.

She bites down on her bottom lip. "Hi, boyfriend."

I exhale, her words giving me the courage to say the words I'd been planning all night. "I need to tell you something, and I need you to listen to me, okay?"

She nods, eyes on mine.

I take one more deep breath before saying, "You told me before that it wasn't possible for me to look at you the same. And you're right. I don't. And I *can't*."

Her gaze drops.

"Because when I look at you now, I see these curls," I say, tugging on a loose strand, "and I picture you when you were little, and I imagine your mom getting frustrated with you because you won't sit still so she can brush it. I bet you were stubborn, even back then."

She exhales a staggered breath, her gaze lifting to mine again.

"And your hands..." I link my fingers with hers. "I used to look at them and just want to hold them, but now... now I see them, I touch them, and I realize how much weight these small hands can hold." I grasp her face, swipe my thumb along her lips. "And these lips... I mean, yeah, sometimes I used to kiss them just to shut you up, but now... now I'll kiss them and wonder what it'll be like to kiss them ten, twenty years from now... And your eyes, I used to look at them, and they'd remind me of the hardwood of the courts, but now... now I look at them, and I see your strength and your courage and your fight to keep them clear. To keep them dry." Liquid hope pools in her eyes, her chest rising with her intake of breath. And when she blinks, I catch the tears with my thumbs and kiss each of her cheeks. "But you never have to hide who you are with me. Because I'm here. And I'll wear your pain as if it were mine. I promise."

"Connor," she whispers. Her entire body envelopes mine, her arms tight around my waist, ear pressed to my chest. Listening to the magic she creates within me.

"But, Ava," I start. "I think what's changed the most is the way I see your *heart*. I used to just feel lucky that you've given me a piece of it. But now... now I know what that heart is capable of. I know the strength and the perseverance and love it carries because I see it in the way you care about your family, the way you protect them. And I'm not just lucky, Ava. I'm..." I pause, take a breath. "I moved here with one thing on my mind. Work hard enough to get noticed so I move one step closer toward the *end game*. But... but maybe fate had other plans for me. *Bigger* ones. Because you're here, with me, and you *noticed* me, Ava, so maybe... maybe the end game was never about basketball. Maybe my end game is *you*."

ava

Ava: Good game, #3.

Connor: Thanks, #1 goat.

Ava: #1 goat?

Connor: #1 Girlfriend of All Time.

Ava: I… *rolls eyes* Dammit, that made me all gooey inside.

Connor: he shoots, he scooooores.

Ava: Hey… I've been wondering. Why #3?

Connor: I don't know. It was the first number given to me. I've just kept it ever since.

Ava: Did you know that in every story, act three is the most important chapter?

Connor: How so?

Ava: Well, it delivers the story's lowest point (me today) and then how the characters cope with that (you today) and then the climax and resolutions.

Ava: I think maybe you're my resolution, Connor.

Ava: So #3 suits you.

Connor: *Unzips*

Ava: what??

Connor: Sorry, I read climax and then... what? Let me go back and read the rest.

Ava: OMG! I hate you.

Connor: Wait. That was actually really sweet. Thank you.

Ava: No, I take it back.

Connor: How far back?

Ava: What?

Connor: Are we still ending on the climax part because if so... *unzips*

Ava: Goodnight, boyfriend.

Connor: Goodnight, goat.

ava

THE KID who messed with me in the cafeteria got a two-day suspension. The first day of his return, he had a little "accident" during gym class and decided to take the rest of the week off. Funny what a handful of laxatives, an underpaid cafeteria worker and two basketball co-captains can achieve. At first, I was mad that Connor and Rhys stooped to that level, but then... fuck that guy.

That was a few weeks ago, and since then, Connor hasn't asked me to do anything besides let him kiss me goodnight every night, to which I comply. And, if anything, what that kid did to cause my little breakdown just brought Connor and me closer together. Made us stronger. So... thanks, shit-stained-ball-sack kid!

* * *

Connor looks up from his phone when he hears my front door open. I should smile or wave or do something, but I'm too busy arguing with Trevor to do anything else.

"You're doing it, Ava," Trevor says, his voice firm, as he opens his truck door. "It's not an option."

I shake my head, my jaw tense, nostrils flaring. "Fine!"

"Fine!"

I stomp my foot. "I said fine!"

"Fine!"

I grunt, "Go to work!"

Trevor scoffs. "Go to school!"

"I am!"

"Good!" he shouts, but there's no malice left in his tone. Instead, he's holding back a smile.

My defenses crack, just a tad, because we're arguing over something so important to him because he thinks it should be important to me. This morning, he handed me a piece of paper with a dollar amount on it, and when I asked him what it was, he told me it was my budget for college applications. I reminded him that it was useless, and he reminded me that I already promised him I'd do it... hence the pointless argument that in the end, I know I'll lose. Because just like everything else Trevor does, he only does it *for me*. "I love you, you idiot."

Trevor laughs and says, before closing his door, "I love you, too, you brat."

Connor's wide-eyed by the time I get to him. "Man, if that's what having a sibling is like... I'm kind of glad I'm an only child."

I mumble, my brow furrowed, "Good morning, boyfriend."

And he responds, "Hmm. Neither your face nor your voice leads me to believe there's anything *good* about this morning."

I kiss him quickly and make my way to the passenger's side of his car, where I get in, slam the door, and *pout*, my arms crossed, nose in the air.

Connor gets in after me. "You know, if you weren't so damn cute, I'd agree with Trevor. You *are* a brat."

"Shut up," I say, but I'm half laughing because I'm so fucking tired, I'm delusional. "I've had, like, an hour's sleep," I say through a sigh. I grab his hand, settle it on my thigh where he usually keeps it. "Sorry, I'm grumpy."

"It's okay," he assures, starting the drive to school.

"My mom kept waking from these horrible nightmares." Or flashbacks, going by how badly she reacted to them. I add, yawning, "I ended up falling asleep on her floor at around three."

"I'm sorry, babe. I can drive you back. You shouldn't be at school."

"No," I whine, pout some more. "It's the only time I get to see you."

"Yeah, but—"

"Shh," I whisper, holding his entire arm to me. "Just let me cuddle your arm and close my eyes. I'll be fine." I let his warmth settle over me and give in to the heaviness of my eyelids. Just a few minutes, I promise myself, and I can get through the rest of the day.

My own snoring wakes me from my sleep. There's a heat pack against my chest and a wetness on my chin. I try to force my eyes open, but I'm too damn exhausted. Then I try to remember how I got into bed... One minute I was getting into Connor's car, and the next... My eyes snap open, and I cower when the bright sunlight hits my eyes.

That heat pack? It's Connor's arm.

And that wetness on my chin? Fucking drool!

I pull away, mortified, only to see my spit all over Connor's arm. "Oh, my God!" I use my sleeve to wipe his arm. "I can't believe I drooled all over your—"

"Weenus," he interrupts.

I'm too humiliated to look at him as I scrub, scrub, scrub. "What?"

"Weenus," he repeats. "That bit of loose skin on an elbow is called a weenus."

"It is not!" I tell him, inspecting his elbow closer, making sure I got everything.

"It is. It's called a weenus."

"Stop saying weenus."

He laughs. "Can I have my weenus back now?"

I release his arm and wipe my chin, then finally look over at him. He's rotating his shoulder as if he'd been in the same position for hours. I look at my watch. "Oh, my God, Connor!" I practically squeal. "You let me drool all over your weenus for three hours?!"

He busts out a laugh. "Say it again but whisper it seductively."

"Shut up!" I laugh out, then look out his window. It's nothing but trees. "Where the hell are we?"

"I don't know," he says, looking around.

"Wait. Did you bring me here to murder me?"

He smacks his lips together. "You know, I left my shovel at home, so no, at least not today."

I take a calming breath, try to regroup. "What the hell happened?"

"I don't know," he says with a shrug. "You were fast asleep by the time we got to school, I didn't have it in me to wake you, so I just drove and found this turnoff and... yeah, I'm going to have to use the navigator to get home."

I take a better look around us. We're in an empty parking lot with only a few spots, surrounded by trees. And because my window doesn't work, I open my door and listen. The sun's out, the birds are chirping, and somewhere in the distance, there's a stream of water. It's kind of beautiful. I look back at Connor, who's focused on a book between the steering wheel and his lap.

"What are you reading?" I ask.

"College essay prep," he sighs out, closing it and tossing it in the makeshift backseat. "It's so overwhelming."

I nod. "I know. Trevor's forcing me to apply."

He smiles, but there's a hint of sadness in his eyes, and I know where it's coming from. We try not to talk about anything beyond *now*, but we both know what's ahead. At some point, we'll have to deal with it.

I ask, "Have you or Coach Sykes or your agent heard any more?"

He shakes his head. "No. Besides that one guy from Duke, nothing. Ross, my agent, thinks I might need more time. He says it's not because I don't have the skill, it's just... I haven't had the exposure."

"So, what does that mean?"

Connor shrugs. "I'll probably get a walk-on at a decent college, but it won't be a D1. At least not yet. He's hoping if I work hard enough freshman year, more options will open up for me." He adjusts so he's on his side, facing me completely. "What about you? Where are you thinking of applying?"

"I don't really know," I murmur. "And I don't even know what Trevor's game plan is. Like, yeah, I get accepted somewhere and then what? I move Mom into the dorms with me? Or I *leave* her?" I shake my head, my cheeks puffing with my exhale. "It doesn't make sense."

"Maybe he's just giving you options," he suggests.

I sigh. "There *are* no options for me, Connor. As soon as I graduate, I become my mother's keeper."

"Is that what you want?"

I stare out through the windshield, then suck in a breath. "It's what she needs," I whisper. And it's true. Because as much as I try to ignore it, she's getting worse, and I don't know how to fix it.

"That's not what I asked, Ava."

I straighten my features and turn to him, my hand going to his hair. "Are you going back to school?"

"Are you going to answer my question?"

"No."

"Then no."

A grin tugs at my lips. "You want to go for a walk?"

We walk through the thick brush, listening for the sounds of the water stream. "Is it weird that I always look around for dead bodies when I'm walking through bushes and trails?" I ask.

"Not weird at all," he says sarcastically.

We walk for a good fifteen minutes before we reach a clearing, and the sight that greets us is nothing less than spectacular. The clear skies reflect off the clear blue water of the calm lake, not a wave in sight.

"You think it'll be cold?" I ask, standing on the water's edge with him.

Connor squats down and runs his hand through the water, then comes up shaking his head. "It's surprisingly warm," he says, then looks up at me, his eyebrows raised. "You want to go for a swim?"

"In what?"

"The water, dummy."

Smartass. "I mean, *wearing* what?"

"I vote nothing."

"I veto your nothing vote."

He laughs, eyeing me. "Well, isn't your underwear the same as a bikini?"

I chew on my lip, nervous. Technically yes, but even if I were standing in a bikini in front of him, I'd still feel self-conscious. "Turn around."

His eyebrows lift. "Why?"

"Because I said so."

He sighs but complies.

I take a moment to breathe, gather my courage. I slip off my shoes and socks first, and then my blouse and skirt. Then I throw them to the side of him, so he's sure of what I'm doing. As soon as he sees the pile of my clothes, he starts stripping out of his own. With my thumb between my teeth, I watch his every move, entranced. It's as if he was born to remove his shirt the way he does, his back muscles flexing, and then he unbuckles his belt, and my mouth goes dry. He drops his pants to his ankles and then kicks his feet to remove them altogether. "Can I turn around now?"

"No."

I take a few steps forward until I'm right behind him. Reaching up, both hands start at his shoulders, then down his back. I marvel at the way his head droops forward, the way his muscles ripple beneath my palms. I kiss the spot between his shoulder blades, his whisper of my name doing nothing to deter me from closing the gap between us, my front to his back. I reach around, my hands on his bare chest, and then down, down, down, to each dip of his abs. I close my eyes, trace each one, and then move lower and lower. "Ava..." He spins in my arms, so quick I shriek a little. "You're so fucking bad," he whispers in my ear, his arousal pressed against my stomach. I bite down on my lip, crane my neck to allow him to kiss me there, his heated hands on my bare back. He moves up with one hand, fingers curling in my hair, gently pulling, forcing me to throw my head back. His mouth is on my collarbone and then on my chest, my breast. He bites down on the top of my bra, tugging just enough that I feel the air against my nipple. He makes a sound from deep in his throat before capturing my mouth with his, warm and wet and open—just for me. With one hand in my hair, the other lowers, curls against the curve of my ass. "So fucking bad," he murmurs. And then he's lifting me off the ground, my legs instinctively going around his waist. Our most intimate parts connect in the most painstakingly perfect way. He grips my thighs as our kiss deepens, our desperation revealed in the sounds we make, the heat emitting between us.

Charged.

Electric.

Magic.

I writhe against him, searching for more.

"Ava," he groans, pulling back.

I suck in breath after breath, needing the oxygen, but needing him more.

His gaze drops to my breasts, rising and falling, frantic and frenzied. "I'm about to..." He clears his throat, then nuzzles my neck. "I'm so fucking close to..." Then he laughs. "We need to cool the fuck down."

I nod, eyelids heavy, hands going to the back of his head.

"You ready to go in?"

"Carry me?"

He rears back, his eyes holding mine. "Always, Ava." And I know what he's saying without saying it—he'll not just carry me physically, but metaphorically, too. He'll carry the heavy weight that comes with all my burdens. *Always.*

* * *

The water is cooler on our bodies than we expected, but we adjust quickly. "If you could be anything in the world, what would it be?" he asks, circling me while I wade around the shallow water.

"Easy. True crime fact checker. No, wait! I'd host my own podcast. Or, like, make YouTube videos, but without me in them. Maybe just my voice. I like my voice."

"You do have a nice voice," he says, stopping in front of me to hold me to him. I instinctively wrap myself around him. He adds, "But you'd definitely get more views if you showed your face."

"You think?"

"Ava, I'm a guy with working eyes. Yes."

"Do you think guys would—*you know*—over me?" I joke.

He laughs. "Also, yes. But I don't like to think about that."

"If I get enough views, I could possibly make an income from it."

"Possibly," he says, amusing my random thoughts.

"Maybe I should get a boob job," I murmur, looking down at my breasts.

He rolls his eyes. "Your boobs are fine, Ava."

"Just fine?" I pout.

He kisses the top of each breast. "They're perfect."

* * *

"Tell me when you fell in love with basketball," I ask him, my chest to his back while he piggybacks me through the water so we can explore what looks like a cave.

He shakes out his hair, flicking droplets all around him. "I don't really know. There wasn't a specific defining moment. I remember being around twelve and... I mean, I didn't really know how well I'd played, but apparently one of the recruits from FSU was there, and he spoke to Dad after the game, told him that I had 'real potential.'" He turns us around so I can climb onto the rocky embankment covered by a low cliff edge. I sit on the edge, listen to him speak. "I swear to God, Dad told everyone about that conversation, even the lady at the gas station on the way home. He was so damn proud." He pulls himself up to sit next to me, his knees bent, elbows resting on them. The sun beats down, making his eyes as blue as the lake in front of us. He smiles when he turns to me, his shoulders lifting. "So... I don't know. I think, for me, it was never about my love for *basketball* so much as it was about my dad's love for *me*."

I hold his arm to me, rest my head on his shoulder. "So... you do it all for your dad?"

He kisses the top of my head. "Kind of like how you do everything for your mom, right?"

* * *

We're farther in the narrow cave, still exposed to anyone in the lake, but hidden away enough that we'd see them first. We spent the first few minutes exploring, finding rocks strong enough to carve our names on the underside of the cliff. I glance at him, at the way his brow dips in concentration as he works on the middle stroke of the letter A. So far, he's written *Connor 4 A*, and it's so sweet and innocent and brings to mind my own innocent insecurities. "Connor?"

"Ava?" he responds, not looking away from his task.

"Why don't you want to have sex with me?"

He drops the rock he'd been using, then curses and picks it back up. He continues the middle stroke, digging deeper and deeper.

"It's just, you've had the chance. You've had me in your bed, and me here, now, and you don't really... touch me... like *that*, I guess..." I mumble, tripping over my words. I sit down, my back against the stone wall.

He rubs the heel of his palm against his eye, groaning.

"You don't need to answer; it's okay. I was just wondering, is all."

He's on the final *A* when he says, his voice low, "I'm scared."

"Scared?" I repeat. "Of me?"

"No," he shakes his head. "I'm just worried that I won't *perform*, I guess. And you're a lot more experienced than I am."

"Not *a lot*," I rush out.

He shrugs. "You've done more than I have. Hell, you've done *all* of it."

I'm quiet a moment, wondering how he knows, but then... "Rhys told you?"

He nods, still refusing to look at me. "He wasn't bragging or anything. I asked him why he cared about you so much and... yeah."

I blow out a breath. "It didn't mean anything. With him, I mean. It would mean something—*everything*—with you."

He finishes our names, then runs a hand over it, blowing the loose dust off, his cheeks puffing with the force. Then he takes a step back, admiring his work. He looks over at what I'd written, a simple #3. His smile widens. After a moment, he slowly sits down next to me, his hand on my thigh. "I want to," he says. "You have no idea how badly I want to. I think about it all the time."

"Do you..." I smirk, do the hand signal for jerking off. "Like my future YouTube viewers?"

He chuckles. "I'm pretty sure you were partially present for one of the hundred times I've done exactly that thinking about you."

I go back to that moment, to the bliss that followed. "What exactly do you think about?"

"You."

"But what about me? Like, where am I? What am I doing?"

His eyes drift shut, his breaths coming out shorter, sharper. He adjusts himself quickly, licking his lips. "You're on top," he whispers.

I get on my knees, carefully, while his eyes stay closed. Then I straddle his lap, whimper when I feel him pressed against my center. His hands find my waist while mine settle on his shoulders. "Like this?" I ask, and he nods, licks his lips again. "And what else?" I ask, breathless as I shift, back and forth, slow, slow, slow.

He grasps my ass, hard, and I moan, feel the throb build in my core. Opening his eyes, his teeth clamp down on my shoulder, then bite down on my bra strap. "And this is gone."

I swallow, reach behind me and unclasp my bra. "Like this?" I ask, releasing the straps and letting them fall to my elbows. He rears back, his lip caught between his teeth. His fingers stroke up my arms, and then down again, taking the straps with them. I'm exposed, in public, but right now, it's just him and me and all the scandalous thoughts racing through my head.

His eyes are fixated on my breasts, first one, then the other. My chest heaves, lifting them, and his mouth opens, so close.

"Connor," I whisper, and he glances up, his eyes hooded. "Please?"

He keeps his eyes on mine when his tongue darts out, flicks at my pointed flesh. I instinctively push my hips down, wanting more, needing all of him. "Shit," I moan when he goes for the other nipple, this time taking the entire thing in his mouth.

"Is this okay?" he asks.

"Please don't stop," I sigh, scooting back an inch. I run my hands down his chest, his stomach, fingers playing with the band of his shorts. I hesitate a beat, not knowing if he wants to go this far...

He makes the choice for me, his hand taking mine, guiding me beneath his shorts until my hand circles his cock. So smooth, so hard, so—

"Move," he says.

"What?" I breathe out.

"Your hand, move it up and down." Every word is a plea, and so I do as he asks, swallow the groan that bursts from within him. He kisses me, his hands tightening on my backside as I stroke him, long and slow. I break the kiss so I can fill my lungs, but he doesn't stop. He goes straight to my breasts again, and my back arches, inviting him, while I try to stay focused on his pleasure. And then I feel him, his fingers at the place I crave him the most. He shifts my underwear to the side, a single finger exploring the evidence of my pleasure. He doesn't stop with my breasts, teasing me, tasting me. I pull on his hair when a single finger slides inside me, again and again, and I can't breathe, can't... the world is a blur, our heavy breaths the only sounds filling my ears.

"Fuck, Ava, I'm so close. And you—you're so fucking perfect."

At his words, I feel the throbbing escalate, two fingers inside me now. I ride his fingers, fucking them without shame, and continue to stroke him. His cock hardens even more, and I build, build, build, until I fly, soar over the edge.

His groan comes at the same time *he* does, his pleasure covering my fist.

My eyes snap open to see him watching me, his mouth wide, breaths harsh, chest rising, falling. "Mmm," he murmurs, then swallows. "Well, that sucked."

I laugh into his neck. "It was horrible."

"The worst."

* * *

Connor lies on his back post-bliss cleanup, stroking the loose strands of my hair while I listen to his heartbeat thump against my cheek. He asks, "Did you and Trevor have a hard time getting along at the beginning?"

"We *still* have a hard time," I joke.

He chuckles.

"Why do you ask?"

"I don't know," he says through a sigh. "Every now and then I get this random thought in my head that my mom's out there, you know? And she has this new family... and that new family is everything she ever wanted. Everything I wasn't." His voice cracks, and I lean up on my elbow so I can look down at him, at his distant eyes and the slight frown pulling on his lips.

I run my mouth along his, but I don't kiss him. "I hope one day you wake up and realize that the mistakes she made are her burdens, not yours. I hope that you'll eventually understand that what she did isn't a reflection of you—of your *three-year-old* self." I'm getting worked up, so I try to take a calming breath, but I fail. "And if she is out there, I hope that one day she'll find you, and she'll see the same man I do. The strong, empathetic, courageous, protective man who cares so much about so many things, who wears other people's pain as if it were his... I hope she sees you and she fucking *hates* herself for not being the one to raise you, to guide you into becoming that person." My nostrils flare with my exhale. "I hope she *hates* herself as much as I hate her." I grind out the last few words, my anger getting the best of me. I sob. I don't mean to, but I do, and as promised, Connor wipes the tears away, his heavy sigh hitting my cheeks.

"It's okay, Ava."

"It's not," I cry out. "It's not okay, Connor. How dare she... how dare she leave you like that—to fucking die—and leave you with these questions and these... these doubts about yourself! God, I hate her so much!"

He leans up a little, lifts his hand to my jaw, his eyes taking me in for a long moment. Then he says, "Do you know the name of that movie with Omar Epps? It's like this guy and girl who live next door to each other, and they're both trying to pursue basketball careers..."

"*Love and Basketball?*" I ask.

He smiles, settles his head back down. "That's pretty much what my life is at the moment." I try to hide my stupid grin on his neck while he brings me closer, my heart racing, flying. Kissing my forehead, he murmurs, "Love and basketball."

We hold on to each other for the rest of the afternoon, talking about everything but tomorrow. We fight, we float, we laugh, and we *fall*. God, do we fall. Deeper and deeper into these reckless emotions.

THE MOMENT CONNOR pulls up in front of our houses, my heart begins to sink. I know it's not reasonable to feel this way, to fear the idea of missing someone so achingly even though it's just one night.

Connor sighs, his head rolling to face me. "I wish today lasted forever," he murmurs.

I take his hand, kiss the inside of his wrist. "Me, too."

A short, sharp whistle has both of us looking up. Trevor's fists are balled, his shoulders squared as he comes down the porch steps. Only they're not my steps... they're Connor's.

* * *

Connor's dad sits on the couch opposite us while Trevor paces the living room, back and forth, back and forth, and I wish he'd stop because it's not *that* big of a deal. "What the hell were you thinking?" Trevor all but shouts. "Ava, I've been calling you nonstop. Where the hell is your phone?"

I try to remember... I'd left it in the car. All day. My pulse spikes. "Oh, my God, is Mom—"

"She's fine, Ava, but that's not the point! Do you know how worried I was? Do you know how many times I tried calling you? And you think you can just cut school for no reason? Do you know how expensive that school is? How hard I work to—"

"I'm sorry!" I cry out, tears welling. "I won't do it again."

"Sorry's not really good enough—"

"What do you want me to say?"

"It's my fault," Connor speaks up. "She fell asleep on the way to school, and I didn't want to wake her so—"

Corey interrupts him. "So you just didn't bother going to school at all? Or not tell anyone where you were or what you were doing?"

"Jesus, Ava!" Trevor yells. "Goddammit, you have that phone glued to your hand twenty-four-seven and all of a sudden it's not—"

"Stop!" I yell back. "Don't take this away from me!" I swipe at the tears refusing to stop and look up at him. "Please," I beg, my voice cracking, my heart breaking. "Today was the best day I've had since Mom got back, and I don't want you or anyone else taking that away from me, okay? I said I was sorry. But I just wanted *one* day, Trevor. Just one day when I could act my age, when I could be careless and reckless and... God, I just wanted to be a seventeen-year-old girl spending time with a boy I love—"

"You *love* me?" Connor cuts in.

I drop my head in my hands, humiliated. I glare at Trevor, imploring him. "Can we just go? *Please!*"

"Ava," Trevor sighs out. "There has to be consequences..."

"I know." I stand and head for the front door. "And I'll deal with them like I *always* do, but please... just enough, okay? I just..."

"Hey," Connor coos, wrapping me in his arms. "It's okay."

Tears blur my vision when I look up at him. "I just..." *I don't want to go home,* I admit only to myself. I don't want to go home and live in the darkness now that I know what it's like to breathe in the light. "I just have to go home."

CONNOR

Dad waits until Trevor and Ava are out of the house and for sure out of earshot before speaking, his tone a lot calmer than Trevor's. "Your coach called. You're suspended for a game, and they assured me that no matter what Ava says or does, this time it has to stick. They're using you to set an example."

I nod, keep my gaze lowered. "That's fair."

Dad sighs. "Connor, if you want to tell me what happened, I'm happy to listen."

"Nothing," I say, looking at him for the first time since I entered the house. "I picked her up this morning, and she mentioned she hadn't slept well because of her mom..."

Dad nods, urging me to continue.

"And by the time I got to school she was fast asleep, and I... I don't know, I felt bad waking her, so I just kept driving."

"What did you guys do all day?"

Shrugging, I give him the truth. "I ended up parking near a lake, I guess, and we just spent the day... just..."

"Being teenagers?" Dad asks, a compassionate smile tugging on his lips.

"Yeah," I confirm through an exhale.

"Well, I'm sure Ava needed that," he says, sympathetic.

"She did. She *does*."

Dad stands, stretches, then starts pacing the living room like Trevor did. I'd ask if we're done here, but I know him... there's more. I just don't know which way he's going to flip it. He sits back down at the spot he left only seconds ago, his elbows on his knees. "You have to start thinking long term here, Connor."

I *almost* fail at hiding my eye-roll. "I know. The end game. I get it, Dad."

He shakes his head, rubs his chin. "It's more than that now," he explains. "If you care about Ava like you seem to and you want a future with her, you need to think about more than just *now*. And while *now* is good for you guys, *great* even, you need to think about the future. Because if you want her in your life for more than *now*, you have to find a way to take care of not only her but her mother... because that girl—she's never going to leave her mom. And as much as she loves you, she loves her mom more, which she should." He pauses a moment, before asking, "So how are you planning on doing that, Connor? Taking care of both of them emotionally and *financially*?"

My head spins while I replay every one of his words, over and over. I think about what I want in my life, in my future, and the only thing I see is Ava. "I go pro," I declare. "I *have* to."

He nods. "So, what you do *now* is going to determine what happens tomorrow. You got that?"

"Yes, sir."

He stands. "Right now, your focus is what?"

I release the only truth that makes sense. "Basketball."

AVA

Krystal offers to stay so Trevor and I can "chat." Luckily, he's calmed down enough to have an *actual* conversation with me. In my room, he sits on my desk chair while I sit on the bed, my fingers gripping the edge of the mattress.

"I understand why you did what you did today, Ava. And I'm sorry I blew up on you like that. I was worried, but I get it. You deserve that time... but you can't be bringing Connor down with you."

"Down *with* me?" I ask, looking him right in the eyes. "I didn't put a gun to his head—"

"That's not what I meant," he sighs out. "What I mean is I know that school. I know the athletic program. He skips class, and it's an automatic one-game suspension."

"I'll write another letter."

"Ava, you're missing the point," he pushes. "Look, that school is lenient with you because of your circumstances. You skip a class here and there, and they allow it. You fall asleep in class, and they send you to the nurse's office so you can sleep some more, but... Ava, it's such a pivotal time in Connor's life right now. He has college scouts and coaches watching his every move on and off the court. What he does off the court is a representation of his character, not his skill, and his character is just as important to them as his contribution to the scoreboard or whatever—" Trevor shakes his head. "Basketball is dumb, but you understand, right?"

"Yeah, I get it," I say, and I do. Truly. I should've made him go back. I should have explained to his coach what happened and fought for him instead of being selfish and only thinking about what I wanted. What I needed. *Him.*

Trevor scratches his cheek, then his head, then his chest, his tell-tale sign of nerves. "So... you... you *love* him, huh?"

"I don't know," I whisper, watching my legs kick back and forth. "I think so."

"You *think* so, or you know so?"

"I don't know, Trevor," I whine. "I have all these thoughts and emotions, and I don't know what to do with them, and I have no one to talk to about them."

He nods, his chest heaving with his heavy breaths. Then he swallows. "Like... like... *sex* thoughts and emotions?" he asks, his voice wavering at the end.

I look to the side. "Maybe."

He's silent a beat, and then another beat, and a whole damn song could play in the time it takes him to react. "Right." I watch him press his lips together, then get to his feet. He jumps up and down on the spot, rolling his shoulders and tilting his head side to side as if he's gearing up for something. "I got this," he whispers... to himself.

My eyes narrow as I watch him, confusion clouding my brain.

"I got this," he says again and then flops back down on the chair.

"Ava," he deadpans.

I eye him sideways. "Trevor?"

"When a man ejaculates—"

"Oh, my God, *NO!*" I throw my pillow at his head. "Get out!"

ava

"I'M NOT HUNGRY," Mom says, her tone flat as she stares at the wall. It's the fifth day in a row she's refusing to eat breakfast, and I really don't know why I bother getting up when I do.

I cower when I drop the spatula and pan in the sink louder than expected. The last thing I want is to wake Trevor. "You have to eat, Mama," I say, turning to her. "Krystal says you haven't been eating much throughout the day." And she's losing weight, fast. I can see it in the hollow of her cheeks and the way her clothes seem to droop against her body. There are dark circles around her eyes from her lack of decent sleep. The doctors had prescribed some sleep meds for her, but she wakes up foggy and out of sorts and her reaction to that is far worse than the constant waking throughout the night. I try to assure myself that it's just a phase and that as soon as they work out the right cocktail of medications to help her both physically and emotionally, we'll be able to move on. I might even get a positive day out of her at some point.

Mom sighs heavily, pushing away the plate I'd just made up for her. "Where are my cigarettes?"

"You don't smoke, Mama."

Her gaze flits to mine before going back to the wall. "Buy me cigarettes on your way home from school, okay?"

"I can't," I tell her, trying to keep my composure. But inside me, something is ticking, ticking, ticking. "I'm not old enough."

She blinks. Slowly. "Then I'll have William get them."

"William—" I exhale, my hands at my sides. I need to calm down. My getting frustrated will just set her off. "William doesn't live with us anymore."

Another slow blink, and then the tiniest hint of a smile. "He'll be back."

I should tell her that he won't. That he's remarried. That he has a new wife and new stepkids and that all of this was too much for him. That it might be too much for me, too. "Can I make you something else to eat?"

"I'm not hungry."

"But you should at least try to get something in your stomach, Mama."

"Where are my cigarettes?"

My head drops forward, my shoulders lifting with the force of my inhale. I squat down beside her, hold her hand in mine. And then I push down the knot in my throat, kiss the scars that created this stranger. "I'll get them on the way home from school, okay?"

CONNOR

I knock on the door of Coach's office and wait for him to look up from whatever he's reading. When he does, his eyes widen, and he looks at his watch. "You're going to be late to first period."

"I know," I say. "I was hoping to talk to you in private."

He settles back in his chair, his arms crossed. "If it's about the suspension—"

"It's not," I interrupt. "I know what I did, and the punishment stands."

Nodding, he motions to a seat on the other side of the desk. "Let's talk."

Nervous energy swarms through my bloodline as I take a seat, my knees bouncing.

"What's got you on edge?" he asks, eyeing me.

"Nothing." I lie. "Well, yeah. *Something.*"

"Spit it out, kid."

"I need your help," I rush out. "I mean, I'd like some *extra* help. Please. Whatever you can offer me. I need to start focusing more on basketball, or else..." I take a breath. "I'm not getting any offers, Coach, and I need to do something about it."

He laughs once, closing the newspaper in front of him. He trashes it under his desk, then opens his drawer, pulling out a pile of envelopes three inches thick. "These are letters of interest," he deadpans.

My eyes widen. "For me?"

He chuckles, killing any form of hope I'd momentarily allowed. "You heard of Graham Sears?"

I nod. "Spurs, right?"

"Yep. He was one of mine junior and senior year. An import, like you. These are the letters he garnered during those two years. You want to see yours?"

I nod.

He reaches into his drawer and pulls out *air*. He pretends to drop it on the desk. "That's your pile."

Discouraged, I look down at my hands.

"Sears was taken third to last in the NBA draft, Connor, and that's the amount of interest he had. So, if you want just a taste of what he had, you better get ready to work."

I look up at him. "I'm here for it, Coach."

"Good," he says, leaning back in his chair. "You know what the main difference is between you and Sears?"

"He was better than me?"

"No," Coach says, adamant. "That's the thing, Connor. He wasn't. But off the court, he was with his team, building relationships and team cama-raderie. He treated his teammates like they were his brothers, and in turn, those men made him *look* better, made him stand out. So, if I were you, I'd start there."

I lift my chin. "Okay."

He picks up his phone, calls the office to excuse me from first period. Then he makes another call, and a moment later, his office is occupied by the entire coaching staff and a few trainers.

All eyes are on me when Coach says, "Son, if we do this, we *do this*, you understand?"

I nod, puff out my chest. "Yes, sir."

AVA

Connor said he had to get to school extra early this morning, so Trevor ended up giving me a ride. I sit in my usual spot first period, my eyes glued to the door, my heart waiting for just a glimpse of what she desires the most. When the bell rings and he still hasn't shown up, I send him a text.

> Ava: Where are you?

"Psst," Rhys hisses from behind me. "Connor said he was meeting with Coach after practice so he might be late, or not show up at all. He said he'll see you at lunch."

Oh. I nod, put my phone away. "Is he in trouble?" I ask.

Mr. McCallister calls out, "Connor's not, but you two might be if you don't stop talking."

CONNOR

We spend all of first period going through a game plan that includes extra practices, one-on-one coaching with all the coaches. More gym time. More studying. More of everything. Coach even puts in a call to an old friend about getting me into a four-day invitational held by some big name pros around Thanksgiving. It would be a dream, but I'm not holding my breath.

At the end of the period, Coach says, "Today, you have lunch with your *team*."

"I spend time with my girlfriend at lunch," I tell him.

He eyes me over the rim of his glasses. "Do you now?"

I shake my head, my heart heavy. "I guess not."

AVA

Lunch comes around, and I spend the first half sitting in the bleachers without my partner in crime. When he does appear, he's grinning from ear-to-ear. "Hey, girlfriend," he says, kissing my cheek. He sits opposite me with the lunch he acquired from the cafeteria. "Sorry I'm late. I had a thing I had to do."

"A *thing*?"

He shrugs. "Just a basketball thing. It's not important."

"It sounds important," I murmur, shoving his knee gently with my foot. "Tell me."

He holds on to my ankle, tugging gently. With a smile, I get down to his level, sit sideways on his lap. He nuzzles my neck. "I missed you," he says, kissing me there.

"I missed you, too."

He exhales, slowly. "Sorry about first period and being late. I know our time together is so limited, but..." he trails off.

I lift his head in my hands, look in his eyes. "It's okay; I know you're busy. What's going on?"

"Nothing." He shakes his head. "Nothing," he repeats. His eyes search mine, his features falling with every second that passes. "I just miss you is all." But that's *not* all, and I can see it in the way he looks at me, the way his lips tremble.

I hold his face in my hands and release the words I've held on to all night. Words I've been looking forward to saying to *him*. "I love you, Connor," I tell him. "God, I love you so much."

CONNOR

I swallow down the pressure that had been building inside me and stare at the soul that causes my heart to beat. Where my world begins and ends. I hold her to me, afraid to let go. "I love you, Ava... with everything I have."

I keep my eyes closed, hiding the fear in my heart.

What if I do all this?

Risk it all.

And still fail?

What happens to Ava?

To her mom?

What happens to *us*?

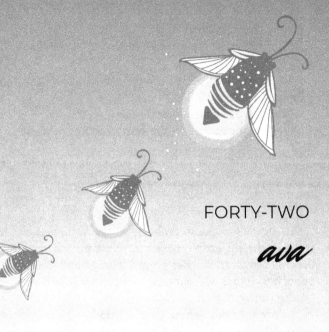

ava

"WE NEED TO DO SOMETHING," Trevor whispers.

I look down at the floor. "I know."

"So... what are we going to do?"

Lifting my gaze, I look at my mother sitting on the couch in the same clothes she's been in for over a week. She's been refusing to shower, and no amount of convincing seems to work. "I don't know."

"It's getting bad, Ava."

"The smell?"

He shakes his head. "That, too, but just... her. She's getting worse," he says, his voice hushed as we stand in the doorway between the kitchen and living room. On the kitchen table behind me, another dinner is left untouched.

"It's fine," I argue, trying to convince myself more than anyone else. "She'll be okay; it's just... a phase."

My phone dings with a text.

Connor: That game just about killed me. About to hop in an ice bath if you want to join me?

"Shit," I hiss.

"What?" Trevor asks.

"I forgot Connor's game." *And the balloon.* "Dammit."

"He'll understand," Trevor assures. "You've been dealing with a lot."

I read over his text again, trying to find a way to respond. And then: "Hey, Mama? What if I run you a bath instead of a shower?"

Her expression doesn't change, neither does the direction of her stare. "A bath sounds nice."

"Thank God," Trevor breathes out.

I rush to the bathroom and start running the water.

> Ava: As bad as that sounds, I wish I could, just to be near you. I'm sorry there was no balloon. Give me five, I'll check the school website and get a rundown of the game.

He doesn't respond, probably in the bath, and so I focus on getting the water to the perfect temperature, filling it with as many scented bath products as I can find. I call her when it's ready, and she comes willingly, stripping out of her clothes without care. "Will you stay with me?" she murmurs.

"Of course, Mama."

I close the door behind us and help her get in. She sits with the water to her neck, her eyes open, staring at the ceiling. She doesn't speak, our breaths the only sound in the small room. I push away all other thoughts—thoughts that seem to invade my mind and ruin me from the inside out.

"Do you..." I start, careful. "Do you want me to wash you?"

Nodding, she sits up and bends over, allowing me to have access. I pour body wash on a loofa and start at her back, ignoring the ailing paleness of her skin, the way her spine sticks out far more than it should. I hear her sniff but stay silent. And then her shoulders... her shoulders start to shake. A single whimper fills the cold, dead air, and I reach up to her shoulder, move her hair to the side. "It's okay, Mama," I say through the knot in my throat. "Sometimes we all need a little help."

She reaches up with her good arm, takes my hand in hers. "Thank you," she whispers, and it's all I need. All I want. For her to know that I'm here for her. Always.

She doesn't say anything more, and neither do I. We finish in the bath, and I help her into fresh clothes and into her bed, pull the covers over her chest. She stares up at the ceiling, and I get on my knees beside her bed, put my hands on her upper arm. "Are you not tired?" I whisper.

Her head lolls to the side, her eyes welling with tears. "I'm scared," she admits.

I sit taller. "Of what?"

She lets out a sob. "To close my eyes."

"Oh, Mama." I settle my head on her chest, my eyes drifting shut when she holds me to her.

"Stay with me, Ava? Just until I fall asleep?"

I wipe my tears on her covers, then suck in a breath, attempt to keep my broken heart bound. "Of course." I get into her bed and try to be her courage while hiding my weakness. She holds me close, using just a portion of the strength of the woman she used to be. The *mother* she used to be.

I lie awake, listening to her breaths settle until I know she's asleep. Then I get out, careful and quiet. I wipe the wetness off my cheeks before opening the door and facing Trevor.

"Is she down?"

I offer the most genuine smile I can come up with. "Yeah, she's sleeping like a baby."

Trevor nods, goes back to watching whatever game is playing. I go to the bathroom and retrieve my phone.

> Connor: I figured something was up when there was no balloon. I hope everything's okay?
>
> Connor: Just got out of the tub. Is everything okay there?
>
> Connor: Can you come out in five? I feel like I haven't seen you in forever.

I look at the time stamp. It was sent over a half hour ago.

> Ava: Sorry, I just got the message.
>
> Ava: I can maybe come out now if you're still up for it.
>
> Connor: Slipping on my shoes.

I tell Trevor I'll just be five minutes, and practically run outside, my heart racing, longing for the only person in the entire world who's capable of letting me forget, even if it's just for a minute.

I wait for him on the sidewalk, smiling when I see his door open. I'm in his arms a moment later, and it should be impossible—that one person can hold so much power in just their embrace—but I physically feel the tension inside me dissolve until it's just him and me and *now*. "I miss you, Ava," he sighs out.

"I know. Me, too."

He pulls away but keeps his arms around my waist, holding me close. Looking down at me, his eyes shift, as if taking me in for the first time. "I promise, once the season's over we'll go back to normal."

Normal. As in one class every other day and lunch breaks and the occasional ride together to and from school. As opposed to what it's been like the past two weeks... when I get to see him in class but not really talk to him, and sometimes he'll show up at lunch, sometimes he doesn't. There are no more rides to and from school. The only reason he gives me is that it's basketball related, but he doesn't give me much else. Any other girl would become suspicious about who he's with and what he's doing. "I understand," I tell him. Besides, he's never once questioned my inconsistencies, and apart from that one time for the pep rally, he's never asked for more of my time than I could give him.

He leans against the chain-link fence of my front yard and pulls me between his legs. I link my fingers behind his neck and just look at him, really truly look at him. He's in dark jeans and a plain gray hoodie, and his hair's wet, or... I reach up... there's product in his hair. I sniff him. "Are you wearing cologne?"

He nods. "You like it?"

"Did you wear it for me?" I ask, half joking.

"Actually..." he starts, grimacing. "One of the guys from the team is having a party tonight, and I said I'd go."

Oh.

"Is that okay?"

"Connor, you don't need my permission to go out."

"I know." His shoulders lift with his shrug. "I just wanted to check anyway."

Well, not really. He's already dressed and ready to go, so he's beyond checking. He's just... *informing.*

"Rhys is coming to get me. He should be here any second."

I get on my toes until my mouth is level with his. "So we only have seconds to get in days' worth of making out?"

His mouth covers mine without a response, his head tilting, getting better access. He pulls me closer again until there's nothing between us. I squeal when his hand covers my ass, squeezing, and then laugh into his mouth. "A little handsy, no?"

Chuckling, he kisses me once more. "I still have a ton of adrenaline. I had a good game."

"You did?" I ask, annoyed at myself for not checking first. I drop down to the heels of my feet. "Shit, Connor, I haven't even had time to check. I'm the worst girlfriend ever."

"You are," he deadpans. But there's a gleam in his eye, a slight smile playing on his lips. "You better make it up to me."

"How?" I ask with a flirtatious lilt.

He's quiet a breath, his eyes on mine, lips parted. "I was talking about that crazy lasagna you make, but whatever you're thinking right now, I choose that."

I tug down on his hoody until his ear is to my lips and whisper, "I want to know what you feel like in my mouth."

Instantly, he has both hands on my butt, lifting, and my legs go around him, holding on to him as he starts carrying me to his house. "Fuck this party," he hisses.

I can't help but laugh. "Your dad's home, and my mom—"

"Get a fucking room," Rhys shouts, pulling up to the curb.

We've barely made it into Connor's yard when he releases me back on my feet. I push him toward Rhys's truck. "Go. Have fun."

He kisses me quickly. "Love you."

"I love you, too."

Rhys says, "I love you both; now hurry the fuck up."

Connor kisses me again. "Can I message you when I get home? Maybe get that goodnight kiss?"

I nod. "Hey. No talking to girls tonight," I joke.

"Yes, ma'am," he says, kissing me again before opening the car door.

"You're so whipped," Rhys remarks.

"I don't mind it." Connor laughs. "Besides, she knows how to dispose of a dead body with little to no evidence. And I like breathing. It's *fun*."

* * *

Mom's stirred twice since I put her to bed, but she hasn't fully woken, which is an improvement from the previous nights.

It's close to midnight, and I'm working on these stupid college applications when a text comes through.

Connor: I is home, woman. Kiss me.

Ava: Are you drunk? Come to my window. BE QUIET.

I open my blinds, lift the window and rest my elbows on the frame, half out, looking for him. He appears, a silhouette lit only by the phone he's looking at. "Connor," I hiss.

"One second." His thumbs are moving, and so is he, closer and closer. When he gets to my window, he finally looks up. "God, you're beautiful," he mumbles at the same time my phone goes off.

Connor: I be there soon.

I drop the phone, reach out and pull him toward me with the ties of his hood. "How much did you have to drink?"

He shrugs, his eyes hooded. "Just a couple beers to take the edge off. I'm not drunk."

I eye him sideways. "How many girls did you talk to tonight?"

"Twelve."

"That's an oddly specific number."

"I made it up. No girls." He shakes his head. Then he reaches up, holds my entire head in his grasp. With his eyes on mine, he says, a seriousness taking over him, "You're the only girl for me, Ava Elizabeth Diana." He kisses me, soft and sweet, and then pulls away. "Can you turn your light on?"

"Why?"

"I always wonder what your room's like, and every time I come here, it's dark. I just want to see... maybe I could come in? Just for a few minutes?"

Biting down on my lip, I hesitate before nodding. "You have to be quiet, okay? My mom's asleep."

He draws a cross over his heart, and I lift my window higher so he can fit through. I step back, watch him climb in, first his arms, then his upper body, and then he's army crawling across my floor with his legs still out the window. When he's all the way in, his feet hit the floor with a thud. "Connor!" I whisper-yell, my finger to my lips as I listen for any movement. I'm not sure what would be worse, Mom waking or Trevor knowing there's a boy in my room.

"Sorry." He grimaces. "That was harder than it looked."

I switch on the light on my nightstand and watch him look around my room. There's nothing in here but my bed, desk, and bookshelf. "It's... different from what I imagined."

"What did you imagine?" I ask, sitting on the edge of my bed.

He sits down next to me, his giant frame almost comical on such a small bed. "I don't really know."

"It was supposed to be temporary," I admit, looking down at my feet, shame washing through me. "We weren't supposed to be here this long. I guess part of me was hoping for a miracle. Maybe William would come back and save us or—"

"Ava," he interrupts, nudging my side. "You forget we live next door. My dad works full-time and only has me to worry about, and that's all he can afford. There's nothing wrong with where we live, and that's not what I was getting at. I just meant that... I don't know. I thought there'd be pictures on the walls or something."

Not in here, I don't say. "Of what? All my imaginary friends?"

He sighs, rubs his eye with the heel of his palm. "Rhys is your friend."

"Rhys feels sorry for me."

"Karen misses you."

I can't help the flash of jealousy that knots my stomach. "You talk to Karen?"

"I mean, sometimes. I talked to her tonight."

My voice cracks when I ask, "About me?"

He settles his hand on my leg, and I can't help but think that his guilt put it there. "She asked about you. About *us*. And I told her how much I love you."

His answer is perfect. *Too* perfect. My old insecurities come back to me, and I swallow the lump in my throat.

"Ava," he says through a sigh. "What's wrong?"

I don't look up when I answer, "Nothing."

He sighs again, this one heavier. "Are you mad that I went out tonight?"

"No."

"Because I needed it, Ava. I need to get the guys on my side so I can... I've just been under a lot of stress, and I just wanted a night out, but the whole time I was there, all I wanted was to be with you, and now I'm here and..."

And I couldn't even be there for him if I wanted to. I'm not able to carry his stress like he carries my pain. I turn to him. "I'm sorry I haven't been there."

"I don't expect you to be, Ava." Even though he said it so matter-of-fact, so innocently... the truth behind those few words shatters any dignity I have left. He adds, "I told you I don't want anything more from you than you, and I meant it."

But it's not enough anymore.

And maybe I'm not enough.

He shifts, getting more comfortable on my bed. His back to the wall, he pats his lap. "Come here."

I ignore the blinding ache in my chest and move to him, straddling his lap.

His hands settle on my thighs while mine go to his shoulders. "I came here for my goodnight kiss, remember?"

Nodding, I close my eyes, hide my doubt, and press my lips to his. His mouth opens, wanting more, and so I give him what he wants. It doesn't take long for his hands to wander, first to my butt, then my breasts, under my top. His kisses move down, down, down, while his hands move up, up, up taking my tank with him. I do the same with him, our bare chests pressed together as he holds me to him, shifts us until I'm underneath him and he's between my legs. He starts to unbutton his jeans and then unzip his fly, and if this is what he came here for... if this is what he wants from me... I'll give it to him. It's the least he deserves, the least I can do. I roll us until he's on his back and make fast work of removing his shoes, then his jeans. I kiss his stomach and move lower to the smattering of hair just above his boxer shorts. His hands find the back of my head, fingers curled, and I pull down on the waistband and don't waste any time. I take him in my mouth, taste him, feel his thighs tense beneath my touch. He whispers my name, and I should feel *something*... aroused or dominant or desired, but I don't.

I feel like a whore.

The sudden sound of glass breaking has us pulling apart. I rush for my top at the same time he quickly covers himself. "Stay here," I tell him, throwing my top back on. I run out of the room, switching on lights, my heart thumping against my chest.

Not again.

Not again.

Not again.

I check the living room and kitchen, but they're empty. Trevor's out of his room, and his panic matches mine. I open Mom's door. She's on the floor, shards of glass around her. "Mama!" I scream, and she looks up, points to her foot.

Blood.

"What happened?" I rush out, moving in on her.

"I knocked over the glass," she deadpans. "Stepped on it." There's no life in her words or her eyes.

I glare at Trevor and shout, "Why the hell is there glass in her room?!"

He rears back. "I must've left it there when I gave her the meds earlier. Shit, Ava, I don't know."

"You know she can't be around this!" I say, dropping to my knees, ignoring the blood pooling around her. There's so much. Too much. Memories flood my brain and I try to push them away, but they're too strong. Too forceful. "How could you do that!" I scream at him.

"It was an accident!" he shouts back.

"Stop yelling!" Mom says, covering her ears. She starts to rock back and forth, and I try to settle my breathing, try to calm myself down. But I can't.

"You can't have *accidents* with her, Trevor! You know you can't!" Tears fall, fast and free, and I open her drawer, pull out whatever I can find to stop the bleeding. I press it to her foot, and she screams, kicks my hands off of her.

"Get away!" she yells, a terror in her voice that has my pulse escalating. I glance at Trevor, and he feels it, too.

"I need to check your foot. There might be glass!"

She kicks my chest and screams, "GET AWAY FROM ME!" And then she looks up, her eyes wide and focused on my doorway. "Who are you?" she breathes out, fear and horror etched on her face.

Connor's in the doorway, his eyes huge. He opens his mouth, but nothing comes out.

"Get away!" She kicks me again. "Go! Go! Go!"

Ignoring Connor, I grab at Mom's foot, blocking her kicks, and now Trevor's on the floor behind her, pinning down her arms. "Connor, a little help!"

Connor steps into the room, alarm evident in his voice. "What can I do?"

I'm still wrestling with Mom's legs when Trevor orders, "Hold her legs down."

"I don't want to hurt her," Connor says, panicked.

"Just do it, Connor!" I plead.

He drops to his knees in front of me and wraps his arms around her legs, holding them together.

Liquid crimson on my hands, I hold on to Mom's foot, but I can't see through the blood. "I can't see!" I cry out.

"Get off of me!" Mom thrashes, trying to get out of all our holds.

Distressed, Trevor says, "We need to call—"

"My dad," Connor cuts in, phone on the floor, on speaker, already dialing.

His dad answers on the first ring, and Connor says, "I need you at Ava's."

"I'll be right there."

For the few minutes it takes to hear the sirens approaching, the only one who speaks is my mom, mumbling words in a language only she understands. Trevor and Connor keep their hold on her while she thrashes around, screaming, then whispering, over and over. Outside, dogs bark, and inside... inside is the world at its darkest, and there's no magic in sight.

I look down at my hands, at the blood dripping from my fingers, and the only thing I can think is... at least she's breathing this time.

I take over holding down Mom's legs while Connor opens the door for his dad and his partner to enter. As soon as they see us, they get down on the floor. Mom screams again, "Get away from me! Don't touch me! Don't touch me! Don't touch me!" She's thrashing around again, harder this time, and I'm too weak... too fucking powerless.

"I think there might be glass in her foot, but I can't... I can't..." I am empty. Void. Running on hopes and dreams that are entirely unattainable.

Corey says, "We're going to have to give her a little something to calm her down so we can—"

"Ketamine?" I ask.

Corey nods. "You've been through this before, huh?" He taps Connor on the shoulder, urging him to move out of the way. Connor gets up, leaves the room completely.

He doesn't want to be here.

And neither do I.

* * *

When it's over, when the glass is out, and the bandages are on and the meds have done their job and Mom's fast asleep in her bed, I stand in the middle of her room while Trevor gives a report, and Connor... Connor stands with me, holding my hand tight in his grasp. "So this is where all the pictures are," he muses.

I look up at him, my eyes dry for the first time since I heard the glass breaking, and then glance around the room. Every inch of every wall is covered in photographs—photographs I put up. From when I was a baby, through to now. Some with Trevor and William and Mom and me, as a family, and some of just us—Mom and me. I inhale a shaky breath, my voice barely a whisper, "Sometimes I hope that she'll one day wake up and see all of this, all of her life, all of *me*, and that's somehow going to be enough for her to... to miraculously snap out of it, as if it's..." I break off, my emotions getting the best of me. "It's so stupid."

"It's not," he whispers, holding my head to him. His heart beats against my cheek, and I close my eyes, listen. I try to hear the magic in there, but my thoughts are too loud, like a constant buzzing of words and memories and pain. So much pain. "It's not stupid to hope, Ava. Sometimes hope is the only thing that gets us through to the next day."

In my mind, I know he's right.

But in my heart, I know the next day will be the same as all the other days. So what difference does it make?

"I should stay," Connor says.

I shake my head, release his hand. "You should go. Try to get some rest. You have early practice tomorrow."

"She's right, Connor," his dad interrupts, standing in the doorway.

"But—"

Trevor stands next to Corey. "I'll walk you out, Connor."

Corey waits until they've left the house, along with his partner, before saying, "This is a lot to handle, Ava. Even for a girl as strong as you."

I don't respond.

He steps farther into the room, glancing at Mom, and then the pictures on the wall.

"Have you thought about putting her in a—"

"I'm not abandoning her," I cut in. Then mumble, "I'm not Connor's mom." Regret forces my eyes to shut the moment the words leave me.

"He told you about that?"

I nod, open my eyes again. "I shouldn't have said that."

Corey offers a reassuring smile, but it doesn't reach his eyes. "You know what I learned early on? Life is a series of decisions. You make them because they feel right at the time, but you're not bound to them forever. She made the decision to leave, and you're making the decision to stay. The difference is, her choices have done irreversible damage. Yours haven't. Yet."

FORTY-THREE

Connor

I BARELY SLEPT after what happened last night and could hardly get through the standard practice this morning. Luckily, most of the guys were hungover, so my lagging didn't seem so bad. Now I'm in the cafeteria, sitting at the "jock" table because I know Ava isn't coming.

> Connor: Just checking in, babe. How is she?

> Ava: She's okay now. She's on painkillers, so she's been in and out all day. Krystal's here. I'm just trying to get sleep in when I can.

> Connor: Anything I can do?

"Are you in, Connor?"

> Ava: No. I'm just sorry you had to witness what you did. A little embarrassed, I guess.

> Connor: What I witnessed doesn't change anything.

"Connor!" Rhys nudges my side. "Earth to Connor."

I look up from my phone, see him motioning to Oscar sitting opposite me. "What?"

"Game tape after school? Our next game is Philips Academy, and they're fucking fierce."

"Yeah, sure," I mumble and look back at my phone. She hasn't responded.

Oscar says, his eyes flitting between me and my phone, "Ava wasn't in AP English this morning. Is everything okay?"

My gaze drifts to him. "She had a rough night."

He nods, and I see the genuine concern in his eyes. "Ava's a nice girl. It sucks what happened to her mom."

I look around the table, see all eyes on us, ears glued to our conversation. "Yeah, it's uh... it's tough."

"If there's anything I can do," he says, "for you or for Ava, just let me know, man."

Rhys adds, "That goes for the entire team, right, boys?"

I look around the table, at my teammates who I've gotten closer to over the past few weeks, all of them nodding, agreeing. And maybe Coach was right, and I was wrong. Maybe it wasn't the worst thing in the world to get to know these guys beyond what they had to offer on the court. Because they all seem sincere, and maybe I'd spent all this time thinking they were judging me when I'd been doing the same thing to them. "Thanks, guys. I appreciate it."

A flurry of "no worries" and "all good" sounds around the table, and then Rhys speaks up. "Here's trouble." He motions to Karen, who's walking toward us. She drops her tray on the other side of me, greets us all with a "What's up, *fuckboys*."

"Was that your mom at the game last night?" Mitch asks her.

Karen nods.

"Did she get new boobs?"

She nods again. "Provided by husband number six."

Mitch chuckles. "If they get any bigger, I might make a play. One day I could be your stepdad."

Karen throws a handful of fries at his head. "Gross, jerk."

Then Mitch waggles his eyebrows. "You can call me Daddy."

I ignore the rest of the banter and check my phone.

Still no reply.

Connor: Ava, I love you. ALL of you.

FORTY-FOUR

Connor

ANOTHER WEEK GOES by in a blur, and my time with Ava is limited, at best. And while we try to make the most of what we have, I can feel the distance growing between us, the disconnect. I convince myself that it's just in my head, that a lot is going on in both our lives and the last thing we need is to talk about my insecurities. Besides, it's only for a few more months. Once I get accepted somewhere, *anywhere*, and the season is over, I can focus all my time and energy on her.

On us.

On the end game.

* * *

The balloon on my porch brings a stupid smile to my face, and Dad says, "I don't get it. Why the *boo!?*"

"Because it's Ava," I tell him, following him to the car. "And it's my good luck charm." Once in the car, I pop the balloon, shove it down my boxer shorts. "And I could use all the luck in the world tonight." Tonight's opponents are currently on top of the leaderboard, a team full of all-stars. Every single person on their roster has already committed to various D1 colleges throughout the country, and *my* team is expecting me to perform, to outsmart, outrun, and outplay every one of them.

"You'll be fine, Connor," Dad says.

. . .

But I wasn't fine. Not even close. I'm double-teamed during every second I'm on the court, and I can barely get a possession, let alone score. My frustration shows in the way I yell at my team, pushing them to go harder, stronger, and then halfway through the third, I hit my fucking limit. I throw my mouth-guard across the court, get a technical and hand the opposition two free throws. I ride the rest of the quarter on the bench with my head between my shoulders and my pulse racing, blood boiling.

It's our first L for the season.

My team lacks any form of responsibility for the way the game played out.

Coach is pissed at me.

Dad is disappointed in me.

And I haven't said a word to anyone since the final buzzer.

For the past few weeks, I've come just short of killing myself to play as hard as I did tonight, and it wasn't enough.

I'm not enough.

While Dad drives us home, in silence, I flip the phone in my hand, jumping every time a notification comes through. Usually there's a text waiting for me when I get to the locker room, *a good game, #3* or something similar. But there was nothing after this game or the last, and it just amplifies all the insecurities I've been trying to ignore.

When Dad stops by the gas station to buy the bags of ice I'll be soaking in later, I hit my limit of patience and send her a text.

Connor: You okay?

Ava: Can I call you later?

My eyes drift shut, my frustration growing.

Connor: Yeah

* * *

I sit in the stupid bath, my teeth chattering, muscles recoiling, and my phone gripped tight in my hand, waiting for Ava.

By the time I get out, she still hasn't called, and I ignore all the other calls and texts from the guys on the team.

I don't need them.

I need her.

After checking that my phone is charging, working and the ringer is set to the loudest possible setting, I settle in my chair, college essay prep notes and applications in front of me. The screen of my laptop is bright against my eyes, the cursor flashing. I type, delete, retype, over and over, but nothing sticks because none of it matters.

An hour passes.

Then two.

Three.

I read over some past essays, make more notes.

Four.

Five.

"Connor?" A hand on my shoulder forces my eyes open. I look up to see Dad standing beside me.

I lift my head off the pile of papers on my desk and stretch my arms, my back, snapping my muscles and bones into place. With a grimace, I ask, "Aren't you supposed to be at work?"

"Son," he says, eyeing me dubiously. "It's morning. You must've fallen asleep at your desk."

"What?" I sit up straight, look at my watch. "Goddammit."

And then I check my phone.

No sign of Ava.

"Maybe you're pushing yourself too hard," Dad suggests.

Disappointed and disillusioned, I don't bother responding.

He adds, "Why don't you take the day off school? Maybe you just need a little reboot."

I nod, already getting into bed.

"You need anything?" he asks.

I stare up at the ceiling. "I'm good."

The second the door's closed, I send her a text.

> Connor: Not at school today. I guess I'll catch you whenever.

And then I switch off my phone because I'm done waiting.

Done *hoping*.

* * *

I wake up to the sound of Dad's voice, and when I peer through my heavy lids, I see him standing in my doorway. "You have a visitor," he tells me, stepping to the side.

In her school uniform, Ava stands just outside my room. I force my eyes to open wider so I can check the time. It's mid-morning. "Shouldn't you be at school?" I mumble.

Ava shrugs, her gaze down, her bottom lip pushed out in a pout. She glances between Dad and me as if asking us both, "Can I come in?"

She's a vision of guilt and remorse, and my chest tightens, but it doesn't give out, and I don't give in. I'm still pissed, and I don't have it in me to hide it. "If that's what you want," I breathe out.

Dad closes the door once Ava's in the room but leaves it ajar—his way of setting rules we haven't yet discussed.

Ava stands at the side of my bed, looking down at me. She's chewing her lip, her eyes on mine. Tears pool there, and I look away.

She fumbles over her words, starting and stopping, and I just want to go back to sleep where time didn't exist, and I don't have to deal with this. Not today. Not after last night. "I've been calling and messaging all morning, and when I couldn't get through, I left school and I... I caught a cab here."

I push down my anger and frustration. "You didn't need to do that. I'm fine."

She sits on the edge of my bed and is quiet a beat, then: "I told you I'd make a shitty girlfriend and you—"

"You're going to blame me?" I face her now. "Dammit, Ava. I waited all night for your call." I sit up. "I *needed* you. You're the only one who can refocus the mess in my head, the only one who can make everything inside me settle and allow me to see straight, and if you were too busy, I understand, but don't tell me you're going to do something and then just forget I exist."

"I didn't forget—" She stops there, shaking her head. Then she blows out a heavy breath. "I'm going to go," she says, standing. "I'm not making things any better by being here, so... I'm sorry, Connor. I'm sorry I disappointed you," she cries out. "And I don't know what else to say."

She starts to leave, but I grasp her hand, my heart and head pounding. I come back to reality. It was one fucking game. Just *one*. And if I want her forever, like I know I do, there are going to be other games, other moments where she can't be there, and I've been selfish. God, I've been so fucking selfish.

I won't lose her over this.

I can't.

She allows me to pull her closer, her back turned. I press my cheek into her open palm, kiss the inside of her wrist. "Don't go," I plead.

She turns to me, her tear-stained cheeks cracking open my chest. "I want so badly to be everything you need me to be."

I pull on her arm until her knees are on my bed, my hands going to her face, thumbs swiping away her sadness. "You are, Ava. And I'm so sorry I made you feel otherwise."

She nods, grasping my wrists.

"Stay?"

Another nod, and I'm shifting until my back's against the wall. She gets to her feet to slip off her shoes while I lift the covers to let her in. Her head on the crook of my shoulder and her hand on my heart, I ask, "Is everything okay with your mom?"

"I don't want to talk about it right now." She leans up to look down at me. "I'm here now. For you. I want to know everything."

I shake my head, push away the past twenty-four hours of my life, and start living for now. "You're right. You're here now. And nothing else matters."

She kisses me, her tongue swiping against my lips, and I'm suddenly awake and alive, and when she moves down to my neck, I stop her. I get out of bed, peek my head out the door to see Dad's bedroom door closed. He's asleep after his shift. I close the door. Lock it. Then strip out of my shirt and get back into bed with the girl I love.

She sits up to remove her blazer, and then she unbuttons her top, dropping them both on the floor by the bed. I hold on to her hips, guide her until she's straddling my lap. I pull at the front of her bra. "Off."

She complies and then lies on top of me, her bare breasts against my chest. I run a hand down her spine while the other settles on the back of her head.

"Thank you for coming," I tell her.

She smiles against my skin. "I haven't yet."

A chuckle erupts from deep in my chest, and she sits up again, starts removing her skirt. I place my hands on hers, stopping her. "Can this stay on?"

She eyes me, questioning.

I don't bother hiding my grin. "And the socks, too."

"Oh, God," she says through a giggle. "Do you have some weird schoolgirl kink?"

I shrug. "I didn't know I had one until you walked into class the first day of school."

"The first day?" she asks, incredulous, eyes widening.

I nod. "I've wanted you since the first time I saw you."

She leans down, bites down on my collarbone. "So now that you have me, what do you plan on doing with me?"

My hands are already under her skirt, pulling down her underwear.

We spend the rest of the afternoon in my bed, under the sheets, in a state of half-naked. We tease, and we touch, and we taste, and we go as far as we can without going all the way. We're lazy and we're carefree, taking breaks to eat or nap, to laugh and to talk and to just *be*. With each other. Within the four walls of my bedroom, we find peace in each other's arms, find solace in each other's touch, and find a *home* in each other's hearts... even if the space is limited.

ava

IT'S the most time I've been able to spend with my boyfriend in weeks, and it's in the form of a giant poster just outside the school gym. I had no idea that it was going to be there. I heard a few girls in my English class talking about it, so I had to check it out for myself.

I sit on the wall opposite with my paper bag lunch and make myself comfortable, smiling at the picture of him with a ball held at his side, standing tall. The poster takes up the entire height of the wall, and I couldn't be prouder.

I take out my phone, snap a picture of myself eating my sandwich with the poster behind me, and send it to him with the caption:

> Ava: If I can't have the real you, I'll have the next best thing.

I don't expect him to respond, because I know he's spending the lunch break on a conference call with his coach and agent.

"Damn, you look good, babe!" I whisper, holding my sandwich in the air as if I'm toasting him.

"What the hell are you doing?" I recognize the voice as Rhys's and look up to see him walking toward me. His gaze shifts between fake-Connor and myself, and I say, "Talking to my boyfriend, who I miss dearly."

Rhys laughs, plants his ass down next to me. "Yeah, he's putting in the work at the moment. No off days for that kid."

I nod.

"It's nothing against you, A. You know that, right? He's just trying to get as much exposure as possible."

"I know," I tell him. "I get it."

He opens my paper bag and peers inside. Then he takes an apple and bites into it. I quirk an eyebrow. "You know I'm poor now, right? That apple was all I had for the rest of the day."

Chuckling, he reaches into his pocket and pulls out his wallet. He hands me a twenty. "I hear that's the going rate for an apple these days."

Shrugging, I shove the cash in my bra. He can spare it.

"How's your mom?" he asks.

I stare up at twelve-foot Connor. "I'm kind of getting over that question, to be honest."

"Fair," Rhys says. "Manage to get your license yet?"

"No." I haven't even gotten my permit. "I should really look into doing that with all the spare time I have."

"You're feisty right now."

"I'm feisty always."

"True. So how are you and Connor doing?"

"I don't know." I turn to him. "How are you and the rotating door of girls doing?"

He chuckles. "It's been slim pickins 'round these parts," he drawls.

"You should head over to West High. I'm sure there are plenty of girls there looking for a sugar daddy."

His nose scrunches. "I'm not that desperate yet."

I shoulder him, shoving him sideways. "You're a jerk."

He straightens up, throws his arm around my shoulders, then looks up at fake-Connor. "Hey, Ledger. I'm making moves on your girl. Whatcha gonna do about it?"

Out of nowhere, Connor appears. "Get your hands off my girl before I rip them off and glue them to your balls."

"Oooh," I tease, giggling. "You're in trouble now."

Rhys removes his arm, slides a good foot away from me. "We were just playing."

Connor sits down next to me at the same time Rhys gets to his feet. "I'd love to stay and be a third wheel and all but... no... I don't really want to. Peace out, fuckers." And then he's gone, disappearing around the same corner from which Connor appeared.

"Guess what?" Connor says, pulling his phone from his pocket. He taps a few times and then hands it to me.

I read the email on the screen:

Dear Connor Ledger,
Please consider this your official invitation to the—

I don't read the rest because I've lost my breath entirely. "Connor!" I squeal. "You got into that—that thing with all the pros and the—" I imitate shooting, even though I'm sure my form is all wrong. "And the dunk thing! *Thing*!"

Connor laughs. "The invitational, yes, I got in!"

"Oh, my God." My grin widens. "That's amazing. That's a big deal, right? What am I asking? Of course it is. It's a *huge* deal." I hug his neck, loving the chuckle that comes out of him. "I'm so proud of you."

When I release him, he says, "Coach had to pull a lot of strings to—"

"No," I cut in. "Don't you dare undervalue your worth. There are only, what, a hundred spots you told me? They wouldn't have sacrificed a single one of those spots if they didn't think you earned it."

"I guess," he mumbles, but he's not as excited as he should be. He's definitely not as excited as I am.

"What's wrong?" I ask, handing back his phone.

"It's just... it's four days over Thanksgiving break, and I was hoping to spend that time with you."

"This is a once in a lifetime opportunity, babe." I smack the back of his head playfully. "And I'll be here when you get back."

He smiles. "Promise?"

My shoulders drop. "Of course."

Smirking, he says, his tone playful, "You're not going to run off with Rhys and have all his babies?"

"Nah... Rhys's genetics are all messed up. His parents are second cousins."

"You're kidding?" he asks, wide-eyed.

"Am I?"

He glares at me a moment, contemplating. Then he gives up on my shenanigans and leans back against the wall, his chin up, looking at himself on the poster. "Damn, Ava. Your boyfriend's pretty."

I laugh, loud and free. "He's modest, too."

"Thank you," he says, sobering.

"For what?"

His head lolls to the side, his eyes on mine. "For being proud of me."

I settle my legs over his and cuddle into him. "You make it easy, Connor." I kiss his lips, and then his jaw, loving the way he brings me closer.

A deep throat clearing has me pulling away, hiding my face in his neck. Connor's shoulders shake with his silent chuckle. "Coach," he says in greeting.

"Ledger," Coach Sykes returns. "Y'all leave room for Jesus now."

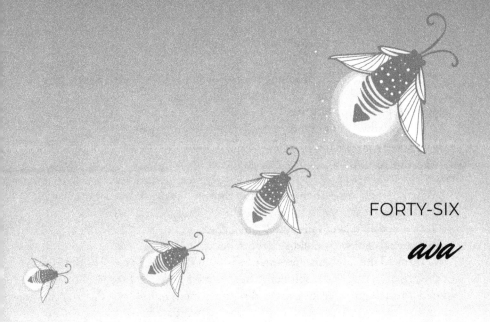

ava

I SWIPE up on my phone, my hands shaking as I rush to read every word on the email Trevor has forwarded to me. It's from our health insurance company about Mom's coverage, but I don't understand what it means. There are too many technicalities, withdrawals, and limitations, and every line, every paragraph has my heart beating faster and faster, my airways tightening.

"Ava!" Connor snaps, and I come back to reality. For a second, I'd forgotten where I was, too embroiled in what the changes to the coverage mean for my mom, for our future.

Connor has one hand on the wheel, his entire body leaning to the side, facing me. "Have you been listening to a word I've been saying?"

We're on our way home from school, I remember that much, and I remember opening the email with the subject: *URGENT* and everything after that was filled with panic. "Sorry, what?" I try to focus on his words over the sound of my pulse pounding in my ears.

His brow lifts. "I was telling you about the tournament this weekend. How there are going to be twenty-five college coaches and eight NBA scouts..."

I peer down at my phone again.

"Ava?!"

"Huh?" My eyes snap to his. "Sorry."

"It's cool," he mumbles, his expression falling. He focuses on the road again. "I was just confessing all my fears and doubts to you, but it seems like you're preoccupied..." Shaking his head, he adds, barely a whisper, "Like always."

"I'm sorry," I rush out, dropping my phone in my bag. I turn to him, give him my full attention. "I'm sorry," I repeat. "Just start again."

He shakes his head. "It's fine."

I grasp his arm. "Connor, no. Just tell me everything again."

He pulls up in front of our houses, his gaze distant as he stares out through the windshield. "I have to get back to school. Coach is waiting for me."

"What?" I huff out. Then realization dawns. "Wait, did you push back practice to give me a ride?"

Connor nods but keeps his eyes trained ahead.

My stomach sinks. "You didn't have to drive me home."

He turns to me now, his movements slow, and just like he stared out the window, he stares at me. Unblinking. But his gaze looks *past* me, and I feel... exposed. I watch him closely, see the disappointment in his eyes, the frustration in his brow. And I hear the defeat in his words when he says, "I just needed to talk to you."

I exhale loudly, try to calm my thumping heart. "Connor, I'm so sorry."

He shakes his head, then reaches across me and opens my door. "I really do have to go."

My stomach is in knots, and I don't want to leave him, not like this. "How long will you be gone?"

Without looking at me, he says, "I don't know, Ava."

"Well, will you call me later?" I'm *trying*. I'm doing my best to fight for his forgiveness, but I don't know how. "You think I can get my goodnight kiss?"

"Sure," he says, but there's no inflection in his tone. No promises.

And while my mind is back on that email trying to process everything it had to say, I get out of the car without another word and leave my heart in the driver's seat, the distance between us growing with every second.

* * *

I spend the rest of the night worrying about Connor, or more specifically, *Connor and me*, when I know I should be more concerned about Mom's insurance. It doesn't escape me that I seem to be focusing on Connor when I'm around my mom and then my mom when I'm around Connor, and I really wish there was a switch for my brain. I wish I could train it to stop and go at the right times. I wish my mind weren't always stuck in a fog. I wish... I wish for so many things. But right now, I wish for Connor. For him to message me and tell me he's home and that he wants his kiss.

It's eleven thirty, and I still haven't heard from him.

Dread pools in the pit of my stomach, because I know how flakey I've been lately. I can see how frustrated he's getting with me, and I want to make it up to him. I do. I just don't have the time or the resources or the... I fight back the constant thoughts attempting to ruin what we have.

That he needs more.

Deserves more.

Ava: How's that goodnight kiss coming along?

It takes him a few minutes to respond.

Connor: I'll be there in five.

I open my blinds and lift the window. And I wait. And wait. And wait. Five minutes turns to ten, and I check my phone. Nothing. I wait some more, the frigid cold air forming goosebumps along my arms as I lean halfway out, searching for him.

After fifteen minutes, he finally appears, but there's no swing in his step, no hint of a smile.

There's no boy who loves me. *All* of me.

"Hi," I whisper, waving.

He gets close enough so he can kiss me, just once. When he steps back, his eyes are on mine, tired and tortured. "Hey."

I swallow the instant lump in my throat, but it just moves lower and lower until it's wrapped around my heart, making it impossible to breathe. "What have you—" I break off when I notice him clenching his jaw.

There's no life in his eyes as he scans my face. "Goodnight, Ava." He turns on his heels and starts to leave.

"Wait," I rush out, grasping for him.

My hand catches air, but he stops anyway.

"Did you..." I want him with me. I want to show him that I care. I want him in my bed, and I want to give him everything he's wanted. And I don't care if it makes me a whore. I just want him to not look at me the way he is. I *need* him to forgive me. "Did you want to come in for a bit?" I say, my entire everything timid and submissive.

Without a second thought, he shakes his head. "I can't."

"Oh." My gaze drops, shame igniting my flesh. "Okay."

He doesn't look back when he says over his shoulder, "I'll see you whenever."

connor

FOUR BALLOONS ARE WAITING for me on the porch, one for each game if we make it through to the final of today's single-elimination tournament. Thirty of the best high school basketball teams in the region all compete for a cash prize that goes directly to the school, but that's not why we play. The arena will be filled with college coaches and NBA scouts, all of them searching for the one hidden gem. That one player who nobody knows about. And today, I'm hoping that one player is me. But so are hundreds of other kids.

I remove the balloons one by one, and I wish they gave me the same knee-jerk reaction as all the other times I'd seen them here. That feeling of elation, of pride, of wanting to do something *great* for someone else.

For Ava.

But it doesn't.

And I don't know if it's because things are rocky with us at the moment or if it's my nerves, because there sure as shit are a lot of those, too. I could barely sleep last night, my mind focused on every play, every opponent. This tournament is my chance to show up. To rise above the rest and make an impact. If this goes well, Coach assures me that colleges will have no choice but to make an offer. And I need that. God, do I *need* that.

AVA

"Trevor!" I call out, sitting on the couch with Mom in front of me while I do her hair. She's having another zero-day, and in a way, I'm glad. Lately, zero days have been the best we can get out of her.

He storms out of his room, his eyebrows drawn, focused on his phone. "What's up?"

"They're streaming today's tournament. Can you connect my laptop to the TV so I can watch it on there?"

Trevor nods, looking up and pocketing his phone. "How does Connor feel about it?"

"Connor," Mom mumbles. "Six-five but is hoping for a growth spurt."

My eyes widen. So do Trevor's. I lean over her shoulder. "You remember Connor, Mama?"

She nods once, staring into the abyss. "Handsome boy."

I can't help but smile. "Do you remember anything else about that day?"

"What day?" she asks.

"The day you met Connor."

"Connor, six-five but is hoping for a growth spurt."

Trevor chuckles, shaking his head as he goes into my room to retrieve the laptop.

"We're going to watch him play in a tournament today," I say, more to myself than anyone else. "He's going to kill it; I just know it."

"Who is?" Mom asks.

"Connor."

"Connor, six-five but is hoping for a growth spurt."

Mom and I spend most of the afternoon in front of the TV watching all the games while Trevor sleeps or works or does whatever it is in his bedroom. When Connor's not on the court, Mom and I do our usual weekend routine: flashcards, speech therapy, basic chores to remind her of daily tasks. She takes long breaks in between, her mental fatigue just as prevalent as her physical.

When Connor's playing, I try to give him my full attention so that I'm *present* when he wants to talk about it all. But sometimes it's hard. When Mom needs me, I have to stop. But it's always on in the background, and I try to retain as much of it as possible. I do my best not to squeal whenever he scores because sudden sounds and movements can set Mom off. So on the outside, I'm still, but on the inside, I'm jumping up and down and screaming and booing, and he's such a phenomenon to watch. And even though I've managed to find shitty-quality live streams on students' social media or post-game highlights online, I'll never not be amazed at his skill, at his level of dedication.

The team flies through the first two rounds, making it to the semis, where their opponents give them more of a challenge. They scrape by with a three-point win and move on to the final.

The camera zooms in on Connor at the end of the game, sitting on the bench with Rhys beside him. He's covered in sweat, his face red with exhaustion. His chest heaves as his lips part, clearing his airways for the stream of water he pours into his mouth from inches above. I stare, fixated, my heart racing, longing for the boy who carried me through the clear blue water and darkened cave. It seems so long ago; that one day of adolescent bliss, and I wish we could go back there. Both physically and metaphorically. I wish we didn't have all this burden and pressure from things outside our control that always fight to pull us apart. Sometimes I think that fight is winning. But then he'll hold me. He'll kiss me. And he'll pull my head to his chest, my ear taking in his existence, a reminder that magic is real, and it lives within him, within *us*.

I whip up a quick dinner between games, and we sit in front of the couch to eat. I don't want to miss a single second. I've thought about messaging him between games, but I don't want to be a distraction.

The final starts and I'm on the edge of my seat, my pulse racing, nervous energy flowing through my veins. The leading score is continually changing, and by the third quarter, it's a draw.

"I think I'll try my prosthetic today," Mom says out of nowhere.

I practically sprint to her room, retrieve it, and come back out, not wanting to miss a thing. I focus mainly on the game while I fiddle with Mom's prosthetic arm, pretending to clean it and adjust it just so I can watch more of the game.

The team they're against, Philips Academy, is at the top on the school district leaderboard and the same team that gave us our one and only loss. And Connor—he's out for blood. I can see it in the way he plays. Everything is amplified. Every step, every dribble, every shot he takes. He's nothing less than perfection, and the opposing team knows that because he's double-teamed, and yet, he's still managing to carry the team. He scores two three-pointers in a row halfway through the final quarter, giving us a three-point lead, and I don't hide my squeal this time. I can't. Mom sits up with a jolt, and I apologize immediately and calm her down. Two minutes to go, and we're up by five, and I focus on the TV while trying to get Mom's prosthetic on. "Ava, you're putting it on wrong."

"Just one second, Ma."

"Ava!" She yanks the prosthetic out of my hands, and I watch, as if in slow motion, as she throws it across the room, smashing the TV square in the middle.

"Mama!"

She shakes her head. Doesn't stop.

I gawk, wide-eyed, at the TV as the picture stutters, and then fades, fades, fades until there's nothing but darkness.

Rage pulses inside me, beats strong against my flesh. "Why would you do that!" I scream, standing over her.

She keeps shaking her head, and she won't fucking quit.

"Answer me!"

"Ava!" Trevor yells, coming out of his room. "What the hell's going on?!"

Mom stands so fast I almost miss it. She pushes past me, sending me back a step, and then charges, full speed, full strength, right into the TV. It falls back, glass shattering. Mom wails, for no other reason than to wail, and I...

I yell, tears blinding my vision, "Go to your fucking room!"

Mom's laughter is hysterical in the most menacing way.

I ball my fists at my sides, my jaw clenched.

"Ava, calm down!" Trevor orders.

Pressure builds in my chest, and I can't... I can't breathe. Through clamped teeth, I seethe, trying to hide my anger, "You need to take her to her room so I can clean up the glass!"

Trevor's throat bobs with his swallow as his eyes bore into mine. He nods once. "Okay."

He helps Mom into her room, closing the door between us. I pick up my phone with only one thing on my mind. *Connor.* I need to show him that I'm here. That I care. That I'm *trying*.

Ava: Good games, #3.

Then I take a moment to put myself back together, to hide my anger and my fear and my self-loathing. I've never yelled at her like that before. Never. No matter how hard things got... I never raised my voice. At least not to her.

I get what I need to clean up the glass, careful not to cut myself. It takes an hour on my hands and knees, making sure there are absolutely no shards left so we don't have a repeat of the last two times she was around broken glass. I go outside to trash what I need to, all the while listening for signs that things will get worse. That we might need to call the crisis team... and it will all be my fault.

I have one hand back on the front doorknob when a text comes through.

Connor: Are you fucking serious?

CONNOR

I choked.

And while the winning team celebrated around me, I collapsed on the hardwood, fatigue setting every muscle ablaze. Failure blocked my airways as I stared up at the arena lights, wondering if this was it.

Some people peak in high school.

And that's as far as they'll ever go.

We were one point down with five seconds on the clock, and I choked. I had time, I had space, I had enough muscle memory to go blind into a simple lay-up. I went for the three-pointer. The rest is history.

I thought all of that was as bad as it would get, and then I opened my locker, reached for my phone, and read her message.

It's ironic, really, because while I was on that hardwood, she was the first thing that came to my mind. I thought if I could just leave, if I could go to her, if I could see her, speak to her, then everything would be better. It wouldn't be perfect, it wouldn't even be *okay*, but it would be *better*.

But I can't get to Ava, don't really want to, and so I search for what I needed from her and find it at the bottom of a bottle of beer. Or six.

Rhys's house is full of kids, and I don't think any of them care that it's a Sunday night and we have school tomorrow. Most of the team are in the pool house watching the highlights from today's games. I watch, too, my lids heavy from the booze. I listen to the guys talk about how good they look on camera and how much pussy they think it's going to get them. And then Karen enters the room, sits on the arm of the couch right next to me. "Tough break, Ledger," she says, ruffling my hair.

My head falls forward, and it's an effort to lift it again.

I focus back on the screen, and my heart drops, my stomach twisting when I see him—Tony Parsons. From Duke. And he's shaking hands with the two guys from Philips who had me covered the entire game. At no point today did he shake *my* hand or even acknowledge that we'd spoken before.

I drop my head in my hands, tug at my hair and groan the loudest groan in the history of groans. Mitch laughs. "It's just a fucking game, man."

I glance at him, my words sloppy. "Hey, guess what? Fuck you."

Karen scoffs, taps me on the shoulder.

I look up at her.

"You want to get out of here?"

Yes.

But *Ava*.

I check my phone. She hasn't replied. Hasn't called. And all it does is heighten my frustration. "Why the hell not?"

I grab another six-pack on the way out and tear into it the second I'm in Karen's coupe. Top down, I welcome the cold chill against my face.

I don't ask Karen where we're going because Karen seems to have a plan. Karen's also got good taste in music. I turn up the stereo to full volume and rest my head on the seat. I close my eyes, get comfortable, and don't bother opening them until the car's stopped. We're parked just outside the sports park gate, and Karen turns off the car, filling my ears with silence.

"Are we breaking and entering, because if so, I should call my dad and warn him about the bail money. We're poor, Karen."

"You're not poor," she tells me, her blond hair blowing in the breeze. "You're middle class. You just live in an area that has too many one-percenters."

"Perspective," I mumble.

"What?"

I heave out a breath. "It's all about perspective. You have good perspective."

"Riiiight," she drawls. "And no, we're not breaking and entering. Stepdad number five owns this place." She hops out of the car, taking her keys with her, and uses them to open the giant padlock on the gates.

"Will you get in trouble?" I ask when she's back behind the wheel.

With a shrug, she says, "He gave me a key for a reason." And then she puts the car in drive and makes her way through the park, around the batting cages, and parks right in the middle of the basketball courts.

Great.

More basketball.

Just what I need.

"Let's go, baller."

I force my body to move. Hand on the door, pulling at the handle. I use all my weight to push open the door. One leg first, then the other. Karen's at her trunk and she pulls out a basketball, and if she wants to play one-on-one, I'm noping the fuck out.

I'm done for the day.

Dee-plee-ted.

She stops a foot in front of me, slaps me across the face. *Hard.*

"What the fuck?" I cry out, hand to my cheek.

"Wake the fuck up, Connor! I'm not here to baby you." She takes the beers from my hand, dumps them in her open trunk. "Let's go."

"I don't want to play," I whine.

She eyes me, hand on her hip. "You have ten minutes to sober the fuck up and get back to reality. If this is how you're going to act after every loss—"

"It wasn't just a normal loss."

She slaps me again.

"What the fuck, woman! Knock it off."

"Ten minutes," she says, setting a timer on her watch. "I'll wait."

I sit my ass on the ground, legs bent in front of me, arms outstretched behind me. And I look up at the stars, breathe fresh air into my lungs, again and again, and I let the coolness of it wash through me, my vision slowly returning to normal.

I ask, because it's something I've often wondered, "Why did you and Ava stop being friends?"

Karen's quiet a moment, and when I glance at her, she's sitting cross-legged, staring down at her hands. "I don't think we ever really *stopped*. Things just got too hard after everything with her mom. We couldn't really hang out, and too many calls went unanswered, and after a while, I just stopped trying to reach out to her." She looks up now, her eyes on me. "I don't think it's anyone's fault. At least I hope she doesn't feel like I'm to blame. I tried, Connor. We all did, but..."

"It got too hard," I finish for her.

She nods. "How are you guys doing?"

I shrug. "I don't really want to talk about it."

"You brought it up."

"Then I'll bring it back down."

Her watch beeps, and she gets to her feet. "Time's up."

Moaning, I stand, catch the ball she throws at my chest.

"Where were you?" she asks, pointing to the three-point line.

"What do you mean?"

She stands around the area where I made my choke shot. "Was it here?"

"About, yeah."

She motions for me to join her at that spot, and so I do. I stand there while she walks off the court.

"Shoot your shot," she says.

I chuckle. "I'm still kind of drunk."

"Do it anyway."

I shoot, sink it.

She grabs the ball, throws it back. "Again."

I do it again.

She returns the ball to me. "Again."

I make the next five shots. Miss one. Then sink the next two.

When I'm done, she takes possession of the ball and holds it to her hip. "Nine out of ten and you're drunk, Connor," she states.

"So, what you're saying is that I should've made the shot, because I know this, *Karen*. But thanks for reminding me."

"No." She shakes her head. Adamant. "What I'm saying is that you miss 100% of the shots you don't take." She throws the ball back.

Dribbling lazily, I retort, "You're just quoting Wayne Gretzky, and that's hockey—"

"Shut up," she laughs out. "Now I've forgotten my point. It was going to be something amazing about 90% of the shots made or... something."

"I get your point," I say through a chuckle. "And I appreciate what you're saying, even if it doesn't really make sense."

She rolls her eyes and moves toward me, hands out asking for the ball. I throw it to her and step aside as she takes over my position. She sinks a three-pointer effortlessly. "Damn. Skills much?"

Her eyes narrow. "You know I'm captain of the girls' basketball team, right?"

"I didn't even know we had a girls' basketball team."

* * *

She asked for no mercy during our one-on-one, so I beat her 21-3. I do a celebratory Steph Curry dance around her. She smirks, then says, "Hey, who am I?" She drops to the ground, on her back, and looks up at the sky. "Boo hoo. I missed a three-pointer under immense pressure, and now my life is over. Wahhh."

I stand over her, brows bunched. "You're kind of a bitch."

"I kind of know this already."

I lie down next to her, the ball between us, and stare up at the darkness above.

"What's your favorite game of all time?" she asks.

"Umm... 1980. Game 6, Lakers versus 76ers."

"Yesss. Magic came to play!" she whoops.

"You?" I ask.

"Without a doubt, 1976, Game 5, Celtics versus Suns."

I shake my head. "Such a weak answer. That's *everyone's* go-to. Do you like the actual game or the fight?"

"I mean, it went triple OT, so it was a good game, but man, I do get all tingly between the legs when I see guys beating the shit out of each other."

"You're weird."

"No, you."

AVA

"Mama, stop, please!" I cry out. "I'm sorry I yelled at you." I hold her head to my chest, try to stop her from banging it against her bedroom door like she has been for the past fifteen minutes.

I can barely see through the tears of frustration constantly filling my eyes, and now Trevor's at the front door letting the crisis workers in. More money wasted.

Mom stops with the headbanging, only to start smacking the heel of her palm against her head. She's rocking back and forth, her knees up between us, and I don't know how much longer I can take this. "Just stop, Mama!"

"I can't. I can't. I can't."

"Yes, you can! I don't understand—"

"What don't you understand?" she screams so loud I release my hold. She continues with the pounding, and I grasp her arm, try to get her to stop. "I don't want to be here, Ava!"

"Don't say that!" I cry out.

She glares up at me, eyes wide. "I. Don't. Want. To. Be. HERE!"

I cower, wiping the tears off my cheeks with the back of my hands, my breaths coming out in puffs. "I know!" I yell, exhausted. Mentally. Physically. All of it. "I know you don't want to be here, but I *need* you here! Why can't you see that?!" I break off on a sob. "Look at me!" I clutch a hand to my chest to stop the pain. So much pain. Years and years of it. "This is killing me as much as it is you!" I try to push down my hurt, but it just grows and grows and grows, every fucking day, and I'm *done*. "I can't do this anymore," I cry. "I just can't."

"I never asked you to!" she screams, her spit flying. "I *hate* you for what you did to me, Ava! I *hate* you."

Everything inside me stops.

My breaths.

My pulse.

My cries.

I look at her, try to find any semblance of the woman I love, the mother who raised me. But she's gone. She's so far gone, and there's nothing left of her. And nothing left of me. "I'm trying," I whisper, getting to my feet. My chest heaves, but I'm breathless. *Lifeless*. "I'm trying so fucking hard, and it's not enough. It never will be."

I grab my phone before storming past Trevor and the crisis workers and run outside.

I need time.

I need space.

I need air.

I need *Connor*.

I stand in front of his house with the phone in my hand, and I remember his text, barely. The phone hardly visible through my tears, I try to calm down, my thumbs searching for the last couple of minutes of his game.

I need to be prepared.

I need to be present.

For him.

I find the video, skim until the end, my heart dropping, lips parting when I watch it back.

I don't think. I just run to his window and knock, guilt building a solid fortress in my stomach. When enough time passes and there's no sign of life, I knock again. Wait. I check for his car, but it isn't there, and I knock again and again and again, getting louder each time.

My heavy breaths create a fog in front of my eyes and inside my mind, and I check the time, 2:27 a.m. I sniff back my cries, dial his number and hold the phone to my ear.

It rings on my end, but it's silent in his room, and I have no idea where he could be. My self-doubt and insecurities fight for a space in my thoughts, and I don't have the energy to push them away. The call connects to his voicemail, and I suck in a breath, try to replace my weakness for courage.

Vincit qui se vincit.

"Hey, Connor. It's me..."

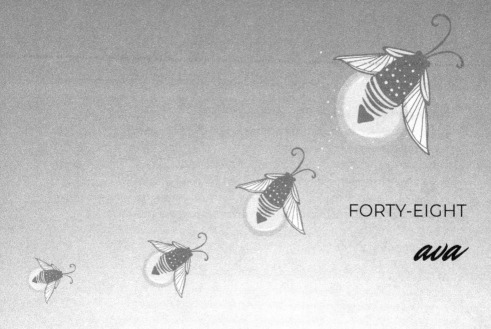

ava

IT'S BEEN a long time since I've just "hung out" in the hallways at school, and maybe that's why I feel like there are even more stares, more whispers than usual. I sit in front of Connor's locker, my legs crossed and my head down, waiting for him. I want to catch him after practice and before psych so we can at least get a few minutes to talk. I need to explain my stupid text.

I have my headphones in, but no music to accompany it. I wear them so I'll be left alone, but I'll still be able to hear Connor coming. Instead, I'm hearing people mock me as they walk past, and then two sets of feet, girls, stop in front of me. I don't look up when they giggle to themselves. Not even when one of them says, "I bet she has no idea what he gets up to when she's not around."

My head spins, my stomach does, too, and I don't... I don't understand what they're saying. All I know is that Connor wasn't home in the early hours of the morning. And so maybe they're right. Maybe I don't know him at all.

Another set of feet stops beside me, and I recognize them as Connor's. "Hey."

I take a quick moment to get myself together before looking up at him. His face is blanched, dark circles around his heavy eyelids. His body's slumped as if it's a task to remain upright, and I get to my feet, say, "Hey." I ignore the ache in my chest when he bypasses our usual morning kiss and goes straight for his locker, throwing his bag in without taking anything out.

He slams his locker shut, then leans against it, his hands in his pockets when he says, "What's up?"

His eyes are on mine, but the soul behind them... it isn't Connor.

I yank the headphones out of my ears and cross my arms over my chest. I feel so little, and I need him to stop making me feel like that. "I've been trying to call you," I murmur.

He shrugs. "I lost my phone."

My eyes widen. "What do you mean you *lost* your phone?"

"I mean," he says, looking down his nose at me, "I misplaced it. I don't know where it is."

"I know the definition of *lost*, Connor. You don't need to berate me."

"I'm not," he sighs out. His eyes drift shut, his shoulders lifting with his heavy inhale. When he opens his eyes again, he says, "Look, I just spent the entire morning running suicides because Coach thinks it's funny to punish a bunch of hungover kids, and so—"

"You're hungover?" I cut in.

He shakes his head. "No, I'm just really fucking exhausted. I've been pushing myself too far for too long, plus the constant lack of sleep—especially last night—and... everyone has their limits, Ava." His gaze bores into mine. "And I think I'm at my peak."

A stillness passes between us, seconds feel like hours, and we do nothing but stare at each other, like we're both searching for something that's no longer there. I look away when I feel the heat burning behind my eyes.

Connor pushes off his locker, his hand reaching up, and I close my eyes, wait for the moment his hand cups my jaw or his finger traces my forehead when he shifts the loose strands away... but nothing comes.

"Thank you," he breathes out, and my eyes snap open as I see him grasp the phone someone's holding up between us. I follow the arm to the person next to me: Karen.

"Where the hell was it?" he asks her.

"You left it in my car, *stupid*."

Connor chuckles. "No, you."

Karen faces me. "Hey, Ava."

All I can do is stand there, fighting back the hurt, the betrayal. I know she's watching me, they both are, and there's no justified reaction to match what I'm feeling, what I'm thinking.

I bet she has no idea what he gets up to when she's not around.

I look back at Connor, willing the tears away. "I'll see you in class."

* * *

Connor and I say nothing to each other as we sit together in psych class. There's no hand on my leg, no witty banter.

There's just him.

And me.

In two very different worlds.

I grasp on to my textbook as I stare ahead, hearing but not listening to everything going on around me. The class phone rings, and Mr. McCallister pauses his speech to answer it. Back turned to the class, the conversation in the room picks up.

"Psst!" Rhys hisses, kicking the back of Connor's chair. "Where the hell did you disappear to last night?"

Connor shrugs but doesn't say anything.

I keep my eyes forward, watching as Mr. McCallister turns to the class, phone still to his ear, and then his gaze locks on me. He's nodding, his lips pulled down in a frown. My chest rises with my shaky inhale, and I sit up higher, my life source pumping rapidly as he hangs up, starts moving toward me. The world around me is silent, bar his heavy footsteps as he closes in.

I shudder an exhale.

And then Connor's hand finds mine on the desk, linking our fingers together.

Mr. McCallister squats down to my level. "Ava, sweetheart, have you got your phone on you?"

I pull it out of my pocket. The battery's dead because I hadn't charged it overnight. I spent the entire night walking the streets aimlessly, and I hadn't been home except to change into my uniform. I didn't plan on staying. I just came here for Connor...

"It's um... it's..." I drop the phone on the desk and look up at him. "What's wrong?"

"You're needed at home."

"Okay," I breathe out, feeling the first panic-induced tear slide down my cheek. I swipe it away. "Can I use the phone to call a cab?"

Mr. McCallister eyes Connor, and Connor says, "I don't have my car here."

Rhys speaks up. "I'll take you, A."

CONNOR

I'd been dreading seeing Ava all morning. When I saw her at my locker, I stood firm. I wanted her to know that she'd hurt me and that I was pissed, and I wasn't going to back down. The past few times we'd been together, I'd needed her, and she hadn't even been present enough to listen to what I was saying.

But when Mr. McCallister started to approach her in psych, I felt her fear, and I realized that I had no idea what had been going on with her. *Not really.* And it's not that I don't ask, but she never opens up about it. She never fully lets me in. Never tells me anything.

During lunch, I ask Rhys to take me to his house so I can pick up my car.

He has no idea why Ava had to go home. He said that she'd been silent on the drive there and he didn't want to push her.

I send her a text, hope she's had time to charge her phone.

Connor: Is everything okay?

Ava: Yes.

I know I should head back to school, but once I'm in my car, the only place I can think to go is Ava's.

I stand on her lawn and send her another message.

Connor: Any chance you can come out for five? I think we need to talk.

The curtains part on Ava's front window, and a second later, she's stepping out and sitting on her porch steps.

I sit next to her, my heart heavy, mind clouded with confusion. I swallow my nerves. "Is everything okay?"

"Yeah, there was just no one available to watch her today," she says, her tone flat, her gaze distant.

I heave out a breath, keep my eyes on her. And I know it's not the right time or place, but I can't keep doing this. Going around and around like we are. "What's going on with us, A?"

"I don't know," she says, her gaze trailing to mine. "Why don't you tell me?"

"What does that mean?"

"Why didn't you tell me about Karen?"

"When?" I snap. "When would I have told you about it exactly?"

"I don't know," she deadpans. "This morning when I was standing right in front of you." She huffs out a breath. "What happened last night, Connor?"

I run a hand through my hair, tug at the ends. This isn't the conversation I was looking for. "With what, exactly? Me choking in the last five seconds of the game or you sending me a message proving you don't care?" There's a hint of anger in my tone that I didn't plan on being there.

"I tried," she whispers. "I watched the entire tournament and then my mom..." Her voice cracks and she sits higher, squares her shoulders. "What happened after the game?"

I sigh. "We went back to Rhys's, and we drank, and some of the guys couldn't drive, so Karen gave us rides home. That's why my phone was in her car." I don't know why I lie, and it's the first time I've ever done it, but none of this matters. That's not why we're here.

She's silent a breath, her eyes lowering. "What time did you get home?"

I shake my head, curbing my frustration in my fists. "I don't know. Like, midnight?" I know it was later than that. Much later. But I don't need her focusing on that because, again, it's irrelevant, and so I tell her that. "It doesn't matter what I did or didn't do last night, and Karen's not the problem. The problem is between us, A. You and me."

"Stop calling me A," she grinds out. "Only Rhys calls me that."

"Yeah?" I snort. "Was that before or after you fucked him?"

"Connor!"

I ignore her and keep at it, getting everything off my chest. "And while we're on the topic of not telling each other things, why is it that everything I know about you, I hear from other people?"

Her eyes snap to mine. "What the hell are you talking about?"

I count off each point on my fingers. "I find out about your mom through my dad. Then I find out about you and Rhys through Rhys. That your mom was a POW through Trevor. And even Peter fucking Parker seems to think it's—"

"My mom was a *what*?" she cuts in, her voice low, shaky.

Fuck. Everything inside me hardens, and I look up to see her watching me, her eyes brimming with tears, her bottom lip trembling.

My mouth opens, but nothing comes out.

"Connor?" she cries, begging for answers. "Was my mom... was she...?

"No, Ava, she—"

"Tell me the truth!"

"Fuck," I spit, pressing the heels of my palms against my eyes. "Fuck, Ava, I wasn't supposed—"

Her sob forces a sharp inhale as she stares at me, her mouth agape. "Why would you keep that from me!" And then she breaks, her shoulders shaking. Those small hands I fell in love with cover her entire face, and she's crying, the loudest, most unconfined cry I've ever witnessed from her, and all the broken pieces of my heart fight for unity again because I remember everything about her, about us, everything I love. I fell in love with her vulnerability as much as I fell for her strength and "I'm sorry, Ava." I sniff back my own tears, watching her shatter in front of me. "I love you. I'm so sorry."

I try to reach for her, to hold her, to show her the magic... but she pushes me away. "Don't fucking touch me." She's on her feet and heading for her door, and I try to grasp on to her, but she's too... everything. She's too determined and too angry and too... too *damaged*. She slams the door between us, and I don't give up. Can't.

I turn the knob and push, but nothing happens. "Ava, please," I beg, my forehead against the door. "I'm sorry."

* * *

I don't bother going back to school, telling Dad that I'm not feeling well, so he excuses me from classes for the rest of the day. I spend the time in my room, my phone to my ear, calling, calling, calling. My thumbs move faster than ever as I write out text after text after goddamn text, each one going unanswered. I stand at her door four fucking times with my fist raised ready to knock, but stop myself, knowing it could make things worse.

When the world around me turns dark and all hope is gone, I try calling her again. This time, she answers. But it's not her on the other end of the line. It's Trevor. "Stop fucking calling, Connor. You've done enough."

I stare down at my phone once he's hung up, anger and fear and disappointment hitting me in waves. Then I notice the voicemail icon and hope spikes in my heart. Maybe she's tried calling at the same time I have, and maybe Trevor's taken her phone because he's angrier at me than she is...

I hit play on the voicemail, listen to the intro timestamped 2:27 am. "Hey, Connor. It's me... It's umm... it's 2:30 in the morning and I'm at your window but... but I don't think you're home and I'm not really sure where you are... I just... I wanted to say sorry about my message. I watched the entire tournament and then with five minutes left in the final, my mom... she broke our TV... deliberately, and God, Connor, I got so angry with her. I yelled at her like I've never done before. And I... I'm just having a really shitty time at the moment. And I know that you are, too, and that's more important right now, so I'm sorry. I'm sorry I wasn't there for you like you've always been there for me, and I know that you're probably sick of hearing me apologize but... I don't know. I just thought... I thought maybe we could spend the night together, or at least a couple of hours. Because um... because I love you, Connor. I just love you... so much."

I throw my phone across the room, watch it fracture. And just like Ava before me, I *break*. As if I've reached my boiling point and the pressure's too much, and I explode. Erupt. Detonate. "Fuck!" I shout. My fist flies, goes through the drywall. Again, and again. And then my dad appears, his eyes wide, and I fall to the floor, my head in my hands. "Jesus Christ, Connor," he whispers, dropping to his knees in front of me. He grasps my hand in his, shifting the blood pooling at my knuckles. "What the hell are you thinking?" He inspects my hand closer, his eyes wide when he looks up at me. "This is your shooting hand."

FORTY-NINE

Connor

I DON'T SEE Ava at school the next day, not that I expected to. But I see her the day after, in psych, walking through the door. I sit higher in my seat and hide my bandaged hand under the table. I need to talk to her, to apologize. I've planned out everything I want to say. I need to tell her how sorry I am for the way I'd been acting, that it was never about her, and that it was all on me. That the pressure became too much, and I took it out on her. And I need to tell her that I love her, that I never stopped loving her, not even for a second.

But she doesn't look at me when she walks in. Instead, she goes to Karen, her mouth moving, but I'm too far away to hear what she's saying. Karen turns to me, her eyes sad, and then back to Ava. She nods, stands, and gives Ava her seat.

My heart sinks, and I look down at the table as Karen settles in beside me. "I'm sorry, Connor," she whispers. "I couldn't say no to her."

* * *

The day is a blur, and I can't focus on anything. Not even basketball. After-school practice is a shitshow, and my injured hand only elevates my piss-poor performance. "It looks like it's healing well," one of the trainers says, inspecting my hand after practice.

"My dad's a paramedic," I mumble. "He made sure it was taken care of. Trust me, no one wants it to heal as fast as he does."

"Where the hell is my deodorant?" Oscar says from behind me. He's opening and closing lockers, searching.

"Just use mine," Rhys offers.

"I have sensitive skin, bruh."

"Check your car," says Rhys.

Oscar sings, "You're not just a pretty face, co-cap."

I watch the trainer wrap my hand again. "Your dad think it'll be good to go by the invitational?"

I nod. "It's just a minor sprain. No fractures."

"Good. Want to tell me how it happened?"

"Not really."

"Connor," Oscar says, his hand on my shoulder. "Your girl's out in the parking lot."

My brow lifts when I look up at him.

He shrugs. "She ain't waitin' on me."

Ava pushes off my car when she sees me approaching, her arms going around her waist. A few spots over, Trevor's in his truck, his eyes on me. Heavy-hearted, I motion toward him. "You bring a bodyguard?"

Ava's looking down at the ground when my gaze moves back to her. "He's just waiting to give me a ride home." Then she notices my hand, and hers reaches across, taking my wrist in her grasp. "What happened?"

I lower my hand so my fingers graze hers, taking hold of them. I say, my voice weak, "A wall came at me. I had to protect myself."

She looks up now, her eyes clouded. I squeeze the ends of her fingers, and it's as if she just realized I was holding on to her. She yanks out of my hold, hiding her hands in the pockets of her blazer. My throat closes in, my stomach twisting. Through narrow airways, I let out a breath and say, "I was hoping I'd get a chance to talk to you. There's a lot I need to say."

"Me too," she rushes out. "And I need to go first so that I don't..." she trails off, and I nod, my eyes on hers, my entire everything drawn to her.

She glances at Trevor, as if needing the courage, then back at me. "When we first started this, I warned you that nothing good can come of it. That there'd be no happy ending to our story..."

"Don't, Ava," I plead. "You're talking as if it's over."

"It *is* over, Connor."

I laugh once, incredulous, and look past her. "So I make one mistake, and that's it? You're done?"

"You didn't make any mistakes," she sighs out. "But we never should've started anything to begin with. We were so selfish to think that it would work." She pauses a beat, her voice dropping when she adds, "I wasn't made for this."

"For what? To be with me?"

"No." She takes a step toward me. Just one. But keeps her eyes downcast. "I wasn't made with the strength to do it all. Taking care of my mom is as much as I can do, and even then, I'm already spread so thin. You told me the other day that you were at your limit, and I think I passed that point a long time ago, Connor. I can't be trying to take care of her and trying to be focused on you and being insecure about us all at the same time."

I kick off my car, take one step forward and retake her hand. "You don't have to be insecure about us," I plead. "Nothing happened with Karen. I swear it, Ava."

Her eyes lift, lock on mine. "Then why did you lie?"

"About what?" I ask, even though I already know. So does my heart, because it's trembling in my ribcage.

"You're the only one who left with her. And you weren't home at midnight, Connor, because I was banging on your window—" Her voice wavers and she clears her throat. "If nothing happened," she says, tears welling in her eyes, "then why lie to me?"

I shake my head, sniff back the burn behind my nose, and look down at the ground, shame forcing my shoulders to drop. "Because I didn't want you to worry," I admit. "Clearly, I had my priorities wrong." I swallow the knot in my throat and peer up at her again. "But this isn't your reason is it, Ava? It's your excuse."

Her sob has me looking up, watching her wipe at her eyes frantically. "It's too hard," she cries out, her entire presence shrinking with defeat. "I can't..." The weight of her cries halts her words, and I exhale, wait for her to finish. "I can't be the person I want to be when I'm with you. I can't forget that... that my mom needs me more than I need you. And I did that. For one split second, I forgot. Because I love you, Connor. And I don't think I'll ever stop loving you..." She falls into me, her arms going around me, holding tight. "But I can't *be with* you."

I take in her words, breathe them into me. "You were my end game," I whisper, knowing she can't hear me through her cries. I wipe the wetness off my cheeks against her hair and clutch her head to my chest, her ear to my life source.

She quiets her sobs.

Waiting.

Listening.

But she won't find what she's searching for.

Because: "There's no magic in a broken heart, Ava."

FIRST AND FOREVER

HEARTACHE DUET BOOK TWO

For my tribe
"I did it for you."

connor

ALL THE DAYS blur into one, and the only thing I care about is basketball. Because never have I wanted a way out of this dumpster-fire of a life more than I do now. Karen sits next to me in psych, Ava on the opposite side of the room, as far away from me as possible. She doesn't talk to me, doesn't even look at me. I spend every lunch break in the cafeteria, suffocating in the stupidity of the people around me.

There are no goodnight kisses.

No knocks on my window.

No lengthy text messages.

No late-night phone calls.

And no game day balloons.

There's just me. Existing in a foreign world, living a life I thought I wanted while loving a girl who *can't* love me back.

And there's also my piece of shit car that decides to randomly stop working on the way home after another back-to-back private coaching session. I have just enough time to pull the car over on the side of the road before it dies completely. Dropping my forehead against the wheel, I crank the engine. *Nothing.* I check the fuel gauge; that's fine. So I flick on the hazards and push open the door with both feet, my frustration making an appearance in the form of a groan. I lift the hood, and then I stare at a hunk of metal because I have no clue what I'm looking at.

I walk around the car, inspecting the tires because... I don't know why. I'm tired, and I'm sore, and I just want to get home and die on my bed and not get up until I have to. I grab my phone from my car and dial Dad's number. It rings out. I try it again. And again. And I'm sure there are other people I could be calling, but I'm drained, physically and emotionally, and so I sit my ass on the gravel in front of the car and take in the silence around me. Appreciate it. It's dark out, but the skies are clear except for a few lonely stars. If a serial killer were to drive by, I'd be the perfect victim. I laugh at the thought and go to message Ava... but then I remember. And then I wonder how it is I could've ever forgotten.

After everything that happened with my mom, my dad thought it would be a good idea to do therapy, both alone and together. I remember sitting next to him when the therapist asked him to describe what it felt like to lose her— his wife. He said—besides his concerns of what it would do to me long-term —losing her was like waking up twice.

First, you wake up and think that everything's normal. Like you're going to walk into the kitchen, and she'll be there making breakfast and playing with your son. And then you realize that that's not going to happen, and you wake up again. To reality. And that reality is your life.

I think, in a way, I'm still at the waking-up-for-the-first-time stage. And maybe it's not fair, or *right*, to compare losing Ava to my dad losing his wife, the mother of his son, but there it is.

And here I am.

Hand out in front of me, I shield my eyes from the oncoming headlights. The car slows and then crosses over, parks in front of me, headlights to head-lights. I recognize the car as soon as my vision clears, and then the long legs and short skirt. Karen stands between both vehicles. "What the hell are you doing?"

I shrug, keep my eyes on her shoes because I know if I look up, I'll see a hell of a lot more than I want to. "I don't know, taking in the scenery?"

"What?" she huffs out, sitting down in front of me, her legs kicked out next to mine.

"My car broke down, *obviously*."

She sighs. "I should start wearing a cape if I'm going to be saving your ass this much."

"You don't have to stay," I tell her. "My dad can come get me. He's just not answering his phone right now."

Karen nods, a frown pulling at her lips. "But you're all pathetic and miser-able, and I feel sorry for you, so..."

I laugh once. "Am I that obvious?"

"Connor," she whines. "It's like you forgot that I lost her once, too."

I look down at my hands, clear the knot in my throat.

"But you're so tragic right now, and I get it," she says with a surprising amount of sincerity. "Maybe it would help if you talked about it?"

"I don't think there's anything to say."

"Well, what happened with you guys? What changed?"

"I don't know..." I find a loose rock and flip it in my hands. "Her mom happened, and my basketball took over any free time we had. We just never seemed to be on the same page at the same time."

"That sucks and all, but it's kind of unavoidable, no?"

I sniff away the memories flooding my mind and ask, "You know what the worst part is?"

"What?"

I look up at her and give her a truth I've kept only for myself. "I was doing it all for her."

Her brow lifts. "What do you mean?"

"My plan was always four years at a D1 college and then hopefully go pro. But then I met Ava and her mom and... and they're struggling so much with everything. I just... I thought if I put in the work now, then I could get the offer I need, do my one year and then declare for the draft and hopefully get a decent enough contract that I could... I could take care of them, you know?"

Karen's quiet as she stares at me, right into my eyes, and I don't look away because I have nothing to hide. Barely a whisper, she asks, "Does she know any of this?"

I shake my head

"Why not?"

"Because I didn't tell her," I sigh out.

"Why?"

I suck in a heavy breath. "Because what if I don't make it? What if all her hopes for her future relied on me and I couldn't follow through?" I throw the rock across the road. "What if I fail?"

Karen's throat moves with her swallow, and she breaks her stare, looks down at her lap. "That's a lot of pressure to put on yourself, Connor."

"But it's not just that," I continue, feeling the weight of my words release the pressure in my chest. "I didn't tell her because I didn't want her to feel obligated to stay with me if or when she ever stopped loving me."

Karen's gaze meets mine again, her eyebrows raised. "She said she loves you?"

I nod.

"And you... do you love her?"

"My heart beats for her."

AVA

Mr. Ledger opens his door, his eyes widening when he sees me. "Hey, Ava. Connor's not home right now."

Good. "Actually, I came to see you."

"Sure," he says, nodding. "Do you want to come in?"

I look over his shoulder to the open door of Connor's bedroom and push away the memories. "I'd prefer to stay out here if that's okay?"

He offers a smile before flicking on the porch light. "What can I help you with?"

"You mentioned before that if I ever needed help with anything I could come to you... and I know that Connor and I are no longer together, but I was hoping your offer still stands?"

"Of course," he says, concern filling his eyes as his gaze flicks to our house. "Is everything okay with your mom?" He moves back a step and starts slipping on his shoes, adding, "Should I get my medical—"

"No!" I rush out, waving a hand in front of me. "No, she's fine. Sorry." I shake my head. "I didn't mean to scare you. She's... she's okay." *Physically.* I raise the stack of papers between us, still warm from the printer. "Trevor and I—we got this letter from our insurance about Mom's care, and I don't understand much of it, or any of it really, but I think they want to make changes and—"

"And you want me to have a look over it?" he interrupts.

"Yes, please," I breathe out. "Whenever you have time. I know you're busy."

"I have time now," he says with a reassuring smile. He takes the papers from me and motions to his porch steps.

I nod, grateful. "Thank you so much, sir," I tell him, sitting down. "You have no idea how much I appreciate it."

He settles in next to me, his eyes holding mine. "It's no problem, Ava. I'll do what I can."

Before he can read the first line, a car pulls into his driveway, and my breath catches. I know the car. I know the girl. I *thought* I knew the boy sitting beside her. "Thanks for the ride," he calls out over his shoulder as he steps out, then shuts the car door. He starts heading toward us, not once looking up. He hasn't seen me yet, and I wish he wouldn't see me at all. I wish it were as easy to hide here as it is at school. My heartache forces a shuddered breath, and I get to my feet. The movement's enough for Connor to look up, deer meet headlights, and he stills. A strangled sound forms in his throat, his eyes wide and fixed on mine. "Hey."

I come to at the sound of his voice, at the way his eyes drink me in. I look away and force myself to remember that *we* no longer exist. It's just him and me... and the world that divides us. "Hi," I offer, my false smile hiding my true agony.

"Ava just had some questions about her insurance policy," Mr. Ledger says, and Connor nods without shifting his stare.

"I should go," I mumble, then turn to Connor's dad. "I put my number on the top there, so just call or message me once you've read over it. And thank you again. I really appreciate it."

He smiles. "It's no problem at all, Ava."

I turn to leave, but a wall of Connor blocks my path. "Can I walk you to your door?"

Nerves fly through my bloodline. "If you want to."

He turns on his heels, waiting for me to step beside him before saying, "My car broke down, and Karen gave me a ride home."

I contain my scoff to a silent sneer. "She seems to be doing a lot of that lately."

Connor's grunt ends in a sigh. Hands shoved in his pockets, he keeps his mouth shut until we're at my porch. "Ava, I need to know that you believe me," he says, and I stop with one foot on the step and look up at him. "I get that you're done with me, and as much as I hate that, I can't force you to be with me if you don't want to be." I chew my lip because I have nothing to say, nothing to add. And so he continues, "I shouldn't have lied to you. Yes, it was just me in her car that night, and yes, I was out longer than I told you. She drove us to the sports park, and after slapping me around for a bit, we played and talked ball all night—"

"And most of the morning," I add, looking down, my arms crossed, shielding him from me.

He sways back a little as if hit by my words. "Yes," he admits. "I lost track of time."

"Because you were so busy enjoying yourself?" He doesn't respond immediately, and so I say through the ache in my chest, "Because it's nice to forget every now and then, to forget the pressures of life and just be a carefree, normal teenager?" When I look up, I see him watching me with anguish in his eyes. Or maybe it's guilt.

He licks his lips, offers a half-hearted shrug. "I guess... I don't know."

"It's kind of worse," I croak out. "You having an emotional connection with someone else." I fight to keep my tears hidden. "I'd almost rather you just fucked—"

"Stop it," he interrupts.

"It doesn't matter anymore," I whisper.

"It does matter because I can't walk away from this knowing you think that of me." He takes a step forward. "I wouldn't do that to you. I *couldn't*. Ava, you *know* me. You know me better than anyone else in this entire world. You know how much I love you," he pleads, his voice cracking with emotion. "You know *me*, Ava," he repeats, and I can feel the layers of protection I've built around my heart start to weaken, to shed, to disintegrate. He taps a finger under my chin, lifting, so I have no choice but to face him. To look at him. To see the sorrow and agony and desperation in his *soul*. He cups my neck, his forehead resting against mine. Breath warm against my lips, he whispers, "Ava, you know my *heart*."

It would be so easy to kiss him.

To love him openly and without regret.

To ignore everything else.

But it would also be greedy.

And foolish.

And *reckless*.

"I believe you, Connor." I push against his chest, forcing some space between us. "But we can't be what you want us to be."

SADNESS CLINGS to Mom's lashes while I cling to hope, and when her eyes close, the tears she sheds merge with the bath water up to her chin. I run the cloth along the scars on her face, then down her neck, and then to her amputated arm. "I'll never be the same," she whispers.

My hand stills. "No. You won't," I tell her honestly. "But only on the outside. Your heart is still the same."

Her eyes open, and she covers my hand with hers. "But my mind isn't, Ava, and that's what scares me the most."

Me too, I don't say, and I hate to think of the demons swarming her mind, continually fighting for ways to escape. Even though I know the excruciating truth of what she experienced, I'll never fully understand the severity of it. "We're going to find a way to get you back." I kiss her temple. "I promise, Mama."

I give Mom her meds before getting into bed with her. And like all the other nights since the first time she asked, I lie with her until she's fast asleep and pray the new cocktail of drugs does the rest. Then I go to my room and ready myself for another long night of homework.

An hour into an English paper and my mind begins to wander. My longing takes over my fingers as they tap away on the keyboard. And even though Trevor's not home, I still check over my shoulder to make sure I'm alone. Shame washes through me as I go to the school website, click on the Athletics tab and scroll down to *Wildcats Basketball*. I watch the highlights of his last game, my lips forming a smile whenever he appears.

"Ava?" Trevor calls out from behind me, and I spin around, my heart racing.

"Jesus, you scared me. When the hell did you get home?"

"Just now." The smile he carries is so big it makes me suspicious. "And I have a surprise for you." He steps to the side, and another figure joins him.

"Amy!" I'm on my feet and hugging her so hard she falls back a step. I didn't even know Trevor was *talking* to his ex, but she has no reason to be here other than to see him. I rear back, my smile as wide as Trevor's only moments ago. "What are you doing here?"

Trevor throws his arm around her waist, then slaps a sloppy kiss on her cheek. "She's here to see her *boyfriend*."

My next squeal is audible, just barely, and I hug them both.

Amy laughs, settles her hands on my shoulders as she takes in my features, her blue eyes squinting. "It's so good to see you, Ava. Gosh, you've grown."

"I didn't even know you and Trevor were talking again."

She shrugs. "Love has a way, you know?"

I nod, even though I *don't* know. The only love I've experienced comes with limits. And those limits have been reached.

My laptop starts to play another video, this one with sound, and Trevor peers over my shoulder to look at it. It's a Connor Ledger highlight reel, and I lower my gaze, waiting for his response.

"Jesus Christ, Ava, I thought you were done with this jerk."

"Don't call him that," I hiss.

He pushes past me, his anger tensing his shoulders, and snaps the screen shut. Then he turns to me. "You shouldn't even be looking at this stuff. You're just going to make things harder for yourself."

"Shut up," I argue. "You did the same with Amy and her new boyfriend. You stalked the hell out of her."

"You did?" Amy asks.

Trevor shakes his head, his nose flaring with his exhale. "That's not the same!"

"Why? Just because we're not together anymore doesn't mean I don't care about his life or his future."

"Yeah, well, you shouldn't. He's a piece of shit for telling you what he did!"

"No! You're a piece of shit for keeping it a secret from me!"

"I was doing it to protect you!"

"Well, a lot of good that did!" I yell, forgetting that Mom's asleep in the next room. "And this is all your fault anyway!"

"*Mine?*"

"Yes. Remember when you said—" I deepen my voice to mimic his. "*You*

can date, Ava. You'd make a great girlfriend." I slump down on my bed, my
brows furrowed. And because I'm a brat, I cross my arms and pout. "I
should've never listened to you!"

Trevor laughs, short and hysterical. "You want to blame me because your
ex turned out to be King Dick?!"

"Get out!" Amy and I order in unison.

Trevor's eyes widen, focusing first on me, then Amy. "*What?!*"

"Get out," Amy says, her tone a hell of a lot calmer than mine. She presses
her hands to his chest, trying to soothe him with her touch. "Let Ava and me
have a little girl chat, okay?"

Trevor grunts, but kisses her anyway. "Fine."

Once Trevor's out of the room, the door closed between us, Amy settles on
my bed, her back against the wall. She pats the spot next to her, so I scoot
back and sit like she is. Reaching across me, she grabs my pillow and hands it
to me. "Scream into it."

"What?"

"Scream into it," she repeats. "Get your frustration out now so you can
talk to me without anger swaying your words."

I scream into the pillow.

"Did it help?"

"Yeah," I lie. It didn't help at all.

"So, this boy... Connor, right?"

I nod. "How much do you know?"

She picks at a rip in her jeans. "Trevor and I have been talking a lot lately.
He's pretty much kept me updated on everything he knows. But I'm sure
there's a lot he doesn't know, so maybe you could tell me those parts?"

It feels so freeing to be able to talk to someone, to be able to share everything that Connor and I experienced. Both the good and the bad, but especially the good, because there was so much of it. And I had no one else to
share that joy with, that excitement. I tell her everything that happened up
till now, and I speak through my disappointment when I tell her of the way I
talked to Mom the day of Connor's tournament and then through my
heartache when I tell her about Connor and Karen.

"Do you honestly believe that something happened with them?" she asks
quietly. It's the first time she's spoken throughout my entire speech, but I
know she's been listening based on her nods, frowns, and smiles at all the
appropriate times.

"I don't know," I admit through a sigh.

"Have you and he...?"

I shake my head.

"Have you *ever*?"

I nod.

"Has he *ever*?"

"No," I murmur. "I know what you're thinking. But, I just... I don't see him doing it just for the sake of doing it." I remember when I brought it up to him when we were at the lake, and he said he was scared, but maybe alcohol and Karen combined... "But I think there's an emotional connection there, one I can't compete with, and I think that's what hurts the most. That and the fact that he lied to me."

Amy huffs out a breath, her blond bangs shifting with the force. "I'm sorry, Ava. You're in such a tough situation and throwing a relationship in the mix, it just makes things so much harder for you." She nudges my side. "Can I see what he looks like?"

Nodding, I reach for my laptop and set it on my lap. Then I lift the screen, find Connor's profile on the school website.

Amy lets out a low whistle. "Damn, girl. No wonder you're having a hard time letting go. He's *hot*."

"I know," I murmur. "I hate him."

She giggles. "You have any of you two together?"

I open up the folder on the desktop titled "Connor 4 Ava" and go through the pictures of us together. Mainly pictures he'd sent me taken on his phone, selfies in his car or at the bleachers.

Amy grabs the laptop from me so she can take a closer look, picture after picture bringing back memories, causing more misery to my heartache.

"You look so happy, Ava," she says.

I push down the knot in my throat. "I was."

"And so in love."

I can't fight back the sob in time. "I was."

"Oh, honey," she coos, wrapping me in her arms. "I wish I could fix this for you."

I sniff back the pain and wipe my eyes on her shoulder. "Thank you for listening," I whisper. "I've missed having you around."

She sighs, strokes my hair. "I'm not going anywhere."

Trevor knocks on the door and doesn't wait for a response. I make sure my eyes are clear before pulling away. "Did you tell her?" he asks Amy.

Amy shakes her head, gets up to stand next to him.

I look up at the both of them. "Tell me what?"

"Amy and her family have asked me to visit over Thanksgiving. Do you think you'll be okay if I go?" He takes Amy's hand in his, and they both watch me, eyes wide. Trevor adds, "Peter's offered to stay with you."

Peter.

I swallow, nervous, unease flowing through my veins. But when I look at them, at the strength of their love and the hope in their hearts, I say, "Of course you can go, you idiot."

IT'S the final period of the last day before Thanksgiving break and every one of my classes has been a washout. Even the teachers are already in holiday mode. The PA sounds with an alert for an announcement, and Principal Brown's voice crackles through the speakers. He starts with the general greeting, followed by a bunch of uninteresting reports, and then he says, "And a special shout-out to our very own Connor Ledger, who'll be spending the break at the Crossland Invitational in Indiana." I bury my head in my hands while everyone around me cheers. Face red with embarrassment, I glance up when he adds, "With only a hundred students from across the country selected to experience this once in a lifetime opportunity, it should be noted how very proud we are of you. Great job, Connor! Everyone else, have a safe and enjoyable break. We'll see you on the other side... well-rested, I hope."

My phone vibrates in my pocket, again and again, but I don't check it. Part of Dad's punishment for throwing my old one at the wall and smashing it was replacing it with a bright pink flip phone from the year *four*. It has physical buttons—ones you have to press numerous times to get the right letter to appear.

When the final bell rings, everyone rushes out the doors, their excitement evident in the cheers and hollers. I head out to the student parking lot to meet up with Rhys, who's been giving me rides to and from school ever since my car died and Dad and I deemed it not worthy of fixing. And even though Dad's car sits in the driveway when I'm at school because he's at home asleep, he refuses to let me drive it—another part of my punishment. This one for damaging my shooting hand. The downside to getting rides is that Rhys likes to hang around after school, shooting the shit with the rest of the guys. Me? I just want to get home.

"Our very own Conner Ledger, everyone!" Mitch announces, his hands cupped around his mouth as I make my way toward them.

I shake my head, narrow my eyes at him.

"Aww, but we're all so proud of you!" Karen says through a giggle, ruffling my hair as I walk past her to dump my bag in Rhys's car.

"That wasn't embarrassing at all," I murmur.

Rhys laughs, pretends to take a crown off his head and place it on mine. "You're the king of the school now."

Mitch scoffs, takes the imaginary crown and throws it on the ground, then stomps on it. "I was always the king, you fuckers."

"King of the asshole patrol," Oscar chimes.

"Fuck off," Mitch huffs.

I chuckle. "Get mad about it, you overcooked six-pack of Chicken McNobodies."

Karen busts out a laugh, her hand going to my shoulder to keep upright.

"Speaking of king of the school," Rhys says, motioning to a car pulling right up to the school steps.

I recognize the car and immediately stand taller.

Rhys adds, "What's Peter Parker doing here?"

"Ava's Peter?" Mitch comments.

My brow dips. "What do you mean *Ava's* Peter?"

Rhys shakes his head. "Not like that. He just means we know him *through* Ava."

"No," Mitch deadpans. "I mean, let's be real. He's probably fucked the daylights—"

"Watch your fucking mouth," I warn.

Mitch laughs. "What's it to you? As if you and Karen aren't—"

"We're *not*," I cut in, shoving Karen's hand off my shoulder. I push off Rhys's car, my eyes searching for Ava. It doesn't take long to find her. Head lowered, she comes down the school steps gripping the straps of her bag. She notices Peter's car and smiles at him the way she used to smile at me. He gets out to greet her with a hug that lasts too long, and I feel the moment my shoulders deflate. He keeps his arms around her waist while she pulls back, her hands pressed against his chest, and I wonder if she feels the same thing there—at the place where life lives—as she felt with me. Finally, he releases her, and then she's on her toes, her eyes wild, searching for something. They land on me, and my pulse becomes volatile. My breaths stop as she walks toward me, and everyone and everything around me is silent. All I hear is the thumping of my heart. One beat. Two. She stops a few feet in front of me, her gaze lowered as she white-knuckles the straps. "Hey."

I manage a "hey" back.

Her eyes lift to mine. "Do you have a minute?"

I swallow my nerves. "Sure."

She takes a step back, implying I follow, and so I do. Because I'd follow her to the ends of the fucking earth if she'd let me. "That was quite a speech Brown praised you with," she mumbles, looking at her feet as we stroll toward Peter's car. He's leaning against the hood, his arms crossed, eyes on us.

"It was possibly the most embarrassing moment of my life."

Her laugh is short. Sharp. "It's kind of a big deal, though, so I get why he wanted to announce it to the world."

I shrug.

"Anyway," she says, stopping halfway to Peter's car. "I um..." She blows out a heavy breath, then shakes her head. "It's so stupid now that I'm here..."

"What's going on?"

Her throat bobs, and she reaches into her pocket. "I got you something." She reveals a handful of bright orange balloons. With her voice low, she says, "You said once that it was your lucky charm." Her eyes meet mine, anguish pooling in their depths. "And I thought you might be nervous, so they're there if you want them or need them—if they mean anything still." She holds them up between us, but I can't move.

Can't speak.

Can't look away.

"I knew it was stupid," she mumbles, turning to leave.

"No. I want them!" I quickly grab her arm. "Please?" I hold my hand out, palm up, and she places them there. I can see the black marker mixed with orange, and the weight in my chest doubles.

"I should go," she says quietly. "Peter's waiting."

I nod. "So, what's with that? Are you guys...?"

"No," she laughs out. "*God, no*. He's staying with me over the break."

"Oh." Jealousy is a bitch. "He doesn't have his own home?"

She's quiet a beat as she chews her bottom lip, and I push away the memories of me doing the same to that lip, in my bed, with her half-naked and on top of me while she looked down at me as if our love knew no boundaries. "Trevor's going away with Amy—"

"His ex?" I interrupt.

Her eyes widen, just a tad. "You remember?"

I nod again. "I remember a lot." I remember *everything*. And a part of me hates that I do.

"They're back together now, so that's kind of cool," she tells me, looking over my shoulder where Peter is waiting for her.

When her eyes meet mine again, I say, "So, what you're telling me is that people can break up, but there's *hope* they can find their way back to each other again?"

Ava stares. Right *into* me. "Good luck at the invitational, okay?"

My heart sinks, and I suck in a breath to lessen the ache. "Yeah, okay."

I look down at the balloons in my hand while she steps around me. And just when I think I can move again, she calls out from behind, "Hey, Connor?"

I spin on my heels. "Yeah?"

She's only two steps away, and with the smallest of smiles pulling on her lips, she says, "I know that things are different between us now, but I'm always going to be proud of you, of how hard you've worked for this, and that's never going to change."

"Thanks, Ava," I tell her, my voice clear. "It means a lot."

It means everything.

connor

Connor: Ur da only 1 I no whod b up @ 4:40 a m, n I jst needed 2 tell u dat my roommate is snoring. & not da ok, I can get thru dis type of snoring. I mean, chainsaw 2 a redwood. My ears hurt.

Ava: Why are you typing like you're 12?

Connor: Bc old fone had fight wid a wall & Dad gave me n old flip fone wid only numbers. I sick of pressing buttons.

Ava: Is this the same wall that came at your fist?

Connor: Maybe

Ava: Idiot

Connor: Thx

Ava: Go 2 sleep. Big day 2day.

Connor: It's hot pink

Ava: What is?

Connor: Da fone

Ava: LOL

Connor: He juz sed TITTIES

Ava: ?

Connor: Snorin roommate

Ava: Connor, you need to get some rest. Throw something at him.

Connor: Shoe?

Ava: Not yours. His.

Connor: K

Connor: He up now. He go for run. I go sleep.

Ava: Goodnight.

Connor: Thx

* * *

Connor: its mixed.

Ava: ?

Connor: There r grls.

Ava: At the invitational?

Connor: yes

Ava: Oh, I bet they love you.

Connor: 10

Ava: 10 girls?

Connor: Yes

Ava: Showed any of them your weenus?

Connor: lol no. grls hv cooties

* * *

Connor: Guess who splurged and got a cheap but much better phone?

Ava: I'm assuming the person who's currently texting me using full words (thank God).

Connor: I feel like a new man.

Ava: Shouldn't you be running up and down a court?

Connor: We're having a break.

Ava: And you're messaging me?

Connor: I needed to tell someone about my new phone.

* * *

Connor: What are you doing?

Ava: Trying to show Peter how to use a washing machine.

Connor: How does he not know how to use one already?

Ava: Life of privilege, I guess. What's up?

Connor: Nothing, just having dinner with a few of the guys.

Ava: Then you should really be present, no?

Connor: We're all on our phones.

Ava: I have to go. Peter's about to wash a red shirt with whites.

Connor: You should let him.

Ava: That would be mean.

* * *

Connor: Ava

Ava: Connor

Connor: Hi

Ava: What's up?

Connor: Can't sleep.

Ava: ...

Connor: I should probably break this habit, huh?

Ava: I don't know, Connor. I think so, yeah...

Connor: Sorry.

* * *

Connor: Dad and I are about to board our flight home. I just wanted to say I'm sorry for contacting you as much as I did. I guess I'm still struggling to get over you, which is my problem, not yours. And I thought maybe the balloons meant something, but obviously, I was wrong. I guess I'll see you around. Sorry again.

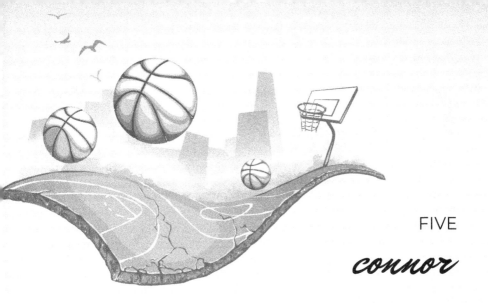

connor

"I'M BEAT," I tell Dad, my head rolling against the passenger's seat of his car as I look up at the familiar street lights.

"Yeah, I bet. You had a full-on few days there, son."

I close my eyes. "Wake me when we get home."

"We're pulling onto the street now," he says through a chuckle.

"Those few seconds will help, trust me."

He rounds the end of the cul-de-sac, then taps my leg. "We're home."

"Already?" I joke.

We're out and unpacking our luggage a moment later when Ava's porch light comes on. She steps out in sweatpants and a too-big Texas A&M hoodie. Jealousy burns a hole in my chest. She puts one earphone in and then sits down on a bench on her porch that wasn't there before I left. Shifting my focus away from her, I grab the last of our bags from Dad's truck.

"Are you going to talk to her?" Dad asks.

I shake my head as I make my way up our driveway. "She made it pretty clear that she wasn't really interested in talking to me much these days."

Dad mumbles, "It's hard to know what women want."

"Tell me about it," I murmur.

He opens the front door, then takes the bags out of my hands. "Talk to her, Connor. If not for her, then for you. You can't be in this miserable limbo forever."

Ava's lying across the bench when I make it to her porch. Her eyes are closed, her fingers laced and resting on her stomach. I start to leave, my nerves getting the best of me, but stop when I see a hint of a smile play on her lips. "Such a creep," she murmurs, her eyes snapping open. She sits up, takes out the earphone, and pats the spot beside her. "How was your flight?"

I sit down next to her. "It was fine. Look, I just came to apologize in person. And I guess... to get some clarity on what I can and can't do when it comes to you. I mean, are we no contact or...?"

Ava's quiet a beat before releasing a heavy sigh. "I don't know, Connor. I think it's going to be hard on both of us to navigate what we do from here. This isn't easy for me, either. And you act like I'm holding all the cards, but I'm not. And it's not like I don't miss you. I do. I still jump when my phone goes off because I'm so used to it being you, but... we can't..."

Turning to her, I see the sincerity in her eyes. I don't know how to respond to what she's saying, so I don't. Instead, I ask, "Where's Peter?"

"Inside. He has some work to do."

I motion to her sweatshirt. "That's a nice hoodie you're wearing. A little big, though."

Her eyes narrow. "You've seen the size of Trevor, right?"

"It's Trevor's?" I ask. "Not Peter's?"

Ava shakes her head, her gaze locked on mine. "Why would it be his?"

"I don't know." I look down at my hands, crack my knuckles. "He's staying with you and—"

"And you think I'm sleeping with him?"

Another shrug. "Mitch said—"

"Mitch is a shit-for-brains, Connor. Don't listen to him."

I push down the knot in my throat. "So you're not...?"

"If I were going to make something work with anyone, it would be—" She breaks off on a sigh, then shakes her head as if clearing her thoughts.

I sit up higher and say, "Can we just talk? I won't bring up *us*. I just want to hang with you for a bit."

"Sure." She smiles, but it's sad. "I didn't know your dad was going with you."

"Yeah," I sigh out. "He wasn't going to go, but then I started thinking about it. I'd never flown before, and the idea of being at an airport... I don't know. I had this whole stupid panic attack over it, which is dumb because—"

"It's not dumb," she interrupts, pouting.

I shrug. "It's incredibly emasculating to have to ask your daddy to fly with you because you can't get over your fucking childhood trauma, you know?"

She stares at me a moment, then lowers her gaze. "I think it's incredibly brave you went at all," she says quietly.

I rub my temples, a tension headache building. "How's your mom?"

Ava heaves out a sigh, her frown all-consuming. "They've got her on so many meds, she's not even my mom anymore. She's *barely* human. I hate it so much."

"I'm sorry."

Ava shrugs. "Krystal's been here during the break, so I've had a lot of free time on my hands." She pats the bench we're sitting on. "I got this."

"I noticed."

"And—" she holds up a baby monitor I hadn't seen yet "—I got this for Mom's room. It's... wait for it... *money*."

A low chuckle builds in my chest, and I look ahead when I say, "I'm never going to live that one down, am I?" That's when I spot a dark car cruising down the street, slowly, no headlights on. "What the hell is this?"

She peers up, sees what I'm seeing. "I don't know," she mumbles.

I get to my feet.

She does the same.

The car turns at the end of the cul-de-sac and slows even more as it starts to pass. I step in front of Ava. "Get down!"

"What?"

I shove her behind me, my eyes narrowed, trying to focus. The back window lowers, and a gun barrel—"Fuck!" I turn, push Ava to the ground and cover her completely. My ears fill with Ava's screams as shot after shot is fired, some hitting the house, some on my back. I hold on to her as she tries to scramble free, crying my name. Tires screech and then silence descends. Heart racing, breaths hot and heavy against the cool night air, I check that they're gone before releasing her. Her eyes wide, mouth agape, she stares up at me, unblinking. I swallow, flick the fucking paint off my arm. "It was just a paint-ball gun," I breathe out.

Ava's shaking her head, her breaths jagged. "Connor." My gaze locks on hers. Her eyes are wild. "There was no way you could've known that was just a paintball gun."

My pulse beats wildly in my chest, but I try to stay calm. For her. I wipe at the paint on the bench, adrenaline tightening my airways. "It should clean up easily."

"Leave it. It doesn't matter." Ava's throat moves with her swallow as her eyes fill with tears. Anger mars her features when she says, "It's the third time this week someone's messed with the house. Sometimes I wish I could just set this whole fucking place on fire and leave and never look back." She takes a calming breath. Two. Then she looks up at me, tears rolling down her cheeks. "Nothing good has come of this place, Connor. There was *you*. And now there's nothing."

I grasp her face in my hands, my eyes soaking in her heartache. "I'm still here," I breathe out.

She grabs on to my jacket, her eyes drifting shut. A heartbeat passes, strong and sure. I lower my mouth, at the same time her front door opens.

"What the hell happened?" Peter asks.

I don't turn to him. I keep my eyes on Ava as she blinks. Blinks. Blinks.

"Fuck," Peter spits. "Get inside, Ava."

My silence begs her to stay.

But her reality forces her to leave.

AVA

"What the hell happened?" Peter whispers, dragging me to my room.

Still in shock, I stare up at him.

His eyes don't stop moving as he takes me in, his hand on my arm squeezing. "Are you okay? Did you get hurt?"

"No," I whisper. "Connor..."

"Connor what?"

I try to breathe, try to calm the hell down. "Connor threw me on the ground and covered me... but he wouldn't have known it wasn't a real..."

"Jesus Christ, Ava," he murmurs, slumping down on the edge of my bed. "Your boy's an idiot."

"What?" I huff out.

Peter laughs. "He's willing to take bullets for a girl he's not even dating."

Peter's words pierce a hole through my chest, and I struggle to stay standing. Struggle to breathe. I sit down next to him, my gaze lowered, hand on my stomach to ease the ache.

Peter throws his arm around my neck, bringing me to him. He adds, scoffing, "The kid's NBA bound, and he just risked his life for what? For *you*?" Bile rises to my throat. "No offense, Ava, but Trevor's already given up his life for you. You don't want another person doing the same. If you're not into him, you need to make it clear. Because he's clearly too dumb to figure it out for himself."

My vision blurs.

"And why the hell do you still live in this shithole of a town with people who constantly abuse you? I don't understand why you can't just let me take care of you."

Guilt swarms through my veins, heating and boiling to anger.

I slip on my shoes and march over to Connor's house. I don't go to his window. I go to his door.

Knock twice.

He answers, dressed in a pair of basketball shorts and nothing else. Welts have started to form where the paintballs had struck him, and I look up and into his eyes, my vision suddenly clear. "You're an idiot!"

His spine straightens.

"You can't be going around risking your life for me."

He sighs. "It was just a paintball—"

"But you didn't know that, did you?"

His lips press tight.

"Jesus, Connor! What were you thinking?"

With a slow head shake, his jaw clenches when he says, "I was thinking that I need to protect the person I love!"

My breath catches at his words, but guilt controls all of mine. "You can't do that! We're not..." I press a hand to my chest, settle the pounding beneath it. "We need to stop."

"Stop what?"

"Skirting these lines. We can't keep doing this. *I* can't keep doing this. I can't keep sending you mixed messages. Shit, you could've—"

"Ava," he sighs out.

"We need a clean break," I declare. Tears prick behind my eyes, and I blink them away, stand firm. "No more texting. No more talking. No more *anything!*"

His chest heaves with his breaths, and I can see the weight of his conflict bearing down on his shoulders. I lift my chin, determined.

Connor licks his lips, his gaze falling. "Is that what you want?"

No, it's what you *need.*

He needs me out of his life.

For good.

"Yes."

Nodding, he leans against the open doorframe. "Karen asked me to go to winter formal with her."

I die on the inside.

On the outside, I stand my ground. "So go."

He heaves out a breath. And then his eyes meet mine, clouded, as if his heartache has shattered all hope.

I look away.

Right before he closes the door on us.

BABY MONITOR ATTACHED to the pocket of my sweatpants, I hold the ladder for Trevor while he searches the garage for the Christmas lights. We haven't used them since we moved here, but Trevor's on this *kick*, influenced by Amy, that we celebrate the holidays just like any other family.

"I'm sure we packed them in clear containers," I tell him.

"No, *I* packed them in garbage bags."

"No, *I'm* the one who packed them. I think I'd know."

"You barely packed anything," he mumbles.

"I did so."

"Did not."

"Did so."

"Shut up, brat."

"How are you twenty-two?"

"How are you your face?"

I bust out a laugh, and God, does it feel good. It's been weeks since I've felt even a semblance of joy, and a part of me wonders if that's the real reason why Trevor wants to suddenly pretend like Christmas is *A Thing* when we haven't celebrated it once since Mom's return.

"Found it!" he announces.

"Oh, look. A clear box," I mock, taking it from him as he starts his descent. "Who would've thought?"

We're making our way out of the garage when a stretch Hummer pulls up to the curb. "What's that about?" Trevor asks.

"Winter formal," I tell him, my heart sinking. It's been impossible not to count the days along with the entire school, but while everyone else is excited about it, I'd been dreading it. And I definitely don't want to be here to see it.

"Let's go," I tell Trevor at the same time the limo door opens. Karen hops out in a tight, red dress, followed by Rhys in a tux. Karen waits by the car while Rhys walks toward us.

"What's good?" Rhys greets Trevor, doing some weird bro handshake that only bros do. Then he turns to me. "Say it."

"Say what?" I ask.

"Tell me I look good."

I scoff, roll my eyes.

He adds, "I have a date in the car, but I can fuck her off real quick if you want to replace her."

Trevor chuckles.

I say, "Sure, give me five minutes to change."

Rhys gives me his megawatt smile that has girls falling for him. Had *me* falling for him. His eyebrows rise. "I'll wait."

"Shut up." I playfully kick his leg, my hands busy holding the lights.

"Just one picture," Connor's dad calls out, his steps fast as he tries to keep up with his son walking down their driveway.

"Dad, no!" Connor whines.

Karen laughs. "Give the man what he wants!"

I stare, fixated, my throat closing in when Connor stands in front of Karen. He's in a perfectly fitted tux, his red tie matching her dress. Connor lifts a corsage between them, the same shade, as if they'd planned all this in advance. Then he takes her hand, places it on her wrist, and she brings that same hand up to rest on his chest: *magic*.

Pain blocks my airways, but I can't look away. Not even when she rises to her toes, her lips pressed to his cheek. "Thank you."

"You're welcome," he replies. "You look nice."

"Ava," Trevor says, but his voice is distant. So far away. "Maybe we should go."

"I'm okay," I rush out, the words burning my throat.

"They're just friends," Rhys tries to convince me. But the way they turn to Connor's dad, the way she holds his waist, the way he settles his hand on the small of her back... a lot can change in a few weeks.

Tears blur my vision.

Trevor says, "Ava, let's go inside."

"I'm okay," I repeat. But I'm not. I'm so far from okay that *okay* is a fantasy. And I know I wanted this. For Connor to move on. For him to let his love live in someone else, but it doesn't stop the ache.

"Rhys, let's go!" Karen shouts, and I know that they'll see me: this pathetic, lonely girl standing in sweats, hands tied up in false magic. And so I turn to Trevor and look into his eyes. Try to find the strength I need to keep from losing it. He stares down at me, pity laced in his expression. A frown tugs at his lips. Rhys kisses the top of my head. "I'll see you later, A."

I hear him leave, but I don't respond. I keep looking at my big brother, searching for courage. Searching for hope. But there's nothing there. "Ava..." he whispers.

And I release the first sob. "I'm *not* okay."

"I know."

I run into the house, discarding the lights by the front door, and go into my mother's room. She's fast asleep, but I crawl into her bed anyway.

I need her.

I need her so much. "I need you, Mama. Wake up."

She doesn't stir.

"Wake up!" I cry out. "I need to talk to you." I shake her, my tears falling fast and free, my heartbreak flowing out in the sound of sobs. "Why can't you just be my mom! I need my mom!"

"Ava!" Trevor's standing beside the bed, trying to pull me away. "Let her sleep. You can't be like this. Not with her."

He grabs me by my waist and carries me to her door, dropping me back on my feet once we're out of her room. I fall to the floor and cry into my hands. And I don't stop. I *can't*. I've worked myself up to the point of hysterics, and I'm breathless, the ache in my chest unbearable. "I want everything they have, and I can't have it!" I break down. Fall apart. Release the emotions I've held on to for too long. My shoulders shake from the force of my cries.

Trevor leaves and returns with a paper bag. He squats down beside me and holds the bag out in front of my mouth, his hand forming the perfect *O*. "Come on, Ava. Breathe," he whispers, bringing it to my lips. I take over his hand and do as he asks and cry harder when he holds me to him, stroking my hair. "I don't know what to do here," he says, his voice cracking. I try to settle my breathing, look up at him through liquid lashes. His eyes are red from holding back his own tears, his breaths short, harsh. His lips quiver when he adds, "I'm out of my depth here, Ava. And I don't know what to do." He exhales a long, shaky breath, his gaze darting to the side. "And I don't know how much more I can take."

CONNOR

We're in the same gym the practices are held, and I'd rather be running suicides for an hour straight. The music is too loud, and the lights are too bright, and I don't want to be here. "Do you want to dance?" Karen asks, sitting next to me.

"I don't really dance," I tell her. I'm a sucky date; I know this. And I should really make more of an effort. "I mean, I don't really know how."

"I can teach you," she offers, and the smile she gives me only makes me feel worse.

"Maybe another time? I don't really feel like embarrassing myself in front of everyone."

"A private lesson." She smirks. "I'm down."

We sit in silence for another five minutes before I hear her loud sigh over the music.

"I'm sorry," I tell her.

"It's okay." She shrugs, and I can see the disappointment fleet across her features, see the genuine frown pull on her lips. She slumps in her chair, her hair curtaining her face, and I feel like the biggest dick in the history of the world.

"Hey," I say, dragging the legs of her chair until she's facing me. I lift her chin, finger a strand of hair away from her eyes. She looks up, sad, sad eyes on mine. And it's not her fault that I am the way I am. Not even a little bit. "I'm sorry," I repeat. "It's just... dances aren't really my thing."

She nods as if she knows me. And even though we've been spending more time together in the past few weeks since Ava crushed my soul, she doesn't *know* me. Not the *real* me. Not like Ava knows me.

"Let's get out of here," she says, standing and taking my hand. I don't know where we're going, but anywhere is better than here, and so I follow blindly behind her as she leads me out of the gym and through the empty hallways.

We end up at the larger gym where the games are played. "Comfortable now?" Karen asks, slipping off her heels.

I nod. "Much."

Giggling, she pulls a flask out of her purse and hands it to me. "You need to relax, Connor. The world doesn't end tomorrow."

She has a point. "You're right. And I'm sorry. I'm sure this version of me wasn't what you were expecting when you asked me to go with you."

With a shrug, she goes to the corner of the court and grabs a ball from the rack. "I just like hanging out with you. It doesn't really matter what we do."

I take a sip of the bourbon she snuck in, wondering why she brought it since she doesn't drink. "Me, too." And it's not a lie. I was wrong to have judged her the way I did, because she's fun to be around. The type of *fun* that lets me forget everything else.

"One-on-one?" she asks, effortlessly spinning the ball on the tip of her finger.

I take another swig, breathe the alcohol straight into me. "Last time we played, I nailed you."

"You haven't nailed me." She smirks. "Yet."

I take the ball from her, go for a simple lay-up, then go after the ball and hold it under my arm as I face her. "I'll give you a fifteen-point head start, just to make it fair."

"Deal."

We play until it's fifteen all, taking breaks for me to sip on her flask. "You gotta give me more than that if you want a chance at scoring," I laugh out.

She narrows her eyes. "So many innuendos, I can't choose one."

I stand under the basket, throw the ball to her while she waits at the free-throw line. I say, "I'll give you a free shot, just because I feel sorry for you."

Smiling, she dribbles for a few seconds, her feet planted to the floor. And then she moves in on me, closer and closer, until she's standing in front of me, her nose to my chest. "Connor?"

I stand taller. "Karen?"

She throws the ball behind her, and I watch it fly in the air, feeling a chuckle build inside me. But it stops when her hands press against my chest, forceful enough for me to take a step back, and then another, and another, until my back hits a wall. I swallow, nervous, and look down at her. Her hands travel down my torso, to my stomach, and my breath halts when she licks her lips. Eyes on mine, she murmurs, "You miss a hundred percent of the shots you don't take, right?"

I nod.

Her eyes drift shut, and I suck in a breath when she leans forward, mouth ready, and it would be so easy to do this. To *be* this. With *her*. I close my eyes...

And I picture Ava.

My eyes snap open. "I can't," I whisper, my hands finding Karen's shoulders to stop her. To stop *myself*. "I'm sorry. I can't."

Karen keeps her gaze lowered. "Because of her?" she asks quietly.

"No, because of me," I tell her honestly, putting more space between us. "Because my heart will always be hers, even if she'll never accept it."

I'M SICK OF CRYING.

I'm sick of hoping.

And I'm sick of my own self-pity.

I promise myself to become the model student (for Trevor) with the perfect patience (for my mom), and I stop letting my emotions drive me, and instead, use my love and appreciation for Trevor to guide me.

Life is a series of decisions, Connor's dad once said. *You make them because they feel right at the time, but you're not bound to them forever.* But *I am* bound to them.

I made a choice to stay for my mom.

And I made a choice to leave for Connor.

I have to stick to those decisions and make the most of what I have.

And that decision is final.

It's Christmas Day, another zero-day in the house. But Trevor and I—we're *trying*, and that's all he asked for. Tomorrow, he takes off to Colorado to spend the rest of the holidays with Amy. Krystal will still be here during the day, and I have the crisis team on speed dial should I need them. Peter will be in town, but he'll only be stopping by every now and then to check in on me.

I walk around the kitchen doing my best to create a Christmas dinner worthy of Trevor's hopes to make the day special. Mom sits at the kitchen table, a whiteboard in front of her. She's practicing writing with her left hand all the words that remind her of Christmas. It brings her neither happiness nor misery.

"Pick one," Trevor orders, walking into the room with two different rolls of wrapping paper. "Purple's her favorite color, but it's not as festive as the red."

I smile. "I'd go purple. For sure."

"Tape?" he asks.

"Do we have tape?"

"Dammit." He rummages through all the kitchen drawers before exiting. Mom writes *wrapping paper* on the board.

"That's a good one!" I encourage.

She doesn't react.

"Would electrical tape be okay?" Trevor calls out.

"No!"

Mom writes down *family*.

My heart bursts. "I like that one," I tell her.

"Mmm," she responds.

Trevor walks back into the room, a stack of papers held in his grasp. His eyes skim one and then another. And my heart stops the second I realize what he's reading. Shoulders tense, I grind out, "What the hell are you doing?"

The muscles in his jaw tick.

I race over to him, try to grab them out of his grasp, but he holds them above his head.

"When in the hell were you going to tell me?!"

"Give them back," I grunt, trying to reach for them.

"No!"

"Why the fuck are you going through my stuff?"

"Stop cussing," Mom mumbles.

He grabs my shoulder and pushes me back, slamming the papers on the kitchen table, making Mom jerk in her seat. She looks up at him, her eyes clearer.

He keeps me at an arm's length, literally, and I try to push him away, but he's too strong. "Texas A&M, University of Florida, UNC. These are all early acceptance letters, Ava!"

"What?" Mom whispers, getting to her feet.

"Trevor, why would you do this?"

"Do what?" he shouts, the loudness of his voice making me cower. "Care about your goddamn future?"

"You said I just had to apply. You didn't say I had to accept!"

"What?" Mom asks again, flipping through all the letters.

"Look what you've done, Trevor!" I cry out. "You've given her false hope!"

"Ava, I swear to God," Trevor grinds out. "If you miss these deadlines—"

"You're going," Mom says, her tone flat.

"What?" I huff. "I'm not going anywhere."

Her gaze lifts, locks on mine. Resolute. "You're going, Ava."

I suck in a breath. Hold it. My teeth clenched. "I'm not leaving you."

"Yes, you are!" she shouts, slamming her hand on the table.

I glare at Trevor. "See what you've done!"

Trevor shakes his head, outrage flaming his eyes. "Your bratty ass is going to college."

I stand frozen, my fists balled at my sides. I look between them, rage building inside me, surrendering in the form of heated tears. "How the hell am I supposed to go!" I cry. "Under no circumstances, in *this* life, is it possible for me to leave. None!"

"Goddammit! I don't know how else to get this through your stubborn little head!" Mom yells. "I don't *want* you here! *I* don't want to be here!"

"Stop it!" I beg, pressing my palms to my ears. My heart aches, drops to the knot tightening in my stomach.

"I gave you an out!" Mom bellows.

I fold in on myself, weak.

"You shouldn't have fucking saved me, Ava!"

I can't breathe.

"You should've let me die like I wanted!"

"STOP IT!" I scream, my throat scratching with the force. I can feel the physical cracking of my heart... right before its collapse.

"Ava," Trevor whispers, his arms going around me.

I fight against his hold and break free, pushing him out of the way. Then I run outside. I need to fill my lungs with air. Because I feel like I'm drowning. Like I've been underwater for almost three years, and I can't—I can't take a breath that isn't liquified heartache or hope, and *I'm done*.

I'm so fucking done.

CONNOR

Dad works a double shift during Christmas because money. And not the "cool" version of money. But real-life paper money to make up for what we spent on the invitational I attended. Rhys invited me to spend the day at his house, and when I mentioned I didn't want to intrude on his family time, he laughed, said that Christmas at his house was the biggest blowout of the year and that most of the team attend after their own Christmas dinners. So, I go. Because really? What else am I going to do? Dad and his work partner, Tony, were invited, too. They came, ate the smorgasbord of food that was offered, but had to leave soon after. Emergencies stop for no one, apparently.

Now it's dark out, and the team plus Karen are hanging in Rhys's room while the grown-ups have a giant orgy downstairs. Not really. But that's the story Mitch keeps telling. "If I were down there, I'd choose Karen's mom," he says.

Karen scoffs. "She'd turn you down faster than Connor turned me down."

"Burn," Rhys laughs.

I turn to Karen, narrow my eyes.

"What?" She giggles. "It's true!"

Things with Karen and me were weird for a hot minute. Then she called me a *fuckboy*, whatever that means, and told me my jump shot was weak. We've been fine ever since.

There's a knock on Rhys's door, and we all hide the alcohol we managed to sneak up. "Yeah?" Rhys calls out.

His mom pokes her head in. "Did you hand out the gifts, pookie bear?"

The entire room burst out in cackles.

"Yeah, pookie bear," Mitch mocks. "Did you?"

Rhys sighs, then offers his mom a toothy grin. "I'll do it now. Thanks, *Mom!*" She closes the door, and Rhys goes to his closet, pulls out a giant garbage bag of gifts. "Have at it," he says, dropping the bag in the middle of the floor.

We dive in like kids at a party when the piñata breaks, fighting and wrestling for gifts we don't even deserve. I rip mine open, my eyes widening when I see what's inside. "Yo, this is a Louis Vuitton wallet. I think maybe—"

"Mine too!" Oscar announces, already transferring his cards.

"Damn," I laugh. "You guys really do live in another world." I move to the window, flick open a gap in the blinds to see all the cars parked on the front lawn—by valets, of course. And that's when I catch sight of her. I'd recognize those loose curls anywhere. She's sitting in front of her old house, just like the day of the cafeteria incident. And I understand that she doesn't want anything to do with me, but seeing her like this, remembering how she was back then, I can't help but go to her. If she needs me, I'm here. Always. I tell whoever is listening, "I'll be back."

I try to make my presence known because I don't want to startle her, but it doesn't seem to matter because Ava's transfixed, chin up, staring at the house she used to call home. "Hey," I croak.

Slowly, she turns to me, and even in her apparent hopelessness, she's still stunningly beautiful.

My heart heavy, I ask, "Can I sit with you?"

Turning back to the house, she nods, a movement so slight I almost miss it.

I sit down next to her, ignoring the icy ground beneath me. "You okay?" I ask.

Ava doesn't respond immediately. She just stares, her blinks slow. "It's so nice, huh?"

"The house?"

"Yeah," she sighs out. "We used to hang colored lights out during Christmas. They only have white ones, but it's still so beautiful."

"It is," I murmur, but I'm not looking at the lights. I'm looking at her.

She inhales deeply, her voice quiet when she says, "Sometimes I come here and just look at it. I try to remember all the good times I had there, the happy memories, but I can never seem to think of anything but... but the blood."

"The *blood?*"

She nods, her lids heavy when she turns to me, eyes clouded. "There was so much blood, Connor," she says, her voice strained with her withheld emotions. Her bottom lip trembles, and I fight the urge to hold her, to pull her into me and love her openly. "There was supposed to be a caregiver with me that day," she says. "But they were ill, and they couldn't come, and I had a test first period." She swipes at the tears with no cry to accompany them. After an audible swallow, she adds, "I had a stupid test, and so I left her there. Alone. I was gone no more than two hours and when I came back..." She shudders a breath, and this time, I ignore what I know she wants. I clasp my hand around hers but keep silent. "It was so quiet. I called out to her, but she didn't answer. And then the stairs. I remember the stairs. I remember the creaks under my feet. And I remember going through every room, feeling the dread escalate with every step." She sniffs back her anguish. "And then the bathroom and the blood and the water and she was in there and she..."

"Ava..." I whisper, wrapping my arms around her. I pull her into me, my heart pounding.

She sobs into my chest. "She wasn't breathing, Connor. Oh, God..." Her shoulders shake, her cries coming louder.

"Shh, it's okay," I whisper into her hair. I sniff back my own tears while I listen to her fall apart, and I do my best to keep it together. "It's okay, Ava."

"But it's not," she cries out, gripping my jacket. "It's not okay. Nothing is okay, and I don't know... I don't—" She struggles to speak, struggles to breathe through her pain. "She hates me because I saved her. She hates me!"

"No, she doesn't," I try to soothe.

"She doesn't, Ava," Karen utters, and I don't know where she came from or how long she's been listening. Ava pulls out of my hold, wiping her cheeks with the back of her hand.

"She doesn't hate you," Karen repeats, sitting on the other side of her. "And I know... I know that this place, this house, brings back all those memories for you, but there are so many good ones," she rushes out. "Like that tree," she says, pointing to a small tree right in the middle of the front yard. "That's Scout's tree, remember?"

Ava lets out a sob.

"And remember when your mom surprised you with him? We got off the bus, and she was standing right on that porch, and you didn't know she was coming home and you ran up the driveway so fast your bag caught on your skirt and you flashed me your bright red undies?"

Ava...

Ava *laughs*... a sound so pure, even if it ends with another cry.

"And you jumped into her arms, and she held you, swung you around as if you weighed nothing. God, I was so jealous of that genuine love she has for you. And then she brought out this mutt of a dog she found at the pound... so old and raggedy and blind in both eyes, and you fell to your knees and you loved that ugly-ass dog as much as your mom loved watching you with him."

Ava's shoulders shake, this time from laughter.

"And your bedroom balcony," Karen continues, nudging Ava's side. "Remember how you and I used to stand out there and pretend like we were performing for a crowd of millions? We'd bust out the *High School Musical* soundtrack as if we could fucking sing, and we truly believed that Troy Bolton was going to somehow climb up there and declare his undying love for us."

I ask, "Who's Troy Bolton?"

"Shut up, Connor," Karen snaps, and Ava giggles, her head down.

"But my favorite memory of all is that tire swing in your backyard."

Ava glances up at her, wordless and breathless.

Karen stares at the house like Ava did only moments ago: gaze distant, mind lost. "I'd just turned fourteen, and I needed to talk to you, but you weren't there. Trevor had taken you out for the day, just you and him. And when your mom told me, I said that I'd wait for you, and I sat in that tire swing. I was probably there for five minutes before your mom came out and told me that she was no Ava, but she'd listen if I wanted to talk. So, I did. I told her about my mom's boyfriend at the time. About how he was creeping on me and touching me." Karen's voice cracks. She clears her throat, sits higher and adds, "Your mom asked if I'd told my mom, and I had, but she didn't believe me. So, your mom—she said she'd take care of it... That guy was gone the next day. Just packed up his bags and left. Never heard from him again. God, your mom was my hero. She's always been my hero, Ava. She was like a mother to me when I didn't have one." Karen sighs. "And I think that's why I took it so hard—what happened to her. And I'm sorry that I couldn't be there for you the way you needed me. I'm sorry I stopped coming around, and I know it's so fucking selfish, but... she was such a strong, powerful force in my life and to see her—" Karen breaks off on a sob, rubbing her eyes. "Seeing her like that killed me, A. And I just couldn't. I don't have your strength. And I'm sorry."

Ava's silent. No verbal response. But she takes Karen's hand in hers. A peace offering.

Behind us, a throat clears. Rhys makes his way around us, saying, "Well, you know what my favorite memory of that house is?"

Ava looks up at him.

"My favorite memory is standing at my window watching you try on bikinis in your bedroom."

"Oh, my God," Ava whispers, shaking her head.

Rhys smirks. "Little boobies out like what."

"Shut up!" Ava kicks his foot.

I say, "I'm about to punch you."

"He's not worth it," Ava says, turning to me. After a heavy sigh, she asks, "Will you take me home?"

"I'll take you wherever you want."

AVA

Trevor's sitting on our porch when Karen pulls up to the curb. I say goodbye to Rhys and Karen in the front seat and wait for Connor to get out first. "I'll see you later, okay?" I ask him.

He nods. "Whenever you need me."

I hug him quickly, then start up my driveway. Trevor stands when I get close. "Jesus, Ava, I've been so worried."

I fall into his open arms, his wide chest rising against me as if it's the first time he's been able to breathe. "I'm sorry," he says. "I'm so sorry."

"I know," I tell him. "Me, too."

I release him and sit on the porch steps, waiting for him to join me before saying, "Trevor, I'm not going to college. At least not yet."

"Okay," he breathes out.

"I feel like all we do lately is fight. You against me. Me against Mom." I push down the knot in my throat. "I don't want you to ever feel like I don't appreciate everything you've done for us. Believe me, I carry so much guilt—"

"Ava," he cuts in, but I don't let him speak, because I need to say what's on my mind.

"I know you miss your old life and your independence, and I don't blame you." I blow out a breath. "I just need to get through the rest of the school year, and I'm going to find a way to fix everything. I promise. But first, I need to fix myself. Because I've been miserable, Trevor, and I just... I want to be happy again."

Trevor smiles, but it's sad.

"And hopefully I can find strength in that happiness so that I can be the person I want to be. Not just for me but for everyone else around me."

With his arm around my neck, he pulls me closer to him. "I want that for you, too, Ava."

"I miss who I used to be," I tell him honestly. "And I miss my old friends."

"Yeah?"

"I miss Karen and Rhys and..."

"Connor?" he asks.

I nod. "I know you're not his biggest fan right now, and it's not like I want to be with him *like that*, but he made me happy, Trevor. Even when we were *just* friends."

"Okay," he breathes out.

"I just... I need to find a balance, and I need to start taking care of myself, because I can't keep going on like this, Trevor. I just *can't*."

EIGHT

ava

I HAD to practically shove Trevor out the door and into a cab so he wouldn't miss his flight to Colorado. He was adamant on staying, worried about how I'd do without him. I had to promise to call three times a day and answer every one of his text messages within five minutes. Peter's come by to check on me every night Trevor's been gone, but things with us haven't been the same since Thanksgiving break... when I told him he needed to stop pressuring me about certain choices I refuse to make.

As for me, I've been trying more to take care of *me*. Of my happiness. And with Krystal around during the day, I've been able to have a little more freedom than what I'm used to. So far, I've taken the first steps to get a learner's permit, walked through the local park, ridden on random buses people-watching, and sat through an entire movie at the theater on my own. I've also been keeping in touch with Karen. Just a few messages here and there. We're definitely not going to have the same level of friendship from years ago, not because neither of us *doesn't* want that, it's just... we grew up and became different people. And then there's Rhys. Rhys will always be Rhys.

Now, I'm trying to do the one thing I've been putting off the entire break.

I walk up Connor's porch steps for the fifth time in the past fifteen minutes. I get to his door, raise my fist to knock, then chicken out at the last second. I walk down the steps, give myself a pep talk, and then walk right back up.

It should be easy: knock, ask if he wants to hang out and see where things go from there. But it's not easy, because...

Because what if he says no?

I run down the steps and make it all the way down his driveway before releasing the breath I'd been holding. I look over at my house, remember what's in there. *Who* is in there. And remember my reason.

I can't be who she needs me to be if I'm miserable. And Connor—he helps take away the misery.

"Come on, Ava," I whisper, shaking out my hands. I practically run up to his door and knock without letting my thoughts overtake me. Only a few seconds pass before the door opens. Connor's in a loose, long-sleeve tee and basketball shorts, and somehow it all still manages to showcase his perfect body. I drop my gaze, try to calm my breathing. He's barefoot, and I've never really paid attention to his feet but, *Jesus,* even they're hot.

"Hey," he says, all cool and calm, as if it didn't take all the courage in the world for me to be standing in front of him. "What's up?"

When I look up, he's biting into an apple, his eyebrows raised.

"I uh…" *I was wondering if you'd want to hang out.* The words are *right* there, on the tip of my tongue, and I should just say it, just blurt it out, but my insecurities get the best of me, so I point behind me to the truck in his driveway. "Is that yours?" Oh, my God. What if it *isn't* his? It's been in his driveway for days, so I assumed he got a new car, but what if… what if he has a girl—

"Uh huh," he says, looking over my shoulder at it.

"It's pretty." I roll my eyes, internally slap myself. "You know… for a truck."

He stands taller, looks down at me, his brow knitted. "Did you need a ride somewhere?"

I nod. A lie. But he won't say no to a ride if he's offering… right? "Just to the store real quick? We're out of… *fruit.*"

"*Fruit*?" he asks, smirking as he bites into his apple again. "I can spare you some fruit."

"And um… bread. And milk. You know…" I shrug. "The necessities."

He steps into his house, slips on his sneakers, no socks. Grabbing a set of keys off the hook by his door, he asks, "You ready to go now?"

"Uh huh."

He closes the door behind him. "Let's go."

The second I'm in his car, my nostrils are inundated with all things Connor, and my mind… my mind floods with all the memories of us sitting in his old car, every conversation, every moment of laughter, every touch of his hand on my leg.

Apple caught in his mouth, he brings his hand to the back of my seat as he looks behind him to reverse onto the road.

"When did you get it?" I ask.

He straightens the car, takes the apple out, and says, "Birthday present from Daddy. I know, I'm spoiled."

My heart skips a beat, and I pout up at him. "It was your birthday?"

He glances over at me, his eyes zoned in on my lips. He licks his own before focusing on the road again. "A few days ago, yeah."

"Sorry. I didn't know."

Connor shrugs. "How could you have?"

True. "Did you do anything for it?"

Another shrug.

"Well, it's a nice truck."

He leans against his door and murmurs, "Yeah, you've said that." There's no humor in his tone, and now that I think about it, he really didn't seem all that happy to see me. And that realization creates a dull ache in my chest. "Did I interrupt something? Were you busy?"

He keeps his gaze forward. "Nope."

"Because if you were, I could catch the—"

"I said no, Ava. It's fine."

"You just seem like... like you're mad at me?"

The heaviness of his sigh has me wanting *out*. Out of this car and out of this entire situation. This was clearly a mistake, and I don't even know why. He stops at a red, and I'm *so* tempted to open the door and run. Anywhere but here.

I swallow the knot in my throat and force myself to try again. "Are you ready for school?"

His gaze flicks to mine, his jaw ticking. Then he reaches over, turns on the radio. And my heartache becomes too strong. "Actually, I forgot my wallet," I tell him, looking out my window. I struggle to speak through the giant lump in my throat. "Can you just take me back home?" He waits for the green and takes off again, but he doesn't turn around. "Or just drop me off wherever. I can walk."

"I can afford what you need, Ava."

But I don't *need* anything besides him, and he's clearly not willing to give me that. "Honestly, it's fine."

"We're almost there."

"We can just—"

He turns the volume up, shutting me out completely.

I turn my back to him, wipe at my eyes before the first tear falls. I don't want him to see them. To *claim* them.

We get to the store, and I grab what I faked coming here for: bread, milk, fruit. He walks with me, but we don't speak, don't look at each other. At the checkout, he grabs a bunch of flowers before paying for everything. I don't ask who the flowers are for because *any* answer would just ruin me more. "I'll pay you back," I tell him, and he shakes his head, looking everywhere but at me.

When we get to his truck, I sit with my back turned to him, my face practically pressed against the window. We don't say a word to each other until we're sitting in his driveway, and the engine's off, and we're surrounded by silence. He asks, "Hey, do you remember that day at the lake?"

I don't know why of all the things he could possibly say, he chooses to say that.

I nod without turning to him. "Of course."

He clears his throat. "That was one of the best days of my life, Ava." He opens his door, and I do the same, but neither of us gets out of the car. After a sigh, he says, "I just wanted you to know that. For whatever stupid reason."

I finally face him, see the anguish in his eyes, and say, my heartbreak forming my words, "It was *the* best day of my life."

His head drops forward, and he rubs the back of his neck, then pinches the bridge of his nose. "Fuck," he spits, hitting the steering wheel.

I cower, grab the groceries, and get out of the car, needing the air, the space. "Thanks for the ride," I call out, closing the door.

I make it to the sidewalk before he grasps my arm. "Ava, just wait."

I suck in a breath, hold it, and reluctantly turn to him.

He's holding the flowers at his side, his jaw tense, nostrils flared.

I stand tall, look up at him.

After a sharp inhale, he lets it *all* out: "I wish I knew what you wanted from me, Ava, because it's doing my fucking head in. One minute you're telling me you want no contact, and the next you're knocking on my door asking for a ride. Why not call Rhys or Karen? Or Peter? Because I know he's in town checking in on you. And you know how I know? Because Rhys told me. Not you. And I know that Krystal's been with your mom all break, which means you've had every chance to come over and hang out with me. And honestly, I've *waited*. For days, I've waited for you to show. And now it's the last day of break, and when you do come, it's because you need something from me. And that's fine. If you or your mom need anything, I'm here. I made that promise to you, and I'm keeping it. I just..." He pinches the bridge of his nose again, then heaves out a breath. "You know, Rhys threw me a birthday party, and he asked if I wanted to invite you and I didn't even know what to say. Like, are we friends or..." He shakes his head, his eyes on mine. "What do you *want*, Ava?"

I listen to his entire speech, agony clenching at my life source. I stare up at him, breathless when I finally find my voice. "I was hoping we could be friends."

He nods, his eyes dimming. "Ava, I..."

"What?" My gaze drops, so does my heart. "Just say it, Connor."

"I don't think I can be *just* friends with you. Not now. Not when I know what it's like to have all of you."

I fight to hold it together. "That's fine."

He sniffs once. "Can you give these to your mom?" he mumbles, handing me the flowers. "I forgot the last time I was over."

* * *

Mom's resting in her room when I get in, and so I unpack the few items I have, then place the flowers in a large plastic cup. Her gaze moves to me when I open her door, her eyes brightening when she sees the flowers. I settle them on her nightstand while I wait for her to sit up. She stares at the flowers, confused at first, and then a hint of a smile plays on her lips. She looks at them closer, entranced, her fingers stroking the petals. "So much color," she mumbles.

"You like the colors?"

"Pretty," she states, not once taking her eyes off them.

I tell her, my voice quiet as I struggle to hold in my heartbreak, "Connor got them for you."

She nods. "Connor, six-five, but is hoping for a growth spurt."

And even through my pain, I can't help but smile. "That's him."

"He's a good boy."

"Yeah," I say, wiping at the tears she doesn't notice. "He is."

connor

"YOU LOOK LIKE ASS," Oscar says, slumping down in the seat next to me.

It's first period, new semester, new year, same shit.

I chose the table at the back corner of the room because I don't even know what this class entails and the less attention I get, the better. "I didn't sleep well," I tell him, and it's true. I spent most of the night staring at my phone, at the blinking cursor of the empty message addressed to Ava. I couldn't think of anything to say. In my mind, I knew that I'd said everything I needed to. But it didn't stop the hurt. And every time I closed my eyes to try to sleep, all I saw was the pain in hers when I told her how I felt.

But I don't regret it.

I can't.

Because everything I said was fact.

Oscar says, breaking through my thoughts, "You better shake that shit off by lunch. We got that pep rally in the gym, remember?"

I groan, slam my head on the desk.

"Welcome to multimedia," Miss Salas announces, standing at the front of the class. "I hope you guys are ready to work this semester because there's a lot to get through!"

The classroom door opens, and it's just like the first time I saw her: a baby bird leaving the nest for the first time, a discombobulation of limbs. "Sorry," Ava mumbles. Her hair's down today, wild curls bouncing around. She hands the teacher a piece of paper, her eyes downcast. "I have a note from Miss Turner."

Miss Salas looks at the note, her nose scrunched. "Will you be late after every session with the school psychologist?"

The class erupts in quiet giggles, and I ball my fists, my jaw ticking. The kid in front of me, Roy, calls out, "At least it's not Alcoholics Anonymous like her mom."

I kick the back of his chair. Hard. He rag-dolls against the edge of the table and screeches out in pain. Then he turns to me. "What the fuck, Ledger?"

I seethe, "How about you watch your fucking mouth?"

"How about you *both* watch your mouths!" Miss Salas shouts. Like she can talk. Who the fuck is she to throw Ava's business out like that?

Okay.

So clearly, I'm still in love with the girl. That's not going to change. I just need to find a way to shut out those feelings so I can move on with my life. And not with or for someone else, but for me. Because I'm drowning in those feelings, slowly, and it's killing me.

"Go on and find an empty seat," the teacher tells Ava.

Ava starts for a seat in the front row.

Good.

Distance.

That's exactly what I need.

Next to me, Oscar stands, shouts, "I forgot my contacts today, so I need to move... to the front." It takes me a moment to realize what he's doing, but by the time I do, it's too late. He's already there, and Ava's making her way toward me.

She sits down next to me, gripping her bag to her chest.

The teacher starts going through the class curriculum for the rest of the year, and Ava lowers her bag to the floor and kicks the back of Roy's seat to get his attention. "Psst. Roy!" she whispers-yells.

He turns to her, a glare in place.

She says, her voice calm and filled with clarity, "Just FYI, my mom's not an alcoholic. She doesn't even drink. She went to *war*, to fight for *your* country, and she was hit with a grenade. It blew off half her arm and half her face, and because of that, she has fucking *brain damage*. And that brain damage is the reason why she slurs her words. Not alcohol." She takes a breath, her nostrils flaring. "So, the next time you want to say something about her because you think it'll get you a few cheap laughs, just... take a moment and imagine if that happened to your mom."

Roy blinks and blinks, and he stares at Ava as if it's the first time he's seeing her.

Meanwhile, I stare at Ava in awe.

"Hey," Roy says, "you're kind of hot when you're feisty."

I kick his chair again. Harder this time.

Ava scoffs. "Fuck you."

We spend the rest of the class listening to Miss Salas talk and talk and talk without ever really saying anything. When the period's over, I turn to Ava, motion to Roy. "That was impressive."

Ava shrugs. "I'm sick of the world dictating how I feel or how I act or what I do," she says, her brow furrowed. "I'm over it, you know?"

"Why do I feel personally attacked right now," I say, half-joking as I pick up my bag and ball.

"Don't feel like that," she assures, walking out of the room with me. "It's not about you, Connor. You just gave me a hell of a lot of perspective."

We stop just outside the room and turn to each other. "How so?"

"I don't know," she murmurs. "I feel like... like my mind is a mess right now, but I'm seventeen, and I'm going to have that same mind for a long time. And that mind is going to make a lot of bad decisions before I learn from them and start making the right ones."

My eyebrows lift.

She shrugs. "I'm not like you. I don't have one goal set for the rest of my life. There is no *end game* for me. But there are two things that I know I want, and the first is to find a way to get out of this shitshow of a town."

"And the second?" I ask.

With a sigh, she shakes her head. "I gotta get to class. I'll see you around, okay?"

* * *

Today's pep rally is the same as all the other ones prior. We watch the cheerleaders' new routine, and then Coach calls us all up one-by-one while we listen to the cheers of our peers. The only thing different with today's is that *Ava is here.*

In the stands.

Standing out.

Out of place.

She doesn't clap or shout or do much of anything. Still, I can't seem to take my eyes off of her. "She promised Trevor she'd make the most of her last semester," Karen says, waving her pompom all over my face.

I swipe her arm away, my eyes finding Ava again. "So that means pep rallies?"

"School spirit, you know. Rah! Rah! Rah! Goooo, Wildcats!"

"Huh."

Karen laughs. "Did you think she was here to support you?"

"No." *Maybe.*

"You sure look butthurt for someone who doesn't even *want* to be friends with her."

My eyes snap to hers. "She told you that?"

Karen nods, a twinkle in her eye.

"It's not that I *don't* want to. It's that I *can't.*"

"Uh huh."

Coach calls out Rhys's name and Ava smiles, claps for the first time. "See that?" Karen says. "She dumped his sorry ass, and they became *better* friends." She pats my head as if I'm a dog. "You should be more like Rhys."

I roll my eyes. "You should be more like Ava."

Karen laughs. "That's one uphill battle I'll never climb."

I face her.

She shrugs. "There's only one Ava in this world, Connor. So, the ball's in your court." She smacks my ass. "You're up."

She's *right*. Jesus, she's fucking right. And even though Ava was the one to break things off, or to ask for a clean break, she had far better reasons—reasons out of her control—than just the simple fact that she *couldn't* be around me because it was "too hard." I suck. In so many ways. For so many reasons. "I don't know how to fix it," I admit.

Karen shakes her head, points to Coach. "No, you're up."

"We don't have all damn day, Ledger!" Coach yells.

Oh. I run up and stand next to Rhys but keep my eyes on Ava. She's smiling, but she doesn't clap like she did with Rhys. Instead, she cups her hands around her lips and mouths, "Boo!"

SURPRISINGLY, the first couple of weeks of the new semester fly by. I don't know if it's the sudden change in my attitude or the fact that I stopped giving a shit about what people say or think about my family, but whatever it is, it's made a difference, and I'm sure as heck not complaining.

I make it to first period earlier than everyone else because I don't want a repeat of Miss Salas's shaming, though I don't think she'd do it again after my little rant to Miss Turner in one of my sessions. Soon enough, more and more students start to file in, and there's a buzz in the air as if something *big* has happened. And as much as I've tried to keep up with all the school news, I'm clearly out of the loop.

From my seat in the back of the room, I see Oscar walk in with a few guys from the team who aren't in this class. Then Rhys shows up with a bag full of something that he hands out to the guys. He sends a few of the girls in the room a smirk, making them weak at the knees, and then winks at me. I roll my eyes. Then Connor walks in, and as soon as he does, the room erupts with cheers. The team sprays him with bright orange Silly String, and Oscar lifts all 220 pounds of Connor off his feet, chanting his name, and what the actual fuck is going on?

I send Trevor a text.

Ava: Did we make the playoffs?

Trevor: Who?

Ava: The basketball team.

Trevor: Ava! I don't know. I don't even go to that
school. And your best friend is a co-captain. So is
your ex. Ask them.

Ava: I don't want to. :(

Trevor: Then leave me alone with your dumbass
questions. I'm trying to earn a living.

Ava: You're grumpy.

Trevor: You're stubborn.

Ava: Once upon a time, you were my favorite brother.

Trevor: Once upon a time, my sister grew the hell up
and stopped being such a brat.

Ava: Fine. Love you. Bye

Trevor: Love you, too. Shithead.

"Okay, everyone!" Miss Salas exclaims, walking into the room. She dumps her stuff on the desk and continues, "Everyone who isn't part of the class, leave immediately."

Oscar puts Connor back on his feet, and the other boys leave. Connor takes a moment to remove all the Silly String from him and the floor—with the help of a couple of girls in the class—and trashes it all. He finds an empty seat in the front of the room, and I bring up my phone again, send him a text.

Ava: Um. What?

I watch Connor sneak his phone under the desk and read the message. He looks behind him, searching, and finds me in the rear of the room. When Miss Salas's back is turned, Connor rushes to the empty seat beside me. "What's up?" he whispers, his mouth so close to my ear, I can feel the warmth of his breath.

"What was that about?" I whisper back.

He pulls away, offers a shrug.

I tap his leg with mine. "What just happened?"

Shaking his head, his eyes forward, he says, "It's nothing."

"You're so full of shit."

Connor chuckles.

I tap his leg harder.

He reaches down under the desk, puts his hand on my knee and squeezes. "Knock it off!"

I ignore the butterflies swarming in my stomach when he shifts his hand higher, his fingers on the inside of my thigh. "Connor," I whisper. "Tell me!"

He moves his hand another inch, and my breath catches. He must notice because he turns to me with a smirk. Biting down on his lip, he quirks an eyebrow. Damn, whatever happened has made him *cocky*. I narrow my eyes, ignoring the repercussions of having my phone out on display, and type his name into the search bar.

Connor's chuckle sends the butterflies *soaring*.

I read the summary of the first site that shows up.

Connor Ledger of St. Luke's Academy, NC, named All-American...

I gasp. Audibly. And turn to Connor, my smile unconfined. I lean into him, whisper in his ear, "Congratulations."

His throat moves with his swallow as he reaches over, takes my phone from me. Under the table, his thumbs fly over the screen. When he's done, he places the phone back down in front of me.

Notes app open.

Cursor blinking.

Five words:

I did it for you.

TREVOR WANTED *me to tell you congratulations for making All-American* Ava writes on a notepad, sliding it on the desk between us during class.

I'd gotten to the room before she did and placed my bag on the seat so no one else would take it. By the time she walked in with another note from Miss Turner, it was the only available spot.

I write:

Tell him I said thanks.

Okay.

Then I take the notepad and set it in front of me, glancing up to make sure the teacher isn't watching. I can't make any mistakes leading up to playoffs.

I write down:

1.

2.

3.

And turn to Ava. She's looking at me, eyebrows drawn, and I can't help but smile. I move in closer to her, our arms touching, and fill in the empty spaces.

1. You've been wearing your hair down lately, and I think it's because you know I like it like that. True or false?

Ava scoffs, circles *false.*

2. You've been coming in late to class after seeing Miss Turner. Is everything okay?

Ava takes the notepad from me and writes on the bottom half of the page:

I'm just going through a lot at the moment, and she's helping me work through it all. In a good way.

I smile when I read her response, claiming the notepad back. And, just to add extra drama to our silent conversation, I turn my back to her, arm shielding her view, and fill in the last number:

3. I, Ava Diaz, forgive one Connor Ledger for being an ass... for being selfish and stupid in saying he couldn't be just friends. Just because he's seen me naked in the past, it doesn't mean that he only ever wants to see me naked every time we're around each other. Because friends don't get naked together. They just don't. Unless, of course, I, Ava Diaz, want to get naked in front of Connor Ledger. Then Connor Ledger is all for it. And I, Ava Diaz, will never, ever, EVER bring up the fact that Connor Ledger got a half-chub during one of Miss Salas's long-winded speeches thinking about me naked. True or False?

I slide the notepad over and watch Ava's eyes move with every line she reads, her smile getting wider, ending on a breathy giggle. She takes the pen from me and crosses out everything after me being an ass, then circles *True*.

Looking up, Ava's already watching me, her face only inches from mine. My eyes explore hers, searching for a semblance of hope. "I want you to look at the person sitting next to you," Miss Salas announces.

Ava and I share a smile.

"Get used to them," she adds.

And Ava's breath warms my flesh when she lets out a silent laugh.

"Because that's going to be the person you work with on your next project."

"Here we go again," Ava whispers.

Miss Salas adds, "And you're going to be spending a lot of time with them."

Smirking, I break eye contact to write down:

Naked?

Under the table, Ava pushes her leg against mine. I clasp her knee, squeeze once. And keep my hand there.

"Who here has heard of podcasts and YouTube?" Miss Salas asks, and the room fills with a mix of groans and giggles.

I shift my hand higher up Ava's thigh and squeeze again. "This is *all* you," I tell her.

"Yes!" she whispers. "Time to get the boobies out."

"WHICH ONES WOULD YOU LIKE?" I ask Mom, sitting at the kitchen table with pictures sprawled out in front of us. She wanted to rearrange the photographs on the wall of her room so she could see them clearer from her bed.

"This one," she says, pointing to one of Trevor and me standing by his car. "And this one." It's another one of us—this one when we were younger, standing out by the pool at our old house, Trevor's dark skin such a contrast against mine. She lifts it up to her nose, inspects it closer. "I took this one."

"You did," I say, trying to hide my excitement. "You remember taking it?"

"Yes."

The front door opens, and Trevor walks in.

"Is that your brother?" she asks.

"Yep."

"Trevor!" she calls out.

"Coming, Mama Jo!" He drops his tools and runs into the kitchen, his expression worried.

"Look!" she says, pointing to the photographs. "I need one of you and Amy."

The smile that overtakes me is instant. So is Trevor's. "I'll send some to Ava for her to print out."

"Good," Mom says, nodding.

I tell him, "Dinner's in the oven. Another ten minutes."

Trevor goes to the fridge for a beer while Mom says, "Wait here." She gets to her feet slowly and goes to her room.

While she's gone, Trevor and I share a look of amazement. "She's doing so well," I whisper.

Trevor nods. "Just don't get your hopes up, okay? She's done this before."

"I know."

"I mean it, Ava."

I press my lips tight, nodding, and wait for Mom to come back in. "Here," Mom says, placing a black velvet box on the kitchen table. She pats Trevor's shoulder. "For you."

"Me?" he asks, eyes wide.

Mom nods as she sits back down.

Trevor opens the box, his brow dipping when he sees what's inside. "Is this the ring Dad got you?" he asks her.

Mom offers another nod. "For Amy."

"I'm not asking her to marry me yet," Trevor says through a chuckle.

"One day," Mom tells him, her lids heavy. She's getting tired, and she'll need a rest soon. "This one," she says to me, pulling another photograph of Trevor and me toward her. "I like this one a lot."

My phone rings somewhere in the living room, and I ask Trevor to grab it for me while I collect the pictures into a pile. "It's Connor," he tells me, walking back into the kitchen.

"Why would he be calling?" I murmur, more to myself than anyone else.

I take my phone from Trevor and answer, "Hello?"

"I got into Duke!"

"*What?*" I squeal, my heart racing, elation rushing through my bloodline.

"What?" Trevor whispers, motioning to the phone

"Connor got into Duke!" I shout, grasping the phone to my ear. "Oh, my God, Connor! You got into Duke!"

"I got into Duke," he repeats, breathy, as if he can't believe it himself.

"Where are you?" I laugh out, unable to contain my exhilaration.

"I'm outside."

"He's outside," I tell Trevor, pleadingly.

"Go!"

I rush out the door, barefoot and bliss filled. Connor's walking down the sidewalk toward my driveway, and I run. I run so fast and so hard and so free, and I crash into his chest, my arms around his neck. "You got into Duke!" I scream, my pride coming out in the form of laughter.

"Holy shit," he mumbles, holding me to him, his arm around my waist while his other hand cups the back of my head. "I can't fucking believe it, Ava."

I release him and land back on my feet. "Well, fucking believe it because it's happening!"

He grasps his hair, looking up at the sky. "This is *insane*."

"No, it's not!" I tell him, tugging on his arm. I lead him back to my porch and sit us down on the steps, my grin splitting my face in two. And it doesn't matter what we are now, or what we were in the past. Dreams are dreams, and no one and nothing should ever take away the beauty of achieving them. I've shed so many tears lately that it feels so much *more* when the tears come from joy. "God, Connor," I cry. "I'm so proud of you."

Connor sits with his elbows on his knees, the letter still grasped in his hand, head down as he tries to settle his breathing.

"Are you okay?" I laugh, wiping the wetness off my cheeks. I know how much this means to him. It's one step closer.

He looks up at me, trying to bite back a smile. "It's happening," he says. "Holy shit, it's actually happening."

"It's just getting started," I tell him, shaking his arm. "You're going to go all the way! I can feel it in here." I press a hand to my chest. "Everything you've worked for... everything you've ever wanted."

He licks his lips, shakes his head. A beat of silence passes as his expression falls. Reaching up, eyes locked on mine, he fingers a strand of my hair. "Not everything, Ava."

My heart strains against the meaning behind his words, and I push back the sudden ache. Because this is *his* moment. His time. And it's bigger than he and I and all the what-ifs we carry. I rear back, plaster on a smile with little effort. "What did your dad say?"

"He doesn't know."

"What?"

He blows out a heavy breath. "I was—I just opened the mailbox and saw the letter and read the first few words and... and you were the first person I thought to call." He swallows, his breaths short. "And I know that's probably bad considering what we are, but—"

I cut in because I don't want this moment to lead to questions about us, "Wait, so you only read the first few words?"

He nods.

I take the letter from him and pretend to read. "Dear Connor Ledger. We are pleased to inform you that you have been selected to join our wait list—"

"Shut up! It does *not* say that!" He grabs the letter from me, his eyes wild as he reads it. "Jesus, Ava." He palms his chest. "You scared the shit out of me."

I giggle, shove his side with mine. "Go tell your dad."

Connor shrugs. "He's sleeping."

"Connor!" I laugh out. "I'm sure he won't care if you wake him."

"I'm scared," he says through a chuckle.

"Of what?"

"I don't know," he admits, rubbing his eye. "I'm nervous to tell him." His gaze moves to mine. "Will you come with me?"

I get to my feet. "Sure."

Taking my hand, I let him set the pace from my driveway to his. He unlocks the door and stands in the middle of the living room. "Dad! Wake up!"

"Connor?" his dad calls out from his bedroom.

"Yeah. And put on some pants! Ava's here!"

I laugh under my breath.

A minute later, Corey appears, his eyes half squinting from having just woken up. He scans Connor's hand linked with mine for only a moment before looking up at Connor. "What's going on?"

Connor seems to stand taller as he gives his dad the letter. "From Duke?" Corey mumbles, then reads it aloud, "Dear Connor Ledger. We are pleased to inform you that..." And that's as far as he gets before his eyes widen, and his entire face lights up as if sleep is ancient. "Oh, Connor!" And then his expression falls, and he covers his face, his shoulders shaking with his cry.

"Aww." I pout up at Connor and rub his arm. "I'm going to go."

"All right."

I lean up, kiss his cheek. "Congratulations."

"Thanks," he says, but he's looking at his dad. I make it to his door before I hear Connor say through a chuckle, "Dad. What's wrong?"

"I'm just so proud of you, son. You earned this. *You* did this."

CONNOR

Dad spends the rest of the evening on the phone to whoever will listen to him go on and on about me getting in to Duke. To say that he's proud is an understatement, and to say that I'm happy to make him feel that way would be the same.

We sit down and have a celebratory feast together, his phone continually buzzing while mine sits stagnant. Besides Ava, I haven't told a soul, and I think I'd like to keep it that way for as long as possible. With playoffs coming up, I want to keep my focus on the team that's helped me get noticed.

Dad's phone sounds, and he answers on the first ring. "He did it!" he almost shouts. "He got into Duke!"..."I know, I'm ecstatic!"..."All on his own!"

I smile at his exuberance, but the fact is, he's wrong. There was no way I could have done any of it without his support or without his final push to do it all for the girl next door.

I pick up my phone.

Connor: Hey, can I come by later?

Ava: Of course! You okay?

Connor: Yeah, I just need to tell you something.

Ava: Should I be scared?

Connor: No, just text me when you're free.

Ava: Ok

It's close to ten by the time Ava messages me.

Ava: I can sit out on my porch now?

Connor: I'll be there in five.

"Hey there, Duke Blue Devil," Ava sings as I walk up her driveway.

"Damn, that sounds good," I laugh out. She's sitting on her porch, a blanket around her, with her hands wrapped around a mug. "Look at you all bundled up."

"It's cold," she says, sliding over a tad so I can sit next to her. She reaches under the bench and reveals another mug, handing it to me. "Hot chocolate?"

I take it from her, blowing at the rising steam. "Thank you."

"Marshmallows?" she asks, digging in under the blanket to get a bag of marshmallows.

Holding the mug out between us, I say through a laugh, "Jesus, what else have you got under there?"

She drops a few marshmallows in and says, "I have one more thing, but it's a surprise."

"Is it a naked surprise?"

"Connor!" she squeals, knocking my side with hers.

The hot chocolate spills over the lip of the mug, burning my hand. "Shit!"

"Sorry!"

I hiss, setting the mug on the floor, and then shake out my hand. I lick the liquid off my fingers and glance up at Ava. Her lust-filled eyes are fixed on my mouth, my hand, her breaths becoming shorter.

Busted.

I smirk. "Can I help you, you creep?"

Ava blinks and comes back to reality... a reality where I'd happily have her lick my entire body. She clears her throat. "Turn around."

"What?"

"Turn. Around."

I shake my head. "No."

"What do you think I'm going to do?"

"I don't know. Pour scalding hot liquid all over me."

She rolls her eyes, then says, "Fine."

Her back to me, she reaches into the blanket again, and I watch her pull out a balloon—this one blue. Her shoulders rise with her inhale, and then she blows into the balloon, making it expand. It takes her a few seconds to knot the end. When she's done, she turns to me, holding the balloon between us. I take it from her and read the black marker.

Connor Ledger

#1 Boo Devil

"I love it," I tell her honestly, my smile stupid. "It's the greatest gift I've ever gotten."

She giggles, takes a sip of her hot chocolate. "Better than that sweet truck sitting in your driveway?"

"So much better," I laugh out, swapping the balloon for my own hot chocolate. I take a tiny sip.

Her front door opens, and Trevor comes out, looking down at his phone. When he lifts his gaze, he says, "Hey, bro. Congrats."

"Thanks, man. Appreciate it." We do the standard—*weird*—universal jock handshake.

He says, "Hey, did you know that according to—"

"Stop," Ava warns.

His eyes narrow at her. "I'm talking to Connor." He switches his focus to me. "Did you know that according to Huffington Post and The Daily Beast, Texas A&M is the *happiest* campus in the nation? The entire nation, *Connor*."

I don't know what his angle is, but my mind's pretty set on Duke. "I did *not* know that," I respond.

"Huh." Trevor nods, then shrugs. "Just thought I'd mention it."

He goes back into the house without another word, and I turn to Ava. "What was that about?"

She's rolling her eyes, her head moving from side to side. "He's trying to get me to go to Texas A&M." She fist pumps the air. "Gig 'em, Aggies!"

"Wait, did you get accepted?"

Nodding, she says, "I got early acceptance to a few places."

"What?! You didn't tell me that."

"It happened, you know, when we weren't really on speaking terms. It caused *a lot* of drama."

"Yeah? How so?"

She sighs, just as a gust of wind blows by, forcing her wild hair to bounce all over the place. She tries to control it, but another gust comes, and her brow dips, frustration forming on her lips.

I set the mug next to me on the bench and take off my hoodie. Then I stand in front of her, order, "Arms up." With a giggle, she does as I ask, and I slip it over her head, making sure her hair is restrained under the hood. I sit back down, glance at her just in time to see her sniffing the fabric. "Why are you so obsessed with me?"

"It smells nice," she says through a laugh. "Like post-shower jock and teen spirit."

"How many jocks have you sniffed?"

"Oh, God," she moans. "Like, *so* many."

"Huh."

Her rumble of a giggle forms deep in her throat.

I tap her blanket-covered leg with the back of my hand. "So, you got early acceptance to a few places...?" I ask, bringing us back.

Nodding, she says, "I kind of hid the letters from Trevor."

"Why?"

"Because," she sighs out, staring ahead. "I didn't want him pressuring me to go. And he did exactly that, and my mom got involved and said some really harsh things. I ran out of the house, and a few hours later you found me sitting outside my old house." She tilts her head to face me, wearing a sad smile.

"I'm sorry that happened."

"It's okay. We're dealing with it all now."

"So, you got a *few* early acceptances?"

"Uh huh," she says as if it's no big deal.

"Where to?" *Please say Duke. Please say Duke. Please say Duke.*

She inhales deeply. "Just Texas A&M, University of Florida, and UNC."

"That's kind of massive, Ava. Like, even if you don't go, that's..."

"Huge," she finishes for me. "And it's not as if I'm not proud of myself, because I am. I know how hard I worked for it. It's just that I'm not ready yet. I have a lot of things to figure out before any of that."

I try to put myself in her shoes. Everything's so simple for me. I have one goal, and there's nothing really stopping me from achieving it besides myself. There are so many factors outside of her control and the fact that she manages to—

"You like the hot chocolate?" she asks, breaking through my thoughts.

I take another tiny sip. "Yeah, it's real nice," I say, my shoulders tense as I rub my arm, trying to ease the chill of the cold night air.

Ava scoots closer, her hands holding the blanket open for me. I squeeze in, gather the ends of the blanket and wrap them around both of us, shielding us from the rest of the world. I use her body heat to keep me warm. She says, "You shouldn't have given me your hoodie, *stupid.*"

"So, give it back."

"Never," she whisper-yells.

I don't mind it, though, because she's in sleep shorts, her bare legs emitting the most heat. I grasp her calves and pull them over my lap. She wriggles around until she's comfortable, taking my free arm and holding it to her. With her head resting on my bicep, she says, "I miss these moments with you. When the world's quiet and we can just *be*... and it doesn't matter what we are. We're just two people who like to be around each other, you know?"

"Yeah," I agree.

"We don't need labels, Connor. Friends or not, you're always going to be the boy who went out of his way to show me that magic is real and that it exists and..." She pauses a beat, her exhale warming my chest. "You'll always be irreplaceable to me."

I let each of her words sink in, inhaling them through my bloodline. "And you'll always be my first."

Her head tilts to look up at me. "But we never..."

"You'll always be my first *love*, Ava. Everything else is insignificant."

She draws in a long, staggered breath, her eyes on mine. Moments pass and unspoken words have never been so loud, so clear. "Connor," she whispers.

"I know," I respond. And I *do* know. I know that the mistakes we've made are in the past and that our love is bigger than that. But our love isn't bigger than *life*. And that life... that life is *too hard* for her right now, and I have to understand that. To accept it. I break our stare and take another sip of the hot chocolate.

"Hey," she says. "Didn't you want to tell me something?"

Right.

I wanted to tell her that she was my end game. That everything I'd done to get myself here was for her. Her and her mom. But I look at her now, and I see the clarity in her eyes. See the way she loves me without being *in love* with me, and even though it causes my heart to ache in ways I never thought possible, I don't want to lose it. Or ruin it. I don't want to let her go. "It was just about that multimedia project. I assume we're going to go with some morbid murder?"

"Is there anything more fascinating?" she mumbles, settling her head on my arm again.

The front door opens, and Ava *growls*. "What now?"

I chuckle.

Trevor pokes his head out. "Two words. *Texas. Barbecue.*"

"Get lost," she laughs out.

Trevor closes the door.

"Texas barbecue *is* pretty dope," I murmur.

"I know, right? It's the first point on my pros and cons list."

"You have a list?"

"Yep."

"What else is on the list?"

"Peter Parker will be there for the next four years earning his master's."

My stomach twists. "Is that a pro or con?"

A heavy sigh. "I haven't decided." Then she sits up, narrows her gaze on the mug I'm holding. "You sure are taking your time with that."

I grimace. "I have a confession."

"What's that?"

"I hate chocolate."

THIRTEEN

ava

> Connor: Thank you. I think I missed your balloons the most.

> Ava: lol. Trevor just saw the message and he thought you were talking about my tits. He wants to kill you now.

> Connor: Oh, yay! Can't wait to see him again.

> Ava: You're welcome about the balloon. Have a good game. :)

> Connor: I will.

> Ava: I mean BOOO! YOU SUCK!

> Connor: lol

"HEY, TREVOR?" I call out, getting Mom settled on the couch with a blanket and a trashy magazine.

He walks out of his room with the phone to his ear.

"Is that Amy?" I ask.

He nods.

"Tell her I said hi."

"And me," Mom tells him.

He says into the phone, "Mama Jo and Ava say hi." He's silent a moment. "She says hi back." Then to me: "What's up?"

I point to the new TV Trevor bought us with the Christmas bonus he earned from his work with the Prestons. "Does that have that AirPlay thingy?"

"I think so, why?"

"Because they're streaming Connor's game tonight and I wanted to see if we could watch it on a bigger screen than my laptop."

Trevor thinks a moment. "When does the game start?"

I check the time. "Like, five minutes?"

He tells Amy, "Let me call you back."

It takes him three minutes to set up the TV so it streams from my laptop, and I get comfortable on the couch next to Mom. "Just tell me if you need anything, okay, Mama? I can stop watching whenever. It's not a big deal."

With a nod, she says, "Okay, Ava. I pwa... pwa—" Her face scrunches with frustration.

"It's okay; take your time," I encourage.

"Pwamise."

"Nice job!" I say, my hand raised for a high five. She's holding a mug of tea in her hand, and so she offers me an eye-roll along with her stump. I high-five it anyway.

I watch the game on the edge of my seat, my eyes glued to the screen. From what I've gathered, the team they're playing is solid third on the leaderboard or ladder or whatever it's called. St. Luke's and Philips Academy continuously vie for first place. The scores are close, but St. Luke's is always a few points ahead. Still, it makes for a decent game. I check on Mom every few minutes, but she seems happy to be reading her magazine. Trevor sits on the other couch, his thumbs continuously tapping on his phone. Five minutes left before the final buzzer, St. Luke's scores twelve points within two minutes and moves even further ahead. Connor scores ten of those points, and then, with three minutes left, something in him switches. He seems to push himself harder, faster, and he puts on a show, amping up the crowd with him. I bite back a smile when I watch him gorilla pound his chest after an insane dunk, his "whooo" heard over the cheers. He's hyped as hell and damn, do I love watching him.

"Jesus, Ava," Trevor says through a chuckle. "Wipe the drool off your chin."

"Shut up."

When the game's over, I think twice about sending him a text. The last time... well, it didn't go so well. Sure, it's different circumstances, but the memories and the fear are still there. I decide to leave it for tonight, and hopefully, I can catch up with him tomorrow.

With the laptop on the coffee table, I sit on the floor in front of it and switch from the stream to my math homework. I'm just getting into it when Mom says from behind me, "Connor, six-five, but is hoping for a growth spurt."

Eyebrows drawn, I turn to her. Then I look out through the closed window, thinking maybe she meant that Connor's here. But he can't be. He'd still be in the locker room. "What about him?" I ask, but she's back to reading her magazine.

A half hour passes, and she says it again: "Connor, six-five, but is hoping for a growth spurt."

Again, I turn to her, confused. "Did you... did you see him on the TV?"

Mom nods, puts down the magazine and stands up. "Tell him to come here."

"What?" I ask, eyes wide. Surely, she didn't say what I think she said.

"Tell him to come here."

"When?"

"Now."

I look at Trevor. He simply shrugs. A lot of help he is.

"Why do you want to see him?" I ask, mystified.

Mom sighs. "Ava. Connor, six-five, here. Now."

I stand, my mouth agape. I try to form a sentence, but nothing comes.

Mom moves to the kitchen. "Now, Ava."

Following after her, I say, "Mama, you know that Connor and I aren't... we're not... he wouldn't be expecting to come here. He's probably out cele-brating with the team."

Mom finishes filling her water bottle from the tap and turns to me. "Ask him."

Ask him... as if it's that simple.

It *is* that simple.

"Okay," I tell her. "I'll ask."

I grab my phone from the coffee table and go to my room. I don't know why I'm so nervous. It's not like he hasn't met her before... but things have changed and *ugh*.

I dial his number, bring the phone to my ear. It rings and rings and rings, and just when I'm about to hang up, he answers, his voice distant. "Shut up, it's Ava! Hello?"

"Hey."

"Hey, what's up?"

In the background, I can hear a couple other boys talking, but he doesn't seem like he's in the locker room. It sounds like he's in his truck. "Are you busy?"

"Ava!" I recognize the voice as Mitch's, and I'm instantly repulsed. "If this is a booty call, just say so."

"Shut the fuck up!" Connor snaps. To me, he says, "I'm just driving a few of the guys to the diner. We're grabbing something to eat. Can I call you after?"

"Um." *After* could be hours from now, and Mom will be too tired. "No, it's okay. I'll speak to you tomorrow."

"No, I'm just parking now. I'll kick the guys out and call you back. One minute, okay?"

"It's fine, Connor. Do your thing."

"I'll call you back."

He hangs up, and I slump down on the edge of the bed, nerves flying through my veins. Less than a minute later, my phone rings.

"Hey," I answer. "Sorry, I didn't mean to—"

"Ava, it's fine. What's going on?"

"Nothing. It's stupid... I'll just tell her you're busy."

"Tell who?"

I swallow, anxious.

"Your mom?" he asks.

"Yeah..."

"Does she... is she okay?"

"Yeah, she's fine. It's just..." I pick at the fluff on my sleep shorts. "She wants you to come over."

Silence.

Followed by more silence.

Finally, he asks, "Really?"

"Yeah," I say through a sigh. "I don't know why, and Mom won't tell me. She just kept saying for you to come over. And, look, you're busy, and I'll tell her so."

His heavy breath causes static through the speakers. "I kind of told the guys I'd—"

"I know," I cut in. "And I don't want you to change your plans. It's *fine*, Connor. Honestly."

"But I *want* to," he says. "Shit. I told Oscar I'd give him a ride home."

"Connor," I laugh out. "It's *okay*. You can't be dropping your life because my mom randomly wants to see you."

"Let me just eat, and I'll ask one of the other guys to take Oscar home. I can be there in half an hour."

"No, it's—"

"Ava!" He almost shouts. "I'm not doing anything I don't *want* to. I *want* to see your mom, and you, too, I suppose, depending on what you're wearing."

"You're a dick."

"I know. I'll see you soon, all right?"

"Okay. And Connor?"

"Yeah?"

"Thank you."

Twenty-six minutes later and Connor's text comes through that he's walking up the driveway. I open the door, anxious and apprehensive, and so I hide those feelings by sniffing him as he enters. "Mmm. Post-shower jock."

He unzips his team jacket and hands it to me, smirking. "Add it to your collection, creep."

I happily take it off his hands and throw it into my bedroom as we pass. It lands on my bed, and I contain my smile as I walk us to the living room. Mom's sitting on the couch, and Connor flops down next to her, his arm resting behind her. "I heard you wanted to see me, Miss Diaz?" he says quietly.

Trevor watches from the doorway between the living room and kitchen, and I sit on the other couch, my heart racing. *People fear what they don't know*, and I have no idea what's about to happen. Connor though—he looks calm. Almost too calm. Maybe it's the post-win adrenaline or the fact that she asked him here. Who the hell knows?

"Connor, six-five, but is hoping for a growth spurt," Mom mumbles, lifting her gaze to him.

Connor's perfect teeth show when he smiles at her.

I say, "It's how she remembers things. Like, recollection words..."

Connor nods. "I know." His eyes soften. "I got this, Ava. Relax."

Mom stands, starts pacing, and Connor keeps his eyes on her. "Connor, six-five, but is hoping for a growth spurt," she repeats.

"Did you have something you wanted to say to Connor, Mama Jo?" Trevor encourages.

Mom nods, taps at her temple. "In here," she says, and she won't stop pacing. "Connor, six-five, but is hoping for a growth spurt."

Connor's gaze flicks to me, and I mouth, "Sorry."

He shakes his head, mouths back, "Shut up."

I glare at him, but he's too busy watching my mother. "Connor, six-five, but is hoping for a growth spurt," she says again. Suddenly, she stops, her eyes wide. Her gaze snaps to Connor. "Weak jump shot."

Trevor busts out a cackle, and I gasp, "Mama!"

Connor's eyes are wide, but his mouth is wider. And then he smiles, the biggest smile I've ever seen on him. Shaking his head, his shoulders bouncing, he asks her, "You think I have a weak jump shot?"

Mom nods. "*Weak*."

"Mama," I admonish.

"No, Ava, it's fine," Connor assures. "How is it weak?" he asks her, that smile still in place.

Trevor—he's lost it. His hands are on his stomach, his eyes watering from laughing so hard.

Mom tells him, "Posture."

Connor gets to his feet, *all six-five, but is hoping for a growth spurt* of him. "Posture?"

"Yes, posture."

"Posture?" Connor repeats.

Mom shakes her head, looks up at him. "Are you deaf? I said it twice."

Connor busts out a laugh, then looks over at me. "Damn, now I know where *you* get it from."

"Jump shot weak," Mom says. "Posture wrong."

Connor rolls his shoulders back, his spine straightening. "All right, Miss D. Show me what I'm doing wrong."

Mom nods. "Okay."

Connor stands in the middle of my living room, adjusting his limbs to mimic what I assume is his jump shot. Legs apart, ass out, arms raised. "What's wrong with this?" he asks her.

She walks around him, her pointer finger tapping her chin as she assesses him.

"This is gold," Trevor says, phone raised in front of him as he takes a picture. And then five more.

I'd be embarrassed... if it wasn't so endearing. I mean, the boy of my dreams, an All-American who just got in to what might possibly be the best basketball college in the nation is standing in my living room allowing my mother to give him tips on his jump shot. *Sigh.* It's kind of adorable.

Mom uses her foot to distance the space between Connor's feet. "Better," she says and starts walking circles around him again. She stops at his right arm—his shooting arm—and adjusts his elbow, then lifts her amputated limb. "Ugh," she huffs. "Sometimes I forget it's gone."

Connor smiles down at her.

"Ava!" she shouts.

I stand. "Yes, Mama?"

"Hold his arm." She taps his bicep. "Right here."

I stand in front of him, grasp his arm where Mom said, and roll my eyes when he flexes his muscles. He smirks down at me, and dammit, I can't help my body's reaction to him—to being this close to him. I remember the way he felt when his entire body was covering mine, skin on skin. The way every muscle shifted when he moved down, down, down, until his shoulders rested beneath my thighs, the way his neck—"Ava," Connor whispers. "You're blushing."

I choke on air and come back to reality. "Shut up."

Mom angles Connor's forearm closer to his head. "Like that."

"Like this?" Connor asks, then mimics taking his shot. "Huh." He stands to full height again, dropping his arms to his sides. "I'll have to try it."

"Yes." Mom nods. "Try it, and when it works, credit me."

Connor laughs. "Absolutely, Miss D."

Mom pats his arm. "Connor, six-five, but is hoping for a growth spurt. I'm going to sleep. Goodnight."

"Goodnight, Miss Diaz."

I ask her, "Do you need me to—"

"No," Mom interrupts. "You stay. Help him with his weak jump shot." She goes into her room and closes the door behind her.

Trevor says, "That's the most entertained I've been in years." Then, following Mom's lead, he goes to his room and closes the door behind him, leaving just me and Connor and, apparently, his weak jump shot.

"I'm so sorry," I say, my voice low. "I had no idea that's why she wanted to see you."

He shrugs. "I don't mind. Honestly, it was fun. She seems like she's doing a lot better."

"She is. We just worry about how long it'll last, you know?"

Nodding, he looks around the room. "Well, I'm here now..."

"You are." I try to hide my nerves. "Do you want to—"

"Yes," he cuts in.

I laugh. "You don't even know what I was going to say."

"Whatever it is, *yes*."

I switch on the TV and motion to the couch. "Do you want a drink?"

He sits down, his eyes on mine. "Sure."

"Water?"

"Thanks."

I head to the kitchen, and when I glance back at him, he hasn't taken his eyes off of me. I return with his water. "I'll be back," I tell him, going to my room to throw on a sweatshirt. I notice his team jacket on my bed, and figure, *fuck it*. I slip it on. Sniff it. *Yum*. When I re-enter the living room, he has the glass to his lips, his entire body frozen except for his eyes. His eyes follow me all the way until I'm sitting next to him, my legs bent beneath me. He tilts the glass, downs the entire thing in two gulps. Then he leans back, throws his arm behind me on the couch. "You know that jacket's got my name on the back."

"It does?"

He nods. "Kind of makes you mine now."

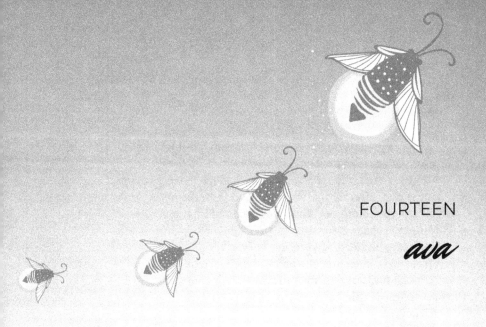

FOURTEEN

ava

I WOKE up this morning in bed, covers up to my chin, with Connor's jacket still on. Which wouldn't be so bad if it weren't for the fact that the last thing I remember was sitting on the couch with Connor's arms around me, my head on his chest, while his hand consistently found a new strand of hair to twirl between his fingers. I remember looking up at him to see him already watching me, and just like that silent moment we shared on my porch, a million unspoken words flitted between us, and the one thought that stood out the most was: *I am in trouble. Deep, soul-shattering, trouble.*

I don't remember falling asleep, and I sure as hell don't remember waking up to go to my room. When my alarm went off, I rushed out to the living room, thinking he might be there, but he wasn't. The TV was off, the blanket was folded up on the couch, and his empty glass of water was washed and put away... and I haven't heard from him since.

The only thing I know for sure is that going by what happened last night, it seems the doctors have finally found the right balance of medication for my mom that helps her get through the night while being able to maintain decent human functionality during the day. I'm so grateful for that because it means I get a little bit of my mother back.

"We're off," I tell her, kissing her on the cheek.

She looks up from the customized crossword puzzle she's working on. "Have a good day, sweetheart."

"I can't wait for you to get your license," Trevor says, slipping on his shoes by the front door.

"I can't wait for you to start teaching me," I retort.

"That's a hard pass." He grabs his keys. "I don't have the patience for your stubborn ass."

Mom laughs.

"Mama!" I whine. "Don't take his side."

"He has a point though," Mom says through a giggle. "And your brother is the most patient man I know."

"Thanks, Mama Jo," Trevor says, standing taller. "See you tonight." He closes the door after us and then just stands on the porch, his gaze distant. "I don't think your mom's ever called me your brother before," he murmurs.

"Sure, she has."

He shakes his head. "Not in front of me."

I stop at the bottom of the porch steps and look up at him. "Is that bad?"

"No," he says, his eyes meeting mine. "It's cool, I guess. Makes me feel like I'm part of the family."

"Of course, you are."

He shrugs. "No, it always felt like you and her, and I was... I don't know."

I shrug. "*I* tell people you're my brother."

"Yeah, but that's different," he says, making his way down to me.

"How?"

"Because that's the way it's always been." His gaze shifts past me. "Hey, it's Connor." He whistles, short and sharp. "Can you give my sister a ride?"

"No!" I whisper-yell, punching his shoulder.

He fakes hurt. "What?"

I keep my voice low. "I'm not..."

"You're not what?"

"Not..." *Ready to deal with my emotions just yet.*

"You coming?" Connor shouts.

"Yeah!" Trevor answers for me, then runs to his truck and slams the door shut, locking himself in from the inside.

I internally groan, walk down my driveway, and meet Connor on the sidewalk. "Sorry. I guess his lazy ass didn't want to go out of his way."

Connor opens my door for me. "I don't mind."

"You sure?" I ask, and because I'm a brat, I add, "The last time I asked for a ride, it didn't end well."

He heaves out a sigh. "God, you're a smartass."

After helping me get in his truck, I tell him, "You were kind of mean to me that day."

He shuts the door and makes his way to his side. Then he reaches into the back seat, reveals a can of deodorant, and sprays me with it. "Get over it."

"Connor!" I wind down his window.

He sprays me again.

"Stop!" I laugh out.

"Are you done sulking?"

"I didn't sulk. You did! Boo hoo. I can't be friends with you because—"

"Because being around you drove me crazy in all the best possible ways, and it still does, but the difference between you and me? I quit sulking about it. Are you *done?*"

I growl at him.

He rolls his eyes, sprays me one more time, then throws the deodorant somewhere behind him. He offers me his pinky. "Truce?"

I link my finger with his. "Truce."

Once we get to school, we walk together to Miss Turner's office before he goes off to practice. "I'll see you in multimedia?" he asks.

Grinning, I nod before entering her office. "Ava," Miss Turner greets, smiling like the Cheshire Cat. "I've been looking forward to this meeting. I have some news..."

CONNOR

Multimedia class has us working in different groups, and so I don't get to speak to Ava as much as I want to. Or *need* to, really.

I'm a goner.

For real.

And I'm not even mad about it.

As soon as the end-of-period bell sounds, I rush to her side and wait until we're out of the room to ask, "Did you want to have lunch together today?"

She leans against the wall just outside the door, her eyes lifting to mine. "I can't." I try to hide my disappointment, but she sees it anyway. Her hand goes to my chest and then drops quickly... as if habit put it there and self-doubt forced it away. She adds, looking down at the floor, "I have a makeup test that I need to take, and I don't know how long it will go for. I don't want you waiting on me."

I shrug. "I'd wait."

"Hey, Connor," says a girl walking past.

"What's up?" I respond without taking my eyes off Ava.

Ava's lips tick at the corners. "Fan of yours?"

I shake my head, offer another shrug. "I have no idea who that was."

"Right." She tugs on my sleeve. "If you're free after school, I could use a ride home."

"Can't. I have back-to-back practice."

"Sucks."

"But after that, I can come to your house if you want."

"We'll see."

My brows knit. "What does that mean?"

It's her turn to shrug. Kicking off the wall, she moves an inch closer. "What happened last night?"

I bite back a smile. "What do you mean?"

"I don't know... one minute I was sitting on the couch with you, and the next I was tucked into bed all cozy and warm."

"And?"

"Did you carry me to my bed?"

I nod.

"That's a little embarrassing."

"Nah," I assure. "You were kind of adorable. Though you did drool all over my weenus again."

A gasp sounds from the open door of the classroom, and Miss Salas is there, her eyes wide. "I would watch what you talk about at school, young man!"

Ava's giggle dies in her throat.

"I think you may have misheard me, Miss Salas," I say.

The teacher's brow drops in fury. "Shouldn't you two be in class?"

"Oh shit," Ava laughs, looking around us.

I do the same.

The corridors are empty.

Ava taps my shoulder. "See you later, *stud*."

I watch Ava walk away for longer than I should, then glance over at Miss Salas still standing in the doorway, her arms crossed. I give her that panty-melting smile Ava used to talk about. "Any chance of getting a late pass?"

* * *

I pick at the food on my lunch tray, wondering how shitty of a person I would be if I offered to *pay* Ava to start bringing my lunches to school. It sounds like a foolproof plan, but it wouldn't work for two reasons. One: I'd almost be forcing her to talk to me, and two: I have no money.

"There's, like, almost 4 billion women in the world, and let's assume 3 billion of those are over eighteen," Mitch says, and I don't know where he's going with this, but I already want out of the conversation. "That's like, 6 billion *legal* boobs."

"Jesus," I mumble, dropping my fork and pushing away my tray.

Next to me, Karen murmurs, more to herself than anyone else, "Why do I sit here?"

"Because you can't resist me," Mitch says, blowing her a kiss.

Karen rolls her eyes at the same time her phone vibrates on the table. "Thank God," she whispers, answering the call. "Hey, Ava."

"What? It's Ava?" That was me, *not* being subtle. I try to listen in on the phone call, but Karen shoves my face away, then holds the phone to her other ear. "Yeah, of course."

My eyebrows kick up.

"I'll be there soon."

She stands, her chair scraping behind her. "Later, fuckwads."

"Wait!" I stand, too. "Is Ava okay?"

"Girlgency. Mind your own business!"

AVA

"Hey, girl!" Karen calls out, climbing the bleacher steps, just like Connor used to do. I sit taller when I hear her and put my phone away, ignoring Connor's message asking if I'm okay.

I'm not okay.

And he can't be the person to help me through it.

I say, "Sorry to call you. I hope you weren't busy."

Rolling her eyes, she sits down next to me. "I was just about to punch Mitch in the face for the third time today, so no, not busy at all, and never too busy for you. What's going on?"

"It's stupid," I admit, regret filling me. I had a moment of panic and thought it would be a good idea to reach out to someone who might actually be able to help me. But now that she's here, I can't form the words.

"Ava," she deadpans. "Spill it."

"It's a... boy thing," I tell her because apparently, I'm twelve.

Karen smiles, and I realize how badly I miss these moments with her. "A *Connor* thing?"

I nod.

"So? Tell me."

"I... I'm scared."

She settles in next to me, her legs kicked out, her arms outstretched behind her. "Of what, exactly?"

"Of history repeating, I guess."

"Well, I don't really know what happened with you guys last time, so..."

"Things just got too hard," I admit. "With my mom and his basketball, it just seemed to take up all our time, and when we were together, it was... I don't know. Bad? Not bad as in we didn't want to be there, but we were under so much stress and..." I puff out a breath. "I'm talking in circles, and this is pointless." I stand, unable to sit still any longer.

"It's not pointless. But just... get it out, A. Whatever you're thinking, just say it."

I look at her, at the genuine concern in her eyes, and so I do as she says and just... *let go*. "The first time we fell in love, it was... *magic*, you know? Like we were two people who just happened to be at the right place at the right time, and there was this undeniable attraction..." I start pacing, my heart beating wildly in my chest. "And we just seemed so connected in so many ways, and then life... life happened, and it tore us apart, and that's okay." I nod to myself, my throat aching with my swallow. "I've come to terms with the fact that it had to happen, but now..."

"Now what?" she asks, her voice low as she watches me.

"Now, it's different."

"How?"

I slump back down next to her. "Now, it's like those feelings have amplified. We're so close to being back there, but I'm afraid because... because things are so much *more* now. They *mean* so much more. I mean, every time he looks at me, I feel this"—I bring my hand to my heart—"this ache in here, like... like something is missing and Connor's it, and last night..."

"What happened last night?" she encourages.

"Last night, he came over and he and my mom—they had this moment together that just killed me in all the best ways."

"So, what's the problem?" she laughs out.

"I—" I take a calming breath, drop my head in my hands. "I want it so bad," I say, trying to collect my emotions. "But I want it forever. And I don't think that's possible. Not under my circumstances. Not even under his."

Karen nods as if taking everything in. She stares out at the field for seconds that feel like hours. Then she blinks, slowly, her gaze moving to mine. "You want to know what I think?"

"Please," I breathe out.

"I think maybe the first time, you fell in love with the *idea* of him, you know?"

I nod.

"And now... now you're in love with *him*."

My breath catches while I let her words sink in. "Yeah," I whisper. "You're right. I am. I'm *so* in love with him, Karen."

She smiles, but it's almost sad. "I love that you're in love, Ava. You deserve it." She links her arm with mine, nudging me gently. "And as far as this fear of forever that you have? Forever's never guaranteed. You know that more than anyone. So, I guess you should ask yourself if forever ended tomorrow, would you rather go out holding on to regret or holding on to Connor."

"Connor," I whisper, facing her. "Thank you."

"You're welcome." She kisses my cheek, then giggles. "I guess I should probably stop hitting on him now."

"I mean, yeah," I laugh. "I'd appreciate it."

connor

"IF YOU PLAN to go pro, you have to get used to this shit," Rhys says after hearing me complain about the open practice we're about to have. It's not that I mind doing stuff like this, and I know how important it is... school spirit and all that, but I'd prefer to be using my practice time doing things that better my skill, especially since playoffs start this week. It just seems like a waste of time. I may as well go home and sit on my porch for the slight chance of seeing Ava. It's been days since I've had any real time with her, and it's getting under my skin. We text every now and then, but it's not the same.

"Let's go, gentlemen," Coach yells.

We file out of the locker room and onto the court, one by one, surrounded by the loud support of our peers. "Just get it done," Rhys says, smacking the back of my head. We start as we always do, with warm-ups, and it's not until I'm halfway through them that I see her. Sitting next to Karen in the front row, Ava's biting back a smile as she watches me. There's a balloon in her hand, bright orange, and she lifts her hand in a wave. I make my way over to her, ignoring everything else. Squatting down to her level, I say, because it's the only thing my brain can come up with, "Hi."

"Hi," she replies through a breathy giggle.

"What are you doing here?"

"Baking." *Smart ass.*

"I mean, how did you manage to—"

"Ledger!" Coach calls.

"One second!" I shout back.

Coach yells, "Now, boy!"

Ava laughs, her head dipping. "Ooh, you're in trouble." Then she pushes on my shoulders hard enough that I have to catch myself on an outstretched arm. "Go! Do your thing, number three!"

I flex, I admit it. But there's something about Ava's presence that makes me want to push myself harder than I usually do. Besides, it's not often she gets to see me in action in real life, and so of course, I give her a show.

I have to.

As soon as the practice is over, I race over to Ava, making sure I catch her before she leaves.

"Hi," I say again.

Shaking her head, she smiles up at me. "Watching you on the court is like watching paint dry. I've never been so bored in my life."

"Sorry," I laugh out. "I'll try harder next time."

She clucks her tongue. "I don't think there's going to be a next time, number three. You were *that* bad."

Karen stands to the side of us, watching our back and forth with a dip in her brow. "So, this is what being in love looks like?"

"Karen!" Ava whisper-yells, her eyes wide and focused on her old best friend.

Busted.

"What?" Karen shrugs. "As if you both don't know."

Ava takes a breath, eyes on me again. "Karen's giving me a ride home. It's just as quick as if I were to take the bus."

"Or me!" I rush out—too loud, too enthusiastic—and point a thumb to myself. "I could give you a ride home."

"I know," she says. "It's just, by the time you shower and—"

"No shower," I cut in. "Let me just grab my things."

"Are you sure?"

Karen speaks up. "He's sure, Ava." Then to me: "We'll meet you outside."

I nod at the same time Ava orders, "Give me your jersey."

I raise my eyebrows at her.

She shrugs. "For my collection."

Without a thought, I reach behind me, pull my jersey off of my back and hand it to her.

Karen lets out a low whistle while Ava stares at my bare chest. Then she brings the jersey to her nose, inhales deeply. "Mmm. Pre-shower jock might be my favorite."

"You're so weird," Karen laughs out, throwing her arm around Ava's neck. "Go get your shit, Ledger," she says, spinning Ava around. They make it to the exit before I realize I'm staring at Ava... and Ava—she's staring back, her neck craned to look at me, her bottom lip caught between her teeth.

I rush to grab my things and put on a sweatshirt. Then I go to the parking lot, where Ava and Karen are standing by my truck. Ava's wearing my jersey, school skirt and knee-highs, and I don't think I've ever gotten a hard-on so fast. She's holding Karen's pom-poms to her chest, and when she sees me, she grins full force. "Ready? Okay!" she yells, the standard cheerleader call. She moves the pom-poms around, her arms and legs kicking out, and I picture every guy in the parking lot watching her and let my growl die in my throat. I close in, seeing her smile fade the closer I get. Her head tilts back to look up at me when I stop in front of her. I take the pom-poms from her, hand them back to Karen. "You don't need these."

Ava giggles. "You don't like cheerleaders?"

Shaking my head, I lead her with a hand on her hip to the passenger's side of my truck and open the door. "I like you as my own personal one, sure," I murmur, helping her step up and settle into her seat.

She eyes me a moment. "That's a little possessive, no?"

I shrug. "Say it again without wearing my name on your back."

"It's just a jersey," she whispers, her gaze locked on my lips.

"If that's the story you're going with."

We're halfway home by the time either of us says anything, the tension in the cab keeping us quiet. I say, "How was your day?" at the same time Ava says, "I know it's not just a jersey." I clamp my lips together, hoping she'll continue, and she does. "I know that it signifies a lot more than that, and I *like* that it does. The thing is, I have some stuff that I need to sort out right now, just a couple of personal hurdles... and I know it's not fair to ask you to wait for me, but I was wondering if maybe when I do have everything worked out if maybe you'd want to try again... with me?"

I glance over at her, my smile unrestrained. "Yes."

"Yeah?"

"A huge fuck yes, Ava, yes," I laugh out, unable to hide my excitement. This is everything I wanted. Everything I needed. "And I don't care how long it takes you to be ready. I'm *so* here for it."

She removes her seatbelt, just long enough to slide in next to me on the bench seat. She kisses my jaw. "Thank you," she says, as if I'm going out of my way to one day be with her. The girl's delusional, and I kind of love that she is.

I pull up outside our houses and cut the engine, but I don't make a move to get out. Instead, I lean against the car door and face her. She's already watching me, a hint of a smile playing on her lips. "So," she says.

"So?"

"Thanks for the ride."

"Anytime."

"And for the jersey," she says, tugging on the fabric.

"Sure."

"Okay," she says through a giggle, sliding across and opening the door.

"Hey," I rush out and then stop because I didn't really have anything to say. I'm just not ready to be apart yet. "You think maybe we can work on that multimedia assignment?"

"Tonight?"

"Or now...?"

She glances over at her house and then back at me. "I don't really know what state my mom will be in."

"Of course, yeah," I reply, nodding as I stare past her, trying to hide my disappointment.

"If you give me a few minutes, I can find out and see..."

"Yeah?"

"Uh huh." She can't seem to stop smiling, and I can't either. And neither of us can take our eyes off each other.

If the world ended and I died right now, I'd be pretty damn happy. I'd be an eighteen-year-old virgin, sure, but still... I'd be *happy*.

I wait out by my truck while Ava goes into her house. She opens the door a few minutes later and waves me in. Exhilaration knocking on my flesh from the inside, I grab my bag from the car and make my way in. "You must be Connor, six-five, weak jump shot," a woman, I assume is Krystal, says in greeting.

"Damn, what's with the women in this house?" I retort.

Krystal laughs, squeezes Ava's forearm as she passes. "Have a good night, sweetheart."

Once Krystal's gone, Ava turns to me. "Mom's having a zero-day, so..."

Ava had explained the rating system of her mom's temperament and emotions to me before. A zero-day means *nothing*. The way Ava explained it, it's as though her mother is a shell, and inside, she is empty. Which sucks, but it's far better than a negative day.

"She's in the kitchen working on her speech words, so is it okay if we sit with her there? Just so I can—"

"Of course," I cut in. I follow Ava into her kitchen, where her mom sits at the table with a bunch of flashcards in front of her. She picks up one. "Cat," she says, looking at the picture.

Ava offers me a sad smile. "Did you want a drink?"

"Sure, thanks." I drop my bag on the floor and take a seat opposite her mom. "Hey, Miss D," I say quietly.

Miss Diaz looks up, then right back down, picks up another card. "Dog." She moves it to the top of a pile on her right at the same time Ava places a plastic cup of water in front of me.

"Thanks," I say.

Miss Diaz picks up another card, and I notice now they're all pictures of animals. "Tuttle," she says.

Ava sits next to me. "Turtle," she corrects.

"Turtle," Miss Diaz states. This card goes to a pile on her left, thicker than the one on her right.

"Do you have any idea what particular murder you want to focus on?" Ava asks me.

"Not really," I answer.

And Miss Diaz says, "Murder."

Ava smiles over at her. "That's not on your cards, Mama. If Connor and I are a distraction, I can ask him to leave."

Miss Diaz shakes her head. "Connor, six-five, but is hoping for a growth spurt." She glances up at me. "Hi, Connor."

"Hi, Miss D."

"Jo. You call me Jo."

"Okay, Jo."

Fixated on her cards again, she picks up a picture of a bee. "Bee." She puts the card on a pile to the right.

"Connor?" Ava says, pulling my stare away from her mom. "Should we start narrowing down our favorite murders?"

"It's so weird when you say it like that."

"Murder," says Jo.

Ava sighs, and her mom goes back to the cards.

Ava and I spend the next couple of hours working on our project, deciding that the current hype around the sudden arrest of the Golden State Killer from back in the seventies and eighties will give us enough resources to create a decent podcast or video. We gather as much information as we can while Jo continues her flashcards. She's moved on from animals to inanimate objects. Ball, ring, bat, all of these go to the pile on her right. Toaster, television, computer all go to the left.

"Hey, Jo," I say, curious. "What is it that you said I needed to work on?"

She looks up at me. "Connor, six-five, *weak jump shot.*"

"My jump shot, huh?"

She nods.

Ava's eyes narrow as she gently nudges my leg under the table. "What are you doing?" she whispers.

I ignore her and ask her mom, "Do you know what sport I play?"

Jo scoffs. "Basketball."

I find a picture of the basketball from her pile and push it toward her with my index finger. "What's this?"

Ava kicks me. *Hard.* I ignore it again.

"Ball," says her mom.

"What kind of ball?"

Jo sighs. "*Ball.*"

"I know it's a ball," I say, and now Ava is grinding her foot on top of mine. "But what *kind* of ball?"

Jo looks up at me, a blank expression marring her features.

I lean forward. "Did you play any sports in college?" I ask her.

She nods. "Basketball."

"One second, Mama," Ava says through gritted teeth. She gets to her feet and tugs on my ear, using that grip until I'm standing up and she's dragging my ass out into the living room. "What the hell are you doing?" she whisper-yells, finally releasing me.

I rub at my ear, relieving the pain. "Your mom's not deaf, Ava. She can hear you just fine."

Her arms cross. "You're making her feel stupid!"

"No, I'm not," I say, matching her stance. "I'm having a conversation with her. Didn't you just see what happened?"

"All I saw was you being a dick, and if you want to keep going, you can leave."

"Ava." I grasp her shoulders, get her to face the kitchen, where her mom's still going with those pointless flashcards. "She has two piles," I start.

"I know this," Ava snaps.

I overlook her attitude and continue, my hands still on her shoulders. "The ones on her right are the ones she gets correct. They're single-syllable words. Everything else is on the left, and they're more than one syllable. But she can *say* those words, Ava. She just can't connect them to the picture. Like when she was looking at the basketball, she didn't say it was a basketball. She said it was a ball, and she got frustrated about it. But when I *talk* to her, when she's having a conversation, she says the word, and she says it easily and clearly."

Ava's shoulders drop as she inhales a sharp breath.

"Those flashcards," I say, "they're useless. You just need to *talk* to her."

After a long moment of quiet, Ava calls out, "Hey, Mama? Do you remember Trevor's pet that he kept in his room? His name was Fetch."

Jo nods.

"Do you remember what animal it was?"

"Turtle," Jo answers, not skipping a beat.

"Oh, my God, Connor!" Ava turns to me, her arms going around my neck. "How did I not see that earlier?"

I don't have an answer, so I don't respond. Instead, I hold her to me, her cheek to my chest.

Their front door opens, and Trevor walks in. Without looking up, he slips off his shoes and demands, "Love me! Feed me! Honor me!" He turns and sees Ava and me, our arms wrapped around each other. "Oh, so we're doing this again," he mumbles.

Ava giggles, releasing me. "Connor's just here to do some homework."

"Oh yeah," he responds, walking past us and into the kitchen. "I remember when I called it 'homework,' too." He places his hand on Ava's mom's shoulder and kisses her right on her scars. "What's up, Mama Jo?"

Miss Diaz taps his hand lovingly. "Connor, six-five is here."

"I see him. You giving him more pointers on his jump shot?"

Jo clicks her tongue. "Weak."

I can't help but chuckle.

Trevor goes to the fridge and grabs a beer, then looks at our homework we have spread out over the table. "What are you guys working on now?"

"Serial killer," Ava responds.

Trevor shakes his head. "I swear to God, one day the FBI is going to come knocking on our door suspicious about your search history, Ava."

Ava shrugs, taking my hand and leading me back to the table.

Trevor says, "So, I assume I'm not being fed tonight?"

Ava grimaces. "Sorry, I lost track of time."

"Pizza?" Trevor asks her.

Ava replies, "Sure."

He points at me. "Pizza?"

"I'm down."

Then he points to Miss Diaz. "Pizza?"

She nods, her arm going up in celebration. "Pepperoni pizza!"

I tap Ava's leg under the table. "See that? *Six syllables.*"

* * *

We sit at the kitchen table downing slice after slice while Trevor and Ava banter back and forth and I do my best to keep up. Jo listens to their conversation, smiling occasionally. I put down my pizza and tell her, "So, Jo, I've been looking at old game tape of myself, and you know what I realized?"

"Weak jump shot?"

"Yep," I lie.

"Because of your posture, right?"

"I guess so. But I can't really tell and your living room—it's not exactly the same as being in front of the basket, you know?"

She nods. "Yes."

"So, I was thinking, maybe we could go to a court, and you could help me out?"

Ava and Trevor are suddenly silent, and Jo—she's looking at me as if I'd just gotten Ava pregnant.

"Connor," Ava whispers. I don't know why she keeps whispering when her mom's *right there*. "You know my mom doesn't leave the house. Why are you asking her?"

I push my plate forward and settle my forearms on the table, leaning in so it's just Jo and me. "Is it because you don't like people looking at you when you go out?"

"Connor, enough," Ava grinds out.

"Yes," Jo whispers.

I suck in a breath, my mind racing when I ask, "What if we go at night when no one can see you?"

Jo blinks and then shakes her head, again and again, and she doesn't stop.

"Connor, you should go," Ava says, getting to her feet.

I ignore her and ask Jo, "And what if I promise you that there'll be no one else there?"

Ava spits, "I mean it, leave!"

"Just let him talk, Ava," says Trevor.

I add, "What if it's just you and me and Ava and Trevor?"

Jo holds onto her amputated arm, hugging herself. "No, no, no, no, no."

Ava physically pulls me up from my chair. Then, with her hands on my back, she pushes me out of the kitchen, through the living room, and right out her front door, slamming it shut after us. "What the fuck is wrong with you!"

I face her, my heart pounding. "What about you? You whisper shit in front of her as if she can't hear. She's not a kid, and you have to stop babying her."

"Who the fuck do you think you are?" she yells.

"She's a Marine, Ava. She's stronger than you think!"

Her nostrils flare. "How dare you!"

"How dare I what? *Try*?"

"How dare you come into our lives and think that you're going to make a difference! I've been dealing with this shit for *three years*, Connor!" She takes a breath, her anger heating her cheeks, burning liquid behind her eyes. "Remember everything I said in the car? I take it back!"

My heart drops. "No, you don't."

"Yes, I do!" she yells. "God, just when I thought things were too good to be true, you—" The front door opens, interrupting her. She cowers, her arms going around her waist.

Trevor pokes his head out and says, "She wants to talk to you."

"I'll be there in a second," Ava whispers, her intake of breath an attempt to regain some composure.

"Not you," Trevor says, looking over at me. "*You.*"

I swallow, nervous, and wait for Ava to step aside so I can move past her. Jo hasn't gotten up from her seat, but her gaze lifts and locks on me when I enter the kitchen with Ava only half a step behind me.

"Pwa-pwa-" She blinks hard. Once. Twice. "Pwamise just you, me, Ava, and Trevor?"

I make a cross over my heart with my finger. "I swear to you, Jo. I would never do anything to make you uncomfortable."

It's silent a long moment, Ava, Trevor and I waiting to see what she says or does next. I can hear Ava breathing heavily next to me, and so I take a risk and grasp her hand in mine, relief washing through me when she lets me.

Jo stands. "Okay."

"Okay?" Ava practically squeals.

Jo nods. "Okay, Connor, six-five, weak jump shot. Tomorrow."

"Tomorrow," I agree.

Her gaze shifts to Ava. "Don't yell at Connor, baby. He's a good boy." She stops in front of me, pats my cheek. "Handsome, too."

Ava lets out a single disbelieving laugh. "Okay, Mama."

"I'm going to bed," Jo says, kissing her daughter on the cheek.

As soon as she's in her room, I turn to Ava. "I'm sorry," I rush out. "I shouldn't have ambushed you all like that, it just came out, and I couldn't stop, but I should have run it by you first. And you're right. I can't just show up and expect to make a difference. It was stupid to think I could."

"Well, technically..." Trevor says, "you kind of have. I mean, Mama Jo even *thinking* about leaving the house is a big deal."

"Trevor's right," Ava says quietly, pouting up at me with those lips I'm dying to kiss. "I'm sorry I yelled at you. I'm just so invested, and I take every-thing personally."

"I know, and I get it."

She sighs. "Mom's right; you are a good boy."

I smile from ear-to-ear. "And handsome, too. Don't forget that part."

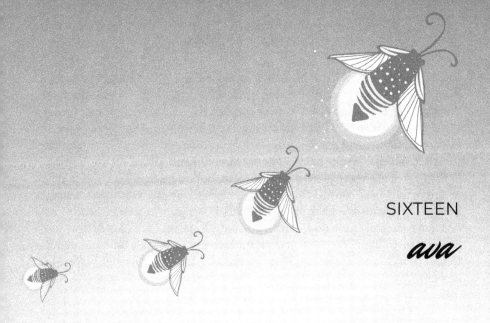

SIXTEEN

ava

"AVA, STOP!" Connor says, grabbing me by my shoulders to stop me from pacing. We're at the bleachers during lunch, and my anxiety over tonight has me on edge. "You need to trust me, okay?" He's trying to bite back a smile, and it makes me want to punch him in the face.

Or kiss him.

I can't fucking decide.

I inhale a huge breath and hold it a moment before releasing it slowly. Looking up at him, I order, "Tell me the plan."

He groans, his entire body deflating. "We wait until it's dark. I'll text you when I'm minutes away. You open the door. We go on a covert mission to get your mom into my truck, which has the darkest legal tint, by the way, and then... we go..."

"Go *where*, Connor?"

He shrugs, all nonchalant like, and it has me leaning toward punching him in the face. "I want it to be a surprise."

"For who? Me or my mom?"

"Both of you," he says, but it comes out a question.

I jerk out of his hold and start pacing again.

Connor laughs. "Relax, would you?"

I turn to him, lift my chin. "Three years, remember?" I say, pointing to me. "I have three years of reasons *not* to relax, and you—"

"Okay," he cuts in, stepping closer to me. "I get it. I'm sorry."

"It just feels like you're not taking this as seriously as you should be."

Sighing, he drops his head, pinches the bridge of his nose. Then he sits down, taking my hand and forcing me to do the same. With his thigh against mine, he says, looking down at his hands, "I've thought of every-thing possible, okay? And if at any time she changes her mind, then we don't go. It's that simple. But I need you to have a little faith in me. It may seem like it's not as important to me as it is to you, but... *your mom* is important to me, and not because she's your mom, but because... she..." he trails off, another heavy breath leaving him. "I don't know, Ava. Your mom —she makes me want to be a better person, and there aren't a lot of people in this world who can do that. And I hate the way the world has treated her. I do." He rubs the back of his neck, his frustration showing. "The thing is, I can't control the world, but I can control *me*. And if I can do this one little thing to show her, and *you* even, that not everybody is made equal, then I will..." He faces me, his eyebrows dipped. "Through *love and basketball*."

* * *

Connor: Dark enough yet?

Ava: Yeah, I think so.

Connor: Money. I'll be there in five.

Ava: Okay. Hey, what's the attire for tonight?

Connor: Attire?

Ava: Like, what should we wear?

Connor: Just make sure your mom is warm and wearing sneakers. As for you, I vote nude, but that would be awkward in front of your family, so...

Ava: Got it. And just for you, I'll be nude under my clothes...

Connor: That's... dammit. Give me ten now. I need to rub one out before we go.

Ava: Connor!

Connor: Say it again but moan it this time.

Ava: And we're done here.

"Connor's going to be here in five," I tell Mom as I look up from my phone.

"Okay," she replies, her voice barely a whisper. I know she's scared; I can see it in her eyes. But she *wants* to do this, to push herself outside of her comfort zone, and I admire that so much. But still, it doesn't take away my own fears *for* her.

I explain, "Connor said that if you change your mind at any time, we can just come back home."

"Nah," Trevor interrupts, walking into the room with Mom's sneakers. He's had to clean and re-lace them because it's been years since she's worn them. "You got this. Right, Mama Jo?"

Mom raises a fist, but there's no inflection in her tone when she says, "I got this."

When I got home today, Krystal mentioned that Mom had brought it up a few times, but it had been another zero-day for her, so it was hard to distinguish how she truly felt about it.

Trevor hands me the sneakers, and I slide them on Mom's feet, then lace them up. "Does that feel okay?"

"Yes."

Trevor returns with a huge puffy jacket for her to slip into. Standing, I zip it all the way up to her chin and put the hood over her head. "You look like a giant marshmallow," I tell her, and she smiles—the first smile I've gotten from her today.

"Connor, six-five, good boy," Mom says, keeping that smile in place.

"He cares about you a lot, you know?" My heart swells when I remember how he spoke of her today. "He says you make him want to be a better person."

Mom gets to her feet, nodding. "I don't want to dis-dis—" She blinks hard, her fist to her temple. I wait, knowing the words are coming. "*Disappoint* him."

"You could never," I tell her sincerely, standing with her just as headlights shine through the living room window, alerting us that Connor's here. He and Trevor had pre-planned that he parks in the driveway, so Mom has fewer chances of being *seen*. It's as heartbreaking as it is necessary. "You ready to go, Mama?"

Mom takes a huge breath and lets it out slowly. "Ready."

Connor's waiting on the porch when I open the door, his goofy smile enough to knock anyone off their damn feet. "Hey, Miss D. I'm ready to be schooled."

Mom settles her hand on the crook of his arm, and he leads her to his truck, her head down, covered by the hood the entire time. And she stays that way the full fifteen minutes it takes for Connor to get to the sports park. He stops just outside the locked gates, and Trevor turns to him. "How did your dumbass not know that this place would be closed?"

Connor flips the visor and catches the keys that fall. "How did your dumbass not think I'd have a key?" He turns to Mom and me sitting in the backseat. "I promised you no one would be around. Did I do good?" He's still wearing that cheesy grin, as if he's so proud of himself, and he should be.

Mom says through a smile, "You did good, Connor."

After opening the gate and closing it after us, Connor drives right onto the basketball courts, his headlights illuminating enough light to see half the court. I help Mom out of the truck while Connor gets a few balls from the bed. Then he comes back, handing me a blanket, thermos and a paper bag. "What's this?" I ask.

His grin broadens. "Hot chocolate and marshmallows."

"I hope you brought some for me," Trevor interrupts.

"Nope," says Connor, walking toward the free-throw line.

"Why not?"

"Because I'm not trying to score points with your dumb ass."

Mom giggles, following Connor.

"All right, Miss D—"

"Jo."

"Jo. Posture, right?" He takes a shot, sinks it. "Better?"

Mom has him move a few steps to the right. "Again."

Connor shoots. Misses. "Dang."

"You practice too much from the same spot," Mom tells him.

Connor moves to another spot a few steps away, tries, and misses again. And I don't know if he's doing this just to make her feel good, but Mom's taking it extremely seriously. "Your feet are wrong."

Connor nods as if listening intently. "Show me."

Mom kicks his feet with hers.

Connor shakes his head. "No. *Show* me," he repeats, holding the ball out between them.

Mom raises both her arms. "One arm, *dumbass*."

Connor chuckles. "You only need one arm to shoot, right?"

Mom sighs. "I'm not the one with a weak jump shot," she retorts.

Trevor laughs, jumping onto the hood of Connor's truck and helping me up. We sit on the edge, watching them.

Connor contemplates Mom's words for a moment before saying, "I'll make a deal with you. We play H.O.R.S.E around the key, and the loser has to cook dinner for the other person. Deal?"

"That's not fair!" I shout.

"You want to play, too?" Connor yells back.

I shake my head, clamp my lips together.

Mom tells him, "You have a whole limb advantage."

Connor rolls his eyes, then drops the ball so he can pull his right arm through the sleeve of his sweatshirt. "Just so we're clear. You're not missing a *whole* limb. Just half of it. So, technically, I'm the one disadvantaged now. Are you going to suck it up or what?"

"Oh damn," Trevor whispers next to me.

"Connor!" I gasp.

His eyes meet mine.

And then Mom—Mom *laughs*. This all-out, carefree laugh that has my heart soaring. "You talk a good game, mister," she tells Connor. "But, boy, you ain't got shit on me." She takes the ball from Connor, moves two steps toward the basket. The ball hits the backboard and goes right in.

Connor's mouth is so wide he could fit his giant ego in there. "Damn."

"*Damn*," Mom mocks. "You forget, I've been using my left hand for years now."

"Huh," says Connor.

"Now go get the ball, kid."

Connor rears back. "What? You suddenly lost your legs, too? *You* get the ball."

Next to me, Trevor is *dying* from laughing so hard.

Mom goes after the ball and calls out over her shoulder, "H.O.R.S.E is for pussies. One-on-one. First to twenty-one, Mr. *Duke*."

Connor stands taller. "I'm not going to go easy on you because you're *old*."

Mom throws the ball to him, then makes her way toward us, unzipping her jacket. "I don't expect you to!" I help her out of her coat, eyeing Connor over her shoulder.

He winks.

I give him the finger... but I'm smiling—the goofiest smile in the history of smiles.

Mom turns back to Connor. "I like my steak medium rare." Connor bounces the ball to her. She returns it, but Connor tries to catch it with the hand trapped in his sweatshirt. "It's not so easy now, is it?" Mom laughs out.

Trevor and I watch what can only be known as the world's weakest one-on-one game ever. They can barely keep the ball in play, and I know that Connor's not going anywhere near his full potential, and Mom would know that, too, but she doesn't call him out on it. Besides, it's hard for her to get a few words in between all their back and forth and *laughter*. So much laughter.

"I don't know what Ava sees in you. You suck with your hands."

Connor busts out a laugh. "You're really going for the jugular now, huh?" He dribbles past her, bouncing the ball between her legs before doing a lay-up and sinking it. "If my calculations are right, it's 20-12." He holds the ball to his waist. "And I'm pretty sure I'm kicking your ass, Miss D."

Mom puts a hand to her hip. "You're right. I guess we'll just have to come out here more and practice."

Connor's face lights up. "Yeah?"

Mom nods. "You think you could spin that ball on my finger with one hand?"

Connor shrugs, approaching her, and mumbles, "With our powers combined..."

Mom lifts her index finger, and Connor places the ball there, tries to spin it. It goes flying to the side, and Mom bursts out laughing. "That was too hard!"

Connor's running after the ball, his shoulders bouncing with his own chuckle. "It's harder than it looks!"

"Swap!" Mom orders when Connor's back in front of her.

They swap tasks, and Mom does precisely the same thing Connor did. Now they've both lost it, their fingers swiping at the liquid joy in their eyes. And me—I'm doing the same. Because never in my life did I ever think I'd hear Mom's happiness come out in this form or see her this free and this blissfully optimistic.

"I need to sit down," she says through a cackle. "I'm not used to *fresh air*!"

Connor smiles as he sits down next to her, then lies down when she does. They stare up at the night sky, the stars bright against the darkness. Mom's head lolls to the side, facing him. "Thank you, Connor, six-five, weak jump shot. I didn't realize how much I needed this."

"You're welcome, Miss D," he replies, pushing his hand through the sleeve and taking hers in his grasp. "It's been an honor."

I try to sniff back another onset of tears, but I can't. And Trevor—he must hear it, or sense it somehow, because he throws his arm around my neck, pulling me to him. He kisses my temple and wipes his own tears across the front of his jacket. Then he clears his throat, his voice low and meant only for me: "When the world is at its darkest..."

I gasp. "...that's when the *magic* appears."

SEVENTEEN

ava

> Connor: Hey, is your mom up?

> Ava: Are we just going to bypass my greetings from now on? I feel used.

> Connor: Good morning, future girlfriend.

> Ava: Good morning. :)

> Connor: Is your mom up?

> Ava: Yeah, why?

> Connor: I have to get to an early practice, but I have five minutes. Can I come by?

I GLANCE up from my phone to see Mom at the kitchen sink, staring out into the yard. She hasn't mentioned last night, and I've been too wary to bring it up.

> Ava: Meet me on the porch.

"I'm just meeting Connor outside. I'll be back in a couple minutes. Okay, Mama?"

Mom doesn't respond, and Trevor and I share a knowing look. We're both used to her short-term memory loss, but Connor... he hasn't had to deal with it yet, and I'm worried about how he'll react.

Connor's already standing on my porch when I open the door, and so I step out to join him, closing the door behind me.

"Hi, future girlfriend," he greets, planting a cold-nosed kiss on my cheek. "How's my second favorite lady doing today?" He's so happy and hopeful and *alive*, and I don't want to break him.

After a sigh, I step closer to him and flatten my hands on his stomach when I look up and into his eyes. "Mom's not having a good day, and I don't know if she's just exhausted from last night or if..." *If this is just a repeat of the many days prior.*

Connor's grin falters, just for a second before his chin lifts. "She'll be happy to see me."

I *can't*.

I don't have it in me to destroy his hope, and so I open the door and step aside to let him in. Mom hasn't moved from her position, and Connor's quiet as he approaches her. "Good morning, Miss D."

Mom spins to face him, her eyes void of any emotion, and there's no inflection in her tone when she murmurs, "Hello." That's it. That's all she gives him before going back to staring outside.

Leaning against the doorway of the kitchen, I let my head rest on the frame, hands behind my back as I watch Connor's expression fall completely. Trevor's loud sigh fills the silence. He gets up from the kitchen table and moves past Connor, patting his shoulder gently. In Connor's ear, Trevor whispers, "Don't let it bring you down, okay?"

Connor's throat bobs with his swallow, but he doesn't respond in words. Shoulders deflated, he looks over at me, and I can see the exact moment hope drowns in his chest, and the liveliness in his eyes flickers and flickers until it dims completely.

"I'm sorry," I mouth, my eyes welling at the sight of him.

He offers a smile—the saddest, most heartbreaking smile—and moves toward me, his chest rising with his heavy inhale. Lips warm, he places a gentle kiss on my forehead and squeezes my hand. "I'll see you at school?"

I drop my head to his chest, my hand to his heart, echoes of magic tapping against my fingers. "Please don't be sad," I whisper, blinking back the heat behind my eyes.

He laughs once, short and sharp. "I'm all right," he assures, stepping away. A moment later, he's out the door, taking his heartache with him.

I roll my head to the side, look at my mother again. She's staring down at the sink. "It's empty," she whispers.

"I did the dishes already."

She shakes her head, slowly, slowly. "Not the dishes, Ava."

"Then what?"

Sighing, she turns around, her eyes finding mine. "Me."

* * *

Connor is a picture of hopelessness when I walk into first-period multimedia class. Head down, forearms on the table, he's ignoring the hype going on around him regarding tonight's game. "Hey," I say, dropping my bag beside his ball and sitting down next to him.

He looks up, a semblance of a smile. "Hey."

"How was practice?"

His cheeks puff with the force of his exhale. "It damn near killed me," he says through a chuckle. "I'm going to feel beaten and bruised after the game."

"Is that why you look so..." I trail off, not wanting to trigger him.

Nodding, he replies, "Yeah. I'm just stressed about tonight."

"Anything I can do?"

A low chuckle builds in his chest and dies in his throat. Leaning in, he whispers, "There's a *lot* you can do to relieve my stress, Ava, but it's not really *friendly*." He rests his hand on my thigh, creeping higher up my skirt.

And, just to mess with him, I whisper back, "Like give you a hand job under the desk?"

His hand stills, his shoulders tensing. When he rears back, his eyes are on mine, narrowed. "You win," he sighs out, his lips curled at the corners. "Honestly, it's a little of that and a little of what happened with your mom."

I pout. "I figured."

"I'll get over it; it's just..."

"Hard?" I finish for him.

His lips thin to a line, his eyes cast downward. "I guess I just really hoped it would make a difference, you know? And I thought—it's stupid..."

"It's not."

And that's all we can get in before Miss Salas enters the room and starts an hour-long diatribe about the effects of social media on our generation.

Connor doesn't take his hand off my leg the entire time.

* * *

"So, how's the plan coming along?" Miss Turner asks, taking a bite of her sandwich.

I'm always telling her that I hate taking up her lunch break, but I have a feeling she prefers my company over everyone else's at this school. "It's kind of at a standstill at the moment. I'm still trying to process it all, to be honest."

"Well, there's not much time left, so you better start making the dream work. Have you told anyone yet?"

I shake my head. "No. I don't want to until everything is in place."

"I'm proud of you, Ava. You've come a long way from the girl who used to come in here fighting the world around you."

"Oh, I'm still fighting," I assert. "But now, I refuse to back down."

She smiles, a hint of pride. "And how are things with Connor?"

I frown. "I think I broke him..."

With ten minutes left of the lunch break, I leave Miss Turner's office, my heart beating fast in my chest. If ever there was a time to find the courage to do what I need to do next, it's now. Because like Miss Turner said, if I truly want what my heart desires, I need to fight for it.

I wipe my sweaty palms on my skirt, pacing the space just outside the cafeteria doors. My eyes drift shut while anxious energy vibrates through my bloodline. "Just do it, Ava," I whisper, then roll my eyes. I talk a big game for someone scared shitless to enter a fucking room.

Without another thought, I enter through the glass sliding doors, my head held high. I don't look around me or stop when the volume drops. Instead, I march over to Connor, noticing Rhys's eyes widen and motion to me. Connor turns his head and then stands slowly. "Sit!" I order. It comes out harsher than intended, but it's too late to take it back.

His eyes soften, the corner of his lips lifting in a smirk.

Pulse in my eardrums, I wait until his ass is back in his chair, and then I sit across his lap, my arm around his neck. I can feel his smile across my shoulder as his hand goes to my waist. Behind me, Karen giggles. "Damn, girl. Way to claim your property." But that's not what this is about, and I hope Connor knows that. I'm here because... because it's time to stop hiding. And because I *want* to be.

His hand drifts up my back, to my nape, and he holds me there, his nose trailing up my neck, lips stopping just under my ear. His exhale warms my entire body, and I shiver when he kisses me there. "Hello," he says, his voice gruff. And that single, stupid word sends a blush right to my cheeks.

I dip my head until my mouth meets his, and I kiss him quickly. "Hello," I return, then bite my bottom lip to stop my smile.

His eyes are bright, a complete contrast to this morning, and this... *this* is the reason I'm here. Because I want to do whatever I can to take away his heartache, just like he'd done for me so many times before.

I pull his tray closer to me and lift an apple. "Are you going to eat this?"

He shakes his head, his smile unrestrained. "Take it. All of it. Anything you want. Whenever you want it."

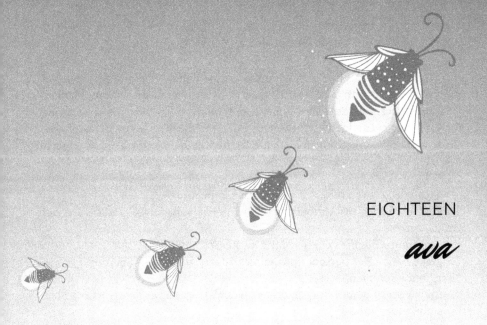

"DO you mind if we watch Connor's game?" I ask Mom as she settles on the couch with a blanket and her tablet. She's started reading for pleasure now, which is a *huge* step, but I wonder how it's possible she can remember what she reads but can't remember the life-changing moment that happened only yesterday.

"Yes, Ava. You don't need to ask my permission to watch your boyfriend," she mumbles, rolling her eyes.

"He's not my—"

"Quit it," Trevor cuts in, setting up the TV for me.

"Quit what?" I huff out.

"Lying to yourself."

He has a point.

The stream starts just as the team walks onto the court, and Connor—he runs out holding the balloon—still inflated—that I'd left on his porch earlier. He squeezes it until it pops, then shoves the remains down his pants. I bust out a laugh at the same time Trevor says, "Your boy's weird."

"You are!"

"You sure feel passionately for a boy who *isn't* your boyfriend."

I sit on the floor between the couch and the coffee table and watch the game. Even Trevor seems interested. Maybe because it's the first game of the play-offs and if they win this and the next, they go to regionals. It's only halftime but St. Luke's is a much stronger team, and the scoreboard proves it. If Connor weren't playing, I'd be bored out of my mind.

When the second half starts, Mom puts down her tablet and pats the spot on the couch next to her. I get up and sit with her under the one blanket. Connor scores the next five points, and Mom shifts next to me, sitting forward, her eyes glued to the screen. She watches the game. I watch her. Because there's something in her stare, in the way her eyes widen just slightly every time Connor appears. "You like watching Connor play, Mama?"

"Mmm-hmm."

Trevor asks, "You think his jump shot's improved?"

"I don't know," Mom murmurs. "But I feel... *something*." She taps at her chest. "In *here*."

My spine straightens, hope filling my heart. "You do?"

"Like um..." Her bottom lip trembles. "Like, *happiness*." She turns to me. "But... but I don't know *why*."

Trevor and I glance at each other quickly. I ask her as gently as possible, "You don't remember?"

Her lips pull down. "No, Ava," she says, shaking her head, her eyes filling with tears. "I don't remember." The first sob comes a second later, and I wrap my arms around her, feel her shoulder shudder against my cheek.

I stroke her hair, the way she used to do for me. "It's okay, Mama."

"It's not!" She pulls back, gaze alternating between Trevor and me. "What else don't I remember?"

"Mama Jo," Trevor tries to soothe, moving to squat in front of her. Hands on her knees, he adds, "It's okay. As long as you remember who you are and who we are, nothing else is important."

Mom's shaking her head, the heel of her palm slapping against her temple. I reach up and try to get her to stop. "Birthdays and holidays and..." She focuses on Trevor. "Why aren't you in Texas?"

Trevor's sharp inhale catches in his throat, and he looks to me for answers.

"Are you here for me?" she asks him.

Trevor's eyes drift shut.

"Are you!" she demands.

"I don't..." Trevor breathes out, his gaze on me, pleading.

Static fills my mind. Mom's never been like this before, never to the point she doesn't understand what's going on around her. "Trevor works here now," I tell her, a half-truth.

She looks around the house as if it's the first time she's seeing it. "Where's William?" It's been a *long* time since she's brought up Trevor's dad, and the last time... it was the onset of too many negative days to count.

On the TV, Connor scores again. Mom's nose scrunches. "Connor," she whispers and taps her heart again. "Happiness." Then her face falls, and the new onslaught of cries begins. She rocks in her place, back and forth, back and forth, her fist moving from her temple to her heart, again and again. "I don't remember. I don't remember. I don't remember..."

* * *

Ava: Hey. I wasn't able to watch the whole game. I'm sorry. It looked like you guys were heading for a W, though.

Connor: Yeah, it was a cakewalk. You okay?

Ava: Call me when you're done celebrating?

Connor: No celebrations for me tonight. I need to rest. About to get in an ice bath. Join me?

Ava: I wish.

Ava: I miss you, Connor.

Connor: I'll call you as soon as I'm out.

True to his word, Connor calls a half hour later, and I can tell he'd literally just gotten out of the bath because he has me on speaker while he moves around his room, opening and closing drawers to get dressed. "I miss you, too!" he calls out as soon as I answer and before I can get a word in. "You said it before, and I didn't say it back, and I didn't want you to think I didn't miss you because I do. Just give me one second."

I wait, phone to my ear, my lips curled at the corners, and it should be impossible to feel the way I do just from hearing his voice or knowing he's close. Especially after the night I've had. A beat passes before his phone crackles, and I know he's taken me off speaker to give me his full attention. "Are you there?" he asks.

"Yeah."

"Tough night?"

With a heavy sigh, I tell him, "I don't want to talk about it. I'd rather talk about you and the game. Will you tell me about it?"

"Um... there's not much to say, but..." He pauses a beat. "Ava, I know something's going on. What happened?"

My lashes dip, my eyes focused on the check I'd pulled out of my drawer.

I can take care of you, Ava.

I'm running out of time. And *options*. "Can you come over?"

"Window or door?"

"Window."

· · ·

I lift the blinds, then the window, and wait for him, my heart somehow racing and settling at the same time when he comes into view. He's in flip-flops, a tank top, and basketball shorts. "Aren't you cold?"

He gets to the window, his teeth clenched. "I didn't really think when I left; I just wanted to see you."

Stepping back, I help him get in as quietly as possible, then close the window after him. "Do you want your hoodie back?" I ask, my back still to him.

When I turn around, he's in my bed, lifting the covers to his chin. "I'm good."

"By all means, make yourself comfortable."

He smirks. "I plan to, but first..." He reaches over, grasps my hand, and pulls me to him as he makes space for me. I get in bed with him, ignoring the iciness of his flesh when he throws his arm around me. "What happened tonight?"

"She's having a hard time remembering things," I murmur, tracing the lines on his palm with the tip of my finger. "And not just last night, but... she didn't understand why Trevor was here, and she kept asking for William." I look up at him, at the all-consuming frown ruining his beautiful face. "I don't know what triggered it, but last time it was this bad... things went downhill so fast. I blinked, and she was..."

"Did I do this? By taking her out last night?"

"No, Connor," I'm quick to say. "This just... this is her *life*."

"But I made it worse?" he mumbles, removing his hand from my grip. The heels of his palms press to his temples, circling. His head tilts, his eyes going to the ceiling for answers. His moan of frustration echoes in the room, in my heart.

I take his hand again, link my fingers with his, and go to kiss the back of it, stopping when I see the black marker there. My eyes narrow when I read the words: *Miss D.*

"What's this?" I ask, and he looks down, traces his handwriting.

After a heavy sigh, he says, "Every time I went for a shot, I'd see her name, and it reminded me of..."

"Of what?"

He licks his lips, focused on our connection. "It reminded me of her... and you. It just helped me push on, I guess."

My heart squeezes at his words, and I lift my gaze to his. "Why are you so perfect, Connor?"

"I'm not, Ava," he replies, shaking his head. "If I were, we wouldn't be here."

"In my bed together?" I try to joke.

But he doesn't find it funny. "You ever think about what happened to us?"

"Of course," I whisper.

But I don't think it was really a question, because he says, "Because I do. I think about it all the time. All the ways I fucked up—"

"It wasn't just you—"

"It *was*, Ava." He clears his throat. "I was impatient and selfish, and I don't think I realized how... how *bad* things were for you. And that night when your mom asked me to come over, I felt like... God, this is going to sound so bad..."

"No, tell me," I encourage.

He sucks in a breath, his chest rising. "I felt like if I was ever going to get you back, it was going to be through her, you know? But now, I don't know; I'm *invested*. And now it feels so much bigger than just you and me." He swallows audibly. "And I think about all the things I did that I regret and how much it hurt you, and now it's twofold. Because I don't want to hurt either of you and I feel like I will. I'll let you both down—"

"Connor, no," I whisper, blinking back the heat pricking my eyes.

"But I'm doing it again—being selfish—because I know you need time, and I want to give that to you. I do." His chest ebbs and flows with every breath. "But it's like... you've invaded every part of me, and I can't get you out of my fucking head. Every time we're apart, there's this ache in my chest. It's like I can't fucking breathe unless I'm with you."

"It's like white noise," I mumble, turning away so I can wipe at my tears without him seeing.

"What?" He gently grasps my jaw, forcing me to face him. "What's like white noise?" he asks, his eyes flitting between mine.

I shrug, fear filling the depths of my words. "When you're not around. It's like white noise inside me, like everything is chaos and nothing makes sense, and then I hear your voice, or I see you and it's as if... as if everything becomes clear and—" I don't get to finish my thought before his mouth covers mine, the warmth of his breath coating every inch of me. His lips part, our tongues colliding. A moan escapes me when his fingers curl in my hair. Every movement, every touch becomes heated. I struggle to breathe, my entire body in flames. I pull back, suck in a breath, but he doesn't stop. Can't. He moves to my neck, kissing there, as his hands fall to my waist. I capture his mouth again, needing more of him. Tongues sliding against each other, he shifts us until I'm on my back, and he's leaning over me, his kisses dominating, claiming me with every second that passes. I reach up, my fingers lacing through his hair as his mouth moves lower, lower, down my neck, to my collarbone. His hand splays across my stomach, the wetness of his tongue leaving a trail on the rise of my breasts. Then he shifts his hand, moving higher, taking my top with it. My fingers tense in his hair when his mouth finds one nipple and then the other. I squeeze my eyes shut, try to do the same with my thighs to relieve the ache building there, but his grip on my leg stops me. His palm cups my sex, and I release his hair, grasp on to the pillow beneath me, my hips rising. "Is this okay?" he asks, his voice hoarse, filled with lust, driving me wild.

"Please," I whisper, spreading my legs wider for him.

His eyes lift, lock on mine, as his hand glides beneath my sleep shorts and underwear, his fingers quick to find the evidence of my desire. A single finger slides into me effortlessly, and my head rolls back when he starts pumping slowly, his mouth open on my taut stomach. I find his hair again, tug with one hand, the other reaching up to cup my breast. With my eyes closed, I can feel every movement, every touch, every vibration when he moans against my flesh. And then it begins, my entire body tensing, my core pulsing. "Oh, God, Connor," I whisper, my hips moving, meeting him thrust for thrust. "I'm going to come."

"No."

My eyes snap open when he pulls away completely. "No?" I almost cry.

He's between my legs now, fingers curled around the top of my shorts. He drags them down slowly, taking my underwear with them. He throws them behind him. "Take your top off," he orders. I start to remove my top, watching him reach behind him to discard his own.

His bare, heated chest crashes against mine when his mouth does the same, and I'm lost. I'm so fucking lost in all things Connor. Gently, he pushes until I'm on my back again, his mouth leaving a heated trail as he slowly makes his way lower down my body. Sweat coats my flesh, my racing pulse beating wildly in my eardrums, throughout my bloodline. I bite my lip, swallow my moan when I feel his mouth at my center, his tongue sliding between my folds. "Oh, fuck." And then he adds his fingers, and it doesn't take long before I'm climbing again, higher and higher, my every exhale filled with bliss. I grasp his hair again, hold him there, my hips jerking, my breaths matching every throb, every ecstasy-filled beat of release. My back arches off the bed, and then my entire body follows as he sucks, devouring my liquid pleasure.

My body erupts.

Right before the world turns white.

Connor kisses the inside of my thighs, in turn, then slowly makes his way up, his mouth finding my neck. "God, I've wanted to do that for—" He doesn't get a chance to finish before I'm pushing on his chest, rolling him onto his back, and straddling his hips, his hardness pressing against my naked core. I kiss my way down his torso, my tongue teasing the spot just above his shorts while my hand slides along his shaft.

"Ava," he whispers, and I look up at him. At the blush burning his cheeks. "You don't have to do this just—"

I lower his shorts and stroke him, skin to skin, feeling his thighs tense against my flattened palm.

"Fuck, babe."

I lick his entire length.

"Ava," he moans, tugging on my hair, forcing my head back to look at him. "Come here."

With my hand still stroking, I make my way up his body again until my mouth's an inch from his. He covers that space, his lips softly parting mine. I taste my pleasure on his tongue, and it only turns me on more. He pulls away before I'm ready, his hand on my nape, eyes searching mine. "I love you, Ava," he breathes out. "I love you more now than I ever have."

"Me too," I whisper through the sudden knot in my throat. "God, Connor, I love you so much." I kiss him again, and again, he breaks the kiss.

"I *want* you, Ava. *All* of you."

"Are you sure?"

He rolls his eyes. "That's the dumbest thing you've ever said."

I giggle a breath, my lips finding his neck. "I have condoms in my nightstand."

"Thank fuck," he rushes out, reaching around him to open the drawer. He finds the unopened box and rips it open within seconds. Then he pulls out the instructions, unfolds them carefully.

I giggle into his chest.

"Are you making fun of me?"

I press my lips tight. "No."

"This is very important, young lady," he mocks in an authoritative tone. "Let me concentrate."

While his eyes dart side to side, reading the instructions, I sit up and remove his shorts completely, then straddle him again, let my wetness glide along him, back and forth, back and forth. He bites his lip as he looks up at me, breathless. "You're so bad," he murmurs, laying the instructions on his chest. He grabs a condom, tears it open, then compares it to the picture diagram.

He starts to put it on, and I finish it for him. "Good?" I ask.

He nods, his hands going to my waist. "All right, I've waited eighteen years for this. It better be good," he jokes.

I rise up on my knees, get him situated, then slowly lower myself, trying my best to hide the slight discomfort at the size of him. It may not be my first time, but it's definitely not something my body's comfortable with. He releases a breath he'd been holding, his grip tight on my thighs now, begging for me to stay put. "Are you okay?" I ask. Maybe I did it wrong.

His nose is scrunched, his bottom lip caught between his teeth. "Uh huh." But his entire face is red, and his breaths are short, sharp.

"Am I hurting you?"

"Nope," he rushes out, then slowly removes his hands from my thighs, his breaths staggered.

I laugh at how hard he's trying to keep it together.

"Don't do that," he says.

"Do what?"

"Laugh. You're, like, clenching around me."

"Okay, I'll stop."

"Good." His throat bobs with his swallow. Then he blows out a heavy breath, his hands finding my breasts. He squeezes once. "So, this is sex, huh? I don't see what the big deal is," he quips.

"No," I say, rising slowly and then taking him entirely again.

"Oh, fuck," he grinds out, bucking beneath me.

"*That's* sex."

He covers his eyes with his forearm. "Jesus, Ava, I'm not going to last long."

"It's okay," I assure. "You'll last longer next time."

He removes his arm, his eyebrow quirked. "You're going to let me do this again?"

"Uh huh," I say, lifting and then bearing down on him. "And again and again and again," I moan, repeating the movement with each statement.

Twelve seconds later, I'm rolling to my side.

I know it's that long because apparently, he counted it in his head. He gets out of bed to clean up and then crawls back in, his arms wrapping around me. "Welp, at least I know I can beat my PB time next round."

I giggle into his chest.

"I'm ready when you are."

I rear back. "No, you're not."

He motions to the space between us, and I lower my hand, feel him hard in my grasp. A stupid smile crosses my lips, and I reach across him, get another condom. This time, he sits between my legs, his gaze intense and on mine. Then he lowers himself, his cock at my entrance. Lips pressed to the spot just beneath my ear, he whispers, "You're my first *everything* now. My first and *forever*." And then he slides into me, and I bite back a moan, my eyes drifting shut when I feel his hand clasp mine above my head, holding me there. He moves, penetrating me. Not just physically. But everywhere. In every way. I find the spot above his heart, feel the magic beating between us, shaking my foundation... turning my entire world dark. "I love you so much, Connor."

NINETEEN

Connor

I WAKE up no longer a virgin. Yes, that's my first thought. My second thought is why I'm waking up at all. "Stay," Ava whispers, planting a gentle kiss on my lips. I struggle to force my eyes open, but I'm glad I do because Ava's barely an inch in front of me, her fingers stroking my hair. Her lips curve at the corners when she asks, "What time do you need to get to school?"

"I don't know," I mumble, pulling her closer to me. Mmm. Warm, naked Ava is The Best. "I have an alarm set."

"Okay, go back to sleep. Come out when you're ready. I'll make you breakfast."

I can't help but smile. "Yeah?"

She nods.

Nuzzling her neck, I mumble, "I sure could get used to this."

With a giggle, she pushes away from me, untangling herself from my limbs. "I have to go."

My eyes drift shut again, and the next time I wake it's because the covers are being pulled off me completely. Trevor yells, "Ava! There's a naked Connor in your bed!"

"Fuck!" I gasp, grabbing what I can of the blanket, and cover my junk.

"Shut up! Leave him alone!" Ava calls back. A moment later, she's at the doorway.

"Good morning, sunshine," Trevor sings, lifting the blinds. I cower against the bright sunlight filtering through the window. "We need to talk," he adds, sitting down on Ava's desk chair.

Ava sighs as she walks into the room, picking up my discarded shorts from the end of the bed and handing them to me. I'm still half asleep, and so I fumble with putting my shorts on without revealing myself entirely to my girlfriend's brother. Ava sits down next to me. "What?" she growls at Trevor.

Trevor looks between us, then settles his gaze on me, his eyes playful. "Well, well, Mister Duke. What do we have here?"

He wants to play games, and I'm here for it. I don't skip a beat. "Your sister took my innocence."

"Jesus, Connor!" Ava laughs out.

I add, unable to hide my smile, "It was pretty *neat*... the whole *sex* thing..."

"Quit it!" Ava cackles.

I keep going while Trevor shakes his head, tries to contain his chuckle. "Between you and me, Trevor, I'm pretty sure I gave her the best twelve seconds of her life."

After getting dressed, I meet everyone in the kitchen. Trevor's downing some bacon and eggs while Ava stands over the stove and Jo wipes down the countertop. "Good morning, Miss D," I greet, hesitant as I stand beside her.

She nods. "Good morning, Connor, six-five, but is hoping for a growth spurt." A second later, she adds, "Weak jump shot."

The fact that she remembers me settles the ache I'd had in my chest through most of yesterday. I lean against the counter, facing her. "I'll have you know, that weak jump shot got me All-American *and* a full ride to Duke. Also... I got that growth spurt I'd been hoping for. I'm officially six-six now, so you're going to have to remember that when you greet me next."

Her gaze flicks to mine. "Connor, six-six." She shrugs. "Weak jump shot."

Trevor chuckles under his breath.

"Eat," Ava orders, dropping a plate of food on the table. I sit opposite Trevor and dig in.

"How come you cut his toast in little triangles?" he asks Ava.

She rolls her eyes. "You want some pepper with your saltiness, you little bitch?"

"Ava," Jo admonishes. "Be nice to your brother."

Trevor sticks his tongue out at his sister.

Then Jo mumbles, "Twenty-to-twelve, twenty-to-twelve, twenty-to-twelve."

We all stop what we're doing and look over at her.

"Twenty-to-twelve, twenty-to-twelve, twenty-to-twelve."

"Are you saying the time?" Ava asks. "Because it's only 6:40."

Jo shakes her head as she turns to us, her fingers tapping at her temple. "Twenty-to-twelve, twenty-to-twelve, twenty-to-twelve."

"It wouldn't be the time," Trevor mumbles. "She'd use military time."

"In here," Jo says, frustrated, as her fingers move from her head to her heart. "Twenty-to-twelve, twenty-to-twelve, twenty-to-twelve."

Trevor adds, "See, she'd be saying 1140 if it was the time."

"Mama?" Ava asks, stepping toward her. "What's twenty-to-twelve?"

"In here!" Jo almost shouts, hand to her chest.

"In your heart?" asks Ava. "Your heartbeat?" Her eyes narrow. "What...?"

Jo shouts. "The *Happiness*!"

Ava's head moves side to side, slowly, slowly. "The *Happiness* is at 11:40?"

Jo's nose flares with her exhale, a frustrated groan forming in her throat.

"Wait!" I stand quickly, my mind racing. "She's talking about the score!"

Ava huffs out a breath. "What score?"

I can't stop smiling as I approach Jo. "The score, right? From our one-on-one the other night?"

"No," Trevor whispers. "It can't be."

"Yes!" Jo nods, her smile huge. "The score!" Her arms go up, victorious. "I remember!"

"You remember!" Ava cries out, laughing.

"Holy shit," Trevor says through a chuckle. He stands, too, lifting Jo in the air and spinning her around.

When she's back on her feet, she laughs out, "Twenty-to-twelve!" Hand to her chest, she adds, looking right at me, "The Happiness. In here. My heart."

"Your heart?" I ask through the knot in my throat, then lean back, my eyes to the heavens as I take a calming breath. "Shit, Miss D. You damn near broke *my heart* when you didn't remember."

Jo laughs. "Twenty-to-twelve."

"That's right." I nod.

She smiles wide. "I won."

"You did not," I laugh. "You owe me dinner!"

Jo giggles. "I don't recall that part."

"Oh, so you have *selective* memory loss. I see how it is."

Behind me, Ava wraps her arms around my waist. I tug on her hand until she's tucked in at my side.

Jo smiles at us, then looks up at me. "She said you're *not* her boyfriend."

"She said that, huh?"

Jo's shoulders bounce with her giggle. "Yep."

I lift my chin, look down at her. "So, what are you going to feed me tonight?"

"Neighbor's dog shit."

Ava giggles into my chest.

I say, "Mmm-mmm. My favorite!"

"What about tacos?" she asks.

"Yes!"

Every phone in the house goes off with an alert. Mine's still in Ava's room, and so I wait for Ava and Trevor to read whatever is on their screens.

"You lucky bastards," Trevor mumbles.

"School's canceled today," Ava says, showing me her phone.

I read the message: *Due to unforeseen circumstances, there will be no classes held at St. Luke's Academy today, February...* Another message comes through, this one from Rhys, and without thinking, I open it. It's a picture of a huge three-foot rubber dick stuck on the main and only doors to the school. I bust out a laugh and show Ava. She does the same and shows Trevor.

"What's so funny?" Jo asks, trying to look at the phone.

Trevor hands it back to Ava without showing her.

"Someone just did a stupid prank at the school," Ava tells her mom.

"Show me."

"No, Mama, it's inappropriate."

"Show me!"

I say, "Show her. It's funny."

Ava sighs, shows her mom the picture. Jo's eyes go wide.

Ava looks up at Trevor. "Well, I guess we can call Krystal and tell her not to come."

"Nah," Trevor says, "the agency needs twenty-four hours' notice, or they'll still charge us."

"Go!" Jo urges.

Ava rears back at her response. "Go where?"

"Anywhere. You two," Jo says, pointing between Ava and me. "You go. Be kids. Have fun."

"Are you sure, Mama?" Ava asks, but I can already hear the excitement in her voice. An entire day for us to spend together, unrestricted. We've only had this opportunity one other time, and it was the greatest day of our lives.

"I'm sure," Jo says, her voice softening. "You need it. You deserve it."

"Thank you, Miss D." I raise my hand for a high five, expecting her to return it.

Instead, she grasps my hand, places it right on her scars, and looks up at me. "You know why I like you, Connor?"

I grin from ear-to-ear. "Because I'm handsome?"

"Because you treat me like I'm human." Her smile lights up her face. "Now promise me you'll go," she says, releasing my hand to tap on her chest again. "Go and find The Happiness in your hearts, just like I did."

"I promise," I tell her through the sudden ache in my throat.

Trevor gets up to put his dishes in the sink and pats my shoulder as he leaves the kitchen, "Damn, Connor, you're like a magician."

Ava gasps, looks up at me, her lips parted, eyes wide. "My *magician*."

ava

IN MY DESK drawer lives a check.
  A check for six figures.
  Signed by Peter Parker.
  The sum is enough to put my mom in a treatment center full-time.
  In my mind,
  I wonder what it would be like not to have to worry as much as we do.
  In my heart,
  I try to imagine what it would feel like to *abandon* her like that.
  The check is made out to me.
  I can take care of you, Ava,
  Peter said.
  But it's our little secret.
  In my mind,
  I wonder why he didn't offer it to Trevor.
  But in my heart,
  I already know.
  In my desk drawer lives a picture.
  Me and Mom surrounded by fireflies.
  When the world is at its darkest,
  that's when the magic appears,
  my mom says.
  So, in my mind,
  I question if the check is a form of magic.
  But in my heart,
  I believe that **hope creates the *magician*.**

connor

AS SOON AS Krystal arrives at Ava's house, we go over to mine and get right into bed. I call Dad, confirming he got the message from school and tell him that Ava's here, and we're probably just going to hang out in my room so that he doesn't get any unwanted surprises when he comes home. As soon as my head hits the pillow, I'm struggling to stay awake, and sure, there are other things I'd rather be doing with my girlfriend in *my bed*, but I'm *that* fucking tired. Even though last night's game was an easy W, I still went hard. I used to show up to get attention from colleges; now I do it for NBA scouts. Ava must sense all this because she kisses the tip of my nose, runs a hand through my hair. "Take a nap, babe."

With heavy lids, I kiss her quickly. "What are you going to do?"

"You got headphones?"

"On my desk."

She gets out of bed and returns with them and her phone. "I'll listen to a podcast or something."

"You sure?"

"Yeah."

Two minutes later, headphones in, she's fast asleep, snoring lightly. I smile as I watch her, take in every single thing I love and missed about her. Her lips curl as if she knows I'm watching, but she doesn't react in words. She simply moves closer, until there's nothing between us.

No space.

No past.

No regrets.

. . .

I wake up to my phone going off somewhere on the other side of my room. At first, I ignore it, because the only person I care about enough to answer is in my arms. But then it rings again, and again, and Ava's slapping my cheek, mumbling into the pillow, "Tell it to shut up."

"Shut up," I murmur.

It stops ringing, and Ava smiles. "Hey, it worked." But then her phone rings, and of course, she sits up immediately and starts searching for it even though it's vibrating *in her hand.*

With a chuckle, I remove it from her grasp. Rhys's smug face takes up the entire screen, and I answer, "What?"

"I tried calling you."

I roll onto my back, my forearm covering my eyes. "Weird."

"Who is it?" Ava asks.

"Rhys," I reply, watching her move to straddle my hips. She flashes a smile, right before she lowers her chest to mine, her mouth going to my neck, kissing me there. "Is this important?" I say into the phone. "Because I'm a little preoccupied right now."

Ava giggles while silence fills the phone line.

"Cool," I murmur after waiting a beat. Then I hang up, my hands instantly latching on to Ava's ass.

She starts kissing down my bare chest, making it to my stomach before she looks up, asks, "Have you got any condoms here?"

Shit. "I don't know."

"Well..." She starts to get off me, but I hold her there.

To mess with her head, I say, "Wait. My dad should be home. I'll ask him."

"What? No!"

"Why not?"

"I don't want him to know what we're doing in here!"

"As if he doesn't already know, and even if he did, he'd rather know we're being safe." I clear my throat, call out, "Dad!"

She covers my mouth, her eyes wide, then rolls to her side when Dad knocks on the door. "Connor?" he asks. "Did you need me?"

"I hate you," she mouths.

I laugh under my breath. "Yeah, I was just seeing if you were home."

"Oh, okay."

Ava's phone rings again, still Rhys, and this time Ava answers, puts it on speaker. "Hey, Rhys."

"Ledger's with you, right?"

"Yep."

"Pool party at my house. Hurry your asses up."

"All right," Ava laughs out. "I'll talk to my *boyfriend* and see if he wants to go."

"He has no choice, A. He pussied out on last night's party, and he needs to show up. He's fucking *captain*."

"Co-captain," I cut in. "And it looks like you're doing enough for the both of us on that front."

"Ava," Rhys deadpans.

"Yeah?"

His tone turns serious. "Tell your boyfriend he needs to at least make an appearance... *for the team*."

Raising her eyebrows, Ava gives me that look that says, *he's right, Connor* without saying a word, and so I tell Rhys, "I'll be there soon... *ish*."

Rhys hangs up without another word, and I turn to my side and ask, "How the fuck is he having a pool party when it's cold out?"

"You haven't seen his indoor pool?"

"There's an indoor pool?"

"Yep. On the west wing."

"They have *wings?*"

She ignores me and adds, "But it's more of a beach than a pool. There's sand and waves, and it somehow feels like summer, like the sun's out even when it's thirty degrees out."

I ignore the nagging question of *how* she knows that and ask, "Do you miss it? The house and money?"

Her gaze fall, eyes moving to the space between us. "The house, yes, but mainly because of the memories it comes with. The money only because it would make our lives so much easier."

"Whose house was it anyway?" I ask, moving closer and placing my hand on her hip. "Was it Trevor's dad's or your mom's?"

"It was my grandparents'. They left it to Mom when they passed. It's old money, like, great-great-great-great grandparents. It sucks that I'm not able to pass that on to our kids when we—I mean *my...I—*" She stops there, pink flushing her cheeks.

I push away the fantasies of a forever with her, even though I've thought about it more times than I'd like to admit.

"Mom told me her parents were pissed when she decided to join the marines. It came out of nowhere. She went to St. Luke's, too."

"Oh yeah?"

Ava nods. "She was the first female student to get suspended for not wearing appropriate clothes, but it wasn't like her skirt was too short or anything. It was because she wore combat boots and pants." Her words falter at the end, a weak giggle taking their place.

"That sounds like your mom," I muse, then ask, "Do you know who your dad is?"

"Nope," she answers, shaking her head. She flips to her back, eyeing the ceiling, her hand covering mine on her stomach. "Mom said he was a guy she dated for a while, but he didn't stick around long enough for her to even tell him she was pregnant."

"You ever want to look for him? What if he could help you out financially?"

"I thought about it for, like, *one* second. But it would be almost impossible. She never told me his name or had it on my birth certificate, and I don't want to ask her now. I don't want her to know how desperate we are, you know?"

I lean up on my elbow, look down at her. "It's that bad?"

"We're doing okay right now, but yeah..." The corner of her lips dip downward. "We'll be going in the red pretty soon."

"So, what do you do then?" I ask.

Ava shrugs, her chest rising with her weighty inhale. Her eyes flick to mine quickly before shifting away. "Just hope everything falls into place."

Her phone chimes with a text, and she rolls her eyes as she reads it.

> Rhys: I'm going to send Mitch to pick your flakey asses up if you don't get here soon.

Ava sighs. "Do you want to go?"

"Do you?"

"I guess, yeah. It should be fun."

"So would staying in bed and beating my PB."

Laughing, she gets out of bed, dragging me with her. "We'll have more time for that later."

"Ava." I stand in front of her, take both her hands in mine. "This is important, and I need you to listen to me."

"Okay."

"Because I don't want to disappoint you."

"Connor." She pouts up at me. "What's wrong?"

I shake my head, suck in a breath. "I don't know if I can beat a minute, forty-eight."

* * *

Ava's in a bikini that shows off *everything*. Well, not everything, but close enough, and I don't know how to feel about it. Luckily, we haven't left yet, so there are no prying eyes.

"Is it too revealing?"

Yes. I clamp my lips together, shake my head. "Nope."

"It's just I haven't bought any new ones since everything with Mom, so these are all, like, from when I was fourteen."

Well, that explains it. "I mean, it's a little... tight."

Standing in front of a full-length mirror, I try to pry my eyes away from her ass as she looks over her shoulder at me. "Too small to wear out?"

Don't be a dick, Connor. Don't be a dick. "It's fine." *It's not.*

"Connor, be honest, and stop looking at my ass!"

I lift my gaze. "I can't help it." I reach out, take two handfuls, and pout when she slaps my hand away.

"Well? Is it too small?"

"Honestly?"

She nods.

"It's not that it's too small. It's just that maybe you've *filled out* a little since then, and I don't know, Ava," I grumble, "I'm already getting stabby thinking about all the guys seeing you in that, and I don't want to stab my teammates because I want to get to state."

"And the jail time would suck..."

"Yeah, I guess that, too."

"I just won't go in the pool."

"But that's *fun*. You said you wanted to have fun." I groan. "Don't listen to me. You shouldn't be letting me tell you what you can and can't wear anyway. But just... keep me away from knives."

She giggles.

"And maybe pens, too; anything I can use to stab someone."

"All right," she murmurs, opening her dresser. She pulls out a pair of denim shorts, and I grip the mattress when she bends over in front of me to slide them over her legs.

I adjust myself in time before she turns to me, and now her boobs are there, and I squirm, the bulge in my pants painfully uncomfortable. "Are you sure we can't just—"

"Have never-ending sex?" she says, throwing in an eye-roll.

"I wouldn't mind it."

Another roll of her eyes, and now I'm starting to feel insecure. "I'll get better."

She opens another drawer. "Shut up, idiot."

"Again, you have the strangest love language."

She pulls out a Wildcats jersey, *mine*, and shrugs it on. "There," she says, turning to me. "Now everyone will know I'm yours. How's that for love language?"

Reaching over, I grasp her hand and pull until she's standing between my legs. Head tilted back, eyes on her, I say, "Tell me."

She offers a smile, so genuine and sincere. "I love you, Connor Ledger."

Then she takes my face in her grasp, kisses me, her mouth already open when it meets mine. Tongue parting my lips, she holds me prisoner to her desire. When she pulls away, she adds, "And you're incredible in bed. The best minute and forty-eight seconds of my life."

* * *

Ava leads me by my hand to the "west wing," even though I could've found my way there by the music blaring and the kids hollering. She wasn't kidding when she said the indoor pool was more like a beach. Take away the obvious painted scenic walls, and I'd think I was down in Myrtle Beach during spring break.

As soon as Rhys makes my presence known, I'm bombarded by the guys from the team and a few girls I've seen hanging around them. Ava's grasp on my hand weakens, and I hold her tighter, making sure she doesn't get a chance to flee. To *hide*. It doesn't take long for the guys to realize that she's here, too, and they greet her with the same enthusiasm. And I don't know if it's honest or if they're doing it for me, because they know how important she is to me, but I appreciate it. Karen shows up next, declares Ava as hers for the day, and I reluctantly release my hold and let them go off together. But I watch her. Closely. Because I *can't not*. I love to see the genuine smile on her face when she sits with a group of girls I assume were once her friends. I love watching her eyes light up when she laughs, the way her head tilts back with the force, and the way her hands move in earnest when she's the one talking. I love the way she glances up every now and then, her eyes searching for me, and the way her lips curve when she spots me.

I even love the way her hips sway when she walks toward me, ignoring the fact that I'm with a few of my teammates. She throws her arms around my neck, drags my face down to hers and kisses me with as much passion and lust as she does behind closed doors. I love the way she looks up at me, her dark lashes fanning those maple-colored eyes, and the way she smiles when she says, "I found it."

"Found what?"

"The *Happiness*."

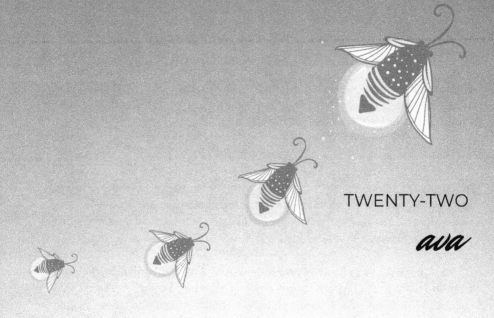

ava

"HOW FUCKING stupid can two dipshits be?" Connor yells, white-knuckling the steering wheel as he drives us home from school.

I don't respond, because there's nothing I can say to make this okay.

The team made it to regionals.

The problem? Mitch and Rhys are suspended. Out of the game. And no amount of their parents' money or offers to build an entirely new building on school grounds is enough to make the school board renege on their decision.

The whole *giant dildo superglued to the door and lubed up to make it impossible to remove* thing? That was done by the two dipshits Connor's referring to. Which means that Connor—he's going to have to carry the entire fucking team on his back to even have a *chance* at winning.

This all went down only a few hours ago. And the regional final is *tonight*. To say he's pissed would be the understatement of the century. His phone's been ringing non-stop ever since we got out of school, and he's ignored every call, besides his coach, who wants Connor to get back to the school right away so they can rework their entire roster together. I told him he could've stayed, that he didn't have to drive me home, but he assured me he needed to get out, to blow off steam. And so this is what he's doing... while driving.

"Over a stupid, useless fucking prank, Ava!"

"I know, baby. I'm sorry."

His nostrils flare, his jaw ticking. I reach over, anxiously place a hand on his leg. His gaze lowers to the touch, and his chest heaves. Without warning, he pulls over to the side of the road, gravel spinning beneath the wheels. My seatbelt catches when he brakes hard. He takes a few calming breaths before turning to me. "I'm sorry, Ava. I'm taking this out on you."

"It's okay," I assure. "I understand." Truly, I do. This is so important to him. After this, it could be state.

"I know you do, but still, I—"

"Connor, I get it. What can I do to help?"

"I don't know," he breathes out. "Besides punching those two in their lopsided nutsacks, I got nothing."

"I could do that," I tell him. "I'd be *happy* to. Especially Mitch."

A hint of a smile plays on his lips, and he leans over to me, places a kiss on my temple. "You're going to watch the game, right?"

"Of course. We wouldn't miss it for the world. I guarantee Mom's already wearing your jersey."

His smile widens. Then he reaches into his school bag, fumbles around until he finds a thick black marker. He hands it to me and says, "Do me a favor?"

"Anything."

"Can you write *Miss D* on my hand?"

I bite back a smile as I do as he asks, his hand settled on my bare thigh.

"And *Ava* underneath that."

My eyes widen when I look up at him. "You want my name there, too?"

He nods once, motions for me to do it. "You're my reason, Ava. You both are."

* * *

"There he is!" Mom shouts, getting to her feet as the stream of the game starts, and Connor appears on the TV. "There's my boy!"

"Um, technically, that's *my* boy, Mama."

"Oh, hush. Don't be greedy now!"

Within minutes of the game, we can see Connor struggling without Rhys and Mitch on the court. He's really the only one on the team worth a dime, and Philips Academy, their opponents, stick to what they've always done when it comes to Connor: they double-team him.

"Jesus Christ!" Mom yells at the TV. "Give the boy room to breathe!"

"Dammit," Trevor grunts, leaning forward, his elbows on his knees. "He can't fucking escape these bastards!"

"Get off him!" Mom shouts.

I stay quiet, watching the boy I love play a game he loves, or at least trying to, but he's so deflated, so hopeless. And I can see it in the way his shoulders sag, see it in the furrow of his brow and the tenseness in his jaw. He's frustrated, and the only people who deserve that frustration are in suits warming the bench.

Fuck Rhys and Mitch.

They ruined this for him.

The buzzer sounds for the end of the first quarter and the score's 30-12 with Philips leading, and while most of our scoring has been done by Connor, it's only due to the constant fouls against him.

Philips is out for blood.

And Connor is their target.

"God, he'll be hating this," I mumble.

"No shit," Trevor responds.

Second quarter starts and his opponents have changed, but there are still two of them, and with fresh legs, they shut Connor out completely.

"Fuck!" Mom shouts. And I feel her frustration to the core. Ten minutes in and Coach Sykes *forces* Connor to sub out. The camera focuses on him as he slumps down on the bench, a towel going to his face. He keeps it there while his shoulders drop, his chest heaving. I can't even imagine how drained he must be. How disappointed. His spirit's crushed, and I can it see it through the screen. When he finally removes the towel, his eyes are red, raw, as if he already knows it's over, not just for the team, but for him, too. A frown tugs at my lips, my chest aching at the sight of him.

"Where's the game being played?" Mom asks out of nowhere.

"At Wyndham Tech."

"How far away is that?"

"It's about fifteen minutes from here."

Mom stands quickly. "Well, go, Ava! He needs you."

My breath catches. I'd give anything to be there with him. For him. But... "How am I going to go? I don't drive. Trevor would have to take me, and you can't be alone."

Mom lifts her chin. "So, we'll all go!"

"What?!" Trevor and I yell at the same time.

"Get your shit," Mom rushes out. "Shoes. Keys. Coat. Quick, quick! Our boy needs us!"

We don't ask if she's sure she wants to go, to be seen in public by *a lot* of people, because she's the one herding us out the door within minutes. "You better drive fast, boy, or I swear..." Mom mumbles, clicking in her seatbelt as soon as we're in Trevor's truck.

To my surprise, Trevor *floors* it all the way to the complex. Thanks to a minor hiccup buying tickets to actually get *into* the game, we're standing courtside (thanks to people's fear of my mom's appearance when she pushes them out of the way) just as the teams are coming back from the half-time break. The moment I see him, my heart begins to race. I cup my hands around my mouth, yell, "Boo!" But the crowd is too damn loud, and he's too focused, and so I suck in a breath, prepare my lungs. "BOO, LEDGER! BOOOO!"

"Why are you jeering him?" Trevor asks.

"Just trust me," I tell him. "BOO, LEDGER!"

Then Mom joins in, "BOO! BOOOOO!"

And I've never loved my brother more than when he mumbles, "I can't believe I'm about to do this." He picks me up effortlessly, and I grasp on to his head as lifts me higher, sitting me on his shoulders. "BOO, LEDGER!" He yells so loud the crowd around us quiets.

"Boo!" Mom screams, and Oscar, Connor's teammate, finally turns around to see what all the crazy taunting is about. When he finds me, a flash of a smile curves his lips, and he backhands Connor's arm, motions his head toward me. Connor looks up, Up, UP, his eyes huge when he sees us. I see him mouth, "one second" to his coach, and then he jogs toward us while Trevor puts me back on my feet.

Connor's shocked, clearly, his eyes shifting between Mom and me over and over. He settles on me first. "What are you doing here?"

"I needed—"

It's all I can get out before I'm in his arms, his hand gripping the back of my head. He holds me to his chest, where magic beats heavily against my cheek. "God, I'm so glad you're here, babe. I'm getting *destroyed* out there."

"I know," I mumble, pulling back to look at him, but he's already focused on my mom.

"You came out for me?" he asks gently.

"Of course, we love you, Connor," she replies, and my heart swells. "But don't you give up," she orders, her tone strict. "Don't you *dare* give up!"

Connor laughs once. "No, ma'am." And then his coach calls him back to join the rest of his team.

"I love you," I tell him, kissing him quickly. I tug on his jersey, the one matching mine and my mother's. "You got this!"

We lose.

We more than lose.

We get *annihilated.*

As soon as the final buzzer sounds, Connor shakes hands with the team, and then...

Then he falls to one knee, his outstretched arm keeping him upright while his entire body shakes with exhaustion. He's wiped. Completely drained. I've never seen him work so hard, push so fiercely. When he looks up, his tired eyes take in the celebrations of players and fans from Philips, no doubt wishing he was part of it. He wanted *state.* He told me so many times how much he *needed* state. And now it was gone, completely out of his grasp. "God, I hate this for him," I mumble.

Mom takes my hand. "He's a strong boy. He'll get through this."

"Ava!" Corey, Connor's dad, calls out, marching down the stands. He looks how I feel.

I raise a hand in a wave, watching the stands clear behind him, and wait for him to stop in front of me before saying, "He gave it everything."

"And more," Corey agrees. He shakes hands with Trevor and introduces himself to my mom, even though he's already met her—though she won't remember the circumstances.

"Your son put up a fight," Mom tells him.

"He's a warrior."

We all turn to look at Connor, the only Wildcat left on the court. He's sitting on the hardwood now, his legs outstretched, knees raised, head between his shoulders. Coach Sykes approaches him, squeezes his shoulder once, and whatever he says has Connor nodding.

Coach leaves him there, and Corey grasps my elbow. "Come with me," he tells me, and so I follow him onto the court, hesitant as I stand in front of Connor. Without looking up, he lifts his hand, and I take it in mine. He tugs, pulling me down to his level. On my knees, I let him hold me to him, ignoring the tightness of his embrace or the wetness soaking through my jersey when he wipes his eyes on my shoulder. His entire body shakes, not from his crying, but from the adrenaline still pumping through him. He presses his lips to my temple, his heavy breaths coating my cheek.

"I'm so sorry, babe. I know how much this meant to you."

He swallows, loudly, before pulling back, his eyes red when they lock on mine. He nods, and I know he can hear me, understand me, but it's not enough to take away his pain. He's so discouraged, so disappointed. So goddamn heartbroken.

Mom stands beside him, her scars highlighted by the gym lights. "Stand up, Connor!"

My eyes snap to her. "Mama, not right now!"

"Stand. Up!"

"Mama!"

"It's okay," Connor murmurs, releasing me to get to his feet. Standing in front of her, he's only half the man she's grown to love. He seems to have shrunk in the time it's taken to lose a single game.

She orders, as if he's one of the privates in her unit, "Goddammit, number three! Chin up!"

Connor inhales deeply, then lifts his chin, looks down at her.

"Shoulders out!"

His spine straightens, shoulders out, just like she commanded.

Mom huffs out a breath. "Now you listen to me, young man! You walk with your head high! You carried that team! All on your own. Not just tonight, but for the entire goddamn season! You have nothing to be ashamed of. *Nothing!* Do you hear me?"

Connor's lashes fall, and he's slow to open his eyes again. "Yes, ma'am," he mumbles.

"I can't hear you!"

Connor's chest rises as he stands taller again. He clears his throat before answering, his voice stronger, "Yes, ma'am!"

Mom offers him a smile. "Good boy. Now give me a hug."

With a crooked grin, he tells her, "I'm all sweaty."

Rolling her eyes, she responds, "I had my arm blown off in Afghanistan, Connor. I can deal with a little sweat."

Connor laughs now, embracing her. "Just half your arm, Miss D. Stop trying to milk it." Mom laughs, too, and she squeezes him tighter. After releasing her, he turns to me. "I should hit the showers."

"Okay," I say, nodding. "You call me whenever you get home, okay? But take your time. I'm sure you want to let loose a little."

"Where are you going?" Mom asks me.

"Home."

"No, you're not. You stand by your man."

"But, Mama—"

She raises a hand, stopping me. "I will go home. I will take my happy, sleepy pills, and I will go right to bed." She looks at Trevor. "Right, Trevor?"

Trevor nods, facing me. "I got it, Ava. You should stay with Connor."

I look up at Connor. "Do you want me to?"

He clucks his tongue. "Second dumbest thing you've ever said."

"I'll see you at home," Connor's dad says, his hand out for a shake. Connor slaps it away and embraces him just like he did my mother. Corey's fingers curl in the back of Connor's jersey. "I'm proud of you, son."

"Thanks, Dad."

I run a hand along his arm. "I'll wait for you out in the lot."

"Okay." Then he eyes the members of both our families, before moving in, kissing me quickly. "Love you. Thanks for coming."

"Thank my mom," I say, just as Connor's main opponent walks past us.

He leers at my chest. "Damn, ho. You ever want to drop that has-been and get with a winner, I'm right here."

Five voices all at once:

"Hey, now," Corey says, the tamest of them all.

I snap, "I'd rather eat shit and die!" at the same time Trevor warns, "Say that shit about my sister again and see what happens," and Connor who grunts, "Watch your fucking mouth."

But Mom—she pulls out the big guns: "Eat a bag of dicks, you cocksucking little twerp!"

* * *

We all walk out to the parking lot, saying bye to Corey first, and then to Trevor's truck. I make sure Trevor knows exactly what meds Mom takes in what order and what time, and he assures me he's got it handled and reminds me that I'm only a phone call away if he needs me, which Mom promises he won't. And while a part of me is fearful that I won't be around if anything does happen, a more significant part of me knows that I need to stay. That I need to be here for Connor.

I watch them leave, all the way to the point of their taillights disappearing in the distance. When I feel safe enough to move, I start making my way to the exit of the locker rooms where Philips' fans are still on a high and the parents and friends of our team stand around, waiting to show their support. Rhys and Mitch are standing by Rhys's car, and I almost go up to them—just so I can punch them in their lopsided testicles.

I don't.

But I really fucking want to.

I stay in the shadows, not wanting to be seen until Connor gets out.

"Hey," a woman says, stopping next to me.

I turn to her, smile awkwardly. "Hi?"

"You're friends with Connor Ledger, right?" She's middle-aged, blonde hair, eyes hidden behind a pair of sunglasses that cover half her face—which makes no sense considering the only sun around here went down hours ago.

My head tilts to the side when I answer, "Yeah, I'm his girlfriend. Can I help you?"

She flashes a smile, but it's weak. "He played really well tonight."

Nodding, I ask, "Are you a reporter, or... a scout, maybe?" Hope builds a home in my heart. "NBA? That would be *insane*. It would sure cheer him up."

"No, I'm sorry," she says through a croaky giggle. "I'm just a fan."

"Right." I look away, focus on the exit, and add, "He has a lot of those."

"Yeah, I'm sure he does." Her voice becomes louder, clearer, as if to say *hear me*, when she adds, "Have you guys been dating long?"

"Kind of. On and off since the start of the school year..." I turn to her again, my brow furrowed. "I'm sorry, what was your name?"

"Oh, it's not important," she rushes out, taking a single step back. "But, umm... can you give him this?" She pulls out a small white box from her bag. "It's just a little present."

I take her offering, still unsure what her angle is. "From a *fan*?" I ask, because if this is her used underwear or something... *gross*. I suppose I should get used to this, though, especially since this is what his future's going to be like.

The woman nods, says, "Yeah. A *fan*. It was nice meeting you....?"

"Ava."

"Ava." She smiles, genuine. "That's a pretty name."

TWENTY-THREE

Connor

AVA and I make a detour to grab food before we go to Rhys's house, so by the time we do get there, it's already packed. She grasps on to my arm the second we enter, and she doesn't let go as we make our way through the crowd to find the rest of the team in Rhys's pool house. A highlight reel of our season is playing on the huge screen, and I don't know whose idea this was, but they're fucking stupid. The last thing I want is to be reminded of what's no longer in my grasp. "Hey, superstar!" Karen greets, hugging Ava first, and then me. Ava still doesn't release her hold on my hand.

"I'm not really feeling like a superstar right now," I murmur.

Karen's eyes narrow, shifting to Ava before settling on me. "Hey, who am I?" She lowers her voice to mimic mine. "Boohoo, I was double-teamed by the best players in the region and I couldn't carry the entire team on my back, on my own, because two dumb shits decided it would be funny to stick a three-foot dick on a door."

Ava lets out a giggle, stroking my arm in comfort.

I turn to her.

"She has a point," Ava says, shrugging.

"Besides," Karen adds, "fuck those guys, Connor. Duke doesn't care about—"

"Shh!" I cut in.

"What?" Karen eyes me sideways. "No one knows you got into Duke?"

I shake my head. "How the fuck do you know?"

Her gaze flicks to Ava for half a second, but I catch it. I face my girlfriend. She shrugs again. "Sorry. I was excited. And what does it matter now? Your season's over, so…"

"I guess," I murmur.

"Hey, everyone!" Ava shouts, releasing my arm finally. All eyes move to her as she throws her hands up, peace signs in the air, and yells, "My boyfriend got into Duke, *motherfuckers!*"

The room erupts in an ear-deafening roar, and then I'm tackled by too many guys at once. My back hits the floor, and I try to escape from under the pile of teenage boys. Ava stands above us, her arms crossed. "So hot."

I push at as many limbs as I can see until it's clear enough for me to crawl out from beneath them. Rhys offers me his hand, his grin from ear-to-ear. I take it, get to my feet. "Congrats, man. You deserve it!"

He's as genuine as it gets, and I push aside the animosity I'd felt toward him because there's nothing I can do anymore. It's done. And Ava's right. I got into fucking *Duke*. "Thanks, man."

"Let's drink to that instead of the loss, yeah?"

I shake my head. "I'm driving."

He looks at Ava. "Damn, you need to get your goddamn license, A."

"I'm working on it," she laughs out, attaching herself to my side again.

A half hour later and not much has changed, but I can tell something's up with Ava. She sits on my lap while we watch the footage. Or she watches, and I watch her. It's not like the last time she was here, when she actually seemed happy to be. She hasn't left my side, and she doesn't engage in any conversations. I lean forward, press my mouth to the part where her neck meets her shoulder, making her squirm. She turns to me, offers a weak smile.

"What's wrong?" I ask.

"Nothing," she tries hard to convince. "Why? Are you not having a good time?"

Honestly? No. I'd rather be somewhere with her, alone, but I know I need to be here for the team. For my friends. Even if the season is over. "I'm fine. But you seem... I don't know... not yourself...?"

She licks her lips, her eyes on mine. Then she sighs. "I'm just worried, is all. Trevor's not used to being alone with my mom, and I know it's stupid considering they're the ones who suggested this, and I want to be here for you, Connor. I do. It's just... I can't stop worrying."

"So let's go home."

"No," she's quick to respond. "Like I said, I want to be here with you. I just wish I could be in two places at once."

"Why don't you call him?" I suggest. "Check in."

"Because I don't want him to feel like I don't trust him."

"Ava." I tap her leg, motion for her to get up. "He'd be expecting you to call."

She gets to her feet. "You think?"

"I know." I stand, too, and take her hand. "Let's go out front and call so you can stop worrying."

The news about Duke must've spread like wildfire because it seemed like I was stopped every few seconds for pats on the back and congratulations while trying to make it to the front door. It takes a good half hour for Ava and me to get to the front yard, down the long-ass driveway, and onto the sidewalk where it's finally quiet enough to hear our own thoughts.

Ava pulls her phone out of her back pocket and dials Trevor's number. When she notices me leaning in to listen to the call, she puts it on speaker and holds it up between us.

Trevor answers with a "What's going on?"

"Nothing," Ava says. "I was just checking in."

"I knew you would," Trevor says through a chuckle. "Everything's fine. Your mom's out like a light. I've checked on her a few times, and now I'm going to bed."

"Okay, she took her meds?"

"Yes."

I squeeze her hand. "And there's no glass—"

"No."

"And has she—"

"Ava!" Trevor cuts in. "Everything's good. Trust me, all right?"

Ava's shoulders drop. "Yeah, I do... I was just..."

"Worried," he finishes for her. "But don't be. We're all good." He pauses a beat. "Hey, why don't you stay at Connor's tonight?"

She looks up at me, her eyes wide and questioning.

I nod, maybe a little too enthusiastically.

"If that's okay with you?" she says into the phone.

"Yeah," Trevor responds. "It's fine. I'll even get up and make her breakfast so you can sleep in."

"Are you serious right now?" Ava mumbles, almost in tears.

"Yeah, and I'll be here until Krystal gets in."

"Trevor..."

"Hey, I'll even call the school and tell them you're sick."

Ava stares at me, her mouth agape. She asks Trevor, "What have you done to my brother?"

He chuckles. "Hey, Ava. I need you to promise me something, okay?"

"Yeah?"

"Have a good night and quit stressing!"

Ava laughs once. "I will."

"Good, I'll see you when I get home from work tomorrow." He hangs up without another word, and Ava's eyes are huge when she looks up at me. "What just happened?"

"I don't know, but don't question it."

"So we have the whole night."

"And all of tomorrow..."

"What do you want to do?"

"The possibilities are endless."

She looks back at the house. "Do you want to drink away your loss until you can't feel your face?"

I chuckle. "Kind of, yeah."

AVA

Back in the pool house, we sit around with the people Connor's spent the most time with since he got here. The only girls here are me and Karen, and it's kind of perfect.

I'm buzzed.

Connor is drunk. And drunk Connor is a hundred times goofier than sober Connor.

Mitch makes a crack about Karen's mom, and Karen threatens to stab him in the dick with a dart she's holding for some unknown reason. Connor removes his arm from around me to fish out his phone, his lids heavy, thumbs slow to move as he goes through his contacts trying to find a number. He gets to Shit-For-Brains-Mitch and dials. I giggle, watching Mitch take his phone from his pocket and hold it to his ear, his eyes narrowed on Connor sitting on the floor opposite him. "What?" Mitch answers.

Connor slurs his words. "Hey, man. I have a question."

"Okay?"

"What has a small dick and hangs down?"

"What?"

"A bat."

"And...?"

Everyone watches the conversation, their heads moving from side to side.

Connor says, "What has a big dick and hangs up?"

"What?" Mitch responds.

Connor hangs up, and the room fills with the kind of laughter that comes with drunken idiots and stupid jokes. "Confirm or deny, Ava?" Oscar asks.

"I mean, I don't have a lot of sources, but I'd say it's pretty fucking big."

"Burn!" Mitch yells, looking at Rhys.

And I'm too late to realize what I've just said. "No, that's not what I—"

Connor covers my mouth with his palm. "That's *absolutely* what she meant."

Rhys glares at Connor. One second. Two. Then he busts out a laugh. "Thank god you're finally getting laid. We'd all started calling you Mary behind your back."

"Mary?" Connor asks, confused as he turns to me for answers.

"Virgin Mary."

"Ohhh." He nods, slowly, his lids heavy.

"How was your first time?" Oscar asks him, and I don't know how we got to this conversation. Is this what guys talk about?

Connor says, "The first six seconds, I was kind of nervous. But the last six... that was fucking *money!*"

I use his bicep to block my cackle, but I'm the only one who tries to keep it together. Everyone else has lost it. "I need another drink," I announce.

Connor stands up. "I got you."

I get to my feet. "I'll come with."

In the corner of the room, a bar cart is set up with as many different spirits as you'd like. Connor grabs a bottle of tequila and a few packets of salt, plus some lemon wedges. He turns to me, his bottom lip caught between his teeth. Then he steps forward, his mouth to my ear. "Would salt hurt on your pus—"

"Connor!"

He ignores me, moves closer again until his front's pressed against mine. "Because I could lick that all night." He puts all the things back on the cart and leans against a wall, tugging on my top until I'm standing between his legs. Dipping his head, he kisses my neck, his lips parted, tongue leaving a trail of wetness across my jaw until his mouth finds mine. His hand slides down my back, resting on my ass. He squeezes once. Hard. And I jerk against his touch, pulling away. Eyebrows raised, he stares me down, taunting, teasing. "You're very handsy when you've been drinking," I say through a giggle.

"I can't help it. You're hot." He kisses me again, his tongue soft when he uses it to part my lips. I tilt my head, get lost in the moment with him. Minutes pass, and I can feel the heat start burning inside me, feel his hardness press against my stomach. He pulls away before I'm ready, his eyes on mine. "Do you think you'd be interested in me if you still lived in a house like this?"

"And *that's* the dumbest thing *you've* ever said."

"Is it, though?"

"My mom was in the military, Connor. It doesn't pay shit, obviously. Otherwise, we wouldn't be in the situation we're in. The house was the only thing her parents left her, and I wasn't raised like"—I circle a finger in the air—"*this.*"

He dips his head again, and I think he's going to kiss me. Instead, he says, "I once had dinner here, and they had two different sized forks."

I laugh under my breath.

"And knives. And spoons, too. And I'm pretty sure I ate a pigeon."

My head tilts back with the force of my guffaw. "You probably did."

His eyes soak me in. "I love watching you laugh."

My heart soars. "I love *you*."

He smiles, standing to full height again. "Did you have a pool house?"

"Yeah, I did."

"Did you have a game room?"

"Uh huh."

"Did you have *wings*?"

I giggle. "None of the houses on the other side of the road are as extravagant as this, but we had the lake."

"The *lake?*"

I nod.

"There's a fucking *lake?*"

I can't help but laugh at his response. "Yes."

"Jesus. In Florida, we had swamps."

"With gators?" I ask.

"I've never seen one."

"You had endless summers."

"And deadly acts of nature."

"Do you miss Florida?" I ask him.

He shakes his head, adamant. "I have everything I need right here." He takes my hand, kisses the inside of my wrist. "Do you miss the lake?"

"Yeah," I admit. "We had a little patio that sat out over the water, and whenever Mom was home from deployment, we'd sit out there, watch the fireflies, and talk all night about anything and everything." A lump forms in my throat. "I miss that patio, and I miss that version of her."

"She's still there," he assures, tapping at his heart. "In here."

I wipe my sudden tears on his shirt, wondering how it is he can make me feel so much in so little time.

"Let's go," he says, dragging me toward the door.

"Where are we going?"

"To your patio."

"Connor!" I dig my heels into the floor, stopping him. When he turns to me, I tell him, "You can't just go onto someone's property and sit out in their yard."

"Bullshit," Connor scoffs. "Watch me."

Only minutes later, we're standing on the porch of my old house. Connor looks down at me with the goofiest grin on his face, before raising his fist and knocking twice.

I grasp on to his arm. "This is stupid. Let's just go." I start to pull him away just as the front door opens.

A middle-aged man pops his head out. Brow knitted, he asks, "Can I help you?"

"Hello, sir," Connor says, tightening his hold on my hand so I don't run. "My name's Connor Ledger, and this is—"

"Who is it?" a woman says from somewhere inside. The man opens the door wider and his, I assume, wife appears next to him. She looks first at Connor, then at me, her eyes widening when she sees me. "Ava?" she asks.

I have no idea who she is or how she knows me. Still, I find myself nodding. "Yes, ma'am."

She places her hand on her husband's chest, moving him out of the way. "I'm sorry, I probably sound crazy right now, but I recognize you from when I went through the house with the realtor. You were here with your... brother?"

I nod.

She adds, "Yeah, you were packing up all your stuff."

Memories flood my mind, darkened moments of that time in my life when nothing made sense, and everything felt like it was crumbling around me. "I don't remember you," I murmur, unconsciously stepping toward Connor. I use his arm to shield me, because if she knows me, then she probably knows everything else about me.

"Did you want to come in?"

"No," I rush out, tugging on Connor's arm. My neck cranes when I look up at him, heat burning behind my eyes and nose. "Can we go?"

"I'm sorry," the woman says. "I didn't mean to cause you any..." *Pain? Discomfort? Heartache?* She could use any of those words, and they'd all be correct because standing here, in front of a door I used to call mine, an entry to a place I used to call home, where music was loud and laughter was louder, until... until all the blood seeped into my hands...

"I want to go," I repeat, stepping back, trying to get Connor to do the same.

Gaze laced with pity, he rushes out, "But the patio and the lake and the memories, Ava. The good ones, remember?"

Tears well in my eyes again. "I don't care," I lie. I *want* to remember the good. I just don't know if I can.

"You want to go to the patio?" the woman asks, nodding. "You can do that." She motions to the side of the house. "Come through the yard if you don't want to come in."

Connor keeps his eyes on mine, eyebrows lifted in question. "It can't hurt," he pushes, and he looks so damn hopeful and eager.

"Okay."

"Yeah?"

I nod.

"Give me five minutes," the woman says. "Meet me at the side gate."

Connor keeps his arms wrapped around me while we wait, no words spoken between us. I don't know how we got from him drowning his losses, to celebrating Duke, to this. Now. And I know I should be grateful, but the truth is, I'm scared.

"We'll go, you'll see it, and you'll know right away if you want to leave or stay, and I'll do whatever you want," he says as if reading my mind. "No pressure."

The side gate opens, and the woman smiles. I should really get her name, but I don't think I could talk through the knot in my throat. "Please," she says, waving us in, "take your time."

"Thank you, ma'am," Connor says, all hints of alcohol in his tone gone. I lead him past the main house, the pool and pool house, and beyond the greenhouse to where the yard opens up. The lake is prettier than I remember, and I stand still, my eyes drifting shut as I inhale a breath, basking in the memories of that scent alone. When I open my eyes again, Connor's watching me, a hint of a smile playing on his lips. "You good?"

"Yeah." I nod, slowly, then look over around him to the patio. The chairs are different from the ones we had, but there are two there, a small table between them. Fairy lights hang from the pillars around the patio, lighting up the small space. We make our way over, noticing the jug of iced tea and slices of pie set out on two little plates. Connor laughs. "Y'all do things so different on this side of town." He sits down on one of the deck chairs and tugs on my hand until I'm sitting on his lap, his hand on my stomach. "It's nice out here," he murmurs, his chin on my shoulder. "Tell me a memory."

I half turn to him. "What do you mean?"

"Tell me something about your mom *before*. What did you talk about *right here*, in this very spot?"

I try to go back to a different time, a different life. Clearing my throat, I adjust on his lap until I'm sideways so I can look at him when I speak. My arm around his neck, I say, "When she was home before her last deployment, we sat out here, and we talked about Karen being boy-crazy."

Connor nods, his smile widening when his eyes focus on my lips, at the way they turn up at the memory. It's so pure—the way he looks at me—as if he's happy just because I am. "What did she have to say about that?"

"She said that we were too young for love," I tell him. "And she said that the only fear she's ever had is that she won't be around to watch me grow, to watch me fall in love for the first time." I choke on the memory and the recollection of what she said next. Because I feel it in my heart. I feel it in Connor's. With my eyes on his, I don't hide my tears when I say, "She said that her hope for me was that I'd find a boy who would hold me through my pain and lift me through my triumphs. Who would love unconditionally. And she hoped that I would understand what that meant—*love*—in every sense of the word. But I didn't know, Connor..."

"Know what?" he asks, his thumbs swiping at my cheeks.

"I didn't know it would feel like this. Like I didn't have a choice."

"In *love*?"

"I don't think we can choose the direction in which our heart beats. Because I didn't *want* to fall in love with you. I didn't want to fall in love *at all*. But then you came along and... and I told you early on that I was falling for you, but I lied. I was already there. And now I can't imagine what my life would be like without you. I can't think or breathe or move or live a single second without you infiltrating my mind, and I know that that's wrong, this... *obsession* I have with you... but there it is." I swallow the outcome of my confessions, keep my eyes on his. "And here *we* are."

connor

WE STAY at the lake for hours while Ava tells me only the good memories she has of her mom, and I listen intently, making sure to pay attention to every word, every syllable that falls from her lips. I watch her smile. I watch the tears fall. I listen to her laugh, and I listen to her cry. And I get lost in all the different sides of Ava; quirky and confident, and vulnerable and sad, and I fall deeper in love with all the different versions of her.

We catch a cab home, both of us knowing what's ahead, at least for tonight, and neither of us can keep our hands and mouths off each other.

When we get there, I walk up my driveway with her on my back as she chuckles into my neck. I say, "My dad's at work tonight, so..."

She jumps down when we get to the door. "So... we can *talk* loudly."

"Yeah." My grin is stupid. "Conversations are *neat*."

We head straight for my room, and I close and lock the door behind me. Ava says, "I thought you said your dad was working?"

I shrug. "Habit."

Ava sits on the edge of my bed, starts removing her jacket, and a glass flask of whiskey falls to the floor. "I'd forgotten about this."

"Did you steal that from Rhys?"

She shrugs. "I got it for Trevor." She looks up at me. "But we could put it to use considering I technically don't have to get home until tomorrow afternoon."

"I'll get the glasses."

When I return, two whiskey glasses in hand, Ava's stripped out of most of her clothes. In only a tank top, bra, and underwear, she holds the lip of the flask to her lips, sipping gently.

"You couldn't even wait for me?"

Another shrug and she offers me the flask. I leave the glasses on my desk and sit next to her. After a swig, I hand it back. Her head tilts back, the muscles in her throat contracting when she swallows. I can't help it; I press my open mouth there, loving the way her back arches to give me better access. She moans, her hands going to my hair as I slide my hand up her top, cupping her bra-covered breast. "Connor?" she breathes out.

I make my way up her neck until my mouth finds hers and I kiss her, my tongue roaming lazily because unlike every other time before, we have *hours* to explore, to tease.

"Connor," she repeats, pushing on my shoulders.

I raise my eyebrows in question.

"I have a question," she says, and I nod, adjusting the bulge in my pants. "Why have you still got so many clothes on?"

I chuckle under my breath and settle back against the wall. I take a swig of the whiskey. "I'm just trying to take my time. Enjoy this moment with you."

She exhales through her nose and then moves to straddle me. Hands linked at my nape, she says, "I'm sorry about your season."

I shrug. "It's done. But hey, it means I have a bit more time on my hands. At least with games. I still want to get some good training time in if that's okay."

"You don't need my permission," she laughs out.

I push off the wall, kiss the top of her breast. "I just want to make you happy, Ava."

She pulls back, takes my face in her hands. "You do."

"Yeah?"

She rolls her eyes. "I mean, you'd make me happier if you took your shirt off." So I reach behind me and pull my shirt off. She runs her hands over my shoulders, down my chest. "Much better."

"Now, you."

She takes off her top, and then her bra, and sits in front of me in all her beautiful glory. I lower my head, flick her nipple with my tongue, loving the way her breath staggers when it leaves her. I keep at it, moving from one to the other, over and over, my hands curled around her waist as she grinds into me. She feels so small beneath my touch, so fucking perfect. I run the back of my fingers down her stomach until I find the top of her underwear, but she stops me, her fingers lacing with mine. I look up at her, eyebrows raised. "No?"

"Not yet."

I exaggerate a pout. "When?"

She starts to slide off of me, and I internally cry, but then she starts undoing my fly, releasing me completely. Her hand curls around my cock, stroking, and I tilt my head back, my eyes closed. I feel her heated breath first, then the wetness of her tongue and everything else is a blur when she starts working me in her mouth. I open my eyes, a moan escaping when I see her watching me, her lips thinned around me. We've never done it like this before, so open, with the lights on. It's always been dark, everything under the covers, and I'm already so fucking close, and I tell her that. But she won't fucking stop. I gather her hair to one side so I can watch it all, my hips rising, thighs tensing, and about to—"Fuck, stop." I pull on her hair, force her away.

"No, I wanted—"

I practically throw her to the side, trying to calm the hell down. She's on all fours when she cranes her neck to look back at me. "Connor!"

I get behind her, slide her underwear down her legs and groan at the view in front of me. And then I go to town, lick every inch of her until she's moaning—my name mixed with God's—again and again, and I flip to my back, bring her back down to me. She grinds against my mouth, her thighs squeezing the sides of my head, while her fingers tug at my hair. She's loud. Louder than she's ever been, and it turns me on more. She *screams* when she comes, her pleasure coating my tongue. My chin. She only takes a second to recover, moving down my body until my cock's at her entrance. I grab a condom from my nightstand and hand it to her, sitting up when she rolls it over me. I kiss her. Hard. And she returns it with the same lust, same passion. I slide into her effortlessly, our moans of ecstasy filling the room. Sweat coats our skin as we find a rhythm, her back arched, arm outstretched, hand on my thigh. I reach behind me, my hand pressed to the mattress, giving me enough leverage to meet her thrust for thrust. I find her clit with my thumb, stroke her once, testing. She loses it, begs for more, and so I do it again and again until she loses her rhythm and falls forward. Her teeth clamped on my shoulder, her release coming in the form of moans that vibrate against my flesh. "Goddamn, Connor. What the hell's gotten into—"

I don't let her finish before I flip her off me. Chest on the mattress, ass in the air, and I can tell she's exhausted, and I should be, but... teenage hormones are one hell of a drug. I get behind her and pull on her hips until she's exactly where I need her. My hand glides up her spine, to her shoulder, and I grip her there. "Is this okay?" I ask because we've never been in this position before and I want to make sure.

"Yeah," she breathes out. I pull back and then enter her slowly, watching every inch of me fill her, then I lean down, my chest to her back. I kiss between her shoulder blades as I start to move again, slowly, but she leans up on her outstretched arms, her neck craned to look back at me. "God, you feel so good inside me," she whispers, and I try to hold off. She grips the top of my headboard with one hand, the other going between her legs, feeling where we connect. "Oh, fuck," she moans, "that's so fucking hot."

I look down, the image in front of me driving me insane, making my dick pulse. "You should see it from my angle."

"Oh, god, I'm going to come again, Connor. I can't—" I reach around, find her clit again. My jaw tenses when she tightens around me. "Fuck, babe. *Fuck me.*" I hold her to me, my hand on her hip, so I can fuck her harder, faster, like she's pleading for me to do.

It's the filthiest, dirtiest sex we've ever had, but it's also the most meaningful. Because we let go of the past, and we let go of ourselves. We find comfort in each other, in asking for what we want. We take our time to explore each other's bodies, to claim them.

The room is constantly filled with the sounds of our sweaty bodies slamming together, of the moans of pleasure, of the screams and grunts of our releases. Over and over. Again and again. We don't stop. Can't. But we take breaks every now and then, and we talk, we drink a little more, we laugh, we shower together, and then we go back to the exploring, and the teasing, and tasting until finally, *finally*, we're done. Spent. We collapse in each other's arms, exhaustion taking over us. "One day," I breathe out, my chest rising and falling, "when I'm in the NBA, we'll live in a house so big that we can do stuff like this all the time, and we can be this loud, and your mom won't hear us."

Ava's head pops up from my chest. "Why would my mom be there?"

"Because she'll live with us." My eyes narrow. "Duh."

"She will?"

I nod. "Who'll take care of the horses?"

"What horses?" she asks.

I flick her forehead. "Her therapy horses, stupid."

She smiles wide. "You're going to buy my mom therapy horses?"

I roll my eyes. "Obviously."

She shakes her head, laughing quietly. "Why do you say all this like it's something we've spoken about so many times before?"

"Oh yeah. I never actually told you." I adjust my head on the pillow. "I've just *thought about* it."

A frown tugs on her lips. "Do you really think about that stuff?"

My eyes drift shut, sleep quick to consume me. "Ava, my future with you is *all* I think about."

connor

I WAKE up to my phone ringing, and my eyes feel like they're burning when I open them. Every one of Ava's limbs is somehow wrapped around me, and it takes me a moment to untangle myself from her to search for my phone. I find it in the pocket of my discarded jeans and cringe when I see Dad's name on the screen. "Hey, Dad."

"Hey. You still sleeping?"

"Yeah, Ava was over last night and uh..." I try to swallow, but my throat's too dry. "Hey, is there any chance you could call the school..." I trail off.

He's silent a beat before answering, "Yeah, I can do that."

"You're the best dad I've ever had," I mumble.

Dad chuckles. "Big night?"

"Kind of."

"No drinking and driving, I assume?"

"No. My car's still at Rhys's, and I'm not going to lie; we had a little here, too. I'm sorry."

"It's okay. I prefer you to be honest, but just remember, you're still a minor, Connor."

"I know."

"Is Ava taking the day off, too?"

"Yeah."

"So, I'll see you both when I get home?"

Next to me, Ava stirs.

"Mmm-hmm," I murmur.

"Should I bring home some breakfast from the diner?"

"*Literally* the best dad in the entire world and I'm not even joking this time."

"I have to use the bathroom," Ava mumbles, climbing over and around me to get out of bed.

"We need to call Ross, too." *My agent.* He'll be *thrilled* to hear how bad my stats were from last night.

"Sure."

Ava skips her pile of clothes and opens my drawers, finding a pair of boxer shorts and an old jersey. She throws them on.

"All right. Well, I'll let you go," Dad says while Ava rummages through her bag. She pulls out her phone and a plain white box. She throws the box on my lap before exiting the room.

"Don't forget to call the school," I remind Dad.

"I won't. I'll see you soon."

"Bye." I hang up and open the lid of the box.

My heart stops.

My breath halts.

Two toy cars.

One red. One blue.

Lightning McQueen and Sally.

My hands shake when I flip them over, a part of me already knowing what's there: the initials CL carved into the metal, so everyone at daycare knew they were mine.

Bile rises to my throat, and I lurch forward, get to the trashcan just in time. Ava rushes into the room, dropping to her knees, her hand on my back. "Damn, how much did we drink?"

Another bout, and this is not how I want her to see me. Or smell me. I wipe my mouth along my forearm, my eyes on hers. "Where did you get that?" I breathe out, my heart racing, panic rushing through my bloodline.

"What are you talking about?"

"The cars!"

"What cars?"

"The box, Ava!" I shout. "Where did you get that box from?!"

"Some lady gave it to me." Her eyes widen. "Why are you yelling at me?"

I take a calming breath because she doesn't know. And I don't want her to. "What lady?"

"I don't know. She was there after the game when I was waiting out in the lot for you." Her chest rises with her sharp inhale. "Why? What—"

"Sorry," I cut in, blinking hard. I pinch the bridge of my nose to alleviate the pounding in my head. "I was just confused, and this hangover..." My words are rushed, just like my pulse, but I don't want her to see it. To start asking questions. Because she will. And I won't have the answers. "I'm sorry,"

I repeat and sit back on my heels. I'd forgotten I was naked. I look up at her; worried eyes look back. "It was so much happening at once," I lie, trying to get out of my head. I *hate* lying to her, but I can't... I can't fucking deal. "With Dad on the phone and my head hammering and you—" I try to smile. "You looking as fucking cute as you do right now."

A hint of a smile. *Good.* It's working.

"I should go clean this up," I say, lifting the trashcan. "And brush my fucking teeth." I put on a pair of boxer shorts before leaving, taking the trash can with me. Then I go to the bathroom, splash water on my face, and urge my body to slow the fuck down. Everything is happening too fast, blood pumping, pulse raging, head spinning—all of it's too swift, too much. I grip the edge of the sink, stare at myself in the mirror.

This can't be happening.

Not now.

Not ever.

Ava.

I just need to get back to Ava, and everything will be okay. Everything will be normal again.

I clean the trashcan, brush my teeth, and make my way back to my room. Ava's in my bed now, lying on her side, the covers pushed down on one side as if she'd been waiting for me. She smiles. "Good morning, boyfriend." And she's *everything*. She's all I need. All I want. She's enough to calm me down, to fill my heart with peace. I pick up the cars, throw them in the trash and get back into bed with her, forgetting everything else. She lifts her head, allowing my arm to find its home around her. "What do you want to do today?" she asks.

"Anything you want."

Ear to my chest, she settles there, her finger tapping at the same rate as the pulse she's listening to. She whispers, looking up at me, "I want to get lost in your magic."

TWENTY-SIX

ava

I'M quick to grab my phone and switch off the alarm, not wanting to wake Connor sleeping beside me. It's been a few weeks now since the team lost regionals, and we've spent almost every night together. Mom and Trevor don't seem to mind it. In fact, the first night he *didn't* stay, Mom was asking for him the next morning, worried that something had happened between us.

Connor groans when I start to get out of bed, his hand finding my arm. "I'm up," he murmurs.

"No, you're not. Go back to sleep."

"No, I'll help with breakfast." A second later, he's snoring.

He hates that I let him sleep in, but he needs the rest. He's still training as often as he can, trying to make the most of what the coaches have to offer before he goes to Duke in the fall. My chest aches at the thought of him leaving, of not being able to have these moments with him every day. But my pride in him quickly kills those thoughts. I kiss him once before leaving the room and going to the kitchen. Mom's already up, sitting at the table with her tablet. "You okay, Mama?" I ask, kissing the scars that *made* her the woman she is today. I used to think they'd made her a stranger, but the meds she's been on lately have given the *real her* back to me, and I couldn't be happier because of it.

"I'm fine, sweetheart, just wanted to get back to my book."

"That good, huh?"

She nods. "Reading has helped me a lot, actually."

"It has?"

"I think it allows me to feel like I'm *living*, you know?"

I switch on the stove and put the pan on the heat before turning to her. "What do you mean?"

"It was starting to get to me—being in the house all day—this allows me to see and feel things without ever leaving."

"Do you want to leave?" I ask. "Because you can, we all can, like we did with Connor and... you went to his game, and that wasn't so bad."

She shrugs. "Maybe one day I'll feel more comfortable. This town isn't very friendly."

"Yeah," I sigh out, my mind lost with thoughts of our future. I just need time, I tell myself. Soon, we'll be out of here for good.

"Hey," she whispers, looking toward my room. "Is Connor here?"

"Yeah, he's sleeping."

"I have a surprise for him."

I smile. "What's your surprise?"

She gets to her feet and undoes the tie of her robe, revealing what she's wearing underneath. I can't help but laugh. "He's going to love it."

A couple of hours later, my bedroom door opens, and Connor appears, rubbing his eyes. He walks into the kitchen, stopping when he sees Mom standing by the sink, her back turned to him. Eyes wide, his instant grin fills my heart with joy. I say through a laugh, "Look what Mama got Trevor to order for her."

Wearing a high school All-American jersey with Connor's name and number on the back, Mom turns around, her smile matching his.

"Hey, it looks good on you!" Connor exclaims, suddenly awake and full of life. He moves to her, kisses her right on the scars like he does most mornings. "Where did you even get this? I don't even have one yet."

Mom giggles. "I have my ways," she says, patting his cheek. "When do you fly out?"

"Just before midday," he answers.

"Is your dad going with you?"

"Nah, he couldn't get the time off work."

"Really?" I ask, cutting into their conversation, my concern evident. "Will you be okay?" I try to ask the question as vaguely as possible because I know about his fear of airports, but Mom doesn't, and I don't know if he wants her knowing.

Connor winks at me, his smile still there. "Yeah, I'm good, babe. I'm a big boy now."

Trevor walks into the kitchen and drops down in his chair, grumbling, "Mama Jo, you never wore my jerseys."

Mom rolls her eyes. "That's because football's for pussies."

Connor busts out a laugh, and I giggle, squeezing Trevor's shoulder as he says, "I feel like I've been replaced by the golden boy."

"Never," Mom tells him, laughing as she walks toward the door.

Connor waits for her to be far enough before baring his teeth, grinning at my brother. "She loves me more."

Trevor shakes his head. "Get out of my house, you Shawn Mendes looking motherfucker," he grinds out, but he's joking... I *think*.

"Shawn's hair is darker," I say, though I do get where Trevor's coming from.

"Who's Shawn Mendes?" Connor asks.

"*Who's Shawn Mendes*," Trevor mimics under his breath.

"Boys. That's enough," I warn, raising the spatula in my hand. "Now you two get along, or I'll beat the both of you to within an inch of your lives."

Trevor shivers. "You're scary," he says, at the same time Connor takes the spatula from me, smacks my ass with it.

I exaggerate a moan as I bite my lip, look up at him.

Connor laughs.

Trevor mumbles, "I do *not* want to know what goes on behind closed doors with you two."

Ignoring him, I ask Connor, "Are you sure you can give me a ride to school?"

"Yes." He takes over cooking his and Trevor's breakfast for me. "I don't want to miss out on any more time with you."

Trevor gags.

Connor adds, "I'll have plenty of time. Enough for me to come home and pack."

"You haven't packed yet?"

Trevor speaks up, "He's a guy, we don't need much."

"It's true," Connor agrees, plating up Trevor's food and serving it to him. He ruffles what little hair's on Trevor's head. "I'll wear your jerseys for you, Trevor."

"Shut up," Trevor laughs out.

Connor gets his own plate and sits opposite my brother. "Do you miss it? Wearing a jersey?"

"Sometimes," Trevor replies, shrugging, "but it was never my end goal like it is with you, so it's not life-defining, you know?"

"What *was* your end goal... or is...?"

I pretend to be washing the dishes, but I'm listening to every word they're saying.

Trevor answers, "I always wanted to be a talent scout."

"Oh, yeah? You'd be good at that."

"You think?"

"Yeah, or an agent."

"What makes you think I'd be good at either of those things?"

"Because you *care*. My agent only really cares about the final numbers. Stats, money. You'd care about the person you're representing, and you'd make sure they get the best outcome."

"Maybe," Trevor replies, and I can hear the contemplation in his tone.

"Would you have to go back to school for it?"

"I guess, yeah. But..." *But this is my life now*, he doesn't say.

The conversation dies there, and soon enough we're all heading out for the day, saying bye to Krystal and Mom at the door.

"What are you doing?" Connor asks, looking over at me on the drive to school.

I turn over a page on my English assignment and answer, "I just wanted to check over this paper real quick. It's due today, and I only finished it this morning."

"*When* this morning?"

"While you were sleeping. Just give me two minutes."

He stays quiet until I finish reading over it and shove it back in my bag. "Can I ask you something?"

"Sure."

"When—how—why—"

"Pick an adverb, any adverb!" I sing.

He chuckles. "I just don't understand *when* you have the time to study as hard as you do, and *how* you managed to get early admittance to all these amazing colleges, and *why* you do it in the first place if you initially never intended on going."

I let his words sink in. "Wow. That's a lot of not understanding."

"I know; there's a lot I don't understand about you." He smiles over at me.

"Like what?"

"Like, why you're with me, for one."

"Your self-deprecation is only cute sometimes."

"Fine," he laughs out. "Then I don't understand how you always manage to deflect every question I throw your way."

I sigh. "I study at night when Mom goes to bed—"

"But I'm there now, and I don't see you—"

"I do it once you're asleep."

"What? How do I not know that?"

"Because you sleep like the dead."

"Fair. So next question, how?"

"Early acceptances?"

He nods.

"I had a killer essay. Pity me, I'm the daughter of a wounded war veteran..."

"Ahh."

"Plus, my grades are good, not great, but good enough."

He nods again. "So, lastly... *why?*"

I suck in a huge breath, let it out slowly. "Because it's always been important to Trevor. There are certain things he doesn't want me missing out on, and education is one of them. A big chunk of the money we got from the sale of the house went to that, and so I don't want it to go to waste, and... more than anything, I don't want to disappoint him. He's sacrificed so much, the least I could do was give him that."

Connor nods again as he chews the corner of his lip, and I know him well enough now to realize that means he's thinking, contemplating.

"What's on your mind, number three?"

He huffs out a breath. "What are your plans for next year or the year after?"

That's the million-dollar question right there, and I really should've seen it coming. "I'm not sure. I'm actually meeting with Miss Turner about it all today. Hopefully, she can guide me."

"Isn't that what the guidance counselor's for?"

"Yeah, but Miss Turner's invested in me. I'm her little pet project. Besides, I like her. She's a good person."

"She is?"

"Yep. You know she grew up around here? She went to West High. I'm pretty sure she loves her job, but she hates St. Luke's. You know she's been asking for funding for three years, and they just keep shutting her down?"

"That sucks."

"It's like no one takes mental health seriously around here, especially at that school. We're the future, and no one gives a shit how we feel. It's like, your brain's an organ, right? It should be treated the same way as if you had pain in your kidneys or something. You'd go get it looked at, and everyone around you would tell you to go see a doctor. But when there's a pain in your brain, these fuckers—"

"You're preaching to the choir, Ava. I get it."

"Sorry," I mumble. "It just sucks for her that no one takes her seriously." I look through the windshield when he begins to slow down, his gaze focused on the green light.

"Why are you slowing down? It's green."

"Go red, go red, go red," he whispers, then smiles when the light turns amber, rolling the car to a complete stop.

"You could've easily made that."

"I know, but I didn't want to." He faces me, a smile tugging on his lips right before he leans across, his mouth pressing to mine, kissing me slowly, openly, perfectly. When he pulls back, he says, "Hi, remember me? I'm your boyfriend, and I'm leaving today for four whole days. I won't be back until Monday night."

"I'm sorry." I hold his arm to my chest while he takes off again. "I know." Believe me, I *know*. It's all I could think about last night while he was sleeping next to me. That, and all the worst possible things that could happen while he's gone. But I don't need him to know those things. I want him to go and make the most of it. "It's only four days," I say, hoping he doesn't hear the forced effort in my laugh. "I'm sure you'll survive." *But* I'll *struggle without you*, I don't say.

"I guess we should get used to it, huh?"

I nod, even though the prospect of being away from him for who knows how long kills me inside.

"Well. Duke's just over two hours away, so if you do stay here, hopefully, I'll be able to come back whenever I can. You'll have to keep your bed warm for me though. I'm pretty sure Dad's planning on going back to Florida."

"He is?"

Connor nods but doesn't say much else. When we get to school, he finds a parking spot and gets out to open the door for me. The whole chivalry thing isn't something I ever thought I wanted—I have arms and legs and can do it all myself—but I kind of love that he does it for me. As soon as I'm out of his truck, he gets bombarded by people wishing him luck for the weekend. I can tell it makes him uncomfortable, but he smiles with every kind gesture, and when it begins to die off, he reaches for me, both his hands linking with mine. "I'll miss you so much," he says, just as the warning bell goes off. He curses under his breath, and I kiss him quickly.

"I have to go," I rush out. Another short kiss. "I'll see you on Monday." Then I shrug out of his hold and start running up the steps, the ache in my chest causing the heat behind my eyes. *It's just four days*, I keep telling myself. *I can do this*. With each step up, each inch I move farther from him, the stronger my emotions become. Tears well in my eyes, and I can't fight them off. And I don't want to. *Shit*. I turn quickly, thankful he's still there watching me. And then I run back to him, faster than I've ever run before. I didn't want him to see me like this, but I can't let him go without saying goodbye properly. He pushes off his truck when I get near enough, his arms open, and I practically jump into his embrace, my arms around his neck while he wraps his around my waist. Feet off the ground, my legs circle him. "I don't want you to go," I mumble into his neck. It's stupid and petty, and I'm *The Worst Girlfriend Ever*.

"Dammit, Ava, don't mess with my emotions like that!"

I rear back, still holding on to him. "I didn't want you to know how badly I'll miss you," I murmur, unable to control my pout.

He sets me back on my feet but keeps me close. "I'm going to miss you, too. Like crazy. But we'll call and message every day."

I nod. "It's *four* whole days."

"It feels like forever."

"I know."

"Don't go getting any other boyfriends while I'm gone."

I scoff, place my ear to his chest so I can listen to the magic that lives only for me. "You're not the one who needs to be worried," I say around the knot in my throat. "There are going to be so many groupies there. Don't go meeting other girls." It's meant to be a half-hearted joke, but I can't seem to hide the legitimate worry that's been building inside me.

He shifts the hair away from my face, holding it to the side of my head so he can look me directly in the eyes. "Ava, *come on.*"

"I know," I sigh out. "But you'll be out there doing *You* things, and I'm the small-town girl you left behind... it's a tale as old as time."

"Stop," he orders.

I shrug. "I'm a little insecure, okay?"

He huffs out a breath, then kisses me once. "What can I do to make you feel better about it?"

Reaching up, I run a finger along his forehead. "Get my name tattooed right here."

He laughs. "Just A V A?"

Nodding, I say, "And Diaz. Just so it's clear. Maybe Ava E. D. Diaz."

"That's a lot of letters, babe."

"Well, lucky you have a giant head."

His head throws back with his laughter, and I smile, pull back a little to give him room to breathe.

"I'm stupid," I admit. "Go and have a good time. The *best* time. Forget me."

"All right. I won't forget you, but I *will* try to have a good time without you."

"Good."

"You're going to be late to multimedia, and Miss Salas has been a raging bitch lately."

"I know." I kiss him again, and this time, I let my tongue do the talking.

When we pull apart, he asks, "Hey, when I get back, will you do that thing with your tongue on my—"

Laughing, I start to walk away from him for the second time and shout, so everyone around us can hear, "Yes, Connor! I promise! When you get back, I'll wax your nipples again! Your asshole, too!"

TWENTY-SEVEN

ava

MY HOUSE LOOKS like the Fourth of July the next day, with red, white and blue streamers and balloons scattered throughout the living room. It was Mom's idea, and I was all for it. Trevor holds on to a lone maroon balloon and raises it in the air. "Gig 'em, Aggies!" He's still butt-hurt thinking we never cared about his games, but it was hard to show how proud we were of him when he was all the way in Texas.

We set up around the TV with popcorn and drinks. Mom wears her All-American jersey, and I wear one of Connor's Wildcats jerseys. Every minute closer to game time, my excitement seems to double. It's his first national broadcast, and I'm so thrilled for him.

I take a photo of the room and Mom and send them both to Connor with the caption:

> Ava: We're just a little excited. Can you tell?

And then one of Trevor frowning with his balloon and write:

> Ava: He doesn't count.

I wait until it's only minutes before the game to send:

> Ava: I know you won't see this until after the game, but I just want you to know how proud I am of you, of everything you've accomplished and everything you are. No matter what happens today, or tomorrow, or a year from now, you'll always be my number one, #3. I love you more than the magic inside you.

"Here he is," Mom says, slapping my leg a little too excitedly.

Trevor turns up the volume as the East team enters the court. They file into a line for the national anthem, and the camera moves past each player. My breath halts when Connor appears on the screen, and then disappears completely when I notice the huge black writing on both his arms. "Did he get tattoos overnight?" Trevor murmurs.

"Go back," I demand.

"It's a live stream, dumbass."

I grunt, wanting to know what the hell's on his arms. Luckily, just a few minutes later while showing the warm-ups, the announcers seem as intrigued as I am. "What's on Ledger's arms?" one of them asks.

"Who knows? Kids with full-sleeve tattoos are *a thing* these days," the other retorts.

"Can we zoom in on his arms?" says the first, and the cameraman must hear because he focuses in on one of Connor's arms while he shoots from the three-point line.

"Is that..." It's clear the first announcer is trying to read it, but I already know what it says, and my heart plummets from the weight of Connor's love.

"Ava E. D. Diaz," I whisper, my smile unrestrained. "Oh, my God..."

"It seems to be a girl's name," the announcer laughs out. "What a lucky girl!"

"What's on the other arm?"

The camera focuses on his other arm, and my grin is so pathetically stupid I can't help but cry. *"First and Forever."*

"Marry him, Ava," Mom orders.

I plan to...

I keep that thought to myself.

CONNOR

> Ava: Oh, you! I don't even know what to say, Connor. You blow me away every damn day. I can't believe you did that!

> Ava: Damn, #3. Way to show up!

Ava: Holy shit of a dunk! That backboard's crying for its mama. I can hear it from here!!!

Ava: Dude, you need to give your opponent a break.

Ava: How the hell were you ranked so low when you're the best player out there!

Ava: Your agent better be watching this. Making calls. Working deals!

Ava: My boy!!!

Ava: Fuck. I think I've lost my voice.

Ava: OMG!!!

Ava: CONNOR LEDGER, EVERYONE!! MV motherfucking P.

Ava: MVP! MVP! MVP!

Ava: Okay, I'm done!

Ava: MVP! MVP! MVP! MVP!

Ava: Okay, now I'm really done.

Ava: You're so getting lucky when you get back. I'll do that thing with my tongue that you like. For, like, a month. Every night. Multiple times.

Ava: MVP! MVP! MVP! MVP! MVP! MVP! MVP! MVP! MVP! MVP! MVP! MVP! MVP! MVP! MVP! MVP! MVP! MVP! MVP! MVP! MVP! MVP! MVP! MVP! MVP! MVP!

Ava: Too much? Too fucking bad!

Ava: I love you. Miss you. Call me when you get done being a fucking MVP! MVP!

My cheeks hurt from the strength of my smile as I read Ava's texts.

Connor: I just got out of the shower. About to shake hands with some NBA scouts. Wish me luck.

Ava: As if you need it.

Connor: lol. I'll call you when I'm done?

Ava: Take your time, MVP.

Connor: You're going to let this get to my head.

> Ava: Oh, I'm going to get to your head. All over it. Drool all over that weenus, baby!

> Connor: You're crazy, and I love you.

> Ava: I love you more.

> Connor: I gotta go. Send nudes.

The few hours after the game are a blur of handshakes and business card collecting. Agents, scouts, even a few pros come out to meet us. I'd planned on showing up and making a name for myself today. I felt like I had something to prove, and so I went out and did it. Never in my dreams did I think I'd get MVP. Not with the caliber of talent that came out to play. It's insane.

I tell the same story to all the reporters in the press conference after, my post-game adrenaline enough to push aside my nerves. When it's all over and I'm walking toward the bus to take us back to the hotel, the first thing I do is go for my phone, read through Ava's texts again, reminding me of my reason, of my end game. My smile widens when I see the few new messages from her.

> Ava: I'm getting your name tattooed on my ass.

> Ava: I'm officially a Connor Ledger groupie. I'm one in a million, sure, but I'm THE one in a million, and I also know where to stab someone for an instant kill and silent death… just in case any other girl gets too close.

> Ava: Shit. Delete that. OMG. I was kidding, FBI! Haha. *shifty eyes*

> Ava: Connor Ledger: St. Luke's Academy, All-American MVP, Duke Alumni, starting point guard for [insert whatever goddamn NBA team you want because YOU GOT THIS, BABY!].

"Connor?"

I look up, my smile falling instantly. My heart stops, and every muscle in my body solidifies.

"Ledger, you coming?" one of my teammates calls from just inside the bus doors.

"I'll uh… I'll catch up with you guys later."

"You sure?" he asks, and I nod.

I wait for the bus doors to close before taking a breath and glancing at the woman in front of me. Anger flares, but it disappears just as fast. "What... what do you want?"

Her gaze drops, so do her shoulders. "You recognize me?" Her hair's lighter than I remember. Her eyes, too. And she's aged. Badly. But she's still the woman my nightmares are made of.

I clear the ball of nerves rising in my throat and mumble the truth I've been holding on to for *fifteen* years. "It's a little hard to forget the person who tried to kill you."

She nods, and it seems like the atmosphere is closing in on us. "I wasn't sure if you'd remember me," she says, just above a whisper.

So many times, I've thought about this moment, right here, and everything I'd say to her if I got the chance. I push aside my hurt and tell her, "I'd probably remember you more if you'd turn around considering the last time I saw you, you were walking away from me."

"You're mad?"

"Should I not be?" I try to take a calming breath, but it doesn't seem to help. "What do you want?"

"Look," she says, glancing at all the people still milling around us. "This isn't the time or place... but can you meet me somewhere?"

"No." I don't want to be here. Not with her. Not *alone*. I grip my phone tighter. As pathetic as it is, I want my dad.

"*Please.*"

I laugh once, look over her shoulder, and hope she can't see the ache through my eyes. "It's funny... I cried that same word over and over in that car... when I felt like I was suffocating. I said *please, Mama*, and you didn't care then, so..."

"I know." She wipes at the corners of her eyes, and my gaze moves there, sees the pain she's carrying. "There's a lot of things we need to talk about."

"*You* need to talk about," I rush out, trying to be strong, defiant. "I have nothing to say to you."

I start to walk away, but she stops me, her hand on my elbow. I flinch. Turn to her.

"You owe me nothing," she says.

"I know this."

"Connor," she sighs out, looking around us. "You don't know how much I'm risking by being here."

I step forward, tower over her, and let that initial anger consume me. "I should have you arrested."

"I know," she whispers, and I can tell she's on the verge of sobbing. And I know that I shouldn't feel the way I do when I hear the single cry escape her. I know I should walk away, just like she did. But...

But I *can't*.

"Here," she says, taking a step back. She keeps her gaze lowered, guarded when she hands me a folded-up note. "Here's my number. I'll be at this address at 7:30 tonight. Show up or don't, but trust me, Connor. It's better to live your entire life with the truth than it is to live with regret."

AVA

I don't hear from Connor for the rest of the afternoon and most of the evening, and so I assume that he's busy. Of course, he would be. I get Mom settled on the couch after listening to her ramble on and on and on about Connor's game, about him getting MVP, and I smile when she says, "You're so lucky to have each other."

I clean up the house a little but keep the streamers and balloons up for when Connor returns. Then I go to my room, grab the large cardboard gift box I keep under my bed and knock on Trevor's door. He doesn't answer, and when I open it, he isn't there. He's not in the kitchen or in the bathroom, and so I check out on the porch. He's sitting on the bench, his phone to his ear. When he sees me, he says into the phone, "I'll call you back." When he hangs up, he focuses on me. "What's up?"

I sit next to him, make sure the baby monitor's on so I can hear if Mom needs me. "Was that Amy?"

"Yeah."

He points to the box. "What you got there?"

I turn to him, my smile soft. "I know that you're just messing around with the whole jealous-of-Connor thing..."

His eyes narrow.

"At least, I *think* you are."

"I am," he assures, and I breathe out a sigh of relief.

I hand him the box. "But I wanted you to know that I'm just as proud of you as I am of him."

He takes the box from me, his eyes thinned in confusion as he opens the lid. He picks up the first scrapbook and flips the page. There's a picture of him and me at his first college game—when I begged Mom and William to let me go with them. He's in all his football gear, and I'm wearing an Aggie jersey with his number on my cheek. I look so young. We both do. He turns the page; sees the article I'd cut out of the Texas A&M Today newsletter about him and where he came from. "You did this?" he whispers, and I can hear the emotion in his voice that he's trying so hard to hide.

"That's just your college freshman year," I say, nodding. I reach into the box, pull out the other five scrapbooks, discarding the additional photographs and articles I didn't have room for but wanted to keep. "These are every year from high school freshman up." Then I point to a photo album. "And that's just of you and me growing up."

He's silent as he goes through every photograph, every article, every printout from every website that ever mentioned his name. He sniffs occasionally, and I know my brother well enough to know he's big and bulky on the outside, but inside... he's a giant softie, and his staggered exhale reminds me of why I love him so much, why I look up to him the way I do. "Jesus, Ava," he mumbles, the heels of his palms going to his eyes. "I had no idea you did this."

"I know," I tell him, shifting when he puts his arm around my shoulders. "And this might sound extra cheesy and super wrong, but... you were the first boy I loved, Trevor, and that won't ever change. You're always going to be my big brother, and I'm always going to be a pain in your ass."

He laughs once, releasing me. Then he drops his head between his shoulders, his heavy sigh deflating his chest. "Ava, I need to tell you something, but I *don't* want to. Especially now."

I grasp his shoulder, force him to sit up so I can look at him. "What's wrong?"

He turns to me, his eyes red, his nostrils flaring with his exhale. "Jesus, I don't know how to say this."

I say through the ache in my chest, "Just say it, Trevor. You're scaring me."

"We're out of money, Ava. And I don't know how to fix it." He looks ahead, his gaze distant, while I try to settle my racing heart. "I tried to get a loan yesterday, and they denied it. I've already borrowed from Mr. Preston, but I can't ask him again, and I lied to you before... I wasn't on the phone with Amy. I was on the phone with Peter—"

"No!" I rush out. "Don't ask him for money."

"I *have* to."

"No." I stand. Pace. "I'll get a job."

"It won't be enough."

"I'll quit school. We're so close. I can still graduate." *Probably.* "And I'll be able to help out."

"The money you'd make could possibly pay for Krystal, but then you may as well stay at home, and even then, we're so far in the red..."

I wipe at the tears too quick to appear.

"I'm sorry, Ava," he chokes. "I thought it would be enough, but—"

"Stop it!" I order, standing in front of him. "You've done more than..." My stomach twists, and I can't breathe.

He looks up, tired, worried eyes on mine. "The changes in her insurance meant we had to pay more for her meds, and now that they've finally found the right—"

"I'll call the doctors to come out on Monday. We'll see what they say."

Trevor nods. "But we still need help, and Peter—"

"No!"

"Why not?"

"Because!" Because with Peter, the debt becomes more than just financial. I calm myself down. "Because we can do this on our own. Just let me call the doctors and the insurance and just… just give me a few days before talking to him, okay? Promise me."

"All right."

"And don't ever do this again."

"Do what?"

"Carry this weight on your own. Don't keep secrets from me."

He nods. "I'm sorry I couldn't do enough."

I sit next to him again, wrap my arms around the solid wall of dependency I've taken for granted. "Don't be sorry, Trevor. Ever."

I just need time, I tell myself again, *and everything will fall into place.*

CONNOR

The world is bright orange as the sun begins to set, and it reminds me of the balloons on my porch, of Ava. I wish I were there instead of standing on the sidewalk, leaning against a streetlamp as I look across the road and into the large windows of the chain restaurant at close to 8 p.m.

She's still there, my mother, waiting for me. Occasionally, she'll check the time and look at the doors, expecting me to appear.

I don't know why I'm here. *Curiosity,* I try to convince myself. *Morbid* curiosity. I pinch the bridge of my nose, try to release the pounding in my head.

Pushing off the post, I take a step forward, and then another, until I've crossed the road and I'm opening the door. My mom sits higher when she sees me, a hint of a smile pulling on her lips. A part of me hates that I've given her that tiny amount of joy. But another part of me flashes to all the moments of joy I remember us having, and I think I hate that more.

"Hey," I murmur the second my ass hits the seat. In a booth, in the corner of the room, I suddenly feel trapped. Anxiety swarms through my bloodline, closing my airways. I shouldn't have come here, but now it's too late. And I know that if I didn't, I'd regret it forever.

"Did you want a drink? Coffee? Hot choco—"

"I hate chocolate."

"Really?" Her brow lifts. "You used to love it."

I keep my eyes on hers when I say, "I used to love a lot of things."

My birth giver shakes her head, her eyes moving to the text written on my arms. She reads it before I can hide what's there. "Ava. She's your girlfriend, right?"

"You already know who she is. You've met her. And I'd appreciate it if you kept her name out of your mouth." *I don't want you to tarnish her like you did me,* I don't say.

Her eyes lift, soften. "I went back, you know?"

I lean forward. "What?"

"I went back for you. Once I'd realized what I'd done, I went back..." Tears form in her eyes, and she's quick to swipe them away. "But you'd already been... *found*... and there were so many people around you and I couldn't..."

"You couldn't deal," I finish for her. "Just like you couldn't deal with being a mother, right?" I swallow the lump in my throat. "Was I that bad of a kid?" It was supposed to come out harsh, but my true emotions fly out with my words, taking my insecurities with them.

"Connor, no," she whispers through a wobbly exhale. "It was never about *you*." She reaches across the table, her hand covering mine, and I let her. I fucking *let* her. "When everyone was gone... I saw your toy cars sitting there. Remember those, sweetheart? You loved them so much, you couldn't go anywhere without them."

I claim back my hand, rest it on my lap, and keep my eyes downcast. "I remember."

"You'd watch those movies for hours, and the soundtracks were always going in my car..."

I don't have anything to say, so I stay quiet.

"Do you still like cars?"

"Not really."

She sighs. "It's all about basketball now, right?"

I nod.

"Or it has been for a while. I think the first time I saw your name pop up you were around twelve."

I look up at her now, my eyes wide in surprise.

"I've been following you for years, watching you grow up from afar." There's a wistfulness in her words, and my heart aches in ways I never thought possible. She's cared about me... but never enough to claim me back.

"Where have you been? And what do you want from me now?" I pause a breath, my voice quiet when I add, "We don't have any money—Dad and me —and if you think you can somehow get some because I'm heading to the league, then... I don't even know what to say to you."

"I don't want your money," she's quick to reply. "And your dad—shit, Connor, no one can know I'm here. If anyone finds out that I exist, I could..."

"I know what could happen to you." And *I* hold all the cards.

"I mean it, Connor. Not your dad, not your girlfriend. No one."

"Why should I give you grace? Did you somehow forget what you did to me?"

"No!" she almost shouts. "I've been hiding out in a cabin in the woods, never leaving my house, living every day with the pain of knowing what I did to you!" She ends on a sob, one so harsh and so loud it has people's heads turning. She cowers, grabs a napkin from the dispenser to wipe at her tears. Barely a whisper, she adds, "I'm protecting you and everyone you love when I tell you that they *can't* know. I'm still a... a *fugitive*." She says the word as if it's acid on her tongue. "And having them know means they could get in a lot of trouble if..." she trails off, and I know where she's going, what she means. I've watched enough true crime documentaries to understand the consequences, but it still doesn't answer my question of what she *wants*.

Confusion fills every nerve of my being, and I hate that I can't control my emotions. I hate that seeing her upset makes my heart ache, but seeing her smile makes me angry. "So why risk it all now?"

She takes a moment, trying to slow her breaths. "My mom's sick."

"Okay...?"

"Do you remember her?"

I shake my head. "Not even a little bit."

She nods slowly. "She's the only person I have contact with, and she's always asking about you. She knows what I did... and she makes it known every day how she feels about it. But..." A frown tugs at her lips. "She's dying, Connor. Cancer. And she doesn't have long. She wanted me to reach out to you, and I *had* to. For her. And maybe even a little for me."

I blow out a breath, stagnant, as I let her words dig deep inside me.

"She's done nothing wrong in any of this, so if you want to punish me, I understand. But don't do it to her, Connor. She's your grandmother, and she loves you very much."

"So, what do you want from me?"

"She just wants to see you again, before... before she dies."

I rub the back of my neck, my mind swarming. "I have to think about it."

"I know. And you have my number. Just... it's time sensitive, you know?"

"I get that."

She smiles.

I start to get out of the booth. "I'll let you know?"

"Okay." She stands, too. "I assume a hug is out of the question?"

I still, bewildered, and find myself lifting my arms, letting her close the distance. Her arms wrap around my torso...

...while mine fall to my sides.

I tell her, my heart heavy, "I already have a mother figure in my life."

She pulls away, her eyes confused when they meet mine.

I add, letting go of every thought I've had since the moment I saw the cars she'd given to Ava, "My girlfriend's mom—she's a war veteran, and she has injuries that caused her brain damage—and even *she* can find a way to love me unconditionally. And my dad... he's done such an amazing job of being both parents to me for so long that after a while, I stopped missing you. Stopped thinking about you completely. And I'm sorry," I say, my chin up, shoulders back just like Miss D ordered the day I lost regionals, "I can't pretend like everything's okay between us, because it's not." I turn for the door, leave her there.

I make it two steps before she calls out my name, and I pause, my eyes drifting shut when she says, "Talk to your dad about what happened back then, Connor. He's not so innocent in all of this."

* * *

I wait until I'm back in my hotel room before checking my phone. Neither Dad nor Ava has called, but there's a message from Dad asking me to call him when I can. Confusion blurs my mind when I hit dial, the question forefront in my mind, on the tip of my tongue. *What does he know that I don't?*

"Connor!" Dad shouts. "I didn't want to call in case I was going to ruin your street cred," he laughs out. "But damn, kid! You made me one proud dad today! I'm kicking myself for not being there. I should've quit my damn job and just gone. Screw dying people, right?"

There's a blinding ache in my chest, in my head, my entire fucking body. I throw myself on the bed, my eyes to the ceiling.

"Are you there, son?"

"Yeah, sorry..."

His voice is filled with excitement when he says, "I heard next door going wild every time you appeared." He blows out a breath, static filling my ears. "Jesus, Connor, even if none of this was happening, just who you are, the man you've become... Honestly, I'm pretty darn proud of myself for raising you." He can't stop laughing, and I picture him sitting on the couch in his sleep clothes, a giant smile on his face, pride lighting up his eyes, just like he did when I got into Duke. But I realize now that it's the exact same way he's looked at me my entire life.

Fuck what my mom had to say. She doesn't know what we are—Dad and me—because she chose not to be there. And how fucking dare she try to take that away. "Dad?"

"Yeah, son?"

"I appreciate you so much." I blink back the tears. "If I've never told you that or made you feel that before...just know that I do. That I'm here because of you. And I love you."

. . .

I wait until my mind's stable enough and finally make the call I've wanted to all day. Ava answers with as much excitement as my dad. "MVP! MVP! MVP!" she hollers, and I can't help but laugh.

"Oh, man, I miss your voice."

"I miss *you*!"

"How's your day been?"

"Oh, you know, just watching my boyfriend make his dreams come true, same old," she says, ending on a laugh. "I'm sorry about all the messages."

"Don't be. They... they were perfect."

"What have you been doing since the game?"

"Just meeting and greeting, making a name for myself," I lie. "Hanging with the guys, you know?"

"That's good, babe! I'm glad you're making the most of it. Are y'all going out tonight to celebrate?"

"They might be. I'm pretty beat, though. Just waiting on you to send those nudes over."

She laughs.

"What about you? What have you been doing? How's your mom?"

"She's good. We're good. Everything's good."

"Hey, Ava?"

"Yeah?"

"Can you just talk to me?"

"About what, babe?"

"Anything. I just want to hear your voice."

I can practically hear her smile through the phone. "Did I tell you about what happened in multimedia yesterday?"

"No."

"Well, Roy was partnered up with that Myra girl in class..." She starts telling me the story, and I listen to her words, and I try so fucking hard to feel the comfort in her voice, but for the first time ever, I can't seem to sense it, to hear it... I can't seem to find it... because I'm lost.

I'm so fucking lost.

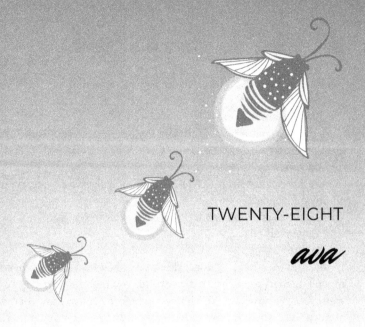

TWENTY-EIGHT

ava

"SORRY, I just need to take this," I tell everyone as I watch Connor's name flash on my phone. I leave the kitchen and move just far enough away that Connor can't hear the conversation Trevor, Mom, and Krystal are having with the doctors.

"Hey, MVP!" I greet, hoping he can't hear my forced smile through the phone.

"Rhys said you aren't at school today..."

"Wow, are you checking in on me all the way from Georgia?"

"No, Ava," he says, his tone serious. "He called about something else and just mentioned it. What's going on?"

"Nothing, babe. Mom's doctors are here—"

"Why?"

"It's just a general check-up; it happens..." I continue to lie because I don't want him worrying. "Did I not tell you? It's been scheduled for months."

He blows out a breath. "No, you didn't," he replies, his voice softening. "So, nothing's wrong?"

"Everything's fine," I assure, and add, "I'm sorry to worry you."

He sighs. "It's all good."

"What are you doing, anyway?"

"I'm waiting around at the airport."

"What time do you land?"

"Five. I'll probably be home around eight. Dad wants to have dinner and then—"

"You'll come over?" I ask, my smile genuine this time. "Please?"

He laughs once. "Yeah, of course."

"Stay the night?"

"I was planning on it."

I sigh, letting his voice fill the void in my heart. "God, I miss you," I tell him, at the same time he says, "God, Ava, you have no idea how much I've missed you."

We both laugh into the phone, a single second of clarity in an otherwise cloudy existence.

"I have to go," I tell him. "But I can't wait to see you."

"Hey, Ava?"

"Yeah?"

He's silent a beat. "I don't think I realized how much I loved you and how much I needed you until this weekend. You mean everything to me. And I just want you to know that." He hangs up before I can say another word and I look at my phone, stare at it, wondering what the hell just happened. I hold a hand to my stomach, try to settle the butterflies there.

"Ava?" Trevor calls out, bringing me back to reality—a reality full of fear and uncertainty.

CONNOR

Dad's as proud of me in person as he was on the phone, and after everything that happened with my mother, it only creates a heavier weight on my chest. I wish I could be as happy to see him as he is to see me, but there are questions, so many of them, and I don't know where to start. But more, I don't know if I want to.

Nothing good could possibly come from opening up the wounds of our pasts.

Nothing.

I sit at the kitchen table, watching him watch me, a smile on his face, his eyes lit up with pride. "You were perfect, Connor. Every second you were out there. Not a single mistake."

I scarf down my meal, not bothering to answer, and look at the clock.

"Damn, did I not give you enough money to eat while you were gone?"

I almost choke on the steak and cough, thump my fist against my chest to clear it. Then I wipe my mouth with a napkin and down my entire glass of water. "Sorry," I tell him. "I told Ava I'd come by after dinner." And as much as I appreciate my dad, he doesn't kill my pain the way she does. But... "I'm being rude. You went through all this trouble, and... I'm being a shit. Sorry."

He laughs under his breath, shaking his head, and pulls the plate away from me. "Go."

"No, Dad," I rush out, bringing the plate back. "She can wait."

"But *you* can't. Can you, Connor?"

I shrug, my heart filling with hope at the thought of seeing her again.

Dad stands, takes my plate with him. "Go, Connor!" he laughs out.

"Are you sure?"

"Yes!"

I don't ask again. Instead, I grab my phone, already texting her when I close the front door.

> Connor: I'm coming over now.

Ava opens the door the second I step foot onto her porch, and she's so much more than I remember. *Four days.* It's only been four days, but it felt like a lifetime, and going by the way her cheeks lift with the force of her smile, the way she pushes me back a step so she can close the door behind her, and the way she jumps into my arms, her mouth going to mine, she felt everything I felt. I tighten my hold on her thighs while her legs go around me, her hands on the side of my face as she tilts her head, her tongue meeting mine, and *this.* This is exactly what I needed to forget everything else.

I just needed her.

She breaks our kiss, her eyes holding more emotion than her words. "I hated every second you were gone, you creep. Don't do that again."

"Me too."

"Never again."

I sigh, lean against her porch railing and put her back on her feet. "How are we going to do that?"

She slaps my chest. "I don't know, Connor! Shrink me and put me in your pocket. Duh!"

I bite back a smile. "What about your mom?"

"Shrink her, too."

Before I can respond, her front door opens, just a tad, and Miss D whispers, "MVP! MVP! MVP!"

Ava laughs. "She's been waiting for you."

Taking Ava's hand, I lead her into her own house and stand in front of Miss D, my smile matching hers. I hadn't realized I'd missed her, too, while I was gone, but here I am... glad to be back in the presence of two of the most important girls in my life. "Are you sick of people telling you how proud they are of you?" she asks.

I shrug. "I could always do with one more."

"Oh, Connor, six-six, I'm so proud of you!" She steps forward, taking me in her embrace, and my arms go around her. One second. Two. And I don't let go when she starts to pull away. I think of the hug my own mother gave me. How it was physically painful to even think about holding her like this. How I couldn't even lift my arms when it was offered...

I look over Miss D's head to see Trevor watching us, a frown tugging on his lips. When he notices me watching, he stands taller, plasters on a fake smile. "You did good, man."

I finally release Miss D, but speak to him, "Thanks." If he's genuinely salty about Miss D's affection toward me, then I'll have to talk to him about it. I turn to Ava; she's looking at her mom the same way Trevor was.

"I'm going to go to bed now," Miss D announces.

"I'll get all your stuff ready," Ava says, her voice barely a whisper. She pats my arm as she passes. "I'll meet you in my room?"

I glance at Trevor, but he's looking down at his feet. I say, "Yeah, sure."

Something's different, *off*; I can feel it in my bones, or maybe it's all in my head because nothing's been clear for days now.

I get in Ava's room, leave the door ajar, and sit on the edge of the bed, my phone burning a hole in my pocket. I take it out, put it on her nightstand. I'd sent my mother a text. Just one. Telling her I needed time. I haven't heard from her since.

On the other side of the door, I can hear Ava and Trevor whispering loudly, a heated exchange, and my eyes narrow when I try to listen harder. "You're not calling him!" Ava whispers.

"We need to do something if we want—"

"We'll talk about it tomorrow," Ava cuts in. "Just let me have tonight, okay?"

"Fine."

When Ava steps foot in her room, she's smiling, but it's not the smile she greeted me with. It's not real. It's not Ava. "Are you ready to get your nudes now?" she asks, sitting next to me.

"I heard you and Trevor arguing just now. What's going on?"

"We weren't arguing," she murmurs, watching her legs kick back and forth.

"It sounded like an argument."

She looks up at me now. "Did it?"

I lick my lips, try to find a response, but I'm tired, and the last thing I want is to fight her on this. She shifts her hair to the side, revealing her neck, and I know what she wants. I press my lips there, moaning when her hand finds my hair. Her head shifts so our mouths meet, and she pushes on my shoulder, lowering me to my back, and everything else fades when I get lost in her touch, in her taste, in the way she feels naked, her body sliding against mine. The world is silent, so are the raging thoughts that had been plaguing my mind. It's just her and me, and her whispered, "I love you so much, Connor. Forever."

When it's over, she lies in my arms, her head on my chest. "So that's what people mean when they say making love," she muses, a single finger running up the length of my torso.

"I guess so," I agree, keeping my voice low, so we don't wake the rest of the house.

She leans up on her elbow and looks down at me. "Connor?"

"Yeah?" I reply, holding her hair away from her face so I can see her clearly.

"Do you think we'll make it? I mean, when you go to Duke, and I... do whatever... Do you think we can do it? Outlast it all?"

"I fucking hope so, Ava."

"Good," she breathes out. "Because I really don't want to live the rest of my life with anyone but you."

"Me, too."

She smirks. "Well, you kind of *have* to live with you."

"You know what I mean, smartass." I roll her off me. "I have to go home."

She sits up, holds the blankets to her chest. Eyes wide, she whisper-yells, "What?!"

I laugh once. "Calm down," I tell her, slipping into my sweatpants, no boxers. "I just have to go grab my toothbrush and stuff. It's all still in my bag." I kiss her forehead. "I'll be back. Don't worry."

She lies back down, settling on her side, and leaves room for when I return.

I rush over to my house, catch Dad just before he leaves for work. "I'm going to stay at Ava's tonight," I tell him, unzipping my luggage to get my toiletries bag.

"Should I be talking to her mom about you staying there as often as you do?" Dad asks, standing in the doorway of my bedroom. "It's not a problem, right? You're not sneaking around?"

"No," I laugh out. "Miss D worries when I'm *not* there in the morning."

"And her brother, Trevor, he's okay with it?"

"Yes, Dad." I find what I need and grab a change of clothes for school tomorrow. "Everything's good."

"Okay." He nods. "And you and Ava, you're being careful when it comes to *intimacy?*"

I chuckle, turning to him. "We're using protection, yes."

"Just one form? Because no contraception is a hundred percent, and I know you love her, and you'd do anything for her—you've proven that—but having a baby in your immediate future..."

I suck in a breath, let his words replay in my mind. "I'll talk to her about going on the pill or something."

"Okay, good," Dad says. "That was a lot easier than I'd prepared myself for."

"Dad, Ava and I aren't normal teenage kids. I'm sure a baby is the last thing she wants. She's already taking care of her mom; adding that to her plate now would just—"

"Of course, yeah..."

"But don't worry." I pat his shoulder as I pass him. "You'll be a grandpa soon enough."

"Jesus, help me," he mumbles.

I laugh under my breath as I close the front door behind me. The idea of a forever with her causes a stupid skip in my step as I make my way back. I enter her house, having left it unlocked, and go straight to her room. She's sitting on the edge of the bed, her head lowered, her phone in her hand. She looks up when I enter, and my heart aches when I see the tears in her eyes. "What happened?"

She hands me her phone, and my heart drops. It's not her phone. It's mine. "Who's Wendy?" she whispers.

My stomach twists, and my breaths halt. I look down at my phone, at the message there.

> Wendy: Thank you for meeting me the other night. I really needed to see you.

"Connor?" Ava cries.

I look up at her, my eyes drifting shut, so I don't have to see the pain in her expression. "She's... *no one*."

"Connor!" she whisper-yells.

My eyes snap open, and I regret it the moment I see her stand, her hand to her heart. She lets out a sob, and then another. "Who is she?"

Anger blazes through me, not at her. But at my mother. That she can ruin everything important to me while *barely* existing. Only she's not here. Ava is. And so I take that anger and aim it at the only person in front of me. "Why are you going through my phone?"

"Get out!" Her fists hit my chest. "Get the fuck out!"

My heart *burns*, regret quick to consume me. "I'm sorry, Ava." I grasp her elbows. "*Please*, I'm sorry."

"Who is she?!" she cries

"I can't tell you," I rush out. *She can't know*, and *I'm not ready*. "But, please, it's not what it looks like; I swear to you. On everything we are and everything we have, I *promise* you." My voice cracks. I don't care that it does. I plead, my hands steepled in front of me. "You *need* to believe me, Ava. Please."

Her nostrils flare, her tears flowing fast and free. "And *you* need to think about what you're asking of me. Because you have a pretty sketchy fucking history of lying to me, especially when it comes to girls! Now get the fuck out, Connor!"

connor

I DON'T SLEEP.

Can't.

Everything inside me is broken.

I regret my initial reaction to Ava reading the text, but I don't regret anything after. The possible legal consequences of her knowing the truth far outweigh the secret. And as much as I want her to be a part of what I'm going through, she can't be. She can't know.

I reach for my phone when the alarm goes off and pray I might have missed a message from her. But there's nothing. The last text is from my mom, and all it does is shatter the already broken pieces of me. I type out a reply:

I hate you.

I delete it right away.

Then I try calling Ava; there's no answer. And so I get dressed for school and wait by my truck. If I can get a few minutes with her just so I can explain without revealing too much, maybe it'll be enough. I push off my truck when her front door opens, but she's not there. Only Trevor. He glares at me, his eyes narrowed, and the last thing I need is a lecture from him. "You waiting on Ava?" he calls out.

"Yeah."

"She already left, bro. She said you had an early practice and she was catching the bus."

She lied. *For me.* "We must've got our wires crossed."

He opens his truck door. "Did you try calling her?"

"I'll do it now."

I get in my truck and dial her number again, and again there's no answer. I get to school just before the first bell. We don't have any classes together today, and I don't see her during lunch or at any time in between. I search for her, though, my eyes always roaming. When the end-of-lunch bell rings, I don't go to class. Instead, I go to Miss Turner's office, knock.

"Come in," she calls out.

I poke my head in, my gaze everywhere at once.

"Mr. Ledger, how can I help you?"

"Have you seen Ava today?"

She shakes her head. "No. Was I supposed to?"

I close her door without a response and head to the student parking lot, my pulse racing, stomach twisting. Everything is a blur once I get in my truck, searching for her everywhere I can think of. I can't seem to keep a single thought in line, and when my phone alerts me to a message, I fumble for it, almost veering off the road.

> Wendy: She's willing to travel. When can you get away
> next?

I ignore the message, my hand forming a fist before it makes contact with the steering wheel. "Fuck!" I drive back home, and I know I should wait, but I can't. Just like I know I shouldn't knock, but I do. Krystal opens the door just enough to peer through the gap. When she sees me, she opens it wider. "Hey, Connor."

"Is Ava here?

"No." Her brow dips in concern. "She should be at school."

I sigh. "We must've just missed each other. Sorry for bothering you."

Miss D appears next to Krystal. "Did you try calling her?"

I don't want to worry them, so I say, "No, my phone's dead, so... I'll see you later?"

Miss D nods. "Why aren't *you* at school?"

"I had a basketball thing." The lies flow, effortless, and I hate that they do.

She asks, "Do you want to wait for her here?"

"I can't. I got some chores I need to get done."

"Such a good boy," Miss D tells Krystal.

She's lying, too.

She just doesn't know it.

. . .

I sit on my porch, constantly checking the time. Ava has to be home soon to let Krystal go for the day. She won't just disappear. At least, I hope not. I plan out what I'll tell her. I'll apologize. Again. And I'll beg her to trust me, that this isn't like before, and that I just need time. I'll plead with her to remember everything we have and everything we share and to look deep inside herself and question whether she truly believes I'm capable of doing anything, *anything at all*, to hurt her. And I pray to a God I don't believe in that my love for her will be enough.

Just when I expect her, she appears, walking down the sidewalk. She has to pass my house to get to hers, and so I run down the driveway. "Ava!"

She jumps when she hears me but doesn't look up. I stop in front of her, blocking her path. "Ava, please." I reach for her hand, but she pulls away. And then she looks up, her eyes puffy, red, completely exposed to the heartache she carries. The sight alone has me taking a step back.

I caused this.

I *did* this.

Every thought, every pulse, every breath flowing through me slows.

Stops.

Dies.

Lids heavy, she lets a tear fall from those maple-colored eyes, the same ones that once held so much strength and courage and fight to keep them clear. To keep them dry. I once told her that she never had to hide those tears from me. But now I wish that she had. Because I can't wear her pain when I'm the one who created it.

"I can't right now, Connor," she says, and I find myself nodding because I can't either. "I just need time."

So do I, I want to tell her. Instead, I step to the side and give her what she wants, what she says she *needs*, in the hopes that soon, she'll give me the same in return.

ava

THERE'S no good morning from my mom the day after I skipped school. No kiss on the cheek. No what's for breakfast? Nope. The first thing she says is: "Is Connor here?"

"Not right now," I tell her, mustering a smile. "But he might come over tonight." I don't want to break her heart and tell her that maybe—maybe she won't be seeing him at all. Ever.

I *tried*.

I went through every possible scenario in my head of who Wendy might be, and I went back to his reaction when I confronted him about it. First was the anger when he realized I'd seen the message, then came the apologies. And it was enough to convince me of what was painfully true, no matter how much it hurt.

I had every intention of going to school yesterday, but the idea of seeing him made my stomach turn. And so I roamed around aimlessly until it was time to go home, hiding in places no one would find me, crying at moments when hope seemed like a dream.

When Trevor wakes up, he asks the same thing. I tell them both, "He's really busy with basketball at the moment, trying to get as much practice in before school's over... and he needs to rest, and my bed's too small for him to get a decent night's sleep." *There*. That should cover everything.

"We should buy you a new bed," Mom says, looking over at Trevor. "We can afford that, right?

"Sure," Trevor lies. Then to me: "Don't worry about making breakfast for me; I'm going to work early."

My brow raised, I ask, "You are?"

He nods, his eyes on mine, a silent message. *He's taken on extra work... for extra cash... and not to buy me a new bed.*

I get ready for school, planning on actually attending because I can't hide out forever. When Krystal arrives, I leave and head for the bus stop, praying Connor doesn't stop me. Halfway there, the sky turns gray, and the heavens open. Thunder claps, followed by rain so thick I can barely see a foot in front of me. "Fuck my life," I grind out, removing my bag and holding it above my head as if it's somehow going to protect me. Luckily, I don't wait long for the bus to arrive, and when I get to the stop around the corner from school, I get off and bolt to the school for some cover. But the gates are closed, padlocked. I grip the iron gates with both hands and shake, cursing at the sky. "What the fuck?!"

I pull out my phone, dial Rhys's number.

"Ava?"

"Why is school closed?"

"Student-free day. Why?"

"Goddammit!" I scream, and he laughs. "Can you give me a ride home? It's pouring out, and I caught the bus."

"Um... I'm a little... pre-occupied right now."

Through the phone, I hear a girl giggle, then say, "Harder, Rhys!"

"Gross!" I hang up, take a second to feel sorry for myself, and then walk at a snail's pace back to the bus stop. There's no point in running; I'm already drenched, and there's no shelter at this bus stop because rich kids don't take buses. They have drivers or their parents' credit cards to Uber everywhere.

I drop my bag on the ground and lie across the bench, letting the rain-drops fall directly on my face, mixing with the tears that can't seem to quit. Cars drive past, splashing dirty road water on me, and I don't even care enough to move.

Then a car approaches, it's engine rumbling as it slows and then stops beside me. I keep my eyes closed, even when I hear the window wind down. I'm about ready to tell them to fuck off, but then I hear Connor say, "Get in!"

I sit up, grab my bag, and get to my feet. "Fuck off!"

"Ava!"

I walk away, my bag gripped tight to my chest. He drives away. Thank fuck. But then I hear his tires spinning as he turns around, yelling at me from the other side of the road. "Get in the fucking car, Ava!"

I almost laugh at the absurdity, but I'm too angry, too tired, and so I hasten my steps. I don't know where the hell I'm going; I just need to be *gone*. His truck turns into the parking lot of a restaurant a few feet ahead of me, and so I turn on my heels, start walking back from where I came. He can drive around as much as he wants, but he's not getting me in there. Arms reach around me, yanking my backpack from me, and I scream, "Help!"

"Shut up!" he yells back.

I turn to see him running to his car with my backpack. He opens the passenger door and throws it in there, then closes it. He stands, rain falling all around him. He's in basketball shorts and a loose tank, and all of it clings to his flesh, exposing the muscles I love running my hands across. *Loved* running my hands across. But so does Wendy. *Probably.*

Fuck him. He can take my bag. I start running, and it doesn't take long before I hear his footsteps behind me. His arms circle my waist, lifting me off my feet. I kick my legs out, scream, "Help!" again. He covers my mouth with his palm while spinning me around, walking us back to the truck. Cars drive by, and no one seems to care that there's an *actual* kidnapping happening right in front of them. We get to his truck, and without pause, Connor opens the passenger's side door and throws me inside. I flip to my back, kick at his chest. He grasps my ankles, pushing me farther across the bench seat. "Knock it off, you fucking brat!" He flicks the child lock on the door, preventing me from opening it, and slams it shut. Then runs to the driver's side just in time to stop me from escaping through there. He sits behind the wheel, his jaw ticking, and starts the car. I try to open the door, but nothing happens, and so I sit, my teeth clenched, arms crossed. The restaurant's closed so there are no cars in the lot, and the rain is too heavy that no one would hear me screaming. Connor seems to take a breath, or ten, trying to calm himself down, and I don't know why he's pissed when I'm the one being held against my will. He steps on the pedal, the tires spinning before we move. He drives, his rage controlling our speed as he goes around the back of the restaurant. "Connor," I scream, grasping his arm when the chain link fence comes into view. He stops a foot in front of it, barely noticeable through the sheets of water falling around us.

"Fuck!" he spits, punching the steering wheel.

Great. *Hulk Connor.* I've only seen this side of him once before, and it was when he concluded that Peter had hurt me. He was wrong then. He's wrong now. I try to look for an escape, see the button for the window and press down on it. The window lowers, and hope fills my bloodline. I start to climb out when Connor curses again, his grip on my hips digging into my flesh when he pulls me back.

"What the fuck is wrong with you!" he yells.

He holds me to him while he winds the window up again from the controllers on his door. Then he locks them, too.

I kick his dashboard.

Because *fuck him.*

"Calm the fuck down, Ava!"

He releases me, his hand instantly going to his face, rubbing at his eyes.

"Why are you making this so fucking impossible!?" he shouts. His chest rises and falls with every breath as thunder cracks above us.

I look around, but I can barely see a foot in front of me, barely hear my own thoughts. But I hear his breaths, each one harsh, until slowly, slowly, they begin to settle. With my back to the door, I watch his throat bob with his swallow, watch his eyes move from his lap to my legs, then up at me. Raindrops fall from his hair, cascade down his high cheekbones and past his jaw. "Ava," he says quietly. "I need you to listen to me." He exhales. "Can you do that? Please?"

I nod, my traitorous fingers itching to touch him.

"I don't want to do this with you," he murmurs.

"Good," I say, lifting my chin. "Neither do I, so just let me go, and we don't have—"

His heavy sigh cuts me off. "That's not what I meant." Another breath. "What I mean is, I don't want to go around in circles with you. I don't want to fight and get back together and then fight and do it all again. I don't want to fight with you. Ava..." He shakes his head, his gaze distant. "You're *it* for me. If there's no you, then there's nothing else. No one else." He laughs once, bitter, and locks his eyes on mine again. "I nearly killed myself for *you*."

"What the hell are you talking about?"

He swallows, his eyes showing his exhaustion, both mentally and physically. "I had one plan in life, Ava. It was four years at college and then the NBA. And then I met you, and I met your mom, and all that changed. I pushed myself so hard and so quickly so that I could get into a decent college and hopefully get the attention I needed so I could do my one year and get drafted and get a decent enough contract that I could take care of you both—you and your mom. I put my mind and body through so fucking much; you have no idea. I never showed you how bad it was, but I nearly lost you once because of it." He pauses a breath, his words filled with clarity. "Everything I've done since the first day I met you has been for *you*. Every sacrifice I've made, every decision..." He holds a hand to his heart. "Every beat of my fucking heart has been *for you*. And I've *tried* so hard to be there for you through *everything*. No matter what was going on in my life, I pushed it all aside so that I could be your strength..." Tears well in my eyes as I listen to the truths that fall from his lips. "And I'm not saying this because I want your pity," he adds, blinking away his heartache as he lowers his gaze. "I'm saying it because I need you to *see* that, to *understand* that. Because right now, I need you to *trust* me. I need you to have faith in me. In *us*." A single tear falls from his lashes, and he holds his thumb there, blocking it.

I shift closer to him, his magic calling for me, and take his hand in mine.

He looks up, his withheld cry ruining me completely. "I'm hurting, Ava, and I *need* you. I need you to be there for me even if… even if I can't tell you *why*."

I hold his face in my hands, kiss away the staggered breath he releases. "Okay."

His arms go around me while I hold him to me, his mouth finding my neck, kissing me there. "Tell me you love me."

I capture his lips again. "I love you."

He chokes out a breath as he pulls away. "Don't abandon me, Ava. Not you, too."

My eyes shift between his, drowning in the vulnerability I'm witnessing. "I swear, Connor."

His mouth claims mine, his urgency forcing me onto my back as his hand slides up my thigh. I part my legs, giving him what he wants.

What he *needs*.

Even if it costs me my pride.

"IS THERE anything I can do for her?" Connor asks, his gaze shifting from Mom, sitting on the couch in the living room, back to me.

I finish up washing the last of the dishes and hand it to him to dry. "Not really, it's just part of who she is." It's a lie, and he seems to realize that going by the way he's staring me down.

It's been a couple weeks now since Connor and I fought and around the same amount of time since the doctors were here. They couldn't find a solution to our financial problems that didn't mean cutting some of Mom's meds and giving her alternatives. They'd hoped the change in her wouldn't be drastic, but it's the third zero-day in a row now, and things are looking bleak, at best. But at least she hasn't hit the negative numbers.

Yet.

"Maybe I should get her back to the sports park. That might help, right?"

I dry my hands on a dish towel and look up at him. "I don't know, Connor. You can ask, but not right now."

He nods, looking out the window. "Fireflies will be out soon. That could help, too." It warms my heart that he's this thoughtful, especially when it comes to her. I just wish it was enough to take away the constant dull ache in my chest. Things with us haven't been the same since Wendy. I still don't know who she is, and I'm not going to ask. But it's there, nagging, always at the forefront of my mind, and maybe that's why I'm struggling with my feelings toward him. Or maybe I'm just placing all the blame for our disconnect on that and not *everything* else that seems to be going on around us.

Headlights shine through the living room window, and I look at the time. It's close to 8 p.m., and Trevor's just now getting home. He enters a moment later, his eyes instantly finding Mom on the couch. He greets her with a kiss on the cheek before making his way to the kitchen. "Hey, man," he says to Connor. Then to me: "Please tell me we have food."

"Yeah. I saved you a plate in the fridge."

"Are you just finishing work now?" Connor asks him.

Trevor nods, his head in the fridge, searching for the plate that's no doubt right in front of him. "Yep. I have to somehow dig myself out of this debt." He looks at Connor. "You know anyone who needs any work done? We're kind of desperate right—"

I clear my throat, stopping him from revealing too much. I don't want Connor to know, to worry.

Trevor's focus flicks between Connor and me, but Connor's the first to speak. "How bad is it?"

"It's not bad," I lie.

Trevor shakes his head at me. "Ava, Connor knows people around here. More than you do. He could probably use some contacts from the team to help us out. Contacts with money."

"Trevor, stop," I sigh out. "It's not his problem."

Connor pushes off the counter. "Wait, it's *that* bad?"

"No." Another lie from me.

"Yes," says Trevor, narrowing his eyes at me. "Would you rather Connor hand out some of my business cards or I make the call to Peter, because—"

"Hang on," Connor cuts in.

I grind my teeth, my lashes lowering.

"What does Peter have to do with—"

"Nothing," I interrupt. "He's got *nothing* to do with this. And neither do you." I look at Trevor. "This is *my* problem. No one else's."

"And mine," Trevor says. "*Mainly* mine."

"I just need time," I whisper, glancing at Mom. She hasn't moved from her spot. In fact, she hasn't moved at all. She's fallen asleep sitting up.

"You keep saying that, but I don't—"

"I'm not doing this right now," I snap, filling a cup with water. I reach up, turn the combination lock for the top cupboard where we keep all Mom's meds, glasses, and anything sharp that could possibly harm her. I gather all the pills she needs at night and turn to Connor. "I'll meet you in my room. Can you set everything up?"

He nods, but he doesn't move.

I go to Mom, wake her gently, and help her to her room, where she downs multiple pills and falls back asleep without any issues. When I get to my room, Connor's sitting on my desk chair, a tripod set up in front of him. He has his phone attached, the camera angled to my bed. We're working on the multimedia project we were given early in the semester. For the past few days, we'd been doing the research and working on the script, and tonight we're supposed to be filming it. "Should I change?" I ask, looking down at my baggy T-shirt and sweatpants.

"I think you look perfect," Connor says, a sad, crooked smile playing on his lips.

I open my drawers, one by one, without really looking at anything in there. I hear the desk chair rolling across the carpet before I feel Connor's touch on my waist. I turn to him, see the anguish coating his expression. "Why are you trying to keep this from me?"

"I told you, it's not your problem." Besides, who is he to question me when it comes to secrets?

"It *is* my problem." He pulls me down until I'm sitting sideways on his leg, my feet between his. "You know how much I care about you, right?" I stay quiet because I don't know how to respond. He kisses my temple, keeps his lips there. "What's happening with us, Ava? I feel like we're falling apart."

Because we are.

"I don't know, Connor. There's just so much going on right now..."

"Why can't you let me be a part of that?"

"You have your own things." *Wendy* things. "We should just do this assignment and call it a night." I get up, sit on the edge of my bed in front of the camera, and start going through my notes. Connor stays where he is, his head lowered. "Or we can do this tomorrow if you want."

"No." He shakes his head, then looks up at me. "We'll do it now."

He sets up behind the phone and presses record. I read off the script, doing my best to perform for the camera, but every time I look up, I see Connor's face. See the way he looks at me through the screen of his phone. Something is missing. The brightness in his eyes has dulled, and he doesn't look at me the way he used to, the way I love.

Gray.

Everything is gray, and there's no color around me, no life.

I pause my speech and clear my throat, try to blink back my emotions. "Maybe now's not a good time for this."

He sighs, his gaze lifting an inch to look at the real me. His hands go to his hair, tugging. Then he gets up to sit next to me. "I can't fix this if I don't know what's broken, Ava."

Me.

I'm broken.

Every time I look at my mother, it breaks me.

Every time Trevor walks through the door, it shatters me.

And every time I'm with Connor, it ruins me.

"I'm fine," I lie. Again. "I just want you to be the same."

He nods, accepting the vagueness of my response, and sucks in a huge breath. "You want me to stay with you tonight?"

I'm quick to shake my head, ignoring the disappointment that fills his eyes. "I'm pretty beat," I tell him. "I'm probably just going to sleep now." He knows it's an excuse, just like every other night since we slept together in his truck. He hasn't stayed over, and we haven't been intimate. Besides, it's hard to give that part of yourself to someone when you're constantly questioning whether he's given that part of him to someone else.

THIRTY-TWO

Connor

THE NEXT MORNING, Ava's waiting out by my truck in her pajamas, not even close to being ready for school. "You left your phone on the tripod," she says, handing it to me.

"Yeah, I figured," I say, tapping on the screen. The batteries dead; not surprising.

"Don't worry; I didn't go through it."

My eyes snap to hers. "I wasn't worried." It hadn't even occurred to me.

With a nod, she looks away.

I sigh. "I take it you're not going to school?"

Still refusing to look at me, she says, "I have some stuff to take care of today."

"Right..."

Her gaze flicks to mine. A single second. "I'll see you later?"

"Sure."

She starts to walk away, but I grasp her hand, pull her into me. I dip my head, my mouth aimed for hers, but she turns away and pulls back. "I haven't brushed my teeth yet. I'm gross."

"I don't care."

"I do." She shrugs me off completely. "I'll see ya."

And then she's gone.

I'm not naive or stupid enough to not realize what's going on or how she's feeling. We haven't had sex in weeks, and any other form of intimacy feels like a blessing. It's a hurdle, I tell myself. A small one. Soon, it'll be over, and we can go back to the way things were. She's giving me time, and I'm giving her space...

Because that's how relationships work...

...right?

* * *

I get to school early, making sure to catch Rhys before first period. "Hey, can I talk to you?"

"What's up?"

* * *

> Connor: When are you getting home from work?

Trevor: Leaving now. I should be there in about twenty. Everything ok?

> Connor: Yeah. Everything's cool. I'll wait for you out front. I need to talk to you.

Trevor shows up a half hour later and pulls his truck into his driveway. I walk over quickly, wanting to catch him before he goes inside. Grabbing the envelope out of my back pocket, I wait until he's out of the truck before handing it to him. His eyes narrow at me, then at the envelope. He opens the flap and glances inside. "This is a lot of hundreds, Connor." He looks around us. "What is this?"

I shrug. "I sold some stuff."

He shakes his head, slams the envelope against my chest. "I'm not taking your money."

I throw my hands up and take a step back, forcing him to hold on to the cash. "It'll help, right?"

"Connor..."

I cross my arms. "One day, you and Ava are going to realize that it's not just you three. I'm part of this, too. Miss D—she's like a mother to me, whether you guys see that or not. I'm just doing my part."

Trevor nods slowly as if contemplating. "It's a loan."

"It's whatever you want to tell yourself."

He sighs. "Thank you."

"You're welcome."

* * *

I wake up the next morning to a knock on the door. No. To someone *beating down* the door. "Connor, I know you're in there! Let me in!"

"Shit," I whisper, pushing the covers off me. I open the door and don't get a chance to say anything before Ava's pushing past me and going to my room. She's moving shit around, looking through my drawers, my closet. She goes through my school bag, takes out the laptop and places it on the bed. Then she looks for my phone. It's there, too. Realization hits, and I know why she's here. I lean against the doorframe as I watch her stand in the middle of my room, already dressed for school. Her hands are on her hips as she looks around, first at the floor, then at the walls, and she won't find what she's looking for, at least not in here. As if reading my mind, she shoulders past me and does the same thing in the living room, turning over the cushions on the couch, checking the TV, and then the stereo. She looks at the floor and then the walls... I groan the moment I notice her shoulders tense.

She pushes past me again, heading for the door. "Do you need a ride to school?" I call out because I'm still half asleep and it's the only thing I can think to say.

"I'm good!" she yells, marching down the steps.

Today is going to be *neat*.

I don't see Ava again until the end of lunch when she storms through the doors on a mission from Satan himself. "Jesus Christ, Connor, what's with your girl?" Mitch laughs out.

I curse under my breath and get to my feet, but she moves past me, curls bouncing around, and goes straight for Rhys. "Give it back!"

Rhys eyes her warily before moving to me, but his words are meant for her. "Give what back?"

"The jersey!"

"What jersey?"

"The signed Larry Bird jersey, you fucking shit-for-brains. Give it back to him!"

Rhys laughs, but I don't, because I don't miss the fury in Ava's eyes like he does. "It was a fair trade."

Ava's jaw clenches and she reaches up, pulls on Rhys's hair until his head throws back. The entire table hisses, a single sound of sympathy for our fallen brother. "Give it back!" Ava yells, but she ends in a sob, and she's lost it. *Completely*. I wrap my arms around her waist and lift her off her feet. "Let it go, Ava."

"No!"

I try to pull her away, but she's still holding onto Rhys's hair, and he moves with us. "Control your fucking woman, Ledger!"

Ava releases his hair just so she can kick him. "Give it back to him!"

"Not here!" I grind out, motioning for Rhys to follow us outside. I carry Ava in the same position while she squirms in my hold, trying to attack Rhys as if this is his fault. It's not. And besides, I like Rhys. I don't really feel like losing him to Ava's raging ninja kicks.

Once out of the cafeteria and away from everyone's cell phones directed at her, I set her back on her feet. She charges at Rhys, and he steps away just in time.

"Ava!" I yell. "Calm the hell down!"

She ignores me, stands in front of Rhys. "Give it back to him now!"

"He sold it to me!"

"So, sell it back!"

Rhys shakes his head, crosses his arms. "No!"

"It's not a big deal," I press. "It's just a fucking jersey."

She spins to me, tears already in her eyes when she says, "It's not just a jersey, Connor!" Her chest rises with her need for air. "You were twelve, and you and your dad drove ten hours for the slight chance that you might meet him! You stood outside that store for five hours before you got to the front of the line! And you told me how it felt for you to be standing in front of your hero and how nervous you were when your dad took a picture of you two! And the smile on your dad's face when that guy shook your hand and told you to follow your dreams! You told me all this when I was lying in your arms one night, and you said it was one of the best days of your life because you got to meet your hero, *with* your hero: your dad! So, *no*, Connor!" she yells through her cries. "It's not just a fucking jersey. It's an amazing memory you got to share with your dad. And you can't take advantage of that because... because you don't get them back! You don't get do-overs!"

My heart sinks, and I realize this isn't about the jersey or the money... this isn't even about *me*.

"You don't get do-overs, Connor, you just—" She stops there, her sobs too strong she can't do anything else.

"Come here," I say, pulling her into me. This time, she lets me. She cries into my chest, her tears soaking through my shirt. I stroke her hair, every part of me grieving the loss of her own moments with her mom. "I'm sorry," I whisper, kissing the top of her head. She looks up, her cheeks wet. Her forceful sob causes a hiccup, and then another, and I frown down at her, place my mouth to hers, inhaling her cries into me. "I'm sorry, Ava. I didn't mean to hurt you."

"I'll give it back," Rhys says, rubbing her back. He offers me a sad smile and then leaves us alone.

"It's not just a jersey," Ava murmurs.

I search her face for a semblance of peace. "I know."

Another sob escapes her, and she places her ear to my chest. "The fireflies might come back, but they won't bring the magic with them."

connor

AVA SITS NEXT to me in multimedia, her head on the desk, her arms shielding her. Miss Salas notices, and I nudge her leg with mine under the desk. Ava looks up, wipes the drool off the corner of her mouth.

She told me she hasn't been sleeping well, and not because of anything her mom's doing. She's just stressed about the uncertainty of her future, and I try to understand. I've offered to stay with her, but she refuses, and so I continue to give her space while she continues to give me time.

The door opens unexpectedly, and Trevor appears. The room gasps and Miss Salas screeches, "Young man! What do you think you're doing?"

"One minute," Trevor mumbles, searching the room for Ava.

When he spots her, she sits taller. "What's wrong?"

Trevor empties the contents of a paper bag he'd brought with him all over the desk. He picks up a plastic crown and puts it on Ava's head. Then he tears open a packet of confetti, tiny bits of paper flying through the air, leaving a mess all around us. He picks up a handful and throws it at Ava. Next comes one of those party horns. He puts the end in his mouth and blows. "Happy birthday!"

I chuckle.

More confetti.

He tells her, "Sorry we forgot this morning."

"It's okay," Ava murmurs, a hint of a smile tugging on her lips.

He pops a party popper in front of her face. "Happy eighteenth." Then he adjusts her crown. "I'll see you at home. I gotta go!" He squeezes her cheeks with one hand, puffing out her lips. "I love you, you little brat."

"I love you, too."

"Get out of my classroom!" Miss Salas yells.

"I'm going," Trevor sings. "Jesus, you haven't changed a bit."

The class erupts in giggles, and I turn to Ava. "Crown suits you."

She smiles. "You think?"

"You could wear a potato sack and still be beautiful."

She moves closer, rests her crown-covered head on my bicep, and hugs my arm to her. "Hey," she whispers. "What time do you leave?"

My stomach turns. "I go to the airport right after school."

She pouts.

"I'm sorry, I know I'm missing your birthday, but it's part of the schedule—"

"I know," she cuts in. "It's all part of being All-American MVP, right?"

It's incredibly painful to force a smile, especially after all the lies I've had to tell. "It's just one night in Georgia."

She nods. "Maybe tomorrow we can do something together. Just you and me?"

My smile widens, genuine this time. "I would *love* that, Ava."

She exhales with a laugh so pure and so her, and she leans up, presses her lips to mine. "I love you."

"I love you, too." I shake my head in disbelief. I've wanted this moment with her for so long, and I finally have it. "I have your present in my locker."

"You didn't need to get me anything."

"You have to promise not to use it until it's dark, okay?"

She squeezes my arm. "I promise."

"Are you two lovebirds done?" Miss Salas calls. "Because I have a class to teach and it's not about unplanned teen pregnancy."

"Sorry," I say, and Ava whispers, "Bitch."

AVA

I hold Connor's gift in my hand and glance out the living room window, watching day turn to dusk. "When are you going to open it?" Trevor asks.

"Connor said to wait until it's dark."

"If you go to your room and close the blinds, it might be dark enough."

"It won't be the same," I murmur.

Trevor grunts. "It's giving *me* damn anxiety; I want to know what it is."

"Connor six-six, twenty-to-twelve," Mom mumbles. Her movements are slow when she faces me. "Happy birthday, Ava."

"Thank you, Mama."

She's said happy birthday numerous times since I got home, and I think it's mainly because I'm still wearing the crown Trevor got me. I haven't taken it off. Connor's is the only real gift I've gotten, and as silly as it is, I'm excited to open it.

When I left the house this morning, Connor was waiting for me with a bunch of flowers. It was only then that Trevor remembered it was my birthday. He's been under a lot of pressure lately, so I wasn't mad about it. "Wait." I sit taller. "Connor said not to *use* it until it's dark; he didn't say not to open it."

Trevor's eyebrows lift, and he shifts forward. "Open it!"

"Yeah, Ava," Mom says. "Open it!"

I rip off the wrapping paper and then tear into the box. It's a plastic jar, like the ones processed fruit comes in. It's painted black, and there's a small switch on top. There's tape wrapped around the lid, indicating that it's not meant to be opened.

"What the hell?" I whisper.

Trevor laughs. "That was so anticlimactic."

"Damn," Mom whispers. "No engagement ring."

"Hey now," says Trevor. "She *just* turned eighteen... I need some time before I picture you walking down the aisle."

"You *walking* me down the aisle, you mean."

Trevor's teeth show when he smiles. "Really?"

I throw the wrapping paper at his head. "Of course, *stupid*."

CONNOR

I wait out in the hallway of the hotel, having just met my grandmother. Or re-met her, really.

I thought maybe once I'd seen her, a memory would come flooding back and I'd recognize at least parts of her. I didn't. And even though my mom warned me that she was sick, that she didn't have much time, I hadn't prepared myself for what was in front of me.

My mom sat in the room while my grandmother choked out questions I couldn't quite comprehend. My grandmother's caretaker was with her, and she was able to translate them for me. I answered them in truth or as much truth as I felt comfortable giving. But when she asked about my dad, I refused. Just like with Ava, I didn't want him to have anything to do with what was happening. This was about me, and it was *for* me. For some form of closure, I guess.

The door opens, and my mother appears, wiping tears from her eyes. "Thank you, Connor. You have no idea how much this meant to her."

I nod, even though I don't really *get it*. Sitting in a room with me for twenty minutes while grilling me about the life I've lived doesn't really seem like it should make up for the fifteen years my grandmother has missed out on. Besides, she could've contacted my dad... if that was ever an option. I really don't know.

Mom rubs a hand down her face and then lets out a sob. "I'm sorry," she cries. "It's so hard seeing her like this."

I can't imagine what it would be like to watch your parent die in front of your eyes, and the way she is now—it reminds me of Ava, of what all she's been through. I find myself reaching out, my hand resting on her shoulder. "I'm sorry you have to go through it."

She shakes her head, her eyes downcast.

I add, "And I'm sorry that I made you guys fly to me." *You kind of gave me a fear of airports*, I don't add. They'd landed while I was at school and had booked two rooms at a hotel near the airport. I thought one was for them, and one was for me. Turns out, my mom expected me to stay with her. That was a hard line I didn't plan on blurring, and so I asked her to get me my own.

She says, wiping at her eyes, "It's okay. You've done everything you can."

I *have*.

And this is all I'm willing to do, I've decided. Because it's caused too many problems and put too much of a strain on the person who matters the most: *Ava*.

"Where's your room?" I ask.

"On the other side of the hotel."

"I'll walk you."

She smiles, but it's sad. "That's very chivalrous of you."

I shrug. "I guess Dad raised me..." I trail off. *He raised me right, even without you.* I look away when I catch the hostility in her eyes.

"Connor, did you talk to your dad about—"

"No," I cut in. "If he wanted to tell me what happened back then, he would've already. And if you think it's something I should know, then *you* need to be the one to say it."

She exhales, her cheeks puffing with the force. "You're very mature for your age."

"I guess it comes with the near-death experience." I regret it the moment the words are out, but I stand tall, act defiant. Because even though I know what I'm saying is hurting her, she needs to see the effect *her* choices have made on *my* life. The hours of therapy, the anxiety, the constant fear of being left alone. For years, I cried, holding on to Dad's leg every morning he left me at daycare or at school, and even now... there are moments when he's not home when I think he should be, and I call just to make sure he'll be back. Fifteen years of this shit, and I...

I don't know why I'm here.

I should go home.

To my dad.

To Ava.

"You know what?" I say. "I think I'm just going to go to my room. It's been a long day."

"All right, son."

"Don't call me that." Aggravation forms a knot in my stomach. "I'm not..." I shake my head. "Bye."

Eyes glazed, she stares through me, nodding. "Goodbye, Connor."

AVA

After what feels like an eternity, I finally feel comfortable enough to "use" the present. I go to my room and use it in private, just in case it's inappropriate, because who the hell knows with Connor.

I sit in the middle of my bed with the jar on my lap while darkness surrounds me. Pathetically giddy, I can't help but giggle when I flick the switch. A buzz sounds from inside the jar, and it takes a moment for something to happen, but when it does, my jaw drops, and my heart soars. Tiny specs of light glow from the jar, hitting the walls of the room, circling all around me. "Fireflies," I whisper, watching them float across the room. And then the music starts, "Fireflies" by Owl City. I'd told him about that camping trip with my mom, but it was so long ago, and how... how did he remember? How did he do this? Tears fill my eyes while elation fills my heart. "Mama!" I leave the jar on my bed and rush to the living room. "Mama, look!" I grasp her hand, force her onto her feet.

Trevor stands, too. "What is it?"

"Look!" I practically drag Mom into my room and wait for Trevor to step inside before closing the door. "Look! And listen."

It takes a second before Mom gasps, "Ava, it's our song."

"It's our song!" I laugh out.

"And fireflies."

"So many of them! Whenever we want them, Mama! Connor—" I break off on a cry, the weight of his gift hitting me right in the chest. "He gave us a do-over."

"He gave us a do-over," Mom repeats, finding my hand in the darkness. "Oh, Ava. It's beautiful."

"I know."

She squeezes my hand. "Let's go!"

"What? Where?"

"Come on!"

Trevor opens the door for the both of us, and I quickly flick off the switch on the jar, not wanting to waste its battery. Now, Mom drags *me* by my arm... through the house and out the front door. She doesn't hesitate, not even for a second as she calls over her shoulder to Trevor, "Open the garage."

Trevor complies, and she starts rummaging through all the stuff we wanted to keep but had no real use for. "What are you looking for?" I ask.

"The tent!"

"The *tent*?" I repeat.

She smiles over at me. "Ava, if we're going to have a do-over, we're going to do it right!"

Trevor chuckles. "I think it's over here." He shifts around some boxes and uncovers our old camping gear.

"Yes!" Mom yells, arms raised in victory.

I laugh, my heart aching in all the best possible ways. "Where are we going to camp, Mama? This is crazy."

"It doesn't matter where, Ava! As long as we're together!" She looks at Trevor. "All three of us. Me and my children!" I don't miss the widening of Trevor's eyes or the way her words have him standing taller. She's always referred to him as my brother, but never as *her* child.

"Grab the sleeping bags," she orders me, and of course, I do as she says, laughing when I see her throw the tent onto the unkempt grass of our front yard.

She tries to unzip the bag for the tent, but she's struggling with just one hand, and she starts laughing—the hysterical kind that has me doing the same. It takes three people over a half hour to put up a tent that's at least thirty years old. It doesn't help that we only have the streetlamps to guide us. We all three stand back when it's up and then burst out laughing at the sight of it. It's obvious rodents have gotten to it since we used it last because there are giant holes where they shouldn't be. "It's so sad-looking," I say through a giggle.

"It's perfect," Trevor says.

Mom nudges my side. "Go get your gift."

I run into the house and grab the jar, then run back out, holding it to my heart. "Got it!"

Mom and Trevor are throwing the sleeping bags into the tent, and I don't know if she plans on all of us sleeping in there for the night, but I don't think it's possible. Still, I crawl in with them and set the jar in the middle, then flick it back on. When the music starts, Mom begins to sing, so loud and so free, and I join in with her. We're off-key and obnoxiously loud, and I look over at Trevor, who shrugs, yells, "I don't know the words!"

The tent vibrates, and I think we're the ones causing it, but then something wet hits my forehead. I look up through the giant hole above me. Another droplet. "Oh, my God, it's raining..."

Mom cackles. "It really is a do-over!" She takes my hand again. "Let's go."

I follow her out of the tent, ignoring the rain now *pounding* on my shoulders. She starts singing again, louder than before, pulling me to her as she sways me in her arms, dancing to a rhythm only we can hear. Trevor stays in the tent while we dance around him, our laughter filling my heart with joy. The rain only gets heavier, until the ground beneath us turns to mud. Mom cackles when she falls to the ground. Lying on her back, she swings her arms and legs back and forth. "What the hell are you doing?" I laugh out.

"Making mud angels!"

I stomp around her, splashing mud all over us, my arms swinging wildly as I continue to sing.

We *needed* this.

God, did we need it.

Just one night. One moment to forget everything else, and just like all the times before, Connor's the one to give it to us... even from all the way in Georgia.

Neighbors turn their porch lights on, opening their doors to see what all the laughing and singing and yelling are about. I don't care what they see, and Mom—she's so blissfully unaware, and I love that she is. It's been eight fucking years since I've seen her like this, and I want to hold on to the moment for as long as I can. Mom starts to sing again, screaming the lyrics as she gets to her feet, mud caked all through her hair, through her clothes. She skips around the front yard, her arms flailing. Our next-door neighbor on the opposite side of Connor comes out of his house, his screen door slamming against the tired siding. "Get your drunk ass back inside! You're disturbing the peace!"

"She's not drunk, you piece of shit!" I yell back.

"Ignore him, Ava," Trevor says, coming out of the tent. He palms the small of Mom's back and holds her hand, and they dance together, a pathetic attempt at a tango that has them both howling with laughter.

The piece-of-shit neighbor's on the phone now, and more people have come out of their houses, watching our joy from the shelter of their porches. I grab my gift, not wanting it to get ruined in the rain, and bring it to the porch, and when I turn back around, the street is lit up by red and blue lights. "Trevor, stop!" I yell, and he's too busy laughing to hear me.

I rush toward them, glaring at my neighbor. "The cops are here!"

Mom's head throws back with her cackle. "What are they going to do, Ava?" she shouts over the rain. "Handcuff me?"

Two uniformed officers get out of the cruiser, while Trevor and I stand side by side, ignoring Mom as she continues to sing.

"Is there a problem, officers?" I ask when they approach.

They're two males. The younger of the two is tall, a solid wall of muscle, and the other one's shorter and rounder around the gut. The tall one says, "We had a noise complaint."

I shake my head. "We were just out here—"

"In the rain?" the short one cuts in.

I nod, wipe the water from my eyes. "Is that illegal?"

"No," says the taller one, and I can already tell he's the nicer of the two. I look at his badge—*L. Preston*—and he must know my brother because he asks, "Trevor?"

"Hey, Leo."

"You know each other?" I ask, looking between them. Behind me, Mom's still singing, still blissfully happy.

"He's one of Tom Preston's boys."

"Oh." *That explains the name.*

"Look," says Leo, "we have to come out if there's a complaint made, but it looks like y'all are just having—"

"They're disturbing the neighborhood!" my neighbor yells. I've never even spoken to him before, and I don't understand what the fuck his problem is. "Look at all the people watching! They're all scared. Who knows what that drunk bitch will do—"

"Don't fucking call her that!" I shout.

"Ava," Trevor sighs, shaking his head. "He's not worth it."

Our neighbor laughs. "Yeah, listen to that—"

I don't *hear* the word, but I know what he said. It's prejudice. Bigoted. Rage fills my bloodline as I take a step forward. "You racist piece of—"

Trevor holds me back, covers my mouth with his palm. But I'm not the one he needs to worry about. Mom screams, pushing past me. Within milliseconds, she has the guy by his collar, his face an inch from hers. "What the fuck did you call my son?!"

"You heard me, you crazy bitch."

It seems so slow—at least in my head—the way her head tilts back... right before she slams it in his face. Blood pools from the guy's nose, and Mom doesn't release him. She does it again. And again. And I can hear the screams of the people around me, see the ones herding their children back into their homes. Trevor releases me, but it's too damn late.

"I want her arrested!" the fucker orders, and fat cop moves around me, his grip harsh on Mom's shoulders. She turns to him. "Don't you dare touch me!" She swings at his head, and it's the moment everything speeds up again. His baton comes out, strikes the back of her leg, and she falls to the ground with a wail of a cry. She's yelling, words incoherent, and my heart falters in my chest. She's kicking, and she's screaming, and *I* know that she's begging, but no one else would, because no one else knows her like I do. A flash of white flickers near her stomach—a taser—and I come to. Scream at the top of my lungs.

"Don't hurt her!" I can't see through my tears, can't hear through my cries as she gets picked up, dragged to the car. Leo Preston is beside me now, cursing under his breath. I rush to the car, trying to pry the officer's hands off my mother. "Leave her. She didn't do anything!"

"She attacked me!" the fucker of a neighbor yells, holding a hand to his nose.

"Fuck you!" I scream.

Trevor's behind me, pulling me away, as the cop gets Mom in the car and closes the door. She sits perfectly still, her chin in the air. But when she turns to me, my blood runs cold. There's no emotion in her expression. No life in her eyes. Another set of lights appears, this one from an ambulance. They stop in front of the cop car, on the wrong side of the road. Connor's dad hops out first, his eyes finding mine. "Ava? What happened?"

I look back at my mother while Trevor releases me slowly. Hand raised, I hold my palm to the window, my vision blurred by the tears, and I croak, breathless, "Mama..."

CONNOR

> Connor: Hmm. I feel like your lack of contact means maybe you hate the present... I hope you realize it's not just an old mayonnaise container.

I stare at the last text between Ava and me. I'd sent it over an hour ago, giving her at least two hours of darkness to open the thing. She hasn't responded yet, and so I send another one.

> Connor: Did you switch it on? Damn, I hope the battery didn't die. It's brand new...

After another solid hour of no response, I call her, but it goes to voicemail, and so I order room service just to take my mind off it. But it doesn't seem to help. Anxious energy flows through my veins, beating hard against my flesh. My brain starts running circles, every possible scenario racing through my thoughts. I know things haven't been the best with us lately, but she seemed better today. At least... I thought so.

It's midnight when I try calling her again, but there's no answer. I lie in bed with the TV on, not really paying attention. Somehow, I must fall asleep, because when I wake next, it's close to 3 a.m. The only alerts on my phone are from my dad. I shoot off a quick text, let him know I'm okay and that I crashed early, and then I call Ava.

It goes straight to voicemail.

This time, I leave a message, my doubt making my voice crack: "Hey, babe. I'm not sure what's going on there, but I've been messaging and calling and... and I hope everything's okay. I'm sorry that I wasn't able to be there for your birthday, and I hope that's not the reason you're... *ignoring* me, I guess. I know that things have been a little... rocky with us lately. A lot's going on in both our lives right now, and maybe that's why we're not *connecting* as well as we should be..." I swallow the knot in my throat. "And I know it might be hard to believe right now given what I've asked of you, but... I just need you to know that I love you." I pause a beat. "God, I love you so much. With everything inside me... forever." Then I heave out a breath, contain my emotions. "Ava, please don't give up on us."

connor

MY MOM WANTS to have breakfast. I tell her I can't, that I'm busy—
it's only a half lie. Truth is, I don't feel like I have anything left to say to her.
And, honestly, after the night I've had, I don't think I could stomach anything.

I couldn't get back to sleep. Not even a little bit. I tried calling Ava all
night, but nothing changed. Either her phone's off or she's blocked my
number completely... and I don't know which one scares me more.

I know I should go home, but leaving early would cause too many questions. I've created a web of fucking lies, and I'm the one trapped. I stay in my
hotel room until it's the time I told Dad and Ava I'd be landing, and I call Ava
first—still nothing—and then Dad. "Are you on your way?" is the first thing
he says, his voice hoarse, weak.

My dread is instant. "Yeah. What's going on?"

"You haven't spoken to Ava?"

My pulse spikes. "No, I can't get a hold of her. Why? What happened?"

He sighs, long and loud. "Come home, son. I'll explain everything when
you get here."

The roads seem to go on forever. Every light is red. Every car in front of me is
going ten miles under the limit. I once told Ava I'd travel through time to get
to her, but time seems non-existent, and the nearer I get, I feel like the
distance between us only grows.

I was a phone call away. A text. I check myself there, because it's not about
me, and whatever it is, Dad *knows*. He's involved. And that can only mean one
thing...

I finally make it home, and my truck has barely come to a stop when I step out, hesitant about where to go first. Looking toward Ava's, I notice Trevor's truck's in the driveway, but besides that, there's nothing to indicate anything's wrong. Dad makes the choice for me by opening our front door, his hand gripping the back of his neck. "Let me to talk to you first, Connor."

I sit on the couch, stand up, pace, sit back down, and with every word that falls from Dad's lips, my heart sinks farther into my stomach, anchored there by the painful twists and turns.

"I should've been there," I whisper. *I could've stopped it.* But I wasn't. Because for one night, my selfish needs outweighed my love for her. It was her fucking birthday; it should've been *magical*.

Dad stands beside me as I knock on Ava's door. Trevor opens it, his phone held to his ear. Eyes tired, he looks up at me, mumbles, "She's in her room."

Without a word, I pass him and go straight to her. I stop when I see her, my hand still on the doorknob. On her bed, she sits in the corner, her back to the wall, knees raised. She looks up, her mouth parting. A lump forms in my throat when I see her expression... as if in a single night, hope lived and died inside her. A tiny hiccup forces movement in her shoulders, and *I hate myself*. I'm quick to get to her, to wrap her in my arms and shield her from the dangers of the world around her. I want to protect her, to love her. She crawls onto my lap, wordless, and places her ear to my chest, listening. And I pray to God she finds what she's looking for, what she needs. Her gaze lifts, her head tilted, brow furrowed in confusion as she looks at me, her hands clawing at my jacket to remove it. With unsteady breaths, she goes back again, her hand shaking as her finger taps, taps, taps. "Where is it?" she whispers, and everything inside me stills.

She removes my sweatshirt now, another layer to help her heal, but when her cheek presses to my chest again, it's still not enough. Lifting my T-shirt until it's skin-on-skin, I watch the rise and fall of her chest, the way her fingers dig into my flesh. Panic forms in her words when she cries, "Where is it?"

The *magic*... it's there. It has to be. "Ava, it's there..."

"It's not!" She pulls away, tears welling in her eyes.

"No," I rush out, my own alarm making me grasp her head, pull her into me again. "I swear to you; it's there."

"It's not there, Connor!" she yells. "It's not there! It's not there! It's not there!"

I bring her closer again, hold her tighter, my heart collapsing in my ribcage. Dad and Trevor are at her door now, watching, waiting. And I recognize the moment Ava falls apart in my arms, the moment the heartache becomes too much, and the cries become so heavy that no sound can accompany them. I rock her gently, whispered hushes floating out with every one of my breaths. Tears blur my vision, and I look up at Dad, fear filling my airways. "I don't know what to do."

He steps into the room and squats in front of me, his hand gentle on Ava's back. "Have you slept, Ava?"

She shakes her head, her face shielded in the crook of my neck.

Dad looks toward Trevor. "Does her mom take any Xanax or anything? Maybe she should have a little? Just a small dose, to help..."

Trevor nods. "I'll grab it."

With the help of the sedatives, Ava falls asleep in my arms within minutes. In the living room, I can hear Dad and Trevor talking, and so I make sure her breaths are even, her features calm, before untangling myself from her embrace and joining them. Trevor looks up as soon as I open her door. His eyebrows raised, he asks, "How is she?"

"She's out."

Dad says, "She needs to sleep... for her own mental health." Then he looks to Trevor. "And so do you, Trevor."

"I know," he sighs out, gripping his phone as if it's his lifeline. "I haven't told Ava yet, but they moved her mom from the jail and admitted her into a psych ward. She kept smashing her head on the..." he trails off.

"Jesus," I mumble, running a hand down my face as I flop down on the couch next to Dad.

Trevor heaves out a breath, low and slow. "My boss—he has a friend who's a lawyer, I guess. He's coming over soon to go through everything. I'm hoping they can settle something out of court. I don't want Ava going through any of that. Not again."

I nod, though I don't really understand what's happening. "What can I do?"

"You're doing it," he assures. "I just need you to take care of Ava so I can take care of everything else."

"And who takes care of you?" I ask.

His eyes drift shut. "Peter's on a flight home right now."

THIRTY-FIVE

connor

FOR THE NEXT TWO DAYS, Ava refuses to get out of bed. She refuses to eat. And she refuses to talk. Even to me. But that doesn't mean I leave her side. Not for a second am I ever more than a few feet away. When she sleeps, I try to, too. But I can't. I worry, and that worry turns to panic, turns to dread. Because what if...

What if they can't cut Miss D a deal?

What happens to her?

What happens to Ava?

Trevor and Peter are in and out of the house, on and off the phone, and I feel useless. I feel like I should be doing more than having one-way conversations with a girl who can barely look at me. A girl who needs magic and can't find it in the person who promised it to her.

She sees me.

I know she does.

But she sees *through* me.

And that's almost worse than being ignored.

I don't go to school, and nobody asks why. They already know. People come by, mainly people I don't know. Trevor closes the door to Ava's bedroom whenever they're here. He doesn't want her hearing what they have to say, and she doesn't seem to care about the secrets they're keeping.

Rhys and Karen show up, too, and they look at Ava, then they look at me, and the only thing we can see in each other is helplessness.

On the third day, Amy—Trevor's girlfriend—arrives. She seems to be the only one who can talk Ava into eating—not much—but it's enough to settle the worry I'd been carrying around for days.

I just wish it could've been me to get her to that point.

Miss Turner comes over, and for the first time, Ava seems to come to.

"Hey, sweetheart," Miss Turner says, standing in the doorway of her bedroom. "I've been waiting for your call. I wasn't sure if you'd want to see me."

"I do," Ava whispers, nodding as her eyes fill with tears. It's the most she's given anyone, and I try to push aside the jealousy, but it's there... bubbling beneath the surface.

"Did you want to talk?" Miss Turner asks her.

Ava nods again, her eyes shifting to me, before going back to Miss Turner.

Miss Turner turns to me, a pitiful smile gracing her lips. "Can you give us a minute, Connor?"

I drop my gaze. "Sure."

She rubs my arm. "Don't take it personally." It's the same thing Rhys told me about Ava when we first met. It didn't help me then, and it sure as hell doesn't help me now.

I look over at Ava. "I'm going to go home and grab a change of clothes. I'll be right back, okay?"

She lowers her gaze.

And then I ask something I've been wondering for days but have been too afraid to ask, too fearful of her answer. "Do you want me to come back, Ava?"

"Of course, she does," Miss Turner answers for her. She sighs and whispers, her words only for me, "This isn't about *you*, Connor. And you need to accept that."

AVA

In my desk drawer lives a receipt.
A receipt for room service.
Signed by one Connor Ledger.
The date on the receipt is the same as my birthday.
In my mind,
I make excuses for why he lied to me about where he was.
In my heart,
I blame myself for not being enough.

The receipt is from a hotel in North Carolina.
It's just one night in Georgia,
Connor said,
It's press for the All-American team.
In my mind,
I wonder how he could so easily lie to my face.
But in my heart,
I already know.
Under my bed lives a plastic jar.
A jar filled with fake fireflies.
When the world is at its darkest,
that's when the magic appears,
my mom says.
So, in my mind,
I wish for the magic to be true, to be real.
But in my heart,
I believe that magic is dead...
Just like Connor's love for me.

ava

MY LIVING ROOM is a constant whirlwind of people, some I barely know. If Mom were here, she'd hate it.

I hate it.

Connor lies in my bed, holding me to him as if he's somehow comforting me, protecting me.

I hate that, too.

"Ava?" Trevor says, poking his head in the door.

It takes everything in me to open my eyes.

"The lawyer's here. Leo Preston, too. They want to talk to you about your mom."

I settle my head on the pillow again, not wanting to talk to anyone.

Next to me, Connor sits up, takes my hand in his. He looks down at me, eyebrows raised. An encouraging smile flickers across his lips. "You should go talk to them, babe. It might be good news." His eyes hold the same amount of adoration and compassion from back when he loved me, and I wonder when it was precisely that he became so fucking good at faking it.

I get out of bed and out of my head, then join my brother in the living room. Amy and Peter are here, too. They stand by the doorway of the kitchen, out of the way, but still in sight.

Again, Connor sits next to me, holding my hand.

"Hi, Ava," a middle-aged man says. His eyes are soft, kind, and I only slightly remember him as the lawyer Tom Preston sent our way. "I'm Nathan Andrews. We met earlier, but I'm sure you—"

"I remember," I murmur and look at Leo Preston. He's out of his police uniform, and he looks so much younger, more *approachable*. "Hi," I say to him.

Leo smiles.

Connor squeezes my hand. "So do you have news about Miss D?" he asks, and I can hear the genuine concern in his voice. Regardless of what's happening to us or what we *aren't*, I know he cares about my mother in ways only a few people do.

And that *has* to mean something.

I hold his arm to my chest, allowing myself this one tiny moment with him.

"I managed to get the judge outside of the courtroom," Nathan tells us. "All charges have been dropped, and your mom can come home today."

My breath falters. "Really?"

"Really."

"How did you...?"

Nathan shakes his head, his eyes shifting. "Unfortunately, in a town like this, it's about *who* you know. And, luckily for you, your brother's made some good contacts over the past few years."

I glance at my brother, but he's averting his gaze, and then I look over at Peter, notice him watching me, his eyes locked on the way I'm holding on to Connor. It's not hard to figure out what's going on here, and I want to be mad. I want to yell at Trevor for bringing Peter into this, but I can't... because my mom is *coming home*.

"Thank you, Peter," I choke out, my withheld sob making it impossible to breathe. I focus on Nathan and Leo again. "All of you. Thank you."

Nathan nods, a sad smile tugging on his lips. "But, Ava, the judge has concerns, and honestly, after looking at your mom's history, so do I."

I ask, fear quickening my pulse, "What does that mean?"

"The state of the mental health care system in this town—"

"I know," I cut in, looking down.

"You know what? What does that mean for..." Connor trails off.

It means she needs more help than we can provide...

"She knows what it means," says Peter.

I can take care of you, Ava.

"I wasn't asking you," Connor grinds out.

But it's our little secret.

Trevor sighs. "So when can she come home?"

"I'm about to start my shift," says Leo. "I'll pick her up and bring her right back."

In the time Leo's gone to pick up my mom, I ignore everyone around me and get to work. I print out new pictures, so many of them, and stick them all on her walls. I clean the living room, the kitchen—making sure to put away any glasses or sharp objects that have been carelessly left out. I check her meds, get them all ready for her. For the first time in days, I shower. I tidy my room, do some laundry, including the jacket I desperately ripped off Connor the second he came back from "Georgia." I needed magic at that moment. I didn't need the receipt that fell from the jacket pocket and all the lies and insecurities that came with it.

Connor follows me around, his words low when he tries to talk to me. It's hard having him here, but telling him to leave and giving him the reasons why I *don't* want him here would be so much harder. Besides, I don't know what state my mother will be in when she gets home, and as much as I hate to admit it, he helps her in ways only the two of them understand.

When I'm done, I sit in the living room and stare out the window.

Waiting.

It's as if I'm fifteen again, and my world is nothing but heartache and hope.

It feels like hours before the squad car pulls into the driveway. Connor's instantly on his feet, taking me with him. He must've been looking out the window, too.

Waiting.

He opens the door for me, and I release his hand, take Trevor's instead. We stand side by side on the porch, watching as Leo opens the back door, his touch gentle as he helps my mother out of the back seat. I bounce on my toes, nerves and anticipation flowing through my veins. I can't hold back when she begins to approach, her head down. I run to her, just like all the times she returned from war. I call for her, my tears making it impossible to see. "Mama!" She feels like home, like her embrace is made of magic... the type of magic that destroys all childhood fears and replaces them with faith and security and *love*. I weep on her shoulder, holding her tight, never wanting to let go.

I feel Trevor's presence before I see him. "Trevor," Mom whispers.

"Don't you dare do that again," he tells her, his voice gruff.

Mom releases me, her hand going to her side as she glares at my brother.

Trevor adds, "Don't go fighting my battles for me. Especially when it comes to *my* race and other people's ignorance."

Mom lifts her chin, her eyes on his as she squares her shoulders. "You are *my* son, Trevor. I would start a fucking war for you."

For the first time ever, I watch my brother break. Shatter. Witness my mother's strength as she holds him through his cries, through his destruction. And it's only now I realize the real effects of my choices. I thought I needed time. If I could just wait, then everything would fall into place. But every second of waiting, our heartache only increases, ruining the people who matter the most to me.

I look over at Connor standing on the porch, watch his chest rising and falling with every one of his breaths.

And then I look at Peter standing beside him.

I can take care of you, Ava...

My eyes drift shut.

Vincit qui se vincit: He conquers who conquers himself.

I flick Mom's ring around my thumb.

I am the conqueror.

I am.

I am.

ava

"TOO MANY PEOPLE," Mom murmurs.

"I know, Mama," I reply, leading her from her bedroom to the living room. "But they're here for Trevor. They worry about him, and he needs the support." God, does he need it.

When she came home earlier today, she bypassed greeting Connor, Peter, and Amy, and went straight to her room. The only thing she wanted to do was sleep, though I don't think she actually did. She just wanted to be alone, and I *feel* that.

I want the same.

Now, the day has turned to night, and everyone is still here, plus Leo and Tom Preston. Leo's finished his shift and is here to check on her. Tom is here to check on Trevor. I've never known this amount of kindness from strangers, and I wish I could portray that to Mom in a way that won't upset her.

"Hey, Miss D," Connor greets, kissing the scars that mar her beauty. He offers her a smile, gentle and warm, and I wish it meant something to *me*, but it doesn't.

Everyone else joins us in the living room while Mom adjusts the hood of her robe to hide her face. Even around Peter and Amy, she gets like this, but around strangers, I fear her reaction.

"How are you feeling, ma'am?" Leo asks her, standing opposite us.

Mom settles on the couch between Connor and me. "Much better," my mom answers, her tone flat. "Sleep—" Glass breaks behind me, and Mom screams. So do I. Another round, and then many more. Shot after shot after goddamn shot flies through the window, shards of glass soaring past me and on me, and then I'm blanketed in warmth, thrown on the floor. Mom doesn't stop screaming, and around me, it's chaos. Feet stomp across the carpet, doors open, and curses fly through the air. Heated breaths land on my neck, and then, after what feels like an eternity, silence descends. Darkness fills my heart, my mind, and my heart is racing, sinking.

"What the hell was that?" Amy shouts, and I finally open my eyes. She's on the floor, too, shielded by Trevor's entire body.

He says, picking something up off the floor. "BB gun pellets."

Next to me, Mom sits with her knees raised, her arms covering her head. Connor's behind her, his back to the window, protecting her. Confused, I look down at the arms pinning mine to my chest. "Are you okay?" Peter asks, his mouth to my cheek.

I watch Leo walk back into the house, his phone to his ear.

"Ava, are you okay?" Peter repeats, shifting until he's in front of me, his concerned eyes locking on mine.

I glance back at Mom, her sobs silent as she looks up at Connor. "Get out!" Her fist slams against his chest, over and over, and I shove Peter out of the way to get to her. "Get out! Get out! Get out!" she yells.

Connor grasps her upper arms, holding them steady, and I should warn him... should tell him that it's a trigger. "Miss D. It's me." He tracks her eyes with his. "Look at me!"

She drops her head, her cries wracking her entire body.

"It's Connor. Remember me?" He peeks over at me before focusing on her again. "Connor, six-five, but is hoping—"

Mom grunts, using all her strength to free her good arm. In my mind, it plays out in slow motion, in reality... it can't be more than a second. She reaches for a broken shard of glass, pools of blood forming around her knuckles when she holds it tight in her grasp.

"Mama, no!"

Connor's quick to switch on, and he grasps her arm again, shaking her entire body until he's practically lifting her off the floor. "The fireflies," he cries, his desperation making his words weak. "The fireflies are back, Miss D." He keeps shaking her arm to try to get her to release the glass, and the blood... there's so much blood. "They're back, and they're right outside your window! We can go out there now! We can go anywhere you want!"

Mom's movements slow, as if his words get through to her. She lowers her hand, finally releasing the shard, and Connor holds her to him, his shoulders bouncing. "I don't want to be here," she whispers, grasping on to his shirt.

I don't want to be here, either, I don't say.

Connor kisses the top of her head like he's done with me so many times before. "But I need you here, Miss D." He takes a breath. "*I* need you here."

connor

THE WINDOWS of Ava's house are boarded up now. I can't see into their house, nor am I invited to step foot in it.

Ava stays home.

Dad forces me to go to school and act as if nothing has happened.

According to Ava, her mom doesn't want to be around anyone.

Not even Krystal.

But Amy is there.

And so is Peter.

It's been a few days now, and every day I get home from school, there's another form of vandalism done to their house.

The neighbor who caused all this shit has gone.

Disappeared.

And nobody knows where.

I lie on my bed, my eyes on the ceiling, my phone resting on my chest. Every call to Ava I've made has gone unanswered, and every response to a text seems like she's giving me just enough to stay within arm's length.

Dad knocks on my door, enters without waiting for a response. He looks at me, pity laced in his stare. "How are you feeling, son?"

I shrug. I don't even know how I'm *supposed* to feel.

He sits on the edge of my bed, his body half turned to me. "Have you heard from her?"

"Not really. I sent her a text earlier, but she hasn't responded," I lie. Because she did respond; she just didn't give me what I needed. "I feel like I've done something wrong," I admit.

"No, Connor, you can't think like that. You can't take it personally."

"Everyone keeps saying that." I sigh. "But I don't know how not to. I get that she's going through a lot, but all I'm doing is trying to be there for her, for *them*, and she just keeps pushing me away."

"Yeah," Dad mumbles, and I can see his mind working. "She's going through a lot, Connor. And sometimes our problems are greater than the need to express them."

I stare at him, right into his eyes, and hope that he can somehow see that I'm going through something, too. But I don't have the heart to tell him. "I guess."

Dad gets up to leave, and I pick up my phone, look at the last message I sent her. I told her I love her. She wrote back: *Ok.*

Dad stops in the doorway, his hand on the knob as he turns to me. "Just give her the time and the space she's asking for. When she's ready, she'll come back to you."

If she comes back at all.

* * *

I wake up to loud knocking on my window, and I rush out of bed, knowing there's only one person in the entire world who would be there. Under a starlit sky, Ava stands with her head down and her arms crossed. Her hair's loose, wet, as if she'd just gotten out of the shower. I'd been so worried and had gotten so worked up about *us* that I'd somehow forgotten how beautiful she is. But she's here, now, and she's everything I've needed, everything I've craved. She's so damn perfect.

When I lift the window, she looks up, those maple-colored eyes clear of the tears that have coated them for days. "Hey, sorry, I tried knocking on the door..."

"Sorry, I must've been... it doesn't matter. Did you want to come in?"

"Can you meet me at the door?"

I smile, giddy. "Yeah, of course."

I'm already waiting at my open door by the time she comes around the front. I open the door wider, expecting her to come in, but she shakes her head, keeps her distance. My smile falls. So does my heart. Right to my feet.

"Connor..." It's just my name. Two syllables. But I'd heard it in this tone once before... It was the last time she gave up on me. On *us*.

"I don't know what I did," I whisper, more to myself than to her.

Her eyes meet mine, and those tears she'd been carrying return. "I'm leaving, Connor."

My stomach *plummets*. "*What?*"

She turns to look behind her, and it's only now I notice Peter's car sitting idle at the curb, headlights on, with Miss D sitting in the backseat. "Ava, what the hell are you doing? Leaving me is one thing, but *leaving*—"

"Trevor has to stay to finish up some jobs," she interrupts as if she's planned this entire conversation in her head, and I wasn't even part of it. "We have to leave tonight to get Mom's placement at the treatment center."

Dread solidifies every organ. Every muscle. "Where?"

"It's in Texas." She blinks, letting a single tear stream down her cheek. "And Peter... Peter's going to take care of me."

"Ava, no," I breathe out, stepping closer to her. I reach for her hand at the same time she reaches into her pocket and pulls out a folded sheet of paper. She hands it to me, her head bowed.

My nostrils flare with my heavy breaths as I take in the scene. Peter has Miss D, and soon, he'll have Ava.

Ava says, "You said you were in Georgia."

"What?"

She motions to the paper, and I quickly unfold it. Bile rises to my throat when realization hits. It's the fucking receipt for the room service. "You said you were in Georgia," she repeats.

"That's not what it looks like," I rush out. "I can explain—"

"You don't need to," she interrupts. "It won't change anything. I still have to leave."

"But—"

A single sob escapes and I try, again, to somehow get closer. But the closer I get, the farther she goes, and I know... I know she's out of my grasp. She wipes at her tears with the back of her hand, her chin lifting, her eyes on mine: a show of strength while I'm drowning in weakness. "Remember that time in your truck, when you told me that you did everything for me?"

I nod, wait.

She swallows. "I got into Duke, Connor."

I whisper a "What?" because it's the only thing that forms in my mind.

"There's a residential treatment facility near there that has a program for people in our situation, but there's a waitlist, and I was doing everything I could to get my mom there. Miss Turner was helping, too. We'd been writing and calling and pleading our case, and I... I just needed time." More tears flow, and this time, she lets them free. "I kept telling myself that if I could just wait, then everything would fall into place. But I can't wait anymore, Connor. Because she's getting worse, and so am *I*. I'm falling apart, and I can't..." She breaks off on a sob, her hands covering her face, and there's an intolerable ache in my chest that won't fucking quit.

"Ava..." I breathe out.

"I did it all for you, too, Connor." She sniffs once. "I should've left a long time ago, but I just thought... if I could get through this..." She inhales deeply, her eyes back on mine. "But maybe it's for the best, you know? Maybe following you to Duke wasn't what you wanted, and—"

"Ava, *please*. Just give me two minutes to explain everything and—"

"There's a place in Texas that can take her right away," she interrupts again. She's made up her mind, and nothing I say or do can fix things. "I'm going to move in with Peter until I can find my own place."

My eyes drift shut as the world around me closes in, and the fragments and happiness of a life I once pictured begin to crumble around me.

"I wasn't going to tell you I was leaving at all," she says, "but that wouldn't have been fair to *us*. And I just came here to say goodbye, and to thank you for loving me, even if—"

Peter honks his horn. "Ava, we have to go!"

She glances at the car and then back at me. "I'm sorry I wasn't enough, Connor."

I'm experiencing it all over again. The moments right before my first death. My body starts to shut down.

To give in.

Give up.

Until I'm drowning in nothing but anguish and despair.

She's at the car now, opening the door, but it's too little, too late. She closes the door on *us*, and I slam my palm against the window, again and again. "Please, Ava! Don't leave!" I kick at the fucking car when Peter revs the engine. "*Please*."

I see her mouth move, see her say a single word that puts the final dagger in my heart: "Go." I watch the car take off, follow it through the night until the lights disappear, and then I run into my house, my heart racing. I grab my phone, dial her number. It doesn't even ring. The automated voice tells me the call can't be connected.

"Two fucking minutes!" I grind out. I just need two fucking minutes to explain *everything*. My legs take me, as if on their own, down the same path I've taken hundreds of times before. I slam my palm on her front door. "Trevor!"

He opens the door, and I'm ready to fight him. To beg him to call her. But the tears in his eyes show the same devastation that's coursing through my bloodline. "She needed to do this, Connor," he says, his voice cracking. "She needed to do this for *her*. And if you love her... you have to let her go."

There'd be no happy ending to our story, she once told me. *There'd be an intense beginning, a shaky middle, and then heartache.*

This is the heartache.

This is The End.

THIRTY-NINE

Connor

I WATCH the night sky outside my window turn to dawn, turn to day. The sun rises, just like it does every day. But today isn't like every other day. There's no warmth that comes with it, no light, *nothing*. Nothing but a reminder of every new day I'll have to live without the person I planned on spending forever with.

Dad comes home, and I don't get up from my place on my bedroom floor. I lean against my bed, stare at the wall opposite. There's a patch of paint a lighter color than the rest of the room from when I put my fist through it the first time she left me. Punching the wall didn't take away the pain then, and it sure as hell won't now.

Dad knocks, and I don't respond, knowing he's going to open the door anyway. I hear the knob turn and the door open, and then Dad's quiet gasp. He'll know—without me having to say a word—that something's wrong... something's changed. "Connor, what happened? Is Ava—her mom—"

"They're gone."

"Who?"

"Ava and her mom, they left overnight. They're gone, Dad."

"Connor," he breathes out, sitting down next to me. "Gosh, son, I'm sorry."

I shake my head, look down at my hands, and sniff back the heat burning behind my eyes. And then I let out the words I've been holding on to for years: "What's so wrong with me, Dad?" I face him, my eyes clouded. "Why do they keep leaving me?"

"Oh, Connor, no..." he sighs out, his arm going around me, pulling me to him. "This is not about you. Ava's pain—"

"And what about Mom's?" I ask around the lump in my throat. "Was Mom's pain so bad that she had no other choice? Because I'm trying to work through all this and I'm trying not to take it personally like everyone keeps fucking telling me to do, but *how*? How the fuck can I not do that?"

"What's happening with Ava is not the same—"

"Are you sure?" I ask, accusing. "Because Mom said to ask you about what happened back then."

His eyes widen in shock. "What the hell are you talking—"

"She found me," I interrupt.

Anger blazes in his eyes, and he releases me. He stands, his fists balled at his sides. I tilt my head, look up at him as he paces the room. Three steps one way, three steps back. "How? When?!"

"Answer me!" I yell, years of withheld anger and frustration and unasked questions pumping through my veins. I get to my feet. "What did you do to make her—"

"Nothing!"

"Then why?" I cry out, unable to hold it in any longer. "Why did she hate me so much she wanted me dead?"

Dad takes me in his arms again, as if I'm three years old asking the same goddamn question.

I push him away. "Your hugs aren't going to fix it, Dad. I'm not a kid anymore. I'm eighteen, and I deserve the fucking truth!"

He swallows, and I can see the fear in his eyes.

"Tell me!"

Dad shakes his head, his eyes drifting shut.

"Dad, *please*. I need to know," I beg. "I need to understand so I can stop feeling *this*." I press a hand to my chest. "Do you know what it feels like to think that something is broken inside you?"

When he opens his eyes again, liquid pain flows from their depths. "It was never about you, son. She did it to hurt *me*."

"Why?"

He grasps his hair, his eyes to the ceiling as his chest rises. Falls. Again and again. "She did it because I told her I was in love with someone else."

My stomach drops. "You were cheating on her?"

His eyes meet mine again, and he nods once. "Yes." Then he seems to release a breath he'd been holding on to for years. "With another man."

Everything inside me stills.

Every memory.

Every moment.

Every laugh.

Every cry.

Everything.

Freezes.

I rear back, unable to look at him.

"Connor, just listen to—"

I shake my head, cutting him off, and lock my eyes on his. Ava once told me we had the same eyes—my dad and me—and I agreed even though I'd never really paid attention before. I just thought I knew him well enough to see them clearly. But now... now I look at him and... "Who the hell are you?" I grab my ball, ignore him calling after me as I leave the house and go to my truck. He stands at the porch, knowing he can't stop me, knowing he can't *save* me.

Not anymore.

* * *

It takes over an hour for me to find the turnoff to the exact parking lot I'm looking for. As soon as I get out of the car, I can hear the stream of water, and I follow the sound to the lake clearing. I'm not sure when it was exactly that I decided to come here, of all places. Having this place bring nothing but memories of Ava is probably the last thing I need, but it's the only thing I want.

We'd both declared the day we spent here The Best Day of Our Lives, and maybe that's why it called to me. To remind me that once upon a time, I had it all right at my fingertips. I sit at the water's edge, my mind spinning with too many thoughts, too fast, and I can't seem to focus on one long enough to steady my pulse.

I think about my dad, and then Ava, and all the moments that led to now, and I still can't make sense of any of it. And then I remember how much Ava had changed in the past couple weeks. I recall her moods, how quickly she moved from angry to happy to sad to loving to devastated, and I wish I'd seen it then; that something bigger was happening. I should have picked up on it when she demanded Rhys give back the jersey I'd sold him. She was so angry and so passionate about it... because she knew how much it meant *to me*. How that memory with my dad was one I hold close.

I picture her sitting next to me while I tell her everything that just went down. And it feels *too* fucking real when I imagine her taking my arm and holding it to her as she looks out at the lake, her eyes glazed, because—I'm too fucking late to realize—my pain was hers, too. I should've seen that, and I should've told her about my mom, but instead, I chose to protect a woman who abandoned me rather than the girl I love. My eyes close when I envision Ava turning to me, her breath leaving her slowly. "He's still your dad," she'd tell me. "He's still the same man who believed in your dreams *more* than you did, who did everything he could to make them come true. He's still that man who held you every morning while you cried because you were so afraid he'd never come back. But he always came back for you, Connor. Always."

I wipe the pathetic tears off my cheeks and suck in a breath. Hold it. Then I get to my feet.

Because she's right.

He always came back.

And so I have to as well.

* * *

Dad looks up when I open my front door, but he's not alone. There's a man I've never seen before sitting next to him. Their hands are locked, fingers laced, and Dad's quick to separate them, quick to stand. "Oh, thank God, Connor. I wasn't sure if you'd come back."

I can't take my eyes off the other man. He's stockier than Dad, with hair so dark it's almost black. His eyes are brown, but light, like Ava's, and when he stands, he stops a few inches short of my dad. He clears his throat, looking between Dad and me, again and again, and all I can do is stand, one foot in the door, one foot out. I want to run, but Ava's imaginary words force me to stay. "I should go," he says, breaking the silence.

Dad nods, and I finally find my voice. "Stay."

The man's eyes widen, and he glances at Dad. "I think maybe you guys should..."

I step into the house, closing the door behind me, and then approach him, my hand out. "I'm Connor."

"Michael," the man croaks out, taking my hand in a firm shake. "And I know who you are. Your dad talks about nothing but you."

I nod and can't seem to stop the movement as I peek over at Dad. He's looking down at his feet, as if ashamed. "Dad?"

He looks up now, guilt and remorse making his lip tremble.

"This doesn't change anything."

Imaginary Ava was right. He's still the same man he's always been, and I can tell by the way his embrace soothes the ache and removes all my insecurities.

Michael stays. He sits next to Dad while Dad and I reveal all our secrets. Fifteen years' worth of them.

I tell him about Mom. Every single detail. From the cars she gave Ava, to the All-American game, and the last meeting we had when I told both him and Ava I was in Georgia. I tell him that in a way, I lied because I was ashamed of my need to get to know her, my need for closure. He says he understands.

That he has to, especially since he can't be one to judge. But he's pissed—not at me, but at her—for going behind his back and using their conflict to get to me.

And then he tells me about Michael.

All of it.

My mom and Michael used to work together, and he and Dad met at one of her work functions. They clicked instantly and became friends, and over time, those feelings grew, changed. Neither of them had ever had a single thought—in *that* way—about another man, so admitting they were *gay* was incomprehensible. Especially to themselves. They were simply in love with someone who just happened to be the same gender. They were never physical back then, but Dad admits that he was emotionally cheating on my mom for months before he told her. He says he "came out to her," because it's the simplest term, but it was so much more complicated than that.

After what my mom did to me, he cut all ties with Michael. He couldn't deal with the reminder and the guilt of his actions, of his *feelings*. And he could never tell me—or anyone else—about his sexuality because of the fear Mom's actions instilled in him.

For fifteen years they had no contact.

None.

Dad never saw anyone else during that time, and neither did Michael. Fifteen fucking years they were alone, and they were lonely, and all because of what my mother did to "hurt" him.

She tried to kill me... as *revenge*.

Bile sits in my throat the entire time he talks, not because of who is here with him or because he's gay or because of anything he did, but because of *her*. Of how much pain her actions caused. And she wasn't even around to witness it.

Coward.

According to Michael, he finally found the strength to reach out, and with the help of social media, he found me first and then Dad. At this point, Dad adds that the "old friend" he reconnected with that helped him see perspective when it came to my relationship with Ava—that was Michael. Michael, who reminded him that we don't get to choose who we fall in love with, and the only way to love openly and love freely is to be supported by those who love us in return.

When they realized that their feelings for each other hadn't changed, Michael moved from Florida to North Carolina to be with Dad.

In secret.

Again.

"That ends now," I tell them both. "And, sure, it's going to take me a while to get used to..."

"We understand," says Dad.

I nod. "I just want you to be happy."

"And what about you, Connor?"

"I'll get there," I say, confident.

Even if it takes me fifteen fucking years.

connor

IT'S INCREDIBLY HARD to make sense of the days post-Ava. I know I wake up every day and I go to school, and then I come home, and that's pretty much all there is to my life. Dad sees my struggle, understands it, and he gives me the time and the space I need to *grieve*. Because that's exactly what it feels like. Like *waking up twice*.

Now, I sit on my porch steps watching Trevor load his truck, his girlfriend, Amy, with him. It feels like forever ago when he was the one to watch me do the opposite. I rub my hands across my shorts, drop my head between my shoulders, because only now do I realize that I haven't just lost the girl I love, or the only woman I ever considered close enough to be a mother, but I'm also losing a friend—the first friend I made when I got here.

Without another thought, I get to my feet and make my way over. The smile I carry is fake, but the words I say are not: "Is it weird if I tell you that I'm going to miss your dumbass?"

Trevor laughs once, shaking his head. Amy rubs his arm, tells him she's going inside to make sure she's got everything. Really, she's giving us a moment alone, and I appreciate it. Trevor watches her leave before turning to me. "Not weird. You've kind of been a staple in my life the past few months. Sitting in my chair, eating my cookies..."

This time, my smile is genuine. "Listen, I know Ava's blocked my number or whatever, but is it cool if I—"

"You know my sister, man. She's going to make me do the same."

I nod. It's true. And I hate that it is.

"It's nothing against you, though," he assures. "It's just easier for her this way. She doesn't need a reminder of everything she loved and left behind."

"Yeah, I guess," I mumble. "So, I guess this is goodbye..."

Trevor looks back at his house and then at me. He leans against his truck, his hands in his pockets. He inhales a breath as if preparing his speech. "I told you when we first met that I thought you had a good head on you, and the more I got to know you, the more I believed that you're destined for great things." He rubs the back of his neck, his eyes downcast. "Look, I don't really know what happened between you and Ava, but I do know that you have *good* in you." He peers up at me, pokes a finger at my chest, right above my heart. "In here, there's *good*. I saw it in the way you treated my sister, in the way you treated Mama Jo. I just... I don't want you to let what happened here take that away. Keep being *good*, Connor. And whatever happens, don't lose sight of your end game, okay?"

I replay his words, let every single one of them sink into me. "Yeah," I say with a nod. "I won't."

He pushes off his truck and offers his hand for a shake. I take it, then grunt when he gets me in a bear hug so tight, I find it hard to breathe. "Don't go near the house tonight," he whispers, his mouth right to my ear.

I pull back just so I can look in his eyes—eyes full of clarity.

It's not a threat or even a suggestion...

It's a *warning*.

It's just after 1 a.m. when I hear the first *pop*, like a single spark in a bonfire. And then a *whoosh*. Seconds later, I smell it. The burn, the smoke.

I throw the covers off me and shrug on a T-shirt before going out to the sidewalk. I get there just in time to watch the curtains ignite and then get set ablaze. Leaning against my truck, I feel the heat across my face while my vision fills with shades of ambers and reds. Soon enough, the neighbors file out of their houses, joining me on the street as whispered gossip overpowers the shock of what's happening.

In the distance, sirens sound.

And this is the part when I wake up for the second time.

To reality.

And that reality is *my life*.

It hurts more now than it ever did before, because I think, deep down, there was a part of me that believed she would come back. She'd change her mind, realize that leaving was a mistake, and she'd come back to me. But now... now she has nothing to come back *to*. And I... I wasn't enough to come back *for*.

"Jesus Christ, Connor," Dad says, rushing toward me, his face switching from blue to red caused by the lights of his ambulance. "Is Trevor in there?"

"No, he's already gone."

My eyes are glued to the house again, and I take in the fire in all its glory, watch as the roof starts to cave in, and then I remember...

I remember what she said the night we sat on her porch and a car drove by and fucking shot up the place with a paintball gun. I remember Ava's screams, Ava's tear-filled eyes when she looked up at me. And I remember what she said...

"Sometimes I wish I could just set this whole fucking place on fire and leave and never look back."

"Jesus," Dad says, "this is terrible for them."

"No," I murmur. "It's kind of beautiful."

connor

FOR WEEKS, the remnants of Ava's house are taped off while the fire marshal investigates the cause of the fire. According to Dad, who shares a station with the fire department, they're leaning toward an electrical fault. Apparently, multiple fires were started at around the same time in different areas of the house, which is how, even though the fire department got there fast, the fire was able to spread quickly, not leaving much of the house behind.

The whispers and the gossip have died down over the weeks. First, it was that Miss D came back in the middle of the night and threw a grenade through the window. Then it was how the ex-neighbor came back and torched the place assuming everyone was still living there. And then the ones about me—the pissed off ex-boyfriend who found out Ava was cheating on me with Peter, and then Trevor, and then Peter *and* Trevor.

This town, man... no wonder they wanted the fuck out of here.

* * *

"Are you sure you don't want to come with us?" asks Dad, flattening a map across the coffee table. He and Michael are here planning a cross-country road trip. They had initially planned to leave once I was all set up at Duke. I tried to convince them to leave as soon as they could, but they worried about me—both of them—and so we met in the middle. The day after I graduate, they're taking an RV and seeing the country until they make it back to Florida and start a new life, where they plan to live freely and openly in each other's love.

So.

Do I want to go with them? *Hell no.*

Do I appreciate them asking? Definitely.

"I think I'm good," I tell them. "I'll just hang here until the lease is over, throw a few ragers, experiment with some heavy drugs, and get arrested."

Dad grunts.

Michael chuckles. "Sounds like a decent plan to me."

"Right?" I like Michael. He's a good guy, and it's pretty damn clear that my dad is *smitten.* And maybe it's because I'd never actually witnessed Dad in relationships with either gender, but it didn't take me long to get comfortable with seeing them together. Though, they do keep any displays of physical affection private, so that probably helps.

"Are you expecting someone?" Dad asks when headlights shine through our living room window.

I shake my head. "No. You?"

He shakes his head too.

We both look at Michael. "Nobody even knows me here," he mumbles.

A car door slams shut, and then another, and I get to my feet, peer out the window. Rhys and Karen are marching up my porch steps. Well, Rhys is marching, and Karen's running after him. I open the door just as Rhys raises his fist to knock.

"I'm sorry!" Karen rushes out. "He's drunk, and he got in his stupid car, and I had to follow him to make sure he got here safe, but he's on a war—"

"You drove drunk?" Dad interrupts.

But Rhys ignores him, too focused on me. Rage forms in his glare as he points a finger at my chest. "You motherfucker!"

"Whoa!" Michael stands. "What's going on?"

"I'm sorry," Karen says again.

But Rhys is too lit, too ready to lay it all out between us. "For years, I've stood by her side. I've been there for her through everything. Whenever she needed anything, she came to *me.*"

"This is about Ava?" I ask, confused.

Karen huffs out a breath. "Of course it's about Ava!"

"And then you fucking come out of nowhere," Rhys fumes, "and she chooses you! I've been on the sidelines waiting for her to—"

I lift a hand between us, shutting him up. "How much have you had to drink?"

"Shut up, *Ledger!*" he roars. "You go moping around school as if you've lost someone you've loved for years. You haven't. *I have!*"

"Fuck you!" I try to slam the door in his face, but he kicks it back open.

"No, fuck you!" He throws the first punch, getting me square in the jaw.

I hold a hand there, waiting for the pulsing to settle down. But there's no fight left in me to retaliate.

Rhys squares his shoulders. "Fight me, you pussy!"

I shake my head, adjust my jaw. "No."

"Rhys, you need to leave!" Dad orders.

But Rhys ignores him and charges at me, his shoulder hitting my stomach until my back lands on the floor. Karen's screaming; Dad's yelling. And I try to push Rhys off me, but he's too fucking outraged, and now we're rolling on the fucking floor, knocking over the coffee table. Water spills on the carpet, and Michael's trying to lift Rhys by his waist. Another blow to my gut, and blood pools in my throat, on my tongue. I cough it up, shielding another blow with my forearms.

"She was *mine!*" Rhys shouts.

"She chose *me!*" I grunt, finding the strength to throw him off me. I get to my feet, look down at him, wondering where the fuck all this came from. How long has he been hiding these feelings? Through staggered breaths, I yell, "She chose me, okay? And I don't know why the fuck she did!"

Rhys sits up now, his head tilted back to look up at me.

"Don't you think I question that every fucking day she's gone! That maybe *I* was the reason? That I *pushed* her to leave?" My chest aches from every physical blow, every verbal admission. "She was fine!" I seethe, my voice cracking with emotion. "When I met her, she was... she was fine, and I—"

"Don't, Connor!" Karen cuts in. "Don't let Rhys's drunk ass convince you that your relationship was anything less than it was. You loved that girl with everything you had, and she—she worshipped the ground you walked on."

Rhys's heavy breaths fill the momentary silence.

She adds, "Rhys is just looking for someone to blame; that's all this is."

I glance down at Rhys, catch the moment his eyes drift shut.

"And if he really loved her the way he's *acting* like he does, then he wouldn't have gone around screwing anything with spreadable legs for the past three years."

Michael gasps. "Is this how kids talk these days?" he asks Dad.

Dad runs a hand down his face.

I squat down in front of Rhys, wipe the blood off my lip. "You're allowed to miss her," I mumble. "But I can't fix this. I can't turn back time and be *better* to her."

"Jesus Christ," Karen sighs out, flopping down on the couch. "You dipshits ever consider that none of this has anything to do with either of you or your giant egos?"

"Girl, preach!" Dad mumbles, handing me a dish towel to wipe off the blood.

"If anyone should be hurting, it should be me," Karen continues. "You're both sitting there all *boohoo, poor me.* She was *my* best friend. You want to talk about who's known her the longest? We've been friends since kindergarten!

And you want to compare who's been there for her the most?" she asks, and I can hear it in her voice... hear the toughness she carries around with her begin to weaken, begin to fade. "That would be me, you assholes! I was there for her when her mom first deployed, and whenever there was something on the news about the war, and she'd get scared, she'd call *me*!" She's crying now, tears are flowing, but still—she holds her head high, her words steady even when her voice isn't. "And some fucking friends you are, because I've been holding both your hands ever since she left, and neither of you—not once— has ever asked if *I'm* okay. And I'm *not*, just so you know. I'm not fucking okay... because she was *my* best friend."

Silence falls, and so does my heart.

"I'm sorry," Rhys mumbles. His eyes shift from Karen to me. "I'm sorry," he repeats.

I sit down next to Karen, throw my arm around her shoulders. "I'm a sucky friend," I admit, kissing the top of her head. "We both are."

Karen nods. "I hate you both and hope you catch chlamydia."

Rhys laughs once. "We'd deserve it."

"No shit," she retorts.

Dad sighs. "I'm so confused."

Michael rubs his hands together. "Can I fix you guys something to eat or drink?"

Rhys shrugs, then starts replacing the coffee table to its original position. "I could eat."

Karen scoffs. "When are you *not* eating?"

Rhys settles on the other couch while Dad and Michael move to the kitchen. "Is that a friend of your dad's?" he asks, his voice low.

I shake my head. "That's Michael, Dad's *boyfriend*."

Rhys's jaw hits the floor. Next to me, Karen gasps. "Your dad's gay?" she whisper-yells. "How did I not know this?"

"I only just found out, but don't make *a thing* of it okay?"

"He's kind of cute," Karen whispers.

Rhys asks, "Who? Mr. Ledger?"

"Well, yeah, him too."

"Don't make this *more* awkward," I mumble.

Dad and Michael return with a tray of drinks and some chips. Michael hands a glass to Rhys, and Rhys says with a toothy grin, "Thanks, Mrs. Mr. Ledger."

I sigh.

Karen says, "I swear to God, Rhys, the shit that comes out of your mouth..."

Rhys chuckles. "No girl's ever complained about my mouth before."

"Why do you—"

A knock on the door interrupts Karen's speech.

Dad shakes his head. "If this is another one of your friends here to throw punches, I'm pulling you out of school and wrapping you in bubble wrap."

I get up and open the door. Just a tad. You know, in case it is someone ready to throw blows.

Mitch stands on my porch, his hands in his pockets. He's never been to my house before, at least not that I know of. "What's up?"

"Hey." He tries to peer into the house, but I step out and pull it closed behind me. I leave it ajar, still wary of his purpose. "You got a second to talk?"

Confusion blurs my senses. "About?"

His throat bobs with his swallow before his gaze drops. "It's just... uh... about Ava and—"

"What about Ava?" I cut in.

He sucks in a breath, holds it, then releases with force. Shaking his head, he looks up at me, his eyes tired. "Look, I shouldn't—I mean, I didn't want..."

I stand taller, alarm hammering in my ribcage. "Just spit it out, man."

His lips part, but nothing comes out, and I raise my eyebrows. Wait. "I uh... it was *me*..."

"The *fire*?" I ask.

He shakes his head. "No. Not the fire, but kind of. I guess I had something to do with that, too. And I feel guilty about that, but..."

"Jesus, man, just say it."

He untucks his hands from his pockets, fists them at his sides. "You ever notice how all of the bad shit that happened to Ava's house happened when Peter Parker was around?"

My eyes widen, and I take a moment to think back. He's right. Apprehensive, I nod, wait for him to continue while a knot forms in my stomach.

"He paid me to do that shit."

I dip my head, lean my ear closer to him because I can't be hearing this right. There's no fucking way. "*What?*"

Mitch nods. "I don't know his angle, or what he expected to get out of it, but he paid me to vandalize her house... the paintball gun, the BB gun, all of it... he paid me to do it all, and I..."

Rage solidifies every muscle, every cell. "And you did?"

His eyes drift shut... just as the door swings open behind me. I get shoved out of the way, and all I can see is a ball of blonde hair and bright red nails holding on to the drink tray as it flies toward Mitch's face. When the contact's made, there's a crack so loud even *I* hiss in sympathy. Mitch's face is nothing but red from his eyes down. Blood pours—no *sprays*—from his nose, his lip, all down his chin, his jaw, dropping onto the porch I never got around to fixing. Before I get a chance to say or do anything, Rhys is lifting Karen by the waist and practically throwing her back into the house. Dad joins Rhys and me on the porch while we take in the mess that is Mitch. Dad's sigh is louder than the fury building inside me. "Let me take a look," Dad says, stepping toward Mitch. He tilts Mitch's head back by his jaw, then clasps the bridge of his nose with his thumb and forefinger. Mitch yelps in pain and Dad squeezes harder. "Yep, it's definitely broken." He releases Mitch completely. "Now get the fuck off my porch before you stain it with your depravity."

FORTY-TWO

connor

I TRIED CALLING Ava to warn her about Peter. I also tried calling Trevor. My calls went unanswered. So did Rhys's and Karen's. We concluded pretty quickly that they'd gotten new numbers and didn't want to be contacted. It all makes sense now that I think about it. Peter was around when all the major stuff went down, and knowing he got what he wanted is one thing but knowing he's with Ava... that's another.

I worry.

I can't not.

Because if he's willing to stoop that low to get to her, then what else is he capable of?

I miss her.

I miss her so fucking much it aches.

What's left of her house has now been cleared. I was able to go there just before the work started and collected what I could of what remained. Mostly, I looked for the photos that were on her mom's walls: the ones of her as a kid, of her growing up, all of them with her smiling that smile that settled so many of my insecurities. I keep them all in a box under my bed and promise myself that one day, I'll look at them, and I'll stop hurting and start remembering. I'll remember the good she brought out of me, the confidence, the ability to love, and to *trust* and to...

Lying in bed, I unlock my phone and start going through all the pictures I'd taken of her.

Nine months.

You can grow an entire human in nine months.

And you can fall in love with an entire human in much less.

I find my favorite picture I'd taken of her. She's in my old car, my arm held to her chest while drool formed a puddle on my weenus. It was the first day I *hinted* that I loved her, and it was the first day she declared it out loud. I keep going through the pictures, moments and memories, and I wish I'd taken more videos because—and I learned after my mom abandoned me—a person's voice is the first thing you forget. You remember the way they look, even if it's blurry; you remember certain parts of their bodies: their eyes, their hair... but you forget their *voice*. You forget what it sounds like when they tell you they love you, and you forget the tones of their voice when they sing. But worse, you forget their laugh, the way they start low and get higher when the single emotion consumes them. You forget the sound of their sigh at the end when the moment's over. You forget the moment when *The Happiness* is so intense it bubbles out of their beings and emits out of their mouths.

I switch to the videos folder and go through them, too, stopping on the last one I'd taken. I'd completely forgotten about it because it wasn't candid and wasn't a display of our love for each other. It's the video for the multimedia project we'd done for school that I'd since been excused from seeing as I didn't have a partner. I hit play, my heart sinking when she comes to life. But it's not the *her* I want to remember. It's not *Ava*.

She's sad.

God, she's so fucking sad, and I see it now, but I didn't see it then. I felt it, I'm sure, but it didn't cut deep like it does now. She's reading off a script, no inflection in her tone, and occasionally she'll look up at me, but her eyes... there's no light in her eyes, no spark, no magic.

I listen to our back and forth, our voices low and melancholy. "Maybe now's not a good time for this," she says.

And I reply, because I'm selfish, "I can't fix this if I don't know what's broken, Ava."

It takes her a moment to respond. "I'm fine. I just want you to be the same."

I replay it all in my head at the same time I watch it play out in front of my eyes. I ask, "You want me to stay with you tonight?"

She shakes her head. "I'm pretty beat. I'm probably just going to sleep now." She gets off the bed, and I recall her walking me to the door, can hear us saying goodnight to each other. No more than a minute later, she's back in her room, on her bed. I sit up higher and watch, my eyes transfixed as she uncaps a bottle of pills and pours the entire content onto her palm.

So many pills.

My heart races as I watch her look up, not at the camera, not at anything really. When her gaze lowers, she lifts her hand, inspecting... and then she tilts her head back, raises her palm to her mouth and I...

I can't breathe.

Can't see through the tears as I watch hope die and heartache unfold...

"Ava?" Trevor knocks on her door.

I let out a breath.

Ava coughs up the pills back onto her palm, then rushes to shove them all under her pillow, hiding them from him. "Yeah?"

I hear Trevor open the door. "Hey, you got an A+ in English?" he asks her.

Ava nods, forces a smile.

"Damn, girl," says Trevor, pride clear in his tone. "I don't know how you do it, Ava. Take care of your mom and *me* and still manage to get these grades. It's ridiculous how proud I am of you."

Ava's blink is slow. "Thanks."

A beat passes before I hear the door latch again, and I see Ava's shoulders drop, her chest rising. She whispers to a Trevor who's no longer there, "I do it all for you." And then she breaks down, and I break down with her as I watch those small hands of hers cover her face, her sobs. Her shoulders wrack with each of her cries, and she reaches under the pillow again, both hands scooping up the pills. She moves off-screen, but I know she's dumped them in her trashcan, and she returns to her bed with her phone to her ear. "Miss Turner?" she sobs. "I'm sorry for calling so late, but you said—"..."I'm having those thoughts again."..."The *dark* ones."

I jolt when my phone vibrates in my hand, cutting off the video. *Wendy* flashes on the screen, and *contempt* flashes inside me. "Yeah?" I answer.

"Hi, Connor." I realize now that I could go the rest of my life never remembering my mother's voice and I'd never miss it. Not for a second. "How have you been?"

Where to start? "What's going on?"

She clears her throat. "I guess we're done with pleasantries, then?"

"Honestly, I don't really have much to say to you anymore."

"Okay," she says. Then pauses a beat. "I accept that."

I stay quiet. *She doesn't really have a choice.*

"Connor," she says with a sigh. "Do you have a lawyer?"

"No. Why?"

"Because you're going to need one..."

FORTY-THREE

Connor

I GET to school early the next morning because I have things to say, and I know the person I want to say them to will be ready to hear them.

It only takes a few seconds for Miss Turner to call out, "Come in," after I knock. She smiles when she sees me, and I don't know her well enough to know if it's genuine or not. After what I saw in the video last night, I wouldn't be at all surprised if she blames me for Ava leaving.

I ask, "Are you scheduled to meet with someone or..."

"Well, this was Ava's time with me, so no." She points to the seat opposite her. "Is this a sit-down or stand-up type of conversation we're about to have?"

I sit down.

She nods once. "Good."

I ask, not wanting to play games, "I know that you're not going to tell me what I want, but can you at least tell me if she's okay?"

"She's okay, Connor. Her mom's getting the care she needs, and so is *she*," Miss Turner answers, her tone gentle. "I promise you that."

I slump farther in my seat, get comfortable. "She said you were trying to help her get her mom into a place near Duke?"

"Yeah, I was," she responds, a smile playing on her lips. "God, Connor, you should have seen her face when she got that letter from Duke. She came in here all excited, and then her reality hit, and she was trying to work out a way to be able to do everything." Pity laces her tone. "Classic-Ava, right?"

I nod, trying to picture Ava's reaction when she got that letter, but I can't... all I can envision is the heartache from the video I watched.

"She would've loved to start with you," she rushes, as if she's been dying to tell me all this but didn't know how. "But she had to make sure her mom was okay and that she'd be settled in her placement. She didn't want to rush things, and that's why she deferred a year."

My eyes widen. "She did?"

"You didn't know?"

"I didn't even know she got into Duke until she told me she was leaving."

Now *her* eyes widen. "Ava just wanted to keep it a secret in case things didn't work out with her mom," she tells me. "She didn't want you to get your hopes up and then..."

I frown at the thought.

"What are you thinking, Connor?"

I shrug. "It's just fu—*messed*—up how we kept so many secrets from each other because we thought we were protecting the other person, and in reality, we were just causing more and more damage."

Miss Turner sits forward, her forearms resting on the table. "What's your secret, Connor?"

I don't hold back. "Remember the first session I had with you?"

"About your mom abandoning you?"

I nod. "She came back into my life recently."

"She did?" Miss Turner doesn't even try to hide her shock. "When? How?"

I tell her everything, just like I told Dad. But I tell her more. I tell her that my mom's name is Claudia, but in order to hide it from my dad, I'd saved her number in my phone under Wendy—because we met up at a *Wendy's* when I was in Georgia for the All-American game. I tell her about my mom and grandmother flying over here to see me, and I tell her about how much I regret choosing to protect her over Ava. I admit that, initially, I had believed my mom's threats about Ava getting in trouble if anyone would *somehow* find out that Ava knew she existed. It took me a while to realize that everything my mom ever said to me was a form of manipulation for her own personal gain. I say all this while looking down at my hands, too ashamed to face a woman who knows Ava more than I do, that saw her at her lowest and embraced her at her peak. "I thought I had time," I say. "With Ava, I mean. I thought I had time to make up for my mistakes, but I didn't, and now... now it's too late."

Miss Turner has stayed silent the entire time I speak, and she's still living in that silence for seconds after I'm done. A steady blink later, as if coming back to reality, she heaves out a breath and leans back in her chair. She grabs a stress ball from her desk and squeezes once. Twice. Then she says, almost singing the words, "I can accept failure; everyone fails at something. But I can't accept not *trying*."

My eyes narrow. "Michael Jordan said that."

She nods. "Are you going to *try*, Connor?"

Baffled, I ask, "With *my mom*?"

"Fuck your mom."

Oh. "With Ava?"

She nods.

I sigh, *hopeless.*

Miss Turner shakes her head. "Here's another one for you then: Hard work beats talent when talent fails to work hard."

"Kevin Durant," I mumble. "Are you saying I'm talentless?"

"No."

I rear back. "I'm confused."

I catch the stress ball she throws at my chest while she says, "I think that quote is about so much more than basketball." She pauses a beat as if contemplating. "When you think about it, *really* think about it, talent is God-given; it's *destined.* And Ava once told me that she thought you were put on this earth for her. That you moved next door, and you saved her, and that you were *destined* to be together..."

The past nine months must've ruined my brain cells because I can't seem to comprehend what she's saying, and she must realize this because she says, "Connor. Replace talent with destiny."

I say, thinking aloud, "Hard work beats *destiny* when *destiny* fails to work hard."

Miss Turner grins when she must see the light switch on in my mind. "I get it," I tell her, a single spark of magic flickering in my chest. "Hey, do you just keep a stack of quotes on file?"

"Pretty much," she replies. "This place does not pay me enough to come up with my own."

I stand, pick up my bag. "Thanks for listening."

"You're welcome."

I stop by the door and turn to her. "Look, I know that there's that whole patient confidentiality thing, but if you do speak to Ava, I'd appreciate it if you told her all that... about my mom, I mean. I don't want her going through the rest of her life thinking that she wasn't enough." I pause a breath. "I've spent the last fifteen years drowning in those thoughts, and I wouldn't wish them upon anyone."

Miss Turner nods, slowly, her eyes lowering. "What are you going to do now, Connor?"

My shoulders lift. "I'm going to start working on me, start giving my dad more reasons to be proud of me, and give my mom even more reason to regret what she did... and then I'm going to work on my end game."

Miss Turner's lips tug at the corners. "And what's your end game?"

Ava.

I tap at my chest, just like Miss D showed me. "The Happiness."

ava

ONE YEAR LATER

"HEY, guys. Just give me a minute. I'll go find her," Brandon, one of the so-called nurses, tells us as he makes his way through the doors behind the reception desk.

"*Find* her?" Trevor says, his eyes narrowed. "What? Did they lose her?"

"It wouldn't surprise me," I murmur.

"Ava," Trevor deadpans.

I roll my eyes. "I'm kidding." *Kind of.*

I watch Trevor as he looks around the waiting room. I come to Mom's treatment center almost daily, but with Trevor back at Texas A&M and working two part-time jobs to try to make a dent in the massive debts he'd accrued over the past few years, he doesn't get to visit Mom as much as he'd like. I try to see things from his perspective: the peeling paint of the walls, the old bright purple showing through the now sky blue. Posters from the late nineties hang in no particular order, all with motivational quotes that are somehow meant to ease the worry of the people who enter. The worst is the buzzing of the fluorescent lights overhead; so neglected, the dead insects in the housing are probably older than I am.

"Where the fuck did Peter find this place?" he whispers, more to himself than to me. It turns out, Peter's promises to take care of me meant me living in his condo while Mom was placed *here*. My living with him lasted all of two weeks, but that's a story for another time. As far as my mom... this is all we can do right now. I've applied for so many places, but the waitlists are insane, and it's not like it's *that* bad—at least that's what I try to tell myself every time I walk through the doors.

Brandon returns and, without making eye contact, tells us, "She's in her room. You can go on back."

Trevor's jaw ticks, his hands fisted at his sides.

"Thanks," I reply, tugging on Trevor's arm until he follows me through the doors. The hallways are just as bad as the waiting room, and I lead us through what feels like endless narrow corridors until we make it to Mom's room. She's in an old plastic chair, her hair matted as she looks out the window.

Zero-days.

Every day here is a zero-day.

And, in a way, I'm grateful she doesn't realize how shitty she has it. Besides, zero-days are far better than negative days.

"Hi, Mama," I edge, careful not to spook her. "Trevor's here."

A hint of a smile plays on her lips as she looks away from the window and notices Trevor standing behind me. "My kids," she muses. "I love my kids."

"We love you, too, Mama Jo." Trevor approaches, kisses her scars. He leaves his hand on her shoulder, waiting for her to reach up and pat it as she always does.

"How's school?"

"Good," he tells her. "One more year and you'll be at my graduation, right?"

Mom looks away.

Trevor's gaze drops.

She hasn't left the building since we got to Texas, too afraid of the outside world, and no amount of convincing can change her mind. "And work, Ava?" she asks. "How's work?"

"It's the same," I reply, fixing the pillows and sheets on her bed. I sit down on the edge, my hands clasped on my lap.

"Same," she repeats. "Everything is always the same."

It is. At least for her and me. I managed to get a job pretty soon after we moved here, washing dishes at an old run-down diner. The pay's not a lot, but it's enough to get me through the week and to cover the rent on my studio apartment, an apartment Trevor hates despite me telling him that *it's fine*.

That it will do.

Everything *will do*.

For now.

I graduated from St. Luke's under "special circumstances." Miss Turner sent my diploma to Amy's PO box. It's the only address I felt comfortable giving out. I'm not really sure what to do with a certificate that says *Congratu-*

lations. You survived. Barely. She's the only one I talk to from back home, and our phone calls have become less and less over the year.

Sometimes, when I get really lonely, my thoughts wander to my old life, to my old friends, to *Connor*. But I'm quick to push them away. I have to be. One thing I've learned from Miss Turner's random emails she sends is that I need to stop punishing myself, and thinking about Connor is the worst form of punishment there is.

"How have you been, Mama Jo?" Trevor asks her.

"Same. Always the same."

Trevor glances at me, and I can see the struggle in his eyes. I shake my head, mouth, "No." Because I know what he's thinking. He wants to give it all up. Again. Quit school and work and find a way to take care of her. Of us. But I won't let him. And it's not that I don't think about it or think of other ways we can do this. Every day I wake up, and it's the first thing on my mind, but we can't go through all that again. We went through so much pain and so much heartache, and it's not our salvation; it's just a band-aid.

We stay for a couple of hours before Mom says she's tired. I get her into bed and then manage to find a nurse so we can get our weekly rundown.

Everything is the same.

Her meds haven't changed.

Her moods haven't changed.

It's always the same.

And that *same* has to change.

I just don't know how.

* * *

Trevor drives me home, walks me to my apartment, his nose scrunched the entire time. From the busted stairs to the rickety hallway, all the way to my door that has to be kicked open with force. "Have I mentioned how much I hate that you live here?"

My neighbor, an old man wearing nothing but striped blue and white boxer shorts, opens his door and peeks outside. "Can I help you?" he growls.

Trevor's brow dips. "Yeah, you can. By getting some damn clothes on."

I pull on his T-shirt until he's in my apartment, then close the door behind him. He jiggles the knob until the lock clicks. "Ava, you need out of this shithole."

"I like it," I tell him, and it's not a *complete* lie. I like that I have my own space and that I can go from my bed to the kitchen to the bathroom in five steps, total. I like the crazy old lady a few doors down who sits out on her balcony every night and tells stories to no one about all the drunken sailors she courted once upon a time. I like the morning sun when it filters through my curtains, and I like the smell of my little herb garden I keep in the corner of the living/bedroom.

He reaches into a cupboard and pulls out a glass—I like that I can keep glasses out in the open and not freak out if it breaks. He fills the glass with water from the tap, then opens the fridge and stares at the contents. "Feed me."

I tap on his shoulder until he moves out of the way and start getting ingredients to make him a stir-fry. Just as I pull out the chopping board, my phone rings. I take it out of my pocket and stare at the number, my heart racing. It's a North Carolina number, but I don't recognize it, and so I do what I do every time an unknown number calls me. I answer, but I stay silent. Trevor watches me, his brow dipped in confusion.

"Hello?" a lady on the other end says.

Trevor motions to the phone, as if to say *talk*, but I press my finger to my lips, tell him to shut up. I made a choice to block *everyone's* numbers for a reason—to help heal my heartache—and I don't want to go backward now.

"Hi, this is Lydia from Sunshine Oak Residential Clinic. I was hoping to speak to Ava Diaz if—"

"Hi," I cut in, my eyes wide. "I'm Ava."

Trevor steps closer, his glare panicked.

"Hi, Ava," says Lydia. "I wanted to speak to you about your mother's care —Joanne Diaz. Are you available to discuss this at the moment?"

"Yes," I breathe out.

Trevor's rolling his hands as if asking for answers. I put the phone on speaker and hold it between us.

"Great," Lydia perks. "Well, I'm not sure if you've heard of us—"

"I have," I interrupt. "I mean, I know of you and your services. You're, like, the best of the best, so..." I exhale. "But... I didn't apply there." At least I don't *think* I did, but maybe I was beyond desperate and wasn't thinking clearly.

"Well, firstly, it's good to hear that you think so highly of our program, and secondly, you *didn't* apply."

"Oh." My heart sinks.

"However," she adds, "we've just had an anonymous donor who wants to start an ongoing program dedicated specifically for people in your situation— for injured veterans and their families—and I mentioned it to a friend of mine who's a director over at Riverside. Do you remember applying there?"

"Yes." I nod, frantic.

"Well, my friend mentioned your case and about how he wishes he had placement available for your mom there, but since they can't and we *can*, I was wondering if you'd like to take us up on our offer?"

"Um..." I look up at Trevor, tears in my eyes, while my pulse races against my flesh. "I mean, obviously, I would love to, but... we're in Texas right now, and I'd need to come up with the money to fly there and... and I'd need to find a place to live..." My mind won't stop spinning. "How—how long can you hold—"

"Ava," Lydia interrupts. "This particular program comes with some very generous extras. It covers all travel expenses and comes with a fully furnished apartment nearby that you can either live in or just stay in whenever you're in town."

"For how long?" I ask, my voice hoarse with emotion.

"For as long as your mom needs the care. It covers all living expenses for her, as well as any and all medication, and we have the best doctors..." She continues to speak while all air leaves my lungs, and I look up at my brother, see the hope in his eyes, feel the *magic* floating between us.

"So, what do you say, Ava?"

I can't speak through the giant lump in my throat, can't see through the tears of relief welling in my eyes.

Trevor grasps my shoulders and then pulls me to him, his arms tight around me.

"Ava?" Lydia asks. "Are you there?"

I wipe the liquid salvation from my cheeks. "How soon can you take her?"

"How soon can you get here?"

FORTY-FIVE

Connor

AUSTIN THROWS a sock at my head, but I manage to duck it just in time. "Why are you trying to ruin my life?" he yells.

Nose scrunched, I pick up his dirty sock from my bed and throw it back to his side of the dorm room. "Why can't you get your own social life?"

His eyebrows lift, and he motions up and down the length of his torso. "Have you met me?"

I shake my head, grab my basketball, and spin it around my finger. "There's nothing wrong with you, Austin."

He sighs, taking the ball from me and hiding it behind his back. "Says the jock who has every girl vying for his attention."

I scratch my head. "What do you want?"

He adjusts his glasses. "Take me to the party with you."

"I'm not going to the party," I reply.

"Thus, you *ruining my life*."

I chuckle. Austin and I were randomly paired to room together in the dorms, and I don't know how Duke decides who gets roomed with who, but you couldn't find an odder match if you tried. At least on paper. He must've felt the same way when we first met because I'm pretty sure he hated me. It took a good few months of us living and breathing in the same space for him to realize that I was nothing at all like the jocks who apparently bullied him all through high school. Now, he calls me his best friend. I'd do the same, except mine is somewhere in Texas, probably living with a guy who managed to coerce her into his home, or worse, his bed.

No, I'm still not over it.

And clearly, I'm still not over *her*.

"I'm never going to get laid," he mumbles, throwing himself on his bed.

"There's nothing wrong with you," I repeat honestly. "You'll find a girl when you least expect it. I was eighteen when I lost my virginity."

He sits up, eyes narrowed, then shakes his head. "So, what are we doing tonight?"

I pick up my laptop. "I don't know what you're doing, but I have to study for finals. We can't all be geniuses like you." Like me, Austin got a full ride to Duke, but unlike me, his is purely academic. I still don't really understand what his end game is or what any of the subjects are that he takes. Something about computers and science and algorithms and I don't know... sometimes I see him on his laptop, his fingers flying across the keyboard, and on the screen is a bunch of letters and numbers and symbols, and then he taps a button and *boom*; he's just made a couple hundred dollars for someone in less than five minutes.

So he says.

Austin groans into his pillow, clearly frustrated. "If I help you study—"

"No."

"Why not?"

"Because every time you do, you make me dumber."

"I make you *feel* dumber. Trust me, being around me has made you smarter, and you don't even know it."

"Probably," I mumble, getting off my bed to sit at my desk. "Hey, is your dad still cool to have me work with him over the summer?"

Another groan from him, this one louder. "Yes, Connor. My dad loves you. He would love nothing more than for a Duke Blue Devil to work with him at our family's junkyard... but why the fuck do you *want* to?"

"Money?" I shrug, lying. Truth is, I've had a shitty year on the court—my focus elsewhere—and I plan on spending the summer getting some extra training and coaching in. "Besides, my dad's going to be in Europe—"

"You mean your *dads*." He snorts, laughing childishly to himself.

"Idiot. They're not married." *Yet.* "And did you say shit like that in high school? Because if you did, it's no wonder you got the shit kicked out of you."

He holds a hand to his heart and jokes, "You're hurting my feelings."

"Uh huh."

He stands beside me, looking over my shoulder.

I open my laptop.

He shuts it. "Are we really not going to this party?"

I open my laptop again and look up at him. "We'll go for a half hour on one condition..."

"What's that?"

I smirk.

He sighs. "This shit *again*?"

I nod, moving to the side so he can reach around me. Fingers swift over my keyboard, he taps, taps, taps at the keys, and with one large inhale, and a final sigh, he taps one more time until the Duke logo appears at the top left of the screen. He'd just hacked—so he says—into the school admissions database like he'd done many times before, and just like all the previous times, I click search, my fingers much slower than his when I type:

A
V
A

D
I
A
Z

And then I smile. "Let's go try to get you laid."

ava

IT'S incredible how much things can change in just a few weeks. Even though Trevor and I had looked up pictures and reviews of Sunshine Oak, we were blown away by the facility when we saw it in person. Sunshine Oak isn't just a treatment facility; it's a *community*, and it's filled with people who love what they do and the patients they care for. Trevor was only able to stay for a few days before he had to go back, but he left more than satisfied; he left *happy*... and a little jealous.

When Lydia at Sunshine Oak informed me that I had a fully furnished apartment, I expected something similar to the one I had back in Texas, so when Trevor pulled up beside the building, we had to just stop and take a moment. It wasn't anything grand, but it was a hell of a lot better than what we'd assumed. "I don't think you're going to have to worry about half-naked old men and crazy old hussies here, Ava," he murmured. And I cackled, so loud and so free, that it had him doing the same, and it felt so good to laugh, especially with him. We were dumbstruck, unable to comprehend the pure luck that had been dropped on us. We needed saving, sure, but this was *beyond* anything I could've ever imagined. And then the apartment itself... two bedrooms, with a bathroom attached to the master, open kitchen and living with dark floors and new appliances. The living room opened up to a balcony that overlooked a communal pool, and I couldn't wait to sit out there with the sun and the stars above me.

It was just a tad better than the apartment—not *room*—Mom has at Sunshine Oak. Hers overlooks the community garden, and every morning she wakes up and looks out the window, and there's *color*. So much color. Not just through her vision but in her *life*. And the doctors... my God, where the hell have they been the past few years?

In a way, I hate that it's taken the help of a random stranger with money to spare to get Mom the care she *actually* needs, but I'm grateful. So very grateful. And so is Mom. I can see it in her smile—because she does that now. She *smiles*. At everyone and everything. She's started taking some classes; painting and gardening, and she's even considering learning a second language.

"There's so much to do here," she tells me, looking through a pamphlet while we sit at the in-house *hair salon*. "Oh, Ava!" she laughs out. "Guess what I did yesterday afternoon?"

"I don't know, Mama," I say through a smile. "What did you do?"

"Pottery."

I glance at her. "You did?"

"I had the room in a fit of giggles when I used my stub to make the opening of a vase," she laughs, unable to control herself. "It reminded me of that night we went to the court with Connor. You remember that?"

My chest tightens. "Yeah, I remember."

Her smile only widens. "Remember when we tried to spin the ball on each other's fingers, and it went flying?" Another laugh, this one louder.

I try to keep my expression passive, but it's hard. "Uh huh."

She sighs, wiping at the tears of joy from the corner of her eye. "God, I miss that boy."

Me too, I don't say aloud.

"What happened to him?" she asks, her eyes serious when they meet mine. "What happened to you two? You were so—"

I cut in, my voice cracking when I say, "I don't really want to talk about it."

She offers another smile, but it's sad. "Okay, baby. I just... he's such a good boy, you know? I wish it had worked out for—"

"I know."

Nodding slowly, she looks back at herself in the mirror. "This place is good for me, sweetheart." She focuses back on me, a hand to her heart. "I can feel it in here."

"Feel what?"

"The Happiness."

Tears well in my eyes, and I reach over, grasp her hand in mine. "I'm glad."

"You've spent too much of your best years taking care of me, Ava. And you know how much I appreciate you, but now... maybe it's time for you to start taking care of yourself."

I inhale a huge breath. Hold it.

"When are you going to be happy, Ava?"

I shrug, look down at my hands. "I am happy."

"You're also a liar."

"Mama," I whine.

"He's at Duke, right?"

"Who?"

She rolls her eyes. "You know who. Connor."

I shrug. "I *think* so," I lie. I *know* so.

"You know I can see Cameron Stadium from my window."

My eyes widen. "You can?"

"Uh huh," she sings. "Wouldn't it have been great if *you had* gotten into Duke..."

I stare at her, right into her eyes, and she stares back, waiting. She knows... she knows *everything*. "How did you..." I whisper.

"I heard everything you had to say to each other the night we left. Damn near broke my heart, Ava. But what could I do? You'd made a choice, and you were doing it for me, and I love you for that, but now... now I'm here, and I'm happy, but I'm not as happy as I could be..."

My heart settles into my stomach, tied there by the weight of what I know is coming next. "You want me to go to Duke, don't you?"

She smiles like mothers are supposed to smile at their children. "I *need* you to go to Duke, Ava. I need you to start living *your* life." She reaches up, cups my face in her hand. "And I need you to start believing in magic again."

connor

"SORRY I'M LATE," I rush out, eyeing Austin sitting behind the desk at his family's junkyard. "My training session ran late."

Austin rolls his eyes. "As if I care."

I grab my employee card from the shelf and clock in, then highlight the time I got in and make a note that I was late. I don't want them paying me for the time I wasn't here. "What are my jobs today?"

"Your job is to look pretty," he mumbles, tapping on the keyboard. He pauses, looks up at me. "Oh, wait. You do that anyway."

I chuckle. "These insults are getting old, Austin."

"I'll stop when my bitterness does," he retorts, his shoulders lifting with his shrug. "And it's quiet today, so there's not a lot to do."

I heave out a breath, calm my racing heart. I hate being late, especially for his parents. They've been so generous with giving me a job and letting me stay at their house for the summer, and the last thing I want is to disappoint them. I lean against his desk, arms crossed, and ask, "Hey, you think I can take you and your parents out for dinner sometime this week? I just want to say thank you for letting me crash with you."

Austin shakes his head. "Man, my parents are just happy I've made a friend. You don't need to do anything for them."

"But I *want* to."

"If you insist, sure, but nothing fancy, okay? We don't own ties."

"Neither do I."

"You wear a tie every game day."

"That's different." He eyes me warily while I pull up a chair and sit next to him. "Austin."

"Yes?" he drawls.

"We're *friends*, right?"

"What do you want?" he deadpans.

I smirk.

"*Again?*"

"Yep."

"Connor, I can't keep abusing—"

"I'll take you to a party when we get back on campus."

His eyes narrow. "Five."

"Three."

He offers his hand for a shake.

I accept, adding, "But I'm going to need a little more this time."

"Dude..."

"I know. Three parties and I'll introduce you to every girl who approaches us."

His teeth show with his grin. "What do you need?"

"Can you see what classes people have registered for?"

He groans. "Really? This is officially stalking now, man."

"No, it's not. It's... *curiosity*."

He sighs, his face scrunched in frustration. "I've been your best friend—"

"No, you haven't."

"Shut up."

I chuckle.

He continues, "I've been your best friend for almost a year now, and I have questions... lots of them... and I've never asked because I figured one day you'd give in and tell me all about this elusive Ava Diaz of yours... but you haven't yet, and that's no way to treat your best friend, Connor."

I stare at him, silent.

Another sigh leaves him. "Is she an ex?"

"Yes."

"From high school?"

"Yes."

"And she broke your heart?"

"Yes."

"And you're a glutton for punishment?"

I shrug.

"Connor, give me something here because I'm risking a lot by doing what I do for you."

My lids lower, and I stare down at my lap, my chest filled with heartache, but beneath that... I feel hope. It's there. It's just not as prevalent. I look back at Austin, my eyes locked on his. "We fell in love at a lake surrounded by reckless ideals, and our lives at the time didn't give us enough grace to allow us to live that love. She left, and I stayed, and every day that you and I have been *best friends,* I work toward getting her back. She was my first *everything,* and I want her—no, I *need* her—to be my *last* everything. I need her to be beside me when all of this is over and everything ends, because *she* is my end game, Austin. My forever."

He stares back at me, unblinking, his breaths shallow. Then he exhales, his cheeks puffing with the force. "Damn, Connor. I thought she was, like, a one-night stand that you couldn't shake... I didn't know..." He shakes his head. "So, this is why you've shown no interest in other girls?"

"There are no other girls for me."

He nods, slowly, then turns to his computer, his fingers hovering above the keyboard. Within seconds, he has Ava's records on the screen and a list of the classes she's registered for. "I have to tell you something," he says, "since we're out here revealing all our secrets..."

"Okay...?"

He faces me again. "I'm not really hacking into Duke's database. I work in their admissions office."

I chuckle. "I know."

"You do?"

"I'm not as dumb as you think I am."

"It made me feel cool for a while there, though."

"I know that, too."

"See?" he almost yells. "I *am* your best friend."

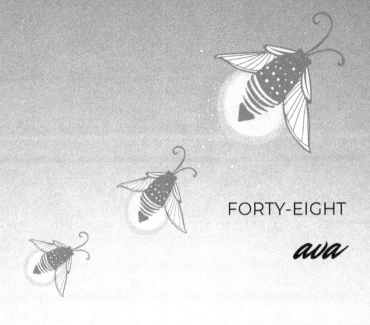

FORTY-EIGHT

ava

I STARE DOWN at the map and then at the door in front of me. I should've paid more attention during orientation, but I was too busy taking everything in. The fact that there's no one else here makes me nervous. I grab my phone, look at the time. I'm not *that* early. At least I don't *think* I am. Maybe I got the time wrong. Pressure builds in my chest, and my hands begin to shake. This is just the first day of the next four years of my life. I'm out of my depth, and I have no one to turn to.

I'm being a brat.

I have Mom, who I can call any time now.

And I have Trevor.

I hold the phone tighter in my hand, and with the other, I press the heal of my palm to my temple. I hadn't slept—stupid, I know—but I'd been excited. Now that excitement has turned to fear and—

"You look lost."

I look up and into the eyes of a boy—no, a man. *You're in college now, Ava. Duke.*

"First day?" he asks, his hazel eyes fixed on mine. They're larger than average, caused by the thick-lens glasses he's wearing. Dark, curly hair flies in all directions, and then he offers a smile, *kind*, and I can't help but do the same.

My airways widen when I exhale a breath. "Yeah. First day and I don't know if I'm lost." I point to the door behind me. "Is this criminal psychology?"

"Yeah, it is."

"Well, good. I can't imagine anything worse than going to the wrong class right off the bat."

He chuckles. "It'd be one of those things that keeps you up at 3 a.m. twenty years from now."

"For sure," I laugh out.

He stands taller, his smile getting wider. "I'm Austin, by the way."

"Ava," I reply.

His expression falls. "Ava *Diaz*?"

My eyes widen. "How did you—"

He takes a single step back. "Oh, my bad."

A hand appears between us, holding a coffee cup. "Here."

It's one word.

One syllable.

But it's enough to flatline my already unstable heart. My eyes shift, slowly, as if afraid of what they'll see. He hasn't changed, not really, but he's *older*, more manly, and his smile... God, that smile. "I got you a hot chocolate," he says to me, handing me a cup. It's warm against my palm, matching the heat in my cheeks. "I hope that's okay?"

I whisper his name as if it's something sacred, something found.

He jerks his head toward Austin. "I see you've met my roommate."

"Hi," I croak out. It was meant for Austin, but I can't take my eyes off Connor's. I clear my throat, dip my gaze—only for a second before I'm back to staring at him. My chest tightens, stomach in knots, and I knew... I mean, obviously I knew that I'd see him, and I'd somewhat mentally prepared myself to run into him at some point, but—

"Is she okay?" Austin asks Connor.

"Yeah." Connor's lips lift at one corner, his smile crooked, and I only now realize that he... he can't take his eyes off me either. "She's *perfect*."

I gasp on a breath and keep it there until my lungs burn with the force.

Austin mumbles, "Are we going to stand out here all day or..."

Connor's the first to break our stare, and he moves around me, his bare arm brushing against mine. He opens the door and waits for Austin to enter. I follow behind, my heart hammering. He stops me, his hand gentle on my forearm. Head dipped, he murmurs, his breath heating my cheek, "I hope you're ready, Ava Elizabeth Diana."

I peer up at him. "Ready for what?"

"Take three... *Act three*."

My eyes narrow in confusion. "The *climax*?"

He stands to full height, shaking his head, and gives me that smile I fell so hard in love with. "The *resolution*."

CONNOR

Okay.

I did it.

I broke the proverbial ice, and now I don't know what to do. I'd woken up confident. I even got to class feeling confident. And then I saw her and everything inside me flipped, switched, and stilled. She was looking down at a sheet of paper, her bottom lip caught between her teeth. Her hair was up in a high knot, a giant mess, but God, she was even more beautiful than I remember.

I told Austin I'd get us coffees and that I'd meet him there. I needed a minute, just one, to calm my racing heart. By the time I looked over again, she and Austin were talking, smiling at each other, and I think I'd missed that smile the most.

It took everything in me not to fall to my knees the second our eyes locked. I played it cool. At least I hoped I did.

Now, I'm sitting in a lecture hall beside the girl I've been "stalking" for too damn long, and I'm *sweating*. The room is big enough to seat at least fifty people, but in my mind, in my heart, it's just her and me... and endless possibilities.

"Hey, Connor," a girl says, walking through the seats in front of us.

Without taking my eyes off the side of Ava's face, I reply, "What's up?" And I can see the slight smile that graces Ava's lips.

I'm going to kiss her there the most.

Next to me, Austin smacks my arm, bringing me back to reality. I look up at the girl, someone I don't recognize, and point to Austin. "Have you met my friend Austin?"

Austin waves, bares his teeth with a grin.

The girl draws out the word, "Hey," and I go back to Ava.

"So..." I start.

"So," she replies. She won't look at me, at least not directly, and by the time I get the courage to say anything more, the professor walks into the room, welcoming the class with a booming, "Welcome to criminal psychology!"

Ava sits up in her chair, her focus at the front of the room.

I pull a notebook out of my bag and tear out a sheet of paper. I write:

Have dinner with me? Yes or no?

I slide it across to her desk while I pretend to be paying attention to the professor's speech. From the corner of my eye, I see her reading my note, then grabbing a pen. Head down, she starts writing away. When she's done, she moves it across the table to me.

There's a circle around *no,* and an arrow pointing down to her writing: *Let me cook dinner for you? Yes or no?*

My grin is stupid. I circle *yes,* hand it back.

She writes: *Tonight?*

And I reply: *I have practice until 7. After?*

Sure. I'll text you my address.

Does that mean you'll have to unblock my number? I hand it to her, watch her grimace while she reads it.

She writes back: *We have a lot to talk about.*

We sure do, but now isn't the time, and so I write, pulling out my false confidence from earlier: *Question: Will dinner tonight end in a kiss? Yes or No?*

She turns to me, her eyes meeting mine, so bright and so sure and so damn perfect. She doesn't respond. Instead, she folds the note until it fits in the palm of her hand, then she shoves it down her top, I'm assuming into her bra, and mouths a single word that turns all my bad days into hope-filled nights: "*Magic.*"

I'M IN TROUBLE.

Deep, soul-shattering trouble.

Because nothing has changed, and everything is the same, and this time, I'm not talking about my mom. I'm talking about my feelings for Connor.

"It doesn't make sense," I tell Amy, my phone on speaker on the kitchen counter. "It's like, I saw him, and everything just came flooding back." I pull out some vegetables from my fridge and grab a knife from the drawer. "And *why* did I ask him to come over for dinner?"

Amy giggles.

"What the hell was I thinking?" I slice a pepper in half, then drop the knife, press my thumb to my temple. "Like, if we went *out* for dinner, at least we could leave separately and whenever we wanted. And going out means *people*, and those people—they would've stopped me from breaking down into tears or, I don't know, humping his leg and licking his face, but *here*, in my apartment... Amy, there are no people in my apartment, and I'm going to make a complete fucking fool of myself. I can already tell."

"Well, if you hump his leg and lick his face..." she says through a giggle.

"You're not helping!" I whine, stomping my foot. "Maybe I should talk to Trevor."

She all out laughs now. "Oh, yeah, he's going to be much more helpful," she sings, and I can hear her sarcasm from a thousand miles away.

"Amy!"

She sighs. "Look, if things get too uncomfortable for you, you can ask him to leave. From what you and Trevor have told me, he's not the kind of guy who would fight you on that. And as far as the whole crying thing, if you feel the need to cry, then cry, Ava. Let it out. And if you want to get angry, then get angry. And if you *really* want to hump his leg, then... I mean, no judgment, but just be careful. Use protection."

"I'm not going to have sex with him!"

"Sure, if you say so. You guys—you have a lot of history, but you've also had a lot of time in between. You're basically walking into unknown territory here."

I groan.

"Ava?"

"Yeah?"

"What are you feeling right now?"

"I don't know," I mumble. "I'm nervous, and I'm scared, but I'm also really excited to see him." I rub the sweat off my brow with the back of my hand. "I just wish I knew how he felt."

"Well, ask him."

Ask him... as if it's that simple.

"It's the only way you'll truly know. So... as soon as he walks in, ask him."

I huff out a breath. "Maybe."

"It's going to be okay, Ava. Hey, your brother just got home, one second." I hear Trevor kiss her quickly, then ask her, "Who are you talking to?"

"Your sister," she tells him. "She ran into Connor today, and she invited him over for dinner."

Trevor chuckles, and it grates on my nerves. Static fills the phone line as if he's taking her phone, and then he says, "Hey."

"Hey."

"So... Connor's coming over?"

"Uh huh."

"Ava, I need to tell you something."

"What?"

"When a man ejaculates..."

"You're such a dick," I snap. "Bye." I hang up just as there's a knock on my door. *Shit, shit, shit.* I look at the clock. It's close to 7:30, and I'm late. Stupid four-hour afternoon nap.

I'm not ready. Not even close. Neither is dinner. I wipe my hands on a dish towel and swing open the front door. "Sorry, I'm running behind. I haven't even started cooking yet, and you're probably starv—"

"Hi," he cuts in, leaning against the door frame all cool and calm and, *Jesus,* he's so ridiculously handsome it makes me sick. "You're flustered." *No shit.* He's smiling down at me as if he's in on a joke only he's privy to... as if *I'm* the joke.

I nod, attempt a calming breath. "A little, yeah."

He returns the nod, peering over my shoulder and into my apartment. I open the door wider, wait for him to step in before closing it behind him. Hands in his pockets, he turns to me, his mouth parting, but before he gets a chance to speak, I say, "How are you... *feeling*?"

His brow lifts. "How am I *feeling*?"

"Yeah, like, right this very second. In three words or less. How are you *feeling*?"

He stares at me, his eyebrows drawn, and Amy is officially the worst advice giver in the world. "I don't know." Hands still in his pockets, he shrugs. "Nervous, scared, excited."

My eyes widen. "How long were you standing outside my door?"

"I just got here. Why?"

I shake my head. "Nothing."

"Can I add an extra one or is there a three-word limit?" he asks, his smirk throwing my mind off balance.

"Sure, add a word."

"Lucky."

"Lucky?" I repeat. "Why?"

"Because you're wearing a dress, and I've never seen you in a dress before."

"Oh." *Oh.*

"You look nice, Ava."

The breath that leaves me is ragged, and I look down at myself. "Thanks."

"You're welcome," he laughs out. "And hi, Crazy. That was one hell of a welcome."

"Sorry." I shake my head, clear the fog. "I've had a long day... and I'm... *flustered*." I point to the counter. "I haven't really started with—"

"It's cool. Can I help at all?"

"No." I motion to the stools beneath the countertop. "You sit. You're probably exhausted."

He takes my advice and sits on the opposite side of me, the counter between us. *Good.* An object that creates distance. That'll help with the whole humping-his-leg thing. "Honestly, I was pretty beat, and then you opened the door in that *dress,* and I got a second wind."

I bite down on my lip to stop my smile and turn away from him, not wanting him to see my blush.

"This is a real nice apartment," he muses.

I open the fridge, a distraction. "Yeah, I like the floors." *I like the floors? What the actual fuck, Ava! Get a grip.*

"Did uh... Did Peter help you with it?"

At the mention of his name, my shoulders tense, and I close the fridge empty-handed. Turning to him, I ask, "Help me with what?"

"The apartment."

"No," I reply, a single laugh bubbling out of me.

Connor's eyes narrow. "Why is that funny?"

"Why would he be helping me—"

"I mean, you moved to Texas with him, so..."

Oh, *that*. I wave a hand in the air, ignore the way his eyes shine extra blue against the overhead lights. "It's a long story."

"Lucky we have all night then, huh?"

Nodding, I ignore the way Connor's gaze dips to my breasts before checking himself and get back to cutting the vegetables on the counter.

His tone turns serious when he asks, "How's your mom, Ava?"

I glance up at him, catch him watching my every move. "You won't believe it if I tell you."

"Try me."

I make quick work of the dinner prep while I tell him everything that's happened with my mom over the past year. He listens intently to every single word, barely ever taking his eyes off me. He asks questions, lots of them, and by the end, his eyes are wide. "So, everything *fell into place*, huh?" he asks, repeating the words I'd used when I told him I was leaving.

After sliding the tray into the oven, I turn to him, nod. "I mean, in a roundabout way, yeah. It did."

"And Trevor?" he asks. "How is he?"

I start clearing the counter to season the steaks I'd gotten us. "Good. He's still a dick," I joke, and he laughs at that. "He re-enrolled at Texas A&M, and he's living with Amy off-campus. Oh, and remember that—"

"I remember everything, Ava."

I can't control the ticking at the corner of my lips. "Um... that conversation you had with him about being an agent?"

Connor nods.

"So, that's what he wants to do now."

"Really? That's awesome."

"Yeah, it is," I say, my voice suddenly cracking with the emotions I've held on to for too long. Feelings I've tried so hard to suppress.

Connor, the boy I met in high school, the boy I fell recklessly in love with, is sitting in my apartment, mere feet away, and he has no idea the impact he's had on me *and* my family. *None*. He'd entered out of nowhere and left footprints wherever he roamed, and our lives are forever changed because of him. And I don't know how to tell him that. How to portray how much his presence in my life has meant to all of us. I realize now, deep down, that it might be the reason I invited him here. Why I offered to cook for him: a small token of appreciation in a vast ocean of what Trevor refers to as *Good*. I'm staring, I know I am, but I can't seem to shake it. I blink back the sudden heat behind my eyes and push down the ache in my throat. "What about you?" I manage to ask. "How's your dad?"

"He's good, Ava," he says, his voice low as he pins me with his gaze.

Now I look away because everything is too much. Too soon. And too *real*. "Is he still living at that house?"

"No, he left after I graduated. I stayed until the lease was over... though for a while I did consider burning the place down."

My eyes snap to his.

He adds, "It's weird, right? An electrical fault when Trevor's an electrician..."

My lips curve while I force out a sigh. "The insurance money sure came in handy," I murmur.

"Oh, yeah?"

I push the steaks aside and move on to the salad. Without looking up, I tell him the truth, "We needed an immediate solution, and Peter helped with that side—"

"Peter," he spits.

I glance up. "Why do you say his name like that?"

"Because I don't like the guy," he grinds out, his hands fisted on the countertop.

I wait a second to see if he'll add any more, and when he doesn't, I say, "Anyway, the insurance money helped with getting Mom's placement and getting Trevor and me on our feet."

He nods, slow. "So, you owe nothing to Peter?"

"Not a cent."

"But your pride, right?"

"Not even that."

"Good."

I drop the knife, drop my pretenses, and shift on my feet. "Why are you so..."

"So what?"

"Your jaw's all tense, and your face is red, and your fists are all punchy." I slide the knife away from him. "And a little stabby."

He chuckles under his breath. "I just don't like the guy, Ava."

"So you've said."

Connor stays silent.

I sigh. "You know, secrets ruined us before, Connor, and I'm not saying that you and I are an *us*, but I'd like to... I don't know... be *friends?*"

He laughs once. Bitter. "You want the truth?"

I nod.

Eyes set on mine, intense, he says, "I don't want to be *friends* with you, Ava. I told you that once, and nothing has changed."

I drop my gaze, my hand floating to my stomach to settle the butterflies there.

He clears his throat. "You know, Peter paid Mitch to do all that shit to your house. The paintballs and the BB gun and... all of it, Ava... it was all Peter."

I gasp, shocked, my chest burning with anger. "That motherfucker!" I exclaim, shaking my head. "Good thing Trevor beat the shit out of him."

Connor's face lights up. "*What?*"

With a nod, I throw it all out there: "For a while, he'd been offering to"—I air quote—"take care of me."

An indescribable sound leaves Connor's lips.

I add, "I don't know when he started looking at me differently, but he did, and it's the reason I held off on taking him up on his offer. He'd given me a check a long time ago, enough to put my mom in care full-time, but I never accepted until... I mean, I always knew that I'd be indebted to him if I took it... in more ways than financially, but I was desperate, Connor."

He takes a moment, his breaths shaky. Then he looks down at his hands, his voice as broken as his demeanor when he asks, "You slept with him?"

"No," I breathe out. My head tilts back, eyes to the ceiling to stop the tears from falling. "I stayed with him, and after a couple of weeks, he crept into my bed one night while I was sleeping and—"

"Ava," he cuts in, pained. "I don't know that I can hear this."

"I was prepared, though," I rush out. "So... I kind of slept with a taser. Got him right in the dick."

His entire everything changes instantly. "No, you didn't," he almost shouts, his laughter music to my ears.

I nod. "I did. And then I left right away and ran to Amy. I told her all about it, and Amy told Trevor and... well, let's just say it took Peter a while to be able to breathe through his nose again."

"Damn," he says through a chuckle.

"Honestly, though, I feel bad," I admit, getting more comfortable in his presence. "He was a genuine friend to Trevor for a long time, even if he saw me as... whatever."

"A genuine friend wouldn't do what he did, Ava," he says, sitting taller.

I grab a glass and fill it with water, then slide it across the counter to him. "Yeah, I know, but there's still guilt there, and I'm trying to work through it all. It's just *one* of the many things I'm working through." I watch, transfixed, as his Adam's apple slides against his throat when he downs the water. Then I swallow, push away the thoughts flooding through my mind: *I could lick him there.*

He lowers the glass, his eyes on my lips, and I blink. Hard. Come back to reality. I say, my words rushed so he doesn't have a chance to speak, "The program that Mom's in—it's pretty extensive in that they offer therapy for family members, too, so I go there once a week and—" he licks his lips "—and um..." I look away. "Yeah."

"That's good, Ava," he says, his voice even. "I'm glad you have that support. You deserve it. Hell, you *earned* it."

I rub my neck with the back of my fingers, feeling my racing pulse beating there. Then I inhale a huge breath, let it out in a *whoosh*. Over a year of holding everything in, and it's time to let go. I'm sure of it. "Connor," I say, but it comes out a whisper. I clear my throat, lift my chin, try to keep it all together. "A lot was going on when I um... when I left, I was in a pretty dark place..."

His eyes soften. "I know."

"No, you don't. There were moments where I gave up hope, not just for Mom, but for me, and—"

"I *know*," he says, reaching across, the tips of his fingers taking hold of mine. Heartache forces my eyes closed. "Ava, look at me." And hope forces them open again. "There was a night I'd left my phone in your room, and we were recording the assignment for multimedia..."

I gasp, low and slow.

"I saw *everything*."

A single sob escapes me, and I cover my face with my hands. "Oh, god..." I hear him get out of his chair, but I turn away, not wanting him to see me like this. Shame floods my bloodline, closing my airways.

"Hey," he says, his hand on my back, soothing. And then he's turning me to him, his arms wrapping around me.

This.

This is all I've wanted.

All I've needed.

And then he holds my head to his chest, my ear over his heart, and I break when I hear it.

When I feel it.

Thump, thump.

Thump, thump.

Magic.

Another sob forms in my throat, and he holds me tighter. "I wish I'd known," he says, his voice shaking. "I wish I could've seen it as it was happening, but I was so consumed with what was going on in my life at the time, and I'm sorry, Ava. Fuck, I'm so sorry."

I wipe my tears on his chest, like I'd done too many times before, and pull back, look up at him, my hands grasping onto his T-shirt. "Miss Turner told me about *Wendy*," I cry. "I'm sorry, Connor. I know that you told me to trust you with all of it, and I should have. I regret it every day. But I can't change it."

His thumbs slide along my cheek, and he stares at me, his eyes clear puddles of devastation. "Would it have changed anything?"

I shake my head. "I don't think so," I tell him honestly. "I think I still would've left. Things were so bad—"

"I get it, Ava. I do." His brow dips. "But if we're throwing it all out there, it took me a long time to accept that you leaving wasn't the same as you *abandoning* me—"

"Oh, God, Connor," I whisper. "I would never—"

"I know, and I don't want that to add to your guilt. I'm sorry I mentioned it."

"No. I *want* you to tell me." I try to shrug out of his hold, angry at myself, but he won't let me go. "God, I'm such a selfish brat, I didn't even consider how that would make you feel."

He shakes his head. "I just needed time to get answers and to process what was happening, and I didn't want it to be a burden on what was already happening with you. We both kept things to ourselves because we wanted to protect each other. Because that's what we thought love was. We did so much to make the other person happy that, somewhere along the way, we forgot about ourselves."

"Yeah, that's true," I say, nodding, and it's clear I'm not the only one who's spent the time apart searching my soul for answers. I ask, hesitant, "So, how is your mom?"

He shrugs. Then he eyes me a moment, as if contemplating his next words. "I lied to you, Ava."

I force a smile. "I thought we just went through all of this. I under—"

"No," he cuts in. "I mean, yeah that, too, but I lied to you earlier than that. A lot earlier. When we first met, you asked if I remembered anything about what happened to me..."

I nod, my heart beating wildly.

"I lied when I told you I didn't. Because I do. I remember it all. I even remember the toy cars I was holding onto..." He watches me, his gaze intense. "You—"

"I met her," I rush out, realization dawning on me like a ton of bricks landing right on my chest. "After the regionals final, that box with the cars? That was her?"

He nods slowly.

Eyes wide, I try to go back to that moment, remembering how she was, how *he* was the next morning when he opened it. He'd thrown up and blamed it on the alcohol, and... "Oh, God, Connor. I'm so sorry."

"Don't be. You couldn't have known, and I didn't want you to."

"Why?" I breathe out.

"I don't know," he answers, his voice cracking. "It just felt like... too much.

We were in such a good place, and I didn't want her coming back and taking that away from me."

My head dips forward, my heart aching for him. And sure, I could relive every moment of the past, redirect every second conversation so that we didn't end up where we were, but that would be pointless, and so I push aside our regrets and ask, stumbling over my words, "Do you... do you guys still talk or...?"

He's quick to shake his head as he gets comfortable leaning against the counter. One hand on my hip, the other wrapped around my waist, he responds, "Not even a little bit."

I pout, my hands flat on his chest. "I'm sorry."

"I'm not," he says, so sure of himself. "She's just as disappointing now as she was back then."

"Did you get the answers you were looking for?"

He nods, clears his throat.

I lean closer to him.

He says, "She um... she left me in the car as *revenge* because my dad was having an emotional affair at the time..."

My eyes widen.

"With another man."

My eyes bug out of my head. "Your dad's *gay?*"

"Yeah, he is," he says, and I don't know how he can fit so much pride in such a small smile. "He's actually with the guy from back then." He reaches up, fingers a strand of hair that's fallen across my shoulder. He fixes his stare there, as he twirls it around his finger. "His name's Michael. I like him a lot. He's a great guy, and he's good to my dad. But... they held on to those feelings and kept quiet for fifteen years, Ava..."

"That's a long time," I struggle to say, feeling the intensity between us growing.

"I know, right? But now they're happy, and they're free, and they're—"

He stops there, suddenly, and I look up at him, my eyes pleading for him to continue.

He releases my hair, glides his palm across my shoulder to my nape. "Ava, I don't want to hold on to my feelings for fifteen—" The smoke alarm goes off, and he gently moves me to the side, grabbing a dish towel on the way to the oven. It's smoking, and how the hell did I not see it? Smell it? *Magic.* I was so lost, drowning in his magic, that nothing else mattered. He lowers the oven door, jerking back when the heat emits. And then he waves the cloth above him, in front of the smoke alarm, waiting for the air to clear.

It starts as a giggle, this *feeling* that takes over me, and ends in all-out, carefree laughter that has him doing the same. He pulls out the tray of vegetables that was supposed to go with the steak. It's charcoal. He laughs harder, turning to me. "I'd still eat it just because you made it."

"I wouldn't make you," I say through a giggle. "We still have the steak and the salad. I'm sorry."

"Don't be." He turns back to the oven, then to me. "How did we not smell that?"

I mouth, my smile wide, my eyes on his, "Magic."

He shakes his head. "Do you want to just order in? Save the steaks for tomorrow?"

"You're coming over tomorrow?"

He smirks. "I could have steak for breakfast."

"Connor!" I gasp. "Who says you're staying the night?"

His expression falls. "I mean, I was talking about *in general* because I love steak... but hey, if you're offering..."

My hands lift, cover the shame pinking my cheeks.

Fingers circling my wrists, he pulls my hands down and links our fingers. "Don't do that."

"Do what?"

"You're too beautiful to be hidden."

I almost lick his face. *Almost.*

"So, we order in?" I ask, releasing his hands to get to my phone. "What's good around here?"

He shoves his hand in his pocket, pulls out his phone. "I got you."

I take his phone, hide it in my bra. "I'm paying!"

"Hmm." He eyes his phone, his hand out to retrieve it, but stops an inch away. "How did my phone get luckier than me?"

With a giggle, I hand it back to him. "Let me pay, though. Honestly. I invited you here; it's only fair."

"Can you afford it?" he asks, genuinely concerned.

I nod. "I don't pay for anything here besides food and travel. The house, all the bills, it's covered. And I get a cut of Mom's benefits."

"A cut?" he asks.

"Most of it goes to Trevor. We're trying to get as much of his debt cleared before he has to start paying off his student loans."

Connor grimaces. "That sucks."

I nod. "So, let me pay?"

"Fine."

We order pizza and pasta and clean the kitchen while we wait for it to be delivered. When it arrives, we sit on the couch, with the Investigation Discovery channel on the TV.

"Did you keep in contact with anyone from school?" I ask him.

He nods, finishes chewing his food before answering, "I talk to Rhys and

Karen, but that's about it, and it's that kind of weak social media conversation, you know?"

I shrug. "Not really."

He chuckles. "Oh, shit. I haven't told you. You know the whole Peter and Mitch thing?"

Anger flares, only for a second, before I nod.

He says, "So Rhys and Karen were over at my house—Rhys punched me a few times because he was still kind of in love with you, by the way—"

"*What?*"

"It's irrelevant," he says, flicking his wrist. "Anyway, Rhys and Karen were at my house when Mitch showed up to confess. Karen heard it all and smashed his face in with a wooden tray. Broke his nose."

"Shut up!" I laugh out, my eyes wide. "That did *not* happen."

"It absolutely fucking happened. Though I'm not sure if the tray broke his nose or if Dad did when he pretended to *look* at it."

"No," I gasp.

His hand settles on my bare thigh. "You are deeply loved, Ava," he says, his tone soft. "And if you ever feel up to it, I think you should reach out to Karen. She misses you a lot."

Without discussing it, we settle in for the evening, his arm on the couch behind me as we watch a stupid amount of true crime. I ask, "How's basketball going?"

He shakes his head. "Last season was kind of a shitshow, to be honest. I wasn't really motivated, and it showed. My agent was pissed. He kind of dumped me."

"*Dumped* you?"

"Yeah, as a client," he says, nodding. "I'm trying to fix it, though. I spent the summer getting extra training." His eyes lock on mine. "I think this season will be different."

"Yeah?"

He nods. "I got my *passion* back."

I bite my lip, break our stare. "Is that why you didn't declare for the draft?"

"How do you know I didn't?"

Shit.

I point to the TV. "Oh, look. *Blood!*"

CONNOR

"What?" Ava whispers, her eyes narrowed. "Why are you staring at me?"

I can't stop smiling. "No reason."

She goes back to watching another person get murdered, and it feels like the first time. Like the time she was in my car and she called me a *good-looking jock*. Back then, what I'd felt for her was nothing more than a crush. I never thought that we'd end up here, that I'd be in this deep.

Because I'm still crazy about her.

Hopelessly.

Endlessly.

Crazy *in love* with her.

Her eyes are wide, unblinking, as she stares at the TV. Loose strands of curls curtain her face. I reach up, pull one aside so I can see her more clearly. I'm ogling, fascinated by every inch, every curve, every quiver of her lips when she inhales a breath. Then she turns to me, slowly, and I can tell that she's nervous, that whatever is going through her mind right now has her hesitant. "So... this place where my mom is..."

I swallow. "Yeah?"

"Um, the doctors and therapists there—they're really great."

"That's good, right?"

Nodding, her gaze drops, her voice quieter when she says, "It only took them a couple of weeks to diagnose Mom with bipolar disorder and mild schizophrenia."

My eyes widen, my breath catching in my throat, but I try to hide my reaction. "Well, at least they know now... it means she can take the right medication and get the right kind of—"

Ava's nodding cuts me off. "Yeah. They suspect that the head trauma caused a lot of it; add that to everything else she was already experiencing..." She inhales a huge breath, lets it out slowly. "It kind of explains a lot, especially with how quickly her moods could switch."

"Yeah," I breathe out, thinking about all the time I'd spent with her, all the different versions of her I'd witnessed. "But she's good now, right? Like, *stable*?" I don't know if I'm using the right terminology, and I hope it doesn't offend her or take away from her mother's mental health in any way.

Ava nods again, then lowers her gaze. "They also diagnosed me with PTSD..." My chest tightens at her words, a lump forming in my throat. I open my mouth to speak, but she beats me to it: "I just thought you should know, because... because you're looking at me a certain way and—"

"How am I looking at you?"

"The way you used to," she says, her voice strained. "And maybe you shouldn't be doing that, because I'm not the same person I used to be, Connor. I'm not that girl you fell—"

"You're right," I interrupt. "You're not that same girl. Not even a little bit. Because you're so much more." I lift her chin, force her to look at me through her tear-stained eyes. "Ava, a label isn't going to change who you are, and it's not going to change how I feel about you or how I look at you," I tell her, sitting taller. "But a label is going to help me understand you more... and, really, it's not *that* surprising." I shake my head. "I mean, after everything you went through and everything you saw, you witnessed..."

"I'm working through it," she croaks, as if trying to convince me.

I settle my palm on her jaw, my heart racing when she presses into it. "I know you, and you'll get there, babe. And I'm going to be *right here*. Whatever you need, whenever you need it. Always."

Her gaze lifts, locks on mine. Seconds feel like minutes. Finally, she says, "It's getting late, and I've got an early class tomorrow."

My heart sinks, just an inch, but I can see it in her eyes. She's afraid of what's happening between us, or what never *stopped* happening. "Okay." I get to my feet, ignore the tightening in my chest as she follows me to her door. She reaches around, opening it for me, and I step out, turning to her as I do. "Thanks for dinner."

She offers a smile. "You're welcome."

"Don't go disappearing on me, okay?"

"I won't. I promise."

I shove my hands in my pockets to stop myself from reaching out and touching her. Anywhere. As long as it's her. "I'll see ya."

"Uh huh."

I rear back when she practically slams the door in my face. Confused, I force myself to step away. One step. Two. A thud sounds from behind her door, and I freeze, wait. She's talking now, and curiosity gets the better of me. I know I shouldn't, but I do. I walk back, my footsteps light, and press my ear to her door.

"Stupid, Ava. Stupid, stupid, stupid!" The door rattles with each of her *stupids*. There's shuffling, and then footsteps fading, and I almost walk away when seconds of silence pass. Then I hear her again: "Amy!" She's almost yelling. "Yeah, he just left."

This is wrong. I shouldn't be listening. But...

"No, I didn't lick his face, but I wanted to!"

My grin is pathetic.

"No, I didn't hump his leg! Quit making fun of me!"

I stifle my laugh.

"God, Amy... he's everything I remember him to be," she says, and I press my ear closer because I don't know if that's a good thing or not. I hear her moving around the kitchen, picture her there with the phone to her ear, trashing the take-out boxes. "I told him everything I wanted to."..."Yeah, even that."..."His reaction was... *perfect*. Everything he said and did was... perfect."... "Dammit, Amy. He's so *good*. Like, everything about him just... he's the peace to my chaos."..."Because I got scared, *obviously*."..."Of course, I didn't *want* him to leave, but—" Hearing that, I find myself raising my fist, knocking twice. "Shit, I have to go."

I step back, act casual. All while my heart beats wild inside me.

She opens the door, her face flustered, just like the first time. "Hi."

"I think I left my keys in here."

"Oh, okay." She steps to the side, opening the door wider for me.

With a smile I can't seem to shake, I go to the kitchen first, pretend to look around. I check the stool I'd been sitting on. "Hmm. I don't know where they could be."

"Maybe the couch," she offers, making her way there. I stand behind her, my eyes glued to her ass when she bends over, reaching in between the cushions. She lifts some throw pillows, searching under there. I'm too late to avert my gaze when she spins to me. "They're not there." And when she realizes *exactly* what I'd been doing, she glares, her eyes thinned to slits. "Pervert."

I shrug.

Then she eyes me up and down, still glaring. "Do not move," she orders.

I lock every muscle in place.

Her hands reach up, settling on my stomach. Holding my eyes captive, she slides them lower, lower, until she brushes an inch above my—"Connor!"

"What?"

She reaches into my pocket, pulls out my keys. "Your keys are right—" That's as far as she gets before I press my mouth to hers, inhaling the gasp that comes from it. I grasp her face in both my hands, pause, hold her there. With her bottom lip caught between mine, I tilt my head, run my tongue along the seam of her lips, asking, *begging* for permission. But she doesn't give in to my desires. In fact, she doesn't move at all. Doesn't breathe. I wait another beat, hope dying in my chest, and then I pull back, my eyes closed, humiliation flooding every cell. "Sorry," I whisper, releasing her.

"No, you're not," she murmurs, and I open my eyes to see her watching me.

I try to hide my disappointment, but fail, because I can't fake it when I say, "I had to shoot my shot, right?"

Her hand comes up, palming the back of my neck, and before I know what's happening, she's pulling me down to her, whispering, "Come here," as she does, and then she *kisses* me. And there's no pause in her kiss like there was in mine. No hesitation. Her mouth opens, her tongue searching mine and when they meet, a million fireflies collide, lighting up the night sky, filling my lungs with magic. I curl my hands around her waist, lift her off her feet, and break the kiss just long enough to sit on the couch, her hips straddling mine. I go back to kissing her again, drowning in the way she feels pressed against me, the way my palms run smoothly along her bare legs. She has her arms around my head, her fingers grasping my hair, pulling, and fuck, I've missed this. She jerks back, gasping for air, and I can't get enough, so I go to her neck, taste her there, all while my hands drift up and down her thighs. I pause a beat, my hand edging beneath her dress, the edge of her underwear right at my fingertips. She pulls on my hair, tilting my head back, and captures my mouth. And just when I begin to lose myself again, she pulls away. "Maybe we should slow down?"

The only thing I can think to say is, "Huh?" Because I'm not really thinking. Obviously.

"Maybe we should wait."

I drop my head on her shoulder, wait a moment for the blood to make its way back up to my brain. "I don't know about you, but I've waited a year and a half for this."

Her eyes roll. "As if you've been *waiting*."

She's delirious. She has to be. "I have."

"Right." She nods once. "So, you're telling me you haven't been with anyone since you and me?"

I lift my chin. "Yes."

"I call bullshit."

I adjust her on my lap, just enough so I can access the phone in my pocket. I dial Austin's number, set it on speaker and hold it between us.

"Hey," he answers.

"Yo, have I been with any girls since Ava?"

"Haven't even looked at one. Why?"

I hang up, my eyebrows raised all: *See? I told you so.*

"Okay," she says, with a brattish lilt to her tone.

"Why? Have you?" Before she gets a chance to respond, I cover her mouth. "Wait. Don't answer that."

Both her small hands clasp mine, and she lowers it for me. "I haven't been with anyone."

"Good." I point between us. "Can we go back to what we were doing now?"

She bites her lip, nods as she murmurs, "Mmm-hmm."

With her mouth open on mine, I ask, "Can I touch your butt?"

She laughs, and I breathe in the sound, let it warm me. "Yes. You can even touch the side of my boob if you want."

"Fuck, yes." I kiss her deeper. "It's my lucky day." My phone rings, and I grunt in frustration. Austin's stupid face lights up my screen. "What?" I snap. Ava laughs into my neck, her hands flat on my stomach. She pushes down, grinding into me as she sucks hard on my neck. "You're so fucking bad," I whisper, grabbing a hand full of her ass to bring her closer to me.

"Why am I bad?" Austin asks.

Ava muffles her cackle on my shoulder.

"What's up?" I say into the phone.

Austin replies, "Are you coming back tonight?"

I tug on Ava's hair until I can see her face clearly and ask, "*Am* I going back tonight?"

She doesn't skip a beat. "Nope."

TWO WEEKS HAVE PASSED since that first night with Ava, and because we weren't really prepared for how things turned out that night, neither of us were *prepared*. We fooled around, got to the point, then she asked me if I had protection, and I looked at her like she was stupid because why the hell would I? I didn't sleep around, and neither did she, so we took care of each other in other ways until we fell asleep on her bed in a mass of sweaty limbs and post-orgasmic bliss.

And now, according to her, she wants to *wait*. Apparently, it's her therapist's advice. Because her therapist wants to make sure Ava is following her heart and not the parts between her legs that might be calling to me. I don't see what's wrong with her vagina calling to me. I wouldn't mind it. Hell, it can call to me mid-game, and I'd go running.

I sound pathetic, but Ava—she makes me that way. And she wears dresses now. All the time. And I take back what I said about her being too beautiful to be hidden because I want to hide her. If I had a basement...

Too far?

Maybe.

But, high school with Ava was one thing. Everyone knew she was mine, and it's not like she was out there, in the wild, wearing *dresses* and looking all hot and adorable all the time. And it's not that I wish she'd go back to being "stuck" taking care of her mom. I just... I get punchy and stabby, and college dudes are far more upfront with their leering, and I hate everyone and everything besides Ava.

And Austin, I guess.

He's okay.

"Connor!" Ava whisper-yells, snapping her fingers in front of my face.
I blink, focus on her.

"You're doing that thing again."

"What thing?"

"That stabby face you make. What is with you?"

"He doesn't like you in dresses," Austin answers for me.

"You don't?" She looks down at her dress.

"No," I tell them both. "*I* like Ava in dresses. I don't like other—"

"How is a dress any different from my old school uniform?"

My dick stirs, and it shouldn't, especially considering we're in the middle of the food court, and I really should start wearing more than basketball shorts because they're bad at hiding certain things and those certain things are happening too often now that Ava's back. "By chance, do you still have that uniform?"

"You're such a dick," Ava says through a giggle, throwing a plastic fork at my head. Then she stands, picks up her bag. She makes her way over to me, kisses me with more passion than my shorts can handle. She bites my bottom lip as she pulls away. "I have to go see Mom."

"Okay."

She hasn't asked me to come with her yet, and even though I'm dying to see Miss D, I know she has reasons and those reasons are pure. She wants to make sure that she and I are solid before reintroducing me into her mother's life. Besides her telling me that she's doing great and that she's happy, she doesn't give me much more.

Which is fine.

For now.

She runs her fingers through my hair, and my eyes drift shut at the touch. "Come over after practice?"

I nod, open my eyes again. "I'll be there."

Austin groans. "I miss my best friend."

* * *

I get through classes and practice and then rush to Ava's apartment because... well, because it's *Ava*. She answers the door in nothing but a towel, and after the initial shock, annoyance takes over. I shove her back in, slam the door shut behind me. "What the hell are you doing? Anyone could be at the door or just walking past, and they're going—"

"Shut up, *Dad*."

"I'm serious, Ava." And then I chuckle. "And it's *Daddy* to you."

Her nose scrunches. "Never." She starts walking toward her room and says over her shoulder, "I was about to get in the shower."

I start stripping out of my clothes, and when she must realize, she turns to me. "No."

"That wasn't an invitation?"

"No."

I shrug my shirt back on. "My bad."

She giggles, kisses me once. "Go wait out in the living room; I'll be quick."

"Fine," I sigh out.

In her kitchen, I reach for a glass from the top cabinet. A tall one. Because I'm thirsty, and not just for water. But I fumble, knocking down a shorter one in front of it. It hits the edge of the counter and falls to the floor, smashing to pieces. "Idiot," I murmur, shaking my head. I pick up all the larger pieces and trash them, then go searching for a broom to clean the smaller shards. I check the hallway closet, the pantry. It's not in any of those, and so I go to her laundry room, stand in the middle. Because I'm a male, and males can't find things that are right in front of them.

I spot her hamper in the corner, my eyes narrowing when I see the familiar black and orange. I make my way there, checking over my shoulder to make sure she's not coming, and lift the jersey. I smile full force when I see the large 3 on the back, my name above. *She still wears my jerseys.* Elation swells in my chest, and I drop the garment when I hear the pipes clank, alerting me that she's done. Remembering why I came here in the first place, I find the only other door in the room and swing it open. I find the broom, but I also find something that has my heart stopping instantly. Orange and black, and white and blue fill my vision. There are pictures of us on the walls of the closet and pictures of me on the shelves themselves. Newspaper cutouts, website printouts. Stacks of DVDs with dates and scores and stats and... I reach up, grab one, and open it. Besides the disc, there's a single balloon— blue—and I inspect it closer, see the black marker. I grab another one. Same thing.

"Connor?" she calls out. "Where are you?"

I can't speak.

Can't breathe.

"Connor?" I hear her footsteps approaching, but I can't... I can't *function.* "What the hell are you doing?" she yells, taking the DVDs from me.

"Ava, what is this?"

"Nothing!"

I finally manage to peel my eyes away from the closet and look down at her. Tears well in her eyes, and she's trying to close the door, but I'm in the way, and her face contorts as she cries out, "You're not supposed to see this! Can you go? Please!"

"Ava..." I reach into the closet again, pull out a stack of DVDs. "These are all my games." I open one, and a balloon falls out and lands on the floor.

She's quick to pick it up, grasping for the DVD cover, but I jerk away, grab a newspaper cutout to inspect that, too. She tries to take it from me. "Stop it!" she begs. I let her take the article while I go back to the DVDs, letting them fall from their stack. "You're getting them out of order!" she sobs. "Stop!" She's pulling on my hands, trying to push me away, and I finally let her. She's crying, tears streaming down her cheeks, her breaths short, sharp, as her hands shake trying to replace everything in some form of order.

I stand behind her, my hands on her hips, my mouth to ear. "Ava, what is this?"

"It's nothing."

I spin her around, force her to look up at me. "It's something."

Those small hands cover her face, and I tug them down, needing her to see me. "What do you want me to say, Connor?"

"I'm not mad about it," I try to console. "I'm just... confused. You had no contact for over a year, and you could have, Ava; I've *been* here." I point to the closet. "You know I've been here. Why..."

"Because... I don't know, okay?" Her hands drop to her sides, and she attempts a calming breath, but she can't seem to keep it together for long. "I *tried*, Connor. I tried so hard to let go of you, to fight those feelings, but I couldn't. I spent every single day away from you trying to convince everyone around me, and even myself, that I was *fine* without you, but I *wasn't*. And this —you seeing this—it's embarrassing, okay?"

"Why?"

"I don't know! Because it's the only way I could deal with how much I missed you, and how much I love you, and I—" She pauses a breath. "My love for you never wavered. Not for a second. And I never stopped being proud of you, of everything you've accomplished and everything you are, but this—" She waves a hand toward the closet. "This is, like, borderline obsession and—"

I kiss her. Without pause. Without heartache. I take everything she is, because right now, all of her is all for me, and it's *always* been like that. Even on her bad days, and even when things got too much, she never stopped loving me. Never.

Her hands form a fist, balling up my T-shirt as she pulls me closer to her, her mouth opening wider for me. Her tongue strokes mine, and I feel the charge between us ignite the second her back hits the wall. Her moan drowns in my inhale, and I grasp her thighs, lift her off her feet until her legs are wrapped around me. Knees bent, I lower us to the floor while she removes my T-shirt, her mouth finding my collarbone as soon as it's off. I lift the hem of her dress, higher and higher until it's gone completely, and my hips jerk up the moment I claim her mouth again. Everything inside me is frantic, fighting for release. She practically rips off her bra and then grasps my head, pulling me there, her hips sinking into mine when I latch on to a breast. Her fingernails dig into my shoulder while she arches her back, grinding into me. I lower my shorts, just enough to free the bulge, and she moans, pushes me until I'm on my back and she's leaning over me, one arm outstretched, hand to my side. The other reaches between us, moving her underwear to the side. She glides against me, her wetness against my length, and my head falls back, hits the floor with a thud. "Jesus, Ava, I need inside you so fucking—"

"Fuck waiting," she moans, and her mouth covers mine while her weight on my hips lightens. I curl my hands around her waist, lift my head so I can watch as she places me at her entrance.

"Wait, we need—"

"I'm on the pill," she breathes out. "I have been for a while because it helps—"

"I don't care *why*." I grip her waist tighter, pull her down until she covers me entirely and, "Fuck!" I breathe through the ecstasy of feeling her heat surround me, feeling her raw. "Don't. Move."

And because she's a brat and she never listens, she moves, sliding me slowly out of her until there's just the tip, then she drops, groaning when I'm all the way in again.

"I said don't move."

"Shut up; I don't care." She starts moving on me, her hands flat on my chest, and I close my eyes, think of every horrible accident my dad's ever told me about. Brains splattered on the road, three-inch nails through hands, legs caught in—"Oh, God, Connor!" I open my eyes just in time to see bliss overtake her, shaking her entire body as she tightens around me. She gasps for air, riding me without apology. When she's done, she falls against my chest, her wet hair matching the sweat coating her body.

I wait only a second before flipping her onto her back and grabbing her thigh, holding it to my hip, and then I *fuck her*. I fuck her as if I've been waiting a year and a half to do it, and tomorrow I'll make love to her. I'll worship her. But tonight... tonight we need the release, both physical and emotional.

We shower together when we're done, laughing at how out of control we were. "You didn't even take your shorts off," Ava laughs, soaping up my chest with a loofa.

"You started it." I kiss her gently, my mouth open on hers.

"Can you get my back?" she asks. Grabbing my hand and placing the loofa on my palm, she turns around, her hands on the wall, ass in the air.

I scrub her back.

She adds, "And how did I start it?"

"With your Creepy Connor Closet."

"Shut up!" she laughs out, reaching behind her to squeeze my hard-on. She starts tugging me, pulling me closer until my front's to her back. I kiss her shoulder, her neck, her jaw, and say, my mouth to her ear. "I stalked you, too."

Her head tilts, her mouth meeting mine. "You did?"

"Austin works in student admissions. I checked every week to make sure you were still enrolled. I think, deep down, that's why I had a shitty season—because I didn't want to leave. I was just waiting for you to come back to me."

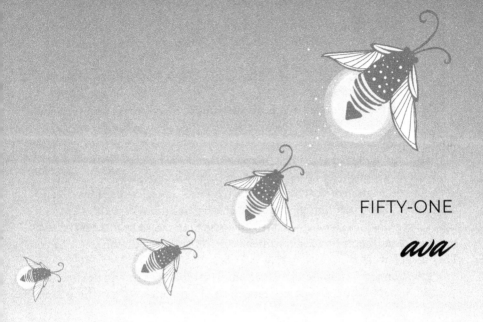

"HOW NICE IS it to have weekends together?" I ask, watching Connor lick his ice cream as if it's his job. A high paying, X-rated job.

He rolls his eyes, playful. "It's *okay*."

I throw my napkin at his head. One month. We've been together for one month, and there's no other way to describe how I feel but *magic*. In every sense of the word. I'd always imagined what it would be like to free myself from the chains of responsibility and just *be* with him, but I never thought it would be like this. We hang out every chance we get, either at my apartment or his dorm, making the most of the time we have before the season starts. Some would think we're finding each other again or falling in love for the second time, but that's not true. We were never lost, always in each other's hearts, and we never stopped loving, not for a second.

"You done?" he asks, standing, his hand out for me to take.

Fingers linked, we walk around the strip mall with no real purpose, no destination in mind. He goes to a sports store, buys a pair of sneakers and another basketball so he can leave them at my place. I go to a few clothes stores and try on some dresses, force him to sit and wait until I'm ready to show him, though I don't think he minds it too much. He offers to pay, and I decline every time, and then I see a furniture store with some housewares and start to walk in. His hand tightens around mine. "What?" I ask, looking up at him. "Are you done shopping?"

"No, I don't mind. But... what do you need from here? Your apartment's furnished."

"I don't know." I shrug. "Maybe a throw or some cute little bits and pieces... why?"

"Nothing." He shakes his head. "Sorry, let's go get your throw—whatever the hell that is."

He holds the door open for me, his brow dipped, and I walk past him, my eyes narrowed in confusion. "Connor, do you have, like, a stalker or something who works here?"

"The only stalker I have is you," he says, taking my hand again.

We walk through the store, and I notice his palm sweating against mine, but I choose to ignore it, just like I choose to ignore the rigidness of his stance. "Hey, look," I say, pointing to a couch. "It looks like mine." I walk over to it, take a closer look. "I think it is mine." I release his hand so I can sit on it, test it. "It is." And then I notice the coffee table. "That's exactly the one I have. They must have—"

"Hey, Connor!" a middle-aged man sings, approaching us. "You're back."

"Who me?" Connor asks, his face flushed. "I think you got the wrong guy."

The guy shakes his head. "No, I remember you. Hard to forget since you—"

Connor clears his throat, cutting the man off. "Seriously, I've never been here before, so..."

The man's gaze trails to me, then back to Connor. "Okay, if you say so."

I wait for the guy to be out of earshot before standing up, whisper to Connor, "That was weird."

"So weird," Connor responds, retaking my hand. We go to the housewares section, where I pick up a vase. "This is cute, right?"

"It's a vase, Ava," he deadpans, his shoulders lifting. Sweat lines his hairline, and his eyes shift. First left. Then right.

"Are you feeling okay, because you look—"

"I'm fine. Get the vase."

The man reappears, waving a stack of papers in the air. "Connor Ledger!" he beams. "I knew it was you! I never forget a face." He stops in front of us, pointing to the receipts in his grasp. "That's you, right?"

Connor swallows.

"See, we take copies of the driver's license for people who come in and spend as much as you did."

Connor's lips thin to a line, and I can see the annoyance in his eyes.

I place the vase back on the table and step forward, my mind spinning. "Can I see that?" I ask.

"No," Connor snaps.

"Sure!" says the man, happily handing it to me.

I look at the receipts, and sure enough, Connor's ID is attached. Then I look at the items, one by one, my chest tightening with every line. Next to the descriptions are images of the products, the same products that fill my entire apartment. My stomach twists, my mind clearing as my heart pounds against my ribs. I look up at Connor, anger forcing the words: "What the hell did you do?"

He swallows, releases a breath. "Ava, it's not—"

I slam the papers against his chest, my voice rising. "What did you do, Connor?!"

He refuses to take hold of the receipts, so they fall to the ground when I march off, my arms crossed. "Ava!" he calls after me, grasping my elbow to stop me from running away. Confusion pulses in my veins and I spin to him, my lip forming a snarl. "Did you get me that apartment?" I shake my head. "No, that apartment came with my mom's care… they told me…" I lower my gaze, my eyes scattered as I try to make sense of everything that's happened from then to now. I look up at him at the same time I release a staggering breath. "You bought the furniture to fill the apartment, but how did you— and why—and where did you get—"

"I'll explain everything, but you just need to calm down."

"Calm down?!" I screech. Shove his chest. "No more secrets, Connor! We agreed!"

The fucker laughs. Right in my face.

"Why are you laughing?"

"Because you're so angry and you don't even know why yet."

"That's not funny!"

He laughs again.

I spin on my heels, walk away. But he's only a step behind me. Air fills my lungs the moment I step outside, and he's talking, begging me to stop, but I won't. *Can't.* Tears of anger fill my eyes. All I can think about is how I forced someone else into financial debt. But it's worse this time, so much worse, because—"Ava!" Connor grasps my elbow again, turning me to him. We're on the sidewalk, blocking other pedestrians, and so he pulls me to the side, leans back against a truck—his truck—and I didn't even know we were back where we started. Figuratively and literally. Hands on my waist, he pulls me between his legs. "Are you done?"

"Fuck you."

He chuckles.

I slam my fist against his chest. "Stop laughing at me," I cry out, hitting him some more.

He grasps my wrists now, holding them to him. "I'll talk when you settle the fuck down."

I *growl.*

He raises his eyebrows.

Then I take a few calming breaths. "I'm settled. Talk."

His mouth parts, but nothing comes. And I wait, one second, two.

"You're an idiot," I snap. "You can't afford to be buying—"

"I can," he cuts in, shrugging, and he's so cool and so calm and why can't he see how much this is affecting me? He sucks in a huge breath as if preparing his speech, and then he says, "My mother came back into my life because her mom, my grandmother, was dying."

Anger's suddenly replaced by sympathy, and I wipe at the residual tears. I pout up at him. "I'm sorry."

"Don't be; I didn't *know* her. I mean, I'm sure I did at one point, but it didn't really affect me. But the point is, my mom was in hiding, and so when my grandmother died, all of her money went to me, and my mom wanted to make sure that she could still access that money *through* me."

"Wait." I struggle to breathe. "She only came back for money?"

Connor nods.

"Okay, so..." I try to clear the fog in my brain, try to wrap my head around what he's telling me. "So your grandmother died, and you got an inheritance?"

He nods again.

"And your mother wanted you to give her some of it?"

Another nod. "I mean, I'm not hard to find, right? You look up my name online, and it shows you what high school I go to. And my mother knew that. My grandmother had lawyers who could easily find me, and that would be it. Done, over. But she wanted a presence in my life so I could drip feed her some cash so she could continue her life as it is."

I ask, hesitant, trying to leave my own feelings about his mom out of it, "Do you give her money?"

"She tried to kill me, Ava. *Fuck her.*"

My lips tug at the corners. "Good." I lean closer to him, unable to control the pull. "So that's it? You got some money, and you decided to furnish the apartment?"

His throat bobs with his swallow.

"Connor," I breathe out. "What else did you do?"

"I kind of... I mean, the apartment's mine, too."

"You *leased* an apartment for me?"

"Actually, I *own* the apartment."

My eyes widen. "You... *what?*"

"Yeah," he says, grimacing.

"I'm still processing," I admit.

"You look so cute when you're confused."

Ignoring him, I ask, "So you came into some money, and you're just out here buying properties?"

He chuckles. "Yeah, actually, I have this neat little portfolio going."

"Shut up," I say through a giggle.

"It's true." He shrugs. "Besides, your apartment's a good investment. But I'd like to get you something bigger—"

"Connor! Stop!"

He clamps his lips shut.

"So... if you have *all* this money, why are you living on campus, and why are you still driving around in this truck?"

"I'm not going to let money change me. I'm still me, and I don't have a reason to live off campus." Then he stands taller, his stance defensive. "Wait. What's wrong with my truck?"

"Nothing," I laugh out, "but why not buy a Mercedes or something? Isn't that what ballers do?"

"Oh, she left me one of those, too... it's in a garage somewhere, I think."

"Jesus."

"Hey, do you want it?"

"No, I don't *want* it."

He smiles. "I don't know, Ava. I'm a simple man with simple needs." Then his brow dips. "No one besides my dad knows about the money," he says, shrugging. "I'd like to keep it that way."

Nodding, I stay silent a moment, still trying to work through everything he's telling me. "Wait. How did you know to buy the apartment and—"

"Because there's more, Ava."

"Oh, God. I need to sit down."

"No, just listen, okay? And please try not to get mad at me."

"Connor! You can't say that and then not expect—"

"Sunshine Oak..."

"No..." My eyes fill with tears again. "You didn't... did you?"

He chews the corner of his lip. "I know you said you were waiting on a place for your mom near Duke, and it took me a while until I found where she was waitlisted, but Riverside... I mean, it's a good place, Ava, but your mom—she deserves the best—and Sunshine Oak—"

I cover my mouth, stop the sob from escaping, but he pulls down my hand, kisses me there.

"Your mom deserves Sunshine Oak, and it took a lot of convincing for them to do what I asked. They were willing to take the money, but trying to get you on board, and anonymously, that was tough, and that's why it took almost a year for them to contact you."

I struggle to breathe, to catch every tear that falls fast and free, and so he does it for me, his thumbs swiping my cheeks.

"And I don't want you to think that your mom's care is mutually exclusive with what happens with us. That's there for as long as you both need or want, okay? I *promise* you that. Even when you get sick of my dumb ass, your mom will always be taken care of."

My shoulders shake with my sob, and he holds me tighter to him, his lips finding my forehead. "Why would you do this?" I mumble into his chest.

He grasps my shoulders, pushing me back so he can look in my eyes. "I told you from the moment I met you, everything I did was for you. My end game was to take care of you and your mom, and that never changed."

"Connor, why didn't you tell me any of this before?"

"Because I didn't want you to feel like you had to be with me for that reason. I wanted to make sure that you'd fall for *me* again." He huffs out a breath, his palm cupping my jaw as he leans in, tastes the tears from my lips. "But, babe, I need you to promise something."

"Anything."

"Two things actually."

I nod.

"I don't want your mom knowing."

"Okay."

"And you owe me nothing."

"Connor, I don't think—"

"Promise me."

I grasp my hair, my palms pressing against my forehead. "This is *so* much right now, and I still... I don't deserve this."

He shakes his head, eyes on mine as he lowers my hands again. "Of course you deserve this. You're my girl, Ava. My first and forever."

My heart beats to the rhythm of his declaration. "I don't even know what to say right now."

"Say you love me."

"I love you, Connor." I press my mouth to his. "I love you so much."

He smiles against my lips, then pulls away. "There is one thing you can do..."

"Is it that thing with my tongue on your ba—"

"No," he cuts in, shaking his head. Then his eyes widen. "But yeah, that, too."

I can't help but laugh.

"Ava, I want to see your mom," he rushes out. "I've been dying to see her, and you haven't—"

"Can we go now?"

His face lights up. "Yeah?"

"She's been *dying* to see you!"

* * *

Mom's out in the garden when we get there, the sun beaming down on her tanning skin. She's wearing a straw hat and a tank top—something she's only now started to be comfortable being seen in. Connor's hand tightens around mine when he spots her, his grin splitting his face in two. "Mama," I call out, and she looks up. Her usual smile for me widens when she sees Connor. "Connor, six-six!" she screams, getting to her feet and rushing over to us. Her laugh fills my heart with hope when she slams into him, throwing her arm around his neck. "Oh, gosh, Connor! I've missed you so much."

"You have no idea how much I've missed *you*, Miss D," he murmurs, releasing my hand to return her hug. His eyes are red, brimming with liquid joy as he smiles down at me. I wipe mine with the back of my hand, my world filling with magic... even in the light of day.

FIFTY-TWO

Connor

"COME WITH ME?" Austin begs.

"No."

"Why not?"

"Because."

"Because... nothing. It's a Friday night, and you have nothing going on tomorrow, so—"

"Because it's a fucking date, Austin. Your *first* date. What the hell—"

"Yeah, you're right," he says through a sigh. "She'll probably take one look at you and forget I exist."

I shake my head. "*She* asked you out, right?"

Austin nods.

"So, what's the problem?"

"The problem is, I'm not built like you, Connor," he answers, his tone serious.

I sigh, getting off my bed to stand behind him as he looks at himself in the mirror. "For someone who calls himself my best friend, you really don't know me at all."

His eye roll makes me chuckle. "You're saying you were this nervous on your first date with Ava?"

"Ava and I never really *dated*. Like, we didn't go out to movies and dinners and stuff. We just... hung out at her house or school. But, yeah, I was nervous around her. I *still* am. I think that's what those feelings are, you know? Those butterflies people talk about..."

He turns to me now, his head craned to look up at me. "Were you her first, too?"

I shake my head.

"Did that bother you?"

"Not really."

He nods, inhales a huge breath. "Okay. I'm going to go, and I'm going to—"

"Be yourself," I cut in. "But lose the blazer."

He looks down at himself. "It's a cardigan."

"Lose it."

"But it makes me look sophisticated."

"It makes you look like a pompous ass."

"You're a pompous ass!"

There's a knock on our door, and I go to open it, saying over my shoulder, "Do whatever you want."

Ava's on the other side, her smile full force when she sees me. "Hey, babe," I greet, kissing her quickly.

"Ava!" Austin shouts, pushing me aside. "I'm going on a date," he announces.

Ava's eyes widen, just a tad. "In that blazer?"

"I told you it was a blazer," I murmur, taking her hand. I start pulling her into the room, but she resists. "What's up?" I ask, confused.

She grins from ear-to-ear. "I have a surprise."

My eyes narrow just as Ava steps to the side and Trevor appears. "Shut. Up," I mumble, my eyes wide.

Trevor's smile matches Ava's, and I can't help my own stupid grin. "What's good?" he asks, his hand out for a shake.

I take it, answer, "Not much."

And then he chuckles, tugging on my hand and embracing me—a little too tight—and with his mouth to my ear, he whispers, "I've missed you, you dumbass."

I laugh, say, "I've missed you, too, you giant fuck."

Behind me, Austin grunts. "You never hug me like that."

* * *

Miss D's reaction to Trevor being in town is similar to mine, although she doesn't bother hiding her genuine emotions. She cries when he hugs her and tells her how much he's missed her. The truth is, I *did* get a tiny bit emotional when I saw him. I'd been hoping that since Ava and I are together again that I'd soon see Trevor, but she always talked about how busy he was and how hard things were for him money-wise. I almost, *almost*, offered to pay for him and Amy to come out because I knew how much she missed them. But I also knew she wouldn't accept... just like all the other times I've offered to pay for things.

"I can't believe it," Miss D says, grasping Trevor's hand on the table. She looks at each of us in turn while we wait for our lunch to arrive, tears at the corners of her eyes. "All my kids are here!"

"Yeah, but I'm your favorite, right?" says Trevor.

Miss D giggles, pats his hand.

"And Connor doesn't count," he adds. "He's not *your* kid."

"Not yet." Miss D winks at me. "But son-in-law sounds good."

Ava chokes on her soda.

I can't help but smile. "Someday, Miss D," I sing, leaning back in my chair. "Someday, your daughter's going to make an honest man out of me."

"Shut up!" Ava whisper-yells, pink blushing her cheeks.

"What?" I shrug. "As if that's *not* going to happen."

"But not for a few years, right?" Trevor says, a threatening lilt in his tone.

I smirk at him.

He adds, "Once she gets her degree, and you're in the NBA, or whatever you decide to do, then maybe..."

I laugh once. "What? Am I going to have to ask your permission?"

"Yes," all three of them say in unison.

Now it's Trevor's turn to smirk at me. "See that?" he says, pointing at me. "*I'm* always going to be the favorite."

* * *

I stay with Ava over the weekend and spend the time showing Trevor around campus, as well as Durham. He spends that time trying to convince Ava and me to transfer to Texas A&M. We visit Miss D every day, sometimes twice a day, and at times in between, we catch up on our current lives, reminisce about the old, and laugh. We laugh so hard, it hurts. And Ava—as much as she'll deny it to his face, she misses him a lot more than she lets show. But I can tell. I can see it in the way she looks up at him, the way her eyes find a sense of calm whenever he's around her. And maybe I should be jealous that I'm not quite *there* yet, that she doesn't look at me like that, but we have something we never had before.

We have time.

And we have *communication*.

I'd told her that first night together that it was important to me that we *both* be open with what we were experiencing and what we were feeling. That if at any time she was feeling a certain way and she needed something from me—time, space, or *me*—that she tell me that up front, and in return, I'd do the same.

No more secrets.

No more hiding what we felt so the other wouldn't feel the weight of it.

We were a team now.

A duo.

Michael Jordan and Scottie Pippen.

I lost her at the basketball reference, but she agreed anyway and said she felt the same. We needed to be solid. A fortress. Then she made an analogy about strands of a rope and something about one fraying, and I told her it didn't make sense. She retorted that Jordan and Pippen didn't make sense. Which is fucking bullshit, and I told her that, too. Then we got into an argument that lasted all of five seconds before she was dry humping my leg again.

Now, we're in bed, and she's fast asleep while I'm wide awake. She stirs beside me, flipping her head from one side to the other. Now her cheek's on the patch of drool on her pillow, and I consider waking her to let her know, but... *eh.*

It's close to midnight and the world is quiet, but my mind... my mind won't rest. I kiss Ava's shoulder before pushing the covers off of me. After throwing on some sweats, I head out of the room, light on my feet, and go toward the kitchen. I stop when I notice Trevor out on the balcony and make my way over, sliding the large glass door as quietly as possible. He looks up at the sound. "Can't sleep?" he asks.

I shake my head. "You?"

"Same."

I take the seat next to him. "You're leaving early tomorrow, right?"

He nods, looks up at the moon. "Yeah. Flying straight to Colorado for Amy's dad's sixtieth." He adjusts in his seat. "I haven't told Ava yet, but Amy landed this killer job in Denver, so she's moving back there in a few weeks. She only stayed in Texas for me to finish up, but this job is... it's too good an opportunity for her to refuse."

"Are you... I mean, are you still going to stay together?"

"Yeah." He nods, sure. "We've done the long-distance thing before so it's not a big deal, but I don't want it to be forever."

"So what are you going to do?"

"I don't know," he says. "I actually wanted to talk to you about that."

"Me?" I ask, my eyes wide.

"Yeah," he breathes out. "I know that Ava and I have been living in different states the past few months, and when Ava told me that you and she were back together... to be honest, it took away a lot of the worry I'd been carrying."

I smile, my chest filling with pride.

"I know you're going to take care of her, of both of them, so... I guess moving back here isn't so urgent."

"You want to move to Denver with Amy?"

Expression pained, he offers a nod.

"That's good, right?" I ask, confused.

"Yeah, but Ava... I don't know how she's—"

"Nah, dude. She wouldn't have it any other way. Trust me. All she wants is for you to be happy."

"It goes both ways," he tells me. "All I want is for her to find The Happiness, and you make her happy, Connor. So, thank you."

"You don't need to thank me," I murmur. "Like you said, it goes both ways."

"I don't *just* mean with her, though. I mean, with Mama Jo, too. You light up something inside them that... I don't even know how to explain it. I just know that I'm grateful for it. For *you*."

There's a knot in my throat that makes it hard to say, "Thanks."

"We should hug again."

I turn to him. "Are you serious?"

"No." He chuckles. Then stares at me, his hand going to his pocket. He pulls out a tiny black box and pops open the lid to reveal a ring.

I blow out a breath. "Are you asking me to marry you? Because I hate to break it to you, but homosexuality isn't genetic, so..."

He busts out a laugh. "I'm going to ask Amy to marry me in front of her family."

"Seriously?" I can't hide my grin. Trevor nods. "That's awesome, man. Congrats."

He closes the lid with a pop, then shoves it back in his pocket. "It's the ring my dad gave Mama Jo."

"Isn't that bad luck?"

His eyes widen. "Is it?"

"I don't know," I backtrack. "I thought I heard it somewhere, but I could be wrong. I'm kind of dumb, in case you didn't notice."

"Shit, Connor. *Is it?*"

I shrug.

"Fuck."

"I'm sorry. I shouldn't have said anything."

He groans, runs a hand down his face. "Dude, we're both athletes; you know how superstitious we are."

I kick myself with the foot that was just in my mouth. "I'm sure it'll be fine."

"No, it won't. And now it's too late. I've told her parents and everything..." He groans again, the heels of his palms going to his eyes. "Dammit."

"Can't you, like, trade it in?"

"It's a little late, *dipshit*."

I sigh. "You and Ava have such strange love languages."

"And even if I could, I wouldn't get much for it, and I don't have the money to buy another one, and what the hell am I doing, Connor? Jesus, I can't even buy her a ring and I'm expecting her to marry me. She's the only one with a job until I find something and—"

"I have a... *proposition*."

He shakes his head. "I'm not sleeping with you."

I chuckle under my breath. "Well, there goes that idea."

"What's your proposition?" He sighs, kicking the balcony railing. "I'm kind of desperate here, and if it's just one night, and we never have to bring it up again, then *maybe*..."

My lips lift at the corners. "Be my agent."

His head dips in frustration. "You have an agent."

"No, I don't."

His gaze lifts, locks on mine. "As good as that sounds, I couldn't do that to you. I haven't even graduated, and I've got no real-life experience."

"But you've got heart," I tell him. "And you *care*. And you're invested in me."

He shakes his head, disbelieving. "What's your angle, man?" His dark eyes flick between mine. "What do you..."

"I'm going to do my four years..."

He nods. "Okay...?"

"And there's only one team I want."

His throat bobs with his swallow.

I add, "And I want *you* to get me on that team. I want to go pro, but I don't care about the money."

"Connor, that's—" He blows out a breath. "It doesn't work like that."

"But you have two and a half years to *make* it work like that."

He licks his lips, his eyes still questioning.

"And I'll give you an advance."

"*What?*"

I nod. "To buy your girl her dream ring."

"*What?*"

"And pay off your student loans."

"*What?*"

"And a house for you and Amy."

"*What?*"

I laugh. "Didn't Ava tell you?"

"*What?*"

"I'm kind of rich now."

"*What?*"

"Say something else."

"No."

"No?"

"No."

"You don't want to be my agent?"

"Connor," he deadpans, his hands going to his head. "My mind is blowing up right now. I can't even comprehend the fact that you *want* me to be your agent, let alone the fact that you're somehow rich enough to—wait, did you take money from someone, because the NCAA—"

"No," I cut in. "It's a long story, but trust me, I can do what I'm offering and not feel a dent."

"Fuck you."

I laugh. "So?"

"It would be a loan?"

"No, it would an advance on whatever you make off of me."

"What if I can't make it happen?"

"Then you're screwed," I joke. Then add, more seriously, "You'll make it happen, bro. I don't know many people in this world who have more perseverance than you."

He stares up at the moon again, cracking his knuckles.

"So?" I ask. "What do you say? You want to take on some nobody from Florida as your first client?"

He turns to me, a puff of breath leaving him. "Okay."

I smile. "Okay."

epilogue

AVA

"OKAY, so what do you need from me? Do you want space, or time, or me? Do you want *me*? Just tell me what you need, and I'll do it."

Connor sits on the edge of the hotel room bed, his head in his hands, his bag by his feet. He releases a long, drawn-out breath before he reaches between us and takes my hand in his. He looks up, his eyes clear. "I need you to calm the hell down, baby. You're making me nervous."

"Sorry," I breathe out, letting him pull me between his legs.

His head settles on my stomach, his arms going around my waist. "You're going to be there early, right?"

"I'll be the first one through the gates."

Connor chuckles. "And you got all the tickets?"

"All of them."

"And you're coming with your mom—"

"As soon as you leave, I'm going to meet her and your dad and Michael in the lobby."

Connor nods. "All right."

"All right."

He turns to me, a smile playing on his lips. "I should probably get going," he says, passing me a black marker. I take his hand, settle it on my bare thigh, and write *Miss D* on the back of his hand, and *Ava E. D. Diaz* below it. Then I reach into my purse and pull out a blue balloon. I blow it up, make quick work of writing *Connor Ledger #1 Boo Devil*. I hand it to him, loving the way his eyes light up when he takes it from me.

Three years.

Three seasons.

And this is what we do before every game.

But we've never had a game like this before.

Duke is in the NCAA Division I championship, and this is Connor's last game as a Duke Blue Devil.

"Okay." Connor stands, and he rolls his neck, his shoulders, then he shakes out his hands, turning to me when I get to my feet. "Say it," he says.

I rise to my toes, my palm above the heart, and kiss him, my mouth open, tongue swiping against his. When I pull away, his eyes are still closed, and so I kiss him again. Just once. "I love you, number three."

He smacks my ass, just as Trevor knocks on the door. Trevor's been staying with us during Connor's finals so he can be nearby when NBA teams call or want meetings with Connor. Because that's happening. *A lot.* And Trevor's Connor's agent—a deal they apparently made three years ago. A deal they didn't tell me about until only recently.

"Can I come in or is my sister naked?"

"You can come in," Connor laughs out, grabbing his bag and swinging the strap around his torso.

Trevor pokes his head in. "You ready to go?"

Connor kisses me once more before meeting my brother in the living room. I stay back, listening to them talk ball and business like they do before most games. When they start for the door, Connor turns to me. "Say it again?"

I stand in the middle of the living room, my hands behind my back. "I love you, number three."

Connor smiles, his chest rising with his inhale. Then he turns to Trevor. "Okay, I'm good now."

The second they leave, I flop down on the couch, my hand to my heart, trying to ease the thumping there. I'm nervous. For him. For the entire team. For three years I've watched the boy I love play a game he loves at the college of his dreams, and now... now he's one step closer to fulfilling every dream he's ever had.

And I *want* this for him.

For us.

But I worry.

Because after this, it's the NBA draft.

And we don't know where he's going.

I still have another year left at Duke, and *I* don't know if I can leave my mom. She's so settled at Sunshine Oak, and I...

I'm scared of the future.

CONNOR

Sweat drips from my brow and into my eyes, and I blink hard, try to clear my vision. We knew it'd be a tough game. Texas Tech always comes out fighting, and we were prepared to go toe-to-toe all damn night. And we have. I can't even count how many times the lead has changed. But now with less than five seconds on the clock, Texas is up by one and we haven't been able to break away from their defense long enough to score. With the ball out of bounds, I take a moment to breathe and press my hands to my knees.

Behind me, I can hear them.

All of them.

Ava, Trevor, Miss D, my dad, and his husband. "Boo, Ledger!" Ava screams, and I inhale that sound into my bloodline.

"You good, Ledger?" Coach calls from the sidelines. "One more play, baby! One more play!"

I nod, more to myself than anyone else, and ignore the ache pinching every nerve, every muscle. I stand to full height, guarding my opponent, my eyes on a Texas Tech player with the ball at the sideline. The ref blows his whistle, and my heart picks up when the ball comes toward me. The world is silent while I wait, every millisecond making a difference. With my pulse the only sound I hear, I lift a hand in front of my opponent, the tips of my fingers making contact with the ball, and then *it's on*. The crowd *roars* and I'm chasing after the ball, pushing off my feet with more strength and determination than I've ever had. The ball meets my palm, and then I'm in control, listening to the world around me erupt. I look up, two more steps. I can make it two more steps, but I can also hear my opponent only half a step behind me. I look at the basket, then down at my hand, and I see it...

Their names.

My reason.

My shoes squeak against the hardwood, my knees bending with muscle memory. Arms come up, elbows bend, and time slows the second the ball's out of my hand.

It spins through the air, hitting the backboard first, then the rim, again and again, and then—

The buzzer sounds, and I'm being tackled to the ground, covered in blue and white.

I didn't see it.

Not with my own eyes.

But when the Duke Fight Song plays, I know I'd sunk the shot...

A jump shot.

AVA

We stay in the arena while most people leave, watching the cleaners start sweeping up the mess of blue and white left behind. Mom's next to me, rehashing every play Connor was somehow involved in with Corey and Michael, and Trevor... Trevor's *somewhere*; I just don't know where.

I alternate between laughing and crying and laughing some more, and my cheeks hurt with the force of my smile. I'd been tempted, so tempted, to run onto the court the second he made the shot, but Trevor held me back. It was Connor's time, he reminded me, and it was important he celebrate it with his team. And he did. For a couple of minutes. And then his eyes found me like they always do, and he approached, his cheeks flushed. He stopped a few feet away, his eyes bright against the arena lights, and he looked at me, shouted over the crowd, "Was I money or what?"

"You were so fucking money!"

His gaze shifted to my mom, and he quirked an eyebrow, cocky. "Weak jump shot, huh?" And then he *whooped*, his back arching, his fists out in front of him, and I loved him so much more at that moment, loved the way he let himself go, let himself *live*.

And to think that once upon a time, someone tried to take that life away from him...

I cried the second I was in his arms, his sweat soaking into my clothes. "Say it," he ordered.

I pulled back, just so I could look at him. "I love you, number three!"

"There he is," Mom says, bringing me back to the present. I stand when I see him. Connor's in his game-day suit, walking toward me with Trevor on one side and a man I've never seen before on the other. The man's talking and Connor has his head down, nodding and listening intently. Trevor—Trevor's wearing a shit-eating grin, and my pulse begins to pound. They all stop in front of us, only a few feet away, but then Connor closes that distance. He grasps me by my waist, lifting me effortlessly over the barrier. I hold on to him when he places me back on my feet. He kisses me once before throwing his hand out between me and the unknown man. "Vaughn," he says, "this is my future fiancée, Ava." I choke on air, my heart swelling at his choice of words. He adds, "Ava, this is Vaughn."

I raise a timid hand, move closer to Connor. "Hi."

Vaughn smiles. "Hi, Ava. I've heard a lot about you."

"You have?"

Behind me, Corey chuckles.

Vaughn nods.

And Connor says, "Vaughn is the president of the Hornets."

My eyes widen, and I look up at Connor. "Hornets?" I breathe out. "As in *Charlotte* Hornets? As in Charlotte, *North Carolina*?"

"Yeah, babe," Connor says, shifting a loose curl from my forehead. "I told you, you gotta work harder if you want to get rid of me."

"So, we're not moving? And my mom doesn't have to... You—you're staying *here*?" I cry, disbelief forcing tears of joy.

"Of course I'm staying." He takes my hand, places it right above his heart, and I feel his life, his *love* beating beneath my fingers. "For *love and basketball*." Then he smiles...

And that smile...

That smile fills my world with *magic*.

bonus epilogue

CONNOR

ONE YEAR LATER

"CONNOR, SIX-SIX!" Miss D sings, getting up from her seat around the table. Next to her, Trevor rolls his eyes jokingly. At least, I think he's joking. Sometimes, it's hard to tell with Trevor. Still, I take the opportunity to give him the finger the second I'm in Miss D's embrace and her back is to him.

He returns the gesture with a chuckle, shaking his head.

Oh, so he *was* joking. *Good to know.* Being an only child, I've never had to deal with sibling relationships, so most of what I know is from witnessing the way Ava and Trevor interact. It's... interesting, to put it mildly. They're affectionate one second, then yelling and throwing things at each other the next. I guess most people would call it a love/hate relationship. But the way I see it, it's all love. They wouldn't be where they are if it wasn't. And that love is why I asked him to be here today... and to keep it a secret from Ava.

Too soon, Miss D releases me from her tight, one-arm hug, and Trevor stands, giving me what my girl calls a "weird bro handshake." And then we hug—far less bro-ish.

We're in a private room at a restaurant close to home, because today, of all days, I don't want to be interrupted. Don't get me wrong; I usually appreciate the Duke and Hornets fans who ask for pictures or autographs, but what I'm about to do... it's not for anyone else's eyes and ears.

"Thanks for coming," I tell them, taking a seat. I focus on Miss D and smile over at the woman who so quickly became a mother to me when my own couldn't. "You look good, Miss D."

Happy.

She looks happy, and there are no words in the entire English dictionary to describe how that makes me feel.

Miss D gives me her classic eye-roll, a trait she definitely passed on to her daughter, and covers my hand resting on the table. "How many times have I told you? You, Connor, call me Mom."

"Funny you mention that..." I trail off, removing my hand from under her touch and swiping both palms along my thighs. I'm sweating. *Bad.* "Is it hot in here?" My voice cracks, my throat suddenly dry, and I pick up the glass of water off the table and down the entire thing in a single gulp. It's a short glass, and it doesn't seem to have any effect, so I reach over for the jug, refill it, and repeat the process.

Twice.

I ignore the way Trevor watches me, confusion pinching his eyebrows. Then I slip a finger in my collar and tug. Hard. "It's hot, right?"

"No," Trevor deadpans; at the same time, Miss D says, "Are you okay?"

Am I okay?

No. And it didn't even hit me until right this moment how *un*-okay I am. I can feel my stomach twist, my chest tighten, and it's too loud in this restaurant. Too fucking bright. I glare at the lights, my eyes immediately watering, and I blink back tears. Oh, God. I'm crying. In front of my girlfriend's family, and who the fuck chose this place?

Oh, yeah. I did.

Stupid.

Why the hell am I so nervous? I'm a professional baller, for fuck's sake. *N.B.fricken.A.* I've come in clutch on buzzer-beater shots that have won career-making games. I've played in front of tens of thousands of screaming fans, done interviews broadcast to millions, spoken on stage, and now *this?* *This* is where I break?

How?

Because Ava was by my side through all the things I listed above, knowing damn well that none of it meant anything without her.

My *End Game.*

And now I'm close to making my dreams a reality, and the two people who can give me that are currently sitting in front of me, staring at me as if I lost my mind, left it on the hardwood at Spectrum Center.

I'd planned out my speech, every word, every damn syllable. Then, on the drive here, I had perfected it, and now... now I can't think.

Can't even breathe.

"Funny I mention what?" Miss D asks, and I have no idea what she's talking about.

"He wants permission to marry Ava," Trevor says, and I glance over at him, his smug smile splitting his face in two.

The walls close in, and I get dizzy when the room spins and spins and spins, and I...

...pass out.

I'm in a tunnel, a small dot of light miles away, and I feel like I've been stabbed in the forehead. There's a voice at the end but no silhouette to accompany it.

"You scared him!" Miss D says, but her words are distant, and they echo echo echo.

"I was just messing with the kid, Mama Jo." My hair is yanked, snapping my neck back, and I try to pry my eyes open. I don't have to work hard when water splashes on my face and I gasp air into my lungs for the first time in what feels like forever.

"Trevor!" Miss D admonishes.

"He's fine," Trevor grumbles. "Look." I don't move away in time for the next glass of water to be thrown at me.

"I'm good!" I almost shout, slapping at his giant behemoth of a hand until he lets go of my hair.

Love/hate *is* real, and right now, I'm on the hate train.

"I'm sorry, bro," he says, moving around the table until he's back in his chair. He leans back slightly while I use a napkin to dry my face, my hair. "It's just... I've thought about this moment a lot," Trevor continues, "and I thought I was prepared, and I know you guys have been together for years now, too many, but she's my little sister, you know? It's been hard watching her grow up, witnessing everything she's been through, and now I have to let her go..."

In my mind, the hate train comes to a halt, and I'm quick to hop off.

Through the knot in my throat, I manage to say, "I get it."

Next to me, Miss Diaz sniffles, and Trevor and I give her our attention. She's wiping her tears using the end of the tablecloth, and the movements shift the glasses on the table, tipping them over. More water spills and no one seems to care. Besides, what's more mess added to the one we already created?

"I'm sorry," I tell her. "I had this whole speech planned. Obviously, me passing out at the table wasn't part of it." I reach up and run my fingertips along my forehead, where a sharp pain still pulses. A row of four tiny indents greets me. "The fuck?"

"You landed on a fork," Trevor chuckles. "Lucky it didn't get you in the eye."

My shoulders bounce with my silent laughter, and I rub my eyes. "God, I'm a mess."

"No, you're not," Miss D coos. "You're perfect, Connor, six-six, and nothing in this world would make me happier than for you to marry my daughter."

I smile at her, loving how the harsh lights somehow soften the scars that made her the woman she is today. I settle in my chair, let go of any expectations of what today was supposed to be, and just give it to her straight. "You know, when I first met you, you wouldn't leave the house, too afraid of how this shitty world has and would treat you," I tell her, my voice cracking with affection. "You've changed so much in the years I've loved you, *Mom*. I am what I am because you are who you are, and I remind myself of that every time Ava writes your name on my hand before every game." I drop my gaze, suddenly too aware of all the emotions swirling inside me. "I appreciate you so much, and I'm forever grateful you trust me with your daughter's heart, but..." I pause for a breath. "It's not you I'm worried about." I chance a peek in Trevor's direction. "It's him."

Trevor stares, and stares, absolutely no emotion on his face. "God-dammit," he finally huffs. Then, suddenly, he's yanking the entire tablecloth off the table, knocking over *everything*. I watch in shock as plates, silverware, and even more water spills to the floor in loud *clanks*. Trevor covers his entire head with the tablecloth, looking like a cheap ghost Halloween costume.

"Trevor!" Miss D shouts; at the same time, I ask, "You good, bro?"

"Yes!" he responds, and I don't miss how his hands cover his face, and is he... is he crying?

"Yes, you're good, or—"

"Yes! You can marry her!" He removes the tablecloth completely, revealing his tear-stained cheeks and red, raw eyes. He glares at me, a finger pointed between us. "And if you ever make me cry like that again, I'll end you."

I laugh, relief washing through every inch of me. "Noted."

"So when do you plan on proposing?" Miss D asks, bringing my attention back to her.

"Soon," I reply. "And I'm going to need your help."

AVA

TWO WEEKS LATER

"Have a good summer!" one of my classmates calls out from across the quad.

"You too!" I wave back, not bothering to tell her that I'll be *here* most of the summer, taking classes to try to get ahead. Turns out, I have no idea what I want to do with the rest of my life. This realization came to me halfway through my senior year. I *thought* I wanted to study criminal justice, but where that led, I didn't know.

Given my past life, I'd never really been one to experience FOMO (Fear of Missing Out), but when I tell you I wept on what should've been my graduation day, I mean it. I cried into my pillow, snot leaking out of my nose, and poor Connor had to walk in on it. He'd stopped at the bedroom door, looked around, then back at me. I could tell he wanted to run, but it's not in my boyfriend's nature. Good or bad, he's by my side. Always. Just like he was then. You can picture it now, right? Connor Ledger—all six-foot-six of professional NBA player, consoling his lowly college non-graduate girlfriend by holding me in his arms and literally rocking me like a baby. We'd already spoken about my future, about my fear of not knowing what the hell I was doing with my life, and his response—bless him—was so simple it almost made me laugh. *Almost.* "So, keep working on finding out," he'd said.

Unlike me, Connor was lucky enough to know what he wanted; fortunately for him, that goal was also his passion. I'm not saying he didn't work hard for it, because Lord knows he did. He worked so hard it almost broke him numerous times, but he never gave up like I've wanted to—multiple times.

"Time isn't a problem," he'd told me then. "And neither is money."

Both were true. Connor had a four-year contract with the Charlotte Hornets. Considering he was probably the highest caliber player on the lowest salary in the entire league, it was unlikely they would trade him any time soon. Besides, he didn't need *their* money. He had plenty of his own, thanks to his late maternal grandma. And, of course, he had no issues spending that money on me, on an education that might be wasted. When I'd told him this, he'd scoffed, said that I'd supported him for five years, getting him to where he is, so the least he could do was give an iota of that same support in return.

So, I decided to take some random classes until I found something that sparked magic inside me. I haven't found it yet, but I'm sure I will. Connor has faith in me, and that's what drives me forward.

Speaking of Connor, I spot him at our usual meeting place, and though I can't actually see *him*, I know he's there somewhere. I keep telling him he doesn't have to meet me on campus when he's free to do so, but he insists. It was bad enough when he was a star Duke Blue Devil, but NBA status is a whole other level. A small crowd surrounds him while he takes pictures and signs autographs, and the smile that tugs on my lips is entirely natural.

I know a part of him hates this attention, but an even more significant part of him appreciates it. As for me, I've always known Connor as two different people—the baller side: confident, proud, and sometimes cocky. Then there's the side of him he reserves only for our families and me: awkward, anxious, and introverted.

Both of them are *real*.

And all of him has my entire heart.

He smiles to the side, his head dipping as he signs something in front of him. I know that smile, that *smirk*. He can sense me moving toward him, and I wonder if he feels what I feel—the sudden increase in pulse, the excitement coursing through my veins. Five years of being his, and this feeling of anticipation just to be with him is still all-consuming. His mouth moves, saying, "Last one, guys, sorry."

He takes a picture with a girl whose eyes drink him in, and for a second, just one, I wonder what would leave less evidence: finding her car and cutting her brake lines or putting her tiny-ass body through a woodchipper.

Hello, intrusive thoughts, go away.

I don't have to do either because Connor takes the picture, his hands an inch from actually touching her like he always does when he takes pictures with females, and then he smiles down at her—fake as fuck—and says, "My girl's here. I gotta go."

The small crowd around him parts like the Red Sea as he turns toward me, his smile all for me. He waits until I'm right in front of him before taking both my hands in his and kissing me quickly. "How was your last day, baby?" If it were up to him, the kiss would be longer, with tongue, until the taste of me lingered on his lips for hours afterward. I know, because he's told me so. Personally, I like to keep a low profile. It's hard enough being a college student while your boyfriend—Connor Ledger—is... well, *Connor fricken Ledger*.

Weeding out the real versus fake attempts for friendships is tough. Add dodging glares from judgmental girls about how Connor could "do so much better," and some days, I don't even want to get out of bed.

First-world problems, sure, but they're problems nonetheless.

I have to remind myself that these people—they don't know me. And they don't know *us*. They have no idea what we've been through to get to where we are.

Besides, there's a reason why Connor still comes to campus to walk me back to our apartment whenever he can. He thinks there's a Mister Steal-

Your-Girl lurking around every corner, and I'm their target. Hilarious. And adorable. And completely false.

One day, we'll grow out of this childish jealousy, but today is not that day.

"Eh," I finally answer him, kissing him again. "It was kind of pointless."

"I told you, you should've skipped," he says, releasing one of my hands and leading me away. Only, he's going the wrong way.

I squeeze his hand, resisting. "Did you need to go train or something?" It's off-season, but Connor still takes advantage of the facilities on campus when he can.

He shakes his head. "Nah, I drove here so we could leave right away."

My brow pinches, and I follow after him, my two steps for every one of his. "Leave to go where? Did we have plans?"

"It's a surprise." He smiles down at me. "I packed your bag already."

"Packed a bag?" *What?* "Babe, I can't go anywhere. I have—"

"It's just a couple nights," he says, squeezing my hand and dropping a kiss on my curls. "Relax, baby."

* * *

"Relax," he says, as if it's that simple, and the farther from home we get, the harder it is to do exactly that. If he's leading me to where I think he's going, I don't know if I'll be able to handle it. Still, I stay quiet, fidgeting in my seat. I *know* Connor. Sometimes I feel as if I know him better than he knows himself, and I know he'd never do anything to intentionally hurt me or even make me the slightest bit uncomfortable. It's taken years to heal from the trauma of my past, and the last place I want to go is back there—to where it all started and where *I* decided to end it... by setting that trauma on fire.

Literally.

Surely, he wouldn't force me back there.

He couldn't.

Fear begins to build a fortress in my chest at the first glance of the sign that shows the distance to Shemeld. It's where Connor and I first met, where our houses sat side by side—where we created memories of late-night kisses and bright orange balloons tied to porch railings... but it's also the place I almost lost my mother. Multiple times. Physically and mentally. Tears blur my vision as I turn to the man behind the wheel, try to keep my emotions in check. "Connor..." It's the first word I've spoken in a while, and it's barely a whisper, but I know he hears me.

He's sitting ramrod straight, both hands on the steering wheel, and he glances at me quickly before focusing on the road again. "You trust me, right?"

With my life. "Yes, but—"

"I love you, Ava," he says, and it's so much more than a simple declaration of his feelings.

It's *I love you, Ava.*

And *I'll never hurt you, Ava.*

And *Please, trust me, Ava.*

He takes my hand, linking our fingers.

You're stronger than you believe, Ava.

I close my eyes, exhale through my nose, and bring his hand to my lips. Kiss him once. "I love you, too, Connor."

* * *

It's almost dark when we get to our destination and pull into the same driveway I spent much of my childhood. The recollections play out like snapshots in my mind, first with my mom, then occasionally with her ex-husband, William, and then Trevor once he got his license. I almost smile at the memories of Trevor sitting beside me, his shoulders up to his ears and a grimace on his face that had me howling with laughter. He often let me choose the music for the drive home when he picked me up from school, and it was always, *always*, One Direction. And, boy, was it loud. "Girl, this makes my ears bleed!" he'd yell, but he never once attempted to lower the volume or switch songs. The day I caught him singing "What Makes You Beautiful" was one of the best days of my life.

Now, I stay put while Connor exits his truck and makes his way to my side. He opens my door, but I don't move to get out, too busy staring at the house in front of me. The brick stairs leading to large white columns and the large balcony hanging over the entrance.

It was so much more than a house.

It was *our home.*

Still, I never expected to come back here, and honestly, I never wanted to.

In that house are *those* stairs, the ones I climbed right before I found my mother—

"Ava," Connor says, his voice quiet as he squats beside me. "Are you coming, or...?"

I could lie and pretend as if I'm not at all affected by being here. "Did you *buy* this house, Connor, because I—"

"No," he says, shaking his head.

I search his face for clues as to why we're here. Blue-blue eyes stare right back at me, giving nothing away. "What are we doing here, baby?"

His smile is slow, spreading wide, and I can't help the way my lips tug at the corners, a short burst of laughter leaving my chest. "You're so cute," I say, taking his offered hand and finally getting out of the truck. "And maybe a little crazy."

"Crazy about you, sure."

"Lame," I retort, holding his arm to my chest.

He laughs once. "You love my lame ass."

"I do," I admit, as he takes us not to the front door but to the side gate that leads to the backyard. The dock. The lake. The last time we were here, we were drunk, both on alcohol and our love for each other. "Are you going to tell me what we're doing here?"

"You'll see," he says, and we bypass the main house, pool, poolhouse, and greenhouse until the yard opens up and the lake... My chest tightens at the unfamiliar fondness that overwhelms my emotions. I miss this house. This lake. But most of all, I miss the joy that lived here, the happiness that faded once my mother returned, wounded and woeful.

She's not that same woman anymore, and maybe that's why... why it feels different now.

"Connor," I gasp when the patio comes into view. Above the lake's stillness, there's a patio table with a large arrangement of flowers, but that's not what has my heart stopping, my breath catching in my throat. The deck is bordered with twinkling fairy lights and Mason jars filled with magic.

With *hope*.

On one of my particularly low days, Connor—as always—had found a way to turn it around. He'd left me in the darkness of our bedroom to cry it out, and when he'd returned less than an hour later, he had dozens of Mason jars, each one filled with water and what looked like different colored fireflies. In reality, they were the liquid from glow sticks, but they'd had the same effect, and then he'd lain beside me on the bed, silently holding my hand as the room illuminated.

Connor Ledger, everyone—my magician.

Now, he holds my hand the same way, silently looking out over the lake.

"This is beautiful, number three," I murmur, and at his non-response, I slowly turn to him.

He smiles, but it's forced.

"What's wrong?"

He sucks in a breath and lets it out slowly. "So... I have a confession..."

I side-eye him. "Speak..."

"I lied earlier."

"About...?"

"I *did* buy this house."

My eyes widen and fill with tears. "Connor..."

"We don't have to live in it," he rushes out. "It can sit here empty for the rest of its days for all I care, but... I don't know, Ava." Only when his shoulders drop do I realize how tense he'd been. I was so deep in my own thoughts, my own emotions, that I never picked up on it. "This was your mom's house. Your grandparents'. Your great-grandparents'. This place is part of your family, your *legacy*. It belongs to you. To you, Trevor, and your mom." His eyes drift shut, and he murmurs words too quiet to make out. When he opens them again, they land right on mine—bright blue against the setting sun. "I know it's not all good memories for you here, so..." He shrugs. "I wanted to replace all those bad ones with one good one." He blows out a breath, his cheeks puffing with the force. "Here goes nothing..." he mumbles, and then he's gone, moving to the patio table and reaching underneath. For a long moment, he fiddles with something there, while I stand in silence, my heart racing, my mind spinning in circles.

He bought me this house. This home. This legacy...

My eyes are so filled to the brim with liquid hope that I can't even make out what he's doing anymore. It's not until he returns to me that I blink, blink, blink, releasing the tears I've been holding on to since I realized where we were going. Only those tears stemmed from fear, while these tears fall from love.

From joy.

Everything becomes clear.

Everything.

He's holding a single orange balloon up between us, revealing the words written in thick black marker. A gasp leaves me, and I take a step back, cover my mouth. "Connor..."

Slowly, carefully, he gets down on one knee. "So..." he asks, motioning to the balloon.

I reread the words: *Be my End Game, Ava?*

I nod without thinking because what's there to think about? "Yes!" I squeal, bouncing on my toes. "Oh, my God, yes!"

His eyes widen. "Yeah?" *Why is this boy even surprised?*

"Yes! Yes! Yes!"

Connor laughs, and I don't miss the way his eyes fill with tears and his chest rises and falls with every breath.

"Here," he says, reaching into his pocket to reveal a safety pin.

I take it from him. "Um..."

"Pop it," he laughs, getting to his feet and holding the balloon closer to me.

"Oh!" I'm so overwhelmed with emotions that I can't even think, and I can't stop laughing. I pop the balloon, but it only falls halfway, the string still in Connors's grasp, and as I watch him fidget with the deflated balloon, I realize why.

Tied to the end of the string, hidden inside the once air-filled balloon, is a ring. *The* ring.

"God, I hope it fits," he breathes out, slipping the ring on my finger.

My hand trembles as I hold it between us, watching the diamonds glint. "It's perfect," I cry out, and it is—both the fit and the ring itself. I don't know much about jewelry, especially engagement rings, but "It's so beautiful, Connor!"

I tear my gaze away from the ring to look up at him just as a single firefly floats between us.

I gasp. Again. And Connor and I remain speechless as we watch it fly around us, wrapping us up in its wonder.

"Ava..." he whispers, and I lift my teary eyes to his. "I love you so much." And then I'm wrapped in his arms, lifted off my feet, and he's kissing me.

In this miraculous moment, surrounded by hope, I kiss the boy who made me believe in magic again.

I wrap my legs around him, kiss him deeper, and he moans against my tongue... just as cheers fill my ears, and I quickly pull away and snap my head toward the sound.

On the second-story balcony, five figures stand, screaming, cheering— celebrating our love with us.

Connor releases me back to my feet, and I laugh through my cries as I catch my mom; Trevor; his girlfriend, Amy; and Connor's dads, Corey and Michael, all here to witness this moment.

I run—*sprint*—dragging Connor behind me. "Mama!" I shout, and I feel like that little girl again, loose curls flying everywhere, running to her mom when she'd returned from deployment. "I'm getting married!"

* * *

"He passed out," Trevor says, his voice super squeaky from the helium he'd just inhaled. *Man-child.*

We're all sitting around on the couches in a hotel suite with orange balloons covering the ceiling, set up earlier by our families. On the drive here, Connor mentioned that he had the poolhouse fully furnished and had planned to celebrate there, but since Amy is heavily pregnant, he wanted to ensure she was comfortable and could rest whenever she needed to.

My future husband, y'all... so incredibly thoughtful.

I smile over at him, about to tell him how I can't wait to have his babies, but he brings the opening of a balloon to his mouth and inhales the gas because he, too, is a giant man-child. Then he says, his voice matching Trevor's, "I landed on a fork." He taps a finger on the middle of his forehead. "*Fucker* got me right here." His eyes widen and shift directly to Amy's huge belly. "Sorry for swearing, baby," he squeaks, rubbing her stomach.

The room erupts with laughter, and my heart fills with bliss.

Also, we might be a little drunk. Well, everyone but Amy, obviously.

"So, I know it's extremely early to ask this," Mom says. "But have you got any idea about timelines? Dates? Maybe just a season?"

I shake my head. "Honestly, I've never even—"

"Tomorrow," Connor squeaks, and we all laugh at the mere thought.

"Sure." I roll my eyes. "Let me just pull an entire wedding—"

Connor coughs a few times, cutting me off, and tests his voice. When he's sure it's back to normal, he repeats, "Tomorrow."

"Connor," I laugh, but the longer I stare at him, the less funny it is.

He turns to me, his eyes searching mine as if we're the only two people in the room. "I've waited five years for this moment, Ava. I don't want to wait anymore. Everyone who's important is here now, and afterward, if you want a big ceremony with all the bells and whistles, you know I'll move heaven and earth to give that to you. But I'm asking you now that *tomorrow*, you give me forever."

I suck in a breath. Hold it. "You're serious?"

He nods, less confident than he was only minutes ago.

He's right. Everyone important is here, but— "We don't have a venue."

"I know a place."

"You know a place?" Mom asks, cutting through my thoughts. "Connor, sweetheart, I love you, but girls dream about their wedding day—"

"Not me," I reply, not taking my eyes off the man in front of me. "The only thing I dreamed about is Connor..."

"You're actually contemplating this?" Trevor asks, but it's not out of worry. It's more... anticipation. Excitement, even. He wants me to do this. *I* want to do this.

It's clear that as much as Connor involved my family in this special moment, it's evident that neither of them knew about this.

"Don't we need a celebrant or something?" It's the only thing I can think to say.

"That's where I come in," Michael chimes in. "Got it online!"

I laugh once, disbelieving, and focus on my fiancé. "You thought of everything, huh?"

He nods, his bottom lip caught between his teeth.

"I don't have a dress."

"I told you I packed you a bag."

"You picked out her dress?" Amy coos. "That's so romantic."

Connor says, "It's not a real wedding dress, but it's white, and it's perfect for where we're going."

My eyes narrow. "Where *are* we going?"

AVA

"This is the place where I drooled on his weenus!"

"Ava!" Both Mom and Trevor admonish, and all I can do is laugh, settle in the car seat.

For such an untraditional wedding, there was only one tradition Connor was adamant on keeping—that we spend the night apart. I wanted to fight him on it, obviously. The boy just asked me to marry him, and I'd wanted to strip him naked and jump his bones the moment he got down on one knee. Instead, I ended the night in bed with my mother.

Fun.

When it was time, I got ready, waiting until the very last minute to even look at the dress Connor had picked out for me. Like he said, it wasn't a "real" wedding dress, but it's so, so perfect. It's V-neck with an open back and an A-line skirt that ends just past the knees. The best part? It has pockets.

But, for all the great there is in Connor, he forgot to pack me shoes, and since I only had the ones I wore to class, white Nikes would have to do.

Also: bless my mother, because I don't think she knows how to feel. How to act. The dress, the shoes, the sudden wedding that she had no involvement in...

If it means that much to her, I'll give her the wedding she wants, but I know—in my heart—it will only be for her. Me? I couldn't be happier with what's about to happen.

Trevor, Amy, Mom and I were told to wait at the hotel until Connor sent a drop-pin of the location Trevor needed take us. According to Trevor, Connor and his dads are already here.

I open the car door just enough to breathe in the fresh, crisp air and look around. Bursts of sunlight filter through the branches above us, and in the distance, I can hear the water flowing freely.

Memories flood my vision of the first and only time we came here, and suddenly, without meaning to, I'm crying. "Ava, if you don't want to—" Trevor starts, but I cut him off.

"It's not that I don't want to," I inform. "It's that I *can't wait* to."

CONNOR

"You guys ever miss touching boob?" I ask and immediately clamp my lips shut, my face burning with embarrassment because what the fuck kind of question is that to ask your dad and his husband. A stupid fucking one, that's what.

Luckily, they laugh at my idiocy. "You're nervous, huh?" Dad asks, fixing my shirt sleeve.

Nervous? "Yes." But I'm also having flashbacks of when Ava and I ended up here and we fooled around. Hence, the dumb boob question.

"Are you sure you don't want to wear a tie?" Dad asks, pointing to his own.

I shake my head. "Nah, I'm good." I opted for a simple look. Cream-colored slacks, a plain white shirt, sleeves rolled up, and buttons undone at the collar. I wanted to be casual today, comfortable. There was no way I was putting on a tux in this heat, and besides, Ava likes my arms. She tells me so all the time.

"You'll be fine, Connor," Michael says, massaging my shoulder.

"Any last-minute words of wisdom?" I ask, shifting my gaze between my dads. "Or, I don't know, something motivational?"

"Mike and I look to you and Ava for motivation, son," Dad chuckles.

"It's true," Michael says.

Dad adds, "You know what you're doing. You always have." Emotion makes his words wobble, and he sniffs once, his eyes turning red.

"Dad…" I say, stepping closer.

"I'm just so proud of you, Connor. For the man you've become, the husband you're about to be, maybe even the father you'll be one day."

I crack a smile, all tension leaving my shoulders. "I'd make an awesome dad," I tell him. "I had the best example."

Want to know what three grown-ass men sound like crying? Comical. That's what it is. And maybe that's why we're all laughing through our tears, or maybe we're just doing that to hide our real emotions because "Holy shit," I laugh-cry. "I'm getting married."

Before I can stew on that thought any longer, my phone goes off with a text. I reach into my pocket and read the notification. "They're here," I say. "They'll be here any second."

Dad pats my back a few times while Michael asks, "What is it you kids say today?" Then hollers, "Let's goooooo!"

I laugh, unrestrained, and get into position. "Let's fucking go," I murmur.

* * *

It feels like I stand there forever, anxiously sweating, looking toward the path's opening for my girl to appear, and when she does, I lose my breath.

Literally.

I got the dress from a shop a few blocks from our apartment, where Ava buys most of her clothes, so they knew her and *me*, considering I like to watch her try on dresses. Ava in sweats and a messy knot is killer as it is. Ava in a dress with her hair down, curls everywhere? Next level.

I had asked the assistants a few months ago to help me—covertly, of course. They'd shown me their "special order only" catalog, and I'd chosen the dress. They came up with an excuse to get her measurements. Even through the screen of a tablet, I could picture Ava in this exact dress, how well it would suit her, how beautiful she'd look.

My imagination came up short.

Ava is... heart-stopping.

And as I watch her walk toward me on Trevor's arm, I feel a sense of ease I've never felt before. I knew from the moment she first held me under those gym lights that I wanted her. Some people can tell you the moment they fell in love with someone—a quirky story about a random Sunday morning—but there was no such turning point for me.

I think, in some ways, I needed Ava before I met her, and once I found her, I loved her with all of me.

It's that simple.

I release the breath I'd been holding when Trevor releases her to stand before me.

"You look..." I start.

"So do you," she replies, and then she smiles, and dang it, I'm crying.

So is she.

I take her hand. "Are you ready, baby?"

"I've been ready, baby."

The vows I'd sent to Michael were short, simple, knowing Ava and I had already said everything we needed to. Still, the words he speaks are a blur, and I can concentrate just enough to listen out for the pauses, so when it's time for me to say "I do," *I do*.

Michael continues, "Ava, do you take..." The more he speaks, the quicker Ava's smile drops, and at the pause, at the exact moment when she's supposed to speak... she doesn't.

Instead, she hesitates, looking around, her breaths short, sharp, eyes brimming with tears.

"Ava..." I choke on her name, and I can feel my knees giving out beneath me.

"I..." *Do. I do. Two words. Come on, Ava....*

I step closer, my words just for her. "It's okay if you don't want to," I whisper. "Or if I pressured you to do it too soon, we can—"

"I just..." She squeezes my hands. "I need to say something."

I catch Trevor's eyes behind her, and I can see the anguish there. He wasn't expecting this. "Go ahead," I tell her, forcing a smile. Internally, I'm readying my heart for imminent obliteration.

Ava takes a few breaths, her head bowed, but she's still holding on to me, and I hold on to hope. She lifts her gaze, her eyes clear now and right on mine. "The first time I spoke to you, I called you self-entitled." She giggles, and relief loosens every muscle within me.

Then she waits for our families' quiet laughter to die before adding, "Little did I know how wrong I was." She pauses to wipe a stray tear from her cheek. "You're the most selfless man I know, Connor. And I know this because... because I was hopeless when you met me. Broken beyond words. I fought you, fought *us*, at every turn, but you never gave up on me. On our friendship. Our love. You sat on my porch and held me through my cries, and then you... you put my ear to your heart until the only thing I could hear was *magic*." Her tears flow freely now, and I release her hands only to cup her face and wipe those tears away.

She sniffs a few times. So do I. So does everyone around us.

"For five years, you've continued to do that," Ava continues, "proving every single time that magic is real and lives and breathes inside you. We've grown so much together, from annoying, bratty little teenagers to..." She giggles again, the sound soothing my soul. "Well, you're a baller, and I'm still a brat, but... you love me, anyway."

"I do, Ava," I say through the knot in my throat. "So much."

"You changed our lives, Connor. You turned all our zero days into positive ones by not just showing but *proving* that... that love is not a noun, love is a verb.... So do I take you to be my husband?" She exhales. "You, Connor Ledger, are absolutely everything my heart and soul desire. All day. Every day. Always. Forever."

Our smiles match, our teary eyes glued to each other.

"I do."

AVA

"What's up, everyone?!" I say into the microphone. "Welcome back to another episode of *'Why Are You Telling Me This?'* with your host, me, Ava Ledger! And beside me, as always, is the real reason y'all tune in." I glance beside me to my husband, shaking his head as he watches me.

"False," he states into the mic.

"My husband, Connor." I clap quietly. "Yay!"

"Hi, everyone," Connor says, waving at the camera set up in front of us.

"Now, for those of you who are new to the channel, the premise of my show goes like this: I tell a different true crime story every episode, and my sweet, handsome-as-hell husband listens in, and during the more... gruesome parts, he'll interrupt with a line that's also the name of the show... *Why are you telling me this?*"

A knock sounds on the studio door, and without waiting for a response, Mom enters with Aria in her arm and Avery by her side.

"Are you recording?" Mom asks, stopping in the doorway. "I'm sorry."

I shake my head. "It's fine, Mama," I tell her while Connor stands, moving toward his girls. Avery will be two in a few weeks, and Aria just turned six months.

Connor goes for Avery first, lifting her off her feet and tickling her sides.

"Daddy, stop!" she giggles, but she doesn't *really* want him to. Avery's a daddy's girl—there's no denying it—and that little finger of hers has Connor wrapped all around it.

After our small, surprise wedding, I could tell that Mama was a little... disappointed. Not that we got married, but that it all happened so fast and that she didn't get to experience the things other mothers-of-brides get to do. When I spoke to her about it, she had admitted that she'd been waiting for the moment she could shop wedding dresses, look at venues and decide on menus with me. Considering there was a point in her life when she couldn't even leave the house, I was surprised that she'd thought that much about it. I told her I was sorry and that I completely understood where she was coming from. She apologized too, because the last thing she wanted was to make it about her. She also understood why I had been so willing to jump in, head first, eyes closed. As long as Connor was the man I was marrying, nothing else mattered.

Still, I wanted to give her that happiness. *The* happiness. So, we started wedding dress shopping. We spent months looking for the perfect dress that we both loved and had it made to my measurements. Only, by the time it arrived at the bridal shop... it didn't fit. Because... well, I was pregnant, and I didn't even know it at the time.

My mom's response when I put two and two together? "Fuck the wedding, Ava!" she'd cried through tears of absolute joy. "I'm going to be a grandma!"

"Ari's about due for her nap," Mom says now. "I thought I might take Avery to see the horses, if that's okay?"

True to his plan, Connor bought us a house with enough room for my mother to live in. And horses. For her therapy, of course. It's close enough to the Sunshine Oak Treatment Center so that she can go there whenever she needs to. Connor even organized a bus once a week to pick up patients to come by and visit the horses. Mom loves showing them off. But, more than anything, she loves showing off her grandbabies.

After we got married, I studied for another year before... I quit. Well, not *quit*, just delayed it until I worked out what I wanted out of life. It turns out, all I really wanted was to be a mother and a wife. And an occasional podcaster and Youtuber, it seems.

Connor had reminded me of the idea and how my seventeen-year-old self had mentioned it at the lake—the same lake where we said *I do*. I told him, "Maybe."

Two weeks later, he'd turned one of the spare bedrooms into a recording studio.

I love it. But, I love even more how much Connor encourages me with it.

"I'll put Ari to bed," Connor says, taking her from my mother. He walks over to me and kisses me once. "I'll be back."

I kiss baby Ari first and then my husband. "I'll be waiting."

I don't think there's a single soul on this earth who would be surprised to hear how great a father Connor is to his little girls. Avery came mid-season, during an *away* game.

Online, you can watch the reel of him getting subbed out in the last five minutes of a game, only for his coach to meet him at the sidelines and speak into his ear. The way Connor sprinted out of that stadium is almost comical. He made it to the hospital with plenty of time to spare. Still, he passed out in the delivery room.

Twice.

But then Avery was born, and he held her in his arms, and nothing else in the world seemed to matter.

They say that being a parent changes you. I don't know that it necessarily changed us. I spent years caring for my mother through sleepless nights and child-like tantrums, and Connor... well, his goal, his *end game*, was to find a way to take care of the people he loved. The difference now is that we're doing it together. And what a difference that makes.

"Grandma and me is going to pick flowers for you, Mama," Avery says, bright blue eyes like her daddy and wild-wild curls like me. I'm pretty sure Connor fell in love with her tiny little curls the moment she was out of me.

"I can't wait to see them," I tell her, getting up and moving in for a cuddle. I look up at Mom. "Will you be okay?"

"Of course," Mom tells me, waving me off before taking Avery's hand and walking away. It was a stupid question. She's been working out with Connor and running the property perimeter most days. She says it's therapeutic. Out here, she's the happiest I've ever seen her. We still go to our old house whenever we have a few days free or Connor's on the road. I've stopped traveling with him since having the girls, but we're there for every home game, all of us, front and center.

I sit back in my chair behind my desk and look at the screen of my laptop. A vision of me stares back.

I'm twenty-five now.

Ten years ago, my life changed dramatically. If you'd have asked that sad, broken little girl how I pictured my life to be, never, *ever*, in my wildest dreams could I even picture the blessings that surround me.

Sometimes, late at night, when the house is quiet and the world is sleeping, I slip away and sit out on the front porch like I did back then. Only, then, I'd keep my eyes open, searching for flickers of hope, because... when the world is at its darkest, that's when the magic appears.

Now, I sit, and I let my eyes drift shut.

I don't need to see the fireflies to know that they're there, just like I don't need to witness magic to know it exists.

In my mind, in my heart, I know magic is real... because I'm living it.

about the author

Jay McLean is an international best-selling author and full-time reader, writer of New Adult and Young Adult romance, and skilled procrastinator. When she's not doing any of those things, she can be found running after her three boys, investing way too much time on True Crime Documentaries and binge-watching reality TV.

She writes what she loves to read, which are books that can make her laugh, make her hurt and make her feel.

Jay lives in the suburbs of Melbourne, Australia, in her dream home where music is loud and laughter is louder.

Connect With Jay
www.jaymcleanauthor.com
jay@jaymcleanauthor.com

CPSIA information can be obtained
at www.ICGtesting.com
Printed in the USA
LVHW041306281222
736018LV00001B/9